THE
COBRA
WAR
TRILOGY

BAEN BOOKS by TIMOTHY ZAHN

THE
COBRA
WAR
TRILOGY

TIMOTHY ZAHN

A Baen Book

Baen Publishing Enterprises
P.O. Box 1403
Riverdale, NY 10471
www.baen.com

ISBN: 978-1-4767-8165-5

Cover art by Dave Seeley

First printing, July 2016
Distributed by Simon & Schuster
1230 Avenue of the Americas
New York, NY 10020

Library of Congress Cataloging-in-Publication Data

Names: Zahn, Timothy, author.
Title: The cobra war trilogy / Timothy Zahn.
Description: Riverdale, NY : Baen , [2016]
Identifiers: LCCN 2016018025 | ISBN 9781476781655 (paperback)
Subjects: | BISAC: FICTION / Science Fiction / Military. | FICTION / Science Fiction / Space Opera. | FICTION / Science Fiction / General. | GSAFD: Science fiction.
Classification: LCC PS3576.A33 C58 2016 | DDC 813/.54--dc23 LC record available at https://lccn.loc.gov/2016018025

10 9 8 7 6 5 4 3 2 1

Pages by Joy Freeman (www.pagesbyjoy.com)
Printed in the United States of America

CONTENTS

COBRA
ALLIANCE

CHAPTER ONE

The warehouse stretched out in front of them, its lights dimmed, its floor and furnishings old and drab. It was obviously deserted, with a thick layer of dust that indicated years of disuse and neglect. For all Jasmine "Jin" Moreau Broom could tell as she gazed over the scene, the place might have been sitting here unnoticed since the founding of Capitalia, or even since the first human colonists arrived on Aventine.

But Jin knew better. The stacks of crates, the parked forklifts, the dangling cables from the ceiling cranes—it was all an illusion. The room had never been a warehouse. Nor had it ever been an aircraft hangar, an office floor, or an alien landscape.

All it had ever been was a deathtrap.

A shiver of memory ran through her, the goose bumps that rippled through her flesh twinging against the arthritis growing its slow but inexorable way through her shoulders and hips. Jin's own Cobra training, thirty-two years ago, had taken place elsewhere on Aventine, as befit the uniqueness of the mission she and her ill-fated teammates had been assigned. As a result, she herself had never had to deal with this room in any of its various incarnations.

But her husband had taken his turn in here. Many turns, in fact. So had both of her sons, and she could still remember the unpleasant mixture of anxiety and pride she'd felt every time she'd stood here on the glassed-in observation catwalk watching one of them in action.

The fear and pride she'd felt in them as Cobras.

Unfortunately, not all of the members of the group here today shared Jin's sense of respect for this place. "You think maybe we could get on with it?" Aventinian Senior Governor Tomo Treakness muttered under his breath from his position two people to Jin's left. "I have actual work to do."

Jin leaned forward to look at him, a list of withering retorts jockeying for the privilege of leading the charge. She picked the most devastating of the options.

And left it unsaid as the man standing between her and Treakness laid a calming hand on hers. "Patience, Governor," Paul Broom said with the mildness and assured self-control that Jin so admired in her husband. "As I'm sure your estate's chief vintner would tell you, a fine wine can't be rushed."

A flash of something crossed Treakness's face. Annoyance, Jin hoped. Politicians like Treakness, who liked to portray themselves as friends of the common folk, didn't like being reminded about their wealth. "Interesting comparison, Cobra Broom," Treakness said. "So you see this as a slow-aged *luxury* beverage?"

"The Cobras are hardly a luxury," Governor Ellen Hoffman put in stiffly from Jin's right. "Maybe you don't need them so much in Capitalia anymore—"

"Please, Ellen," Treakness interrupted, his tone cool with a hint of condescension about it. "You know perfectly well I didn't mean the Cobras themselves."

"If you disparage the Sun Advanced Training Center, you disparage the Cobras," Hoffman countered. "Without the center, there *are* no Cobras."

"Really?" Treakness asked with feigned incredulity. "I'm sorry—did the MacDonald Center burn down when I wasn't looking?"

Hoffman's face darkened—"That's enough," the fifth member of the group, Governor-General Chintawa, put in firmly from Hoffman's other side. "Save the fireworks for the Council chamber. We're here to observe, not debate."

"If there's ever anything *to* observe," Treakness said.

"Patience, Governor," Paul said again, pointing to the left. "Here they come now."

Jin craned her neck to look. Fifteen shadowy figures had appeared around the side of one of the stacks and were marching with military precision toward the section of floor in front of the observation catwalk. Keying her optical enhancers for telescopic and light-amplification, she took a closer look.

Another shiver ran up her back. The alien Trofts who occupied the vast stretches of space between the Cobra Worlds and the distant Dominion of Man had been trusted friends and trading partners as long as Jin had been alive, plus quite a few years before that. But she knew her history, and the sight of the creatures who had once been mankind's deadliest enemies never failed to stir feelings of not-quite distrust.

This particular group of Trofts were even more impressive than usual, she decided as she watched them marching along. Their gait was military-precise and as fluid as their back-jointed legs could manage. Their hand-and-a-half lasers, the size and power currently favored by the Tlossie demesne's patrol forces, were held in cross-chest ready positions. Their eyes continually swept the areas around them, their pointed deer-like ears twitching as they did their own auditory scan, and the wing-like radiator membranes on the backs of their upper arms fluttered in and out to maintain their internal temperature and distinctive infrared signatures.

They were so perfect, in fact, that they might have been real.

"They get better every year, don't they?" Paul murmured.

Jin nodded . . . because the figures marching along down there were not, in fact, living Trofts. They were robots, designed as the ultimate test of new Cobras and seasoned veterans alike.

And like all ultimate challenges, this one carried the ultimate risk.

"Finally," Treakness grumbled. "Now how long are going to have to wait for them to get to their hiding places before the Cobras can move in?"

The words were barely out of his mouth when the brilliant spear of a Cobra antiarmor laser beam slashed across the warehouse, slicing into one of the lasers in the center of the enemy formation. "Not long at all," Paul said calmly. "This is an ambush exercise."

The robots scattered madly for cover as three more Cobra lasers joined in the attack. Two of the enemy went down in that first salvo, as did a third whose laser exploded in its face as the Cobras' attack shorted out the weapon's power pack. A moment later, the remaining Trofts had made it to cover, and the battle settled into a slower but no less deadly game of hide-and-seek.

Jin gazed down at the operation, another set of memories rising from the back of her mind. She'd fought the Trofts herself once, the only person since the First Cobras to have ever faced the aliens in actual combat. She'd taken on a cargo ship full of them on the human breakaway colony world of Qasama, more or less single-handedly. Not only had she lived to tell the tale, but she'd even managed to pull a quiet but genuine victory out of the situation.

And had then returned to Aventine and watched helplessly as that victory was snatched from her fingers by truth-twisting politicians.

She leaned forward for a surreptitious look past her husband. Treakness was watching the battle closely, visibly wincing every time one of the robots was knocked out of action. With Treakness it was always about money, and Jin could practically see the calculator tape running through his brain. Fifteen robots at roughly a million *klae* each, plus the costs of the techs running the exercise, plus the maintenance costs of the Sun Center, plus the creation and training of the Cobras themselves—

"They're not actually being destroyed, you know," Paul commented.

"No, the lasers are just chewing up their outer ablative coating material," Treakness said tartly. "I *do* read the reports, thank you."

"I just thought it might be worth mentioning," Paul murmured.

"I also know that it still costs a minimum of fifty thousand for each refurbishing," Treakness continued. "That's a *minimum* of fifty thousand. If the internal works get damaged, that bill can quadruple."

"And it's worth every *klae*," Hoffman put in. "The statistics on Cobra survival in the field have gone up tremendously since the Sun Center opened."

"You get a lot of Troft warriors in the fields of Donyang Province, do you?" Treakness asked pointedly. "I must have missed those reports."

Paul looked sideways at Jin; she rolled her eyes at him in silent reply. For some reason that she couldn't fathom, the military concept of *deterrence* still managed to elude some of the allegedly brightest minds in the Cobra Worlds. *Yes,* for most of the Worlds' existence the Cobras had served mainly as frontier guardians, policemen, and hunters, working hard to clear out the spine leopards and other lethal predators from newly opened territories so the farmers and ranchers and loggers could move in. And *yes,* the three Troft demesnes nearest the Worlds had been as peaceable as anyone could ever hope for, even if they did always tend to press their trade deals a bit harder than they should and wring out every brightly colored *klae* possible.

But *some* group of Troft demesnes had once felt themselves capable of attacking the Dominion of Man and occupying two of its worlds. If there was one thing every governor-general since Zhu had understood, it was that the Trofts needed to know that the Cobras were the finest, nastiest, deadliest warriors the universe had ever seen, and that the Cobra Worlds were most emphatically not to be trifled with. Why Treakness and some of the others couldn't understand that simple point Jin had never been able to figure out.

Perhaps it was simply the natural way of things. Perhaps when people were too far removed from immediate, visible threats they began to doubt that such threats could ever exist again. Or, indeed, that they had ever existed at all.

Maybe people periodically needed something to shake them up. Not a war, certainly—Jin wouldn't wish that on anyone. But it would have to be something dramatic, immediate, and impossible to ignore. A sudden influx of spine leopards into Aventine's cities, maybe, or a small but loud uprising among some group of disaffected citizens.

"Jin," Paul said quietly.

Jin snapped out of her reverie. There had been something in his tone... "Where?" she asked, her eyes darting around the warehouse.

"That one," Paul said, nodding microscopically to the far left toward one of the Troft robots moving around the crate stacks.

A hard knot settled into the pit of Jin's stomach. The robot had half a dozen laser slashes across its torso and head, enough damage that it should have shut itself off in defeat and collapsed onto the floor. But it was still wandering around in aimless-looking circles, its laser hefted across its burned torso, its head turning back and forth as it searched for a target. "I think I can get to my comm," she murmured.

"Don't bother—I already hit my EM," Paul murmured back. "The malfunction must have scrambled the local comm system."

And the techs in the control room, their attention occupied with other duties, hadn't yet noticed the problem. "You think we should risk trying to wave at one of the cameras?" Jin asked.

And then, before Paul could answer, the robot's head turned and tilted back a few degrees, its eyes coming to rest on the three men and two women standing on the catwalk.

"No one move," Paul ordered, his voice quiet but suddenly carrying the crisp edges of absolute authority.

"Don't even blink," Jin added, her mind sifting rapidly through their options. At this distance her fingertip lasers were too weak to do any good, especially since they'd first have to punch through the catwalk's glass enclosure. The antiarmor laser in her left calf was a far more powerful weapon, theoretically capable of slagging the robot where it stood, assuming she could hold the laser on target long enough to penetrate the layers of material protecting the robot's expensive optronics. The targeting lock built into her optical enhancers and the nanocomputer buried beneath her brain could easily handle such a task, but only if the robot didn't make it to cover before the laser finished its work. Neither her arcthrower nor her assortment of sonic weapons would operate through the glass, and her ceramic-laminated bones and servo-enhanced muscles were of no use whatsoever in this particular situation.

She was still trying to come up with a plan when the robot lifted its laser toward the observers.

"Stay here," Paul ordered, and with a sudden smooth motion, he ducked past Treakness and took off into a mad dash along the catwalk in the direction of the rogue robot.

"What the—?" Treakness demanded.

"He's trying to draw its fire," Jin snapped, her heart thudding hard in her throat. Just like a real soldier, the robot was programmed to see an enemy moving rapidly in its direction as a greater threat and therefore a higher-priority target than four other enemies standing motionless and unthreatening.

Only now that her husband had gotten the robot's attention, the only thing standing between him and death were his programmed Cobra reflexes. In the tight quarters of the enclosed catwalk, those reflexes were going to be sorely limited.

But there might be another way. Getting a grip on the handrail in front of her, Jin braced her feet against the catwalk floor, her eyes on the robot as its laser tracked along its target's vector. Paul was perhaps a quarter of the way to the distant door at the far end of the catwalk when Jin saw the subtle shift of robot musculature as the tracking laser found its mark. "Stop!" she shouted to her husband.

And pushing off the floor, she sprinted full speed after him.

For a terrifying fraction of a second she was afraid Paul hadn't gotten the message, that he would keep running straight to his death. But even as Jin dodged around past Treakness her husband braked to a halt.

And with that, it was suddenly now Jin, not Paul, who represented the greater threat. Without even pausing to squeeze off a shot at its original target, the robot swung its laser around toward Jin.

Jin clenched her teeth against the arthritic pain jabbing into her joints as she ran. *Well,* she thought. *That worked.*

Or had it? To her dismay, she suddenly realized that with the bouncing inherent in a flat-out run she could no longer see the subtle warning signs that would indicate the robot had acquired her and was preparing to fire. She tried putting a targeting lock on the machine, hoping it might steady her eyesight. But it didn't. She kept running, trying to coax a little more speed out of her leg servos—

"Stop!" Paul shouted.

Jin leaned back and locked her legs, gasping at the sudden flash of pain from her bad left knee. Even as she skidded to a halt she saw Paul break again into a run.

Jin focused on the robot, watching as it disengaged its attention from her and once again shifted to the more immediate threat. This would work, she told herself. It would work. She and Paul could just tag-team their way to the door, get off the catwalk and through the door into the rest of the building and yell to the oblivious techs to hit the emergency abort.

She spared a fraction of a second to glance down the catwalk. Only it wouldn't work, she realized with a sinking sensation. The closer she and Paul got to the rogue robot on their angled vector, the faster it would acquire its new target, and the shorter the distance each of them would get before being forced to stop again. Worse, since Paul was closer to the robot than Jin was, his window of opportunity would get shorter faster than hers would, which meant she would slowly catch up to him, which meant they would eventually end up within range of a quick one-two from the robot. At that point, their only two choices would be to stand still and hope the robot lost interest, or go into an emergency corkscrew sprint and hope they could beat its fire.

The robot twitched—"Stop!" Jin shouted, and started her next run.

She got no more than two-thirds her last distance before Paul's warning brought her to another knee-wrenching halt. Two more sprints each, she estimated, maybe three, and they would reach the dead-end killing box she'd already anticipated. They had to come up with a new plan before that happened.

But she hadn't thought of anything by the time she called Paul to a halt and started her next run. She watched him out of the corner of her eye as she ran, hoping he'd come up with something.

But he merely shouted her to a stop and took off again himself, with no indication that he was trying anything new. Either he hadn't made it to the same conclusion Jin had, or else he had and had decided their only chance was to try to beat the robot's motion sensors to the punch.

The robot's motion sensors...

It would be a risk, Jin knew. The chance that even a damaged robot's sensors would lock on to something so much smaller than a human target was vanishingly small. More ominously, what she was planning could easily throw off Paul's stride enough that the robot would finally get in that lethal shot.

But she had to try. Turning her chest toward the glass wall in front of her, gripping the handrail for support, she activated her sonic disruptor.

The backwash as the blast bounced off the glass nearly ripped her hands from the rail and sent her flying backward into the wall behind her. Grimly, she held on, her head rattling with subsonics as the weapon searched for the resonance of the target it had been presented.

And with an earsplitting blast, the glass shattered.

Not just in front of Jin, but halfway down the catwalk in both directions. Through the lingering rattling in her head, she dimly felt herself being hammered by flying objects.

But her full attention was on the robot, whose laser was even now lining up on her husband. The robot which had suddenly been presented with a hundred small objects flying through the air in its general direction.

The robot which was just standing there, frozen, its laser still pointed toward the human threats as its deranged optronic brain tried to work through its threat-assessment algorithms.

The gamble had worked, Jin realized, an edge of cautious hope tugging at her. All the flying glass had distracted the robot and bought Paul a little time. If he could get to the door and call for help, they still had a chance.

And then, the motion at the edge of her peripheral vision stopped.

She shifted her eyes toward Paul, her first horrifying thought that the shattering glass might have sliced into an artery or vein, that her move might have in fact killed her husband instead of saving him.

She was searching his form for spurting blood, and opening her mouth to shout at him to get moving, when a flash like noonday sunlight blazed across her vision and a clap of thunder slammed across her already throbbing head.

Paul had fired his arcthrower.

Reflexively, Jin squeezed her eyes shut against the lightning bolt's purple afterimage, simultaneously keying in her optical enhancers. In the image they provided, she saw that the high-voltage current had turned the robot's laser and right arm into a smoking mass of charred metal and ablative material.

But the robot was still standing... and with its threat assessment now complete it was reaching for the backup projectile pistol belted at its side.

Jin could do something about that. Keying for her own arcthrower, she lifted her right arm and pointed her little finger at the robot. The arcthrower was a two-stage weapon: her fingertip laser would fire first, creating a path of ionized air between her and the robot that the current from the arcthrower's capacitor could then follow. She curled her other fingers inward and set her thumb against the ring-finger nail.

And broke off as a pair of human figures appeared, sprinting into view from behind different stacks near the damaged robot. The two men leaped in unison, one of them hitting the robot at neck height, the other at its knees, unceremoniously dumping the machine at last onto the floor. The dim overhead lighting abruptly shifted to bright red, the signal of emergency abort.

It was finally over.

"About time," someone said.

Jin turned to look at the other three members of their group, still huddled together in stunned disbelief a hundred meters behind her. She wondered who had spoken into her ringing ears, realized it must have been her. At the far end of the catwalk, behind the politicians, the door flew open and a line of Sun Center personnel came charging through.

It was only then, as Jin wiped at the sweat on her forehead, that she realized she was bleeding.

Paul and Governor-General Chintawa were deep in conversation in the waiting area when Jin emerged from the treatment room. "You all right?" Paul asked, bouncing to his feet and hurrying toward her, his eyes flicking over the fresh bandages in her forehead and cheeks. "They wouldn't let me come in there with you."

"I'm fine," Jin assured him as he took her hands in his, gripping them with that unique combination of strength and gentleness that she'd fallen in love with so many years ago. "They had to use cleansing mist to get some of the bits of glass out, that's all. By the time you'd have gotten suited up, it would have been too late to watch anyway."

"I'm glad you're all right, Cobra Broom," Chintawa said gravely, rising from his own seat in old-provincial politeness as Jin and Paul came over to him. "That was quick thinking, on both your parts. Very impressive. Thank you for risking your lives for us."

"You're welcome," Paul replied for both of them. "After all, protecting civilians is what we're all about."

"Indeed." Chintawa's lip twitched. "Unfortunately, some would say otherwise." He gestured toward the door. "But we can discuss that on the way back to Capitalia."

Chintawa's aircar was waiting on the parking area where they'd set down four hours ago. "Where are the others?" Paul asked as the driver opened the rear door for them.

"They left an hour ago," Chintawa said, gesturing Jin into the car ahead of him.

Jin shot a frown at her husband as she climbed in. The group had only brought two aircars: Chintawa's and Treakness's. "Governor Hoffman was actually willing to get in an aircar with Governor Treakness?" she asked.

"Neither of them wanted to wait for you two to get patched up," Chintawa said. "It was either share an aircar or one of them was going to have to walk."

"It's so nice to work for grateful people," Jin murmured as Paul sat down beside her.

"Sarcasm ill befits you, dear," Paul murmured back.

"Unfortunately, in this case sarcasm is a close match for reality," Chintawa said as he sat down across from them and signaled the driver to take off. "Did Governor Hoffman tell you why she wanted you to join us in observing today's exercise?"

Jin pricked up her ears. She and Paul had been trying to figure that one out ever since Chintawa issued the invitation the previous afternoon. "No, she didn't."

"She's submitted a proposal to have a second advanced training center built in Donyang Province," Chintawa said. "Her argument is that it would be closer to the expansion regions where the Cobras are needed. And of course, it would also be closer to where most of the recruits these days are coming from."

Jin rubbed her fingers gently across one of the bandages on her forearm, feeling the brief flicker of pain from the cut beneath it. She'd been looking at the recruitment numbers only a couple of weeks ago, and had noticed the ominous downtrend in new Cobras coming from Capitalia and Aventine's other large cities. "We could certainly use another center," she said. "I understand Esqualine and Viminal still haven't gotten the quotas the Council voted them."

"Not to mention Caelian," Paul added.

"Yes, let's not mention Caelian," Chintawa said darkly. "At any rate, Governor Hoffman wanted you two along to add a little weight to today's proceedings. She was hoping that a particularly impressive showing might help convince Governor Treakness that moving the center out there would be a good idea. Now, though—" He shook his head.

"Actually, what happened was far more impressive than a simple by-the-numbers Cobra exercise," Paul offered mildly. "It showed Cobra initiative, courtesy of Jin and me, as well as the quick assessment and response on the part of Cobras Patterson and Encyro."

"You're preaching to the choir, Cobra Broom," Chintawa said sourly. "I doubt most of the rest of the Council will see the event much differently than Governor Treakness, either. We'll be lucky if we don't lose a few more Syndics to his side of the argument."

At her hip, Jin's comm vibrated. Pulling it out, she keyed it on. "Hello?"

"I just heard the news," the tight voice of their younger son Lorne said without preamble. "Are you and Dad okay?"

"We're fine," Jin assured him. Paul was looking at her with raised eyebrows; *Lorne,* she mouthed silently at him. "A few scrapes and cuts. Nothing serious."

"Are you sure?" Lorne persisted. "The prelim report said the whole observation catwalk had been destroyed."

"Since when do you believe prelim reports?" Jin asked, keeping her voice light. "No, really. Some of the glass got broken, but the catwalk itself held together just fine.

"*Some* of the glass?" Lorne retorted. "Come on, Mom—they *had* pictures."

"Okay, maybe more than just some," Jin conceded. Out of the corner of her eye, she saw Paul pull out his own comm and quietly answer it. "But your dad and I are okay," she went on. "Really."

There was a pause, and Jin could imagine that intense look on Lorne's face as he sifted through her tone and inflection. Of their three children, he was the one most sensitive to the quiet currents underlying people's words. Back when they were children, both his older brother Merrick and his younger sister Jody had occasionally been allowed to stay home from school solely because Lorne had thought he'd heard pain or sickness in their voices. Usually, the sibling he'd fingered had wound up running a fever within a couple of hours. "Okay, if you say so," he said at last. "But I'm coming in."

"That's really not necessary," Jin protested, wincing again. The thoughtful, sensitive type Lorne might be, but he nevertheless had a bad tendency to drive way too fast, especially when he thought there was trouble in his family. "Besides, aren't you on duty?"

"I'll get Randall to cover for me," Lorne said. "They've postponed the spine leopard hunt again, so it's not like I'm really needed."

"In that case, you might as well stay for dinner, too," Jin said, conceding defeat. "We should be back home in a couple of hours. If you get there first, let yourself in."

"I will," Lorne said. "See you soon. Bye."

"Bye." Jin closed down the comm and put it away, noting as she did so that Paul had also finished with his conversation. "Lorne's coming to the house for dinner," she told him.

"I hope he's learned to cook," Paul said. "We're going to the Island tonight."

Jin frowned. "That was Uncle Corwin?"

"Merrick, actually," Paul said. "He said Uncle Corwin had called and invited all of us to dinner."

A tingle went up Jin's back. Uncle Corwin never called dinner parties on the spur of the moment this way. And if he had, he would have called Jin, not Merrick, to make the arrangements.

Which meant this family get-together was Merrick's idea, with the Uncle Corwin connection having been thrown in simply for cover.

Jin looked at Chintawa. He was busily leafing through some papers, but she could tell he was listening closely to the conversation. "Sounds good to me," she told Paul. "All I have at the house is leftovers anyway. I'll call Lorne and let him know."

"No need," Paul said. "Merrick was going to call both him and Jody as soon as he got off the comm."

"Okay." Settling back against the cushions, Jin closed her eyes. And wondered uneasily what was going on.

It couldn't have anything to do with today's trouble at the Sun Center. Merrick had inherited his father's cool unflappability, and he wouldn't have even started worrying until he had something besides an initial report to go on. He'd been planning to stop by the house today and drop off some of Jody's new azaleas—could something have happened to their house?

But then why hadn't he just said so? Surely he wouldn't have worried about either Chintawa or the two governors hearing that the plants were dying or that someone had driven a car into their living room.

"Think of it as an early Thanksgiving," Paul said into her musings. "It'll be a nice treat to have the whole family together again, even if only for one evening."

"Absolutely," Jin murmured. "And you all know how much I love surprises."

CHAPTER TWO

Merrick Broom closed the comm and looked across the desk at the silver-haired man sitting there. "They're coming," he confirmed. "Dad said they'd be home in a couple of hours. Add in time to clean up and change, and they should be here by six or so."

"Good," Corwin Moreau said, thoughtfully fingering the paper Merrick had brought to him half an hour ago. Those fingers, Merrick noted, were thin and age-stained, but still strong and flexible.

As was Great-Uncle Corwin himself. Eighty-seven years old, he was still hale and hearty, with every indication that he still had ten to twenty years of good life left in him.

A hundred years, or even beyond, whereas Merrick's own grandfather Justin, five years Corwin's junior, had barely made it to sixty. A sobering reminder of how drastically the implanted Cobra weapons and equipment shortened the lives of all those who committed themselves to that service.

A list which included both of Merrick's parents and Merrick's younger brother Lorne. Not to mention Merrick himself.

"What do you think she's going to do?" Corwin asked, lifting the paper slightly.

Merrick pulled his thoughts back from the dark future to the equally dark present. "You really think there's a question?" he countered. "She's going to go for it, of course."

"I'm afraid you're right," Corwin conceded. "Your mother's always been the damn-the-consequences sort."

Merrick raised his eyebrows slightly. "I understand it runs in the family."

Corwin's wrinkled face cracked in a wry smile. "Don't believe everything your mother tells you," he warned. "Even at the height of my political career I never took a single step without making sure the floor was solid beneath me."

"I'm sure you didn't," Merrick said. But he knew better. The last step of Corwin's political career, thirty-two years ago, had been made knowing full well that the planks beneath that step were riddled with dry rot. Corwin had taken that step knowing it would destroy him, but also knowing that it was the right thing to do. Outsiders who remembered the Moreau family at all tended to forget that part of it.

But Merrick hadn't forgotten. Neither had the rest of the family.

There was a hint of sound somewhere behind him. Merrick notched up his auditory enhancers, and the sound resolved into a set of soft footsteps on the hallway carpet. "So I guess the question is whether or not we're going to let her," he said, lowering the enhancement again.

Corwin snorted. "You really think you'll be able to talk her out of it?"

"*I* won't, no," Merrick said. "But I think Dad can." He raised his voice. "Hello, Aunt Thena."

"Hello, Merrick," Thena's voice came from the vicinity of the footsteps behind him. "Corwin, in case you missed it, the timer just went off on whatever you had running downstairs."

"Oops," Corwin said, looking at his watch. "Thanks, dear—I'd forgotten about that." He stood up and came around the side of his desk. "Come on, Merrick. As long as you're here, I might was well put you to work."

"What have you got cooking this time?" Merrick asked, standing up as well.

"It's a new ceramic the computer simulation says should be as strong as the stuff you're currently wearing," Corwin said, gesturing toward Merrick's body. "It's also supposedly less reactive than standard Cobra bone laminae, which may help delay the onset of anemia and arthritis."

"Sounds good," Merrick said. After his stormy departure from politics, Corwin had gone back to school, earning a degree in materials science and launching into his own private crusade to try to solve the medical problems that had been shortening the lives of Cobras since the very beginning of the program a century ago.

Though even if he succeeded it would do Merrick himself no good. He had the same equipment that had sent his own father to an early grave.

"I wouldn't get my hopes up *too* high, of course," Corwin warned as he walked past Merrick. "But you know what they say: fifty-something's the charm."

Merrick fell into step behind him, noting the hint of stiffness in his great-uncle's gait. His own parents, three decades younger than Corwin, had that same stiffness, especially first thing in the morning. Another sobering reminder, if he'd needed one, of how rapidly the clock was ticking down for them.

"Before you take Merrick away to the dungeon, never to be seen again," Thena said as Corwin reached her, "I wonder if I might borrow him for a quick menu consultation."

"Sure," Corwin said, his hand brushing hers as he passed. "Come on down when you're finished."

"I'll be right there," Merrick promised. "Oh, and I need to call Lorne and Jody, too."

"Take your time." Corwin headed out into the hallway and turned toward the stairway that led down to his private lab.

Merrick stopped beside Thena and raised his eyebrows. "The *menu*?" he murmured.

"It seemed plausible," she said, handing him a pad.

"I don't know why you even bother," Merrick said as he took the pad. "You know he's not fooled in the slightest."

"No, but he enjoys playing the game."

"If you say so," Merrick said, running his eyes down the list she'd made. Drogfowl cacciatore, sautéed greenburrs, garlic long-bread, and citrus icelets for dessert. Nothing he couldn't handle with his eyes closed. "You have everything, or will I need to go shopping?"

"It's all here," she said. "I've got the drogfowl defrosting, and the longbread dough should be finished rising in half an hour." Thena lowered her voice. "Merrick, you can't let her do this."

"Have you ever seen my mother in full gantua mode?" Merrick asked dryly.

"Actually, I have," Thena said grimly. "But I'm not talking about the inherent danger of this whole insane thing. You have to stop her because she'll be doing it for the wrong reason."

Merrick frowned. That was not where he'd expected Thena to be going with this. "You mean she'll be doing it to justify herself?"

"Not at all," Thena said. "I mean she'll be doing it to justify Corwin."

Merrick winced. Thena was right, he realized suddenly. His mother had never truly forgiven herself for her perceived role in wrecking her uncle's political career. The fact that everyone else in the family—Corwin included—agreed that she didn't bear any of the responsibility was completely irrelevant. "Is that what Uncle Corwin thinks, too?"

"I don't know," Thena said. "But if it hasn't occurred to him yet, it will soon enough."

"And of course, he can't mention that to Mom, because she'd just dig in her heels and insist he was imagining things."

"Exactly," Thena said. "In case you hadn't noticed, there's an incredible streak of stubbornness in your family."

"Hey, don't look at me," Merrick protested. "*I* was drafted for this outfit. *You're* the one who volunteered."

Thena smiled, a whisper of fondness penetrating the taut concern in her face. "Willingly, even," she said quietly. "I don't know if you ever knew, but I was in love with your uncle for many years before he finally figured out there was more to life than politics."

"The public spotlight can be pretty dazzling sometimes."

"And the Moreau family has somehow always managed to be in that spotlight," Thena agreed. "Right in the center of Cobra Worlds history." Her smile faded. "But you've paid a huge price for it."

Merrick sighed. "Mainly because so many of us over the years have chosen to be Cobras."

"And because even those like Corwin who haven't have usually ended up directly under the fallout from those decisions," Thena said. "Don't get me wrong—I'm proud of the family I married into. Immensely proud. You've done great things for the Cobra Worlds, whether anyone else remembers or not." She looked away. "I just don't want to see that fallout claim another victim."

"I agree," Merrick said. "Let's see how the evening goes." He pulled out his comm again. "Meanwhile, I need to touch base with Lorne and Jody."

"Go ahead," Thena said. "I'll go pull out the spices and measuring spoons."

"And don't worry," Merrick said, reaching out to touch her shoulder as she started to leave. "You never know. Mom could decide to be reasonable."

The twitch of Thena's cheek told Merrick what she thought of that possibility. But she merely nodded. "Let's hope so," she said.

Lorne Broom put away his comm and turned to the sandy-haired man standing a couple of meters away. "Mom says they're okay," he told the other. "Of course, she'd probably say that if she and Dad each had a limb hanging on by scraps of skin."

"Yeah, my mom hates it when I worry, too," Randall Sumara agreed. "You'd better get going if you're going to beat the Capitalia traffic."

"You sure you don't mind?" Lorne asked. "I know you and Gina were planning to make a long weekend of it."

"So we make a short weekend instead," Randall said with a shrug. "She'll understand. I'll have her drive out early tomorrow and we'll take off as soon as you're back."

"Which will be tomorrow evening at the very latest," Lorne promised. "Sooner if I don't see any actual blood."

"Take your time," Randall said. "Like I said—"

Across the room, the intercom warbled. "All Cobras: assembly room," Commandant Ishikuma's voice came tartly.

"Uh-oh," Randall muttered. "You think they've changed their minds about the hunt?"

"I hope not," Lorne said, wincing. The spine leopard hunts were vitally important to the citizens out here in Aventine's expansion regions, and being a protector of those citizens had been his main reason for joining the Cobras in the first place.

But his parents' health was important, too, and for his own peace of mind he needed to personally make sure they were all right.

The other seven men in their squad were waiting when Lorne and Randall arrived at the assembly room. Ishikuma was standing behind the display table, flanked by four civilians Lorne had never seen before.

And laid out on the table in front of them all were four rifles.

Not just any rifles, either. They were high-tech, super advanced gizmos: top-heavy with lightscopes, darkscopes, and needle-sensors, bottom-heavy with dual power packs and redundant emitters, and topped with an ominous-looking double walnut shape nearly buried beneath all the hardware.

Lorne sighed. *Not again,* he thought wearily.

"Have a seat, Cobras," Ishikuma said briskly, nodding Lorne and Randall to a pair of vacant chairs. "The gentleman to my left is Dr. Emile Belain, from Jaland City's Applied Tech Institute. We've been asked to assist him and his team in their final field test of a new scheme for hunting spine leopards. Dr. Belain, perhaps you can give us a quick thumbnail of your technique."

"Thank you, Commandant," Belain said, and launched into an enthusiastic description of his new guns and their computerized ability to identify, target, and fire at the number-one scourge of expansion-region citizens.

Lorne and the other Cobras had often speculated as to when the bulgebrains in their nice safe ivory towers would figure out that none of the elaborate weaponry they kept coming up with could replace live soldiers. The recognition software was too iffy, the range of spine leopard physiques and colorations too variable, and the simple inertia of the guns worked against the kind of quickness that was critically important to the gunner's survival. Not to mention the fact that the combat and hunting abilities of the citizens who were supposed to use the guns were literally all over the map.

The bulgebrains knew that, of course. Surely by now they knew it. But they kept hammering at the problem anyway. There were just too many people in the civilized regions of Aventine who disliked or feared the Cobras, and who would grasp at any straw that might lead to their ultimate elimination.

Still, even if the visiting bulgebrains never had the right answers, they could always be counted on for a good dog-and-puppy show. Belain waxed bafflegabbily poetic about the capabilities of his new guns, with plenty of reasons why they were so much better than the efforts of those who had gone before. Lorne listened with half an ear, trying to put the image of maimed parents out of his mind.

At least that latter task was made a little easier when, midway through the briefing, his comm keyed in with a message: Merrick was inviting the whole family to Uncle Corwin's estate for dinner. That was a good sign, Lorne knew—if they were gathering at the Island instead of the hospital, his parents must genuinely be doing all right.

Finally, after ten interminable minutes, Belain ran out of superlatives and wind. "All right, Cobras, listen up," Ishikuma said. "As you know, the usual procedure is to start these things in the practice cage. However, Dr. Belain has requested something a little more realistic, so we're going to head to Sutter's Creek and the glade where Dushan Matavuli reported signs of a way station. Questions? Then get to the transports—we're taking One and Three. Broom, stand clear a moment."

Silently, the Cobras got out of their chairs and headed for the door. Belain and his civilians joined the stream, their new superweapons resting in the crooks of their elbows and pointing proudly at the ceiling. Lorne stayed out of the crowd, and as the last of the group vanished out the door, Ishikuma left the table and came over to him. "I hear there was some problem at the Sun Center this afternoon," the commandant said.

"Yes, sir," Lorne confirmed. "But my mother says she and Dad are all right."

"The aftermath film looked pretty nasty," Ishikuma said, watching Lorne's face closely. "I also hear that you've arranged with Sumara to take the first half of your weekend shift."

"Yes, sir, I have," Lorne said, wondering how the hell Ishikuma always knew so much about everything. He must have the whole station wired. "He said he'd log it for me."

"I'm sure he will once we're back from this exercise," Ishikuma said. "Meanwhile, you're dismissed. Check out an aircar and get your tail to Capitalia."

"Thank you, sir," Lorne said, briefly fighting the temptation to salute, turn around, and obey the orders he'd just been given. "But we're going on a hunt. I need to be there."

Ishikuma snorted. "This may come as a shock, Cobra Broom, but we were doing just fine out here before you came along, and we'll do equally well after you leave. We'll handle the hunt. You get to Capitalia and check on your parents."

"I appreciate the offer, sir," Lorne said. "I'll head out as soon as the hunt is over."

For a moment Ishikuma eyed him. "As you wish, Cobra Broom," he said. "Get to your transport."

It was a ten-minute trip to the Matavuli spread and the section of Sutter's Creek where the rancher had spotted the spine leopard way station. Sumara and Werle put the transports down on the nearest halfway-reasonable landing area, and the group headed in.

"Did the local who reported this way station mention its size?" Belain asked quietly as the group walked through the tall grass and thickening woods toward the sound of running water. He was holding his gun in a more or less horizontal position, swinging it gently back and forth in a thirty-degree arc. All four of the civilians were doing that, and the Cobras had responded by fanning out mostly behind and beside them in hopes of staying out of their lines of fire.

It wasn't simply paranoia. Two Cobras over in Donyang Province had been seriously hurt three months ago by a different group of bulgebrains and their weapons.

"He didn't get close enough for a good look," Ishikuma said from Belain's side. "But this close to water, it's probably a good-sized one."

They had gone another ten meters, and Lorne had just caught sight of the matted reeds and splintered bones that marked a spine leopard way station, when they were attacked.

The spine leopards came in two groups, the first consisting of four males leaping from the tall grass beside a big obsidian rock, the second group of three males half a second later coming from beneath the edge of the drop-off beside the creek bed.

Lorne snapped his hands up, his eyes tracking through the sudden deluge of laser fire coming from both the civilians and his fellow Cobras. The first group of spine leopards collapsed to the ground, the black stitching of laser burns along their sides and bellies. Apparently, Belain's weapons were holding their own. Lorne shifted his attention to the second group, targeting one of the as-yet-untouched predators.

He had just fired a volley from his fingertip lasers into the creature's head when his enhanced hearing caught a soft rustling from the reeds behind him.

Instantly, his nanocomputer took control of his body's network of implanted servo motors, breaking off his attack and throwing him into a long slide-leap to his right. He rolled half over onto his back as he hit the ground, twisting his head around just in time to see another pair of spine leopards slice through the space he'd just vacated. He twitched his eye to put a targeting lock on the nearer of the two and fired his antiarmor laser, his body twisting awkwardly around as his servos brought the weapon to bear.

The laser flashed, cutting into the leopard's flank. Without waiting to see if that single shot had done the job, Lorne shifted his eyes to the second predator, who had hit the ground and bounded out into a second leap toward the party. Before he could fire, another antiarmor laser blazed across the leafy background, taking the spine leopard's head off at the neck.

Lorne rolled up onto his feet, his fingertip lasers again held at the ready as he rapidly scanned the impromptu battlefield. But the only ones still on their feet were the humans.

Minus one.

He hurried over to the group crouching or standing guard around the fallen civilian. "What happened?" he asked as he took a spot in the defensive circle, sparing a single glance at the writhing body Ishikuma and de Portola were hunched over.

"Same as always," Randall said bitterly. "The guns all targeted just fine, only they all targeted the first wave, three of them alone on the first spine leopard who poked his nose into sight. By the time the computers disengaged and retargeted, it was too late to shift to the second wave."

Lorne nodded grimly. And without a Cobra's servos and programmed reflexes to protect them, the civilians had been sitting ducks. If they'd been out here alone, all four would probably be dead now.

He looked at Dr. Belain. The other was staring down at the injured man, his face pale, his jaws tight, his hands gripping his rifle as if it was a magic totem.

Lorne turned his attention back to the woods around them. When would they learn, he wondered. When would they ever learn?

"That's all we can do here," Ishikuma said briskly, getting back to his feet. "Broom, Sumara—get him to one of the transports and take him to Archway. Be sure to call ahead and make sure they've got a trauma room prepped."

"Yes, sir," Sumara acknowledged for both of them.

"And when you've done that," Ishikuma added, his eyes boring into Lorne's face, "you, Broom, are to get yourself out of my jurisdiction as per my previous order. Understood?"

"Yes, sir," Lorne said.

"Then move it," Ishikuma said, his voice marginally less severe. "And give them both my best wishes."

"I'll be there," Jody Moreau Broom promised into her comm. "Bye."

She closed the device and put it away. "Well?" Geoff Boulton asked anxiously, his eyes flicking back and forth across the display screen in front of him.

"Merrick says they're both fine," Jody assured him. "Mom picked up a few small cuts from flying glass, but that's about it."

"I don't know," Geoff said doubtfully, fiddling with the view on the display. "Near as I can tell from this, whatever happened left a real mess."

"Merrick wouldn't lie to me," Jody said firmly. "Besides, he's already talked to Lorne, who talked to Mom. You can't hide anything from Lorne."

"If you say so," Geoff said, still not sounding entirely convinced. "So. Where were we?"

"She was showing us her new trap design," Freylan Sonderby spoke up from beside the workbench. He frowned slightly, as if something had just occurred to him. "Unless you were wanting to go to the hospital, I mean," he added awkwardly to Jody. "I mean, you *did* just say you'd be there, right? There being—wherever *there* is. Or is going to be?"

Jody suppressed a smile. That was Freylan, all right. He was the tech end of the team, with the analytical and biochemical skills necessary for taking Geoff's visionary ideas and translating them into reality.

He was also the stereotypical socially inept bulgebrain, with a sometimes astonishing lack of ability to put coherent sentences together. Another good reason why they let him do the lab work while Geoff handled the grant-application pitches that had kept the team going for the past year and a half.

Jody herself possessed neither set of skills. Fortunately, she had other things to bring to the table. "That was just a dinner invitation," she assured Freylan, stepping around the desk to join him at the table. "Whenever you're ready, Geoff?"

"Ready now." Geoff took one last lingering look at the pictures of the Sun Center damage, then shut off the feed and got up from his chair. "Ready," he said again, stepping to Jody's side. "Nice little rabbit trap, anyway," he commented.

"It *is* just a model," Jody reminded him, running her eyes over the device. It didn't actually look like much, she had to admit: a flat, rectangular tangle of mesh, thirty centimeters by fifteen, sitting in midair and supported by a pair of meter-long bars extending outward along each of the rectangle's long sides. One set of bars was currently resting on the end of the table, the other on Geoff's desk. Between each set of bars were a set of five slender crossbars with what looked like thin medicine bottles extending a few centimeters upward from their centers. To the side of the central rectangle was another rectangle, similarly sized, though the mesh in this one was neatly arranged instead of apparently tangled. "We'll have plenty of time to construct a proper one on the way to Caelian," she added.

"Assuming we ever get there," Freylan muttered.

"We will," Geoff promised. "So how's it work?"

"The whole thing gets buried under a couple of centimeters of dirt or leaves," Jody explained. "With a much deeper hole under the central section, of course. Little Rabbit Foo-Foo comes hopping along the trail—" she pulled out her comm and bounced it, rabbit-like, along the desk toward the arms and crossbars "—and comes upon a nice little morsel of food." She stopped at the first medicine bottle and nuzzled the comm against it. "Being a smart, hungry little bunny, she of course scarfs it right down."

"Question," Freylan said, half raising his hand. "How do we make sure that only Little Rabbit—what was it again?"

"Foo-Foo," Jody supplied.

Freylan frowned slightly, but apparently decided to take it in stride. "That only Little Rabbit Foo-Foo takes the bait?"

"Good question," Jody said. "We'll need to figure out how to tailor the bait to whatever animal we're after at the time. Hopefully, the settlers will be able to help us with that once we're there. Anyway, once Foo-Foo has taken the first bite, we keep her going the right direction by having the rest of the bait cups open up in sequence, once at a time, drawing her onto the main part of the trap." She bounced her comm along the bars, stopping briefly at each bait cup, and onto the main part of the trap.

And as she dropped the comm with a little extra force in the center of the rectangle, the entire structure collapsed, the tangle of mesh dropping down and resolving itself into the sides and bottom of a deep box. Simultaneously, the screen that had been sitting next to the box flipped over onto the top, forming a lid and sealing the comm inside. "And presto—one trapped test animal," Jody said, gesturing at the enclosed comm like a magician concluding her act.

"Very neat," Geoff said approvingly. "You come up with this yourself?"

"Hardly," Jody said. "The basic design's been around for centuries. My main contribution is here."

She pointed to the mesh on the sides and bottom of the cage. "Note the little cylindrical free-spinning tubes around each of the main mesh wires. That means that, instead of the animal just lying there, highly annoyed and using every claw and tooth it's got to try to tear through the mesh—"

"I get it," Freylan spoke up suddenly. "If you make the mesh wide enough and the hole deep enough, when it lands its legs will slide on the rollers and go straight through so that it ends up lying on the mesh on its belly."

"Exactly," Jody said. "For most of the animals we'll be looking at, that'll immediately put their claws out of action."

"And even if it manages to chew through the lid, it still won't be able to climb out," Geoff said. "*Very* neat."

"Thank you," Jody said. "And of course, the lifting bars let us pick the whole thing up like a sedan chair and trot it back to the lab without having to open the cage out in the open, risking those same aforementioned claws and teeth."

"Amen to that." Geoff grinned at Freylan. "See, buddy? Let that be a lesson to you. When you hire the best, you get the best."

"Thank you kindly," Jody said, inclining her head. And pretending to believe him.

But she knew better. Her ability with animal traps wasn't the reason Geoff had insisted on hiring her. Neither were her newly minted college degrees in animal physiology and management. No, Geoff had something else entirely in mind.

But it wouldn't do to bring it up. Not here. Not in front of courteous, earnest, naive Freylan. If this worked out, the three of them would be spending a good deal of time together on the hell world that was Caelian, and there was no point in revealing to him the full depths of his buddy's deviousness.

"So how long will it take you to build a full-sized one?" Geoff asked. "Wait a second—hold that thought," he interrupted himself, pulling out his comm. "This could be it." He clicked it open. "Hello?"

Listening to his end of the conversation with half an ear, Jody unfastened the lid on her trap and retrieved her comm. She put it away, then pushed the bottom and sides up again, fastening the bottom with the quick-release hooks that had held it in place until it was sprung.

"You really want to do this?" Freylan asked quietly at her side.

She frowned at him. "What do you mean?"

"Caelian," he said, his dark, earnest eyes boring into her face. "I know everyone calls it a hell world. But most of them just say that just because everyone else says it. They don't really know what they're talking about. But I do. My uncle spent eight months there a few years ago, and it nearly killed him."

"You and Geoff are going," Jody reminded him. "Assuming you get permission, that is." She nodded toward Geoff and his quiet conversation.

"Yeah, but Geoff and I are crazy," Freylan said, an uncertain smile briefly touching his lips. "You aren't. So why do you want to go with us?"

Jody looked over at Geoff, who was now pacing the room the way he always did in the midst of deep comm conversations. "There are just over three thousand Cobras on Aventine," she said. "Roughly one for every four hundred people. You know how many Cobras there are on Caelian?"

Freylan huffed. "Some ungodly number, probably."

"Seven hundred," Jody told him. "That's one for every *six* settlers. When people say the Cobra project is too expensive and that they want to shut it down, what they really mean is that *Caelian* is too expensive."

"I know," Freylan said heavily. "I also know you and your family have a long history with the Cobras."

"Never mind the history," Jody said shortly. "We need the Cobras, Freylan. The Trofts aren't our friends. We trade with them, and we have good diplomatic relationships with maybe three or four of the demesnes. But even those three or four aren't really our friends. And there are hundreds of demesnes out there."

"And there's Qasama," Freylan murmured.

Jody felt her throat tighten. Qasama. There was a lot of family history tied up in that world, too. Way too much history. "And there's Qasama," she agreed. "The point is that we can't afford to stop the Cobra project. Ever." She ran her fingertips gently over the stainless steel of her trap. "That's why we need to solve the problem of Caelian. If we can find a way to finally tame that world, it'll knock a lot of the props out from under the anti-Cobra argument. Some of the Caelian Cobras could be retasked, the world could be opened up for new colonization, and we could start pushing out the boundaries on Viminal and even here on Aventine. It's not the Cobras themselves the public doesn't like, it's the feeling that the whole program's become nothing but a sinkhole for everyone's hard-earned money—"

"Hey, hey—steady," Freylan said, holding up his hands in a gesture of surrender. "We're on your side, remember?"

Jody made a face. "Right. Sorry."

"That's okay," Freylan said, a little awkwardly. "Passion is good. That's what Geoff always says, anyway. Passion is why people do stuff like this."

Jody cocked an eyebrow at him. "You mean aside from the fame and fortune parts?"

His smile this time was a lot more relaxed and genuine. "Aside from that, sure," he agreed.

Across the room Geoff gave a sudden war whoop. "We're in!" he shouted, lifting his comm in triumph. "That was Governor Uy's office. The project's been approved. We're going to Caelian!"

"That's great," Freylan said, his eyes lighting up. "Jody—we're in."

"Yes, we are," Jody agreed. "Congratulations."

And hoped that her own smile looked as genuine as theirs.

CHAPTER THREE

Uncle Corwin had moved to his estate at the southern edge of Capitalia nearly thirty years ago, a week after his fifty-seventh birthday and less than two years after his political enemies had forced him out of his governorship. That loss had ended his political career, a life he'd led as long as Jin had been alive, and even after all these years she still couldn't think about that without feeling a twinge of guilt for her part in the whole thing.

Corwin didn't blame her, she knew. Never had, for that matter. But knowing that was only minor consolation.

The gate opened as she and Paul walked toward it. Either Corwin had set it on automatic or else someone inside was keeping close watch. "Did you ever get hold of Jody, by the way?" Jin asked as they passed the gate and started down the twinkle-lit walkway toward the dark, looming structure ahead.

"Yes, while you were showering," Paul said. "She doesn't know what this is about, either. But I do know she's been trying to talk Corwin into coming in on her side on this proposed Caelian trip of hers."

Jin grimaced. Caelian had been the third world settled by the Dominion colonists who had come here nearly a century ago, right after beachheads had been established on Aventine and Palatine. The first two worlds, despite occasional bumps along the way, had eventually become unqualified successes.

Caelian, unfortunately, hadn't.

The planet had a hundred different bitter-edged epithets among the Cobra Worlds' population, most of them variants on the words *money pit, home of damn fools,* or *hellhole.* Out of a high-water population of nearly nineteen thousand, only forty-five hundred still remained, all of them too stubborn or stupid to give up and move back to Aventine or to one of the two latest additions to the Worlds.

But though most Worlders had written off Caelian as a dead loss, not everyone had. Every year or two some group of young visionaries would surface with a new plan for dealing with the deadly plant and animal life that was so determined to choke mankind off their world. Jody's friends Geoff Boulton and Freylan Sonderby were merely the latest in that long parade of idealists. "If she thinks Uncle Corwin's going to help her visit Caelian, she's sorely underestimating his senility level," she said.

Paul shrugged. "Perhaps."

The estate's grounds were compact but well gardened, and Jin could smell the delicate scent of budding bablar trees as they walked toward the house. Some gardens of this sort included pools, fish ponds, even small waterfalls, additions Corwin hadn't bothered with.

So why then did he call it the Island?

No one in the family knew, but that hadn't kept them from speculating about it. Jin had always thought it was a reference to the ancient *no man is an island* aphorism, but had never been able to coax a yes or no out of her uncle. Jody's theory was that it was a reference to an old Earth classic book, while Lorne believed it to be a not-so-subtle jab at the five islands in the lake west of Capitalia and their rather snobbish inhabitants. Merrick, typically, hadn't bothered with the question, declaring that his great-uncle would tell them when he was good and ready.

Jin and Paul reached the house, to find Jody waiting for them just inside the main door. "Mom; Dad," she said in greeting. She was silhouetted against the hall light, but Jin's optical enhancers were able to pick out the tension lines in her daughter's face. "I hear you had a bad day."

"It could get worse," Jin warned her, "depending on what's happening with your project."

"I showed Geoff and Freylan my trap design today," Jody said. "They liked it."

"What about your application?"

Jody shrugged. "You know governments. These things take time."

"But Uy hasn't denied it?" Jin persisted. She'd been hoping against hope that Caelian's governor would shut down the project at his end.

"Sorry," Jody said.

"I think," Paul put in wryly, "the day's just gotten worse."

"It won't be that bad, Mom," Jody insisted. "We really *do* know what we're doing."

"Do you?" Jin countered. "Do you really?"

"Yes, we do," Jody said. Her voice was low and earnest, matured and reasoned.

And grown-up. Despite all her emotional expectations to the contrary, Jin couldn't ignore the fact that her little girl had grown up.

"I imagine we'll be discussing it further tonight," Paul said. If he was feeling the same surge of emotion, Jin thought resentfully, he was hiding it well. "Meanwhile, you have your mother and father standing out in the cold Aventinian evening air."

"It's not *that* cold," Jody said, a hint of her little-girl dry humor peeking out through the adult she'd become. Nevertheless, she stepped aside out of the doorway. "Come on in—dinner should be ready soon."

"Who's cooking?" Jin asked. "Uncle Corwin, or Aunt Thena?"

"Merrick, actually," Jody said. "He said that as long as he'd called this dinner, it was his responsibility to feed all of us."

"As long as it's Merrick and not Lorne," Paul murmured.

"Trust me," Jody promised. "*No* one wants the day to get *that* bad."

When Merrick had first become a Cobra seven years ago, Jin remembered fondly, he'd sworn the whole family to secrecy about his culinary skills. Not because he'd been afraid the other Cobras would rib him about it, but because he'd been on enough field maneuvers during training to fear that he might be designated official unit cook and chained to the stove while the others dealt with the real Cobra work. So far, he'd managed to keep his secret.

The dinner conversation was as pleasant as the food. Jody, who'd always been good at taking hints, avoided any mention of Caelian, instead focusing her end of the conversation on the last few remaining details of her upcoming graduation ceremony. Lorne, after once again confirming that his parents had emerged from the Sun Center trouble mostly unscathed, shifted his part to news of the expansion provinces and the various social and business doings out in those hinterlands, peppering each story with the dry humor he shared with his younger sister.

Merrick himself, Jin noticed, was being especially quiet tonight, carefully cutting precise pieces from his cacciatore and adding little to the table talk. At the head of the table, Corwin and Thena were equally restrained.

Finally, the meal was over. "Excellent, Merrick, as always," Corwin complimented the young man as the group stacked the dishes together. "A man who can cook will always be surrounded by friends."

"Thank you, Uncle Corwin," Merrick said gravely. "Coming from someone who gets to sample Aunt Thena's cooking on a regular basis, I count such praise very highly indeed."

"Diplomatic as always," Thena said with a smile. "Do bear in mind, though, that your uncle Corwin survived on his own cooking longer than he has on mine."

"*Survived* being the operative word," Corwin said, reaching over to take his wife's hand.

Jin watched them, feeling another twinge of guilt. Uncle Corwin hadn't married Thena until his fall from power, and while Jin couldn't see anything but good having come from their marriage, she still couldn't help wondering if Corwin saw the life of a husband and father as something of a consolation prize.

Especially now that their son Rave was himself grown and out of his parents' house. All Corwin had left was his wife, his home, and his memories.

"So cooking's the secret, huh?" Lorne put in. "I've always thought the best way to keep friends around you was to owe everyone money."

"Whatever works for you," Merrick said equably. "Speaking of debts, I did all the cooking. That means it's up to you two to go load the dishwasher."

"That seems fair," Corwin agreed. "Go ahead—we'll wait on dessert for you."

"Not a chance," Jody said, folding her arms across her chest. "I know this trick, and we're not falling for it. Whatever you and Merrick have cooking, Lorne and I are going to be in on it."

"Jody, that's no way to talk to your great-uncle," Paul warned.

"It is when he's trying to send us to the children's table," Jody countered. "In case some of you haven't noticed, the baby of the family is twenty-one now. We're full-fledged members of this family now."

"Which isn't to say there aren't things that concern one member and not another," Jin said.

"It's all right, Jin," Corwin said. "She and Lorne can stay."

"I respectfully disagree, Uncle Corwin," Merrick said firmly. "Not because we're trying to hide anything from you," he added, looking back at his brother and sister, "but because we're trying to protect you."

"I'm sure we both appreciate the thought," Lorne said. "But as a twenty-four-year-old, I sort of resent the implication that I need protecting." He looked over at his great uncle. "As a twenty-four-year-old Cobra, I *definitely* resent the implication."

"Resent it all you want," Merrick said. "We're not talking about jaywalking or disturbing the peace here."

"What *are* we talking about?" Lorne countered.

"Treason," Merrick said flatly.

Lorne seemed to draw back in his seat. "What?" he asked, his voice suddenly subdued.

"You heard me," Merrick said. "What we're talking about tonight is borderline treason."

"Only *borderline*?" Jody said. "Well, that's not so bad."

Merrick turned toward her—"It's all right, Merrick," Corwin said again. "Go ahead—give your mother the letter."

For a moment Merrick hesitated. Then, with a sigh, he reached into the inner pocket of his jacket. "I was unloading Jody's azaleas at the side of the house today when a courier came to the door," he said, pulling out a long, thin envelope. "He marched up to me and said, 'Cobra Broom?' I of course said yes, and he handed me this. I'm afraid I've already opened and read it." He held out the envelope toward his mother.

"Tell her the rest," Corwin murmured.

Merrick's lips compressed briefly. "The courier," he said, "was a Troft."

Jin froze, her fingers a millimeter from the envelope. "A *Troft*?"

Merrick nodded. "A Tlossie, I think. Like I said, I thought it was for me, so I opened it. Three minutes later, I was on the comm to Uncle Corwin."

Jin shot a look at Corwin as she took the envelope from her son. She opened it and pulled out the single slip of paper inside.

The note was short, consisting of just two handwritten lines in precise Qasaman script:

To the Demon Warrior Jasmine Jin Moreau:

Urgent you return at once to Qasama. Crisis situation requires your personal attention.

There was no signature.

"What is it?" Lorne asked.

"Sort of a party invitation," Jin murmured, handing the note to Paul.

"It's *what*?" Lorne demanded. He half stood, reaching across the table and trying to snatch the note from his father's hand.

Without even looking in his direction Paul twitched the paper out of the other's reach, his forehead wrinkling as he read the note. Lorne stayed where he was, his hand outstretched, and after a moment his father handed it across to him. "Interesting," Paul said thoughtfully as Jody leaned close to Lorne to read over his shoulder. "I wonder how he got it to the Tlossies."

"How who got it to them?" Lorne asked, frowning at the note the same way his father had. "Who's it from?"

"Daulo Sammon, I assume," Paul said, cocking his head at Jin. "That *is* his handwriting, isn't it?"

"Actually, I don't know," Jin said, struggling to keep her mind focused as memories three decades old came flooding back. Daulo Sammon, Obolo Nardin and his treacherous Mangus plot, the earnest but deadly young Shahni agent Miron Akim—

"What do you mean, you don't know?" Lorne asked.

With an effort, Jin pushed back the memories. "The only thing I ever saw him write was an order at the family mines," she explained. "It was written very quickly, on a pad balanced on his arm in a blustery wind. I never saw what his writing looked like when he was being careful."

"On the other hand, who else down there ever knew your full name?" Jody pointed out. "It has to be Daulo, doesn't it?"

"There were a few others who knew my name," Jin told her. "But I doubt any of them would want to see me again."

"Except maybe for revenge," Merrick said.

"Thirty-two years later?" Jin shook her head. "Highly unlikely."

"But not impossible?"

Jin grimaced. "No."

"Let's try it from the other direction," Corwin suggested. "Any idea what the crisis situation might be that the note mentions?"

Jin snorted. "On *Qasama*? It could be any of a hundred things."

"Give us a couple of possibilities," Paul said.

"Well, there was a strong tension between the cities and the villages when I was there," Jin said. "Largely because the cities had mostly gotten rid of their mojos while the villages still held onto some of theirs."

"Using the birds as bodyguards?" Merrick asked.

"Partly that, and partly as added protection against the krisjaws and spine leopards," Jin said.

"Though if the plan worked, I would assume the mojos will

have deserted even the villagers by now," Corwin reminded her. "And of course, once the local spine leopards all have them as symbionts, the predator attacks should also stop, making mojo bodyguards unnecessary."

"Lot of *if* and *should* in there," Lorne warned.

Corwin shrugged uncomfortably. "Life is uncertain," he conceded.

"Actually, I think the shift was already starting," Jin said. "But even if you write the mojos out of the equation it doesn't necessarily follow that the cities and villages will have started getting along."

"Witness the tension between our own cities and expansion regions," Merrick murmured.

"Exactly," Jin said. "And feelings and memories run a lot deeper on Qasama than they do here."

"What other possibilities for trouble might there be?" Paul asked.

"Like I said, it could be any number of things," Jin said. "Obolo Nardin's effort to subvert the Shahni with his Mangus Project might have had a resurgence somewhere. Some Troft demesne might be poking around Qasaman internal affairs again. Or someone might have been inspired by Nardin and be trying his own plan for revolt or subversion."

"So far, none of this sounds like a problem they'd want your help with," Lorne pointed out.

"Except maybe the Troft thing," Jody said. "The Qasamans can't know nearly as much about the ins and outs of Troft culture and politics as we do."

"Not necessarily," Jin said. "They've obviously made contact with at least the Tlossies." She gestured toward the paper Lorne was still holding. "Or at least Daulo has. And Qasamans learn *very* quickly."

"Yes, let's talk about the Tlossies for a minute," Paul said. "Merrick, did this courier say anything about how he'd obtained this note?"

"Not a word," Merrick said. "I had the impression he had no idea what the envelope was, that he'd simply been hired or ordered to deliver it. He did give me a card with contact information, but it wasn't for him personally."

"How do you know?" Lorne asked.

"The status curlies around the card's border didn't match those on his abdomen sash," Merrick explained. "Not nearly as elaborate, either, which means the card is from someone considerably higher in social rank."

"I spent an hour earlier trying to match the curlies to known Tlossie traders, but the search came up dry," Corwin added. "Whoever the card's from, he's apparently no one who's done serious business here."

"Have you tried contacting him?" Jody asked.

Merrick shook his head. "I assumed that whether or not we went that far would be up to Mom."

A brief silence settled over the room. Jin stared at the note lying beside Lorne's dessert fork, acutely aware of the precarious ledge she was now standing on.

The ledge *all* of them were standing on. Merrick's earlier warning that they were edging onto treason hadn't been hyperbole—the Cobra Worlds Council had imposed a strict interdiction on travel to Qasama, and they meant it. Even getting on a starship with intent to travel there could conceivably land Jin a multiyear prison term.

And the knowledge that she was planning such a trip could likewise land everyone in this room in that same prison on conspiracy charges.

But the legality of the matter wasn't really the question. The question was what was the right thing to do.

Qasama...

They were still waiting for her, she realized suddenly. "Well, it can't hurt to ask," she said, motioning to Merrick as she pulled out her comm. He hesitated, then slid a small business-sized card from his pocket and handed it to her. Jin glanced at the number and punched it in.

It was answered on the fifth ring. [The evening, it is good, Jasmine Moreau Broom,] a recorded Troft voice said, the alien cattertalk as crisp and precise in its way as the Qasaman handwriting on the brief note. [The voyage, if you intend to make it, will depart from Pindar three days from the delivery time of the package. All that is necessary, it will be provided.]

There was a click, and the connection was broken. "Well?" Paul asked as Jin closed the comm again.

"It was a recording," she said. "I'm to leave from Pindar in three days, at—Merrick, what time was the note delivered?"

"Just after two."

"Three days from now at two o'clock," Jin said. "He says he'll provide everything I need, which I assume will include proper Qasaman clothing and accessories."

"Sounds good," Lorne said briskly. Briskly, but with an undertone of tension beneath the words. "Three days should give me enough time to get myself on the off-duty roster. I'll collect my stuff—"

"Whoa, whoa," Jin interrupted. "The invitation was for *me*."

"So?" Lorne countered.

"So I'm going alone," Jin said firmly.

"You most certainly are not," Paul said, just as firmly. "But you *are* right about Lorne not going with you. We can—"

"You're not going, either," Jin said, forcing herself to look into her husband's eyes.

Haunted eyes. Worried eyes. Loving eyes. "Jin—" he began.

"No," Jin insisted. "You don't know the Qasamans, Paul. One Cobra sneaking onto their world is bad enough. Two of them will be interpreted as an invasion."

"So we make sure they don't see anything that jumps them to that conclusion," Paul countered. "I can stay in the background, or be your loyal servant, or whatever you need."

Jin braced herself. "What I need," she said as gently as she could, "is for you to be willing to stay behind. I have to do this alone. I really do."

"What is this, mass insanity?" Lorne demanded. "Jody's going to Caelian, you're going to Qasama—"

"*Caelian?*" Jin cut him off.

"Lorne!" Jody bit out, her stunned expression edging rapidly toward fury.

Lorne winced. "Sorry," he apologized.

"Never mind sorry," Jin said sternly, her stomach suddenly doing flip-turns inside her. "Jody?"

"I was going to tell you after dinner, Mom," Jody said, her expression managing to be repentant and stubborn at the same time.

"We got the call this afternoon from Governor Uy's office. We're leaving on the *Freedom's Fire* in—" she grimaced "—in three days."

"From Capitalia?" Paul asked.

"Yes," Jody said. "But maybe I can get the time changed."

"Don't try," Jin said, feeling the heavy weight of irony settling across her shoulders. The same time Jin would be leaving Aventine... only they'd be leaving from spaceports a thousand kilometers apart. The universe wasn't even going to let her say a proper dock-side farewell to her daughter. "They'd only want to know why, and we can't afford anyone asking awkward questions."

"I'm sorry, Mom," Jody said. "I know you didn't want this."

"No, I didn't," Jin said quietly. "But I doubt your grandfather really wanted me going to Qasama, either. Sometimes we just have to face the unpleasant fact that our children do, in fact, grow up."

She looked at Corwin, wondering if he would point out the obvious difference in their situations: that Jin's father, at least, had sent her off to Qasama with a group of other Cobras.

But her uncle remained silent, and after a couple of seconds she turned back to Lorne. "Your cue, Lorne," she invited.

"My what?" he asked, frowning.

"A minute ago you were all set to come to Qasama with me," she reminded him. "Time to offer to accompany your sister to Caelian instead."

"Go for it, kiddo, because *I'm* sure not going," Merrick spoke up before Lorne could answer. "Capitalia patroller duty may not be as glamorous as hunting spine leopards, but my commandant takes our duty rosters very seriously."

"Well—okay, sure," Lorne said, fumbling a bit. "Jody—"

"Sorry, Lorne, but you're not going to Caelian, either," Paul spoke up. "You have a duty to the citizens of the expansion region."

Jin turned to her husband in disbelief. "Paul—"

"Luckily," Paul continued, looking over at his daughter, "I just happen to have an opening in my own calendar."

Jin felt her lower jaw drop open, her planned protest strangling into silence in her throat. "Paul, you are *not* going to Caelian," she insisted.

"Why not?" Paul countered calmly. "No, let me put it more strongly: I'm not going to sit home and water the azaleas while my wife and daughter travel to the two most dangerous places in the known galaxy. If I'm not going to Qasama with you, I'm going to Caelian with Jody."

Jin stared at him, momentarily at an uncharacteristic loss for words. And yet, as the emotional fogbank cleared away, she realized he was right. Even at fifty-three, with arthritis and anemia starting to make themselves felt, Paul was still a Cobra. Moreover, he had the maturity and experience and coolheadedness that Lorne still lacked. There could be no better protection for Jin's little girl.

She grimaced. No, not her little girl. Her young lady.

She looked at her two sons in turn. Lorne seemed midway between annoyed and frustrated, no doubt as a result of the ground being cut out from under him twice in two minutes. Merrick merely looked his usual stolid self, with no hint of embarrassment or shame at how quickly he'd refused to even consider going to Caelian with his sister.

Or maybe he'd simply realized before the rest of them that his father was heading in that direction and had made certain he wouldn't be standing in the elder Broom's way. "I guess it's settled, then," Jin said, forcing some false heartiness into her voice. "Paul and Jody will go to Caelian, I'll head to Qasama, and Lorne and Merrick will hold down the fort here."

"And try to maintain the illusion that you're still on Aventine," Merrick put in.

Jin frowned. She hadn't thought about that part of it. "Yes, good point. Any ideas on how we do that?"

"One or two," Merrick said. "But we can work on that later." He raised his eyebrows at Corwin. "After dessert, perhaps?" he prompted.

"That is the direction we were headed, wasn't it?" Corwin agreed. "Perhaps, *now,* Lorne and Jody, you'll be kind enough to clear the table for us?"

"Sure," Jody said as they both obediently pushed their chairs back from the table and started collecting the dishes.

"So is that it for the evening's surprises?" Paul asked, looking at Corwin.

Corwin cocked an eyebrow. "Isn't that enough for one night?"

"Very much so," Paul said dryly. Reaching under the table, he took Jin's hand in his. "I just wanted to make sure. *And* to make sure that everyone had a say."

"Everyone who wanted a say has had one," Corwin assured him. "For now."

The group was midway through dessert, and the conversation had shifted to Jody's plans for the Caelian study, when Jin suddenly realized that Aunt Thena hadn't said a single word throughout the entire debate.

The next three days went by quickly. Far too quickly.

The Troft recording had said that everything Jin needed would be supplied aboard ship. But she couldn't and wouldn't simply assume the Trofts knew what a proper infiltrator needed to do her job.

On the other hand, she could hardly go to the hardware store and ask the clerk to assemble a standard-issue commando backpack for her, either. Fortunately, the standard Cobra survival pack was a good place to start, and she knew its contents by heart. She bought enough supplies to stock two such packs, making sure to shop in a half dozen different stores across the city so as to muddy the backtrail a bit. Once those were prepared, she added a few other odds and ends as they occurred to her, and then decided she was as ready as she was going to be.

She spent the rest of the time she had left with her family. Those hours went by even faster.

The sky was beginning to cloud up as she stepped off the intercity transport and headed on foot toward the long, sleek Troft freighter squatting on its pad across the Pindar landing field. She'd done everything she could; had given Paul and Jody their final hugs earlier that morning, and then had called from the transport for a last good-bye as her husband and daughter watched Jody's two colleagues load the last bits of gear aboard the *Freedom's Fire*. But the farewells had been sorely inadequate for the occasion, and Jin could feel her mood filling with its own dark clouds as she walked wearily toward the ship.

The danger she had long ago accepted. The loneliness she hadn't counted on.

"Carry your bags, ma'am?"

She spun around, feeling her eyes widen with shock. Merrick was back there, smiling solemnly as he strode toward her, a survival pack of his own settled across his shoulders. "What are *you* doing here?" she demanded.

"What do you think?" he countered, stopping beside her and getting a grip on the straps of one of his mother's packs. "I'm coming with you."

"You most certainly are *not*," she insisted, trying to snatch her pack away from him. It was a waste of effort—his servos were every bit as strong as hers were. "Now get out of here and back to Capitalia before someone sees you."

Merrick shook his head. "Sorry," he said. "I'm on temporary detached duty, assigned to watch over one of the legendary heroes of the Cobra Worlds."

"What legendary hero?" Jin asked, thoroughly confused now.

"You, of course," Merrick said. "In case you hadn't noticed, you've gone into a tailspin of depression over Jody and Dad's plan to go to Caelian. Lorne and I have been very worried about you, especially when you announced you were going out to the wilderness north of Pindar to, quote, think things over."

"So what, I'm a strap-stretcher case now?" Jin demanded, not sure whether she was more outraged or embarrassed by the story her sons had concocted.

"Oh, I'm sure you'll pull out of it after a while," Merrick said. "The point is that I'm on indefinite leave, and we're off in the wilderness all alone where no one's likely to notice us."

"Brilliant," Jin growled. "But your poor, aged mother is perfectly capable of, quote, thinking things over on her own."

Merrick took a deep breath. "Mom, remember back at the Island three days ago, and the talk Uncle Corwin and Aunt Thena had with you after dinner?"

Jin grimaced. Like she would ever forget. Corwin had grilled her for nearly an hour about her motives for wanting to go to Qasama, trying to get her to admit that she was doing it solely to vindicate him. Which she wasn't. "I remember it very well," she said. "And how exactly do *you* know about it? I thought you were all off in the billiards room at the time."

"I know because Uncle Corwin, Aunt Thena, and I planned the talk long before you and the rest showed up, of course." A brief flicker of grim amusement touched his eyes. "When did you think Dad, Lorne, Jody, and I cooked up the rest of this scheme? The only safe time to do it was while you were busy defending your honor."

"Only you'd already made up your mind about this, hadn't you?" Jin asked, thinking back to that evening. "That's why you were so quick to take yourself off Jody's escort list."

"Uncle Corwin and I had already run the logic," Merrick said. "Dad was too old to go with you—he's got the same health limitations you do. Lorne is too young, plus he really *is* needed in the expansion regions. That leaves me."

"Or it leaves me going by myself," Jin said. "Or don't you think I can handle it?"

Merrick sighed. "If you insist. No, we *don't* think you can handle it. Not if worst comes to worst."

"Because I might be going with the wrong motives?"

"Because you're fifty-two years old," Merrick said bluntly. "You're not exactly in prime fighting condition anymore, you know."

"Bring me a couple of spine leopards, kiddo, and I'll show you what condition I'm in," Jin retorted. "Besides, the idea is to avoid *any* fighting."

"Amen," Merrick said fervently. "But if it *does* come down to a fight, you know as well as I do that two Cobras will always have a better chance than one."

"Unless it was the presence of that second Cobra that precipitated the fight in the first place," Jin said. "As long as we're remembering conversations, do you remember *that* one?"

"Certainly," Merrick said. "But as I recall, the Qasamans are very family-oriented, and I as your son am the kind of close blood relation that even Dad can't match. The Qasamans will respect that."

He was right, Jin had to admit. Even if they discovered he was a Cobra, they would more likely interpret his role as that of his mother's protector than as an invader.

And as she gazed at the determination in her son's eyes, she realized suddenly that she really *didn't* want to do this alone. "There's no chance I can talk you out of it, is there?" she asked, just to be sure.

"None," he said in a voice that left no room for argument.

"Then let's do it," she said, turning toward the ship. She paused and let go of the bag he was still holding. "And yes, you *may* carry my bag."

Besides, this was just a friendly visit between old acquaintances, she reminded herself. There wouldn't be any fighting. Surely there wouldn't.

CHAPTER FOUR

The last time Jin had traveled to Qasama, the ship had been running on a fuel-conserving course and had taken two weeks. She was therefore somewhat surprised when, barely five days into the trip, the Troft captain announced that they would be arriving at Qasama within the next twelve hours. Even granting three decades' worth of advances in starship efficiency and the fact that this was a modern Troft freighter instead of the older models the aliens typically foisted off on the Worlds, the captain clearly wasn't all that concerned about his transportation costs. Either he had an important schedule to keep, or else the crisis on Qasama was as critical as the mysterious note had made it sound.

Not that Jin was able to find out which. The captain and crew were polite enough, as befit the long trading history the Tlos'khin'fahi demesne had with the Worlds. But the veneer of hospitality had a steel wall behind it, and five days' worth of gentle probing and wheedling had gained Jin exactly nothing in the way of new information. Merrick, who had inherited his father's calmer and more diplomatic wheedling approach, came up equally dry.

Jin had also hoped the captain might have further information on the logistics of the operation, particularly some advice on how to sneak into Daulo Sammon's town of Milika without attracting unwelcome attention. But the captain assured her he'd been given nothing but the original note, a small collection of old-smelling Qasaman clothing, and an easterly approach vector that would hopefully slip his passengers into the forest west of Milika without tripping whatever radar coverage the Qasamans had set up to guard the Great Arc region where most of their people lived.

Which meant that as far as actual penetration of the Qasaman populace was concerned, Jin and Merrick were on their own.

They made a final check of their gear, including the Qasaman clothing, and loaded it aboard the freighter's shuttle. Designed as it was for cargo transport, the shuttle had no actual passenger seating. But the cockpit was designed for a crew of four, and the captain assured them that the engineering and supercargo stations could be left open for a trip this short.

They dropped over the nighttime side of the planet, the freighter pulling up and away as the Troft pilot sent the shuttle skittering toward the dark mass below. Five minutes into the flight they hit the first noticeable wisps of upper atmosphere, and the shuttle began to shiver, then tremble, then shake as the air around them grew steadily more dense.

Jin spent the trip staring at the mass rushing up toward them and consciously forcing herself not to dig her fingers into her seat's upholstery. Occasionally, she sent a furtive glance at Merrick, noting with a small nugget of wry resentment that her son showed no hint of the tension Jin herself was feeling. The buffeting hit a teeth-chattering peak, then began to subside again as the shuttle slowed to subsonic speeds. The ground below remained a mostly featureless inky black, but as they headed eastward toward the western arm of the Great Arc Jin began spotting little clusters of lights nestled among the forests that dominated the western part of the planet's inhabited regions. She watched the lights as they went slowly past, her muscles taut as she waited for a repeat of the attack that had killed her first team.

But no attack came. An hour after leaving the freighter, they touched down in a small clearing at the edge of their planned landing zone.

Jin and Merrick and their gear were at the edge of the clearing in ninety seconds flat. Thirty seconds after that, the shuttle was back in the air, clawing for altitude. Ten seconds more and the red glow from its gravity lifts had vanished over the treetops.

Hopefully, the captain's information about this area being outside any likely radar coverage had been correct. If not, Jin and Merrick would be getting some company very soon.

But for now, at least, they were alone, and Jin took a moment to stand beneath the tree canopy, the sounds and scents of Qasama whispering through her senses and echoing back from her memory. Suddenly, the last thirty-two years of her life seemed to vanish. She was once again the young Cobra all alone on a distant and hostile world...

"Spine leopard at three o'clock," Merrick murmured from beside her.

As quickly as they'd gone, the lost years came crashing back onto Jin's shoulders. Activating her optical enhancers' light-amplifiers, she looked to her right.

The spine leopard was standing motionless in the shadows, its eyes staring at the two rash humans who had intruded on its territory. The quills on its forelegs were quivering as the creature apparently mulled over whether or not this would be a good time for lunch.

"So that's a mojo," Merrick murmured.

Jin shifted her gaze from the spine leopard's forelegs to the silver-blue hawk-like bird perched on the spine leopard's back behind its head. The mojo, too, was watching the humans, gazing at them with a disconcerting alertness and perception that Jin had never quite gotten used to. "That it is," she confirmed. "The question is, has he figured out that we're not someone he and his companion want to mess with?"

"Maybe we can help him out a little," Merrick suggested. "Watch your eyes."

Jin switched from light-amp to infrared, watching as the images of the spine leopard and mojo shifted from pale green to flowing shades of red and orange. "Go."

Lifting his right hand, Merrick fired a brief low-level burst from his fingertip laser into the tree trunk beside him.

The spine leopard dropped into a crouch, its quills flaring outward. But the mojo showed no such agitation, merely fluttering its wings as it got a fresh grip on the predator's back. For perhaps half a second both of them continued to gaze at the humans. Then, with a shake of its head, the spine leopard straightened out of its crouch, its quills resettling themselves along his forelegs. It turned away, and without a backward glance strode back into the forest.

"Smart bird," Merrick commented.

"Luckily for us," Jin agreed, the warm scent of burned wood from her son's laser shot drifting across her nose. And luckily for the animals, too, she added silently. The spine leopard and mojo made up a symbiotic pair, with the bird functioning as the primary decision-maker of the team. On its own, the spine leopard would probably have leaped blindly to the attack and been dead by now.

Once, the mojos had served a similar purpose for the humans of Qasama, calming natural aggression with guidance so subtle that the inhabitants had never recognized it for what it was. Jin's own father, grandfather, and uncles had helped create the scheme for seeding Qasama with spine leopards, hoping that the mojos would be lured away from their human hosts and onto the more useful—from the mojos' point of view—predators.

Unfortunately, the Qasamans hadn't seen it that way. The introduction of new and deadly predators onto their world had driven much of the hatred they felt toward the Cobra Worlds.

Distantly, Jin wondered if the people here would ever truly understand that the plan had been for their ultimate good. Or whether such understanding would make any difference.

"It's about thirty kilometers east, right?" Merrick asked.

"East by north," Jin said, shaking the thoughts away. Standing in the middle of the Qasaman forest at night was hardly the time and place for deep philosophical contemplations. Shifting back to light-amp, she checked her compass. "That way," she added, pointing.

"Assuming, of course, Daulo Sammon is still living in Milika," Merrick warned as he adjusted his pack across his shoulders.

"He will be," Jin assured him. "Qasaman families stick very close to their hereditary land."

"Let's get to it, then," Merrick said.

Jin frowned at him. His expression had the same oddness she'd just heard in his voice. "Something wrong?" she asked.

"No, nothing." Merrick nodded in the direction the spine leopard and mojo had gone. "I was just thinking that Qasaman birds seem to understand the concept of deterrence better than some of our own politicians."

"No argument there," Jin agreed sourly. "But then, mojos don't have political agendas muddying their thinking. All they care about is survival." She took a deep breath. "Which is something you and I should also keep in mind. Quietly, now. And from this point on, we speak only Qasaman."

The trip wasn't nearly as difficult as Jin had expected. There were plenty of natural hazards along the way, with the complete range of tripping vines, thorn bushes, and leaf-covered roots that a healthy forest had to offer. But their optical enhancers gave them fair warning of most of the pitfalls, and even when the forest did manage to trip one of them their bone laminae and strengthened ligaments protected them from sprained ankles or worse.

More interesting to Jin was the fact that the only animals that gave them any trouble along the way were the six-limbed monkey-like baelcra, the gliding-lizard monota, and a few varieties of annoying insects. They saw a handful of spine leopards and a couple of the native krisjaws, but those larger, more deadly predators merely watched the two humans go past without interfering with them.

But then, none of the baelcra had mojos watching over their best interests. All of the spine leopards and krisjaws did.

Jin and the Troft captain had worked out the landing place and time to give them about six hours of darkness in which to cover the thirty kilometers to Daulo's village. With the lack of serious predator problems, they made it in just over five, emerging beside the main road leading to the village's high wall and closed gate. The gate itself wasn't visible from their exit point, but a bit of the wall could be seen about half a kilometer away through the trees around the next curve in the road.

It would have been convenient if they could simply march up to the gates and knock. But that was out of the question. The last time Jin had been here few people traveled the Qasaman forest at night, and none of them outside of sturdy vehicles. That might have changed in the past three decades, but it wasn't a risk she wanted to take.

Instead, she and Merrick retreated fifty meters back into the forest and settled in to grab a few hours' rest, each taking a turn on watch.

It was midmorning when Jin decided it was time. Her enhanced hearing could pick up the faint sounds of activity from Milika's direction, and it took no enhancement at all to hear the vehicles passing along the nearby road. She and Merrick cleaned themselves up as best they could, then changed into their Qasaman clothing. Their half-empty packs went into a shallow hole that Merrick had spent an hour of his time on watch digging, which they then covered with a generous helping of dirt and dead leaves.

And with that, the final stage of their journey was before them. "Remember that men are very much the dominant gender here," Jin reminded her son as she gave his outfit a final check. "Naturally, you'll show respect to me as your mother, but you're the one who'll approach other citizens, who'll ask all the questions, and who'll make all the decisions. And don't forget the sign of respect."

"I won't," Merrick said, and Jin winced a little at the slightly strained patience in his voice. They'd only been over this a million times on the transport, but he was far too polite to remind her of that. "I make the sign first to superiors, and inferiors make it first to me." He touched his bunched fingertips to his forehead in demonstration.

"And you can assume that most of the people in there will be our superiors," Jin said. She paused, searching for anything she might have missed. But nothing came to mind, at least nothing she hadn't already told him another million times already. "Okay," she said, making sure the pouch of wild *charko* leaves she'd picked during an hour of her watch was securely tied to her sash. "We left early this morning to get *charko* leaves for a stew I'm making, we had a little trouble finding a good patch, and we're only just now getting back to town. Got it?"

"Yes, Mother," Merrick said, as calm and patient as ever.

"Right." Jin took a deep breath. "Okay. Let's do it."

With the aid of their optical enhancers, the trip through the predawn had been relatively easy. In broad daylight, it was even easier. Still, Jin approached the edge of the tree line cautiously, waiting for a momentary lull in the road's vehicular traffic before she and Merrick stepped out of the woods and headed at a brisk walk toward Milika.

The last time Jin had been here, Milika's gates had stood open throughout the daylight hours, with a pair of armed guards on duty in case some krisjaw or spine leopard was foolish enough to try to attack that many people at once. That part of village life, at least, hadn't changed, she saw as she and Merrick rounded the last curve in the road and came within sight of the gates.

Still, the guards did look more relaxed than they had in days gone by. Apparently, rogue predators weren't nearly the problem they'd once been.

There was more traffic on the road now than there had been thirty years ago, too. A large number of vehicles were on the move, some of them heading down the road she and Merrick were using, with a somewhat larger number making a hard right turn just outside the wall onto a road that hadn't been there before.

As for pedestrians, the village beyond the wall was teeming with them, striding along about their business, browsing the small shop stands near the gate, or engaged in animated conversations with their fellow citizens. Clearly, Milika was prospering.

Jin keyed in her optical enhancers' telescopic capability as they approached, paying particular attention to the pedestrians' clothing. To her relief, it all seemed reasonably similar in style to the outfits she and Merrick were wearing. That had been one of her major concerns, that the Trofts might have brought them clothing that was so out-of-date it would instantly finger them as foreigners.

Keying off her opticals, she picked up her pace a little. All was as well as could be expected, certainly as well as she could make it. The goal now was to get to Daulo's house and out of the public eye before she or Merrick made some dangerous social blunder.

She had keyed her audio enhancers on low-power, listening to the nearest conversations to remind herself of the region's accent, when she heard a sudden catch in Merrick's breath. "Mom—one o'clock," he murmured. "Those two men in gray and blue."

Jin shifted her gaze and audio enhancers in the indicated direction. The two men seemed to have just started an animated conversation about animal pelts. "What about them?" she asked.

"Just watch," Merrick said, his voice dark. "There—that other one coming toward them. Watch him." The newcomer stepped up to the other two, smiled, and lifted his right hand to make the sign of respect.

Only it wasn't the same sign Jin had learned thirty years ago, the one she'd just coached Merrick on. Instead of touching bunched fingertips to forehead, the newcomer touched only his first two fingertips to his forehead and then touched his lips.

And the two other men answered, not with two fingers, but with *three* fingers to foreheads and lips.

The Qasamans had changed their mark of respect.

Jin shot another look around the people beyond the wall, a jolt of sudden panic running through her. She'd expected clothing styles to have changed over the years, and had been relieved that she and Merrick had the right versions. It had never even occurred to her that something so basic as the mark of respect might similarly have been modified.

And if the mark of respect had changed so drastically, what else might have changed along with it?

She didn't know. What she *did* know was that she and Merrick were in big trouble. There were new rules to Qasaman social interaction, and neither of them had the faintest idea what those rules were.

Merrick had obviously tracked the same logic. "Not good," he murmured.

"Extremely not good," Jin agreed tightly, focusing her attention back on the gate area. A few steps behind the two armed guards she'd already noted were four more men, two on either side, who she'd originally dismissed as common loiterers.

But now that she was concentrating on them, she realized their faces were too alert for that, their eyes lingering just a little too long on each passing vehicle as it entered the village.

Milika wasn't the haven she'd expected it to be. Milika was a trap.

And she and Merrick were walking right into it.

"We have a plan?" Merrick asked.

"Working on it," Jin gritted out, forcing herself to keep walking. One of the four non-obvious guards had spotted the two incoming pedestrians and was watching them closely. The last thing she and Merrick could afford was a guilty-looking break in their stride. "You want to try running?" she asked her son.

"To where?"

"Exactly," Jin agreed. "Fighting is out, too—way too many people around."

Merrick huffed a thoughtful breath. "So we bluff?"

"We bluff," Jin confirmed reluctantly. "Okay. Best guess, and it's only a guess, is that the number of fingers used indicates rank. I just wish I knew whether two fingers is the minimum or whether it goes all the way down to one."

"Or if women use different signs entirely," Merrick added.

Jin winced. Unfortunately, that was a distinct possibility. "Could be," she conceded. "Haven't got a clue what it would be, though."

"Well, all we can do is try," Merrick said calmly. "Let's both stick with the two-finger version. If they call us on it, maybe we can convince them we're social idiots who grew up in a barn."

Not likely, Jin thought grimly. But at the moment she didn't have anything better to offer. "Okay," she said. "But if it blows up—if they want to search us or even toss us into holding—just go along with them. Whatever happens, do *not* do anything to show who you really are."

"Understood," Merrick said. "And don't *you* forget to be a nice, quiet, submissive little woman."

Jin grimaced. Sticking with that role had been one of the toughest parts of her previous visit here. This time, with her pride and ego presumably tempered by age and maturity, maybe it would be easier.

"Hey!" a gruff male voice called from behind them.

Jin turned, forcing herself not to lift her hands into combat positions. A boxy brown car was coming up along the road toward them, its driver steering with one hand as he gestured out the window with the other. "Hey, cousin!" he called again.

Jin keyed in her enhancers, trying to cut through the midmorning glare off the windshield. The driver was a young man, Merrick's age or a bit younger, with black hair and a short, neatly trimmed beard. His eyes were locked on her and Merrick, his expression hard. "Mom?" Merrick asked quietly.

"Better answer him," Jin told said as the car came to a stop beside them.

Merrick nodded microscopically and touched two fingers to his forehead. "Good day—" he started.

"Did you run out of fuel *again*?" the man in the car interrupted. He was clearly trying for a wry tone, but the darkness in his face effectively negated any humor that might have been in his voice. "That *was* your car I saw two kilometers back, wasn't it?"

Out of the corner of her eye, Jin saw that the gate guards were watching the conversation. "Mm-mm," she grunted softly, hoping Merrick would pick up on the cue.

He did. "I'm afraid so," he told the driver. "We decided to walk instead of—"

"You have to stop doing that," the other young man said. "Get in—I'll take you in. You can send someone back for the car later."

Merrick started to look questioningly at Jin, remembered in time that he was supposed to be the one making these decisions, and nodded. "That would be most kind," he said, stepping behind Jin to the car's rear door.

For a second his fingers fumbled as he tried to figure out the mechanism. Then, he got it, pulled the door open, and ushered Jin inside. Motioning her to move over, he started to get in beside her.

"You come up here," the driver said softly.

Obediently, Merrick closed the door and started around the front of the car. Jin tensed, wondering if the driver was planning to suddenly gun his engine and try to run him down. Maybe this was some elaborate trap designed to reveal Cobra reflexes.

But the car didn't move as Merrick finished his circle and climbed into the front passenger seat. "We thank you for your hospitality," he said as he closed the door behind him.

"Save your gratitude," the driver growled. Now that the gate guards couldn't hear, he'd abandoned even his half-hearted attempt at levity. He looked Merrick up and down, shaking his head in disgust, and started the car rolling again. "I just hope that no one with actual eyes saw you in those outfits."

Jin watched the guards closely as the driver maneuvered them through the gate. The two armed men merely glanced at the driver, but sent hard gazes at her and Merrick. The four non-obvious guards, in contrast, seemed to divide their time equally between all three occupants. Still, none of the six seemed to show any more suspicion than they had with any of the other cars that had passed their positions.

And then the car was past the gate and into Milika. Jin thought about checking behind them, decided that would look suspicious if the guards were still watching, and forced herself to continue facing forward. "Where are we going?" she asked.

The driver scowled at her in the mirror. "If you can't figure even that much out, you must not be much of a spy."

"You're welcome to believe that," Merrick murmured.

The driver shot him a look, and then fell silent.

Milika didn't seem to have changed much in thirty years, Jin decided as they crossed the Great Ring Road and continued inward toward the center of town. Several buildings were clearly new, but the shops and the people seemed much as they had back then.

Of course, she reminded herself, she hadn't had *that* much time to really observe the village. There were probably a lot of smaller changes she was simply missing.

They reached the center of town and turned left onto the Small Ring Road, circling the large park area known as the Inner Green. Jin leaned forward, her heartbeat picking up as she watched for her first glimpse of the Sammon house.

And then, there it was: a high privacy wall surrounding the courtyard, with the top of the house visible beyond it. Memories flooded back: the family's unhesitant hospitality when they thought her merely an injured stranger; their cautious but firm support when they learned who she really was; Daulo's willingness to risk his life for her. Not just his life, but also his family's honor.

A shiver ran up Jin's back as the driver maneuvered the car beneath the archway into the courtyard. The Sammon family had risked everything for her... and now her very presence on Qasama was once again putting them at horrible risk.

Whatever Daulo had summoned her here for, it must be something incredibly important.

"He's expecting you," the driver said as he pulled the car in front of the ornate door and rolled to a stop. "Do you need someone to show you the way?"

"No, I remember," Jin said. "Thank you."

The driver didn't answer.

The house struck Jin largely the same way the village itself had. It was basically the same as she remembered it, but there were enough differences in furnishings and décor to show the passage of years and the presence of a new owner. Feeling her heart once again speeding up, she climbed the stairs and went down the hallway to the room that had once been Kruin Sammon's office.

The door to the office stood open, with no guards in evidence. Jin keyed in her audio enhancers as she and Merrick approached, concentrating on the quiet sounds of breathing ahead of her. There was only one person in there, she decided. She started to step ahead of her son—

His hand brushed her arm. "I'll go first," he murmured. Before she could reply, he lengthened his stride and crossed in front of her through the doorway. Grimacing, Jin followed.

She rounded the door jamb to find Merrick standing a little to the right just inside the room. Seated at the desk across the room, his eyes steady on his visitors, was a heavyset man with a roundish face and white-flecked black hair. He wore an elaborate red-and silver robe, with a dual-patterned scarf tied casually around his throat.

Jin took a deep breath. "Hello, Daulo Sammon," she said, hearing the slight trembling in her voice. After all these years...

"I greet you, Jasmine Moreau," Daulo replied, his own voice dark and steady and without a single trace of genuine welcome that Jin could hear. His eyes shifted briefly to Merrick, measuring the younger man with a single glance. Then, laying down the stylus he'd been working with, he rose to his feet. "In the name of God," he demanded, "what are you *doing* here?"

Daulo lifted his eyes from the letter and shook his head. "No," he said. "I didn't write this. Nor did anyone in my household."

"Yet your driver quickly identified us and brought us in," Merrick pointed out. "Obviously, he was expecting us."

"First of all, the *driver,* as you refer to him, is in fact my son Fadil," Daulo said acidly. He ran his eyes up and down Merrick's clothing. "As to identifying you as strangers to Qasama, anyone who came within five meters of you would have known that instantly."

"What's wrong with our clothing?" Jin asked, glancing down her front. "It looks close enough to what I saw the villagers wearing."

"The design is close enough," Daulo agreed. "But the material is wrong. We stopped using it over two years ago."

"You're saying it hasn't been *sold* for two years?" Merrick asked, frowning.

"I'm saying we *stopped using it,*" Daulo growled. "By order of the Shahni. All Qasaman clothing had to be remade in this new material, with older garments destroyed."

"But that's crazy," Merrick protested.

"Hardly," Jin said, wincing as she suddenly understood. "In fact, it worked exactly the way they intended."

"What—oh," Merrick broke off, his face changing as he got it. "Right."

"Indeed," Daulo said. "The real question is whether anyone else saw you."

"The gate guards were watching us," Jin said. "I don't know whether they could spot something as subtle as clothing material from a moving car, though."

"Well, we can't afford to take chances," Daulo said heavily, standing up and coming around the corner of his desk. "I'll take you to rooms and have fresh clothing brought to you."

"Thank you," Jin said. "I'm sorry, Daulo. I really did think the message was from you. The last thing I want is to bring more trouble down on your household."

"May God grant that we can avoid that," Daulo said. His voice was still grim, but Jin caught a hint of a smile at the corners of his mouth. "I'm no longer as young and reckless as I once was, after all. I'm a respectable member of the community, who would very much prefer to avoid scrutiny from the Shahni or their agents."

"That goes double for us," Jin assured him. "Don't worry—as soon as we have that new clothing, we'll be gone."

"Gone where?" Daulo asked as he gestured them toward the door. "You said you had no way to contact the alien ship."

"No, but it'll be back in two weeks to pick us up," Jin said. "We'll just find somewhere safe to hide until then."

Daulo was opening his mouth, undoubtedly to argue that there *was* no such place on Qasama, when the door was thrown open and Daulo's son Fadil hurried in. "Father, they're coming," he panted, his expression tight. "The Shahni agents. They're coming.

"They're coming *here*."

CHAPTER FIVE

Jin shot a look at Merrick. His eyes went briefly wide, then calmed down again as he recovered his balance. "From the front?" she asked Fadil.

Fadil gave her a half-astonished, half-scandalized look. "I wasn't speaking to you," he bit out.

"Answer her anyway," Daulo ordered.

Fadil looked at his father with the same look he'd just given Jin. "Yes, from the front," he managed.

"Go and stall them," Jin said. "Daulo, we'll need those fresh clothes, *now*."

"I'll get them," Daulo said grimly. "Meanwhile—"

"What do you mean, *stall them*?" Fadil cut in. "These are agents of the *Shahni!*"

"Which is why we need to stall them," Jin explained, fighting hard for patience.

"And how exactly do I do that?" Fadil persisted. "Tell them you've gone?"

"Don't tell them anything," Merrick said. "Welcome them in, ask about their families, get them some refreshments—you *do* still do those things, don't you?"

"Yes, of course," Daulo said. "But that will only gain us a few minutes."

"That's all we'll need." Merrick visibly braced himself. "Get me some new clothes, and I'll go down and talk to them."

"Out of the question," Daulo said firmly.

"He's right, Merrick," Jin agreed. "If anyone's going to talk to them, it'll be me."

"What, a woman?" Merrick countered. "You don't think that'll raise their suspicions?"

Jin squeezed her hand into a fist. Unfortunately, he was right. "Merrick—"

"I need those clothes, Master Sammon," Merrick said. "And you, Master Fadil, need to get downstairs and entertain our guests."

"Father?" Fadil asked in a strained voice.

Daulo grimaced. "Do it," he confirmed.

Fadil hesitated, then gave a jerky nod and headed back down the hallway. "But I don't think either of you should face them," Daulo continued. "Let me first go see what I can do."

"With all due respect, I think running interference for us will only add to any suspicions they already have," Merrick said. "No, the faster one of us comes out and spins them a soothing story, the better." He looked at Jin. "It also occurs to me that if the Shahni have been updating their facial-recognition software, they may have a fairly good idea what my mother looks like."

Jin looked at Daulo, found him looking at her. "Jin?" he asked.

"I don't like it, either," Jin admitted reluctantly. "Unfortunately, it really is probably our best shot. At worst, all he'll do is confirm suspicions they already have. Merrick, do you know yet what you're going to say to them?"

"I've got a couple of ideas," he assured her. "While I'm changing, perhaps Master Sammon can give me a quick update on the new mark of respect and anything else they've changed since you were here."

"I'll do what I can," Daulo said grimly. "Come with me. Jin, can you find your way to the women's section? If they ask where you are, it might be useful to be able to say you're in a bath."

"I can do that," Jin said, acknowledging the advice without in any way stating she would follow it. In actual fact, she had no intention of getting out of earshot of her son right now.

She squeezed Merrick's shoulder, her fingers lingering perhaps a bit longer than really necessary. "Good luck."

From the way Fadil had been talking, Merrick had expected all four of the men from the village gate to be in the house, accompanied by the two official gate guards and possibly a few other armed friends. It was therefore something of a surprise when he descended the staircase to find that only one of the four men was actually present.

The youngest of the four, in fact, if Merrick was judging the other's face properly behind his closely trimmed beard. The young man's tunic was mostly brown, with dark red and blue highlights, tied with a tan sash. His trousers were a darker brown, with low, age-scuffed boots completing the ensemble. He would have looked perfectly at home beside any of a dozen other young men Merrick had noticed on the way into Milika.

He and Fadil were in the greeting room just off the foyer, Fadil watching stiffly as his visitor studied the refreshment trays being held for him by a pair of servant girls. The young man looked calm and perfectly at home, considerably more so than Fadil himself.

Merrick took a deep breath. *Showtime.* "Master Sammon, your father said I'm to—oh; excuse me," he said, bringing himself to a slightly jerky halt a couple of steps into the others' sight. "My apologies. I didn't realize you had a guest."

"Greetings to you, friend," the stranger said, waving away the trays with a double flick of his fingertips and lifting his right hand to touch bunched fingertips to his forehead.

Merrick suppressed a smile. That one had to be the oldest trick in the book. "Greetings to you," he replied, responding with the more proper two fingers to forehead and lips that Daulo had just taught him. "I am Haiku Sinn."

"Ah! My apologies—I keep forgetting," the other man said, lifting his hand again and giving the proper mark of respect. As he did so, his sleeve fell back, and Merrick caught a glimpse of a scaled gray undersleeve beneath the tunic. "I am Carsh Zoshak. Please; join us."

"Thank you," Merrick said, starting forward again. As he walked, he keyed in his optical enhancers' infrared, and a patterned red haze appeared superimposed over everyone in the room. One of the servant girls offered her tray to him, and he selected the minced *poofoo* strip that Daulo had recommended. "Are you a friend, or a business acquaintance of Master Sammon's?" he asked Zoshak as he took a bite. It tasted a little like spiced shrimp, he decided.

"Neither, actually," Zoshak said. "I'm an inspector for the Shahni."

"Really," Merrick said, letting his eyes go a little wider. "May I ask what such an illustrious personage seeks in such a modest village as Milika?"

"I am hardly an illustrious personage," Zoshak said wryly. "My job is simply to travel around Qasama monitoring compliance with current social norms. You may have noticed me at the gate when you came through?"

"I'm afraid I wasn't paying much attention to individuals," Merrick admitted, peering closely at him. "It was my first visit to Milika, and I was eager to see what the village was like."

"Really?" Zoshak asked in a tone of polite disbelief. "A cousin to Fadil Sammon, and this is your first visit?"

"A *cousin*?" Merrick echoed, frowning. "No, not at all. What gave you that impression?"

"One of the other gate guards heard him call you his cousin," Zoshak said, his eyes steady on Merrick's face.

Merrick held his puzzled frown another second. Then, letting his face clear, he gave a short laugh. "Oh, how funny," he said. "No, he didn't call me cousin. He simply called my name: *Haiku Sinn.*"

For a moment Zoshak looked blank. Then, slowly, he smiled as well. "Haiku Sinn," he repeated. "Yes, I can see how that could have been misheard. How funny, indeed."

"I only wish I were related to the Sammon family," Merrick went on, giving Fadil a rueful smile. The other didn't smile back, but merely continued looking tense. "If I were, perhaps it would be easier to persuade them to combine our two mining operations."

"You deal in metals?" Zoshak asked.

"Mining and refining, yes," Merrick said. "We're particularly interested in the new deposits of iridium and platinum they've uncovered." He grimaced. "Unfortunately, so are many others."

"Indeed," Zoshak agreed. "Tell me, who is the older woman who was in Master Sammon's car with you?"

"My mother, Lariqa Sinn," Merrick said. He'd thought about trying to come up with another identity for her, but there was too much risk that someone might have noticed a family resemblance. "She knows a great deal more about my father's business than I do."

"But is perhaps not an expert on fashion?" Zoshak asked pointedly.

"Oh. Yes." Merrick winced. "Yes, I know—those old clothes we were wearing."

"Clothing which should have been destroyed two years ago," Zoshak said, his voice dropping to the tone Merrick often heard from Aventinian bureaucrats quoting rules and regulations.

"I know," Merrick said again. "We usually just wear them when we're inspecting mines—we don't mind if they get damaged, you see. Unfortunately, in our haste to get to Milika after we received Daulo Sammon's invitation, we didn't bother to change."

"Or to check your fuel gauge?" Zoshak suggested, his tone lightening a couple of shades.

Merrick winced again. "Indeed," he confessed. "If we're trying to impress Daulo Sammon with our efficiency, we're not doing a very good job of it."

"Perhaps you may yet redeem yourselves in his eyes," Zoshak said. "You will, of course, destroy that clothing immediately."

"Of course," Merrick hastened to assure him. "And all the rest, too, as soon as we return home."

"Yes," Zoshak said, his tone making it clear it wasn't a suggestion. "Where *is* your home, by the way?"

"Patrolo," Merrick said. He knew nothing about the town other than that it was midway down the Eastern Arm of the Great Arc, that it had a decent mining and refining industry, and that Daulo had suggested it as Merrick's supposed home town. "You've probably never even heard of it."

"Actually, I have," Zoshak said. "I understand it has decent mining facilities and several small refineries."

"Yes, that's it," Merrick confirmed. "Also several fine restaurants, if I may be so boastful. We would he honored to have you visit us someday." He dared a small smile. "And I promise you'll find nothing illegal when you do."

"I'll hold you to that, Master Sinn," Zoshak said, smiling back. "Thank you for your hospitality, Master Sammon. With your leave, I'll be on my way."

"Of course," Fadil said. He and Zoshak made the sign of respect, Zoshak and Merrick did likewise, and then the young Shahni agent headed out again into the midmorning sunlight.

Fadil exhaled a shuddering breath. "Leave us," he said tartly to the two servant girls. "You—upstairs," he added to Merrick as the girls bowed and headed silently toward the kitchen.

Daulo and Jin were waiting at the top of the stairway. "What do you think?" Merrick asked.

"You sounded convincing enough," Daulo said. "Whether or not he *was* convinced, of course, is another question entirely."

"He wasn't," Fadil bit out, glaring at Merrick. "How could he have been?"

"Merrick?" Jin invited.

Merrick shrugged. "If he recognized me for who I was, it had to have been right at the beginning," he said. "I saw no indication of sudden surprise or excitement."

"A man could hardly become an agent of the Shahni without control of his face," Fadil said contemptuously.

"True, but I doubt even Shahni agents can control their heartbeat and the subsequent changes in their heat output," Merrick told him. "I was monitoring his infrared signature the whole time, and I saw no change."

"You can read body temperature that subtly?" Daulo asked, frowning. "I never knew that."

"It's something that was added to Merrick's generation of Cobras," Jin explained, her voice oddly distant. "My own enhancers aren't nearly so sophisticated."

"Still, it's certainly possible that I misread him," Merrick continued. "Qasaman reactions may be different from those I'm familiar with."

"Especially given the range of enhancement drugs available to us," Daulo agreed grimly. "And as you say, he may have been convinced of your true identity from the very beginning."

"He was also wearing something odd under his tunic," Merrick said. "Something gray and scaly that I've never seen before."

"Probably a krisjaw-hide armband," Daulo said. "It either means he's a good hunter, or that he likes to pretend he is."

"Never mind that," Fadil asked impatiently. "What do we do?" He jerked a thumb at Merrick and Jin. "They've been seen in our house."

"I think all we can do now is minimize any potential damage," Merrick said, "which means us getting out of here as soon as possible. If Zoshak tries to make trouble, you'll just have to claim that our story fooled you—"

"There's one other possibility," Jin said.

Merrick eyed his mother. There was an odd look on her face, even odder than the tone she'd used a moment ago. "What's that?" he asked.

"We assumed that Daulo Sammon sent me that note," she said slowly. "Only we know now that he didn't." She seemed to brace herself. "What if it was actually sent by Miron Akim?"

Merrick felt his mouth drop open. "The Shahni agent?"

"I know it sounds crazy," Jin admitted. "But I can't think of anyone else on Qasama aside from the Sammon family who ever heard my full name."

"Obolo Nardin did," Daulo said, his face darkening with memory. "I distinctly remember you telling him who you were. Rather proudly, in fact."

"Not that it made any impression on him," Jin said. "But no, I only gave him the name Jasmine. The note refers to me as both Jasmine *and* Jin." She looked at Merrick. "In which case, it's possible Carsh Zoshak showed no reaction because he wasn't here to capture us, but merely to report on our arrival."

"Ridiculous," Fadil said with a snort.

"Fadil," Daulo said warningly.

"I apologize for any disrespect, my father," Fadil gritted out. "But it *is* ridiculous. What in the name of God would the Shahni want with enemies of Qasama?"

"We aren't your—" Merrick broke off at a gesture from his mother.

"I don't know what he would want with us," Jin said calmly. "I'm simply following the logic trail."

"To a completely erroneous conclusion," Fadil insisted.

"Possibly," Jin said calmly. "I'm open to other suggestions."

For a moment no one spoke. "I have to say, I agree with my son," Daulo said. "Such a suggestion is so unlikely as to border on the completely impossible." He made a face. "Unfortunately, I have nothing more probable to offer."

"Well, then, I guess it's time Merrick and I finally paid a visit to the Shahni," Jin said. She was trying to keep her tone light, Merrick knew, but he could sense the quiet concern beneath it. The Shahni, after all, were the ones who had declared Qasama's national hatred for the Cobra Worlds in the first place. "Where do they make their headquarters these days?"

"Where they always have: the city of Sollas," Daulo said. "You understand now why your arrival on their very doorstep fifty-five years ago was such a shock and concern to us all."

"If it makes you feel any better, the choice of the team's landing zone was purely coincidental," Jin assured him. "All the official records—as well the stories I heard from my father and uncle—agree that they picked Sollas only because it was more or less in the center of the string of Great Arc settlements."

"Which is precisely why it was made the capital to begin with," Daulo said. "Which makes you capable of predicting and anticipating our actions, which offers us no comfort at all."

Merrick felt his throat tighten. *Qasaman paranoia.* He'd heard his mother and grandfather talk about it, but until now he'd never truly understood the full implications of the phrase. "So Sollas it is," he put in, hoping to turn the conversation away from supposed Cobra Worlds omniscience. "We can get a bus to there, right?"

"Buses are hardly the transport of choice for fugitives," Daulo said heavily. "No, I'd better drive you."

"We can't let you do that," Jin said firmly. "Just let us have a vehicle and a map and we'll manage it ourselves."

"Have either of you a proper license?" Daulo asked. "I didn't think so. We may be a bit casual on the point of personal identity papers—a long and very deep part of our heritage—but we are *very* firm on allowing only those so authorized to drive our roads. Among other matters, you can't purchase fuel without one."

Jin threw Merrick a helpless look, then reluctantly nodded. "I have no right to ask such risks of you, Daulo Sammon," she said. "But I see no other way. Thank you for your offer, and we accept with humble thanks. How long a drive will it be?"

"If we leave within the next hour, we should be there around dawn," Daulo said.

"Can we do that?" Jin asked. "I mean, travel at night?"

"Of course." Daulo smiled humorlessly. "Interestingly enough, the number of predator attacks has been dropping steadily over the past half century. I suppose we have your people to thank for that."

"I have a question," Merrick said, trying to visualize the Qasaman maps he'd looked through. "I can't see how we can make a trip that long without driving straight through."

"Were you wanting to stop and sightsee along the way?" Daulo asked.

"I was thinking more about driver fatigue," Merrick said. "Unless you're planning to let Mom or me drive for a while."

"Weren't you listening?" Fadil snapped. "You can't drive here."

"It'll be all right," Daulo said. "If I get tired, we can stop for a brief rest."

"Which will look highly suspicious to anyone passing by," Fadil argued.

"We'll just have to risk that." Daulo eyed his son. "Unless you have an alternative to offer."

For a long moment Fadil glared at his father. Merrick flicked on his infrared again, watching with interest as parts of the young man's image shifted between red and orange with his fluctuating emotional state. "You know what the only alternative is," Fadil said at last. "We drive them together."

Daulo inclined his head; acknowledgment or thanks, Merrick couldn't tell which. "Do you have any other equipment, Jasmine Moreau?"

"We have some packs buried off the road about half a kilometer south of the village," Jin said. "But we can hardly pick them up in broad daylight with the gate guards already suspicious."

"I'd rather not wait until nightfall to leave Milika," Daulo said. "Can you make do without them?"

"Easily," Jin said with a nod. "There's nothing in there we can't do without."

Merrick grimaced. Nothing except their camo night-fighting suits, their compact medical kits, their rope and climbing gear, and a few small smoke-and-shock diversionary devices. But she was right. If Zoshak was still suspicious, parking alongside the road while someone went for a short walk would be a suicidally stupid thing to do.

"Then as soon as we've collected some spare clothing for you, we'll be under way," Daulo decided. "Fadil, we'll take the green truck. Go make sure it's fueled—" he smiled tightly "—and add a few small boxes of recent ore samples from the mine."

Fadil frowned. "*Ore* samples?"

"If we're going to go to Patrolo to discuss joint operations with the Sinn family refining facilities, we'll need to show them samples of our output," Daulo said. "Go."

"Yes, Father." Fadil gave Daulo the sign of respect and then, grudgingly, Merrick thought, repeated the gesture to him and his mother. Turning, he went back downstairs and disappeared down a corridor leading toward the rear of the house.

"Come," Daulo said, gesturing to Jin and Merrick as he headed the opposite direction down the corridor. "We'll see about food for you while we pack a few essentials."

Merrick and Jin fell into step beside him. Behind Daulo's back, Merrick caught his mother's eye. *I hope you know what you're doing,* he mouthed silently to her.

Her lip twitched. *So do I,* she mouthed back.

CHAPTER SIX

The truck Fadil brought up was a relatively small one, about the size of an Aventinian personal transport vehicle, with a cab in front and an enclosed cargo area attached behind it equipped with front, rear, and side windows. The cab only had two main seats, but the slightly enlarged space behind it included two inward-facing fold-down jump seats.

From the gate guards' point of view, of course, the vehicle made perfect sense. With the visitors' own car supposedly waiting a couple of kilometers down the road, there was no reason for Daulo to bring a larger vehicle. He would theoretically simply drop his guests at their own car, refill its fuel tank, and then the four of them would continue on to Patrolo in a two-vehicle convoy.

But of course there was no such car conveniently waiting for them. As the four of them settled into the truck, and Merrick tried to find a comfortable position for his feet that wouldn't involve kicking his mother's, he reluctantly concluded that this was going to be a very long trip.

But at least their exit from Milika was satisfyingly anticlimactic. None of the gate guards gave them so much as a second glance as they headed out of town. Carsh Zoshak himself, in fact, wasn't even present, and Merrick dared to hope that the Shahni agent really *was* in Milika merely to check on social detail compliance.

The first major population center along the southward road was the city of Azras. There they stopped for fuel and a meal before turning northeast onto the main road that linked Qasama's five major Western Arm cities. By the time the sunlight faded away behind the forest and the stars began to appear, they were alone on the road.

Merrick spent most of the night staring out the cab window past his mother's head at the stretches of forest and plain rolling past them, or out the windshield at the winding road ahead. Occasionally, just for a change of pace, he took in the view out the rear window, looking through the mostly empty cargo area and out the cargo area's own rear window, watching the red-lit landscape disappear behind them.

He caught occasional snatches of sleep, too. But the seat and his position were uncomfortable enough that those interludes of oblivion didn't last very long. Seated across from him, his mother seemed to be having a much easier time of it, as did Fadil at Merrick's right in the front passenger seat.

A little after midnight Daulo found a long, open, and deserted stretch of highway and pulled off to switch drivers. Merrick and Jin got out as well, glad of the opportunity to stretch their legs for a minute. The forest had been cleared well back of the road at this point, and as Merrick paced back and forth he used his optical enhancers to check the tree line on both sides for predators. He spotted a single spine leopard lurking among some thorn bushes, but if the creature even noticed the humans it made no sign. A few minutes later they were all back in the truck and, with Fadil now at the wheel, they continued on their way.

The glow of approaching dawn was reddening the sky ahead when Merrick first noticed they were being followed.

"Mom?" he murmured, just loud enough to be heard over the road noise.

"I know," she murmured back. "He's been there for at least the last half hour."

Merrick stared at her. "Half an *hour*? And you didn't say anything?"

"Who's been where for half an hour?" Fadil asked, frowning at them in the mirror. "What are we talking about?"

"We're talking about the person or persons following us," Jin told him.

"We're being followed?" Daulo asked, straightening up in the passenger seat and throwing a quick look over his shoulder.

"Yes, but so far that's all he seems interested in doing," Jin said.

Fadil muttered something under his breath. "More Shahni agents?"

"Unlikely," Daulo said. "Half an hour would have been more than enough time for an agent to call for a roadblock or an air strike."

"Unless they merely want to watch us," Fadil growled.

"Again, unlikely," Daulo said. "Instead of following us, it would be much more effective for them to put a SkyJo combat helicopter directly overhead at an altitude where we would never notice it."

"Maybe it's just another traveler heading to Sollas," Merrick suggested.

"I don't think so," his mother said. "There was that half-kilometer of bad road about fifteen minutes ago where Fadil had to slow way down. A normal car would have maintained his speed on the good road until he hit the patch himself, which would have meant temporarily closing the gap between us. Instead, he slowed to match our speed, staying as far back as he could while still maintaining visual contact. *And* he also didn't slow down through the rough patch, again maintaining visual in case we turned off on one of these side roads."

"So then who *is* he?" Merrick asked.

"Probably part of a local gang of thieves," Daulo said contemptuously. "We're probably heading for their roadblock right now."

"Well, we can't have that, can we?" Merrick said. "I'll take care of it."

"How?" Jin asked suspiciously.

"I'm going to give him some car trouble," Merrick said. "Master Sammon, do we have any left-hand curves coming up? Preferably something with forest or other cover close at hand."

There was a soft glow from the front seat as Daulo consulted his map. "There's a fairly sharp left curve about five kilometers ahead," he reported. "But the nearest trees to that spot are almost twenty meters back from the road."

"Any depressions or pits anywhere along the curve?" Merrick asked.

"There's a drainage channel running along both shoulders the whole length of the curve," Daulo said. "But they're not likely to be more than half a meter deep."

"Good enough," Merrick assured him. "Can you keep the overhead light from going on when the door is opened?"

"What exactly are you planning?" Daulo asked as he reached up to the dome light switch.

"As I said, I'm going to give him some car trouble," Merrick said, swiveling his legs around the front side of his jump seat. "Lean forward, please, and crack the door open a few centimeters."

"Wait a minute," Daulo said, his tone suddenly ominous. "You're not planning to *jump*, are you?"

"Don't worry, I'll be fine," Merrick assured him. "Low-altitude aircar quick-exits are something we do all the time."

He looked at his mother, waiting for her to raise the point that, although the quick-exit was certainly taught at the academy, Merrick himself hadn't done one since graduation. But she remained silent. "As soon as I'm out, close the door and keep going at the same speed," Merrick continued. "Mom will tell you when you should slow down so that I can catch up with you."

"Understood," Daulo said. "Be careful."

He hitched his seat forward and opened his door a crack. Merrick got one hand on the seat back and the other on the doorjamb and waited.

They reached the curve, and as they turned into it Merrick eased himself alongside Daulo's seat and pushed the door open half a meter, balancing himself partway out the door. The wind buffeted hard against his face, and he closed his eyes against the onslaught as he keyed in his optical enhancers to give him some vision. For a few seconds he crouched beside Daulo, waiting for just the right moment . . . and as they approached the midpoint of the curve, he shifted his weight and dropped out the door.

He barely had time to get his legs pumping before his feet hit the pavement. For a second he thought he wasn't going to make it, that his feet would be swept out from under him and he would end up being dragged along the road.

Then his nanocomputer got his servo-driven legs into the rhythm, and he had his balance back. He released his grip on the door, angled toward the edge of the shoulder, and started to slow down. For another couple of seconds he fought the same fight against speed that he'd just won, only this time in reverse.

And as the truck continued past him down the curve, Merrick threw himself headfirst into the drainage channel beside the road, tucking his forearms against his face to protect it as he slid off the remainder of his momentum.

He'd half expected his Qasaman outfit to disintegrate under the stress, leaving him with a few bad scrapes at the very least. But the clothing was tougher than he'd realized, and it came through the ordeal with only some minor rips. Even more fortunately, the channel was dry, which meant no huge spray of water to warn the trailing car that one of their quarries had flown the coop. Ignoring the handful of bumps and bruises his landing had beaten into his arms and chest, Merrick rolled up onto his back and waited.

From his new vantage point, he heard the tailing car well before he saw it. He focused on the edge of the road, his right hand curling into firing position. The car flashed past, and in a single motion Merrick sat up, glanced a target lock onto the nearer rear wheel, and fired his fingertip laser. There was a muffled *pop* as the tire blew.

And suddenly the car was all over the road, its tires screeching as the driver fought to bring it back under control. Merrick swung himself around and rose up into a low crouch, watching the car swerving back and forth. As soon as it came to a halt, he would slip away, cut across the landscape, and catch up with his mother and the Sammons.

He was still watching when the driver abruptly lost his battle with momentum. The car shot across the center line, angled across the shoulder, and slammed down into the drainage channel on the far side.

"Damn!" Merrick bit out as he leaped up and sprinted toward the car. The idea had been to quietly and peaceably stop the vehicle, not wreck it and injure or kill everyone inside. He reached the car and bent down to look inside.

The driver was draped over the steering wheel, his head and arms limp, his face turned away. Swearing again, Merrick hurried around to the driver's side and pulled at the door. It resisted, probably knocked out of shape by the crash. He tried again, this time putting his servos into the effort, and with a horrible grinding noise the door came open.

The driver didn't move. Gingerly, Merrick reached in and touched his fingertips to the other's neck. To his relief, he found a slow but steady pulse. At least the man wasn't dead. Merrick focused on the other's face, notching up his light-amps.

And a sudden chill ran down his back. This wasn't just some random member of some random gang.

It was Carsh Zoshak.

There was the sound of tires on pavement, and he looked up to see the Sammon truck back up to a jerky halt in front of the wrecked car. "What happened?" Jin called as she jumped out of the truck.

"He lost control when I popped his tire," Merrick said grimly. "And it's not a thief. It's Carsh Zoshak."

"What?" Daulo demanded as he got out of his side of the truck and hurried to join them. "But—"

"I guess he wasn't senior enough to call in a SkyJo," Merrick said. "Mom, can you help me get him out of the car?"

"You think that's wise?" Jin asked as she leaned into the car and checked Zoshak's pulse for herself.

"Well, we can't exactly leave him here," Merrick said tersely. "I don't see any blood, but there could be a concussion or internal injuries."

Daulo came up beside them, his expression tense. "God in heaven," he breathed, looking at the unconscious Shahni agent. "What did you *do*?"

"I just popped one of his rear tires, that's all," Merrick told him. "It should have brought him to a stop and kept him there. Instead, he lost control."

Daulo snarled a word Merrick's Qasaman classes had somehow never covered. "What do we do?"

"We get him to a hospital," Jin said. "Merrick, I'll take his head. You lean him out and get his torso and legs. Daulo, is there a medical kit in the truck?"

"Yes, but only a simple one."

"We'll take whatever you've got," Jin said as she and Merrick eased the unconscious man out of the car. "I'll ride in back and see what I can do for him."

Merrick grimaced. "No, I'll do it," he said. "My training is more up-to-date than yours."

"You sure?" Jin asked, peering closely at him. "I thought you hated the sight of blood."

"So what?" Merrick growled. "Besides, I'm the one who wrecked him."

His mother hesitated, then nodded. "All right. Daulo, can you get the back of the cargo area open?"

The cargo area had a very low ceiling, and getting Zoshak inside without jostling him proved to be a delicate operation. But between them, Merrick and Jin managed it. Merrick climbed in beside the wounded man, accepted the first-aid kit Fadil handed him, and settled himself into a cross-legged position as Daulo closed the rear door.

Zoshak's teeth were chattering quietly as Merrick pried open the kit and took a quick inventory. Bandages, cleaning cloths, painkillers, a few patches of unknown purpose, and a handful of small color-coded hypos whose contents consisted of medical-looking words that Merrick had never learned. As the truck headed off again, Merrick set the kit aside and carefully eased open Zoshak's outer robe and tunic.

Back at the Sammon house, Daulo had suggested that the gray scaly material Merrick had spotted under Zoshak's sleeve was a krisjaw armband. To Merrick's surprise, it wasn't.

Beside him, the connecting window to the truck's cab slid open. "How's he doing?" Jin asked, looking through the opening.

"His teeth are chattering," Merrick said, shifting his eyes to Zoshak's face as he took off his own robe. "Well, they were a minute ago, anyway. His skin doesn't feel cold, so I'm guessing it's shock."

"You need to keep him warm."

"Already on it," Merrick assured her, laying his robe across Zoshak's legs and abdomen. "Where's Lorne and his magic health-ometer ears when we need him?"

"You're the one who insisted on inviting yourself along on this trip," his mother said.

"Don't remind me," Merrick said. "By the way, you can tell Daulo that this krisjaw armband of his goes all the way up. *And* down."

"What do you mean?" Jin asked, frowning.

"I mean he's got a whole suit of the stuff," Merrick said. "Shirt, trousers—the works. Might have socks, too, for all I know. Either he's one heck of a hunter, or else he has serious compensation issues."

"Never mind his issues," Jin said. "What can you tell about his injuries?"

"Not much," Merrick admitted, gently kneading the usual places on Zoshak's torso. "I don't feel any swelling in his major organs. No broken ribs, either." He shifted his hands to Zoshak's arms. "Arms seem okay, too. That just leaves his head."

From the front seat, Daulo said something Merrick didn't catch. "Daulo says you can use the green hypo to wake him up," Jin repeated. "It's a mild stimulant."

"I'd rather not pump any chemicals into him if we don't have to," Merrick said, eyeing the hypos dubiously as he sealed Zoshak's tunic and robe again. "As long as he seems stable, I vote we just watch him and let a real doctor handle the treatment."

"That's probably best," Jin agreed reluctantly. "I just hate to sit here and do nothing."

"'The patient heals; the doctor collects the bill,'" Merrick quoted. "How much farther?"

Jin glanced over her shoulder. "We're here."

Merrick ducked his head and looked between Daulo and Fadil. There, rising up from the plain ahead, framed against the red fire of the rising sun behind it, was Sollas.

The first mission to Qasama had spent the bulk of their time in and around Sollas, and Merrick had studied all the pictures they'd brought back of the city. The skyline had changed a little since then, he noted, with a few new buildings and some extra height on some of the others. But the most striking change—"Is that a *wall* around the city?"

Jin turned around again. "Certainly looks like one," she confirmed, her voice sounding odd. "Daulo, when did they put *that* up?"

"Quite a few years ago, actually," Daulo said. "A few years after your visit. You didn't know?"

"Not even a hint," Jin said. "Our observation satellites all started dying shortly after I left, and with the . . . new political climate the Council decided not to replace them."

"Probably because they would have showed that the Moreau plan had worked," Merrick put in sourly.

Fadil shot a glance over his shoulder. "The *Moreau* plan? The razorarms were *your* idea?"

"Partly," Jin told him. "Well, mostly, I suppose. But the people who opposed it wanted to smear our family, so they dubbed it the Moreau plan and worked hard to make the name stick." She turned back to Merrick. "Any change?"

Merrick looked down at Zoshak. "Nothing obvious," he reported, checking the young Qasaman's neck again. "Pulse and breathing are still steady."

"Keep an eye on him."

"I will." Merrick shifted to a side-sitting position, easing the strain on his leg muscles, and glanced out the cargo area's rear window. Thoughts of Zoshak had suddenly sparked the thought that the Shahni agent might not have been alone. But the road behind them was empty of vehicles. With a sigh of relief and fatigue, Merrick started to look away.

And paused. The road itself was clear, but there was something in the distance above it: a black spot, moving rapidly toward them out of the darker part of the sky. One of the SkyJo attack helicopters that Daulo had mentioned? Hoping fervently that it was something else—*anything* else—he keyed in his telescopic enhancers.

The next instant his vision exploded into a violent back-and-forth sway, the unavoidable price for using telescopics inside a moving vehicle. Merrick clamped down on his sudden vertigo and let his head and neck float, compensating as best he could for the bounces. An image flashed into view and then back out again before he could identify it. He set his teeth, fighting to bring it back.

And as he did, he felt his breath catch in his throat. The vehicle back there wasn't a SkyJo. It was a Troft spaceship. "Are we expecting company from the Trofts?" he called toward the cab.

"What do you mean?" Daulo asked, turning in his seat.

"There's a ship coming in from the west," Merrick told him, working furiously to maintain his hold on the image. "It's definitely a Troft, but it isn't a type I've ever seen before."

"Can you describe it?" Jin asked, bobbing her head up and down as she tried to look out the back. "It's too high for my angle."

"Looks sort of like a wrigglefish," Merrick said. "Tall but thin, at least from the front. It's—well, it's longer than it is tall, but it's too far away for me to get a definitive scale. There are two sets of short wings on each side . . . wait a minute."

"What?" Jin asked.

"He's not coming in on gravity lifts," Merrick said, frowning as the strangeness of that suddenly struck him. Troft spacecraft *always* came down on gravity lifts. "He must be using airfoils." Blinking, Merrick shut off the telescopics, trying to give his brain a brief rest.

And stiffened as his field of view expanded back to normal again. The strange Troft ship wasn't alone. There were at least fifty of them, coming out of the darkness in a wedge formation, none of them running grav lifts.

Running without the telltale red glow of grav lifts.

Merrick keyed in the telescopics again, focusing on the lead ship . . . and this time he spotted the cluster of objects nestled up beside the hulls beneath the stubby bow and stern wings. "Oh, hell," he murmured.

"What is it?" Jin asked tautly.

With an effort, Merrick found his voice. "Tell Fadil to punch it," he said, marveling at how calm his voice sounded. "Those are Troft warships. Fifty to a hundred of them."

He turned to face his mother's suddenly widened eyes. "Qasama's under attack."

CHAPTER SEVEN

"God in heaven," Daulo breathed. "Are you sure?"

"Trust me," Merrick said, looking back and forth between the various incoming ships. "There are at least twenty more of the wrigglefish ones, but also a few that look like flying sharks. I see a couple of wider ones in back too—whoops; there go their grav lifts," he said as red glows appeared in unison beneath each of the incoming ships.

"Coming in for a landing," Jin said tightly. "Looks like Sollas is the target."

"Like there was any doubt," Merrick said. "What do we do?"

"We have to warn the Shahni," Daulo insisted.

"Right," Jin said. "You have any kind of comm or radio? Ours are still in our packs back at Milika."

Daulo hissed viciously between his teeth. "Unfortunately, the only radio equipment simple villagers like ourselves may use are the short-range sets we use to communicate into the mines," he said. "Everything else is reserved for the Shahni and military."

"Maybe Carsh Zoshak has something with him," Jin suggested. "Merrick?"

"I'm on it," Merrick said, running his hands quickly over Zoshak's tunic and robe. But there was nothing. "No good," he said. "If he had something, we must have left it in the car."

"Any idea where any of the Shahni live?" Jin asked. "If we can't call them, maybe we can go pound on someone's door."

"They and their families all live together in the Palace in the center of Sollas," Daulo said. "Unfortunately I doubt we can reach it before the invaders do."

"Depends on how smart the Trofts are," Jin said. "If they decide to secure the airfield area first—which is what I'd do—we might have time to get to the Shahni and at least help them get to cover."

There was a soft noise from Zoshak, and Merrick looked down to see that the other's teeth were chattering again. "We may have to postpone any door-knocking," he warned. "I think Carsh Zoshak's going into shock again."

"Daulo, check and see where the nearest hospital is," Jin said. "Someplace that can handle—"

She broke off as the forward edge of the invasion force shot past overhead, filling the air with a deep, throaty roar. For a long minute the sound continued, the truck rattling as Fadil fought the buffeting slipstream of the ships' passage.

And then the wave was past, and the sound faded away into the tense stillness of the predawn landscape. "Someplace that can handle possible head trauma," Jin finished her sentence. "Doesn't look like they're all headed for the airfield, does it?"

"It would appear they mean to take the entire city at once," Daulo agreed tightly. "But we won't be destroyed without a fight."

"Fortunately, mass destruction doesn't seem to be part of the Trofts' playbook," Jin said. "At least, not the Trofts the Dominion of Man ran into a century ago. They prefer to conquer planets and peoples in more or less working condition. Did you find us a hospital?"

"The closest is just inside the southwestern gate," Daulo said, holding up the map for her to see. "Once he's there—"

A hand brushed Merrick's knee. "Hold it a sec," Merrick interrupted, looking down.

Zoshak's eyes were open, though just barely. "Where...?" the young man whispered. "What...?"

"You were in an accident," Merrick told him, feeling a fresh flash of guilt at having been the one who'd caused the wreck. "We're taking you to—where are we going?"

"The Everhope Hospital," Daulo said.

"The Everhope Hospital in Sollas," Merrick repeated. "We'll be there in just a few minutes."

Zoshak closed his eyes. "Lodestar," he murmured. "It must be Lodestar."

"What's Lodestar?" Merrick asked.

"It's another hospital," Daulo said, studying his map. "But it's near the city center. Even at this time of morning it would take an additional quarter of an hour or more for us to reach it."

Merrick nodded. "The Everhope's closer," he told Zoshak. "We'll take you there."

Zoshak shook his head weakly. "Lodestar," he insisted, his voice almost too weak to hear. "Specialist. Kambuzia."

"He says there's a specialist there named Kambuzia," Merrick repeated.

"Not smart," Daulo objected, looking over the back seat at the cargo area. "The first rule of emergency care is to obtain it as quickly as possible."

"Kambuzia," Zoshak whispered. "Kambuzia."

"Yes, but he clearly wants this Dr. Kambuzia," Merrick said, touching his fingers to Zoshak's throat. "Pulse is still good," he said, gazing down into the other's face. Zoshak's eyes had opened a little again, and behind the drooping lids Merrick could sense an unbending insistence. "I don't think he's going to be happy with anyone else."

Daulo muttered something under his breath. "Probably some relative," he muttered. "Fine. Fadil, at the Ring Road swing north toward the western gate instead of continuing on to the southwest entrance."

They reached the ring road and turned north. Merrick tried to see what might be happening in the city, but the wall blocked everything but the tops of the nearest buildings.

But at least there was no sound of gunfire or lasers. Yet.

The western gate was standing wide open when they arrived. It was also deserted, with no guards or other travelers anywhere in sight. "This isn't right," Fadil muttered as he drove through. "Where is everyo—?"

The rest of his question was cut off by the abrupt screech of tires on pavement as he slammed on the brakes. Merrick grabbed for a handhold and ducked down to look past his mother's head out the windshield.

And found himself gazing at the tall side of one of the Troft ships.

It was squatting on wide landing skids in the center of the intersection just beyond the gate, positioned with its longitudinal axis along the wider southeast-to-northwest avenue and its flank toward the narrower street the Sammon truck had entered by. "Regular air field not good enough for them?" Merrick muttered.

"First rule of urban occupation is to control or block major intersections," Jin said tightly. "Looks like they've decided to do both. Look at the firepower they've got under those wings."

Merrick craned his neck and grimaced. Now that the ship was close by and standing still, he was able to get some detail on the weapons mounted on pylons beneath the stubby wings. "Looks like lasers *and* missile launchers," he said.

"All mounted on individual swivels on those pylons, you'll notice," his mother said. "Makes it easy to fire in any direction."

Merrick nodded. And with Qasaman city avenues nice and straight and wide, a single gunship's weapons would command a lot of territory.

"God in heaven," Daulo murmured.

Merrick tore his gaze from the ship. Striding toward them with hand-and-a-half lasers held at the ready were four Trofts.

He felt his muscles stiffen, a sudden flood of claustrophobia gripping his heart. Each of the aliens was wearing a thick armored leotard with heavy knee-high boots and a belt that sported a small sidearm, a long knife, and half a dozen gadgets that Merrick didn't recognize. Their helmets were of an odd, almost flowing design that curved down behind them to protect the backs of their necks, with a thick plastic or glass faceplate covering their faces.

And here Merrick sat, trapped in the back of a truck, with his mother and her friends blocking most of his field of fire. If the

Trofts decided to mow them all down, there was nothing he could do to stop them—

"Merrick, do you recognize the demesne pattern?" Jin asked quietly.

With an effort, Merrick forced down his fear. His mother was right—this was the time for thought and planning, not panic. Anyway, if the Trofts wanted them dead, they would have already opened fire. "I think I can see some elements of the Pua demesne," he said. "But taken as a whole it isn't any combination I've seen before."

"That's what I was thinking," his mother agreed. "Which may imply the attack isn't coming from any of Qasama's immediate neighbors, or at least not the ones who first told us about their presence here."

"What does it matter where they came from?" Fadil snarled as the Trofts continued toward them.

"I don't know yet," Jin said calmly. "But all information is eventually useful."

"*If* you live through it," Fadil bit back. "You're the brave demon warriors. *Do* something."

"Patience, my son," Daulo said. His voice, Merrick noted with a flicker of resentment, was as calm as Jin's, and far calmer than Merrick himself was feeling. "Jin Moreau, how do you wish to play this?"

"As low-key and truthful as possible," Jin told him. "We were coming to Sollas to shop around some ore samples, found an accident victim on the road, and are trying to get him to the hospital."

"We'll try it," Daulo said. "Remember to let me do all the talking."

Five meters from the truck the Trofts shifted formation, one of them approaching the driver's side while the other three fanned out sideways with their lasers covering the occupants. At a murmured word from Daulo, Fadil rolled down his window. "What's the meaning of this?" Daulo demanded, his voice stiff and even a bit haughty. "We are citizens of Qasama—"

Behind the faceplate, Merrick saw the Troft's beak moving as he said something in cattertalk. "You will remain silent," a round pin on the alien's left shoulder boomed out the Qasaman translation. "State your business in Sollas."

"We bring ore samples to the refineries." Daulo nodded back toward Merrick and Zoshak. "More importantly, we also have an injured man we found on the road. He needs to be taken to a hospital."

The Troft looked past Fadil's head into the cargo area. Merrick crouched low over Zoshak, putting as much concern into his face and his body language as he could. He had no idea whether the Troft could even read humans that closely, but there was no harm in trying. "Where was this accident?" the alien asked.

"About twenty kilometers back along the Azras road," Daulo said. "Go look for yourselves if you don't believe me."

Merrick felt his stomach tighten. If the Trofts examined the wreck closely enough to find the laser damage to the car's tires . . . but that was pretty unlikely. If they did anything, it would be a quick flyover to see that an abandoned car was, in fact, where Daulo said it was.

"Where is this hospital?" the Troft asked.

"Four blocks down that street," Daulo said, pointing toward the Troft ship blocking the road.

The alien seemed to consider. "You may take him," he said. "But on foot. No vehicles are currently permitted on the streets."

"He's *injured*," Daulo repeated, in the tone someone might use when trying to explain something to a small child. "The extra time that would take could be fatal."

"No vehicles are currently permitted on the streets," the Troft said again. "Take him, or leave him here."

"Fine," Daulo shot back scornfully. "Fadil, pull over there."

"Do not move the vehicle," the Troft said, gesturing sharply toward Fadil with his laser as the younger Sammon started to put the truck into gear. "Shut off the engine and give me the starting mechanism."

"Why?" Daulo demanded. "This is *my* truck. You go find your own."

Fadil shot his father a nervous look. "Father—"

"Quiet," Daulo cut him off, his glare focused on the Troft. "You want me to beg? Is that it? Fine, then—I'll beg. May I *please* drive the injured man to the hospital?"

The Troft gestured again. "Get out of the vehicle," he ordered. "Give me the starting mechanism."

Daulo snorted, an angry, contemptuous sound. "Give him the keys, Fadil. Everyone else, out."

A minute later they had Zoshak out of the truck, Jin supporting the unconscious man's head while the other three carried his body horizontally on their forearms like a living stretcher. "You take terrible chances, my father," Fadil murmured tautly as they headed down the street.

"I'm a Qasaman, my son," Daulo countered, his voice still simmering with anger. "These invaders might as well know from the very start who we are whom they have challenged. Jin Moreau, do we go around the front of the alien ship, or around the rear?"

"The front," Jin said. Merrick could see from her expression that she didn't agree with Daulo's in-your-face attitude, but it was also clear she wasn't about to call him on it. Certainly not in front of the man's own son. "I want to see what the forward weapons and sensor clusters look like."

Another pair of Trofts stepped into view around the ship's bow as the stretcher party approached, their lasers not quite pointing at the humans. But they made no effort to stop or even challenge. Apparently, the word had been passed from the checkpoint that this group was to be allowed past. Jin led the way around the ship, glancing casually up at the gleaming metal as they walked. Merrick looked up, too, but he could make little of the orderly array of bumps, nozzles, pits, and intakes.

And then they were past the ship and the watchful Trofts and were heading down the deserted street. "Another three blocks, you said?" Jin asked.

"Yes," Daulo confirmed. "It should be that eight-story white building just ahead, the one with the half-circle drive for emergency vehicles."

Jin half turned, taking care not to jostle Zoshak's head as she did so. "I see it," she said, turning back. "I don't suppose the Palace would happen to be somewhere along the way?"

"Not on the path, but not far off it," Daulo said. "Two streets down and half a block to the left."

"About a block away from the hospital?"

"Correct," Daulo said. "It might be possible for me to make a short side trip while you continue on with Carsh Zoshak."

Merrick looked behind them. The two Trofts they'd passed were standing together beside the ship, their attention clearly on the four humans carrying their burden down the street. "How well is the place marked?" he asked.

"There's no large illuminated sign, if that's what you mean," Daulo said. "Why, you think the invaders may not have found it yet?"

"It's possible," Merrick said.

"But unlikely," Jin warned. "If they've done their homework, they know where all the centers of government and industry are."

Daulo muttered something under his breath. "We'll know soon enough," he said.

They reached the cross street Daulo had identified, to discover that the Trofts had indeed done their homework. Midway down the block, a large but unpretentious four-story gray-stone building had been completely encircled by armed aliens, with support from a handful of tripod-mounted heavy lasers and a pair of panel-truck sized armored vehicles. Two of the soldiers were crouched by a tall front door, fiddling with something Merrick guessed was probably some kind of explosive. "So much for our lending assistance to the Shahni," Daulo muttered.

"Don't give up yet," Jin said. "If they haven't gotten the door open by the time we've turned Carsh Zoshak over to Dr. Kambuzia, there may still be something we can do."

They were at the hospital's main door when the flat crack of an explosive charge came from around the corner they'd just passed. "So ends your hoped-for options," Daulo growled. "And so ends freedom for the Shahni."

"Don't count them out yet," Jin warned. "If there's one thing I've learned about your people, it's that they always have a trick or two up their sleeves."

They reached the hospital and went inside. To Merrick's uneasy surprise, the reception lobby was as deserted as the street outside. "Hello?" Jin called. "Anyone here? We need a doctor. Where *is* everyone?"

"I don't know," Daulo said, nodding toward a group of gurneys lined up along the side wall. "Let's put him down over there."

They got Zoshak onto one of the gurneys. His teeth were chattering again, and Merrick took an extra few seconds to wrap the other's robe more snugly. "One of us could try to get into the hospital computer while the others search for the staff," he suggested as he checked Zoshak's pulse. "Maybe we can at least find out where Dr. Kambuzia is supposed to be."

"Good idea," Daulo said. "It should be—*God in heaven.*"

Merrick jerked his head up. Five armed Trofts had appeared around the corner from of one of the two hallways leading off the lobby and were forming themselves into a wide V-shaped wedge. "Humans, stop," the Qasaman words came from the leader's translator pin.

"We have an injured man—" Daulo began.

"You carry a radio transmitter," the Troft interrupted him. "You will submit to an immediate search."

Out of the corner of his eye Merrick saw his mother turn a sharp look on him. He gave her a microscopic shake of his head in response—as she'd already said, both their comms were still back at Milika. And Daulo had already said he and Fadil weren't allowed such devices.

Which meant that Merrick must have missed something when he'd searched Zoshak's clothing. Now the Trofts were going to give it a go, and they were likely to be a lot more thorough than Merrick had been. Wherever Zoshak's transmitter was hidden, they would find it.

Merrick didn't know what would happen after that. But he was pretty sure it wouldn't be pleasant. "You don't have to search," he spoke up impulsively, digging beneath his tunic. "I have it."

He held his breath as Daulo and Fadil turned astonished faces toward him. But Jin, at least, was instantly on her son's wavelength. "Yes, give it to them, " she put in before any of the aliens could respond. "While he does, we need to get our friend to the doctor." Without waiting for permission, she started pushing Zoshak's gurney toward the hallway leading off the other end of the lobby.

She'd gotten three steps before the Troft leader apparently recovered from his surprise at such chutzpah from a mere human. "Stop!" he snapped.

Jin frowned at the alien, managing to get two more steps before coming to a confused halt. "What's the problem?" she asked, glancing back at Merrick. Her hands came casually together, her left forefinger tapping the little finger of her right hand. "I said he would give it—*God in heaven*—" She broke off, her eyes going wide as she focused on the empty corridor behind the Trofts.

And as the two Trofts in the rear of the V started to turn around, she activated her sonic disruptor.

The disruptor wasn't really an antipersonnel weapon, having been designed mainly for shattering glass and brick and crystalline-based electronic equipment. But at close range, its effect on living beings was also nothing to sneer at. The two Trofts closest to the center of the blast jerked as if they'd been punched in the face, while the ones at the edges staggered like drunkards, all of them clearly fighting to hold on to their balance long enough to deal with this unexpected attack that had apparently sneaked up from behind them.

They were still trying to make their uncooperative bodies turn the necessary hundred eighty degrees to look behind them when Merrick lifted his right hand and activated his stunner.

A short, low-power laser blast shot out of his little finger, its frequency carefully tuned to expend most of its energy on the air instead of on the Troft at the other end. An instant later, a high-voltage, low-amperage lightning bolt shot out of the electrode beside the laser emitter, the current riding the partially ionized pathway that the laser flash had just created.

A full-power arcthrower blast from that same electrode would have fried the Troft where he stood, even through battle armor. The much less energetic stunner, or so the theory went, would merely knock him out.

The theory turned out to be correct. Without even a gasp, the Troft collapsed to the floor and lay still.

He was still falling when Merrick shifted his aim to the next alien in line and again fired his stunner. Four more shots, and it was over.

"Backup," Jin murmured, nodding toward the corner where the Trofts had appeared.

Merrick nodded and headed across the lobby, his hands curled into fingertip-laser firing position, his heart thudding painfully with reaction. He'd never used his stunner outside the Sun Center practice range, certainly never against another living being.

And suddenly the old family stories and histories had come boiling off their nice, neat pages. This was real. This was combat.

This was war.

"God in heaven," Daulo's shaking voice came from behind Merrick. "What *was* that?"

"Stunner," Jin told him. "Something else Merrick has that I don't. Merrick?"

Merrick reached the corner and paused, his audio enhancers reaching out ahead of him. *A spine leopard hunt,* he told himself firmly. *Just think of it as another spine leopard hunt. With really weird-looking spine leopards.*

There were no sounds of footsteps coming from the hallway. Cautiously, he eased an eye around the corner.

"Clear," he called back softly. There *were* faint noises of a sort coming from down there, though. Not Trofts, but soft, tense Qasaman voices. "I may have found the doctors and staff," he added, turning his enhancers off again." He turned back to look at his mother. "Do you want me to check—?"

He broke off, his eyes refocusing on the gurney behind his mother and the two Sammons, the gurney where they'd laid Zoshak.

The *empty* gurney where they'd laid Zoshak. "Mom!" he snapped, jabbing a finger.

The others turned to look. "What in—? Where did he *go*?" Daulo demanded.

"No idea," Jin said grimly as she hurried to the far corridor where she'd been heading when the Troft stopped her. "He's not down here," she reported, peering around the corner. "But there's a stairway just off the lobby. Just a minute."

She paused, and Merrick spotted the twitch of cheek muscles as she keyed in her audio enhancers. "He's on the stairs," she said. "Moving fast." She threw an unreadable look at Merrick. "I guess he wasn't as injured as he looked."

"That's impossible," Merrick protested. "He had a slow heartbeat. How do you fake a slow heartbeat?"

"Forget the *how* and concentrate on the *why*," Jin said, waving him forward. "Daulo, Fadil; go check on the hospital staff. See if they need any help. Merrick and I will go find Carsh Zoshak."

The stairway was quiet as Jin and Merrick went in. "You sure the footsteps were in here?" Merrick asked as he looked upward through the gap between the switchback flights of stairs.

"Yes, I could hear the echo," Jin said. "Sounded like he was taking the steps three at a time, which means he could have made it all the way to the top floor by now."

Merrick frowned. *Three* at a time? Not only had Zoshak not been injured, he'd been in a lot better shape than Merrick had guessed. "What do we do?"

"He seemed to be going for speed, not stealth," Jin said. "That implies distance, which implies a high floor. Let's start at the eighth and work downward."

They headed up, their servos allowing them to also take the steps three at a time. At the top, Jin listened briefly at the door, then opened it and slipped through. Merrick followed, and found himself in a long, light-blue corridor lined with numbered doors.

He keyed in his audio enhancers. Above the general background murmur that seemed to pervade any center of human activity, he could hear what sounded like two different nearby voices. They were too quiet for him to distinguish individual words, but there was no mistaking the underlying urgency. "Left side," Jin murmured. "Four or five doors down."

She headed off. Merrick keyed off his enhancers' and followed.

They were within a few meters of the door when Merrick began to make out actual words. "—easy, Your Excellency," Zoshak was saying. He did not, Merrick noted a bit resentfully, sound even dazed, let alone seriously injured. "Lean on me—I can take your weight."

Jin glanced back at Merrick, crossed the last two steps to the doorway, and strode into the room. Merrick followed.

And came to a sharp halt beside his equally motionless mother. Across the room, standing beside an elaborate recovery bed, Zoshak had a supporting arm around an old, frail-looking man dressed in a hospital gown, a robe, and a pair of soft boots. Between the two of them and the door, facing the two Cobras, was another young man, his tunic partially open to reveal the same scaled gray outfit Merrick had seen on Zoshak.

Only this man was also wearing a matching set of gloves, and both hands were raised to point at the intruders, his little fingers extended, the other fingers curled back over his palms with his thumbs resting tautly against the ring-finger nails.

The same position a Cobra would use to fire his fingertip lasers.

Merrick felt his stomach tighten. What in the Worlds had he and his mother gotten themselves into?

"Step away, enemies of Qasama," the young man bit out, his eyes blazing defiance and anger and a complete absence of fear. "Step away, or die."

CHAPTER EIGHT

"Take it easy," Jin said, lifting her hands to show their emptiness, her heart and bad knee throbbing in unison as she stared at the positioning of the young man's hands. No—it wasn't possible. The Qasamans *couldn't* have created their own Cobras. Not from scratch, not even with the bodies of her former teammates to examine. This had to be some kind of bluff. "Just take it easy," she said again. "We're not your enemies."

"You are the demon warrior Jin Moreau," the other ground out. "You are here, and we have been invaded. What conclusion *should* we draw?"

"Those are *Troft* ships out there, not ours," Jin pointed out.

"From which we conclude that you and the Trofts are in league," the Qasaman countered.

"We're not in any sort of league," Jin said. "We trade with some of them, but that's all."

"And we don't even trade with this bunch," Merrick put in. "Their demesne markings aren't like any we've ever run into before."

The Qasaman spared a quick glare at Merrick, then turned his eyes back to Jin. "Then why are you here?"

Jin winced. This was going to sound incredibly lame. "I was invited."

"By whom?"

"I don't know," she had to admit. "I received a written but unsigned message urgently requesting my presence on Qasama."

"Most likely from Daulo Sammon," Zoshak spoke up, an edge of urgency in his voice. "Ifrit, we need to leave this place. If His Excellency is taken, this will all have been for nothing."

"There's no profit in escaping enemies who stand before us if other enemies stand at our back," the other Qasaman countered, his face hardening even further. "And liars are ever enemies."

"I'm not lying," Jin insisted as calmly as she could. There was a narrow tube running along the outer edge of the little finger of each of the Qasaman's gloves, she noted, the tubes extending all the way back to his wrists. Dart throwers with compressed-air propulsion, most likely, possibly modeled after the palm-mate gun Decker York had used during the Cobra Worlds' first Qasaman mission. That was probably what she and Merrick were facing, not Cobra-style fingertip lasers.

But why then was the Qasaman holding his hands that way? Had they deliberately adopted Cobra-style triggering for their dart guns? "And it wasn't Daulo Sammon who asked us here," she added.

"Someone else, then?" the Qasaman suggested, his voice carrying the subtle undertones of a hidden trap. "Someone else you might have met during your last intrusion onto Qasaman soil?"

Jin hesitated. It was a trap, all right. Only which way did it point? Would invoking Miron Akim's name help her or damn her? She had no idea what had happened to Akim in the past three decades, whether he had worked his way up the ladder or whether his brief and reluctant association with her had completely ruined his career.

But she had no choice. The Qasaman was angling for a name, and she had only one to offer him. "It's possible the invitation came from a former Shahni agent named Miron Akim," she said.

The Qasaman smiled tightly, and Jin could practically hear the sound of the trap snapping shut. "No, Jin Moreau, it didn't," he said. "Miron Akim did *not* invite you here."

"How do you know?" Merrick demanded. "*We* don't even know who sent the message. How could you?"

"Because, demon warrior," the Qasaman bit out, "I am Siraj Akim, *son* of Miron Akim."

Merrick felt his mouth drop open. "You're his—?"

And then, abruptly, something flashed past the room's window. "Watch it!" Jin snapped, dropping into a crouch.

"What was it?" Zoshak demanded. He, too, had dropped lower, bringing the old man down into a crouch alongside him. "I saw something go by the window."

"Some kind of aircraft," Jin said. "Looks like the Trofts have started a serious search of the hospital."

"And so now your mission is plain," Siraj accused coldly. "You led them here against us."

"It wasn't them, Ifrit," Zoshak said, his voice respectful but firm. "The attackers detected my communications with you and the Nest."

"That is claimed to be impossible," Siraj insisted.

"Let's figure out later how they did it," Jin said. "Right now, it's obvious you're trying to get this gentleman out of here before the Trofts find him. Merrick and I can get out of your way, or we can help you. Your choice."

Siraj snorted. "And why would you wish to help us?"

"In the name of God, Ifrit," Zoshak snapped. "We have no time for this. You have two options: kill them, or trust them." He looked at Merrick. "For myself, I trust them."

For perhaps five of Jin's accelerated heartbeats Siraj continued to stare at her. Then, to her relief, he slowly moved his thumbs away from the curled fingers and lowered his hands. "Very well," he said. "But we travel under *my* command."

"Absolutely," Jin assured him, feeling some of the tension drain out of her. The reprieve was only temporary—that much was obvious from his expression and tone. But at least they weren't going to have a firefight here and now. "What do you want us to do?"

Siraj gestured to Merrick. "You: help Djinni Zoshak."

Jin felt her eyebrows creeping up her forehead. *Djinni, Ifrit*— both names were echoes of ancient Earth Middle Eastern spirit mythos . . . and the Qasamans had always called Cobras *demon warriors*. Another coincidence, like the dart gun triggering?

"We might do better to lay him flat," Merrick suggested as he crossed to Zoshak's side.

"We can't," Zoshak said. "There's still residual healing fluid in his lungs, and his torso must be kept upright. You and I will form a cross-seat, our hands interlocking with each other's wrists to form a square."

"Yes, I know that one," Merrick said. "But we really don't need both of us. I can carry him by myself, which would free you up in case there was trouble."

"You will both carry him," Siraj ordered before Zoshak could answer. "We travel toward the rear stairway, at the end of the hall most distant from the lobby. You—Jin Moreau—see if the corridor is clear."

Jin nodded and turned back to the room's doorway, the skin between her shoulder blades crawling with unpleasant anticipation. If Siraj meant to kill her, now was his best chance to try it.

But nothing came poking or stabbing or burning into her back, and she reached the hallway to find it still deserted. "Clear," she called softly, looking both ways and then stepping out into the center of the passageway.

The others stepped out of the room to join her, Siraj first, then Merrick and Zoshak with the old man sitting on their intermeshed forearms, his arms draped loosely over the younger men's shoulders. The soft plastic water bottle that had been sitting on the table beside the bed, Jin saw, was now resting in the old man's lap. "Rear door, you said?" she murmured.

"Yes," Siraj said. "You have spearhead."

Spearhead? Probably their term for *point*, Jin decided. With a nod, she set off down the corridor, her audio enhancers searching for sounds of movement ahead.

"Where *is* everyone?" Merrick asked softly from behind her. "The Trofts didn't put the whole staff downstairs, did they?"

"The doctors and attendants on this floor have taken shelter in the various patient rooms," Siraj said as he came up beside her. "I ordered them there when I first arrived." He gave a short, low hiss. "If I'd known how quickly the invaders would focus on this place and the Palace, I would have risked bringing him out alone."

"So His Excellency is one of the Shahni?" Jin asked.

Siraj darted her a dark sideways look. "His identity is none of your concern," he said stiffly.

"No, of course not," Jin agreed. "My apologies."

For another two steps they traveled in silence. "I am told the other demon warrior is your son," Siraj said.

"Yes," Jin told him, wondering how he'd known that. "My eldest."

Siraj grunted and again fell silent.

They were halfway to the brightly-lit EXIT sign at the far end of the hallway when Jin's enhancers picked up the faint sound of hurrying footsteps ahead of them. "Someone's on the stairs," she warned, stepping sideways to the nearest door and trying the knob. It was locked; with a boost of strength from her wrist servos, she snapped it open. "In here," she said, swinging the door wide.

"No," Siraj said, motioning her back to the center of the corridor. "We meet them here."

"I meant that Merrick and Carsh Zoshak can go in there while you and I—"

"We meet them here," Siraj repeated tartly. "All of us together."

With a supreme effort, Jin kept her mouth shut. Didn't Siraj see that facing an enemy with half his force burdened with an invalid was a stupid thing to do? Even worse, with one of his two available *Cobras* burdened that way?

But she couldn't say anything. Not a woman. Not in this society.

But Zoshak could. Jin opened her mouth to suggest he do just that—

The door ahead slammed open, and five armed Trofts boiled into the corridor. They'd been closer than Jin had realized. "Stop!" the leader's translator pin barked.

Siraj motioned, and the group of humans came to a halt. "Is that all they can say?" Merrick muttered.

"What now?" Jin asked quietly as the Trofts strode toward them, sorting themselves into the by-now-familiar wedge formation.

"Follow my action," Siraj murmured back. "And do not reveal your true nature."

Jin shot him a frown. Beneath the other's cold eyes, a hint of a grim smile was tugging at the corners of his mouth.

And suddenly she understood. The old man being carried by two of their number, the whole group being caught in the middle of an open hallway—it wasn't simply stupidity or carelessness. Siraj had deliberately staged the scene in order to lower the Trofts' expectations and therefore their guard.

It was a good and subtle plan, and now that she knew about it Jin could appreciate the tactic. Nevertheless, as the Trofts approached, she took a moment to put targeting locks onto each of the aliens' foreheads behind their transparent faceplates. Whenever she next fired her fingertip lasers, her servos would move her arms and hands to make sure those targets would be the first ones hit.

There wasn't much point in looking harmless, after all, if it ended up getting you killed.

The lead Troft put a finger over his translator pin as he walked, and Jin notched up her audio enhancers. [Five humans, we have them on the eighth floor west,] she heard the murmured cattertalk over the relative thunder of the aliens' footsteps. [Weapons, none are visible.]

"Take his weight," Zoshak murmured to Merrick.

The lead Troft acknowledged something Jin couldn't hear and lowered his hand from his translator. Taking the cue, Jin also lowered her audio enhancement. "Where do you take the old human?" the Troft asked as he and his squad stopped two meters in front of Siraj.

"To a treatment room," Siraj said, pointing toward one of the doors the Trofts had just passed. "That one, right there."

The two Trofts in the rear turned to look where he was pointing. As they did so, Siraj abruptly leaped forward, grabbed the lead Troft's laser, and twisted it effortlessly out of the alien's grip. [Soldiers—!] the Troft yelped, his outburst cut off as Siraj slammed the laser's butt hard against the side of his helmet.

Jin sprinted toward her side of the wedge as the stunned Troft collapsed to the floor. The other soldiers were already in motion, two of them swinging their lasers toward Siraj, the other two lining up their weapons on Jin. Jin dodged sideways out of their line of fire, hoping to draw the muzzles far enough away from the old man that when she fired her fingertip lasers there would be no chance that any of the aliens would get off a dying shot in that direction.

Something caught the corner of her eye as it shot past over her shoulder from behind her. It was the old man's water bottle, arrowing toward the two Trofts on her side of the wedge and sending the aliens reflexively jerking back from the incoming missile.

And as they did, Siraj fired a casual-looking sideways burst from his captured laser that sliced the bottle open and flash-heated the water just as it splashed across the Trofts' faces.

Their faceplates protected them from any actual injury, of course. But the simple fact of having liquid splashed violently and unexpectedly in front of their eyes distracted them for a fatal half second. One of them managed to get off a shot, the burst going wild.

And then Jin was there, ripping open the first Troft's faceplate and throwing a servo-powered punch into his throat bladder. Snatching the laser from his suddenly limp grasp, she hurled it sideways it at the farther of the two Trofts on Siraj's side, hoping to take him out or at least distract him as Siraj waded into his own battle. Another pulled faceplate and punch finished off her second opponent, and she turned to help Siraj, her hands curling into laser-firing position.

Her help wasn't necessary. Jin's two Trofts had barely thudded to the floor when Siraj's pair joined them.

"My father was right, Jin Moreau," Siraj commented as he tossed his captured laser disdainfully onto the body of the nearest Troft. "You are indeed a capable fighter." Half turning, he motioned to Zoshak. "Quickly, now."

The group resumed its journey down the hallway. "I trust you're not expecting to push the innocent routine any farther," Jin warned. "You can bet there are already backup troops on the way."

"They are welcome to the exercise," Siraj said coolly as he came to a halt well short of the stairway door. "Djinni Zoshak?"

Jin blinked as Zoshak brushed past her and pulled open a halfmeter-wide panel set into the wall, a panel labeled *Laundry*. "You're kidding," she said.

Neither Qasaman bothered to answer. Zoshak climbed feet-first into the shaft, maneuvering himself all the way to the rear and turning to face the others, sliding down until only his head and upper chest were visible. "Ready," he said, holding out his arms.

"Mom?" Merrick asked uncertainly.

Jin peered at the shaft. It was considerably deeper, front to back, than it was wide, which left plenty of room in front of Zoshak for a second person to join him. But that didn't make the idea any less lunatic.

But by now, all other exits from the floor were undoubtedly blocked. "Go ahead," she told Merrick. "They seem to know what they're doing."

Still looking doubtful, Merrick eased the old man's legs through the opening. Siraj moved in to assist, and together they worked their burden into Zoshak's waiting arms. Gripping the old man firmly around his chest and waist, Zoshak began a rapid but clearly controlled slide downwards. "You next, Jin Moreau," Siraj said, nodding toward the shaft. "Use the pressure of your feet against the sides to control your descent." His eyes narrowed. "Do *not* lose control and fall."

"I won't," Jin promised as she climbed into the shaft. It felt narrower than it looked, and she sent up a quick note of thanks that she wasn't claustrophobic.

Unfortunately, she quickly discovered that her servos hadn't been designed with this sort of maneuver in mind, and that her own leg muscles weren't nearly strong enough on their own to apply the pressure needed to control her descent. Fortunately, some of her upper-body servos *did* work in the proper direction, and pressing her elbows and upper arms against the sides of the shaft did the trick.

She'd made it a couple of meters down when the shaft darkened as Merrick came in above her. There was a moment of soft scraping as he figured out the necessary technique, and then silence as he joined her and Zoshak in their mass slide. Another few meters, and the shaft went completely dark as Siraj brought up the rear, closing the flap behind him.

A minute later, they reached the bottom of the shaft and a

bin half full of white sheets. Jin held position until Zoshak had extricated himself and the old man from the bin, then followed.

She found herself in an institutional laundry facility of the sort she'd seen a hundred times in thrillers and comedies. This was the first time she'd ever actually been in one, though, and she found her nose crinkling at the crisply intense smells pervading the place. "What now?" she asked when Merrick and Siraj had joined them.

"That is your decision," Siraj said, eyeing her coolly. "You may leave now, and we shall most likely not meet again. Or you may come with us and ensure that His Excellency arrives safely at his destination."

Jin snorted. Her and Merrick, alone in hostile territory, with an even more hostile enemy having just invaded? "Not much of a choice there, Siraj Akim," she said. "We're with you. How exactly do we get His Excellency out?"

"There is a secret exit from this level that we can use." A ghost of a smile flickered across Siraj's face. "We have been preparing for war for many years, Jin Moreau."

"Only you've been expecting the wrong opponents," Jin pointed out.

"Perhaps," Siraj said, his voice neutral. "You will again take spearhead—" he looked at Merrick "—and you will carry His Excellency." He started toward the laundry room door.

"Wait a minute," Jin said with a surge of sudden guilt. In the excitement of the past few minutes, she'd completely forgotten about Daulo and Fadil. "We first have to go get our friends."

"No," Siraj said flatly. "We must go now."

Jin braced herself. "I understand," she said. "Merrick, you go with them."

Merrick's jaw dropped. "*What*? Mom—"

"Help them get him to safety," she cut him off, working hard to filter her apprehension out of her voice. "I'll catch up with you later."

"Mom, this is *crazy*," he growled.

"You want me to just leave Daulo and Fadil to the Trofts?" Jin countered.

Merrick clamped his mouth shut. "Of course not. Fine—I'll come with you."

Jin looked at Siraj. There was a watchful look in his eye, the same look she'd seen there earlier when he'd asked who else she knew on Qasama. "No," she said. "I can get Daulo and Fadil out myself. You help Siraj Akim and Carsh Zoshak."

"But—"

"They're our allies now," Jin said firmly. "This is war, Merrick. Follow your orders."

He took a deep breath. "Where do we meet?"

"Two blocks south of the gate where we came in," she said. "Show yourself for two minutes at fifteen and forty after each hour until we make contact."

He nodded, still clearly unhappy with the arrangement but knowing it was useless to argue further. "Good luck," he said.

"God be with you," Zoshak added.

"Thank you." Jin nodded to Siraj. "And with you." She turned toward the door.

"Wait," Siraj said; and to Jin's surprise he stepped to her side. "I will accompany you."

"I appreciate your offer, Siraj Akim," Jin said, frowning at him. "But I thought we just decided it would be safer if His Excellency had a three-man escort."

"Djinni Zoshak knows the route," Siraj said. "He and your son can follow it without significant danger." He smiled humorlessly. "Allow me to put it more bluntly: I trust them with His Excellency more than I trust you alone in Sollas."

Jin suppressed a grimace. So much for being allies. "As you wish," she said. "Merrick, I'll see you later."

The hallway outside the laundry room was deserted. Zoshak turned to the right; with a final nod at his mother, Merrick followed, the old man balanced across his forearms. "Stairs are this way," Siraj said, pointing to the left.

"Just a second," Jin said as a rack of freshly washed white medical coats caught her eye. "A little camouflage might not be a bad idea."

They each took a coat and slipped it on. "You might want to take off those gloves, too," Jin added. "They don't exactly look hospital-issue."

"This will do," Siraj said, taking three more coats and folding them into a bundle that would hide his hands. "Take spearhead."

Jin's enhanced hearing was picking up sounds of hurrying feet and rapid cattertalk well before she and Siraj reached the top of the stairs. It was thus no surprise when she stepped out into the corridor to find it full of Trofts. Two of them stopped abruptly at the sight of the humans, leveling their lasers as one of them moved his beak in inaudible cattertalk. "What are you doing here?" the Qasaman translation came.

"Don't shoot," Siraj gasped, his eyes wide, his face taut with astonishment and fear. Whatever else the man might be, he was a competent actor. "My name is Rajeem Tommarno. Lanara Summel and I are laboratory technicians. We were asked to bring some spare coats to the doctor's station on this floor."

"Why?" the Troft asked.

"I don't know," Siraj said. "Three coats—that was all they said."

For a moment the Troft eyed him. Then, taking one hand from his laser, he gestured Siraj over. Siraj hesitated, then stepped gingerly up to him and held out his bundle for inspection. The Troft pawed systematically through the coats, clearly searching for anything that might be hidden inside the folds of cloth. Finding nothing, he stepped back, shifting his laser back into a two-handed grip "This soldier will take you," he said. "You will stay there until other notice is given."

"Yes, of course," Siraj assured him, backing hastily away. The other Troft took a step down the corridor and paused expectantly. "Yes, of course," Siraj said again, and started off. Jin joined him, the Troft soldier falling into step a cautious couple of paces behind them.

"They seem upset," Siraj murmured to Jin.

Jin grimaced. Twenty Trofts in this corridor alone, plus who knew how many dozens more elsewhere in the hospital. "Having their soldiers beaten into the sand does that to military types," she murmured back. "I guess I should have insisted you get out with the others while you could. This isn't going to be easy."

"It may turn out to be not quite the challenge you believe," Siraj said calmly. "In here."

He led the way under an archway into what appeared to be

a patient receiving and processing area. The alcove was deserted except for a pair of Trofts flanking a door at the rear of the area. Jin eyed the various desks and computer stations as they maneuvered their way through, noting that the chairs were all facing different directions, without a single one being tucked neatly beneath its desk. When everyone had left, they'd left in a hurry.

"Go to the door in the rear," the Troft behind them ordered.

The two guards eyed the group as they approached. One of them started to speak, and Jin notched up her audio enhancers. [These humans, why are they here?] the guard demanded.

[The two civilians inside, to them they bring disguises,] the Troft behind Jin said. [The enemy combatants we seek, perhaps these are the ones.]

The door guards' expressions went a little harder. [Yet these disguises, they bring *three* of them,] the spokesman pointed out.

[An additional and unknown enemy, such may lurk nearby,] the escort agreed. [Watchfulness, we will maintain it.]

[The humans, we will watch them closely,] the guard assured the escort grimly.

The Troft behind Siraj nudged the Qasaman with the muzzle of his laser. [The door, go through it.] "Go inside."

"Yes, of course," Siraj said. He reached the door, pushed it open with his forearm, and went through. Jin followed, once again lowering her enhancers.

The room beyond the door was a lounge of sorts, with computer monitors scattered among the couches and cushions to allow the doctors and staffers to keep an eye on what was happening with their patients. There were about a dozen men and women in the room, some pacing nervously, the rest sitting alone or in quietly conversing pairs. Flanking the inside of the door were another pair of watchful Troft soldiers.

And seated on a couch at the rear of the room, painfully conspicuous in their non-medical garb, were Daulo and Fadil.

Siraj nudged Jin to their right, away from the door. "I will take Daulo Sammon the coats," he said. "As the soldiers watch me, you will move behind you to the fire alarm."

"*If* they watch you," Jin warned, glancing casually over her shoulder at the Trofts. Out of the corner of her eye she spotted the alarm Siraj had mentioned: a small red plate set into the wall with a thumb-sized lever set into it.

"They will," Siraj assured her. "There are two civilians, yet I have *three* coats. They will watch closely to see what I do with the third."

"If you say so," Jin said frowning. Either Siraj was making a monumental leap of logic, or else he'd eavesdropped on the conversation outside and understood enough cattertalk to know the Trofts were already thinking in that direction. "When do you want me to set off the alarm?"

"You do not set off the alarm," Siraj said. "The alarm is activated by pushing the lever downward. You will, instead, push the lever in—it will resist, so push firmly—and once it is in you will pull it *upward*."

"Which will do what?"

"It will help us," Siraj said. "Go now."

Jin looked around the room, pretended to notice someone she recognized and started over toward him. Halfway there, she pretended she'd changed her mind and drifted instead to the side, coming to a halt a pace away from the wall and the fire alarm. Siraj had meanwhile crossed to Daulo and Fadil and was whispering urgently to them. From the two villagers' expressions, it was clear they had no idea who this man was and weren't particularly happy at having extra attention being drawn their way. *So far, so good,* Jin thought, and looked over at the two Trofts by the door.

To find that Siraj's plan had worked exactly halfway. One of the Trofts was indeed thoroughly engrossed in Siraj's inaudible conversation. Unfortunately, the other was gazing just as intently at Jin.

She shifted her attention back to Siraj. He was gazing sideways at her, his eyebrows cocked in silent question. She gave him a tiny shrug, followed by an equally microscopic tilt of her head toward the Trofts. Siraj inclined his head slightly in reply and turned back to Daulo. There was another short conversation, and this time it was Daulo who looked a question at Jin. She gave him a small nod, wondering uneasily what Siraj's new plan was and what the

Trofts were thinking about all this. She was hardly an expert on alien body language, but she'd seen enough annoyed Trofts to have the unpleasant feeling that the one focused on her was looking for an excuse to shoot something.

Across the room, the quiet conversation ceased and Daulo and Fadil stood up. Siraj handed a lab coat to each of them, and the two villagers headed toward opposite rear corners of the room.

And with that, the two Trofts now had *four* humans they needed to keep a close eye on. Jin held her breath, waiting for her personal watchdog to shift some of his attention to one of the others. Half a second's worth of inattention, maybe less, and she would be able to get to the fire alarm without being shot.

She was still waiting for that half-second window when the door opened and the two Trofts who'd been standing guard outside strode in.

Jin grimaced. So much for that approach.

So much, too, she decided suddenly, for letting Siraj call the shots here. The Trofts were probably still a little off-balance after the brief battle upstairs, but that confusion wouldn't last long. She and the others had to get out of here before the invaders got their balance back. Focusing on each of the Trofts in turn, she set up targeting locks on their heads, starting with the one watching her. It was risky—if her watchdog decided she was making suspicious movements he could probably get off a shot before she could take him down. But if she didn't do something—

And then, Siraj raised his hands and pointed both of them at Jin. "Now!" he shouted.

Jin froze in disbelief as all four of the Trofts spun around, their lasers tracking toward her. With that single barked word, Siraj had just quadrupled the odds she was already facing. Was he *trying* to get her killed?

Maybe he was. Maybe that was why he'd insisted on accompanying her up here in the first place.

And then, to Jin's astonishment, all four lasers changed direction in midtrack as the Trofts turned their attention back to Siraj.

All of the Trofts, including Jin's own guard.

Jin didn't waste time wondering why they would do something so foolish. Stepping to the wall, she pushed in the lever and pulled it up.

Nothing happened.

For a fraction of a second she just stood there, staring at the alarm. She'd expected something instantly lethal or at least instantly dramatic: targeted lasers or machine guns, flash-bang grenades, or at least stun-strobe lights. But nothing.

Nothing, that is, except that her sudden movement hadn't gone unnoticed. The four Troft lasers changed direction again in mid-turn, this time tracking back toward Jin. She turned toward them, bringing up her own hands, consciously relaxing her muscles to let her nanocomputer and its programmed evasion reflexes to take over the instant it became necessary.

Her hands were halfway to firing position, and the first Troft's laser was nearly lined up on her torso, when a pair of brilliant blue flashes lanced out from Siraj's hands and blew off the side of one of the other Trofts' helmets.

Jin's fired her own lasers even as she turned to look more closely at Siraj's hands. So those slender tubes, which she'd earlier pegged as dart guns, were in fact real Cobra-style lasers.

But there was no time to consider the ramifications of that now. She turned back to her own target.

To find to her dismay that his laser was now pointed directly at her chest.

Unlike Siraj's lasers, hers hadn't even penetrated the Troft's helmet.

Reflexively, she fired again, cursing under her breath as her arms swung of their own accord to send another ineffective shot at the second Troft she'd targeted instead of the Troft she really wanted to shoot at. She threw herself to the side, canceling the rest of the targeting locks as she did so.

The Troft in front of her fired, the shot burning past her shoulder. Desperately, she flashed a new targeting lock on him, slamming to the floor just as Siraj took out another of the aliens with a second pair of shots. Wincing as the jolt of her landing drove spikes of pain through her arthritic joints, she fired her antiarmor laser, her nanocomputer wrenching her joints still further as it twisted her body around to bring her left leg to bear on the designated target. She half closed her eyes, watching the Troft swinging his own weapon toward her, wondering who would win the race.

She did, but just barely. This time, her more powerful antiarmor laser blasted with gratifying speed though the armor her fingertip lasers had failed to penetrate. She targeted the last remaining Troft as the first collapsed to the floor, firing again as her swinging leg continued its arc.

Her shot and Siraj's got there at the same time. The alien went down, his head effectively vaporized.

Jin rolled back to her feet, her joints still throbbing from her barely controlled fall. Siraj's hands, she noted uneasily as she straightened up, were still curled in firing positions, his face unreadable as he gazed across the room at her. "Nice job," she said as conversationally as she could into the room's sudden deathly silence. "What now?"

For a moment Siraj didn't move or speak, his hands still ready, his little fingers not quite pointed at Jin. Perhaps wondering if this was the chance he'd been waiting for to deal with this other enemy of his world. Jin stood equally motionless, her heart pounding, keeping her own thumbs away from her fingernails...

And then, to her relief, Siraj lowered his hands to his sides. "Check the corridor," he said, his voice brisk and businesslike as he started across the room, gesturing to Daulo and Fadil to join them. "Confirm that it's safe."

Safe? Frowning, Jin stepped to the door and cautiously pushed it open.

And felt her jaw drop. Three humans and five Trofts were visible out in the corridor, lying in crumpled heaps. "What in the—?" She broke off, throwing a stunned look at Siraj. "Did I just—?"

"They are merely asleep," Siraj assured her as he and the two Sammons joined her. "A quick-acting gas, released into every part of the hospital except the room where the system is activated."

"Nice," Jin managed, feeling a whisper of relief. Relief, and a little embarrassment that she'd automatically assumed the worst.

Surely even the Qasamans wouldn't indiscriminately slaughter this many of their own people without absolute need.

"But the reprieve is only temporary," Siraj warned, sweeping his gaze around the rest of the room. "You—return to your homes, or seek shelter in those of friends. Go now. In the name of the Shahni."

The staffers glanced at one another. Then, without question or protest, they made their way calmly to the door. Siraj stepped aside, motioning Jin and the Sammons to do likewise, as the staffers filed though the doorway and disappeared in both directions down the corridor. "You realize, of course, that the Trofts outside will see them," Jin said quietly.

"And may stop them for questioning," Siraj agreed as he started across the receiving area. "They will say nothing."

"What if the Trofts insist?"

"That will take time," Siraj said. "At this point, time works to our advantage."

Even at the possible cost of their lives? With an effort, Jin kept her mouth shut. Maybe her earlier assumption about the lengths the Qasamans would go to hadn't been all that far off the mark. "Where are we going?" she asked instead.

"We follow Carsh Zoshak," Siraj said. "Daulo Sammon, you and your son stay close behind me." He hesitated, just noticeably. "You, Jin Moreau, will guard our back path."

He headed off at a brisk stride toward the stairway. Daulo threw Jin an unreadable look, then turned back and concentrated on keeping up with Siraj. Fadil, for his part, seemed intent on pretending Jin didn't exist.

The exit from the laundry room level was hidden behind a tool rack near the end of the hallway. The small landing behind the door was only dimly lit, but with her optical enhancers Jin could see there were three or four floors' worth of narrow switchback stairways leading down into the gloom. What was at the bottom of the stairs she never found out; midway down the second flight, Siraj opened a hidden door in the side wall and led the group into another dimly lit tunnel heading off at right angles to the first.

The road didn't end there, either. There was a whole warren of tunnels beneath the city, with a bewildering array of cross-tunnels, stairways, descending ramps, and occasional booby traps that Siraj carefully deactivated and then reactivated once they were past. Several times Jin considered asking where exactly they were going, but each time decided there was no point. Even if Siraj was willing to tell her, the name or location would probably be meaningless to her anyway.

The trip seemed to take forever, but according to Jin's nanocomputer clock they were in the tunnels for only seventeen minutes before Siraj opened a final door and led the way into a well-lit room whose only furnishings were a pair of Qasamans seated behind transparent body shields and armed with nasty-looking machine guns. Siraj exchanged a set of countersigns with them, then led the way past to one of three doors leading off the room.

"What is this place?" Daulo asked as they walked down another corridor.

"A refuge prepared against the onslaught of war," Siraj told him. "There are many such as this beneath the cities and larger villages. In here."

He opened one of the doors and gestured the others inside. Jin stepped through the doorway.

And came to an abrupt halt. Five other Qasamans were standing silently along the walls of the room, all of them wearing identical grim expressions above their scaled gray bodysuits.

Seated in a wooden chair in the center of the room, his hands manacled behind him, his ankles similarly fastened to the chair legs, was Merrick.

"What in the *Worlds*?" Jin bit out, her eyes flicking around the room. "Siraj Akim, what is the meaning of this?"

Siraj remained silent. So did the other Qasamans. "Merrick?" Jin asked, looking at her son.

"You know that old gag, Mom?" Merrick asked, his voice taut. "The one that goes, 'I could tell you, but then I'd have to kill you'?" His lip twitched. "I think our hosts may be taking that seriously."

CHAPTER NINE

Jin looked around the room, her pulse once again pounding. The five gray-suited Qasamans were standing casually enough, with their arms hanging loosely at their sides. But all five were wearing the same laser-equipped gloves as Siraj, and all five had their fingers curled almost into firing position. All they needed to do was twist at their wrists and squeeze their fingernails, and she and Merrick would be in the center of a kill zone. "All right," she said as calmly as she could. "You've made your point."

"What point would that be, Jin Moreau?" Siraj asked.

"You didn't bring us all the way here just to kill us," Jin said. "You could have done that anywhere along the way."

"What, with you standing behind me?" Siraj countered. "That would have been difficult."

"The marching order was your choice," Jin reminded him. "You could have put me in front of you at any point. Certainly long enough to dispose of me."

Siraj's lip twitched. "We may yet do that."

"Why?" Jin asked. "What have we done against you or the Qasaman people?"

"You are a demon warrior," a new voice said from behind her.

Jin turned to see a gray-haired man enter the room through another door. His face was lined, his walk the careful gait of someone with sensitive bones. Probably somewhere between eighty and eighty-five years old, she estimated. "Yes, my identity's been established," she said. "And you are . . . ?"

He smiled tightly. "Come now, Jin Moreau," he admonished. "Have the years been so unkind to me?"

Jin blinked. The years had, actually—the man looked to be a good thirty years older than she was, and she still couldn't reconcile his face with her memories. But his *voice*—"Miron *Akim*?" she asked.

"Of course," he said. His smile faded away. "Why else do you think you and your son are not already dead?"

Jin took a careful breath. "I received a note," she said. "I assumed—"

"Yes, I've heard of your story." The elder Akim held out his hand. "Show me."

Jin reached inside her tunic, noting the extra wariness of the gray-suited guards as she did so. "It was delivered to my home on Aventine," she said, pulling out the paper and handing it over.

Akim took the note and studied it briefly. "Convenient," he said, handing it back. "Also conveniently unsigned." His gaze hardened a little more. "Why are you here?"

"I've already told you," Jin said. "The answer isn't going to change just because you keep asking."

"No, I suppose it won't." Akim eyed her thoughtfully. "My people don't trust you, Jin Moreau. My own son doesn't trust you. Why should I let you live? You *or* your son?"

Jin took a careful breath. His people and his son didn't trust them . . . but Akim had rather conspicuously left his own name off that list. Maybe there was still enough doubt in his mind for her to talk their way out of this. "Because you've just been invaded," she told him, "and because you need all the assets you can get. Merrick and I can be two of those assets."

"Or you could be two more of our invaders," Siraj put in.

"We just helped you rescue someone out from under the Trofts' noses," Jin reminded him. "Why would we do that if we were allied with them?"

"Perhaps in order to infiltrate this facility," Akim said, gesturing at the room around him.

"Oh, please," Jin said scornfully. "You would hardly have brought four strangers to a place you genuinely wanted kept secret. This can't be anything more important than a minor staging area."

"Perhaps you hoped we would take you deeper," Siraj said.

"Knowing how you feel about us?" Jin asked. "Now you accuse us of being not only enemies, but *stupid* enemies."

"Or very clever enemies," Akim said. "What would *you* do in our place?"

Jin studied his face. But it was giving nothing away. "I'd try to find a way to split the difference," she said. "You don't trust us, and I can't think of any way we can prove we're genuinely on your side."

She looked at Siraj. "And to be honest, I can't blame you for that attitude," she conceded. "Not after the mistakes our people have made with yours."

"'Mistakes'?" Siraj bit out. "Is that what you call them?"

"Call them whatever you want," Jin said, turning back to Akim. "So as I say, let's split the difference. You take Merrick and me back up to street level, and you'll never have to see us again."

"Where would you go?" Akim asked. "Back to Milika with Daulo Sammon and his son?"

Jin looked at Daulo. His face was just as wooden as Akim's. "No," she said. "Not even if Milika was willing to accept us. A Cobra's greatest strength is subterfuge, and for that we need a population base large enough for us to blend in. No, our war against the Trofts will be much more effective here in Sollas."

"*Your* war?" Akim asked.

"You are our people, Miron Akim," Jin said. "Whatever our differences in the past, you're part of humanity. We aren't going to sit by and let some group of Trofts think they can pull off a stunt like this."

"And so you propose to challenge the invaders to single combat?" Akim asked. "How long do you think you would survive against a force this size?"

"I don't know," Jin admitted. "But I think we might all be surprised."

"Perhaps," Akim said. "But the question is moot. We cannot allow you to rampage through Sollas under no authority but your own."

"Then let us fight with you," Jin offered.

"Not without proof of your loyalty," Siraj interjected.

Akim inclined his head. "Unfortunately, my son is right. We seem thus to have arrived at an impasse."

"What if we could prove you can trust us?" Merrick spoke up.

"How do you propose to do that?" Akim asked.

"You've had me in this chair for over half an hour," Merrick said. "My mother's also been here for several minutes now, and you've spent most of those minutes threatening our lives. If we're on the Trofts' side, why haven't we taken out the whole bunch of you and escaped?"

Siraj snorted. "Against six Djinn? You boast overmuch of your strength, demon warrior."

"It's not boasting if you can do it," Merrick countered. "And you've never seen a Cobra in action before."

"*I* have," Akim said. "And you *are* boasting, Merrick Moreau. I know all of your weaponry, and where those weapons lie hidden within your body. With your ankles manacled to the chair, and your hands fastened behind you with your thumbs blocked from your fingers, you are indeed helpless."

"You boast in turn of your own cleverness, Miron Akim," Merrick said calmly. "Do you really think it's this easy to restrain a Cobra?"

Jin winced. This was not a good direction to be taking this conversation. "Merrick—"

"Quiet, Mother," Merrick cut her off, his gaze steady on Akim. "How about it, Miron Akim? My mother spoke of us being an asset to you. Shouldn't you at least see what Cobras are capable of before you decide whether or not to throw us away?"

Akim folded his arms across his chest, one thumb stroking thoughtfully across his lip. "An interesting challenge, demon warrior," he said. "What exactly do you propose?"

"Before your men can get their hands into firing position, I'll be out of this chair," Merrick told him. "I'll have my own hands pointed at the ceiling, as proof I intend no harm against any of you."

"You court serious danger," Akim warned. "What if my Djinn are faster than you realize?"

"I'm willing to take that risk," Merrick said. "At the very least, we'll find out what kind of soldiers they are. Do we have a deal?"

Akim cocked an eyebrow. "Very well," he said. "Djinn, arms at your sides. Let us make this a fair competi—"

Right in the middle of the word, Jin was rocked backward as a terrific blast from Merrick's sonic disruptor hammered through the room.

Even knowing that would be Merrick's first move, she was still nearly knocked off her feet. The Qasamans, taken completely by surprise, had it far worse. They staggered backward, grabbing for sections of wall or each other as they tried to keep their feet under them.

The blast was still reverberating when, in the center of the chaos, Merrick straightened convulsively in his chair, his back arching, his legs snapping upward against the shackles binding his ankles to the chair legs. For maybe half a second nothing happened; and then, with a multiple snap of breaking wood, the chair shattered beneath him, dropping him onto his back on the floor.

He rolled over the wreckage onto his stomach, and Jin got her first clear look at his shackles. They were like regular wrist cuffs, except that the chain connecting the loops had been replaced with a thick metal bar. There was also some kind of flange stretching up from each cuff across his palm, blocking his fingers and preventing him from bringing his hands into firing position.

But Merrick didn't even bother trying to bring his fingertip lasers into play. Stretching his arms as far away from his back as he could, he bent his left leg tightly at the knee and fired a blast from his antiarmor laser that vaporized the center of the bar. Pushing off the floor with his now freed hands, he leaped to his feet.

Someone across the room spat something, and Jin saw that one of the Djinn had gotten his balance back and was swinging his arms up into firing position. Merrick glanced over his shoulder at a spot on the ceiling behind him, bent his knees, and jumped. There was a blur of motion punctuated by two rapid-fire thumps as his nanocomputer executed a standard Cobra ceiling flip, first turning him halfway over to hit the ceiling feet first, then turning him another hundred eighty degrees to land upright on the floor.

And an instant later Merrick was standing behind Akim, his arms raised in the air. "Done," he called.

The Djinni ignored him. Still weaving with the aftereffects of the sonic, he brought his hands up in front of his chest. Squinting furiously, he cocked his thumbs against his ring finger nails.

"Hold!" Akim snapped. He looked a little unsteady himself, but his voice was rock-hard. "Djinni Ghushtre, stand down."

For a long moment Jin thought the younger man was going to ignore the order. He held his posture, his expression thunderous as he glared at Merrick. Merrick himself didn't move, his hands still pointed harmlessly upward, his body half shielded behind Akim.

"You heard Miron Akim," Siraj said into the brittle silence. "Stand down."

Slowly, reluctantly, Ghushtre lowered his hands. "That was not fair," he growled. "He cheated."

"Do you expect an enemy to play by rules of your choosing?" Akim countered. "Do you count on him to inform you of his plans before launching them?"

"This was not to be combat, but a test," Ghushtre insisted. "Tests *do* have rules, and you had not finished stating them."

"Then *I* am the offended one, not you," Akim said, his voice hardening. "And I choose to take a larger view than my own honor and pride."

Ghushtre snorted. "What can be higher than honor?"

Akim looked him squarely in the eye. "What is higher than honor," he said quietly, "is victory."

He turned to Jin. "Come, Jin Moreau," he said, gesturing toward the door he'd come in through. "You and your son. We need to speak."

The room Akim took them to was the size of a mid-rank Aventinian politician's office, only with a much smaller desk and six chairs facing it rather than the standard two that Jin was used to. There were no pictures or frames on the walls, either, the only decoration being two rows of video monitors, all currently blank. Possibly some kind of ready room, Jin decided as she followed

Akim toward the desk. Maybe they were deeper into the Qasamans'
secret labyrinth than she'd thought.

"Please; sit down," Akim said, gesturing to the row of chairs.
He circled the desk and sat down behind it. "May I call for some
refreshment?"

"No, thank you," Jin said, frowning at him. The cold, distrustful
Qasaman from the other room had suddenly become calmer, even
marginally friendly. *Who are you,* the old half joke ran fleetingly
through her mind, *and what have you done with the real Miron
Akim?* "You said we needed to speak?"

"If you truly wish to assist us, yes." Akim hesitated. "I should
first apologize for our behavior out there." His lip twitched. "For
my behavior out there."

"Not a problem," Merrick assured him. "We understand you
had to play to your audience."

"Who, the other Djinn?" Jin asked, frowning. "I thought you
were in charge of them."

"I was referring to the private audience," Merrick told her. "The
ones watching on the hidden cameras."

Jin blinked. "There were *cameras* in the room?"

"Of course," Merrick said, as if it was too obvious even to mention. "Middle of the wall to my left and somewhere behind you.
Probably the doorjamb."

"So the cameras weren't as undetectable as I was promised,"
Akim commented thoughtfully. "Interesting."

"Oh, I didn't actually see them," Merrick said. "But when one's
host glances at a couple of blank sections of wall two or three
times in the same conversation, it's obvious what's going on." He
raised his eyebrows. "From which I gather escaping from my cuffs
really *was* a test?"

"Very good," Akim said with a wry smile. "You are indeed your
mother's son."

Jin felt her cheeks warming. No, Merrick was his *father's* son on
this one—quiet, calm, and with Paul's eye for detail. Jin herself, in
contrast, seemed to have lost whatever limited combat sense she'd
once had. She'd better get with the program, and fast.

"Yes, it was indeed a test," Akim continued. "Not for my benefit, as you've already surmised—I know perfectly well what you demon warriors are capable of."

"Cobras," Merrick corrected him mildly.

Akim inclined his head. "What you Cobras are capable of," he said. "But the Shahni had to be convinced of your abilities." He grimaced. "Convincing them that you're worthy of trust is another matter."

"Wait a minute," Jin said, fighting to get her brain back on line. Why was it so hard to think tactically anymore? "It was the *Shahni* who were watching? I thought the Trofts had them trapped in the Palace."

"What, with this whole rabbit warren underneath the city?" Merrick countered. "I doubt they set it up just so people could sneak out of hospital laundry rooms."

"In theory, you're correct," Akim said. "In practice . . . your mother has always thought of us as being paranoid, Merrick Moreau. Unfortunately, when the test came, we weren't paranoid enough."

Merrick threw Jin a sharp look. "You mean they're still *in* there?"

"Seven of the nine escaped," Akim said. "But all were slow to move, and those seven barely made it to the secret exit in time. The two who remained behind hoped to send out an alert to the rest of the planet and then sabotage the communications system. They were still performing that task when the invaders entered the Palace and cut off their escape."

"Do the Trofts know who they have?" Jin asked.

"The invaders don't actually *have* anyone," Akim corrected. "The Shahni were able to reach a hidden safe room, which the invaders haven't yet located."

"But it can only be a matter of time," Merrick said.

"True." Akim's lips compressed into a thin line. "Which is why I'm asking you to go into the Palace and bring them out."

For a moment, even Merrick's calm cracked. "You *what?*" he asked. "*Us?*"

"You're the only ones who can do it," Akim said heavily. "The only ones who can take the invaders by surprise."

"What about your own Djinn?" Jin asked. "If your son Siraj is any indication, a few of them should be more than capable of taking on a group of armed Trofts."

"If a commando raid was feasible, we would certainly mount it," Akim told her. "Unfortunately, such is not the case. We were forced to shut down the Palace escape route after the Shahni left, lest the invaders discover the entrance and find their way into the subcity. The only routes into or out of the Palace are now through the main doors."

"And your Djinn can't go in that way," Merrick said slowly, "because the Trofts would spot their power suits."

Jin frowned. "Their *power* suits?"

"Of course," Merrick said, looking puzzled. "How else did you think Carsh Zoshak and Siraj Akim made it down the laundry chute that way?"

"I just assumed—" Jin broke off in embarrassment. Her brain just wasn't working today. She must be more tired than she realized. "They're not Cobras?" she asked, turning back to Akim.

"That's indeed what we hoped to create," Akim said ruefully. "But even with—" He broke off.

Jin felt her throat tighten with memories. "With the bodies of my companions available to study?"

"As you say," Akim conceded. At least, Jin noted distantly, he had the grace to look pained. "Even so, we haven't been able to master the technique of adding ceramic to the bones and laying down the necessary array of optical control fibers. The creation and programming of the small subbrain computer also remains a mystery to us."

"So since you couldn't go inward, you went outward," Merrick said, nodding. "Hence, exoskeleton fighting suits."

"Exactly," Akim said. "The suits are made of treated krisjaw hide—extremely strong and resilient, with a fiber stiffening meshwork added throughout the longer sections to provide additional support. Servo motors similar to yours are situated at the major joints, which react instantly to the Djinni's movement in order to enhance his strength."

"And, of course, they've got metalwork lasers in the gloves," Jin said. "How are those aimed?"

"Each Djinni has small sensors implanted in his eye lenses," Akim said. "Wherever he looks, that's where the servo motors will aim and fire the lasers."

"Nice," Merrick said approvingly. "Not quite as versatile as our targeting locks, but a lot better than simple dead reckoning. Where's the computer that does all this?"

"In the collar and extending downward along the spine." His lip twitched. "It was thought that an attack strong enough to destroy the computer would probably also destroy whatever was beneath it."

Jin grimaced. And since a computerless Djinni was probably a soon-to-be-dead Djinni anyway, the two events might as well be simultaneous. "Do they have any other weapons?" she asked.

"They have a short-range sonic weapon designed to induce nausea and loss of balance," Akim said. "Dangerous to use in an enclosed space, as it may backfire on the Djinni himself." Akim inclined his head toward Merrick. "Unlike, apparently, the weapon you used. If I may ask, how did you successfully aim and fire your large laser at your restraints?"

"Actually, I cheated a little," Merrick admitted. "When the Djinn first brought the restraints into the room, it was obvious where they were going to go. So I simply put a target lock on the center of the bar."

"And your laser was able to fire without you being able to see it?"

"The servos give kinesthetic feedback positioning data to the nanocomputer," Merrick explained. "Once the target lock is on, I could hit the target with my eyes closed."

Akim shook his head. "Remarkable."

"We like it," Merrick said. "Anything else in the Djinn bag of tricks?"

"Their visual tracking method also permits them to accurately fire other weapons besides their glove lasers," Akim said. "They also carry small gas canisters for use in enclosed spaces, with filters already surgically implanted in their nostrils."

"What about their radios?" Merrick asked. "I assume that's what the Trofts zeroed in on back at the hospital."

"They have a transmission system copied from those used by the first visitors from your worlds." Akim grimaced. "We'd hoped they would prove as undetectable for our use as they'd been for yours."

"That would have been nice," Merrick said. "Unfortunately, you had no way of knowing that those particular gadgets came from our local Trofts."

"And so the invaders can detect them with ease," Akim said grimly. "That'll pose a serious problem."

"You still have that rock-layer waveguide system under the Great Arc, don't you?" Jin asked.

"Yes, but it only works for hard-wired communications between cities and villages," Akim said. "Mobile signaling between combat units cannot use it. Unless you have something newer we might be able to use?"

Merrick shook his head. "Most of our combat these days is against spine leopards, the things you call razorarms. Not much need for private communications with that."

"No matter," Akim said, his dark eyes flashing sudden fire. "If necessary, we'll fight the invaders without communications. If necessary, the Djinn can and will launch a massive frontal assault against the Palace."

"Of course they will," Merrick said hastily. "We understand that."

"We ask for your help only to prevent unnecessary and useless deaths," Akim insisted, almost as if he was trying to convince himself as much as he was Jin and Merrick.

"We understand," Merrick repeated. "Do you have a plan for getting me inside?"

"Wait a minute," Jin protested, feeling her chest tighten. "Shouldn't we at least think about this a little longer?"

"There's no time," Merrick told her. "The Trofts aren't just sitting around congratulating each other on a job well done. They'll be going through the place with a fine-mesh strainer, hunting up official papers and military data and anything else they can find. Sooner or later, they're going to find the safe room."

"I know that," Jin said, struggling to find the words that would express what she was feeling. This wasn't some carefully planned, carefully coordinated operation like those her grandfather had run during his own war against the Trofts. It wasn't a quick hit-and-hit against a group of inexperienced Troft merchants, either, like the little adventure she herself had survived three decades ago. This was a full-blown invasion force, with real soldiers and real military weapons. Couldn't Merrick *see* that?

"Mom, we have to do this," Merrick said quietly. "Remember what Carsh Zoshak said back in the hospital, that the Qasamans had to either trust us or kill us? Well, that works both ways. Either we prove we're trustworthy, or we can't ask them to risk giving us their protection."

Jin stared at him. At the grimness in his face, but also the underlying excitement behind his eyes.

And slowly, she understood. Of course he could see the terrible danger he was facing. But he didn't care. The people of Aventine had all but rejected the Cobras, with many in the government trying to marginalize them, phase them out, or shunt them off to Caelian where they could be ignored. Merrick had watched in frustration as his chosen profession—indeed, his entire family history—had been increasingly brushed aside by people who hadn't the faintest idea what Cobra commitment and sacrifice had meant to their own safety and security.

But that wasn't how the Qasamans saw it. Right here, right now, Merrick was both appreciated and needed. After years of suffering beneath the contempt of people like Governor Treakness, that had to feel good.

And on top of all that, this was the first chance her eldest son had ever had to show what the Cobras were capable of. Down deep, Jin knew that he wasn't going to let that chance pass him by. No matter what stood in his way.

Not even if it was his own mother.

"I just meant we can't go off half-cocked," she said, trying hard to keep the sudden surge of emotion out of her voice. "We'll need schematics of the building, the location of the safe room, pictures of the two Shahni so that we can identify them—" she looked at Akim "—and anything else Miron Akim has undoubtedly already thought of that I haven't."

"Upper-class clothing, for one thing," Akim said. His expression was controlled, but Jin could hear a new hint of hope in his voice. "I also have the schematics if you wish to look at them. But that won't be critically important, since I'll be accompanying you the entire way."

"Very kind of you," Jin said. "But hardly necessary."

"On the contrary," Akim said. "The Shahni won't trust two strangers who come in asking them to leave their sanctuary. Besides, our best chance of entering is to announce ourselves as diplomats intent on negotiation with the invaders. Neither you nor your son can carry off such a charade, but I can."

He gestured. "Come. I'll take you to a place where you can change your clothing and have a bit of refreshment while you study the schematics."

There was food and drink waiting for them when they reached the preparation room. Merrick's stomach was growling, but he was too exhausted from his mostly sleepless night to do more than sample each selection.

Fortunately, the room had also come equipped with a cot, and after obtaining his mother's promise that she would wake him in half an hour he lay down and fell deeply asleep.

He awoke to that dazed, sluggish sensation that always accompanied a short nap on top of a serious sleep deficit. The sluggishness vanished when he discovered that, instead of the half hour he'd requested, he'd been allowed to sleep for nearly two hours.

"You needed the rest," Jin told him, not even looking up from the schematics Akim had spread out over the table. "And there wasn't really anything you needed to do."

"Except maybe learn a little about where we're going?" Merrick growled, trying to put some righteous indignation into his words. But it was a waste of effort. She was right—he'd been way too tired to even tackle spine leopards, let alone armed Trofts. All the preparation and strategy sessions in the Worlds wouldn't do him any good if he was too fuzzy to shoot straight.

"Miron Akim and I both know the layout," his mother assured him. "It's highly unlikely all three of us will end up getting separated."

"And if we are, it will likely be because we're in the midst of combat," Akim added. "At which point your job will be to clear out as many of the invaders as possible while I attempt to reach the Shahni."

"Your new clothes are in the bathroom," Jin said, nodding toward a half-open door. "Get dressed and we'll give you a quick summary of the plan."

The plan turned out to be considerably more wide-ranging than Merrick had expected. "Teams of Qasaman soldiers will be attacking five different locations throughout the city once the two Shahni have been moved to safety," Akim said, pointing to circled locations on a map of Sollas. "The Palace itself, the airfield control tower, the Southfield underground manufacturing facility, the western gate where you entered Sollas, and one of the city's eastern market areas."

"What's in the market area?" Merrick asked, eyeing the map over Akim's shoulder.

"Nothing," Akim said, a grim amusement in his voice. "But if we attack the invaders there, they may assume there's something of military value in the area and waste effort and resources trying to locate it."

Merrick grimaced. A neat little red herring, that. He wondered if the locals would be equally amused when hoards of Trofts descended on their neighborhood. "The troops will be assembling in the underground tunnels, I assume?" he asked.

"No, the main assaults will come from nearby buildings," Akim said. "But there will be small squads of Djinn waiting in the subcity to attack from within once the invaders' eyes are turned outward."

"And after the Shahni are out?" Merrick asked.

"None of the forces move until then," Akim confirmed. "Have you any further questions?"

Merrick slid the Palace floor plans out from beneath the city map and gave it a quick scan. There were actually two safe rooms, he saw, one on the second floor amid the administrative offices and one on the fourth in the living areas. Both rooms were well hidden, each nestled into a few square meters of floor space that had been subtly carved out from the rooms around them. "No, I think that's it," he said. "I assume we won't be using our real names."

"I will, though my title will be that of Senior Administrator to the Shahni," Akim said. "You are Haiku Sinn, my driver and assistant. Your mother is Niora Kutal, a specialist in law and procedure. We're requesting a meeting with the invasion leadership in order to open communications regarding their occupation of Qasaman territory."

Merrick looked at his mother. "You spent my nap time getting a law degree?"

"Hardly," Jin said. "But I think I can guarantee I know more about Qasaman law than any of the Trofts will."

"You're ready, then?" Akim asked.

Merrick nodded. "Let's do it."

"One final thing," Akim said, looking suddenly uncomfortable. "Understand that I say this not of myself, but at the direction of the Shahni." Visibly, he braced himself. "Daulo Sammon and his son Fadil will be held as hostages to your good behavior. Should you betray us, they'll be immediately put to death."

Merrick felt his jaw drop. Of all the underhanded—"Of course they will," Jin said calmly.

Merrick stared at his mother. "You *knew* about this?"

"No, but once he said it, it was obvious," she said. "Probably why Siraj Akim offered to help me rescue them in the first place."

"Of course," Merrick said, trying to sound as calm as his mother despite the hard knots in his stomach. *Paranoid culture*... "Anything else?" he asked Akim.

"No," Akim said, clearly relieved that that particular task was now behind him. Or maybe he was simply relieved that the Cobras had taken it so calmly. "Follow me."

Akim led the way through another maze of tunnels that eventually led back to the surface in a part of Sollas Merrick didn't recognize. They emerged from a set of row houses to find a black limousine waiting for them at the curb. Merrick got behind the wheel, giving the controls a quick scan while his mother and Akim got into the back seat. The limo was considerably fancier than the Sammons' truck, but the important controls and gauges seemed to be in roughly the same places. Akim gave him a minute of instruction on the specific protocols of Qasaman city driving, then another half minute's worth of directions back to the Palace, and they were off.

There were no other cars on the city's streets to hinder travel, but the Troft barriers and checkpoints more than made up for it. Every third intersection or so was blocked by a handful of armed Trofts, many of them supported by an armored vehicle with a mounted swivel gun fastened to its roof. At each stop Akim lowered his window, gave his name and new title, and demanded he be permitted passage to the Palace to speak with the Troft commanders. Each time, the Trofts conferred by radio with someone higher in authority, and the car was passed through.

They also encountered two more of the tall, slender gunships along the way. Merrick, who'd never particularly liked city driving, found himself sweating as he carefully maneuvered the car through the narrow gap between gunship and curb under the Trofts' watchful eyes. Whether by luck or unexpected skill, he made it both times without even scratching the limo's paint.

And then, sooner somehow than he'd expected, they were back at the Palace. "Looks like they're setting up camp," he commented as he eyed the wide canopy the Trofts had erected beside the Palace entrance. Beneath the canopy, a handful of the aliens were setting up long tables and portable computer equipment.

"Most likely preparing to interview and register the citizens," Akim said. "An invader's first task is to control the movements of the people he's invaded."

One of the Trofts standing guard by the curb stepped into the street and held up a hand toward the approaching car. Merrick eased the car to the curb, and once again Akim rolled down his window. "I am Senior Administrator Miron Akim—" he began.

"You are known and expected," the Troft's translator pin boomed. "The commanders have agreed to meet with you."

"Excellent," Akim said briskly, popping open his door. "My assistants—"

He broke off as the Troft pushed the door closed again. "You will follow that vehicle to their location," he said, gesturing with his laser at an armored vehicle that had pulled out into the street in front of them.

"Follow it where?" Akim demanded, a sudden edge beneath the official arrogance in his voice. "I told you I wish to speak to your leaders."

"You will follow that vehicle to their location," the Troft repeated, his own tone hardening as he gestured again. As he did so, Merrick noticed the alien's hand dip into a pouch at his waist. "Go now, or their invitation will be rescinded."

Akim glared at the Troft. "Very well," he said icily. "Haiku Sinn, follow the vehicle as instructed."

He rolled up his window as Merrick shifted the car back into gear. As he did so, out of the corner of his eye he saw the Troft reach his hand up past the window, and there was a soft thud as he slapped the roof.

Ahead, the armored car pulled away and headed down the street. Grimacing, Merrick followed. They were going to see the Troft commanders, all right.

Only they were going to see them in the wrong place.

CHAPTER TEN

"Great," Merrick muttered as he drove. "Now what—?"

"Quiet," his mother said. "Miron Akim, change places with me."

Merrick frowned, watching in the mirror as the two of them exchanged seats. His mother partially rolled down the window Akim had been sitting beside and slipped her hand up through the opening. For a moment she seemed to feel around; then, with a brief grimace of effort, she pulled against something, and Merrick caught a glimpse of a small object falling past the window onto the pavement. "All right, it's off," she said, pulling her hand back inside and closing the window again.

"What was it?" Akim asked. "A bomb?"

"I doubt it," Jin said. "Not much point in subtlety when they've got all those guns. My guess is that it was a bug so they could listen in on us, maybe get a preview of who we were and what we want."

"So what *do* we want, now that Plan A is blown?" Merrick asked.

"There may still be opportunities," Akim assured him. "Let's first see were we're taken."

"Looks like we're heading toward the airfield," Merrick suggested as the Trofts at the next checkpoint waved the two vehicles though. "Maybe the commanders are still aboard one of their ships."

"Perhaps," Akim agreed. "Though they'd be foolish indeed to allow three potentially dangerous persons into one of their vessels."

"The airfield control tower, then?" Jin offered. "It gives a good defensive view of that end of the city, not to mention the airfield itself."

"I agree," Akim said. "The control tower is definitely the most likely destination," Akim agreed. "If we're taken inside..." He trailed off, and in the mirror Merrick saw him grimace. "We'll have only one real option," he continued reluctantly. "One of us will have to escape from the invaders' custody and confirm to the Shahni that the rescue plan is no longer viable." His eyes locked on to Merrick's in the mirror. "That will be your task, Merrick Moreau."

"Shouldn't it be you?" Merrick asked. "I mean, you're the one they'll listen to."

"Unfortunately, the route you'll need to take will be dangerous for a man of my age," Akim said. "We'll have to trust that they'll accept your word and instructions."

Merrick looked at his mother in the mirror. But if she had objections she was keeping them to herself. "You're the boss," he said with a sigh. "What do I do?"

"There's a trapdoor in the rear corner of each elevator in the tower," Akim told him. "It will drop you into a net, which will then drop you through the false floor of the shaft to a landing below. The trip will be stressful, but not lethal."

"That's good to hear," Merrick said dryly. "What happens once I'm at the bottom?"

"From the landing a door leads into the subcity," Akim said. "There should be a squad of Djinn waiting there, and you'll instruct them that Plan Saikah must be initiated."

"What's Plan Saikah?" Merrick asked.

"Our best hope for throwing off the invaders," Akim said. "There's no need for you to know the details."

Merrick felt a chill run through him. An all-out assault on the Trofts? "All right," he said. "What do I do after I deliver the message?"

"That will be your choice," Akim said. "You may assist the Djinn, if they're willing to accept your aid, or you may step aside."

"I have a question," Jin said. "What happens to the Shahni in the Palace during Plan Saikah?"

"They'll serve Qasama in their own way," Akim said. "There—our destination."

Merrick shifted his full attention back to the view through the windshield. Sure enough, the airfield tower loomed ahead, with one of the wrigglefish-like sentry ships flanking it on either side. "How do I trigger the trapdoor?" he asked.

"I'll do that," Akim said. "Just make sure you stand in the right rear corner of the elevator as you face the doors."

Their pilot car led the way to a set of large doors and came to a halt. Four of the six Trofts guarding the entrance detached themselves from the others and strode toward the limo, their lasers covering the vehicle. "Prepare yourselves," Akim said. "And allow me to do the talking."

For the immediate moment, though, there wasn't any call for talking. With a handful of curt orders from one of the Trofts, the aliens herded the three humans into the tower and down a hallway to what had probably originally been a conference room. Over the past few hours, the Trofts had transformed it into a clearing station, complete with bolted-down interrogation chairs and a full staff of techs and armed guards.

They started with Akim, two of the guards firing questions at him about his family and background as one of the techs ran a handheld scanner over his clothing. After that it was Merrick's turn, and he could feel sweat collecting beneath his collar and in his armpits as he answered the questions and watched the tech's face for signs of surprise or confusion. Cobra gear was supposed to be undetectable unless someone was specifically looking for it, but as far as Merrick knew that theory had never been tested. Certainly not under conditions like these.

It was thus with a huge sense of relief that he watched the tech finish his sweep and step back without shouting a panicked warning. Whatever trouble they were expecting to find, Cobras apparently weren't on the list.

"What is your purpose here?" one of the Trofts asked after Jin had also been cleared.

"To speak to your commanders," Akim said, his voice the

controlled stiffness of someone carrying out an errand he hadn't particularly wanted. "The Shahni wish to know why you have invaded Qasaman territory, and to open discussions leading to your departure."

The Troft covered his translator pin and started murmuring in cattertalk. Merrick ran his auditory enhancers up—[The humans, our presence they wish to discuss,] he said. [The leader, the garb of a senior Shahni official he wears.]

He received a reply and lowered his hand from his pin. "Follow," he said, and strode out of the room. Akim followed, with Jin behind him and Merrick behind her. Behind Merrick, two more Trofts brought up the rear.

Twenty meters later, they arrived at an alcove and a pair of elevators guarded by four more Trofts. One of the latter punched the call button as the party approached, and both sets of elevator doors slid open. The Troft leading the way turned and backed into the leftmost car, his eyes and laser trained on the humans. "Come," he said.

Akim nodded, but instead of following the other inside he stopped at the door and gestured Merrick to enter ahead of him. Merrick nodded and continued forward, hoping he could get inside before the Trofts started wondering about the sudden change in marching order.

But the Trofts merely stood impassively by as Merrick walked into the elevator. The lead Troft, to Merrick's relief, hadn't taken the corner above the trapdoor, and he casually crossed the car and took up position there. One of the other Trofts stepped into the elevator behind him and touched the lowest button on the control panel.

And to Merrick's stunned disbelief, the doors slid closed and the car started down.

"Wait!" he yelped, lunging toward the doors. Or trying to lunge, anyway; he managed only a single step before the first Troft swung the muzzle of his laser around and jabbed it warningly into Merrick's ribs. "We can't leave—Senior Administrator Akim is still outside."

[Fools, you think we are they?] the Troft at the door spat. [Spies, we do not understand that you are?]

The Qasaman translation had barely begun when Merrick grabbed hold of the laser barrel poking into his ribs and twisted it hard, shifting the muzzle out of line with his side and trying to pull it out of the Troft's grip.

But the Troft didn't let go, not even as the unexpected tug pulled him off his feet. He hung on grimly, his beak clacking unintelligibly as he fought for possession of the weapon. Merrick tried twisting the laser in the opposite direction, but the alien still kept hold of the weapon. The other Troft leaped forward, shoving at Merrick's arm with one hand and jabbing the muzzle of his own weapon into Merrick's face with the other.

And in that frozen fraction of a second, Merrick's body moved.

He let go of the laser he and the first Troft were fighting over, shrugging off the second Troft's grip on his arm and following through with a blindingly fast sweep of his hand across the weapon to knock it out of line. The momentum of the sweep twisted Merrick's shoulders around; and as his whole body did a quick corkscrew to the right his left hand swung up, little finger extended, the other fingers curled tightly toward his palm, and fired a burst of laser fire at each of the two Trofts' foreheads.

Only neither alien dropped over dead. Instead, the transparent faceplates blackened at the points of impact, blocking off the main brunt of the blasts.

But enough had gotten through to send a shock of pain through both aliens. Merrick grabbed again at the first Troft's laser, and this time he was able to wrench it from the alien's grip. Spinning it around, he jammed it upward beneath the lower edge of the alien's faceplate and fired.

There was a brilliant flash, and the soldier dropped to the floor. Merrick spun the weapon around, elbowing the remaining Troft's laser aside, and fired a second shot under that one's faceplate, sending him crumpling to the floor beside the first.

Merrick stared down at the bodies, his heart thudding in his ears, his breath coming in short gasps. *My God*, the thought flashed across his numbed mind. *Was that me?*

Of course it had been him. It had been his body, his combat reflexes, his Cobra weaponry.

He closed his eyes, fighting the sudden urge to vomit. Never before had he used his power against another person. Never before had he even been tempted by anger or frustration to do so.

He'd killed two people. Not spine leopards, mindless predators who would cut a murderous swath through someone's ranchland if they weren't eliminated. He'd killed two living, sentient beings.

He clamped his teeth tightly as a second wave of nausea swept through him. Up until now he'd thought only about the fear-edged respect Miron Akim had shown for him and his mother, a respect in stark contrast to the disdain that radiated from so many of Aventine's people. Thoughts of combat had been little more than a hazy backdrop to that warm glow of vindication, a vague and sanitized mural consisting of images of fire and triumph and glory. This blood and stillness and stench of burned flesh wasn't what he'd expected. Wasn't at all what he'd signed up for.

He took a shuddering breath. Only it was, he knew. He'd signed up willingly, even eagerly, and it was too late to back out. Not when there were people out there who were counting on him.

People like Miron Akim . . . and Merrick's mother.

Merrick winced. Jasmine Moreau, daughter of Justin Moreau, granddaughter of the legendary Jonny Moreau. She wouldn't panic in this situation. *Hadn't* panicked, in fact, when she'd found herself facing similar danger all those years ago.

You boast overmuch of your strength, demon warrior, Miron Akim's son Siraj had scoffed. Maybe he'd been right.

It was time to find out.

Merrick gave his head a sharp shake, and as the haze in front of his eyes vanished he realized that the elevator was still heading downward. Apparently, the fight and his brief surge of horrified introspection and self-pity had lasted only a few seconds.

He checked the elevator indicator, noting that they were passing the second subbasement, and tried to think. With Jin and Merrick stuck here at the airfield, it was clear that Akim assumed the two Shahni trapped in the Palace would have to be abandoned.

Probably he was right. But maybe he was wrong.

Reaching down, Merrick picked up one of the Trofts' lasers. So far, the invaders had no idea that there were Cobras on Qasama.

The longer that ignorance could be maintained, the better. Steeling himself, he pointed the laser at the black spot he'd made in the first alien's faceplate and squeezed the trigger.

The Troft weapon was considerably more powerful than Merrick's fingertip lasers, and the blast had no trouble getting through even the darkened faceplate and through the mass of skin and bone behind it. A reminder, Merrick thought grimly, that he'd better make damn sure he didn't end up at the receiving end of any future blasts. Shifting aim, he repeated the camouflage on the second Troft, then lifted the weapon toward the side of the car. He had no idea how to trigger the secret trapdoor Akim had told him about, or whether the net would deploy properly if he simply blasted the floor open. He certainly wasn't ready yet to just throw himself blindly down a Qasaman elevator shaft. Aiming at a spot about chest height, he shifted the laser to continuous mode and squeezed the trigger.

The beam lanced out, sizzling like cooking breakfast meat as it sliced through the relatively thin metal of the car wall. Merrick carved out a human-sized opening, then dropped the weapon back onto the floor and peered through the hole he'd created.

A meter away, the wall of the shaft was sliding past, its surface covered with cables and protrusions. Bracing himself, Merrick picked out a suitable spot and jumped, grabbing on to a convenient set of handholds. He locked his fingers around the cold metal and looked down in search of similar purchase for his feet.

Just as the elevator car settled to a stop a meter below him.

Merrick blinked, embarrassment and chagrin sweeping across him as he saw the elevator shaft floor no more than half a meter below the car. The Trofts had been taking him to the tower's lowest level, and he'd now arrived.

But the chagrin at his unnecessary derring-do vanished as a far more urgent thought belatedly gripped him. When the car doors opened, and the reception committee saw the two dead bodies in there . . .

There was a faint creak as the doors started to open. Merrick looked frantically around, but there was nowhere he could see where he could hide. From the corridor beyond the elevators came a sudden explosion of startled cattertalk—

And even knowing how stupid and predictable it was, but unable to think of anything better, Merrick stepped onto the car's roof and dropped silently onto his stomach.

Just in time. Against the shaft wall he saw a multiple flicker of shadows, and with the scraping of leathery armor against metal a pair of Trofts climbed out of the car through Merrick's newly blasted hole. Merrick pressed himself as flat onto the roof as he could, wondering tensely if the Trofts would be able to jump high enough to catch a glimpse of him up here.

Fortunately, they didn't seem interested in trying. From the sounds of their footsteps, they were instead working their way around the car, easing cautiously around the rear toward the larger open area on the far side. Possibly hoping to get a better view of the car roof from over there?

Abruptly, Merrick tensed. No, of course the searchers weren't going to bother with the top of the car. Not when the Trofts one floor up could simply open their own elevator doors and look directly down on him.

He looked up. Those doors were still closed, but they wouldn't stay that way for long. No exit for him that direction. Meanwhile, the two roving Trofts were still poking around the shaft on the far side of the car.

Which left Merrick only one option. Getting a grip on the edge of the car, he rolled his legs over the side, making sure not to come anywhere near the hole and any more Trofts prowling around in there. He took half a second to let his swing dampen out, then dropped as quietly as he could onto the shaft floor. Dropping flat onto his stomach, he slid underneath the car.

The gap between car and floor was smaller than it had looked when he'd been hanging on to the wall a few moments ago, and he found the space an ominously snug fit. But at least he was finally out of sight.

But again, probably not for long. He could see the roving Trofts' feet as they continued to move around, the sizes and angles of their shadows now indicating that they were shining lights up along the inside of the shaft. Unless one of them had already looked beneath the car, they would surely eventually get around to doing so. And if there was one guaranteed fact in the universe right now, it was that Merrick wasn't going to be doing any serious fighting from under here.

But if he was lucky, he might not have to.

The trapdoor will drop you into a net, Akim had said, *which will then drop you through the false floor of the shaft to a landing below.* The floor beneath him certainly didn't *feel* false, Merrick observed as he wriggled his way over to the car's rear corner. It felt as solid as any other floor he'd ever been on.

But Merrick had studied all the records from Grandpa Justin's mission half a century ago, and he knew that the airfield tower elevators went a lot deeper than just a couple of subbasements. This had to be the false floor Akim had talked about, which meant there had to be a way through it somewhere.

But if the rabbit hole was directly under the trapdoor, Merrick couldn't find it. He ran his hands over the grimy concrete, keying in his light-amplification and infrared enhancements to help in his search. But he couldn't find a single trace of anything that seemed out of the ordinary.

The muffled footsteps across the shaft changed tempo. Merrick looked in that direction, to see that the two Trofts were retracing their path around the rear of the car, heading back toward the hole.

And if they decided to check under the car one more time before they gave up their search...

Cursing silently, Merrick frantically renewed his search. But there was still nothing. He rolled up onto his side facing the Troft feet, raising his hands into firing position. A futile gesture, he knew—the minute he fired, everyone in the shaft, the car, and the corridor would know instantly where he was. If they decided they still wanted him alive, they could recapture him with ease. If they didn't, all they had to do was open fire through the floor of the elevator car.

The Trofts were at the rear of the car and starting around the last corner when Merrick heard a soft snick.

And without a whisper of warning, the floor beneath his elbow suddenly gave way.

He grabbed for support as his upper body started to fall into the large, irregularly shaped hole that had magically opened up in the thick concrete. He looked for the missing section of flooring, saw it swinging gently from hinges at the far end. Getting a grip on the edge of the hole, he pulled himself forward and down into the opening.

For a moment he hung there, studying the underside of the floor in the dim backwash of light from the elevator shaft. The false floor was constructed on long metal I-beams, one of which ran right along one edge of the trapdoor. Shifting his grip to it, he held on one-handed as he reached over and pulled the trapdoor back up into place. It closed with another soft snick.

And then all was silence.

For a long minute Merrick just hung there, listening to the indistinct sounds of activity overhead. It was hard to tell through the thick floor, but he couldn't hear any of the extra urgency that might mean his escape had been spotted. Within half a minute, all of the sounds had faded away. The hunt, apparently, had moved elsewhere.

Merrick took a deep breath, painfully aware of how close he'd just come to his own death. Something else that hadn't entered into his calculations when he'd volunteered to join this war. He took a few more deep breaths, sternly ordering his heart to calm down, then keyed his light-amps to full strength.

It was a waste of effort. The shaft extension stretching down around him was completely and utterly dark, without a single bit of light coming in from anywhere that even his optical enhancers could detect. He shifted to infrared, hoping his own body might be radiating enough in that wavelength that he could at least see *something*. But aside from giving him a view of the two or three square meters of false floor directly above him, that didn't work either.

Switching back to his light-amps, he let go with one hand and aimed his little finger into a random section of the darkness. He touched his thumb to his forefinger nail—the laser's lowest setting—sent up a silent prayer that he wasn't aiming at anything important, and fired.

The shaft below him stretched deep enough that even the laser flash wasn't bright enough to show where it ultimately ended. But it was more than adequate to show the semicircular platform five meters below the spot where he was hanging. Bracing himself, he let go.

He hit the platform with a solid, metallic thud, bending his knees as he landed to absorb some of the impact. The shaft was still pitch black, but his glimpse of the platform had also shown a door in the shaft wall across from where he now stood. Moving carefully forward, one hand extended in front of him, he made it to the wall.

He pressed his ear against the metal and held his breath, his auditory enhancers keyed to full power. The wall was alive with the hums, thumps, and rumblings of distant machinery, but there were no sounds of human activity that he could detect.

Still, Akim had said there would be Djinn down here somewhere. Turning his enhancers back down again, he tried the knob and found it unlocked. Pushing the door open, he stepped through into a space filled with the soft mustiness of dust and age and long neglect. Unlike the shaft, this place had a little light, a faint glow coming from somewhere to Merrick's left. Closing the door behind him, he started to activate his light-amps.

And suddenly, a blazing white light exploded in his face.

He jerked back, squeezing his eyes tightly against the blaze as he reflexively threw one arm up to protect his face. "Well, well, well," a voice growled from somewhere behind the light. "What have we *here*?"

The Troft stepped into the elevator behind Merrick...and to Jin's stunned horror, the doors closed behind him, leaving her, Akim, and the other five Trofts still outside.

Wait! Ruthlessly, she stifled the word before it could make it past her lips. She was a woman in a patriarchal society, and it would look suspicious if she spoke up instead of Akim.

Only Akim wasn't speaking up. He was just standing there, not even looking at Jin, apparently without a single shred of concern that their little group of infiltrators had just been split up. One of the Trofts gestured toward the right-hand elevator, and Akim merely nodded and stepped inside, leaving Merrick to whatever fate the Trofts had planned for him.

But whatever those plans were, they were about to be canceled. Glancing casually around, Jin set a targeting lock on each of the five Trofts' foreheads. Her fingertip lasers were useless against their faceplates, but a drop onto her back and a sweep of her antiarmor laser would leave her free to pry open the elevator doors and either drop onto the top of Merrick's car if they'd taken him down or else to jump up to the underside if they'd taken him up. Either way, another blast from her antiarmor laser would get her inside—

"Niora Kutal."

Jin jerked out of her frantic train of thought. Akim was standing in the elevator, gazing at her with the mix of authority and aloofness she'd seen on so many Qasamans as they dealt with female subordinates. "Yes, Miron Akim?" she managed.

"Attend," he said, making a small gesture toward his side.

But what about my son? "Of course," she said instead. Lowering her eyes like a good Qasaman woman, her jaw tight as she fought to control her pounding rage and fear, she stepped into the elevator. Akim was right. Whatever the Trofts had planned for Merrick, blowing their cover now wouldn't do him any good.

And he wasn't seven years old anymore, either, she reminded herself firmly. He was a competent, capable adult.

And a Cobra.

She stepped to Akim's side. The five Trofts piled in behind her, lasers leveled and ready, their sheer numbers and bulk forcing the two humans all the way to the rear of the car. The doors slid shut, one of the Trofts punched a button, and they headed up.

"To whom do you take us?" Akim asked into the silence.

No one bothered to answer. In the close confines, Jin heard a faint voice coming from somewhere, and keyed up her auditory enhancements. [—of his presence,] the cattertalk whispered. [A full search of the elevator shaft, it is being made.]

Jin felt her muscles tense. Were they talking about Merrick? Had he escaped?

[The other humans, under close guard hold them,] the voice continued.

None of the five Trofts stiffened, gasped, or showed any other visible reaction to the report. But it seemed to Jin that the ring of lasers moved perhaps a centimeter or two closer to her and Akim.

She took a careful breath, feeling her heartbeat slow a little. But only a little. Merrick had apparently escaped, and escaped alive. But had he taken that action on purpose, as Akim had ordered, so that he could go warn the Djinn of the change in plan? Or had he panicked, as his grandfather Justin had when facing an eerily similar situation?

There was no way for her to know. She could only hope that either way, he would make it safely to the subcity.

She raised her eyes to one of the Troft faces gazing at her above his leveled laser. The double sets of eyes gazed back through the faceplate, the main eyes a dark blue, the three tiny compound eyes grouped around each of the main ones largely colorless in the elevator's artificial light. She lowered her gaze, taking in the vaguely chicken-like beak, the double throat bladders, and the flexible radiator membranes on his arms. The Troft's outfit was similar to the usual leotard-like garment the traders on Aventine wore, except that his was festooned with various equipment pockets and hooks and was clearly armored.

Why were they here? The Qasamans had had contact with the local Troft demesnes—that much had been obvious fifty years ago, when the Trofts had provided the Worlds with a Qasaman translation program prior to their first mission here. Had the Qasamans annoyed someone enough to invite this kind of response? Had some Troft demesne decided it was running out of room, and Qasama offered the most convenient and attractive expansion?

The elevator came to a stop at the topmost floor, and the doors opened to reveal another group of five Trofts with weapons at the ready. Apparently, the aliens weren't taking any chances that their other two human visitors might make a break for it. The Trofts in the elevator filed out, the two groups of aliens forming themselves into a sort of double receiving line out in the corridor. It was, Jin thought as she and Akim passed between the lines, very much like the honor guard she'd sometimes seen at official Aventinian receptions.

Except for the drawn weapons, of course. And the way the lines re-formed into a guard behind them.

"To whom do you take us?" Akim asked again.

Again, the Trofts ignored him. The two humans were escorted through a couple of turns and arrived at last at an open door. At a gesture from one of the aliens, they went inside.

The room was clearly an executive office, complete with a large expanse of carpeted floor and a panoramic window that opened out onto the city of Sollas stretching out to the south. But unlike most offices, the only furniture here was a pair of metal armchairs sitting back to back across the room by the window.

Armchairs with wrist and ankle shackles attached and ready.

"Sit down in the chairs," one of the Trofts ordered.

"What is this?" Akim demanded, not moving from the doorway.

The muzzle of a laser prodded against the small of his back. "Sit down in the chairs."

"I was sent to speak with your commanders," Akim insisted as he moved with clear reluctance into the room.

"You were sent to spy," the Troft countered. "Sit down in the chairs."

"This is a breach of all proper diplomatic protocol," Akim continued stiffly as he seated himself with strained dignity, nodding to Jin to do likewise. "Do you now propose to interrogate us like common criminals?"

"No," the Troft said him as four of the aliens moved in and fastened the shackles around their wrists and ankles. "If you are high enough in your leaders' counsels to negotiate, you are high enough to be sorely missed by those same leaders."

His arm membranes fluttered. "You are no longer negotiators. You are now hostages."

CHAPTER ELEVEN

"Get that light out of my eyes," Merrick snapped. "You trying to ruin what little night vision I have left?"

The light didn't waver. "Who are you?" the voice demanded. "What are you doing here?"

"My name is Merrick Moreau," Merrick told him. "I was sent with Miron Akim—"

"Merrick *Moreau*?" a new voice cut in, the source moving as someone apparently came forward from the rear of the group. "What are *you* doing here?"

This voice Merrick recognized. "Greetings, Carsh Zoshak," he said. "As it happens, I'm on a mission for Miron Akim. Come on—vouch for me and get them to turn off this light."

"Not so fast," the first voice said darkly. "If you're Merrick Moreau, you're supposed to be at the Palace."

"Unfortunately, the Trofts didn't get that memo," Merrick said. "They intercepted us outside the Palace and sent us here to the airfield."

"'Us'?" Zoshak asked. "Is Miron Akim also here?"

"Yes, somewhere up in the tower," Merrick said. "At least, I think he's still there. The Trofts separated us."

"Where did they do this?" Zoshak asked. "At the elevators?"

"Yes, but I don't know if Miron Akim and my mother were put in the other one or just taken somewhere on the ground floor."

"The other elevator is currently on the top floor," a third voice reported. "That's probably where they were taken."

"Is that where the Troft commanders have set up their head-quarters?" Merrick asked.

"The supreme commanders are not here," the first voice said. "Only local commanders."

Merrick grimaced. So much for the Trofts taking them anywhere within close reach of any of the invasion's chief organizers. Still, he shouldn't have expected the aliens to be that naive. "Miron Akim sent me with a message," he said. "He said that since we hadn't been able to get to the trapped Shahni you were to initiate Plan Saikah instead."

There was a moment of silence. Then, to Merrick's relief, the blinding light went out. "Plan Saikah?" the first voice asked carefully. "Are you certain?"

"Very certain," Merrick assured him. "Why? What is it?"

There was a soft sigh. "It is a sentence of death."

A shiver ran up Merrick's back. "For you?"

"We are not concerned with our own deaths," the other said stiffly. "Facing danger for Qasama is our duty and our honor. I was speaking of the Shahni who will soon be lost to us."

"We cannot simply condemn them to such a death, Jol Najit," Zoshak said urgently. "Not without at least making an attempt to rescue them."

"And how would you do that, Carsh Zoshak?" the first voice—Najit—countered. "Would you have us chew through the barriers like demented rodents?"

"What kind of barriers are we talking about?" Merrick asked. His eyes were recovering now, enough for him to see that the glow he'd noticed when he'd first arrived was coming from the display and controls of a small monitor built into the elevator shaft wall. In the dim light, he could see that besides Zoshak and Najit there were three other Djinn in the room. "Because maybe if we—"

"We are talking about barriers that cannot be breached with the necessary speed and silence," Najit cut him off. "Now be quiet—we have work to do."

"I'm just trying to help," Merrick said doggedly, trying to visualize the Palace floor plans he'd glanced at earlier. Given the location of the safe room, even if Plan Saikah was a brute-force assault the Shahni should still have a pretty good chance of surviving long enough to be rescued. "If we could open up a pathway—"

"I said be *silent,* demon warrior," Najit bit out. "You are not part of this."

"I understand that," Merrick said, trying to keep his voice calm. What part of *I'm trying to help* didn't Najit get? "Since I'm not part of your group, there's no particular place I have to be."

"An excellent point," Najit growled. "Go somewhere else, and be out of our way." He turned his back on Merrick and headed toward the monitor station.

"So I guess I'll just pop over to the Palace and get the Shahni out," Merrick called after him.

Slowly, Najit turned around, and even in the dim light Merrick could see the rigid set to the other's face. "Let me make this clear, demon warrior," he said. "You are to stay out of our way. *Completely* out of our way. You will not go to the Palace, you will not return to the airfield tower, you will not stand or sit or lie in the path of any Qasaman forces. Do you understand?"

"Yes, I understand," Merrick said quietly. "You've been given a mission. Well, so have I. And though you may find this hard to believe, I feel as strongly about mine as you do about yours."

For a long moment the two men locked eyes. The other four Djinn were listening silently, their hands not quite curved into laser firing positions. "The only remaining way into the Palace is through the outer doors," Najit said at last. "Attempting to enter that way will prematurely alert the invaders to our intentions."

"It might also draw more of them inside the Palace," one of the other Djinni murmured.

Najit's expression changed subtly. "True," he said thoughtfully. "That might be useful."

"I wasn't really thinking about running the gauntlet they've got set up outside the Palace," Merrick said. "I was hoping for something a little more subtle and less exposed."

Najit shook his head impatiently. "I've already told you. There is no other way in."

"There has to be," Merrick insisted. "Come on, think. The building has plumbing outlets, air system intakes—there must be *something* that a human body can squeeze through."

"What about the communications conduit?" Zoshak suggested, pointing toward a large metal cylinder about two-thirds of a meter in diameter running vertically from floor to ceiling beside the monitor console.

"Too small," Najit said. "And the plumbing and air systems were specifically designed to keep intruders out."

"Wait a second, not so fast," Merrick said, eyeing the cylinder. "Is this the same sort of conduit that runs down from the Palace?"

"Yes, but it is filled with bundles of shielded communications cables," Najit said.

"Cables can be dealt with," Merrick said, crossing to the cylinder and running a fingertip thoughtfully along the metal. If the cylinder's wall wasn't too thick, there ought to be plenty of room for him to climb up the inside. He'd have to come up with something to use for hand- and footholds, but it could be done. "I assume these are the cables that carry signals down to that basalt waveguide you use for intercity communications?"

Abruptly, the room behind him went deathly quiet. Carefully, he turned his head around.

None of the Djinn had moved. But all five of them were now wearing Najit's same stiff expression. "What?" Merrick asked.

"How do you know about the waveguide?" Najit demanded, his voice low and dangerous.

"Oh, come on—we've known about it since our first visit," Merrick said, keeping his own voice calm. Busy facing down Qasaman stubbornness, he'd almost forgotten about Qasaman paranoia. "I'm sure my mother mentioned that to Miron Akim when she was here last."

"We cannot let the invaders learn about that," Najit said.

"Are you suggesting I might run off and tell them?" Merrick asked.

"Perhaps," Najit said. "Or you might be captured, and offer a trade for your life."

Merrick's thoughts flashed to Daulo and Fadil Sammon, locked up somewhere by the Shahni as hostages to the Cobras' good behavior. "I'm not offering them any deals," he told Najit icily. "I'm not taking any, either. Get this through your skull, Jol Najit: I'm on your side. As far as I'm concerned, until the Trofts are off this world, I *am* a Qasaman."

There was another short silence. Then, beside Najit, Zoshak stirred. "He won't find his way through the subcity to the Palace without assistance," he murmured. "I request permission to accompany him."

Najit's lip twisted, but there was no surprise in his face that Merrick could see. Clearly, he wasn't happy with any of this. Just as clearly, he'd already figured out which way it was going and had bowed to the inevitable. "Plan Saikah will take one hour to prepare," he said. "It will *not* wait upon you."

"Understood." Zoshak turned to Merrick. "You still wish to take this risk upon yourself, Merrick Moreau?"

The doubts and fears from the elevator flickered like dry lightning through Merrick's mind. No, he *wasn't* sure. But someone had to do it, and it might as well be him. "We're wasting time," he said.

Zoshak nodded. "Follow me."

He slipped past Merrick, breaking into a jog as he passed the door leading into the elevator shaft, and headed down an increasingly darkened corridor. With a controlled burst of speed, Merrick caught up and fell into step behind him, keying in his light-amps to make as much use as he could of the monitor glow receding in the distance behind them.

A few meters later they rounded a corner into almost complete darkness. Merrick thought about pointing that out, decided that if Zoshak could stay on his feet and not run into a wall, so could he.

Fortunately, Zoshak wasn't interested in playing that kind of game. "Are you all right?" he called softly as he flicked on a small light attached to his collar. "Is this light bright enough?"

"It's fine," Merrick assured him, keying back his enhancers a couple of notches. "How far is the Palace? I got a little turned around on the drive."

"At this pace, perhaps fifteen minutes," Zoshak said. "But we should try to go faster if possible."

"I can if you can," Merrick said. "Are we in that much of a rush? I assumed that if the Shahni had stayed hidden this long, they would probably be good for another hour or two. And I'm thinking that Plan Saikah might kick up a nice diversion for us."

Zoshak threw an odd look over his shoulder. "Didn't Miron Akim tell you?"

"Tell me what?" Merrick asked.

"About Plan Saikah," Zoshak said. "The first step is the detonation of the explosives built into the Palace walls."

Merrick felt his mouth drop open. "No, he damn well did *not* tell me that," he ground out. "Are you saying you're going to blow the Palace with two of the Shahni still inside?"

"The Shahni, and many of the invaders," Zoshak reminded him. "Perhaps some of their highest leaders. It's a fair gamble."

"Only if you're the one standing outside pushing the button," Merrick said. "Who came up with this crazy plan, anyway?"

Zoshak looked him straight in the eye. "The Shahni."

Briefly, Merrick tried to envision a situation where Aventinian governors like Tomo Treakness would deliberately sacrifice their lives in order to inflict unknown levels of damage against an invader. But his imagination wasn't up to it. "In that case, you're right, we might want to step it up a little."

"Agreed," Zoshak said, picking up his pace. "Let me know if I go too fast for you."

"Don't worry about me," Merrick said, matching the Qasaman's speed as he turned the bulk of the work over to his leg servos. "I'm right behind you."

The door closed behind the Trofts, and Jin heard the click of a lock.

And she and Akim were alone.

"Well, *damn*," she muttered, looking around. The room had seemed empty enough a minute ago when the Trofts had led them in here. Now, on closer examination, it looked even emptier.

There were nail holes in the walls where paintings had once hung, decorative hooks in the ceiling that had once supported planters or hanging artworks, and deep indentations in the carpet marking the former positions of desk, chairs, and other furniture. It looked rather like a student apartment, hastily and carelessly abandoned at the end of the term.

She frowned as the oddness of that belatedly struck her. Why would the Trofts have bothered to take down the paintings and planters? Had they been afraid their soon-to-be prisoners would somehow break free and find something in the room to use as a weapon? In that case, they'd missed the most obvious bet of all: the metal chairs she and Akim were shackled to, which weren't even bolted to the floor.

Or had the Trofts removed everything so that the prisoners wouldn't suspect hidden cameras or microphones lurking among the palm fronds? Smiling to herself, Jin keyed in her telescopic enhancements and took another, closer look at the nail holes.

There they were: a pair of tiny cameras nestled into two of the holes on opposite sides of the room. It was a little hard to tell, but one of them seemed to be angled slightly toward the door, while the other was angled toward the two prisoners. The Trofts hadn't skipped the audio, either: hanging in the near corner of the room, masquerading as a plant hook, was the telltale perforated plastic of a small microphone.

"All you all right, Niora Kutal?" Akim asked from behind her.

Using her assumed Qasaman name, which meant that he also knew or suspected they were being monitored. "I'm unharmed, Miron Akim, but highly offended," she replied stiffly. "We're ambassadors, and not to be treated in this way."

"Agreed," Akim said, and beneath his own tone of controlled outrage Jin could detect a hint of approval for her quick pickup of the situation. "The invaders will have a great deal to answer for when this is over."

"If they think this will frighten us or the Qasaman people, they're gravely mistaken," Jin agreed. Bracing herself, she activated her omnidirectional sonic.

A tingle ran through her, an unpleasant vibration as the speakers buried inside her body slipped through harmonics of natural body resonances. The pitch altered as the sound dug into the walls, seeking out similar resonances with the cameras and microphone...

"Are we under attack?" Akim asked quietly.

Jin didn't answer, focusing instead on counting down the seconds. It was supposed to take about a minute for the sonic to find all the possible resonances and vibrate the bugs into paralyzed uselessness. She let the minute tick by, then gave it another fifteen seconds just be on the safe side. "No, that was me," she said, answering Akim's question. "The hidden cameras and microphone shouldn't be picking up anything now."

"Excellent," Akim said. "But speak toward the window, please."

Jin obeyed, noting out of her peripheral vision that he'd also turned his face in that direction. "Nice view," she commented, gazing out at the city stretched out in front of them.

"I was thinking about the cameras," Akim said. "In case your attack wasn't entirely successful."

"Ah," Jin said. "Okay. We also should keep our mouth movements as small as possible. They may also someone out there on a rooftop with a telescope and a computer that can read human lips."

"Ah," Akim said. "Yes—good point."

"As to the cameras, they're not actually destroyed, just gone way too fuzzy to see anything useful," Jin continued. "And the mike should be delivering nothing but a low-pitched hum right now. So how do we play this?"

For a moment Akim was silent. "How much do you know about Troft military doctrine?"

"The Dominion of Man had more experience with it than anyone wanted," Jin said. "But that was over a century ago. I assume their tactics and strategy have undergone a lot of change since then."

"Yet their basic psychology has likely remained essentially unaltered," Akim pointed out. "From our admittedly limited understanding of them, I wouldn't have expected them to so eagerly take hostages."

Jin gazed out the window at the Troft ships and the brilliant morning sky beyond. Now that she thought about it, she realized Akim was right. The records from the Dominion's war against the Trofts had indicated that *hostage* wasn't a term the aliens generally applied to living beings.

Still, the Troft Assemblage was made up of hundreds of demesnes. Maybe different rules applied to the particular group that had invaded Qasama. "Maybe they've learned to adapt to their particular target," she suggested.

"No," Akim said flatly. "Basic psychology is by definition basic. It doesn't change that drastically."

"You know the Trofts well, then?" Jin asked, a flash of annoyance running through her. The Cobra Worlds had been trading with Trofts for multiple decades, dealing with the aliens on a regular basis. Yet Akim presumed to tell *her* what the Trofts could or couldn't do?

"We've studied them as best we could," he said. "Trading vessels have occasionally come and gone over the past fifty years, though we've given them no encouragement to return." He snorted gently. "And of course, there was the group you and I dealt with."

Jin frowned. "I thought all of them made it off-planet before your people arrived."

"They did," Akim confirmed. "But their interactions with the Qasamans they had dealt with left detectable changes. Studying those changes gleaned for us a fair amount of useful information."

A shiver ran up Jin's back. "I don't even want to know what you had to do to get that."

"The subjects of the study were in no danger."

"I wasn't thinking about them," Jin said. Over the years the Qasamans had built up a large pharmacopoeia of mind-enhancing drugs, each one individually tailored to temporarily improve memory, perception, observation, or reason. The Qasamans had also developed a tradition—a borderline insane one, in Jin's opinion—of using those drugs.

Insane, because however effective the drugs might be they also demanded a terrible price. Habitual users could suffer anything from premature aging to brain damage to a quick and probably painful death.

In fact...

Jin felt her throat tighten. Miron Akim had been a young man when Jin had first visited Qasama, no more than ten years older than she was. Yet when they'd met again a few hours ago in the subcity, she'd guessed his age to top hers by at least thirty years.

She turned her neck a little farther around, taking a good, long look at his profile. His face was calm enough, but now that she was looking for it she could see a brightness and intensity in his eyes that she hadn't noticed before.

He hadn't come along on this trip just to play native guide to her and Merrick while they freed the trapped Shahni, she realized with a sinking feeling. He was here for some other purpose entirely.

"So if we're not hostages, despite their words, we must assume we're here for some other purpose," Akim went on. "We must discover or deduce that purpose."

I thought you already knew everything about Troft psychology. With an effort, Jin held back the words. "Let's start at the beginning," she suggested instead. "We were allowed in on the pretext of meeting their leaders, but were instead chained up without any of those leaders making an appearance."

"Chained *after* our party had been split up," Akim said slowly. "And then locked in an empty room without guards but with hidden monitors."

"*And* right in front of a window," Jin said as that odd fact suddenly struck her. "Where we can see across the whole city."

"And can be seen in turn by everyone outside." Akim snorted. "We aren't hostages, Jin Moreau. We're bait. They wish to see what a Qasaman rescue operation looks like."

"I think you're right," Jin agreed, her face warming with embarrassment that she hadn't figured that one out on her own. It was exactly the same trick the Trofts had pulled on her grandfather, after all, only in reverse: they'd set him up to escape from a fortified base so that they could gather data on Cobra weapons and techniques in a more or less controlled environment. "They're going to be sorely disappointed, though." She looked sideways at Akim again. "Aren't they?"

"I don't know," Akim admitted. "Plan Saikah makes no provision for the rescuing of hostages. But in this case . . . some of the Djinn may take it upon themselves to seek us out."

"Terrific," Jin muttered. "Either we let the Trofts see Djinn in action, or we tip them off that there are Cobras on Qasama."

"Neither of which is acceptable," Akim said flatly. "We must find a third alternative."

"I'm game," Jin said. "How much time do we have?"

Akim hissed thoughtfully between his teeth. "From the time our forces are alerted as to the change in the operation . . . perhaps an hour."

Jin grimaced. That wasn't much time. "Then we'd better get busy," she said. "Let's put our heads together and see what we can come up with."

The room Daulo and Fadil were taken to was small but pleasant enough. There were three cushioned chairs, a water dispenser, a small fruit grouping, and an equally small basket of travel-style snack and meal packages. It was, for Daulo, an unexpected courtesy, given how less comfortable a cell the Djinn could have chosen to put them in.

Fadil, though, didn't seem to see it that way. For the first hour of their incarceration he paced the room like a caged krisjaw, answering his father's comments and questions with terse replies just barely within the bounds of courtesy. A few minutes into their second hour he abandoned his pacing and dropped into one of the chairs, staring at the fruit as if he expected it to explode at any moment.

Daulo's first thought was that his son was fighting between the desire to eat and the conflicting desire to avoid showing the weakness of hunger in front of the Djinn. It was only when the elder Sammon got up and picked out a pomegranate for himself that he discovered Fadil wasn't actually gazing at the fruit, but at something far more distant, something only he could see.

In someone else, such a state might have indicated meditation or focused thought. But Daulo knew better. In Fadil, at least in his younger days, such concentration had usually followed a deliberate insult by a member of a rival family, and the concentration had subsequently led to the boy's carefully planned response to that insult.

And villager that he was, he almost couldn't help but see their incarceration at the hands of city people as such an insult.

But he'll think it through, Daulo tried to assure himself. *He'll realize that behavior in time of war isn't the same as in time of peace.*

And if he didn't, it would be Daulo's job to convince him of that. Hopefully before the boy did something foolish.

He had finished his pomegranate and was dozing in his chair when a sudden pounding startled him awake. He looked up to see Fadil standing at the door, pounding on it with the heel of his hand. "Someone!" he called. "Someone come!"

"Fadil!" Daulo snapped. "What are you—?"

"Someone come!" Fadil called again.

There was the click of a lock and Fadil stepped back as the door swung inward to reveal a gray-clad Djinni. "What do you wish?" the Djinni asked.

"I wish to see someone in authority," Fadil said, his voice respectful but firm.

The Djinni shook his head. "All such are occupied."

"Then let me see the man from the hospital," Fadil countered. "The one your companion Carsh Zoshak was so eager to free."

"Just a minute," Daulo put in as he hastily gathered his robe about him and scrambled to his feet. He had no idea who the mysterious old man was, but the fact the Shahni had sent two Djinn to get him out ahead of the Trofts implied he was *not* the sort of person from whom a simple villager demanded an audience. "Fadil—"

"Quiet, Father," Fadil said calmly. "We brought two Cobras here to help with the war, Djinni. You owe us for that."

"And an audience with His Excellency is what you wish in repayment?" the Djinni asked. Despite the seriousness of the situation, Daulo could nevertheless hear a hint of amusement in the Djinni's voice. A city dweller, speaking down to a villager, and Daulo could only pray that his son wouldn't also hear the telltale tone.

If the younger man did, he made no sign. "If that's how you choose to see it, yes," he said.

Timothy Zahn

The Djinni cocked his head. "Very well," he said, taking a step back out of the doorway and gesturing Fadil forward. "Do you wish to speak with him as well, Daulo Sammon?" he added as Fadil strode past and disappeared down the corridor.

Daulo absolutely did not, and he very much wanted to say so. But Fadil was already on his way, and Daulo could hardly leave his son to face the results of this strange insanity alone. "Thank you," he said, and hurried from the room.

He caught up with Fadil a few paces from a door flanked by two more Djinn, both of whom were eyeing the approaching villagers with uncomfortable intensity. "Fadil, what are you *doing*?" Daulo murmured tautly into his son's ear.

"Showing these city dwellers that villagers will not simply stand by and take what is handed to them," Fadil said.

Daulo winced. "Fadil—"

And then there was no more time for talk, because one of the Djinn pushed open the door and Fadil strode inside. Cursing under his breath, Daulo followed.

The room beyond the door was the same size as their cell, but much better furnished. Instead of chairs, the entire rear quarter of the room was piled with large cushions, on which sat a frail old man with a lined face and sunken cheeks. His piercing eyes were focused on a pair of computers sitting on a low table in front of him, and wafting through the air was the faint scent of a mild incense. "I bid you welcome, Fadil Sammon," the old man said, raising his eyes to his visitors as Fadil came to a halt a respectful three paces away from the computer desk. Like the guards outside, his gaze was intense, but he didn't seem bothered or even surprised by the intrusion. "And you, Daulo Sammon," he continued. "I am Moffren Omnathi, advisor to the Shahni. How may I be of service?"

Daulo felt his breath freeze in his throat. *God above.* This wasn't just some important old man. It wasn't even some random Shahni advisor, or even one of the Shahni himself.

This was *Moffren Omnathi.* The man assigned to escort the first Aventinian mission around Qasama, and the one who had first detected their deception. The man who had thrown together a plan for their capture on the fly, and had caught on to their second and more subtle deception, and who would have taken the entire group of them captive had it not been for the unexpected power and weaponry of the Cobras. The man whose quick military action years later had succeeded in capturing a great deal of Troft equipment after Obolo Nardin's failed bid for power.

Moffren Omnathi was more than just a hero. He was a legend.

And Daulo and his son had just barged in on him.

Daulo looked sideways at Fadil. The other recognized Omnathi's name, all right, and for a second his resolve seemed to falter. But then he took a deep breath and squared his shoulders. "Forgive the intrusion, Your Excellency," he said, making the highest sign of respect. "But a grave injustice has been done to us, which I pray you will see fit to rectify."

"And what injustice is this, Fadil Sammon?" Omnathi asked.

"Our home has been invaded, Your Excellency," Fadil said. "Yet my father and I have been forced to sit idly doing nothing."

He drew himself up. "I request your permission to be given a weapon, assigned to a unit, and allowed to fight."

Daulo stared at his son, feeling the universe tilt around him. Of all the things he had imagined Fadil might say, this was one possibility that had never even crossed his mind. "Fadil, what—?" He broke off, looking back at Omnathi. "I beg your pardon, Your Excellency—"

"Peace, Daulo Sammon," Omnathi said calmly, his bright eyes boring into Fadil's face. "Yet you already provide an important service to Qasama, Fadil Sammon."

"Only that of hostage, Your Excellency," Fadil said. "A guarantee for the behavior of Jin Moreau and Merrick Moreau."

Daulo felt his throat tighten. He'd hoped Fadil wouldn't figure that out.

"But two such hostages are hardly necessary," Fadil continued. "Especially since my father is the only one Jin Moreau truly knows and truly cares about. Let him stay here and be guarantee of her loyalty. Give me a weapon and let me fight for my world."

Omnathi studied him a moment in silence, then shifted his

gaze to Daulo. "You disapprove of your son's offer, Daulo Sammon?" he asked.

"Not at all, Your Excellency," Daulo hastened to assure him.

"You are surprised, then?"

Daulo looked at his son. "Yes," he admitted. "But also proud."

"Indeed." Omnathi looked back at Fadil. "You are willing, then, to give your life for your people?"

"If need be, yes." Fadil drew himself up. "But hopefully not before I've given the Trofts ample opportunity to do the same."

Omnathi smiled. "So be it. Can you handle a weapon?"

"We of the villages still mount razorarm and krissjaw hunts," Fadil said with an edge of pride. "I've killed one of each within the past six months. I doubt the Trofts are nearly as quick on their feet."

"We shall soon find out." Omnathi looked over Fadil's shoulder to the Djinni who had taken up silent guard in the doorway. "Take Fadil Sammon to the simulation range," he ordered. "Assess his ability with a weapon, and assign him accordingly."

"Yes, Your Excellency." The Djinni stepped out of the doorway and gestured. "Master Sammon?"

Fadil gave Daulo a brief nod. "Father," he said, and strode from the room.

"And you, Daulo Sammon?" Omnathi asked.

With a start, Daulo realized he was still staring at the doorway where his son had disappeared. "Your Excellency?" he asked, turning back to Omnathi.

"Do you wish to follow your son into combat and danger?"

Daulo frowned. "I stand where the Shahni so order," he said formally. "But I understood I was to remain as hostage to the Moreaus' behavior."

Again, Omnathi smiled. But this time, there was no humor there. "The Moreaus' behavior is based on their belief that you and your son are under threat of death," he said. "Whether such a threat actually exists is irrelevant."

Daulo stared at the old man, his blood running suddenly cold as he focused on the other's shining eyes and the other marks of enhancement drug use. Omnathi was pushing his intellect to the fullest as he prepared Sollas for war.

And if he was willing to give even a pair of untried villagers guns... "We don't have enough men, do we?" Daulo asked quietly. "This attack isn't going to succeed."

Omnathi lowered his gaze to the computers in front of him. "Every hour we delay a response is an hour the invaders will use to settle themselves ever more firmly into their defensive positions," he said. "We have no choice but to attack as quickly as we can, with all the strength we have, and to trust to God for victory."

"I understand," Daulo murmured. It wasn't, he noted, exactly an answer to his question. Or perhaps it was. "I haven't been on a hunt in several years," he continued, "but I still remember how to use a rifle."

"Then the Djinni outside will take you to the range," Omnathi said gravely, his shining eyes still on the computers.

Clearly, he was dismissed. "Your Excellency," Daulo said, making the sign of respect. Turning, he left the room.

CHAPTER TWELVE

Merrick's first journey through the subcity earlier had left him with the impression that it had been designed by cross-eyed moles. Now, as he headed toward the Palace with Zoshak, he concluded that those same moles had also had one set of legs shorter than the other.

Still, even as he privately cursed the unexpected jags in the passageway and the uneven footing, he could understand the military logic that had gone into the system. With all the curves, drops, and angles in the corridors, any enemy who got in here could be held off for days by a relative handful of defenders. The attackers would have to use explosives or smart missiles to break free, which Merrick guessed would merely collapse the local tunnel area, blocking further access to the system and possibly burying attackers and defenders alike.

Twice along the way he heard Zoshak making the same odd teeth-clicking sound he'd heard while the group in the Sammons' truck was coming toward Sollas. Then, he'd assumed Zoshak was going into shock; now, he knew it was part of the Djinni's radio comm system.

It was definitely a good thing to let any defenders in the subcity know that he and Zoshak were coming. It wouldn't be so good if the Trofts on the surface were able to pick up the transmissions, as well.

But if the aliens heard the signals, they were too slow on the uptake to do anything about it. Eight minutes after leaving the airfield tower, the Cobra and the Djinni arrived beneath the Palace.

The monitor room, a duplicate of the one beneath the tower, was deserted. "Where is everyone?" Merrick asked, looking around as Zoshak busied himself with the monitor.

"Why would anyone be here?" Zoshak countered as he ran quickly through a set of images. "The Palace situation appears as we expected."

"Trofts?" Merrick asked.

"Didn't you see them?"

"You went through the images pretty quickly," Merrick pointed out.

"Yes, there are Trofts." Zoshak stepped over to the vertical cylinder. "Can you get this open?"

"Sure," Merrick said, going over to join him. Curving his fingers over into firing position, he aimed at a spot about knee height and gave the cylinder a blast with his fingertip lasers. To his surprise, the metal merely sputtered and sizzled without breaking open. "Uh-oh," he murmured.

"What do you mean, *uh-oh*?" Zoshak demanded. "Can't you cut through it?"

"Not like this." Merrick backed up, targeting-locking a horizontal line across the tube at about waist height. "You don't care about the cables inside, do you? Never mind—the whole place is going to blow anyway. Move away and watch your eyes." Putting a forearm over his own face, he lifted his left leg and fired his antiarmor laser.

A brilliant beam of blue light lit up the room, accompanied by a much louder sizzling from the cylinder. Merrick finished his sweep and shut off the laser, then lowered both his leg and his arm.

The metal that had successfully resisted his smaller lasers had succumbed without fuss to the larger one. The cylinder now sported a neat two-centimeter-wide gap, the cut edges glowing a dull red. "That's better," Merrick said as the stink of vaporized metal tingled his nostrils. "I'll make another cut, and we'll be good to go."

"One moment." Stepping forward, Zoshak wrapped his arms tightly around the cylinder above the gap. "Sound carries well in confined places," he added. "We don't want something this heavy crashing to the floor."

"Good point," Merrick agreed, targeting another cutting line half a meter above Zoshak's head. "I hope that suit of yours is good against hot metal sparks."

"It is," Zoshak said dryly. "Do be careful not to miss."

"Don't worry." Again protecting his eyes, Merrick lifted his leg and fired.

Again, the room lit up with blue light, and with a muted clunk of breaking metal the section came free. "You need a hand?" Merrick asked.

"No," Zoshak said. Sliding the section out of line with the rest of the cylinder, he set it down on the floor. Merrick stepped up beside him and peered into the opening.

To his surprise, it was completely empty. "Aren't there supposed to be cables in here?" he asked quietly.

"You mean the ones you just cut through?" Zoshak suggested as he straightened up.

"I don't think so," Merrick said, stepping aside. "See for yourself."

Zoshak ducked his head into the gap, shining his collar light upward. "You're right," he said. "The Shahni must have cut all of them."

"Of course they did," Merrick said as one of Miron Akim's earlier comments suddenly came back to him. "The Shahni who were left behind were trying to sabotage the equipment. Cutting all the cables and letting them fall a hundred meters would pretty well cover that." He reached up into the cylinder, running his fingers along the slightly rough metal surface. "Should be able to get decent traction," he decided, looking over at Zoshak's gloved hands. "I don't suppose you have a spare set of gloves I could borrow?"

"I'm sorry," Zoshak said. "Will your hands be all right?"

"Hopefully, I can do most of it with my elbows and knees," Merrick said. "Let's go." He stepped up onto the lip of the cylinder and pressed his elbows against the sides.

And stopped as a horrible thought suddenly occurred to him. "Oh, hell," he said softly.

"What?" Zoshak asked sharply.

Merrick looked up into the darkness. "Do you know if there's a cap on the tube somewhere inside the Palace? Or does the cylinder go all the way up into the roof?"

"There's a cap at the fourth-floor communications room," Zoshak said. "Why?"

"How sturdy is it?"

Zoshak stared at Merrick, his expression hardening as he got it, too. "It's quite substantial," he said. "Certainly as substantial as the cylinder itself."

"Then we're in trouble," Merrick said, a tightness settling into the pit of his stomach. If the top was capped, and his fingertip lasers weren't powerful enough to cut through the metal...

"No, it just means you'll have to travel upside down," Zoshak said briskly. "Sit down and slide your feet upward into the cylinder."

Merrick made a face. But the other was right. Sitting down beside the cylinder, he lifted his legs up into the opening, straightened his hips and back, and pushed himself up into a handstand with his legs as far up the cylinder as he could get them. He got his balance, then walked backwards on his hands and got his palms up onto the cylinder lip. "This is as far as I can go on my own," he told Zoshak, blinking against the dizziness as the blood rushed to his head.

"Hold still." Zoshak squatted down facing Merrick and got his hands underneath Merrick's shoulders, squeezing his palms into the narrow spaces between neck and arms.

And to Merrick's astonishment he lifted the Cobra the rest of the way out of the gap up into the cylinder. "Can you hold there a moment?" Zoshak murmured.

"I'll try," Merrick said, pressing his forearms and shins as tightly against the cylinder walls as he could. "How's this?"

"Perfect." Quickly, Zoshak let go of Merrick's shoulders and climbed into the shaft beneath him. With his feet straddling the lip, he reestablished his grip. "All right. Hmm. This will be difficult."

"Hang on—let me try something," Merrick said. Shifting around so that his back was pressed against the tube, he tried pushing against the wall with his forearms. To his mild surprise, he slid upward a few centimeters. "Looks like you won't have to push me the whole way," he said, sliding himself up another few centimeters.

"Try using your feet, too," Zoshak suggested. "Press with the edges or soles and then bend your knees inward."

Merrick tried it. This time he moved nearly twice the distance of his first two tries. "Probably as good as it's going to get," he said, resetting his elbows and knees and repeating the operation. "Okay. Let's go."

The trip was agonizing. Merrick was able to turn most of the work over to his servos, which at least relieved the strain on his muscles. But there was no such protection for his hands, and the rough metal slowly but steadily rubbed them raw. Combined with the constant thudding of blood in his head, it made for a more miserable experience than anything he'd gone through since graduating from the Academy. Closing his eyes, trying to focus on his forearms instead of his slowly disintegrating hands, he kept going.

It was therefore something of a shock when he stretched out his legs that last time and bumped his feet into something solid. "We're here," Zoshak whispered.

"Right," Merrick said, settling himself against the wall and trying to clear his head. First step, the thought seeped through his pounding skull, was to see if any Trofts were nearby. Pressing his ear against the metal, he keyed in his auditory enhancers.

And found himself in the center of a soft but bewildering tangle of sounds and voices. "Well?" Zoshak prompted.

"Quiet," Merrick said, fighting to untangle the cacophony. From the sheer number of conflicting noises it almost sounded like the Qasamans and Trofts were having a dinner-dance party. Yet everything was oddly muted, as if the partygoers were afraid the neighbors would hear.

And then the obvious answer penetrated his numbed brain. The metal cylinder was funneling sounds to him from all four levels of the building. More importantly, the fact that everything sounded quiet even with Merrick's enhancements going implied that the fourth-floor area around him and Zoshak was in fact deserted.

Or it just meant that the Trofts babysitting that particular communications room were being very quiet.

There was only one way to find out. Keying down his audio

enhancements again, Merrick tucked his right leg down as far as he could out of the way and aimed his left heel at the edge of the cylinder's cap. "Watch your eyes," he warned Zoshak, and fired.

The familiar blue light blazed, and a second later a rain of metal sparks began to burn into Merrick's legs and hips, joining the pressure in his head and the throbbing in his palms. Squeezing his eyes shut, ignoring this fresh source of pain, he swept his leg around the edge of the lid, slicing it free of the cylinder. The blue light vanished as he shut down his laser.

And without warning Zoshak put his hands on Merrick's shoulders and shoved, and Merrick found himself flying straight up out of the cylinder like a cork from a champagne bottle, his feet knocking aside the severed lid on the way. He had just enough presence of mind to grab the upper edge of the cylinder with one hand as he passed, checking his upward motion before he could slam feet-first into the ceiling and swiveling himself into a circle that landed him more or less upright on the floor.

Fortunately, his nanocomputer was more alert than he was, and bent his knees to absorb the impact. Snapping his hands up into firing position, blinking to clear his vision, he looked around.

He was in a small room with an electronics-laden wraparound desk pressed up against two of the walls. Above the desk were rows of monitors like the ones he'd seen down in Akim's subcity command center, all of them currently dark. The cylinder lid he'd knocked off had landed on the desk, hopefully with a minimum of noise.

Still, even if the Trofts had finished checking these upper floors, it was unlikely that they'd simply abandoned them. "Where's the entrance to the safe room?" he asked Zoshak as the latter pulled himself out of the cylinder.

"Two rooms to the left, behind a blue and white tile mosaic," Zoshak said, pointing. "I just hope the Shahni are up here, and not in the second-floor safe room."

"Well, this is where they cut the cables, anyway," Merrick pointed out as he crossed to the door. "Otherwise we'd have run into dangling cable ends two floors down. Be quiet a second."

He pressed his ear to the door and keyed his enhancers. Nothing. "Sounds clear," he said. "I'll go check it out."

"Be careful," Zoshak warned. "There may be a roving patrol."

"Probably," Merrick said grimly. "You find the Shahni and get them ready to travel."

The Shahni apartment levels, as Merrick had noted earlier from Akim's floor plans, had been designed with an open layout: wide hallways opening smoothly into lounges, dining areas, and media rooms, with only the various sleeping rooms closed off from the general space. What the floor plans hadn't shown was the fact that the wide corridors were liberally sprinkled with sculptures on carved or molded pedestals, many of them partially recessed in half-cylindrical or semispherical wall niches. Other sections of wall were covered with colorful, intricate tapestries or more of the tile mosaics that Zoshak had mentioned. Quietly, Merrick moved along the colorful displays of the main corridor, his senses alert for trouble.

He was halfway to the elevators when he heard the soft sounds of rhythmic footsteps coming his way.

He looked around. To his left was one of the hanging tapestries, to his right a large vase on a pedestal within a half-cylindrical floor-to-ceiling niche. Getting a grip on the pedestal, he pulled.

The combination of vase and pedestal was heavier than it looked, and he had to brace one foot on the wall and use his servos to get the thing to move. He pulled it about fifteen centimeters out into the hallway and then slipped around behind it. Set into the ceiling directly in front of the vase was a directed light, which a quick fingertip laser shot blasted into darkness, putting Merrick's hiding place into partial shadow. Another quick slash with the lasers cut a vertical line in the tapestry across from him and then added enough of a horizontal cut at the top to suggest a hidden doorway had been opened and then hastily and imperfectly shut. Crouching down, he set one palm against the vase and the other against the midpoint of the pedestal and prepared himself.

Ten seconds later, the footsteps grew louder as the Trofts came around one of the corners, then faltered as the aliens spotted the dead light and the damaged tapestry. For a moment the footsteps stopped completely, and there was a moment of indistinct muttering as one of the soldiers called it in. *Be overanxious,* Merrick urged them silently. *Be overanxious, and just a little bit careless.*

The soldier finished his report. Merrick held his breath; and then they were there: two Trofts, dressed in the same helmets and armored leotard outfits Merrick had seen on the aliens at the airfield control tower. Both had their lasers pointed at the tapestry, ready for something to come jumping out at them from behind it. One of them turned his head to check out the niche across the hall.

And as he jerked with surprise, Merrick shoved with all his servos' strength against the pedestal and vase, hurling them across the hall.

The impacts knocked both soldiers off their feet, slamming them into the tapestry and the solid wall behind it. One of them managed to get off a wild shot before he hit that burned harmlessly into the floor.

And then Merrick was beside them, ripping open their faceplates and punching hard into their throat bladders. Hefting the heavy pedestal up into his arms, he hurried down the hallway toward the elevator. If the backup hadn't been coming before, it was definitely on its way now.

The stairwell door beside the twin elevators was alive with the sounds of racing Troft feet when Merrick reached it. He set the pedestal against the door, using another nearby pedestal to help wedge it in place. The elevators showed no sign of activity, but he gave each of the doors a quick spot-weld just in case, then headed back toward the safe room.

The camouflaged door was standing partially open as he came around the final corner. He was nearly there when Zoshak slipped out of the safe room, a compact but deadly-looking submachine gun gripped in his hands. "What was that noise?" he asked, peering past Merrick's shoulder.

"That was the roving patrol," Merrick said. "It's not roving anymore." Stepping past Zoshak, he pulled the door all the way open. "Are our guests about ready to—?"

He broke off. Akim had said that two of the Shahni were trapped in here. Only it wasn't just a pair of old men standing silently in the hidden room. The two old men were accompanied by an old woman, a young man and a young woman, and two boys of perhaps six and eight.

"What the—?" Merrick grabbed Zoshak's arm as the other came up beside him. "I was told we were rescuing two Shahni."

"We are," Zoshak said grimly. "And yes, they're ready."

"What about the others?"

"There's no time," Zoshak said stiffly. "They must remain behind."

Merrick stared at him, his mouth dropping open in astonishment. "They're *what?*"

"There's no time," Zoshak repeated. "Quickly, now, before more aliens arrive. Your Excellencies?"

One of the Shahni stepped forward. The second paused to squeeze the old woman's shoulder and then followed. "Wait a minute," Merrick protested. "We can't just leave these people here to die."

"We have no choice," the second Shahni said firmly. "There is insufficient time to bring everyone through the escape route Djinni Zoshak has prepared."

"Then we'd better find some other way out for them," Merrick said harshly. "Plan Saikah starts with blowing up the Palace, remember?"

"And so we will serve our people," the young man said. His hand, Merrick noted, was tightly gripping the young woman's.

"Are the children to serve the same way?" Merrick demanded.

"They are sons of Qasama," the young man said, letting go of the woman's hand and resting one hand on each of the two boys' shoulders. "They will do what is necessary."

"There *is* no other way out," the first Shahni said impatiently. "And we waste time."

Merrick focused on the boys' faces. Both were trying very hard to be as brave and determined as their parents, but the younger one was clearly teetering on the point of tears.

The only route now into or out of the Palace is through the main doors, Miron Akim had said, and the first Shahni had now confirmed it. Unfortunately, it was an exit currently blocked by multiple layers of armed Trofts.

Merrick's old spine leopard hunting squad might have been able to cut through them all. But the squad wasn't here, and Merrick didn't have a hope of defeating that many enemies, especially not once the element of surprise was gone.

Which meant he had to somehow get the Trofts to leave on their own.

"Can you get the two Shahni out by yourself?" he asked, turning back to Zoshak. "Piggyback them down on your shoulders or something?"

"What nonsense is this?" the first Shahni growled. "You have been ordered to bring us out. You will obey that order. *Now.*"

Merrick kept his eyes on Zoshak. "Carsh Zoshak?"

Zoshak looked at the two children. "It would be difficult for the one directly above me," he said hesitantly. "He would carry much of the weight of the second upon his own shoulders."

"We waste time—" the first Shahni said.

"What are you proposing?" the second Shahni interrupted.

"I'm proposing that Djinni Zoshak bring you both out," Merrick told him, "while I attempt to do the same with the others."

"You think you can carry all five of them upon *your* shoulders?" the first Shahni scoffed. "This is foolishness. I insist you carry out your orders."

Merrick turned to face him. "Technically, Your Excellency, I'm not—"

"It can be done," the second Shahni again interrupted. "I will take center position, above Djinni Zoshak's shoulders, with Shahni Melcha's weight upon me."

"Thank you, Your Excellency," Merrick said, turning back to Zoshak. "Can you do it?"

Zoshak's lips were pressed tightly together, but he gave a short nod. "I believe so," he said.

"Then get them to the cylinder and get in," Merrick said. "I'll be there in a minute to help them in behind you. Any idea how long before Plan Saikah starts?"

"Approximately ten minutes," Zoshak said, motioning the two Shahni toward the door.

"Can you find out more exactly?" Merrick asked.

"It would require me to transmit the request," Zoshak warned. "The invaders have already shown they can detect those signals."

"That's okay," Merrick assured him. "In fact, at this point, the more transmissions out of here, the better." He gestured to the young man. "I'll need some kind of timer," he continued. "It doesn't have to connect to anything, but it has to have a visible countdown display. Is there anything in here you can rig up to do that?"

The young man glanced at the two Shahni, as if for confirmation that he was allowed to talk to this upstart stranger. "There's an assembly timer in the lounge," he said. "It calls the Shahni to meetings, marking the time remaining until the opening prayer."

"But the display has repeaters throughout the building, including the lower floors," the young woman put in. "The invaders may see it."

"Perfect," Merrick told her. "Carsh Zoshak?"

"Twelve minutes and thirty seconds," Zoshak reported.

"Set the timer to hit zero twelve minutes and thirty seconds from now," Merrick instructed the young man. "Then return here, and leave the door open so I can get back in. Come on, Djinni Zoshak—let's get you and the Shahni out of here."

They headed back toward the communications room. "I hope you have a plan," Zoshak warned quietly. "I don't know how you see things on your world, but here we're expected to obey orders precisely. We were told to rescue the Shahni. That's all that matters."

"And you *are* rescuing them," Merrick reminded him. "As for how we do things on the Cobra Worlds, we absolutely do *not* abandon anyone if there's a chance of saving them."

"Even at the risk of your own life?"

An echo of the brief battle in the control tower elevator flashed through Merrick's mind. Before that, he'd never fully appreciated the ramifications of the fact that war meant he would have to kill.

Just as he had never before appreciated on a gut level that he might also have to die.

But he certainly couldn't confess such fears and doubts in front of a dedicated soldier like Zoshak. Personal and national pride both demanded Merrick maintain some shred of dignity here. "Yes, even then," he said, trying to sound strong and fearless. "What other purpose does a soldier have?"

For a moment Zoshak was silent. Merrick winced, wondering if the other had penetrated his deception and was wondering what kind of coward he was traveling with. "We've been told you demon warriors come from a soft people," the Qasaman said at last. "It appears we were wrong."

Merrick snorted quietly, Governor Treakness's contempt for the Cobras flashing to mind. "Don't fool yourself—my people have plenty of softness," he said grimly. "But we still have a few pockets of strength left."

The two Shahni were waiting in the communications room when Merrick and Zoshak arrived. The first was gazing down into the open cylinder, an incredulous look on his face. "You expect us to travel through *this*?" he demanded.

"It is passable," Zoshak assured him as he hopped up onto the desk and slipped his legs into the cylinder. Pressing his feet firmly against the sides, he stood upright and slid smoothly downward until only his head was visible. "Shahni Haafiz, you'll need to climb up onto the desk and place your feet on my shoulders," he said. "Mind your hands—the cylinder edge is sharp in places."

Haafiz looked at Merrick. "Your assistance," he ordered.

"Certainly." Merrick stepped forward and held out a hand. "Lean on me, Your Excellency."

Haafiz took hold of Merrick's forearm and hoisted one foot up onto the desk.

And suddenly a small knife flashed in his other hand, driving straight at Merrick's heart.

CHAPTER THIRTEEN

It was so unexpected that for that crucial fraction of a second Merrick's eyes and brain refused to grasp the fact that he was under attack by a man he was risking his own life to save. But his nanocomputer had no such emotional limitations. Even as the knife tip drove through Merrick's clothing and into his skin his servos were twisting his torso away from the blade while at the same time shoving him backward.

But even Cobra reflexes could move a man only so fast from a dead stop. As Merrick twisted and fell onto his back he could feel the throbbing pain in his chest and the warm spreading wetness of his own blood. "What are you *doing?*" he gasped, pushing himself desperately backward along the floor on his torn palms.

"You think I do not know who and what you are, enemy of Qasama?" Haafiz bit out, jabbing his knife toward Merrick, an edge of bright red now coating the gleaming metal. "Better for my family to die together in honor than to allow them to fall into your hands and those of your allies."

"I'm not working with the Trofts," Merrick protested, clutching at his wound. The sudden pressure sent a dazzling stab of new pain through the torn skin. "I came here to help you."

"And here is where you will die," Haafiz said. Shifting the grip on his knife, he started toward Merrick. Merrick braced himself, flicking a target lock on to the knife.

And then, through the open doorway behind him, he heard a dull thunderclap and the crackle of scattered debris hitting tiled floor. "You hear that?" he demanded as the Shahni came to a sudden halt. "That's the Trofts getting through the barricade I set up to slow them down."

"That *you* set up?" Haafiz scoffed.

"There is no time for foolishness," Zoshak snapped. His face was rigid, his eyes staring in horror and disbelief at the spreading stain on Merrick's tunic. "Shahni Haafiz, you must come to me now, or die."

The Shahni hesitated another moment. Then, contemptuously tossing the knife to the side, he turned and climbed up onto the desk. Zoshak slid farther down the cylinder and Haafiz put his legs in. As he slid downward, the other Shahni climbed in on top of him, this one not even bothering to glance in Merrick's direction. Another moment, and he, too, was out of sight.

Leaving Merrick, bleeding and alone, to face the Trofts.

"Damn," Merrick muttered, pressing his hand to his chest as he carefully got to his feet, the throbbing agony in his chest momentarily eclipsed by an equally throbbing rage. What the *hell* did Haafiz think he was doing? And who the hell did he think he was doing it to? Staggering on suddenly wobbly knees, Merrick made his way across to the cylinder. He would like nothing better than to jump up onto the desk, aim his antiarmor laser down the cylinder, and give His Exalted Excellency Shahni Haafiz one last second of wisdom-enhancing pain before he died.

He couldn't do that, of course. Not even if he could guarantee that such a blast wouldn't kill two innocents in the process.

But he would remember Shahni Haafiz. He would remember him well.

The metal lid he'd burned off earlier was still lying on the desk. Setting it back on top of the cylinder, Merrick fired three quick shots with his fingertip lasers, spot-welding it into place. Then, pressing one hand against his chest wound, wondering how deep the Shahni's blade had gotten and how fast he was losing blood, he headed back toward the safe room.

He was nearly there when five Trofts suddenly appeared, their lasers pointed at him. "Human, stop!" the translator pin boomed.

"We have to get out of here," Merrick gasped, putting a weaving stagger into his walk as he continued toward them, trying to look like a man on his last legs. "They wouldn't listen—they wouldn't stop it. He stabbed me—"

"Human, *stop!*" the Troft repeated, more emphatically this time.

"He tried to kill me," Merrick said, finally coming to a shambling halt. "He stabbed me, and then they left."

"Who left?" the Troft demanded.

"The Shahni who were hiding here," Merrick said. There was a sudden commotion behind the Trofts and another group of aliens appeared, pulling and dragging the five Qasamans who Merrick had left in the safe room. "They were hiding with them in that secret room," Merrick added, pointing at the newcomers. "They're going to blow up the building and kill us."

One of the Trofts stepped to the side, covering his translator and muttering urgent-sounding cattertalk into his radio. "Didn't you hear me?" Merrick pleaded, putting some desperation in his voice. "They're going to blow up the building. You have to get us out of here."

"How do they plan to do that?" the lead Troft asked. "With artillery?"

"The bombs are already built into the walls," Merrick said, wondering dimly whether the aliens were serious or just humoring him.

But the tone of the soldier still talking with upper command was anything but light-hearted. Even more telling, all the aliens were exhibiting the telltale fluttering of radiator membranes that was the mark of serious emotion. They believed him, all right.

And only then did it occur to him that Shahni Haafiz's sneak attack might have something to do with that. A human in the Shahni's palace would almost certainly be lying to Qasama's invaders. A human who those same Shahni had tried to kill might not be.

"Which walls?" the Troft demanded.

That was, Merrick realized with a sinking sensation, a damn good question. He'd hoped to sell this story to the Trofts, but had never really expected to get even this far with it. Apparently his bloody tunic, plus the ticking countdown timer the young Qasaman man had set up, had convinced someone to take the whole thing seriously.

Only now he was expected to point out some actual explosives as confirmation. Without any such proof, the Trofts would probably put his story down to an elaborate hoax and go about their business.

At least until the building turned to fiery dust eight and a half minutes from now. "I don't—" Merrick began.

"Traitor!" the Qasaman man shouted suddenly. "Don't tell them!"

Merrick jerked, the movement sending a fresh wave of pain through his chest, the words themselves digging deep into his soul. Couldn't these people understand that he was trying to help them? Were they all so full of unthinking rage at what his parents and grandparents had done that they couldn't see anything beyond that?

And then he took another look into the young man's eyes. Eyes that were holding steady on Merrick even as the rest of his face twisted with rage and contempt. Eyes that waited until Merrick was looking straight at them, and then flicked to his right.

And with that, some of the frustrated weariness lifted from Merrick's shoulders. The young man was onto Merrick's plan ... and despite Qasama's corporate institutional rage at the Cobra Worlds, he was willing to cooperate. "You want to die?" Merrick demanded, throwing every bit of acting ability he'd ever had into selling it.

"I will die with honor," the young man snarled, again twitching his eyes to his right. "Let them die, too, like the dung worms that they are."

"You die however you want to," Merrick bit out. "I'd rather live." He pointed at the wall the Qasaman had indicated. "You want to see some of the explosives? You can start with that wall right there."

The lead Troft snapped an order, and one of the soldiers grouped around the Qasamans stepped across the hallway, sprung a long knife, and stabbing into the wall between a pair of standing sculptures. He twisted the knife hard over and pulled, and a half-meter chunk of some plaster-like substance came free.

And behind it, nestled into the space between the a pair of

thick wooden supports, was a square meter's worth of a plastic-wrapped gray clay.

The lead Troft didn't waste even a second gawking. [The prisoners, take them below,] he snapped, loud enough for Merrick to hear even without using his enhancements. [Their bindings, fasten them along the way. The commanders, warn them immediately.]

"And that's just one of them," Merrick said as the Trofts grabbed the Qasamans' arms or jabbed lasers into their ribs, getting the group moving down the hallway toward the elevators. A second later Merrick bit back a gasp of pain as his own arm was grabbed and he was hustled off after the others.

And as they hurried along, one of the Trofts wove in and out of the Qasamans, fastening their arms behind them with chain-link wrist shackles. Merrick watched the operation closely, studying the restraints and trying to figure out where best they could be broken. Unlike the solid-bar shackles the Qasamans had used on him earlier, chains were harder for his nanocomputer to pinpoint when it didn't have any optics available for positioning data. The place where the chain was fastened to the right wrist cuff, he decided, would be his best bet.

The Troft finished with the Qasamans and headed toward Merrick with one final set of shackles in hand. Merrick glanced a target lock onto the spot he'd chosen, and silently let the alien pin his arms behind him.

The elevators were both waiting when the group arrived. The five Qasamans and their escort were guided into one, while Merrick and his own five-Troft guard took the other.

Merrick took a careful breath as the elevator started down, his nose tingling with the subtle scents of Troft and metal and armored leotard, his mind's eye flashing with unpleasant images from his last time in an elevator with Qasama's invaders. But this wouldn't be a replay of that other deadly ride. This time, he was going to cooperate fully with the Trofts. Right up to the moment when he stopped.

"Three minutes," the sergeant called softly from the hallway. "All gunners, stand ready."

Lying flat on his belly on one of the Lodestare Hospital's beds, Daulo took a moment to reflect on the irony of the whole situation. Earlier, Jin Moreau and Siraj Akim had gone to tremendous lengths to get him and Fadil out of this very place. And yet, now here they were again, joining a dozen other Qasaman soldiers preparing to throw this invasion down the enemy's throat.

On the face of it, moving troops into a building that the Trofts had already sequestered could be considered the height of foolishness. But on the other hand, bypassing the guards the Trofts had set up at the hospital's entrances had been simplicity itself, thanks to the subcity passages. And Daulo had to admit that after Jin and Siraj Akim had put the Lodestone into the center of Troft attention it was probably the last place the invaders would expect the Qasamans to come back to.

It was also unarguable that this particular line of eighth-floor rooms gave a perfect view of the rear of the Palace and the enemy soldiers guarding that section of the perimeter.

"Uh-oh," Fadil murmured from the bed beside Daulo's. "Look there, Father, at the group heading toward the street."

Daulo shifted his gaze to the street running along the front of the Palace. There were two different groups there, one consisting of five Qasamans and a half-dozen Troft guards, the other composed of a single human and five more of the aliens. "What about them?" he asked.

"Look closely at the singleton," Fadil said. "I believe we know him."

Frowning, Daulo swung his rifle around, centering the scope on the man Fadil had indicated.

It was Merrick Moreau.

"You suppose this is part of his plan?" Fadil suggested, his tone making it clear that he thought exactly the opposite.

"Enough chatter," the sergeant crouched beside the window growled. "If you villagers can't keep your minds and eyes where they're supposed to be, I'll find something else for you to do."

"Our apologies," Daulo said, his face warming with embarrassment and annoyance. *Villagers.* Not fellow soldiers, or fellow snipers, or even fellow Qasamans. Just *villagers.*

He stole a final look at the street as Merrick Moreau and his guards filed through the massive rear doors of the first of the two armored trucks the aliens had pulled to the curb, while the group of Qasamans were ushered into the one behind it.

He could only hope that being taken prisoner *was,* in fact, part of Merrick Moreau's plan.

"It's time," Miron Akim murmured from behind Jin.

With a start, Jin jolted out of a light doze and checked her nanocomputer's clock. Fifty-eight minutes of Akim's estimated hour to Plan Saikah had passed. "Right," she confirmed. "Let me get turned around."

Looking casually over at one of the room's two hidden cameras, she put a targeting lock on it. Then, gripping her chair's armrests, she started rocking her body back and forth, steadily walking her chair around toward the window.

"You still wish to destroy the window first?" Akim murmured.

"It's our best chance of hiding who I am," Jin reminded him. "At least for a little longer."

"And every minute that truth is concealed is valuable," Akim agreed with a sigh. "Very well. Proceed."

Jin continued to walk the chair around until she was facing the window. As she settled herself into place, she glanced behind her across the room and put a targeting lock on the second hidden camera. Then, turning back to the window, she lifted her arms off the armrests as high as the shackles permitted and began curving her hands into a series of sign-language configurations.

Not genuine ones, of course. Or at least, nothing that would make any sense to anyone watching her. She'd learned some of the gestures when she was a girl, mostly so that she and her sister Fay could talk together at family gatherings without the adults eavesdropping on their conversation. Once Fay had married and moved off Aventine, though, Jin's abilities had waned to the point where she could now barely even remember the finger-spelling letters.

But the Trofts had no way of knowing that. For all they knew, the random set of gestures she was making might be an esoteric Qasaman battle code. If they were good little soldiers, they would be recording her every move and trying to figure out what she was trying to say.

And with their attention now hopefully pointed in the wrong direction, she activated her sonic disruptor.

She started the weapon at low power, giving its sensors time to search for the window's resonance. In principle, this was no different than the trick she'd pulled back at the Sun Center when she'd shattered the glass surrounding the observation catwalk. In practice, though, the size of this window made the whole thing considerably less certain. Not only would the resonances be harder to hit, but it would take a lot more power to actually shatter the glass.

And if she couldn't make that happen, her hoped-for diversion wasn't going to happen.

Deep within her, she felt a subtle change in vibration as the sonic locked onto the window's resonance. Still making her nonsense hand signals, she fed more power to the weapon. Ten seconds, she decided. If she couldn't break the glass in ten seconds she wasn't going to break it at all. Out of the corner of her eye, she saw Akim join in the fun with hand signals of his own.

Her mental countdown had reached nine seconds when, without even a warning crack, the window blew up in their faces.

The explosion was so unexpected and so violent that Jin nearly missed out on the opportunity she'd been trying to create. But then her brain unfroze, and as the flying glass swirled past her and Akim she twisted her hands into cross-fire positions and fired her fingertip lasers.

Her nanocomputer responded with its usual deadly efficiency, gouging a pair of black-edged holes in the walls where the hidden cameras had been, hopefully fast enough that the Trofts would assume they'd been taken out by shards from the exploded window. Shifting aim, Jin cross-fired at her own wrist shackles, blasting apart the metal and freeing her hands. Another pair of shots freed her legs, and then she was out of her chair, turning toward the door. If the Trofts had left guards out there, they would be charging in any second now.

But the door remained closed. Keeping one eye on the panel, Jin cut Akim free of his chair, and together they headed across the room.

They were nearly to the door when it finally slammed open and a pair of Trofts charged through.

A blast from her antiarmor laser could have taken them out instantly. But Jin had something a bit more subtle in mind. Putting a targeting lock on the lead Troft, she bent her knees and shoved herself off the floor straight toward him.

The combination of targeting lock and leap kicked Jin's nanocomputer into the programmed ceiling flip that Merrick had performed earlier for Akim and the other Djinn. Only this time, it wasn't a sturdy ceiling that took the impact of her feet, but the Troft, who gave an agonized cough of expelled air as he went flying back into his companion. Jin herself bounced back from the impact, again turning halfway around as her nanocomputer tried to finish the ceiling flip, and landed on her side on the floor. She scrambled up into a crouch as Akim grabbed one of the Trofts' lasers and did a quick one-two slam to their helmeted heads. "Come," he snapped to Jin. Flipping the laser around into firing position, he stepped over the unconscious aliens and out into the hallway.

And threw himself to the floor as a pair of laser shots blazed through the air from down the hallway to the left.

Biting out a curse, Jin again bent her knees and leaped forward. Her arcing path shot her just through the doorway, her momentum breaking as she grabbed the door jamb with her left hand and brought herself to a sudden halt. She caught a glimpse of four Trofts at the far corner, two of them in kneeling positions in front of the other two as another pair of shots cut through the space where she would have been if she'd let her leap carry her all the way into the hallway.

The Trofts were busily correcting their aim as Jin fell flat onto her back on the hallway floor beside Akim and slashed her antiarmor laser across them, collapsing them into crumpled heaps.

"Quickly," Akim murmured from her side as he scrambled to his feet.

"Shall I clear us a path?" Jin asked, eyeing the corner beyond the dead Trofts. There were bound to be more of the aliens gathering somewhere on the far side.

"No need." Akim crossed to the wall across from the office

they'd just broken out of and rested his hand against a decorative wall-mounted plaque.

And two meters to the right, a section of the inner wall popped open. "Quickly," he said again, nodding Jin toward the opening.

Jin threw a final look at the dead Trofts. So much for not revealing who she really was. But maybe the Troft commanders would assume someone had simply used one of their own lasers on the victims. Stepping behind Akim, she slipped into the narrow entryway.

From the way Akim had described the elevator escape route earlier, Jin had expected to find herself in some kind of emergency drop shaft. To her surprise, the hidden door led instead into a narrow corridor that stretched away to her left, its far end hidden by a gentle inward curve. She took a couple of steps into the passageway, pausing there until Akim had joined her and closed the secret door, plunging them into total darkness.

Or rather, nearly total darkness. Activating her optical enhancers, Jin discovered there was a faint light coming from around the curve ahead. "Where are we?" she whispered.

"On the outer rim of the central monitoring room," Akim whispered. "Follow the corridor, but make no noise."

Jin looked past Akim's shoulder at the hidden door behind him, wondering what they would do if and when the Trofts found the way in. With Akim between her and any intruders, she would be severely limited in her ability to fight off any such attack.

"Don't concern yourself with pursuit," Akim said. He did something, and a section of the wall rotated silently to seal off the passageway behind him. "Should the invaders find the door, the passage will now lead them in the opposite direction. Now go."

They were nearly to the curved section when the whole building gave a gentle shake around her. Jin looked back at Akim, her stomach suddenly tightening. "The Palace?" she whispered.

His expression in her amplified eyesight was tight and grim. "Yes," he confirmed. "Hurry—the attack here will begin very soon."

Jin nodded and continued on. The adrenaline rush of the earlier activity had worn off, and she could feel a dozen points of stinging pain and the warmth of trickling blood where shards from the exploded window had dug a new set of wounds into her face and arms and chest. Ignoring the injuries, she reached the curve and walked around it.

And came to a sudden halt. She'd expected to find some kind of secret exit that would get them out of this place. Instead, clearly visible behind a layer of tinted plastic on the corridor's inner wall, was the central monitoring room Akim had mentioned.

A monitoring room currently filled to the rafters with Trofts.

Jin twitched back from the dark plastic, feeling horribly exposed. "Go further in," Akim whispered, pressing a hand impatiently into her shoulder. "Don't be concerned—we aren't visible."

Jin wasn't nearly so sure about that. Still, from the Trofts' frantic hand and head movements, not to mention their vibrating radiator membranes, it did appear that they had other matters occupying their attention at the moment. Keeping her movements slow and smooth, she sidled farther down the corridor, studying the room and its occupants as she went.

Not all of the Trofts appeared to be line soldiers. Not even most of them, she realized as she focused on the unarmored leotards most of the aliens were wearing. The only actual combat troops were a pair of armed Trofts standing guard by each of the room's two doors, plus another four standing at the sides of a large curved glass window that opened out onto the airfield and the rows of Troft ships parked across the open space. "What now?" she whispered as Akim moved into view of the room.

"We wait," he said. "And we watch."

Jin frowned. Watch? For what?

And then, through the window, she caught the flicker of gunfire. The Qasamans were attacking the airfield.

She took a deep breath, methodically target-locking the eight armed Trofts in the control room and preparing herself mentally for combat. "I'm ready," she murmured. "Just tell me when."

There was no answer. "Miron Akim?" she prompted, turning to look at him.

And felt a shiver run up her back. Akim wasn't looking at her. He was instead gazing into the room, his eyes bright and unblinking, his lips making small movements as if he was talking silently to himself.

Earlier, Jin had wondered if he'd had come on this mission with some other purpose in mind than the ostensible one of freeing the two Shahni trapped in the Palace. Now, she finally understood what that purpose was.

Akim wasn't here to fight. He was here to observe. To see how exactly the Trofts would react to Plan Saikah.

Jin looked away from him back into the monitor room, fighting back a reflexive flicker of anger at having been lied to this way. She should have known there would be layers of other motivations lurking behind the obscuring veil of the Qasamans' distrust of her and Merrick.

Still, if Akim's goal had been observation, he'd certainly found a good place to do it. As the gunfire picked up outside, the monitor room burst into quiet but frenetic activity. The unarmored Trofts hunched over their consoles, their radiator membranes fluttering like crazy, their beaks snapping in rapid-fire cattertalk. The soldiers were equally tense, the ones at the window gazing tautly out at the battle that had been joined, the ones at the doors taking up full defensive positions, their lasers leveled against possible intrusion.

And unless Akim had lied to her about the extent of the Qasaman attack, there could be Djinn coming through those doors at any minute. "Do you want me to take them out?" she murmured. "Miron Akim? Shall I eliminate the soldiers?"

She counted ten seconds before Akim finally stirred. "We're finished here," he murmured. "The wall behind you. Give it a gentle push."

Jin turned around, studying the smooth wall. "Where?" she asked, looking in vain for the subtle clues as to where the wall ended and the hidden door began.

"There," Akim said, tapping his fingertips on an otherwise unremarkable section of the wall, his eyes still on the activity in the monitor room. "Push there."

Bracing her feet against the floor, Jin placed her palms against the wall and pushed. Nothing happened. She reset her feet and hunched her shoulders in preparation for another try, wondering if the whole wall was supposed to move, and wondering too why such an escape route was even here when obviously only someone with Cobra or Djinni strength could operate it.

"Enough," Akim said. He took a step backward, squatted down, and pulled up a thick section of floor, revealing a narrow shaft leading downward into darkness. Attached to one side of the shaft were a set of metal rungs. "Follow," he told Jin as he took hold of the top rung and lowered himself into the shaft. "Pull the door closed behind you—it will seal automatically."

A moment later they were heading downward, the faint sounds of voices and running feet drifting in through the shaft's walls. Jin tried her audio enhancers, but there was too much distortion and echo for her to tell whether the voices were Troft or human. Occasionally she also heard what sounded like volleys of laser fire.

They had gone perhaps three floors when a sudden surge of dizziness swept over her.

Reflexively, she looped her right arm through the nearest rung, crooking her elbow around the cold metal as she gripped her forearm with her left hand to make sure she didn't fall. The blackness of the shaft seemed to spin around her, twisting her brain into a hard knot and threatening to empty her stomach right where she stood.

"Jin Moreau?" Akim called softly from beneath her. "Are you all right?"

"I don't know," Jin said, clenching her teeth against the waves of vertigo.

"Do you need me to carry you?"

Jin took a careful breath. The dizziness was fading, as inexplicably as it had begun. "I'm all right," she said. "Just let me catch my breath a minute. Keep going—I'll catch up."

"We go together," Akim said firmly. "What happened?"

"I don't know," Jin said. "It felt like I'd been hit with a sonic weapon—dizziness and nausea and all that. You felt nothing?"

"No," Akim said. "And we certainly wouldn't have installed any such traps in these exits. Those most likely to use them would be poorly equipped to find and disable such barriers."

Jin nodded. That was pretty much the same conclusion she'd already come to.

Of more immediate importance, the simple act of nodding hadn't threatened to take off the top of her head. "I think I'm all right now," she said, cautiously readjusting her grip on the rung. "Go ahead—I'm right behind you."

They continued downward. Jin took each rung carefully, making sure she had a solid grip with one hand before releasing the other. The voices and running feet and gunfire still echoed through the shaft, and she wondered vaguely if the Qasamans were winning.

And tried not to wonder what was happening to her.

CHAPTER FOURTEEN

Merrick's first indication of how seriously the Trofts were taking their new prisoners was the sheer thickness of the rear double doors on the truck they marched him up to. The doors were dauntingly thick, heavy with the sort of armor that would have worn well on a frontline urban assault tank.

It was only as he stepped into the vehicle and got a look at the interior that he understood why it had such security overkill. Instead of the plain benches and equipment racks or attachment rings he would have expected to find in a troop carrier, the vehicle was instead equipped with padded walls, monitor and communications screens, and a half dozen luxuriously upholstered and padded couches.

This wasn't a simple troop carrier. It was a senior officers' transport.

"Sit," one of the Trofts piling in behind him ordered, punctuating the order with a poke from his laser.

"Watch it," Merrick growled, striding past the rear couches and sitting down on the rightmost of the two front ones. And suppressing a grim smile.

Because the Trofts had made a mistake. A big one. A normal troop carrier would probably have had a personnel section that was sealed away from the driver's cab. A prisoner transport certainly would have.

But not this vehicle. This vehicle was for VIPs, who would want to see what was going on as they drove along, studying terrain and troop positions through the thick glass windshield.

Which meant there wasn't even a partial barrier between where Merrick was sitting and the driver sitting on the left side of the cab.

He'd barely gotten himself settled when the rear doors thudded shut. The driver apparently already had his orders, and immediately shifted into drive and pulled away from the curb. A moment later, they were lumbering down the street.

"Where are we going?" Merrick asked, turning back toward the Trofts behind him.

None of them bothered to answer. None of them had made any move to settle onto the fancy couches, either, Merrick noted, instead propping themselves against the walls or bracing themselves into the rear corners. Despite the vehicle's slight roll and occasional bounce, though, all five lasers were holding remarkably steadily on Merrick.

"Well?" Merrick tried again, shifting his gaze to each of the Trofts in turn as he put a targeting lock onto each faceplate. His fingertip lasers hadn't done much good earlier against those faceplates, but his more powerful antiarmor laser shouldn't have that problem. "Come on—how about a little consideration?" he continued. "I just saved all your skins from the self-destruct, you know."

"That remains to be seen," one of the Trofts finally said. "If you lied, it will go badly for you."

The words were barely out of his mouth when a thunderous blast slammed into the truck from behind, lifting its rear end momentarily off the street and sending the whole vehicle into a violent swerve.

And as the Trofts grabbed at the walls for balance, Merrick opened fire.

It would have been better if he could have tackled the soldiers first, while the element of surprise was still with him. But the first targeting lock he'd set up, back inside the Palace, had been on his shackles, and that was where his first shot had to go. He triggered his left fingertip laser, hoping the Trofts bouncing around the transport would be too preoccupied to notice what was happening.

His hand twitched and curled as the nanocomputer shifted it into position, and with a flash of heat across his wrist the cuff broke in half and Merrick was free. Rolling over onto his side on the couch, he lifted his left leg and triggered his antiarmor laser.

But the Trofts had indeed noticed that first blast. Even as Merrick's laser began to blaze its precision shots across the open space, all five aliens opened fire.

Merrick's nanocomputer took over, swinging his shoulder violently backward, twisting his torso to send him rolling off the couch onto the floor. But in the cramped space even programmed reflexes could only do so much. As Merrick fired his final shot, a brilliant flash stabbed across his vision and a burning stab of pain lanced across his right cheek.

Clenching his teeth against the agony, he pushed himself shakily back up onto the couch. His cheek felt like it was on fire, and his right eye could see nothing but a giant purple blob. Switching to his optical enhancers, he peered forward into the cab.

The driver was still fighting the wheel as the aftershocks from the Palace explosion continued to shake both the vehicle and the ground beneath it. Whether the Troft was aware of what had just happened behind him Merrick couldn't tell, but he had no intention of giving the alien time to react to it. Shoving himself off the couch, he staggered across the weaving vehicle into the cab, grabbed the driver's arm and pulled him out of his seat, then threw him across the cab to smash headfirst into the window on the opposite side.

To Merrick's surprise, the soldier didn't simply bounce back off of the obviously strengthened glass, but instead went straight through as the impact popped the window neatly out of its frame and onto the street. The Troft himself ended up half in and half out of the cab, hanging limply through the window with his legs dangling inside. Dropping into the seat behind the wheel, Merrick pressed his foot on the accelerator to get back up to speed and gave the controls a quick once-over. Everything seemed simple and straightforward enough.

He peered into his side-view mirrors. The other transport was still following closely, apparently with no idea that anything was wrong. For a moment Merrick wondered why the driver was ignoring the Troft hanging out though the window, then realized that part of the transport's exterior wouldn't be visible from the other driver's position.

But the soldier would be extremely visible to any other Trofts they might happen to pass. Whatever Merrick was going to do, he had to do it before they ran across a patrol or vehicle and the alarm was raised. Taking a deep breath, he pressed the accelerator to the floor.

With a muted roar from the engine, the transport leaped ahead. The sudden change in speed seemed to take the other driver by surprise, but a second later he also began to speed up. Merrick continued to accelerate, watching as the transport behind him slowly closed the gap.

And as it settled into place a few meters behind him, Merrick braced himself against the wheel and jammed on the brakes.

Once again, the other driver was caught completely by surprise. This time, though, the results were immediate and cataclysmic. Even as Merrick fought the sudden yawing from his own transport, the other vehicle plowed full-tilt into the rear of Merrick's.

There was a horrendous grinding of metal and both transports jumped forward, the impact jamming Merrick's back and head into the thin seat cushion and the unyielding metal behind it. He wrestled the vehicle to a halt, jammed the gearing into park, and wrenched open the door beside him. Jumping out, he headed back.

The Trofts had built their transports well, he found as he reached the other vehicle. Despite the force of the collision, neither was badly damaged, with the hood of the rear vehicle merely showing some external crumpling and the doors of Merrick's bent inward slightly at the point of impact. Jumping up onto the top of the rear vehicle's hood, Merrick peered in through the windshield.

The collision might not have affected the vehicle itself much, but the same couldn't be said of its passengers. The driver was draped over the steering wheel, his torso twitching with some kind of reaction Merrick couldn't identify. Behind him, both the prisoners and their guards were sprawled on the rear compartment floor, some of them motionless, the rest making the slow movements of dazed people fighting their way back toward full consciousness.

Jumping back down onto the street, Merrick tried the door handle. It was locked, of course, but he already knew the way in. Aiming his little fingers at the lower edge of the window, he fired his lasers, methodically vaporizing a line through the metal lip protecting the thick glass.

And then, without even a hint of warning, his peripheral vision caught a flicker of movement from the transport's rear.

Once again, his nanocomputer took over, shoving him back from the door and toward the ground as it swung his hands up to aim at the unexpected threat.

But it wasn't the Trofts from inside the transport, as he'd assumed. Sprinting silently toward him were two Qasamans in gray Djinn outfits with matching gloves and soft helmets. "Moreau?" one of them called.

"Yes," Merrick confirmed, scrambling to his feet again. "There are prisoners in the back—"

"We know," the Qasaman cut him off as they stopped beside him. "Carsh Zoshak sent us. I am Narayan—how can we assist?"

"We need to unseal this window," Merrick said, turning his fingertip lasers on the frame again. "It pops right out—their idea of an emergency exit, I suppose."

"Understood," Narayan said, stepping up beside Merrick and adding his more powerful glove-mounted lasers to the operation. "Baaree: see to the rear."

The second Qasaman nodded and headed back along the transport's side. "Wait—come back!" Merrick called after him. "Waste of time—you can't get in that way."

"He knows that," Narayan said calmly. "His purpose is to provide a diversion."

Merrick swallowed, a flush of embarrassment warming his face. "Oh."

Sure enough, a moment later the transport began to vibrate as Baaree began pounding with loud uselessness against the rear doors. Merrick kept his eyes on his work, trying to ignore the throbbing pain in his cheek and chest.

Ten seconds later, he and Narayan had finished. "Now we need to pop it out," Merrick said, wincing as he eyed the narrow gap beneath the window. It was barely wide enough for his fingertips, with burning hot metal all around it. But without anything handy that he could as a pry bar, his fingers would have to do.

He was steeling himself for the task when Narayan deftly shouldered him out of the way, brandishing a thick-bladed knife he'd produced from somewhere. "I'll do it," he said. "Take a moment and assess the enemy threat."

"Right," Merrick said, his knees suddenly starting to tremble with fatigue, shock, and probably loss of blood. Stepping back to give Narayan room to work, he looked around.

Earlier, when he and his mother and Miron Akim had driven to the control tower, it had seemed like the area was crawling with Trofts. Now, in contrast, the aliens were conspicuous by their absence, at least in and around the couple of blocks within Merrick's view. Whatever else Plan Saikah had or hadn't accomplished, it had certainly cleared the enemy troops off the streets.

But the lack of ground troops didn't mean the Trofts didn't still control the city. As Merrick stepped out of the transport's shadow, he found himself gazing at one of the Trofts' big wrigglefish sentry ships as it squatted on guard two blocks away.

A shiver ran up his back. The weapons clusters beneath the stubby forward wings were tracking back and forth, a constant reminder of the death and destruction ready to be unleashed at the touch of a button. So far the operators of those weapons didn't seem to be reacting to this particular drama, but Merrick doubted that would last much longer. Once the aliens realized what was happening, they would certainly try to do something about it.

There was a sudden crackling thud, and Merrick turned back to see the transport's window pop neatly out of its frame. "Come," Narayan called, reaching in through the gap and opening the door. As Merrick hurried back to join him, the Djinni grabbed the twitching Troft driver, pulled him out onto the street, and bounded inside. Merrick grabbed the edge of the door and started to follow.

And nearly lost his grip as a blast of reflected sound slammed

over him from inside the transport. "Djinni Moreau!" Narayan
called, his voice suddenly slurred. "Assist!"

Shaking his head to clear it, Merrick pulled himself up into the
cab and around the seat into the transport's main compartment.

When he'd looked through the windshield right after the two
vehicles had crashed, he'd seen the passengers and their Troft guards
sprawled on the floor where the impact had thrown them. But in the
minute since then, the situation had changed dramatically. Four of
the six aliens were back on their feet, one of them battling for his
laser with the young Qasaman man who had tangled the chain of
his wrist shackles around the weapon's muzzle and was trying desperately to keep the aim away from himself and the other prisoners.
One of the other Trofts was pounding at the young man with the
butt of his laser, trying to knock him away from the first soldier. In
the car corner the young woman was standing with defiant helplessness between her children and the lasers of the other two conscious
aliens. To Merrick's left, the old woman had thrown herself on top
of one of the Trofts who hadn't yet made it back to his feet, trying
to hold him down with the sheer weight of her body.

It was a scene that should have been vibrant with violent activity, but at the moment no one was doing much of anything at all.
Everyone in the vehicle, human and Troft alike, was staggering
with the effects of Narayan's sonic blast.

Everyone except Merrick.

He took out the two Trofts facing down the woman and children first, wrenching the laser from the nearest alien's grip and
slamming it hard into his faceplate, then repeating the action with
the second. He turned next to the aliens grappling with the young
man, only to find that one of them had recovered enough from the
sonic blast to try to bring his weapon to bear. Merrick responded
by locking on to the alien's faceplate and blazing an antiarmor laser
shot that dropped the Troft to the floor.

And then suddenly there was a movement to Merrick's left, and
he spun around as Baaree, the Djinni who'd been providing the
diversion at the transport's rear, bounded in through the driver's
door, his glove-mounted lasers blazing away at the remaining Trofts.

Merrick shifted his attention to the alien still trying to shove the old woman off him, targeted his helmet, and silenced him with another antiarmor blast.

Seconds later, it was over. "Nicely done," Merrick said, stepping over to the still shaky young man and blasting off his wrist shackles as Narayan helped the old woman to her feet. "We have a plan for getting out of here?"

"There's an escape tunnel three houses behind us," Narayan said, his voice still a little slurred as he gestured Baaree toward the transport's cab. Baaree nodded and stepped into the cab, sitting down behind the wheel. "We'll back the transport there and escape into the subcity."

"Sounds good," Merrick said, going over to the young woman and children and getting to work on their shackles. "Let's hope the engine still works."

His answer was a sudden jerk as the transport wrenched itself free of the other vehicle and began rolling backward. "No problem," Baaree called.

"Excellent," Narayan said, crouching down to peer out the side windows as the transport began to pick up speed. "As quickly as possible," he added. "We don't know when the invaders will—"

And without warning, the interior of the transport suddenly lit up with brilliant flash of blue light and a thunderclap and wave of superheated air that slammed Merrick up against the rear doors. Once again his nanocomputer took over, throwing him sideways toward the floor in an attempt to get him out of the line of fire. Both eyes were dazzled into uselessness, and he keyed in his enhancers to try to see what was going on.

He almost wished he hadn't. The entire windshield had been shattered by the sheer intensity of the blast, and everything in the cab that was flammable was ablaze with roiling flames and a thick, foul-smelling black smoke.

Baaree himself was no longer burning. There was nothing left of him to burn.

The Trofts in the sentry ship two blocks away had found their shot.

"Djinni Moreau!" a voice gasped through the crackle of flames. "Djinni Moreau!"

"Here," Merrick called back, closing his eyes tightly against the smoke and turning in the direction of the voice. Narayan was crouched at the side of the transport, the old woman coughing violently at his side, the Djinni's body curled half over hers to protect her as best he could.

"Can you see the others?" Narayan called back. "My eyes are blocked."

Merrick looked around, keying in his enhancers' infrared to try to penetrate the thickening smoke. The young couple and their children were huddled together in the rear of the transport, their bodies wracked with silent coughs. "They're okay," he reported. "We're going to need a new plan."

"Did they shoot through the windshield or the transport roof?" Narayan asked.

Merrick looked back at the front of the vehicle. The windshield, as he'd already noted, was completely gone. But the metal roof of the cab, though blistered, was still quite solid. "The windshield," he reported. "But we can't stay in here forever."

"We won't," Narayan said. "The rear doors are the same—" He broke off into a fit of coughing.

"Are the same material," Merrick finished for him, turning and targeting the three hinges on the left-hand door. Making sure the Qasamans were all out of splatter range, he lifted his leg and fired three quick shots.

With a screech, the door broke free, its outer edge sagging outward against the lock that still held it to the pillar between the doors. "One away," Merrick called. "Come on."

A handful of seconds later Narayan was at his side, feeling his way with one hand as he led the old woman with the other. "I still can't see to shoot," he said.

"I got it," Merrick said. He crossed to the young family, led them away from the door on that side, and blew that set of hinges. "Can you get one of them?" he asked.

In answer, Narayan moved to one of the doors, fumbling a bit as he got his hands through the crack beneath it. "Ready."

Targeting the door's lock, Merrick blasted it free, severing the last connection with the rest of the transport.

The door sagged suddenly in Narayan's grip, but the Djinni's power suit was up to the task and the heavy panel didn't fall. Grunting with the strain, Narayan manhandled the door back up to his level, leaning back to balance it against his chest and cheek. Then, stepping carefully out onto the street, he half turned to put the door between himself and the distant Troft ship's lasers. Merrick winced as the sudden cross breeze sent an extra wave of heat washing over them from the fire still blazing in the transport's cab. "Beside me," Narayan ordered.

The young man helped the old woman down from the transport's rear and positioned the two of them behind Narayan and his new shield. "You will bring the others?" the Djinni added.

"Of course," Merrick said. "Go."

"Stay close," Narayan said. With the two Qasamans close behind him, he began backing rapidly down the street.

Merrick looked at the young woman, her two children clutched close to her sides in the choking smoke. "You ready?" he asked.

"We are in your hands," she said simply.

Turning back, trying to ignore the flashes of laser light sizzling over his head as the Troft sentry ship fired shot after shot at Narayan's shield, Merrick blew the lock, sending the remaining door slamming to the ground with a dull thud. Jumping out beside it, he got a grip on one edge, angled it to the side, and got his other hand underneath it. He locked his finger servos solidly in place and levered the door upward. "Now," he called to the woman.

She was already out of the transport, still holding the boys tightly to her sides, and at Merrick's order she moved them all behind the shield, coming close enough to Merrick for him to feel her breath on his neck. "Crouch down," Merrick warned her, taking a moment to look over his shoulder. Narayan and his two charges were just disappearing into a narrow walkway between two of the houses, their shield battered and warped by the Trofts' attacks but apparently still solid. Turning back, Merrick hunched over, lowering the door to provide as much protection as he could to their legs and feet. "Now," he ordered.

The door had been rocked with four blasts of laser fire by the time they reached the walkway. Merrick held the shield in place against the side of the nearest house, letting the woman and children slip away and hurry down the passage. Then he followed, dropping the half-vaporized door behind him.

Narayan was waiting by an opening in the side of one of the buildings along the walkway. "Hurry," he called, gesturing to Merrick as the woman and boys disappeared through the door.

Merrick nodded, clenching his teeth as the scene in front of him began to waver. The adrenaline of the battle and mad-dash escape was starting to fade, and the shock and blood loss were starting to make themselves felt again. *Just get to the door,* he told himself. *That's all you have to do. Just make it to the door.*

He had made it through the door, and Narayan had closed it behind them, when the blackness finally took him.

"*Fire!*" the sergeant at the hospital window snapped.

Pressing his cheek against his rifle stock, Fadil held his breath and gently squeezed the trigger. The rifle bucked against his shoulder, and as he brought the weapon back to position he had the satisfaction of seeing the Troft he'd targeted sprawled on the ground. All around him, his father and the others were also firing, dropping the invaders like the vermin they were. Grinning tightly, Fadil lined up his sights on the next Troft in line.

And with a sudden buzzing sound, something came flying in through the window. It hit the sergeant full in the chest, the breaking-stick crack of its explosive not quite loud enough to cover the man's agonized scream. Clenching his teeth against the sound, Fadil checked his aim and fired his second shot, dropping another enemy soldier.

He was lining up the muzzle on his third target when he heard the sound of multiple buzzings coming toward them.

And then, with a multiple blast of a hundred carefully placed explosives, the entire Palace disintegrated in a cloud of fire and smoke and debris. Fadil flinched back, reflexively lifting his rifle in front of his face to shield his eyes.

The roar of the Palace blast was still hammering his ears when the rifle shattered in his grip.

Fadil heard himself cry out as shards of metal and wood sliced into his arms and shoulders and the side of his face. Dimly, he felt a hand grab his arm and yank him sideways, pulling him off the bed he was lying on and tumbling him onto the floor.

And then the entire room seemed to explode, and as the flame and agony and noise rose all around him, he fell into darkness.

CHAPTER FIFTEEN

The room around Merrick was ablaze with light as he dragged himself back toward consciousness. He winced away from the glare, trying to turn his head, trying even harder to close his eyes. But nothing seemed to do any good.

It was only as he untangled his arm from some kind of obstruction and brought his hand up in front of his face that he came awake enough to realize that his eyes *were* shut, and that the light was coming in via his optical enhancers. Apparently, he'd never gotten around to shutting them off after the battle.

He shut them off now and carefully opened his eyes. He was lying on a bed in what seemed to be a long, wide corridor with rows of beds on both sides. Some of the beds were empty, but most were occupied by figures wrapped in the same kind of hospital gowns the old man they'd broken out of the Lodestar Hospital had been wearing.

And the obstruction Merrick had had to free his arm from turned out to be a small group of thin tubes and wires that were connected to various places on his arm and torso. He frowned down at them, trying to trace them out and hoping he hadn't pulled out anything important.

"Welcome back," a familiar voice said from his left.

Merrick twisted his head around. Carsh Zoshak was sitting on a chair behind him and beside a rolling equipment table. "Thanks," Merrick said. "How long was I out?"

Zoshak shrugged. "A couple of days," he said. "You were in pretty bad shape."

"I was, wasn't I?" Merrick agreed, the memory of all his injuries flooding back to him. He'd been so busy checking out his surroundings over the past minute or so that he hadn't even thought about checking out himself. Carefully, he touched his cheek where the Troft laser had burned it.

To find that it was completely healed.

He frowned, pressing a little harder against the skin, and then gently sliding the finger up and down. The skin felt a little leathery beneath the growth of beard stubble, but it wasn't the hard leather of scar tissue. More importantly, there was no pain.

Nor was there any pain in his chest where Shahni Haafiz had tried his best to knife him open. He slipped a hand beneath his gown and touched the skin, to find the same slightly leathery consistency and no sign of torn flesh.

He looked back to find an amused smile on Zoshak's face. "I gather you're impressed?" the Djinni suggested.

"Very much so," Merrick assured him, a sudden coolness dampening his initial excitement at his remarkable healing. For all this to have happened so quickly..."I assume this means you used some of your drugs on me?"

Zoshak's smile faded. "Of course we did," he said. "Would you have preferred to spend weeks in a recovery room?"

"No, of course not," Merrick said. He touched his cheek again, thinking about the stories he'd heard about the Qasamans' drugs and their sometimes dangerous side effects.

Still, the Shahni were surely taking care not to damage their soldiers. *Any* of their soldiers, even interlopers like himself and his mother.

Speaking of whom—"Have you heard anything about my mother and Miron Akim?" he asked.

A shadow seemed to cross Zoshak's face. "I have," he said. "They were both able to escape their captors and return safely to the subcity."

"How safely?" Merrick asked, something ominous stirring inside him as he tried to read the other's expression. "Were they injured? Lightly? Seriously? Dangerously?"

"Neither was injured in their escape."

"After their escape?" Merrick persisted. "Before their escape? Come on, Carsh Zoshak—I need to know."

Zoshak's lips compressed briefly. "Your mother may have some other medical problems," he said reluctantly. "Problems unrelated to their mission."

Merrick grimaced. She had medical problems, all right. All Cobras her age did. "Are they going to check her out?"

"I believe they've already done the tests and are studying the results," Zoshak said.

"Can I see her?"

"Certainly, after the doctors discharge you," Zoshak said. "That should be later today, or tomorrow at the latest."

"Can't we sneak over there right now?" Merrick asked. "I promise to be good and keep the meeting short."

"Not until you're discharged," Zoshak said firmly. "Until then, you must remain in the ward."

Merrick peered down the line of beds, hoping to spot a doctor or nurse with whom he could argue the point. But he couldn't see anyone who seemed to be in charge.

But he'd had enough experience with doctors on Aventine to know that he'd probably be wasting his breath anyway. "Fine," he said with a sigh. "Can you at least tell me how the battle went?"

A muscle in Zoshak's cheek twitched. "The part you and I played was very successful," he said. "Those we rescued are safely in the subcity, where they've joined in the fight against the invaders. Mali Haafiz, in particular, asked me to extend her gratitude for your service to her and her family. She was the older woman," he added. "The wife of Shahni Haafiz."

"Who was the one who tried to kill me."

Zoshak grimaced. "Yes."

"I take it he has no more doubts about me?"

Zoshak's eyes slipped away. "Shahni Haafiz is very busy with the city's defense," he said obliquely.

Merrick felt a stirring of anger. "Meaning he still thinks I'm your enemy?"

"Keep your voice down," Zoshak warned, glancing almost furtively at the nearby beds. "Keep your words and your identity to yourself."

Merrick's budding anger vanished. The look in Zoshak's eyes... "Did something go wrong?" he asked quietly.

For a moment Zoshak didn't answer. Then, his shoulders seemed to droop. "Everything went wrong, Merrick Moreau," he said quietly. "We thought we were prepared for anything. We weren't. We thought we could take on any enemy who dared attack us. We couldn't."

Merrick felt his throat tighten. "How bad?"

Zoshak seemed to brace himself. "Thirty percent casualties, killed and wounded, among the Djinn who were deployed." He hesitated. "Among the regular soldiers, sixty percent."

Merrick stared at the Djinni in disbelief. Even in his great-grandfather's war against the Trofts the casualties hadn't been *that* bad. "But some of the wounded are going to recover, aren't they?"

"If their lives on the other side can be considered recovery," Zoshak said, an edge of bitterness in his voice. "Many will be crippled, or at the very least severely limited in what they can do. But that's not the point. The point is that what should have been a staggering blow against the invaders failed."

"I'm sorry" was all Merrick could think of to say.

"As are we all," Zoshak said with a sigh. "Ironic, isn't it, that the only clear successes all day were those that you and your mother were involved in." His gaze flicked to Merrick's left leg. "Those long lasers give you a strong advantage over even the Djinn."

"They're definitely handy," Merrick agreed. "But your glove-mounted lasers are no slouches, either. They're certainly stronger than our fingertip versions."

Zoshak hissed. "For all the good that did us."

"It did a lot of good," Merrick insisted. "For starters, I can't shoot through the Trofts' faceplates, with that instant black-block system of theirs. You can."

"The faceplates, perhaps," Zoshak conceded. "But our glove lasers aren't nearly powerful enough to penetrate their main armor." He snorted again. "I'm told the designers of our combat suits considered putting such a laser along the left calf, but ultimately rejected it as being too difficult to aim."

"It *is* a little tricky," Merrick agreed. "But you already have implants on your eye lenses for targeting, right? Couldn't they have tied an antiarmor laser into that system?"

"I don't know," Zoshak said. "Perhaps it wouldn't work because our system requires both eyes to be on target. The positioning of a calf-mounted laser would normally require us to fire it with only one eye on the target."

So either the Qasamans' computers couldn't handle the kind of targeting system Cobras routinely used, or else their power suits' servos weren't up to the necessary fine tuning. "So we got nothing out of the attack except a couple of the Shahni and their families?"

"The invaders took casualties," Zoshak said. "But we didn't permanently recover any buildings, nor did we inflict any serious damage on their weaponry or ships before we were pushed back. Particularly the ships."

"Yes, I saw what those sentry ships could do," Merrick said, grimacing at the memory of Djinn Baaree's fiery death.

"Yet the shipboard and vehicle weaponry was only a small part of our defeat," Zoshak said. "Many of our casualties were caused by small, self-homing missiles that seemed to seek out the sound of the soldiers' gunfire."

"I remember stories about things like that from my great-grandfather's war," Merrick said ruefully. "Not much you can do about them except try not to let the Trofts get close enough to use them."

"What do you mean, close enough?" Zoshak asked, frowning. "Some of the missiles were launched from over two blocks away."

"Two *blocks?*" Merrick asked, frowning. "They were able to lock on to gunfire noise from that far away? Accurately?"

"Accurately enough to kill and wound our soldiers," Zoshak said grimly.

Merrick scratched at his cheek stubble, trying to remember everything he'd ever learned about what little the Cobra Worlds' trading partners had let slip about Troft weaponry. Gunshots *did* have a fairly unique sound pattern, he knew. But for a missile to make that identification, then have enough sensor scope and memory to figure out the proper vector and guide the weapon there was starting to sound awfully complex. Especially for something small enough for antipersonnel use.

Unless the gunfire had come as a barrage, which would give the missile current-time data and allow it to take its electronic time locking in on the sounds. "Were the soldiers using machine guns or single-shot weapons?" he asked Zoshak. "And do we know how big the missiles were?"

"I don't," Zoshak said, standing up. "But if you feel up to a short walk, we could go speak to one of the field officers."

"I thought I wasn't supposed to leave the ward."

"You won't," Zoshak assured him. "Several of the wounded officers are in this facility. Perhaps one of them will be awake and willing to speak to you."

"It's worth a try," Merrick said, eyeing the tubes still poking into his arm. "Though come to think of it, I'm not sure how portable I am at the moment."

"Very portable," Zoshak assured him as he walked around the end of the bed. "Give me a moment, and I'll extend the medical stand's wheels."

A minute later they were walking down the corridor between the twin lines of beds. Merrick found himself feeling a little light-headed, and made sure to keep a firm grip on the rolling stand to help maintain his balance. At the end of the corridor they turned in to a much longer corridor that had likewise been equipped with beds and patients. As in Merrick's ward, most of the beds were occupied, and Merrick found his stomach churning as he noted how many head and chest wounds seemed to be in evidence.

He was passing yet another bed when the occupant's half-bandaged face suddenly leaped out at him. "Hold it," he said, grabbing Zoshak's arm and peering at the sleeping man. "Is that—?"

"Merrick Moreau?" a strained but familiar voice spoke up from the next bed over.

Merrick tore his eyes away from Daulo Sammon's closed eyes.
Sure enough, Daulo's son Fadil was peering up at him from the
next bed. He didn't look much better than his father, but at least
his face seemed mostly undamaged. "What in the Worlds are you
doing here?" he demanded as he stepped to the young man's side.

"What does it look like we're doing?" Fadil countered. "We're
two of the casualties of the great Plan Saikah."

"Yes, but—" Merrick shot a look at Zoshak, who was standing a
couple of paces away with a stony expression on his face. "I meant,
why were you wounded in the first place," he said, turning back
to Fadil. "Miron Akim told us the Shahni were keeping you and
your father as hostages for our good behavior."

"And so they were, until I asked permission to join in the
battle." Fadil smiled weakly. "They graciously allowed us to do so."

Merrick winced. "I'm sorry."

"You need not apologize, Merrick Moreau," Fadil said. "It was
my decision, and that of my father, that put us here." He looked
over at Zoshak. "And I would make the same decision again," he
added, an edge of pride or challenge slipping into his voice.

"You may yet have that opportunity," Zoshak said. "You and
every other villager on Qasama."

"We stand ready," Fadil assured him.

For another moment the city dweller and villager continued to
stare at each other. Then, Zoshak stirred. "Merrick Moreau wishes
information about the invaders' anti-personnel missiles," he said.

"They were fast, and they were deadly," Fadil growled. "What
more do you need to know?"

"I want to figure out how they were aimed," Merrick said, trying to keep his voice calm. "Djinni Zoshak suggested they might
have homed in on the sounds of your gunfire. Were you actually
shooting when the missiles arrived?"

"We opened fire on the sergeant's command," Fadil said with
the air of someone who's told the same story way too many times
already. "The first missile struck him—I don't know how soon
afterwards. Not long. The rest of the missiles came in a group.
One of them hit my rifle, and then my father pulled me down

on the floor as all the rest began exploding. Everyone was killed except us. Does that tell you anything?"

"Maybe," Merrick said. "You say the sergeant was hit first. Was he firing like everyone else?"

"I already said he was."

"And how far away were the Trofts you were shooting at?"

"We were in the hospital from which you and I escaped earlier," Fadil said. "Top floor. Our targets were the Trofts on the Palace grounds. Do a calculation, or ask someone to loan you a measuring tape."

Merrick scratched his cheek thoughtfully. At least a block's worth of distance, then. "And the main group of missiles arrived together?"

"I already said that, too," Fadil said impatiently.

"And you all had projectile rifles?" Merrick persisted. There was something here, something he could sense but couldn't quite get a handle on. "No lasers?"

"No," Fadil said.

"But teams using lasers against the invaders suffered the same fate," Zoshak put in.

"Really?" Merrick asked, frowning. "But lasers don't sound anything like projectile guns. How did the missiles home in on them?"

Zoshak shrugged. "Possibly through their heat signatures."

"Maybe," Merrick said, thinking back to the rescue of Mali Haafiz and the others of her family. "But in that case, why didn't the Trofts use them against Djinni Narayan and me? We were using our lasers like crazy out there."

"There may have been no one nearby who carried the launchers," Zoshak pointed out. "The Palace explosion and the multiple attacks drove most of the ground troops to cover." He grimaced. "At least briefly."

"I suppose," Merrick said, getting a firmer grip on his med stand as his head started to swim a little. "I still don't think that's the whole answer."

"Are you all right?" Zoshak asked.

"Just feeling a little dizzy," Merrick assured him. "Two days of no food, probably."

"Or two days on healing medication without time to purge the drugs from your system," Zoshak said, stepping forward and taking his arm. "Time you were returned to your bed."

"Wouldn't argue the point even if I could," Merrick agreed. "Thank you for your time, Fadil Sammon. And thank you, too, for your willingness to risk your lives."

Fadil snorted gently. "As if risking our lives for Qasama means anything to you."

"It does," Merrick told him. "Whether you believe it or not."

He turned away, paused a moment to wait for the spots in front of his eyes to fade out, then headed back the way they'd come. "I'm okay," he assured Zoshak as the other continued to hold his upper arm. "You don't have to hang around if you don't want to."

"It's not a problem," Zoshak assured him. "I'm happy to assist you."

"And I'm happy to have your company," Merrick said. "But you surely must have better things to do than visit the troops in the recovery ward."

Zoshak was silent for another two steps. "You misunderstand, Merrick Moreau," he said. "I'm not your visitor. I'm your guard."

Merrick swallowed. "Oh," he said.

They made the rest of the trip in silence.

Jin looked up from the report, her throat tight. "Thirty percent," she murmured.

"Yes," Miron Akim confirmed, his back unnaturally stiff as he sat in a chair beside Jin's hospital bed. He looked tired, Jin thought, his facial skin sagging, his eyelids clearly being held open by sheer force of will.

Jin herself had spent the past two days resting up after being healed from the glass cuts she'd received when she blew out the tower office window. Distantly, she wondered how Akim had spent those two days. "I don't know what to say, Miron Akim," she went on, laying the report on the bed beside her. "Is that the end, then? Do you have any fighting force left at all?"

"Of course we do," he assured her. "Less than a quarter of our soldiers and Djinn were committed to this first battle, and many of the wounded will recover enough to fight again." He grimaced. "The true horror of this loss was that we brought to it both the coordination of a preplanned attack and the element of surprise. That combination should have been sufficient to at least stagger the invaders, if not defeat them outright. To have instead paid so high a cost for so little gain is a disaster."

His eyes bored suddenly into hers. "A disaster which we have no intention of revealing to the general populace."

"Understood," Jin said with a shiver. It was a given that secrecy and censorship were a necessary part of any wartime effort...but whether even a government as strict and powerful as the Shahni could keep something like this quiet remained to be seen. "Which leads directly to the question of why you're telling *me* about it."

"Because I come with two questions I must ask," Akim said. "The first...we have never trained for this sort of war, Jasmine Moreau. What we *have* trained for has clearly been ineffective. Your people, on the other hand, have fought against the Trofts. More importantly, *you* have fought against the Trofts. My first question, then, is whether you can offer advice and insight that will enable us to mount a more successful resistance."

Jin let out her breath in a huff. "That's a tall order, Miron Akim," she warned. "And understand that I'm not as well trained in combat as I wish I was. I'll have to think on the matter, but a couple of thoughts do come immediately to mind. First off, Cobras weren't designed for use as regular frontline troops. Our mission has always been one of harassment and sabotage, using small groups and infiltration tactics. I think that's also the direction your Djinn need to go."

"And the tactics themselves?" Akim asked. "You're familiar with them?"

"I had the standard Cobra course in military theory," Jin said. "But it was brief and largely theoretical. You and your military planners are undoubtedly far more knowledgeable than I am."

"Still, you have the advantage of having worked with such groups," Akim said. "But I understand that you need time to contemplate. Take what time you need, but no more than necessary."

"I'll be as quick as I can," Jin promised. "And the second question?"

Akim cocked his head slightly. "This may sound strange, but is there a value to razorarms that we're unaware of?"

Jin blinked. A value to *razorarms?* "What sort of value?"

"That is precisely the question." Abruptly, Akim stood up. "Come. I'll show you."

He waited until Jin had pulled on a robe and slippers, then led the way out of the private room into the subcity's maze of seemingly identical hallways. Jin walked carefully, favoring her bad left knee, trying to read the mood of the soldiers and civilians moving briskly back and forth down the hallway on their various errands. If any of them was worried about the failures of Plan Saikah, they weren't showing it.

Or perhaps they simply didn't know just how bad a failure it had been.

A few minutes later they reached a door flanked by a pair of armed soldiers. Akim gave them a hand signal as he and Jin approached, then stepped between them and pushed the door open. Pausing on the threshold, he gestured Jin inside.

Jin had expected an ordinary conference room. Instead, she found herself in a duplicate of the airfield tower control room. An exact duplicate, in fact, or at least exact within the limits of her memory.

"Over here," Akim said, brushing past her and heading across the room, circling the Qasamans who were gathered in twos and threes around the monitor stations.

Jin followed, glancing at the various monitors as she passed. Each display seemed to be active, with either a single image or else a short loop of words or images or track lines. It was, she realized with an eerie feeling, a complete reconstruction of the handful of seconds she and Akim had been standing in the hidden corridor.

Earlier, she'd wondered what Akim had been doing for the past two days. Now she knew.

"Here," Akim said as he stopped by a monitor no one else seemed to be interested in at the moment. "Sit down, and tell me what you see."

Jin slid into the chair in front of the monitor, wincing a bit as her bad knee gave a last twinge, and skimmed the display. It appeared to be a status report on—"Spine leopard captures," she murmured, frowning.

"In the forested areas to the north and west of Sollas," Akim said, tapping a list of latitude/longitude pairs. "Reports from the villages in those regions confirm the presence of large invader transports moving back and forth."

"Yes, but *spine leopards*?" Jin objected, frowning at the display. If she was reading the numbers correctly, the Trofts had already captured twenty of the predators by the time Akim took his mental snapshot of their activities, only a few hours into the aliens' occupation. If they were still at it, she could only guess how many they might have picked up since then. "What do they want with them all?"

"That was my question to you," Akim reminded her. "You've stated that your worlds have trade dealings with the Trofts. You've also been studying the creatures far longer than we have. So again I ask: are razorarm pelts in demand? Or is there something in their nature or biochemistry that would make them valuable to the invaders?"

"Nothing I've ever heard of," Jin said, staring at the display with a mixture of horror and revulsion. Could this whole invasion—all the death and destruction the Trofts had rained down on Qasama—be nothing more than a bizarre resource grab?

No—that made no sense. Qasama was as big as any other inhabitable world, with the Qasamans themselves occupying only a relatively small fraction of its land area. In the sixty years since the Cobra Worlds had brought the first spine leopards here, the animals had surely spread out far enough into uninhabited regions that anyone wanting to harvest them could simply travel out into the wilderness and do so.

But if the Trofts didn't want the predators as trophies, what *did* they want them for?

Unfortunately, there was only one reason Jin could think of, and it wasn't a pleasant one. "I think the people of Sollas are about to get some unexpected company," she told Akim grimly. "Best guess is that the Trofts are planning to release them into the cities and villages in the hope of keeping your soldiers and Djinn busy shooting something besides them."

"Yes, that was our thought as well," Akim said. "But it's been nearly three days since the invasion began. If the invaders intend to flood our streets with predators, why haven't they done so? What are they waiting for?"

"You're right, that doesn't make any sense," Jin said, grabbing for the edge of the desk. Suddenly, without warning, the dizziness she'd felt on the airfield tower escape ladder was hitting her again. "Maybe they're . . . waiting until they have . . . enough to—"

"Are you all right?" Akim asked sharply. "Jasmine Moreau?"

The last thing Jin remembered before the darkness took her was Akim's hand closing around her arm.

CHAPTER SIXTEEN

The dishes from the evening meal had been cleared away, the ward lights had been dimmed for the night, and Merrick was starting to drift off to sleep when he heard the sound of measured footsteps coming his direction.

He rolled over, grunting like a sleeping person might, and activated his optical enhancers. Six Djinn in full combat suits were marching quietly down the corridor toward him.

Merrick turned his head slightly to give his enhancers an angle behind him. The chair Carsh Zoshak had been occupying for most of the day was vacant. Time for the changing of the guard?

He looked back at the approaching Djinn, this time concentrating on their faces. The enhancers had limited detail sensitivity, but as near as Merrick could tell every man in the group was wearing the same grim and wary expression. And all eyes were definitely focused on him.

He continued to play asleep as the Djinn arrived at his bed. One of them stepped to Merrick's side, waited until the other five had fanned out into a semicircle at the foot of the bed, then carefully touched Merrick's shoulder. "Merrick Moreau?" he murmured. "Djinni Moreau?"

Merrick inhaled sharply, the way his brother Lorne always did when woken out of a deep sleep, and opened his eyes. "What is it?" he asked, blinking in feigned surprise at the group gathered around him. "Is something wrong?"

"You are summoned," the Djinni beside him said. "Your clothing is in a drawer beneath the bed. Dress quickly."

"Where are we going?" Merrick asked as he pulled the blanket aside and sat up, bracing himself for a fresh bout of the dizziness he'd experienced earlier in the day. But this time there was nothing. Maybe the healing drugs were finally out of his system. "Has something happened?"

"Dress quickly" was the only reply.

Two minutes later, they were all heading back between the rows of sleeping patients in the direction the Djinn had come from. His escort, Merrick noted uneasily, had fallen into step around him in a two-in-front, four-in-back formation, the same setup Cobra units typically used with civilian VIPs in spine-leopard-infested areas. It allowed the Cobras to focus maximum firepower to the front and sides, while protecting the group's rear with their own bodies.

Only there weren't any spine leopards in the subcity. And Merrick was hardly a helpless civilian.

Maybe that was the point.

The corridors were quiet and mostly deserted, with only the pairs of guards at each corridor intersection as evidence that the citizenry hadn't simply picked up and left. Occasionally someone else would come by, either walking with the briskness of someone on an errand or else plodding along with the weariness of someone long overdue for sleep.

The trip ended at a door guarded by two pairs of armed guards and another pair of Djinn. One of the guards opened the door as Merrick and his escort approached, revealing a darkened room beyond. Merrick keyed in his infrared enhancers as he walked inside and spotted three figures seated behind a long, curved table about ten meters away at the far end of the room. His rear guard filed in behind him, the door was closed, and a set of low-level lights came on.

The figures Merrick had seen turned out to be three old men, dressed in what were obviously some kind of ceremonial robes.

The two on the ends were men Merrick had never seen before, but the one in the middle was someone he recognized all too well.

"Step forward, Merrick Moreau," Shahni Haafiz ordered, his voice stiff and unfriendly.

Merrick glanced at the Djinn standing on either side of him. Their full attention was on Merrick, their expressions unreadable.

Turning back to the Shahni, Merrick walked forward until he was a meter from the table. "If you wanted to apologize to me, Shahni Haafiz," he said, "a nice note would have been sufficient."

"Hardly, enemy of Qasama," Haafiz growled. "You were summoned here for judgment."

Merrick felt a chill run through him. "For which of my actions is judgment called?" he asked, flicking a look at each of the other two men. Their eyes were hard, their expressions as studiously neutral as those of the Djinn guard.

"Disobeying the direct order of a Shahni of Qasama in time of war is by itself punishable by death," Haafiz said. "Other charges include—"

"And the fact that I brought your family out alive instead of leaving them to die counts for nothing?" Merrick interrupted.

"It does indeed count for something," Haafiz said darkly. "If you had let them be as you were ordered, dozens of the invaders would have died inside the Palace. Instead, your warning allowed most of them to escape."

"And that would have been a fair trade for you?" Merrick countered. "A few enemy soldiers for your wife and family?"

Haafiz didn't even flinch. "Yes," he said flatly.

Again, Merrick looked at the other two Shahni. Again, there was nothing there but cold detachment. They meant it, he realized with a shiver. All three of them.

What kind of soulless people *were* these, anyway?

"In that case, I must offer my apologies," Merrick said, not quite managing to filter all the contempt out of his tone. "I obviously misunderstood the relationship of Qasama's rulers to Qasama's people."

"I have not finished," Haafiz said, ignoring both the comment and the underlying sarcasm. "Other charges include putting Qasaman citizens unnecessarily at risk, forcing us to permanently seal away at least two entrances to the subcity, and forcing us to demonstrate the window booby-trap system to the enemy."

Merrick frowned. "What booby-trap system? I didn't break any windows."

One of the other Shahni leaned toward Haafiz and murmured something, and Merrick activated his audio enhancements. "—against the other one, the female," the other was saying.

"No matter," Haafiz murmured back. "They act in concert. Their crimes are thus shared."

The other Shahni nodded and straightened up again, and Merrick notched down his enhancements, feeling a frown creasing his forehead. Clearly, they'd been talking about his mother and something she must have done during her own escape from the airfield tower.

Which led immediately to a question that hadn't occurred to Merrick until just now: namely, why wasn't she here? Did Haafiz have a separate kangaroo court planned for her? Or was this just his ham-handed way of getting back at Merrick for the unforgivable sin of making him look foolish by getting his family out alive after Haafiz had declared that to be impossible?

"For these actions, and the secondary effects stemming from them, you are hereby ordered into custody," Haafiz intoned. "Such custody will continue until the invaders are thrown off our world, or until you prove yourself trustworthy and of no further danger to the Qasaman people."

"How do you suggest I do that?" Merrick asked, fighting back a sudden surge of anger. Even under the truncated rules of wartime courts-martial, this whole thing was a joke. "Or would I be wasting my time to even try? I get the feeling there's no proof of any sort that would satisfy you."

"Of course there is," Haafiz said. "But what that proof will consist of, you must discover for yourself." He picked up a gavel from in front of him and lightly double-tapped it against the tabletop. "Sentence is passed. Guard: escort the prisoner to his cell."

Merrick turned around as the six Djinn started toward him. He could take them, the thought flitted through his mind. He'd already proved that in front of Miron Akim and that first group of Djinn. A burst from his sonic, a quick ceiling flip to get behind Haafiz and the other Shahni, and he would have the leverage he needed to get out of this whole insane mess.

He took a careful breath. *Steady,* he warned himself. Because Akim and the Djinn *had* seen that trick, and if there was one thing his mother had impressed on him it was that Qasamans learned fast. The Djinn would be ready for it this time. And if Haafiz's plan was to goad him into proving that he *wasn't* trustworthy, that would be the fastest way for Merrick to hand himself over on a silver platter.

The group of Djinn stopped in front of Merrick, again positioned for a two/four arrangement. "Merrick Moreau?" the leader prompted, gesturing back to the door.

Merrick looked back at Haafiz. "My mother and I are trustworthy, Shahni Haafiz," he said, keeping his voice calm and measured. "We're also the best weapon you have against the Trofts. Until you understand those two things, more of your people are going to die. Consider that when you start placing guilt."

It was as good an exit line as any. Turning his back on the three old men, Merrick stalked toward the door.

The cell block was several corridors away from the midnight court room, roughly the same distance as the recovery ward but in the opposite direction. The cell they ushered him into was about as bare-bones as possible: a windowless concrete-walled room, three meters square, equipped with a bolted-down bed, a sink/toilet combination, and an overhead light which was currently giving off the same low, nighttime glow as he'd seen back in the recovery ward. The door was three-centimeter-thick metal, with a peephole at eye level and a narrow flap at the bottom, the latter presumably for delivering meals. "Nice décor," Merrick commented, glancing around the cell as he stepped inside. "I don't suppose you'd let me give my mother or Miron Akim a call and let them know where I am?"

None of the Djinn bothered to answer. One of them swung the door closed, and there was a muted thunk as the lock engaged. Pressing his ear to the door, Merrick heard the footsteps fade away into the silence of the night.

He held that pose for the next few minutes, his audio enhancements at full strength, trying to determine if he was all alone in the cell block or if there were other prisoners. But he heard nothing. He repeated the experiment at the room's walls and back, and then at the sink/toilet's plumbing. He was able to pick up a few sounds from the latter, but the noises were soft and unidentifiable.

Finally, with nothing better to do, he went to the bed and lay down. The cell door, which would be an imposing barrier to the average prisoner, would probably collapse within minutes against a Cobra antiarmor laser. He could think of at least two other scenarios that would similarly leave him on the outside of the cell and his jailer or jailers on the inside.

But he knew better than to try any of them. Chances were good that Haafiz had put him in here precisely in the hope of goading him into breaking out, thereby vindicating his own belief that the Cobras were a danger to the Qasamans.

Of course, there was also the possibility that breaking out was the way to prove he *wasn't* a threat. If he broke out, then deliberately didn't harm anyone . . .

But he'd already done that for Akim, and it obviously hadn't impressed Haafiz in the slightest. No, the grouchy Shahni had to be angling for something else.

But what that something was, Merrick hadn't a clue.

With a sigh, he closed his eyes. His dizziness hadn't returned, but that didn't mean he was completely recovered from the quick-healing regimen the Qasamans had put him through. A good night's sleep to flush the rest of the drugs out of his system, and maybe he would be better able to figure out what the hell the Qasamans wanted from him.

Resting his forearm across his eyes to block out the last of the overhead light, he settled down to sleep.

❖   ❖   ❖

The attendant had just brought Fadil's breakfast when he spotted the Djinni Carsh Zoshak striding toward him along the ward corridor.

Quickly, Fadil grabbed his spoon and dug into his breakfast stew, pretending to be engrossed in his meal. The last thing he wanted right now was to have to speak or even nod a greeting to a city dweller who didn't even try to hide his contempt for villagers like Fadil and his father. If he was lucky, the Djinni would be busy on some errand and would likewise pretend not to notice Fadil. Spooning up a mouthful of the thick stew, he shoved it into his mouth.

"Fadil Sammon?"

Fadil sighed. On the other hand, if he was lucky he wouldn't have ended up in the middle of an alien invasion in the first place. Lifting his gaze from his bowl, arranging a neutral expression across his face, he gave Zoshak the sign of respect. "Good morning, Djinni—"

"Have you seen Merrick Moreau this morning?" Zoshak interrupted.

Fadil suppressed a grimace. Apparently, Zoshak wasn't even going to bother with common courtesy. "Why would I have seen him?" he countered. "He and I are barely acquaintances."

"He's missing," Zoshak said. "The nurse said he was transferred out of his ward in the middle of the night, but there was no destination point listed."

"Again, why should this have anything to do with me?" Fadil countered.

Zoshak grimaced. "My mistake," he said. "Forgive the interruption." He lowered his gaze briefly to Fadil's bowl. "Return to your meal," he added, and strode off.

Fadil watched him go, a sourness tightening his stomach. But at least the other had made it short.

"Fadil."

Fadil turned his head. His father was lying motionless in bed, clearly still weak after his own medical ordeal. But behind the drooping lids his eyes were alert and accusing. "You bring dishonor upon our house," he said.

"How?" Fadil demanded. He wasn't in the mood for this. "The man asked a question. I answered him."

"And you don't care what might have happened to Merrick Moreau?"

Beside him, out of his father's sight, Fadil curled his hand into a fist. He *really* wasn't in the mood for this. "Why should I be concerned?" he asked. "Merrick Moreau is about as non-helpless a person as I've ever met."

"And you owe him nothing?"

Fadil forced himself to meet his father's gaze. "No, I don't," he said flatly. "Neither do you."

The elder Sammon made a sound that seemed half cough and half grunt. "His mother saved my life," he reminded Fadil.

"And you in turn saved hers," Fadil said. "It seems to me that you and she are even."

For another moment Daulo gazed at his son in silence. Then, with a twitch of his lip that might have been a grimace, he closed his eyes. A minute later, his chest had settled into the slow rhythm of sleep.

With a sigh, Fadil turned back to his interrupted breakfast. But the stew no longer tasted as good as it had a minute ago.

Blast Merrick Moreau, anyway. And blast Jasmine Moreau, and the Shahni, and the city dwellers, and the Trofts. And while he was at it, blast his father, too.

His father was still sleeping when Fadil finished his breakfast. He set the tray aside, then carefully got to his feet. The attendants and nurses at his ward's main station should have records from all the other wards, as well as this one. Maybe the right questions, asked in the proper way, would give him some idea of what the city dwellers had done with Merrick Moreau.

The other eleven Djinn in Zoshak's squad were already in their chairs when Zoshak arrived at the briefing room. So were the members of two other squads. So were the men of a full unit of regular Qasaman soldiers. Whatever was in the works, it was big.

Miron Akim, standing on the low platform in the front, gave Zoshak a somewhat cool look as he slipped into his chair, but didn't say anything. Zoshak's squad leader, Akim's son Siraj, wasn't so restrained. "You're late," he muttered as Zoshak slipped into the empty seat beside him.

"My apologies, Ifrit Akim," Zoshak said, bowing his head to the other. "I had an errand, and misjudged my time."

"Misjudging time in the midst of war can be fatal," Siraj countered. "And not only to yourself. You need to—"

"Enough," a voice said quietly from behind Zoshak.

Zoshak turned, and felt his breath catch in his throat. Seated alone in the far back corner was Senior Advisor Moffren Omnathi. "The point has been made," Omnathi said in the same measured voice. "Marid Akim, you may begin."

"Thank you, Advisor Omnathi," Akim said, bowing his head to Omnathi and shifting his attention back to the gathered Djinn. "The Shahni have selected a mission for you," he announced. "You will be attacking the invader sentry ship currently standing guard at the intersection of Barch and Romand Streets, with the goal of neutralizing its external weaponry and thus permitting an attack force to overwhelm its forces and capture or destroy it."

Zoshak nodded to himself as a map came up on the display behind Akim. The intersection was on the city's western side, a block north of the Freegate market area and far removed from the airfield tower or any other critical area. If the invaders suspected an attack on one of their ships, that particular one would be low on their list of possibilities.

"In the aftermath of Plan Saikah, the invaders are undoubtedly feeling very safe," Akim continued, his dark eyes drifting across the assembled warriors. "We intend to shake that feeling of security."

"Understood," Siraj said briskly. "Have you and the Shahni a plan?"

"We do," Akim said. He touched a button, and a position/movement overlay appeared on top of the street map. "It will be a sundown attack, just as the market is closing and the customers are returning to their homes."

Zoshak felt his stomach tighten. "So there will be civilians in the fire zone?" he asked.

"There will be as few as possible," Akim assured him. "But some will necessarily have to be there. The Djinn will need to dress as civilians and mix with them in order to get within attack range of the ship and the ground troops guarding its base."

"We'll do whatever we have to," Siraj said, throwing a warning look at Zoshak. "When is the attack to take place?"

Akim seemed to brace himself. "Tonight."

A murmur rippled across the room. "*Tonight?*" Siraj echoed carefully. "With less than a day to learn the plan and practice it?"

"I regret that you weren't given earlier notice," Akim said. "But the Shahni deem it necessary to send this message as soon as possible."

Though it won't be much of a message if we all end up slaughtered, Zoshak thought darkly. But he kept his mouth shut. His commander was annoyed enough with him as it was.

And surely the Shahni had considered that possibility when they'd set the attack's timetable.

"I will begin by detailing the plan," Akim went on. "After you've asked any questions, we'll adjourn to the arena for practice."

As Djinn plans went, this one was fairly straightforward, certainly more so than the complexities and cross-city timing of Plan Saikah. It was actually feasible, Zoshak decided, that they could pull it off with only a day's worth of practice.

"Very well, then," Akim said after he'd finished and a few questions had been asked and answered. "The arena should be set up. We'll assemble there in ten minutes for practice. Djinni Zoshak, remain behind a moment."

Zoshak stayed seated, wondering uneasily what Akim wanted, as the rest of the Djinn and soldiers filed briskly from the room. Akim waited until they were all gone, then left the platform and came to stand directly in front of Zoshak. "I understand you were looking for Merrick Moreau this morning," the older man said. "Why?"

"I was concerned for his well-being," Zoshak said. "He fought bravely for Qasama, and I wanted to make sure he was being properly cared for."

"No other reason?" Akim persisted.

Briefly, Zoshak wondered if Moffren Omnathi was still sitting behind him. But he didn't dare turn to look. "I also wondered when he would be able to fight again," he said. "He's a powerful and capable warrior, a great asset to our effort against the invaders." He paused. "In fact, if I may speak freely, I would suggest he could be a great asset in the mission you have set before us."

Akim cocked his head. "Are you suggesting that Qasaman warriors and Djinn are not capable of dealing the necessary blow to our enemies' confidence?"

"I suggest only that the blow will be stronger and more memorable were he to assist us," Zoshak said, picking his words carefully. Usually, he had no trouble reading the thoughts and intentions behind people's words. But Akim's thoughts were hidden behind a mask he couldn't penetrate. "I also suggest that he is able and willing to serve Qasama."

"Merrick Moreau will indeed serve Qasama," Moffren Omnathi's voice came quietly from behind him. "But not in the way you suggest."

Zoshak swallowed. Senior Shahni advisors had better things to do with their time than sit in on the briefing of a single military mission. They *certainly* had better things to do than stay on after that briefing to watch a very minor warrior being lectured by the Djinn's supreme commander. "In what way *will* he serve, may I ask?" he said.

"That is none of your concern," Akim said stiffly. "The fate of Merrick Moreau and his mother rest now in the hands of the Shahni."

"And you will make no further inquiries as to their whereabouts or condition," Omnathi added. "Nor will you mention either of them again. Do you understand?"

A cold lump settled in Zoshak's chest. "Yes, Advisor Omnathi," he said.

"Good," Akim said. "Dismissed."

Making the sign of respect, Zoshak stood up and turned back toward the door. Omnathi was looking down at some notes, ignoring the Djinni, but Zoshak gave him the sign of respect anyway.

No, he wouldn't inquire about Merrick Moreau, Zoshak thought grimly as he hurried down the corridor. Nor would he mention either of the Cobras again. He was a good Qasaman, and obedient to his leaders.

But no one could stop him from thinking about the Moreaus. Or prevent him from wondering what exactly the Shahni were up to.

CHAPTER SEVENTEEN

The sun had disappeared behind the western line of buildings, and the sky overhead was starting to take on a hint of darkness, when the loudspeaker in the center of the Freegate market area boomed the five-minute tone. "Five minutes," Zoshak said quietly to the young woman beside him as they pretended to search through the nearly empty bins of vegetables.

"I'm ready," the woman replied.

Zoshak studied her profile. She wasn't ready, of course. There was no way she could be. There were no female soldiers on Qasama, which meant Iuni hadn't had any training in combat technique or contingency thinking or any of the other skills that prepared a warrior for the sort of situation that was about to happen. Iuni was simply an average citizen who'd volunteered to risk her life today in defense of her city and her world.

Beyond that single fact, Zoshak knew nothing about her except her first name, and he wasn't even sure about that. The Shahni insisted that any soldier who might be captured was to carry as little potentially useful information within him as possible. Iuni might be just an ordinary citizen, but she could also be the daughter or wife of someone in authority. Either way, it wasn't something anyone wanted the invaders to learn.

Three minutes to go. Zoshak looked over at the baked goods

booth next to the vegetable stand, to find the vendor looking back at him. Zoshak gave the other a microscopic nod, got one in return, and touched Iuni's arm. "Hurry and make your selection," he told her. "I'll go get the bread."

He headed toward the booth, throwing a brief glower at the pair of armored Trofts standing ten meters away as he walked. A dozen of the aliens had been wandering around the edges of the market area for most of the hour Zoshak had been here, not quite intruding on the shoppers' space, but nevertheless keeping a watchful eye on the proceedings.

From the snatches of conversation Zoshak had overheard from his fellow citizens, he gathered the prevailing theory was that the Trofts were playing mind games: trying to make their presence felt, or else emphasizing that the Qasamans no longer owned their city or their world. Zoshak's own theory was that the diversionary attack three days ago on the invaders in the Sunrise market area across town had led the aliens to believe there was something of military value hidden in *all* of Sollas's market areas.

In theory, that was all to the good. Forcing the Trofts to waste time and energy looking for soldiers among the vegetables was time and energy that couldn't be used elsewhere on Qasama. In practice, though, he wished that the Trofts had picked a different market area to concentrate on today.

The man at the baker's booth gave the sign of respect as Zoshak came up to his counter. "Good afternoon," he said as Zoshak returned the gesture. "How may I help you?"

"A loaf of bread, please," Zoshak said, making sure to pitch his voice at a normal conversational level. The idea was to keep all of this looking perfectly normal to any of the invaders who happened to be watching or listening.

"I'm afraid this is all I have left," the man said, stooping down behind the counter and bringing out a long, spindly, splotchy loaf of French bread. "Not one of our best, as you can see," he added, cradling the loaf almost tenderly in both hands. "It's four and a half, if you want it."

Zoshak hissed out a sigh. But after three days of alien occupation, that was indeed the current inflated price for a loaf that size, and any Trofts who'd been paying attention to the day's transactions would know that. "Very well," he said.

Pulling a handful of coins from his pocket, he sorted out the proper ones and laid them on the counter. "Careful, now," the baker warned, leaning the loaf over the counter to him.

Not careful because the loaf looked on the verge of shattering into a dozen pieces, Zoshak knew, but careful because the thing was far heavier than any actual bread could possibly be. Zoshak took the loaf, wincing a little as his wrists momentarily tried to bend the wrong way. He got the joints back under control, pulling his hands up and in where the servos in his combat suit could take more of the weight. "Thank you," he nodded to the baker, and retraced his steps to the booth where Iuni was waiting.

She looked up as he approached, only a slight tightness around her eyes betraying her tension. "You bought *that?*" she asked with obvious disapproval.

"And we were lucky to get it," Zoshak told her, wishing briefly he knew whether or not the Trofts were even paying attention to them. It would be a shame to go through this whole prearranged scene if they weren't.

The loudspeaker gave its final double boom, signaling the end of the shopping day. "Fine," Iuni said. "Better carry it like that—it's not going to fit in any of the bags. And *don't* let it break."

"I won't," Zoshak promised, pulling the loaf close in to his chest. "Come on, let's get home."

Iuni nodded and turned their collapsible shopping cart around, pushing it away from the market plaza and toward the Troft sentry ship looming over the street to the northwest. Several of the other patrons, Zoshak noted peripherally, were heading in that same direction, some singly, others in couples. On the far side of the street, half a block ahead, two of the couples were chatting together as they pushed side-by-side baby carriers. Behind them, Zoshak could hear the sounds of moving boxes and closing doorways as the merchants closed up shop for the night.

Zoshak gave the sentry ship a casual once-over. It was a good

three meters taller than the buildings immediately around it, domi-
nating the entire area. Grouped around its base at both ends were
squads of Troft soldiers, their laser rifles held ready across their
armored chests. The ones nearest Zoshak and Iuni were giving a
close look to each Qasaman who passed their positions. A few of
the pedestrians returned the aliens' gazes, but most of the others
just ignored them.

The apartment building Zoshak and Iuni had come out of earlier
was across from the sentry squad and almost directly beneath the
ship's stubby starboard wing and its assortment of mounted weapons.
Iuni pushed the cart to the building's outer doorway and stopped,
digging through her handbag for the key. Zoshak, still clutching
the loaf to his chest, turned a haughty look on the aliens.

The look didn't go unnoticed. Two of the Trofts shifted position
slightly, turning their bodies so that they had merely to drop their
muzzles from their cross-chest positions to target him. Zoshak
responded by adjusting his own stance and hefting the loaf exactly
the same way the Trofts were holding their lasers.

That earned him the attention of a third alien, this one not only
turning in his direction but actually lowering his laser into firing
position. Zoshak ignored the silent warning, his eyes still on the
Trofts, his loaf of bread still held rifle-style across his chest. The
more aliens who were watching him when the timer ran down,
the fewer there would be to shoot at the Djinn working their way
along the other side of the street.

From the receiver buried in the bone behind his right ear came
the quick double-click of a fifteen-second warning. "You have that
door open yet?" Zoshak called behind him, pitching his voice
loudly enough for the Trofts to hear. "Hurry up—the air's starting
to stink out here."

"I've got it," Iuni said, her voice suddenly taut as she caught
the cue and knew the attack was about to begin. "Can you help
me with the cart?"

Zoshak continued to stare at the Trofts for another few seconds,
then turned his back on the aliens. Iuni was standing in the open
doorway, tugging on the front of the cart as she tried to pull it

over the threshold. Zoshak stepped up to the rear of the cart and began nudging it with his forearms as if attempting to help without breaking the loaf of bread.

With his body blocking the Trofts' view, he set the loaf upright in the cart. Keeping his movements small, he reached into his tunic and retrieved the combat suit gloves that had been hidden there. He slipped them on, feeling a brief tingle as the gloves' servos connected to the power and control surfaces in the sleeves, and this time he was able to pick up the loaf without any strain at all.

There was a final double-click from his implanted receiver. Turning back to face the Trofts, he stretched out his arms, holding the loaf vertically as if offering the bread to the aliens, and squeezed the center.

And as the street around him suddenly erupted in gunfire from the buildings and laser fire from the other Djinn surrounding the sentry ship, the missile burst from its bread coating and blasted upward toward the under-wing weapons cluster.

Zoshak leaped to the side as the brief jolt of exhaust fire washed across his face. Lifting his hands, he fired a pair of bolts at the nearest Troft sentry's laser. The weapon blistered and then shattered, blowing out a cloud of metal splinters and sending its owner staggering backward. Simultaneously, one of the other sentries jerked and fell to the pavement as a combination of projectile and laser fire took him down.

There was a brilliant flash from above him. Zoshak looked up to see the missile he'd just launched disintegrate five meters from its target, blown apart by one of the weapon cluster's point-defense lasers.

Unfortunately for the Trofts, Miron Akim and the other tacticians had anticipated that. Instead of the muffled pop of vaporized explosives and electronics, the missile erupted with a spray of evil-looking green liquid. Even as the lasers continued to fire uselessly at it, the liquid continued upward on the missile's original trajectory and splattered against the cluster.

Zoshak didn't wait, but leaped away to the side, pushing his leg servos to their limit. The liquid was reasonably viscous, but he had no intention of being anywhere nearby when it started dripping back to the ground. He landed fifteen meters away just as the first few drops began to rain onto the street, sizzling violently as the concentrated acid burned through the paving material.

A laser bolt burned past Zoshak's side. Dropping into a crouch, he snapped off a couple of shots of his own, catching the Troft soldier across his faceplate. At this range the bolts probably wouldn't penetrate the self-shielding, but at least the plastic's protective blackening would interfere with the alien's vision. Before the Troft could do more than fire off a couple more wild shots in Zoshak's general direction a heavy machine gun somewhere above him sent a short burst across the alien's helmet and torso, sending him flying backward to slam up against the sentry ship's bow. Another alien raised his laser toward the Qasaman gunner, and Zoshak stitched another pair of black lines across his faceplate.

And then, as Zoshak grabbed for one of the throwing weights at his belt, a brilliant beam of light slashed through the air above him, and the Qasaman machine gun went abruptly silent.

Reflexively, Zoshak threw himself sideways, looking up in disbelief and dismay as a second blast of laser light shattered the pavement where he'd just been standing. The acid wash *had* hit the cluster—he'd seen the impact himself. Every one of the weapons up there ought to be out of commission.

But they weren't. None of them. All six of the lasers were firing, targeting the Djinn still engaging the ground troops, as well as those running toward the ship's fore and aft hatches. The heavier missile launchers hadn't yet fired, but the tubes were tracking back and forth as if looking for a worthy target. One of the machine guns farther down the street shifted aim toward the weapons cluster, and once again the Trofts' lasers lashed out. For a long moment the machine gun continued to fire, and Zoshak held a brief hope that the gunner would survive. But the lasers continued to fire, and a few seconds later the machine gun finally went silent.

And then, Zoshak's receiver implant gave the triple-click order for retreat.

God in heaven, he thought viciously. But there was no other choice. With the weapons clusters still operational there was no hope of success, and to continue would simply cost more lives without any gain. He clicked back an acknowledgment and straightened up, looking around for any of his fellow Djinn who might need assistance—

His only warning was a slight flicker of motion from the corner of his eye. He threw himself to the ground beside the slabs of broken pavement the Troft laser had gouged into the street as a wave of tiny antipersonnel missiles shot past, exploding like a volley of firecrackers against the wall behind him. Another wave was right behind the first; grabbing the biggest piece of shattered pavement he could reach, he rolled half over, holding the slab up as a shield. A half-dozen of the missiles exploded against it, blasting off splinters and chunks. He rolled back to his feet, still holding the slab for protection, and began backing through the chaos toward the alley where the closest emergency exit was located.

He was the first of the Djinn to make it through the hidden door and into the safety of the subcity. A Djinni from one of the other squads was the second. Siraj Akim was the third.

There wasn't any fourth.

Jin was gazing up at the hospital room ceiling, listening to her rumbling stomach and wondering when the evening meal was going to be delivered, when she heard the sound of running feet outside her door.

She frowned, activating her audio enhancers. There appeared to be two different groups of footsteps out there: one group running to her left, the other, heavier group heading to her right.

And the group heading right was accompanied by occasional metallic clinks. The kind of clinking that weapons and military equipment made as they bounced against belts and chests.

Reaching to her left arm, she carefully disengaged the two IV tubes that still remained after the battery of tests the doctors had put her through. Then, slipping into the soft boots and robe beside her bed, she padded to the door and opened it a crack.

A line of civilians was running to her left, some of them carrying small equipment consoles or record boxes. Others, mostly hospital staff, were pushing wheelchairs or assisting the more ambulatory patients. Down the hall, she could see other doors opening in sequence as the staffers systematically cleared out the rest of the patients.

On the opposite side of the hall, heading to Jin's right, was a line of grim-faced soldiers.

She pulled the door open all the way. One of the passing soldiers caught her eye and jerked his thumb silently in the direction the civilians were going. "Wait," Jin said quietly. "I can—"

He didn't even pause, but just kept going. "I can help," Jin muttered under her breath. She lifted a hand to the next soldier back, but he merely gave her the same thumbs-back gesture.

Jin grimaced. But there was clearly no time to argue the point, even if she could find someone to argue it with. Spotting a gap in the traffic flow, she left her room and joined the civilians heading to the left.

She'd gone only about fifty meters when she spotted a familiar face: Fadil Sammon, hurrying toward her behind two burly soldiers. "Fadil!" she called, holding out a hand toward him. "Fadil Sammon!"

He jerked at the sound of his name, then finally noticed her. "There you are," he said, stepping out of the soldiers' line and falling into step beside her. "I was on my way to see you. I can't—"

"What's going on?" Jin interrupted. "Are the Trofts coming in?"

"Sounds that way, yes," Fadil said grimly. "There's been some kind of breach, anyway. The Shahni have ordered this area evacuated."

Jin half turned to look at the departing soldiers. She should be back there, she knew. She should be on her way to the breach, helping to defend the people of Qasama—

"No," Fadil said firmly, grabbing her arm and turning her back around front. "They can do it themselves."

"Who can?" Jin asked. "The Qasamans? Or the city people?"

Fadil muttered something under his breath. "Come on—the seal is just ahead."

Jin had noticed several seals during her travels around the sub-city. They would have been hard to miss, actually: red-rimmed slabs of stone or reinforced concrete set into the sides of strategically placed corridors or doorways, ready to be slid into position to block off any further access. Some of them had gunports or firing niches nearby that guards could use, others had red-striped ceilings just behind the slabs marking something ominously labeled as avalanche zones.

This particular seal had no such backups, just a pair of Qasaman soldiers waiting tensely by the slab as the refugees streamed past. One of them, a few years older than the other and wearing sergeant's insignia, frowned hard at Jin as she and Fadil slipped through with the others—

"Jasmine Moreau?" he called suddenly.

Jin stopped, stepping to the side out of the way of the hurrying civilians. "Yes," she confirmed.

"A message from Miron Akim," the sergeant said. "He asks if you will remain here until all have passed."

"Why?" Fadil demanded. "She's not a soldier."

"It's all right," Jin said, touching his shoulder. "Go on."

Fadil hesitated, then gave a snort and rejoined the line of civilians. "Did Miron Akim say what he wanted me to do?" Jin asked the sergeant.

"The seal will need to be closed when everyone's past," he told her, his voice tight. "That duty usually goes to a Djinni, but we've received word that none are available in this sector."

A cold knot settled into Jin's stomach. "Did they say why not?"

"No," the sergeant said. "Just that none was available." He looked back over his shoulder at her. "Miron Akim said that you were here, and that we were to stop you when you came through and ask for your assistance."

"No problem," Jin assured him.

The flow of refugees had faded to a trickle of hospital workers when the faint sound of gunfire began to echo down the hallway.

The other soldier snarled something under his breath. He was young, Jin noted as she studied his profile. Actually, neither of the two was all that old. Certainly neither could have had any experience in the sort of warfare their world had suddenly been plunged into.

Or had they? The city/village rivalry that Jin had seen and heard of on her first visit to Qasama was clearly still going strong three decades later. Could that rivalry have occasionally boiled up into actual shooting combat?

Daulo hadn't even hinted at any such violence on his world during their conversations. But then, he wouldn't have. Not to her and Merrick.

"It's time," the sergeant said quietly.

Jin frowned. The gunfire was still going strong. "What about the soldiers?" she asked.

"They will return to the subcity by a different route." The sergeant hesitated. "Or not at all."

Jin clenched her teeth. *Let me go to them,* the words and plea flashed through her mind. *I can help.*

She took a deep breath. "What do I do?" she asked instead.

"Pull up on this," the sergeant said, indicating a long lever set into the wall just inside the slab. "More than once, I think."

With Jin's first tug on the lever it became clear why Djinn were generally tasked with this job. Even with the gearing that was obviously built into the system the lever took a lot of effort to pull. The first hundred-eighty-degree rotation moved the slab perhaps a centimeter into the corridor; ratcheting the lever back down, she hauled up on it again, and again, and again, until the slab completely blocked the corridor.

"What now?" Jin asked as she released the lever and stepped away from it.

Both soldiers were staring at her with a mixture of awe and uneasiness. But the sergeant merely nodded back down the hallway. "This way," he said. "Miron Akim wishes to speak with you."

Given all the civilians and medical personnel that had just come through the area, Jin had expected it to be crowded with masses of displaced people. To her surprise, though, the corridors didn't seem much busier than she'd usually seen them. Wherever the refugees had gone, they'd gone there quickly and efficiently.

The soldiers led her through the usual maze of corridors to a door guarded by a single soldier. "Jasmine Moreau?" the guard asked formally as Jin and her escort came up to him. "Miron Akim offers his regrets, and states that he was called away on urgent business," he continued, reaching over and opening the door. "He asks that you wait for him inside, and that you examine a file he has left for you."

"Thank you," Jin said. "And thank you," she added to her escort, giving them the sign of respect.

Neither of the soldiers returned the gesture. Either she'd done it wrong, or else word had spread that the visitors from the Cobra Worlds weren't worthy of the sign.

The room was typical of what she'd seen in the subcity: small and sparsely furnished, with a desk and computer terminal and two wooden chairs. Lying beside the terminal was a single dusky-red file folder. Circling around behind the desk, wondering briefly if the door would be locked from the outside, she sat down and opened the folder.

The sheet of paper on top was a report of some sort, a listing of Troft activities from one of the villages, complete with alien troop numbers, types of air—and spacecraft observed, and a time-line that indicated it was a single day's report. She leafed briefly through the rest of the papers, noting the differing times and village names but that all of them followed essentially the same format. Leave it to the Qasamans, she thought with a touch of grim amusement, to be organized even down to their paperwork.

She was skimming the fourth page when a particular entry belatedly caught her attention: *razorarms captured.*

Frowning, she settled down to read.

It was an axiom of war, she'd heard once, that numbers quoted in the heat of battle or delivered by civilians should never be taken entirely at face value. But if the numbers in the various villager reports were even halfway accurate, the Trofts had been incredibly busy. In the three days since their invasion they'd already hauled nearly four hundred razorarms out of the forest and loaded them aboard cargo carriers. The reports were a bit vague on the techniques involved—apparently none of the observers had managed to get very close to the scene of the action—but it seemed to include multiple small aircraft as spotters and some kind of tranquilizer gas bombs.

Of even more interest was the fact that the Trofts were apparently leaving the razorarms' mojos behind.

She was midway through the papers when Akim arrived. "My apologies," he said as he closed the door behind him. He had a folder of his own, Jin noted, a light green one. "No—please," he added, waving Jin back to her seat as she started to rise and seating himself in one of the other chairs facing her. "Did you finish reading the file?"

"I only made it through about half the reports, but I was able to skim the rest," she said, studying his face. His expression was under rigid control, but there was a dark tightness around his eyes, a darkness she hadn't seen even on the day of the invasion itself. "They've been busy, haven't they?"

"That they have," Akim said. "The question remains: why?"

"I see two possibilities," Jin said. "One, they mostly want the razorarms. Two, they mostly want to leave mojos in the forests *without* symbiotic companions."

"An interesting possibility, that last," Akim said. "Yet if they wanted the mojos to be alone, why not simply kill the razorarms out from beneath them? Why bother taking the animals away alive?"

"A good point," Jin conceded. "Are we sure the razorarms haven't shown up in any of Qasama's cities or villages?"

"Not that we know of," Akim said. "Of course, there are many smaller villages and settlements outside our communication range. Still, if sending razorarms into those villages was the goal, why not do their hunting in those same areas? Why choose animals from near Sollas and transport them the entire distance?"

"No reason I can see," Jin agreed. "So it would seem they're simply taking the most convenient animals, the ones that are near where all their heavy transports are already located."

"Here at Sollas," Akim said, nodding.

"Right," Jin said, frowning as something else occurred to her. "The transports *do* leave those areas once they have their razorarms, don't they?" she asked. "I didn't see that in the reports."

"Yes, they invariably leave," Akim confirmed. "But where they go, we have no idea." He cocked his head, and Jin thought she saw a subtle change in the man's expression. "Could it be that the invaders want them for the same reason you brought them to Qasama in the first place? That they wish to seed an enemy's land with quick-breeding predators?"

Jin stared at him, a horrible sensation rippling through her. There it was, staring her suddenly in the face.

And it was so terribly obvious. How in the *Worlds* had she missed it? "That's it," she said, her throat tightening against the words. "You're right, Miron Akim. That's exactly what they're doing.

"Only the enemy you mention isn't Qasama. The enemy is us."

Akim nodded, his expression going even darker. "So indeed I have suspected from the first," he said, an edge of accusation in his tone. "All the more so since you never suggested the possibility."

"Because I didn't think of it," Jin said, embarrassment and chagrin flowing in around the sudden heartache. Her worlds—her people—her family, under Troft attack. "I don't know why not. It's so obvious."

"Perhaps," Akim said, his voice a shade less angry. "But even if true, it cannot be the entire truth. If your world is their target, why invade Qasama at all? There are many unoccupied territories where they could hunt razorarms with little effort and less resistance."

Jin sighed. "They invaded you because you're here," she said quietly. "And because you're humans."

Akim's eyes bored into hers. "Explain."

Jin took a deep breath. "A century ago there was a war between the Dominion of Man and an alliance of demesnes at that end of the Troft Assemblage. The reasons for it are muddled, but they don't really matter. What matters is that the first the Dominion knew about Troft animosity was when the alliance's troops landed and occupied two of our worlds." She lifted her arms slightly. "We were the Dominion's response."

"Forces who could move easily among the occupied peoples," Akim said, nodding. "And could fight back from that concealment."

"Keeping them distracted and softening them up until they could be ultimately driven off," Jin said. "The problem was that once the war was over, there was nowhere for the surviving Cobras to go. They didn't really fit in with their old homes anymore, a good percentage of the general populace was terrified of them, and the political leaders simply wanted them to go away." She smiled tightly. "It was my grandfather's brother, actually, who came up with the answer: send the remaining Cobras past the Assemblage as guardians and police for a new group of human colonies."

Akim frowned. "And the Trofts actually agreed to this?"

Jin shrugged. "The demesnes who'd lost the war didn't have a lot of say in the matter," she reminded him. "The rest of them didn't seem to particularly care one way or the other whether humans went zooming back and forth through their space." She grimaced. "Or maybe they all just recognized the opportunity buried inside the apparent humiliation."

Akim straightened suddenly, as if a missing piece of the puzzle had just fallen into place. "Because you were now hostages to the Dominion's good behavior."

"Exactly," Jin said. "The Dominion's idea, I think, was that having a group of Cobras out here would be a nice two-front threat against the Trofts to keep them from further mischief. But if it was, it backfired. Badly. Barely twenty years after we got here the corridor we'd been using was closed, cutting us off from the Dominion."

"You must have been perturbed, to say the least," Akim murmured.

"Actually, it was our idea," Jin told him. "My grandfather's, to be specific, worked out along with his brother. They forced the closure of the corridor, ending the Dominion's threat of a two-front war."

"So the Dominion lost the lever it had hoped for," Akim murmured. "But the Trofts didn't."

"The Trofts didn't," Jin agreed, her stomach tightening. "And apparently someone's decided it's time to cash in."

"Apparently," Akim said grimly. "I wonder what the Trofts have done to your Dominion this time."

"Or what the Dominion has done to them," Jin said. "But from this end of the universe, it doesn't much matter who started it or why. What matters is that someone has decided we're a potential threat that needs to be neutralized."

"And they believe Qasama to be your allies?"

"They probably don't care whether you are or not," Jin said. "Remember, these are most likely Trofts from the Dominion side of the Assemblage who don't care a damn about our political relationships. They've come here to punish the Dominion by suppressing human colonization, period."

"I see," Akim said. "It would have been nice to have known this sooner."

Jin winced. "I know," she said. "I'm sorry, Miron Akim. I don't know why I didn't think of it before. I just can't seem to think like I used to. Old age catching up with me, I guess."

"No apologies needed," Akim said, an odd tone in his voice. "And I wish it was merely old age." Reaching to his lap, he picked up the green folder. "I have the results of your last group of tests."

"And?" Jin asked carefully.

Akim visibly braced himself. "You have a brain tumor, Jasmine Moreau," he said quietly. "A highly virulent one.

"In two months, perhaps three, you will die."

CHAPTER EIGHTEEN

Jin stared at him, feeling the blood draining from her face. Her strange inability to think straight, her unexplained blackouts... "Are you sure?" she heard herself ask.

"Very sure," Akim said. "I'm sorry. I wish it were otherwise."

"Is there anything that can be done?"

Akim pursed his lips. "The doctors will study the data and see if there are any options." He hesitated. "But you have to understand that they have other matters occupying their attention at the moment."

"Of course." Jin took a deep breath. Two months. "All right," she said. "What can I do until then?"

"There are dietary techniques that may slow the process," Akim said. "Bed rest may also be of some use."

Jin shook her head. "You misunderstand. What I meant was, until the doctors have time to study my case—and probably haul me in for more tests—what can I do to help in the war?"

A muscle in Akim's cheek twitched. "I appreciate your offer," he said. "But I'm afraid your service to Qasama is at an end. Aside from anything else, we can hardly risk you having a blackout during a combat operation."

"I suppose," Jin conceded, marveling at how calm she was. Or perhaps how numb she was would be a more accurate description.

Even on Aventine, doctors had little chance against a brain tumor. On Qasama, in the middle of a war, the odds were undoubtedly far worse. "I'll need to tell Merrick. Can I see him? Or hasn't he recovered yet from his injuries?"

"No, he should be recovered by now," Akim said, the odd note back in his voice. "I'll see if I can locate him. Wait here, please, and continue reading through the file."

Like she would really be able to concentrate on Troft troop movements now. *Two months to live...* "All right," she said.

She'd been trying to focus on the papers for nearly an hour when a knock finally came on the door and a tall young man in a gray Djinni combat suit and shocking—for a Qasaman—red hair stepped into the doorway. "You are Jasmine Moreau?" he asked formally.

"Yes," Jin said.

"Marid Miron Akim sent me to bring you to him," the Djinni said shortly. "Follow me."

"May I know your name?" Jin asked, making no move to stand up.

The other glared. Perhaps he didn't like being in the presence of an enemy of Qasama. "I am Ghofl Khatir, Djinn Ifrit of Qasama," he said shortly.

"Honored to meet you, Ifrit Khatir," Jin said, nodding to him as she got to her feet. "Please; lead the way."

She crossed the room, but to her mild surprise, Khatir remained in the doorway blocking her exit. "We will be meeting with your son on a matter of intense importance," he said. "Miron Akim requests that you do not speak of personal matters at this time."

"Will there be a time provided for such a conversation?" Jin asked, resisting the impulse to simply pick him up by the arms and move him out of her way.

"You must ask Miron Akim about that," Khatir said, finally stepping back out into the corridor. "Follow me."

The room he took her to was larger than the one she'd just left but only slightly better furnished. Three men were waiting: Miron Akim, Carsh Zoshak, and Merrick.

Merrick was on his feet even before she was all the way into the room. "Mom!" he said, hurrying toward her and gripping her arm. "Are you all right?"

Jin glanced at Akim, noting the stiffness in his face. "I'm fine," she said, giving her son a quick once-over. "*You're* the one who got all shot up."

"I'm fine," Merrick assured her, dismissing his condition with a quick wave of his hand. "They did a good job of patching me up."

"Save your personal conversation for another time," Khatir said brusquely as he stalked past them. "We have work to do."

"Courtesy, Ifrit Khatir," Akim admonished him mildly. "But he's correct. The hour is late, and we have much to discuss. Please; be seated."

Gripping Merrick's hand, Jin stepped to the row of chairs in front of Akim and sat down in one of them. Merrick sat beside her; to her mild surprise, Zoshak took the seat on Merrick's other side. Khatir, in contrast, pointedly moved one over from Jin's other side, leaving an empty chair between them.

"We suffered a serious setback today," Akim began, his eyes touching each of their faces in turn. "More importantly, many Qasaman lives were lost." He gestured toward Zoshak. "Djinni Zoshak was the only survivor not currently undergoing medical treatment. He'll describe what he saw and experienced from the ground."

Jin listened silently as Zoshak related the attack on the Troft sentry ship and its aftermath. "Have any of you any questions?" Akim asked when he had finished.

Jin looked at Merrick. He looked back and gave her a small shake of his head. "I have one, then," Akim continued. "The acid Djinni Zoshak and the others used should have quickly destroyed or at least seriously damaged any alloy of the sort the invaders are known to use in their ships. Do you, Jasmine Moreau or Merrick Moreau, have any idea why it didn't do so?"

With an effort, Jin dragged her mind back from images of carnage. "Your statement implies you've examined Troft ship construction," she said. "May I ask when and where you did this?"

"That information is classified," Khatir put in.

"Over the years we've had the opportunity to take spectroscopic samplings from four Troft trading ships," Akim said, ignoring Khatir's comment. "The alloys were all very much of a kind, with only slight variations in the percentages of the admixed metals."

Jin looked at Merrick. "Any ideas?" she invited.

He shrugged. "Those were probably local Troft traders," he pointed out. "This bunch seem to be from some other demesnes. I suppose they could use entirely different hull materials."

"Maybe," Jin said doubtfully. "But unless my high-school physics has been completely outdated, hullmetal is pretty much basically hullmetal. You need certain characteristics for the hyperdrive to haul the whole ship along with it instead of just blasting its way through the bulkheads and taking off on its own."

"Unless the Trofts have come up with a new alloy that also works," Merrick said. "Neither of us is exactly an authority on these things." He turned to Zoshak. "Did the acid do *anything* to the weapons? Slow them down, set the barrels drooping— anything?"

"Not that I could see from the ground," Zoshak said grimly. "They were certainly functional enough to kill our soldiers and Djinn."

"With lasers," Akim said suddenly.

Jin looked at him. "What?"

"The invaders fired at our soldiers with lasers," Akim said slowly, his eyes on Zoshak but his gaze focused somewhere more distant. "But I don't believe they ever fired their missiles. The small anti-personnel missiles, yes, but not the larger ones from the clusters. *Any* of the clusters."

"Perhaps they saw no need to spend them," Khatir suggested.

"No," Zoshak said, a sudden new edge to his voice. "I remember a specific instance, when a machine gunner was firing at the weapons cluster. A missile would have made quick work of the gunner, possibly bringing down the entire building and reducing all resistance from that direction. But instead the invaders fired a barrage of laser shots until he was silenced."

He looked at Merrick. "And yet the launchers *were* tracking. I remember seeing them swinging back and forth as if looking for targets."

"Maybe they wanted to limit the amount of destruction they were causing," Jin suggested, a bit hesitantly.

"That's not one of their concerns," Akim said firmly.

"He's right," Merrick seconded. "I saw some of what they did during Plan Saikah. They might not be ready to nuke Qasama back to the stone age, but you attack them and they'll fight back just as hard as anyone else." He frowned. "Though come to think of it, they didn't use missiles against Narayan and me, either, when we were rescuing Shahni Haafiz's family."

"Because the missile launchers on that sentry ship were occupied elsewhere," Akim said. "You were perhaps unaware that other forces were attempting to distract the invaders so that your rescue could succeed."

Merrick winced. "Oh," he said. "You're right. I didn't see that."

"The question remains as to why the missiles weren't used this evening," Zoshak said. "Could the acid have done some damage, but not enough for us to notice?"

"But if the lasers worked—" Merrick broke off. "Do those weapons clusters retract?"

"You mean into the ship?" Akim shook his head. "No, I don't believe so. There's no place for them to retract into, and the pylons seem permanently attached."

Merrick grunted thoughtfully. "Did you pick up the Troft ships on radar as they were coming in toward Sollas?"

"We don't normally use active sensor equipment," Akim said, studying Merrick closely. "Such techniques run the risk of betraying the observer's location."

"That they do," Merrick agreed. He turned a tight smile on his mother. "But the Trofts wouldn't have known that. Especially not Trofts from this far out of town."

And suddenly Jin saw where he was going. "The ships are sensor-coated," she breathed.

"Bingo." Merrick turned back to Akim. "She means there must be some kind of coating on the hullmetal that deflects or absorbs

radar signals," he explained. "Something thin that wouldn't interfere with hyperspace travel, but would help protect them from
unfriendly eyes while they were here."

"Is this a technology your own warships use?" Khatir asked.

"We don't *have* warships," Merrick told him. "And our handful
of transports *want* to be visible to radar when they're coming in
for a landing. The point is, the coating is what the acid attacked,
not the alloy you were expecting."

"And how is it that this material is impervious to acid?" Zoshak
asked, sounding confused.

"Oh, I'm sure it's not," Merrick said. "But Miron Akim implied
the acid you used was specially tailored for hullmetal. Regardless,
whatever punishment the acid did was absorbed by the coating,
leaving the hullmetal itself mostly undamaged."

" 'Mostly'?" Khatir asked.

"Yes," Akim said, his voice suddenly thoughtful. "Because the
interior of the missile tubes wouldn't have been treated with that
coating. Enough acid must have penetrated into those areas to
render them unsafe to use."

"Then we have our solution," Zoshak said, a growing excitement
in his voice. "We mix a two-stage acid, the first to eliminate the
coating, the second to destroy the metal itself."

"And how exactly do you propose we create this new acid?"
Khatir asked with exaggerated patience. "Shall we ask the invaders
for the chemical parameters of their radar-absorption material?"

Zoshak seemed to deflate. "Oh," he said in a more subdued
voice. He looked at Merrick. "Unless *you* know something about
this material?" he asked hopefully.

"Sorry," Merrick said. "But we may not have to be that clever.
Whatever the stuff is, it's not likely to be able to absorb radar *and*
also hold up to intense laser fire." He looked at Akim. "In fact, I'd
bet that a Cobra antiarmor laser could easily take it out."

One of Akim's eyebrows twitched. "Are you volunteering to
participate in the next attack?"

"A moment," Khatir spoke up. "As designated Djinn commander
of the next assault, I wish to state that I do not *want* Merrick

Moreau along. We have lasers of our own, which we're quite capable of using."

"It would be a foolish warrior indeed who would turn down expert assistance out of pride," Merrick countered.

"I do not turn down assistance out of pride," Khatir snapped, glaring at Merrick. "Take offense as you choose, but the fact is that I do not trust you."

"Yet I've proven my willingness to work for your freedom against the invaders," Merrick reminded him. "And I've proved my capability, as well." He looked at Akim. "Shahni Haafiz suggested I need to find a way to prove my trustworthiness. I submit that helping Ifrit Khatir and his men take out a Troft sentry ship is as good a way of doing that as any."

Jin frowned at him. She hadn't heard anything about any Shahni demands. "When did you speak to the Shahni?" she asked Merrick.

"It was an informal little meeting," Merrick said, a flick of his eyes warning her to drop it. "Miron Akim?"

"It may be possible," Akim said, his eyes shifting back and forth between Jin and Merrick. "I'll submit your proposal to the Shahni." He paused, shot a look at Khatir, then turned back to Merrick. "In the meantime, we now have a direction for our new attack plan," he continued. "Thank you all for your time and insights."

"Do you have a planned timing yet for the attack?" Merrick asked.

"Certainly not before tomorrow night," Akim said. "Possibly not until a day after that. I want Djinni Zoshak and the other survivors from his squad to join with Ifrit Khatir's squads, and their medical treatment and recovery is not yet complete."

"What do you want us to do until then?" Merrick asked.

A faint smile twitched at the corners of Akim's mouth. "For the next few hours, at least, you should probably sleep. You've been assigned a bed in Djinni Zoshak's barracks. He'll show you there."

Jin braced herself. "Before he goes," she spoke up, "I wonder if I might have a little time alone with him."

For a moment, it looked to her like Akim was going to say no. But then he bowed his head. "Of course," he said. "You may use this room if you'd like. I'll leave a soldier outside to show him to his quarters." He smiled faintly. "And another to guide you to your new hospital room, as well," he added. "Ifrit Khatir, you'll come with me."

"As you wish, Marid Akim," Khatir said. Sending one last glower at Merrick, he rose and followed Akim out of the room.

"It's good to see you again, Jasmine Moreau," Zoshak said, smiling uncertainly at Jin as he also stood up. "Merrick Moreau, I'll see you later." With a nod at each of them, he headed out.

Merrick turned to Jin. "You have a *hospital* room?" he asked.

Jin took a deep breath. This was not going to be easy. "I've had some tests done, Merrick..."

It was nearly two hours later when Merrick finally arrived at the bunk the soldier pointed out to him.

It felt more like it had been two years.

He was too weary to bother undressing farther than just fumbling off his shoes before curling up on the hard mattress, his mind a swirl of anger, fear, and a horrible, horrible grief. A parent, he'd heard someone say long ago, shouldn't have to bury his or her children.

Neither should a twenty-seven-year-old son have to bury his mother.

And it would be his responsibility to do that, he knew. His responsibility alone. They were trapped on Qasama, with no hope of getting back to Aventine before the end.

Which meant his mother wouldn't have a chance to say a proper good-bye to Lorne or Jody. Or even to her husband.

Merrick closed his eyes against the tears welling up and spilling out onto the pillow. *It's not fair!* he screamed silently at the universe. *Not her. Not now.*

But the universe didn't care. Or rather, the universe had its own unbending laws to adhere to. Thirty-two years ago Jasmine Moreau had made the choice to follow in her family's footsteps, knowing full well what the cost would be. Now, the price had come due.

Merrick pressed his face against the pillow, feeling his tears soaking the case and spreading out to chill his cheeks and forehead. Had she really, truly understood the full consequences of that decision? For that matter, did any of those who chose to become Cobras really understand? Could any normal, healthy teenager or twenty-something genuinely comprehend their own death?

But ultimately, willingness or ignorance didn't matter. All that mattered was that Merrick was going to lose his mother. And farther down the road, he himself would lose half of his own life's potential span.

Or even more. He was, after all, in the middle of a war.

And the most hateful and painful irony of it all was that the people for whom they were making this sacrifice didn't even appreciate it. The people of the Cobra Worlds watched the Cobras' deaths with indifference or resentment. The Qasamans would watch with distrust and hatred.

"Are you all right?" a whisper came from Merrick's side.

With an effort, Merrick forced back the tears. This wasn't Zoshak's concern. "Sorry," he whispered back, striving to keep the emotion out of his voice. "Sinus trouble. I didn't mean to wake you."

Zoshak was silent long enough that Merrick thought he'd fallen asleep again. "I've cried myself, you know," he said quietly. "There's no shame in being afraid."

A flash of anger shot through Merrick. "Is that what you think?" he bit back. "You think I'm a coward?"

"I didn't say you were a coward," Zoshak said. "Do you wish to talk? We can go to one of the briefing rooms if you want privacy."

Merrick sighed, ashamed of his burst of anger. Zoshak was only trying to help. "There's nothing to talk about," he said. "Maybe later when . . . never mind."

"Never mind what?" Zoshak persisted. "We're comrades in war, Merrick Moreau. I'd like to think that we're also on the path to becoming friends. Whatever it is you need or want, please tell me."

Merrick shook his head. This was going to sound so stupid. "I was just going to say that I don't know anything about Qasaman burial customs," he said. "Maybe you'd be willing to help me when the time comes."

There was a sound of shifting sheets, and in the darkness Merrick saw Zoshak sit up. "*What's happened?*" the Djinni asked, his voice suddenly tight.

Merrick closed his eyes. It wasn't fair to share this burden with Zoshak, he knew. But Zoshak had asked.

And to be honest, Merrick didn't want to have to face this alone. With the rest of the Moreaus light-years away, Zoshak was the closest thing to family or friend that Merrick was likely to find. "My mother's dying," he said quietly. "Miron Akim says she has no more than two or three months to live."

"God in heaven," Zoshak breathed. "What is it? What's wrong with her?"

"Cancer," Merrick said. "A brain tumor. Maybe some side-effect of our Cobra implants—God knows there are enough of them."

"A brain tumor," Zoshak repeated. Even in a whisper his voice suddenly sounded odd. "And it's inoperable?"

Merrick swallowed hard. "Miron Akim said the doctors would be studying the possibilities. But I know the doctors on Aventine have a lousy success rate with tumors like that. I can't imagine your doctors just casually go in and cut them out, either."

"Why not?" Zoshak asked, still in that same odd tone. "They do."

Merrick stared across the darkness at the vague shape that was Zoshak. "What?" he asked carefully.

"Qasaman doctors routinely remove brain tumors from cancer victims," Zoshak said. "Did Miron Akim say anything about this one that would make it inoperable?"

Merrick blinked at the last tears still leaking from his eyes, reflexively fighting against this sudden new hope. No—it was too easy. Zoshak had to be mistaken. Surely Akim wouldn't have left such a sense of doom hanging over his mother's head otherwise. Surely he would have given her hope...

"Merrick Moreau?" Zoshak asked, his voice suddenly a little uncertain. "Did Miron Akim say anything about your mother's tumor?"

"No," Merrick said, once again struggling to keep the emotion out of his voice. Only this time the emotion wasn't grief. This time, it was pure, white-hot rage.

Because now he knew what was going on.

The bastards. The stinking, rotten, ice-hearted *bastards*.

"I need to speak to Miron Akim right away," he said as calmly as he could. "Do you have any idea where he might be?"

"At this hour? I would assume he's asleep in his quarters."

"I don't think that guy ever sleeps," Merrick said, trying to think. If he were a ice-hearted, stinking bastard, where would *he* go? "Are there any tactical or strategy-planning rooms nearby?"

"Not that I know of," Zoshak said.

"What about a high-level conference room?" Merrick asked, his mind flashing back to yesterday's confrontation with Shahni Haafiz and his two cohorts. "The one they took me to wasn't too far from the recovery ward I was in."

"Yes, I think I know the one," Zoshak said. "What's going on?"

"Miron Akim's betrayed me," Merrick said bluntly. "Or at least, I see it as a betrayal. Maybe you wouldn't."

For a long minute Zoshak was silent. "Let's find out," he said at last. "Give me a moment to get dressed."

There were more people moving about the subcity than had been in evidence the previous night, Merrick noted as Zoshak led the way through the maze. But fewer of them were civilians, and more of them were grim-faced soldiers.

Briefly, he wondered if the Trofts had managed another breakthrough like the one he'd heard about from earlier that evening. But even with his audio enhancers at full strength he could hear no sounds of gunfire. The soldiers were probably there to make sure the Trofts didn't make it deeper into the Qasamans' refuge.

Ten minutes later, they arrived at a door flanked by two soldiers standing at parade-ground attention. "Looks promising," Merrick said. "But then, all these doors look alike."

"By deliberate design, of course," Zoshak murmured back. "It doesn't look like they want company, though."

"We don't always get what we want," Merrick said. "Thank you for your assistance, Carsh Zoshak. You'd better head back to the barracks. After tonight you won't want to be too closely associated with me."

"Yet if I leave now, how will I ever know whether I consider Miron Akim's actions to be betrayal?" Zoshak asked calmly. "Besides, without me you won't be able to get in." Out of the corner of his eye Merrick saw the other flash him a wry look. "Without harming someone, I mean. Follow me."

He picked up his pace, moving a couple of steps out in front of Merrick. "Greetings, warriors of Qasama," he said formally as they approached the guarded door. "We have urgent business with those within. Step aside, and allow us to pass."

Merrick saw the soldiers' eyes flick down to Zoshak's gray Djinn combat suit, then to Merrick as he trailed behind, then back to Zoshak. "I'm sorry, Djinni," one of them said in the same formal tone. "Shahni Haafiz gave word they were not to be disturbed."

Merrick felt his throat tighten. Haafiz. Why was he not surprised?

"We have important business," Zoshak insisted, not slowing as he continued toward them. "Stand aside."

"We have orders," the soldier repeated, his hand getting a grip on his shoulder-slung rifle.

And suddenly, Merrick had had enough. "Let me talk to them," he said, lengthening his stride and stepping past Zoshak.

The soldiers' faces had gone stone-like, and both were starting to swing their rifles up into firing positions, when Merrick lifted his hand and fired his stunner.

The first soldier jerked as the high-voltage current slammed into him, scrambling nerve pathways and collapsing him into an unconscious heap on the floor. The second soldier had just enough time to widen his eyes when Merrick sent him to join his friend. Without even breaking stride Merrick grabbed the doorknob, twisted it and shoved the door open.

Once again there were three men seated at the curved table at the end of the room, with Shahni Haafiz again at the center.

But this time the rest of the cast had changed. Instead of two more Shahni, Haafiz had Moffren Omnathi at his right and Miron Akim at his left.

And standing in front of them, in the place where Merrick himself had been standing only hours earlier, wide eyes turned toward the unexpected intruders—

"Merrick," Jin gasped. "What are you doing here?"

"Step aside, Mother," Merrick told her shortly, his eyes steady on Akim. "Miron Akim and I have some business to conduct."

CHAPTER NINETEEN

Jin felt her heart catch in her chest as Merrick strode across the room toward her. *No,* she pleaded silently. *Not now.* "Merrick, go back," she said with as much firmness as she could pull together on the spur of the moment. "You don't understand."

"Oh, I understand," Merrick told her, his voice dark and simmering with rage, the natural calmness he'd inherited from his father gone like leaves in a gale. "I understand just fine."

"Stay where you are," Shahni Haafiz snapped, his voice betraying no hint of Jin's own fear. "There are Djinn to both sides of you."

"Really?" Merrick said, still moving forward. Jin saw her son's eyes twitch—"Then I suggest you warn them to be very careful," he continued. "I've locked up on the three of you, and Moffren Omnathi there will tell you that we Cobras are very hard to kill. One of the Djinn opens fire, and all three of you die." He pointed at Haafiz. "You first, of course."

"You didn't come here to kill," Omnathi said quietly. His face, unlike Haafiz's, showed no sign of emotion. "Else we would be dead already."

"True enough," Merrick agreed as he came to a halt beside his mother. Zoshak, Jin noted peripherally, had stopped a few paces back from them, silently watchful but making no attempt to interfere. "Two points. First, I came to let you know that I'm on to what you did to me, and what you tried to do to my mother."

"Merrick—" Jin tried again, laying a warning hand on his arm.

"And second," Merrick said, shaking off her hand, "I came to make a deal."

For a long moment the room was silent. The three Qasamans gazed hard at Merrick, and Jin held her breath. Then, to her relief, Haafiz stirred and made a small hand gesture. "Very well, Cobra Moreau," he said. "Speak."

"It didn't make sense," Merrick said, his eyes shifting back and forth among the three men behind the table. "Why spin me this big prove-yourself-trustworthy line and lock me up to think about it, and then just open the door and let me out a few hours later?"

"Perhaps it was an act of mercy," Omnathi suggested. "A chance to spend some time alone with your mother to hear of her medical condition."

"Yes, and we'll get to that in a minute," Merrick said, the sudden darkness in his tone sending a shiver up Jin's back. "But if that was the case, why not lock me up again afterward instead of sending me to a regular barracks? No, the only way it made sense was if you no longer needed whatever it was you'd originally wanted from me."

He looked at Jin. "And then, lo and behold, I find out that this whole terminal brain tumor thing is nothing but a scam. That you could go in there tomorrow and pull it out if you wanted to." He looked back at the three Qasamans. "And you *do* want to... because while you're in there, you can pull out something else. The thing you were hoping I would think to offer you while I was rotting away in solitary.

"You want a Cobra nanocomputer."

Once again, the room fell silent. "Very good, Cobra Moreau," Omnathi said at last. "Did I not warn you, Shahni Haafiz, that they were not to be underestimated?"

"Perhaps," Haafiz said calmly. "But their cleverness is irrelevant."

"I don't think so," Merrick said. "You see, I happen to know that you had access to Cobra nanocomputers once before." He looked at his mother, and to her relief Jin saw that his uncharacteristic anger was fading away. "You had the bodies of my mother's team, which

is where you got the Djinn glove lasers and trigger mechanisms."
He looked at the men again. "So if you have all of those, why do
you still need one of ours?"

"Why waste our time asking questions to which you already
know the answers?" Haafiz growled. "The nanocomputers you
speak of had degraded by the time we were able to study them."

"Yes, they had," Merrick said. "By deliberate design, of course.
Which brings me to the deal." He drew himself up. "You operate
on my mother, remove the tumor and heal her completely. In
return, I'll let you take out my nanocomputer and tell you how
to keep it from degrading."

"An interesting offer," Haafiz said, smiling thinly. "Unfortunately,
you're too late."

Merrick's eyes narrowed. "What's that supposed to mean?"

"He means," Jin said gently, "that I've already made them the
same offer. Only they'll be getting *my* nanocomputer, not yours."

Merrick turned startled eyes on her, and in his face she could
see his sudden chagrin as he belatedly realized he'd been so preoccupied with his confrontation that it hadn't even occurred to
him to wonder what she was doing here in the first place. "No,"
he said flatly. "They get mine, or they don't get either of them."

"Perhaps we should simply take both," Haafiz said.

"*Or* you don't get either of them," Merrick repeated, glaring at
him. "I can play games, too."

"This isn't a game, Merrick Moreau," Akim spoke up quietly.
"This is survival."

"That's your excuse for manipulating us this way?" Merrick bit
out. "After we've both risked our lives to help you?"

"We manipulated you because we had no choice but to do so,"
Omnathi said. There was no pleading in his voice that Jin could
detect, nor any regret or even embarrassment at having been
caught out in their scheming. "The fact is that the defenses we've
so carefully prepared over the years have failed. Without the new
possibilities represented by your nanocomputers, we have no chance
of victory against the invaders. We'll continue to throw ourselves
uselessly against their might until attrition takes the last of us."

Merrick looked at Jin, then shifted his eyes to Akim. "What about your Djinn?" he asked. "They've got the capability to be nearly as good as any Cobra. In fact, in some ways, they're better than we are."

Akim shook his head. "Their training and tactics are based on real-time squad coordination," he said. "But the invaders' ability to lock their antipersonnel missiles on to our radio signals renders that coordination impossible."

Merrick grimaced. "I wondered about that," he said. "I heard stories that they were tracking gunfire noise, but the ranging distances seemed way too big."

"In actual fact, they do track gunfire sounds, but only once they're within two or three meters of a target," Akim said. "The point is that your nanocomputer's programmed movements give you a far better capability of working alone than any Djinn possesses. We need that capability if we're to mount an effective defense of our world."

"Maybe," Merrick said. "But even once you have a working nanocomputer—"

"The other point is that it's not just Qasama that's in danger," Jin put in, silently pleading with her son not to say anything more. "The Trofts have been out in the forest since the invasion began, capturing spine leopards and loading them aboard transports. We think they're planning to take them back to the Cobra Worlds."

Merrick snorted. "What, we don't have enough of them there already?"

"They're not going to be dumping them in the wastelands," Jin said tartly. "They're going to turn them loose inside the cities."

Merrick stared at her. "You're jok—" He broke off, glanced at Akim, then looked back at Jin. "You can't be serious."

"Why not?" Akim said. "If you wish to neutralize the police, create a massive accident that draws them to the scene. If you wish to occupy warriors, give them something more urgent to do battle with."

"We also think they may not have launched their attack yet," Jin said. "They wouldn't want to just dribble the predators into

Capitalia or Pindar and give us time to figure out what they were up to. They have to be planning to dump them all in at once so that everyone will be running around in panic while they consolidate their positions."

"Yes," Merrick murmured, his eyes narrow with thought. The last of the anger was gone, Jin saw with relief, and he was finally thinking again. "Which means we still might have a chance to warn them," he said. "Get hold of a ship somehow and get back to Aventine. *If* we can move fast enough."

"Which is the bargain Jasmine Moreau has just made with us," Omnathi said. "She'll give us her nanocomputer. In return, we'll provide you with transport back to your world."

"Really," Merrick said. "Did Qasama develop spaceflight capability when we weren't looking?"

"Who is to say we have not done exactly that?" Haafiz asked loftily.

"Please, Your Excellency," Omnathi rumbled. "No, Merrick Moreau, we obviously haven't. But there are always ways." He eyed Merrick closely. "Provided, of course, that both parties to an agreement truly intend to honor their commitments."

Merrick looked at Jin. "Mom—"

"We have no choice, Merrick," Jin cut him off firmly. If she couldn't convince him that this was the only way, the questions and doubts would haunt the rest of his life. Just as her own questions and doubts had haunted hers. "I can't do any more here. Even after the tumor is removed it'll take me weeks to recover to the point where I could do any fighting. You, on the other hand, *can* still fight. If you give them yours, they won't have either of us to help them."

Merrick swallowed. "And if I decide the cost is too high?"

"You're talking about the price of freedom," Jin reminded him. "Both of us proclaimed ourselves willing to pay that price when we put on the uniform."

Merrick closed his eyes. "Have I ever told you how much I hate your sense of logic?"

"Everyone always has," Jin said, wincing as an unwanted memory from thirty-two years ago flashed across her mind's eye: her arguments to her father and Uncle Corwin that, despite years of precedent and custom, she was the best possible person to become a Cobra and go on the Qasama mission. "But only because I'm usually right."

"Mom—"

Jin stopped him with a hand to his cheek. "My husband, daughter, and other son are back there," she said quietly. "They'll have no warning of what's about to happen unless we make this deal. Please let me serve them in this one last way."

For a long minute he just gazed at her, and Jin could see the swirling emotions fighting themselves across his face. "When?" he asked at last.

Jin felt some of the tension fade from her throat. "As soon as possible," she said.

"But not until after you've assisted with the attack on the invader sentry ship," Omnathi put in.

Merrick gave him a look that was half disbelief and half disgust. "What, sacrificing the rest of my mother's life isn't enough for you?" he demanded. "You want me to fight, too?"

"Have you not sworn to protect Qasama from its enemies?" Haafiz countered. "Have you not stated that until the invaders are off this world that you *are* a Qasaman?"

"At any rate, it'll take time to prepare for your return to your worlds," Omnathi added. "As short a time as possible, of course."

"Of course," Merrick said stiffly. "Fine. Miron Akim, have you chosen your attack plan yet?"

"It'll be ready by nine tomorrow morning," Akim promised. "At that time you'll join Ifrit Khatir and his team for a briefing." His eyes flicked over Jin's shoulder. "As will you, Djinni Zoshak," he said, raising his voice. "I suggest you both return now to your barracks for sleep. One way or another, tomorrow is destined to be a busy day."

"Understood." Merrick looked at Jin. "You want me to walk you back to your quarters?"

"I'll do that," Akim said, standing up. "I have a few other matters to discuss with her."

"I could walk with you," Merrick persisted.

"You have been ordered to your barracks, *Qasaman*," Haafiz cut in. "You have already spoken of the price of freedom. Do not force me to demonstrate the price of disobedience."

For a bad moment Jin thought Merrick was going to argue the point. But he'd apparently had enough conflict for one night. "As you wish, Shahni Haafiz," he said with all the formality anyone could want. "Until tomorrow, Miron Akim."

"Tomorrow, Cobra Moreau," Akim said with a nod.

Squeezing Jin's hand once, Merrick forced a strained half smile and headed back toward the door. Zoshak, still without saying a word, also turned as he passed, falling into step beside him.

"Jasmine Moreau?"

She turned to see that Akim had circled the table and come up beside her. "We'll use this door," he said, gesturing toward an unobtrusive exit tucked away behind a display board. "It'll bring us more quickly to your room."

Jin didn't speak until they were walking down yet another of the subcity's corridors. Unlike all the others she'd been in, though, this one seemed completely deserted. A special parallel corridor system reserved for the Shahni and other high-ranking officials? "We *could* have let Merrick come along, you know," she commented as they walked. "I doubt we're going to talk about anything he shouldn't hear."

Akim made an odd sound in the back of his throat. "Actually," he said reluctantly, "we are."

They were halfway back to the barracks when Merrick finally couldn't stand the silence anymore. "Well, come on," he growled at Zoshak. "*Say* something. Even if it's just to lecture me on how I shouldn't be rude to one of the Shahni."

"What do you want me to say?" Zoshak asked calmly. "You *shouldn't* be rude to the Shahni."

Merrick grimaced. "Yeah, I know."

"But the ultimate fault lies with Shahni Haafiz and Advisor Omnathi, not with you," Zoshak continued. "They shouldn't have tried to manipulate you that way. Not when you'd already proven your willingness to serve our people."

Merrick grimaced again. Perversely, Zoshak's support only made him feel worse about the whole confrontation. "I suppose you can't really blame them," he said. "They've grown up hating us. A person doesn't toss all that aside just because someone lets the bad guys take a few shots at him."

Zoshak was silent for another few paces. "One thing I don't understand. I thought your equipment enhanced your normal abilities without being a substitute for them. Yet you state that your mother will die without her nanocomputer?"

Merrick sighed, the whole situation once again wrenching at him. "She won't literally die," he said. "But the condition she's going to end up in might as well be death. Our nanocomputers control our servos, not just their extra-strength capabilities but also the normal everyday movements. Without that control, the servos won't function. Every movement she makes will be against little motors that don't want to move and will have to be forced. Throw in the inherent extra weight of our ceramic laminae, and it'll be like she's wearing exercise wraps all over her body. Add in the arthritis and anemia that are already starting to affect her, and you have a prescription for a living hell."

"Is there nothing that can be done to help?" Zoshak asked. "Perhaps implant a new computer?"

"In theory, I suppose that could be done," Merrick said. "But the equipment to do that is forty-five light-years and a long visit to a Qasaman brain surgeon away. The point is that she'll have to go through her surgery and recovery in that state." He shook his head. "I'm just worried about what it'll do to her."

"And so you volunteered to take her place," Zoshak said, his voice thoughtful. "Willing to sacrifice yourself for your family."

Merrick shrugged. "Probably sounds a little selfish," he admitted. "After all, without my nanocomputer, I'd be pretty much out of the war. That's a lot safer than going out in the streets and getting shot at."

"I hardly consider such a sacrifice to fall under the heading of selfishness," Zoshak said. "I was merely noting that you're perhaps more like us than you realize."

An hour later, as Merrick finally began to drift off to sleep, he was still wondering whether being like the Qasamans was a good thing or a bad thing.

Jin sighed. "Merrick won't like this," she said. "Neither will Shahni Haafiz."

"Nor will probably anyone else on Qasama," Akim agreed soberly. "But my concern right now is for you, Jasmine Moreau. What do *you* think?"

Jin looked away from him. What *did* she think of Akim's plan?

Perhaps more importantly, what *could* she think with a tumor grinding inexorably away at her brain and mind? Merrick had commented earlier on her sense of logic, but she wasn't at all certain she could even trust her thought processes anymore. Especially not when it concerned something this potentially explosive. "You're the one putting your life on the line here," she pointed out instead. "You're the one who told me thirty years ago that on Qasama treason is punishable by death."

"Oh, they can't afford to execute me," he scoffed, waving a studiously nonchalant hand. "Not in the middle of a war. I'm far too important to them."

"That's an assumption," Jin warned. "And Shahni Haafiz in particular seems to be largely driven by pride."

Akim smiled sadly. "Aren't we all driven partially by pride?" he asked. "Even you, with your desire to warn your people of the Troft attack."

"That's not pride," Jin insisted.

"Isn't it?" Akim countered. "Tell me, how were you treated when you returned home from your last time on Qasama? Were you honored for your service in helping to eliminate a threat to our world? Or were you vilified for that action?"

Jin grimaced. "The latter, I'm afraid. In fact, my uncle lost his political position because of me. Is it that obvious?"

Akim shrugged. "You came here with only your son," he reminded her. "An honored and respected warrior would have answered the summons with a full contingent of warriors."

Jin stared at him. "Then you *did* send the message."

Akim shook his head. "Not I," he said. "Perhaps it came from one of the Shahni, though who that could be I can't even begin to guess. More likely the note was from Daulo Sammon, who is now simply lying about it. My point was that I was treated much the same way you were. On the surface I was honored for my role in eliminating Obolo Nardin's threat. But beneath that layer of gratitude lay a quiet anger and suspicion for my having cooperated with you. That distrust lasted long after most of the Shahni had forgotten even my name, let alone what specific crimes I was accused of committing."

He smiled tightly. "So I'm not a stranger to charges of treason, Jasmine Moreau. And if preventing my people from beating themselves mindlessly against an enemy they can't defeat is treason, then I'm willing to wear that badge."

"I admire your courage, Miron Akim," Jin said. "You rather remind me of my uncle that way."

"I'll take that as a high compliment," Akim said gravely. "Then you'll do this?"

"Yes," Jin said, a tingle running up through her. With that word, and that promise, the deal was made. There would be no going back. "You know the real irony here? Two weeks ago, back on Aventine, I was wishing something dramatic and dangerous would happen to our worlds. Something that would remind them that the Cobras are still a vital part of our society." She shook her head. "As the saying goes, one should be careful what one wishes for."

"We have that saying here, too." Akim took a deep breath and exhaled it in a tired-sounding sigh. "I'll escort you back to your room now. Get as much rest as you can."

Jin felt her stomach tighten. "It's set for tomorrow, then?"

"Barring any last-minute problems, yes," Akim confirmed. "The Djinn can be made ready in time, and delay only favors the invaders."

"I suppose so," Jin said. "Will I be seeing you again before then?"

Akim shook his head. "I'll be occupied all day with other matters."

And even if he wasn't, he probably wouldn't want to be seen with her anyway. "Understood," Jin said. "Good luck to you, Miron Akim."

"And to you, Jasmine Moreau," he said. He hesitated, then touched his fingers to his forehead and lips in the sign of respect. "Travel with God."

Ten minutes later, the nurse bade Jin good night and closed the door to her room. Listening to her heart pounding in her ears, she closed her eyes and tried to go to sleep. And wondered if she would ever see Miron Akim again.

CHAPTER TWENTY

The rooftop beneath Merrick was cold and hard, the warmth of the day's sunlight long gone. Above him, the Qasaman stars glittered in a cloudless sky, their patterns subtly different from the ones he'd grown up with on Aventine. Beside him, Zoshak and the other three Djinn of their squad huddled together in the radar and infrared shadow of the building's heat-plant chimney.

And directly in front of him, past the edge of the building's roof, was the Troft sentry ship, the same one Zoshak's team had attacked the previous day. Theoretically, or so Akim had said, now that the Trofts were alerted to possible attacks on their ships, one that had already repulsed an attack would be thought unlikely to be the target of a second one.

Theoretically.

"Two minutes," Zoshak murmured.

Merrick checked his nanocomputer's clock circuit. One minute and fifty-eight seconds, according to his count. "Check," he murmured.

"You ready?" Zoshak added, hunching his shoulders to resettle the heavy backpack he was wearing.

Merrick grimaced. Crouching in the middle of a Qasaman rooftop, dressed in a Qasaman Djinn combat suit—which the techs assured him would alter his infrared signature to something non-human, should the Trofts happen to pick up on him—surrounded by Qasaman warriors, preparing to take on an alien warship. Was anyone, he wondered, ever ready for something like that? "As ready as I'll ever be," he murmured back.

"This time we'll succeed," Zoshak said firmly. "I have no doubts. We'll show them that Qasamans—" He gave Merrick a lopsided smile. "That *humans* aren't to be trifled with."

"Let's hope they get the message," Merrick said, studying the shimmery mass of alien metal in the distance and doing one final ranging check. The wing supporting the weapons cluster was three meters above the level of the rooftop, plus another three from the edge.

An impossible jump for a normal human. Also well beyond the range of a Djinni in a combat suit, though Merrick doubted the Trofts knew enough about Djinn to have positioned their sentry ship that deliberately.

No problem at all for a Cobra.

Assuming, that is, that Merrick's borrowed combat suit didn't get in the way. The techs had also assured him that the built-in computer had been disconnected and that there would be no residual resistance or sluggishness from the suit's servos. But Merrick had had only limited opportunity to experiment with his new outfit between the day's practice sessions, and he couldn't quite shake the feeling that it might suddenly turn against him at the worst possible moment.

He peered across the rooftop again, where Siraj Akim and his squad were supposed to be waiting on the rooftop on the far side of the avenue, ready to provide cover fire for Merrick's team. Siraj had insisted on being included in this second attack on the sentry ship, and his father and the other team leaders had signed off on it, but that was yet another bad feeling Merrick couldn't shake. It had been barely a day since Siraj had led his original squad in the first disastrous attack on this same target, and Merrick wasn't at all sure Siraj was up to trying it again this soon.

Oddly enough, he had no such doubts about Zoshak. The Djinni crouched beside him seemed to have come out of that experience stronger, more determined, and somehow more optimistic than he'd gone into it. Siraj Akim, though, seemed to have come out darker and grimmer.

Merrick had seen that sort of response a few times before, in Cobras whose mistakes during a spine leopard hunt had gotten someone killed. Sometimes it took months or even years for them to fully snap out of it.

Which led to the even more interesting question of why Siraj was not only aboard, but had also been put in charge of Ghofl Khatir's team.

That one bothered Merrick a lot. True, Khatir had been decidedly unenthusiastic about having to work with the offworld Cobra, and it was possible that Miron Akim had decided he wasn't right for the job after all.

But for him to then replace Khatir with his own son was even more ominous. Was this Akim's version of the old get-back-behind the-wheel philosophy, that the best therapy for Siraj's dark mood would be to lead the charge on the return engagement?

Certainly Siraj seemed determined to do it right this time. Even after Merrick's team had been declared fully prepared, Siraj had insisted his own squad stay in the arena for more drills. The question was whether the Djinn was being driven by thoroughness, or obsession.

"One minute," Zoshak murmured.

Merrick took a deep breath and tried to put his concerns about Siraj out of his mind. It hadn't been his place to question Miron Akim's authority in these matters before, and it wasn't his place to be second-guessing him now. Long ago, Merrick's mother had trusted her life to Akim, and it had worked out all right. He would just have to hope that thirty years hadn't dulled the older man's judgment. Getting a fresh grip on the heavy rope bridge coiled up beneath his left arm, he watched his clock circuit count down to zero.

Exactly half a second later, the neighborhood exploded with the thunder of automatic gunfire.

It was an awesome display of firepower, particularly given that no one had any illusions that it would do any good against the sentry ship's thick armor. The entire point of the attack was to draw the Trofts' attention away from the small groups of men huddled here on the rooftops. The crucial question was whether or not the aliens would really let themselves be fooled this way.

And then, beneath the wing, Merrick saw the lasers and missile launchers of the weapons cluster swivel around and began spitting their deadly fire toward the impertinent humans who insisted on fighting against their new overlords.

"Five seconds," Zoshak announced tensely.

Merrick squeezed his hand into a fist. Over the years the Qasamans had slowly built up a profile of the basic Troft mind, and had concluded that it would take five seconds from the opening salvo of their counterattack until they were mentally and emotionally committed to that course of action.

But even five seconds was an eternity when you were at the business end of an enemy barrage. There were Qasamans behind each of those chattering machine guns, and the delay that would help protect Merrick's team would cost some of them their lives.

"Go!"

Merrick shoved himself out of his crouch, leaning forward into an all-out sprint toward the edge of the roof. The under-wing lasers were still firing at the other attackers, the Trofts apparently still unaware of this new threat closing in on their flank. Merrick kept going, waiting tensely for the moment when someone aboard the ship would suddenly notice him and bring one of those lasers to bear...

And then, sooner somehow than he'd expected, the edge of the roof loomed directly ahead. Gauging his distance, giving his stride one final tweaking, he ran to the very edge, and jumped. There was a tense half second as he soared toward the sentry ship, a half second of ballistic flight where no programmed reflexes could do him a damn bit of good if the Trofts locked up on him—

And then he was there, landing neatly on the center of the wing's two-by-three-meter expanse. He braked quickly to a halt, then spun around and hurled the coiled rope bridge back toward the rooftop. Zoshak was in position; catching the coil, he snapped out the bridge's anchoring spikes and jabbed them hard into the rooftop. Getting a firm grip on his own end, Merrick dropped onto his back, bracing one foot against a small ridge at the wing-tip and the other against the wing's trailing static discharge wick. He stretched the bridge tight and locked his arm servos in place.

And with a multiple thud that jarred him with each footstep, the rest of the Djinn ran single-file up the bridge and onto the wing.

Zoshak was the last one up. As he stepped past Merrick onto the wing, Merrick tossed his end of the bridge to one of the other Djinn, waiting beside him for that purpose, then bounded back to his feet and followed Zoshak toward the line where the wing joined the hull. Out of the corners of his eyes, he saw the remaining two Djinn climb up onto the crest of the hull and crouch down into guard positions.

Zoshak had his backpack off by the time Merrick arrived beside him. "Ready?" Merrick called over the noise of the gunfire.

Zoshak nodded. Lifting his left leg, Merrick aimed at the wing's inner edge and fired his antiarmor laser.

The sizzle of vaporizing metal was lost amid the cacophony still going on around them. But the shimmery flash as the laser cut into the wing was all Merrick needed to know that his guess had been correct. There was some sort of radar-absorption material coating the metal, a coating that was burning off with gratifying speed in the laser's focused heat.

The metal beneath it was another story. It was thick and strong, and as Merrick tracked his laser slowly along the edge of the wing he saw he was barely managing to carve a shallow groove. If the Qasamans' fancy acid didn't work, this whole exercise was going to be for nothing.

He was nearly finished when a flash of something caught the edge of his eye. He looked up—

To see a flicker of brilliant blue light coming from somewhere on the other side of the hull crest.

He felt his chest seize up. It was the Trofts over there. It had to be. They'd gotten up there somehow, and were coming for him and his team.

And the two Djinn up there who were supposed to be watching for that kind of flanking maneuver were just *standing* there?

"Move it!" he snapped to Zoshak. Without waiting for acknowl-edgment, he leaped up from the wing onto the crest. In the pulsating light from the laser he could see a handful of figures gathered on the other weapons wing. Cocking his ring fingers into laser firing position, wondering if he could get all of them before they took him down, he threw himself into a shallow dive onto the wing.

He was midway through his jump when it suddenly registered that the figure he could now see standing at the inner edge of the wing wasn't actually *holding* the laser that had caught his atten-tion. The beam was, instead, blasting downward from the figure's left foot...

Even with his mind frozen with stunned disbelief, his nanocom-puter was up to the task of landing him safely on the wing. But the figure had spotted him. It reacted instantly, throwing itself flat onto the metal surface and spinning around on its back to bring its laser to bear—

"Mom!" Merrick barked. "Don't shoot!"

"Merrick?" his mother's voice came from the Djinn-suited figure as she jerked her laser away from him. "What are you doing here?"

"That's *my* question," Merrick gritted out. "You're supposed to be on an operating table somewhere."

"I meant, what are you doing on this side of the ship?" Jin demanded as she scrambled back to her feet. Even in the dim light, Merrick could see that her face was pinched with pain from the quick-dodge maneuver his sudden appearance had forced her into.

"Get back over there," Siraj Akim snapped, coming up beside Merrick. "This operation depends on everyone following the plan as ordered."

"He's right," Jin seconded. "Get over there and let me finish up here."

"Right," Merrick said through clenched teeth as he stepped past her and hopped up onto the hull again. Like he could be expected to follow a plan that he didn't know half of. If he made it through this alive, he promised himself darkly, Miron Akim was going to have some *very* serious explaining to do.

Zoshak was crouching beside the groove Merrick had carved

in the wing when he made it back to his side of the ship. "What's
going on?" the Djinni asked.

"We've got company," Merrick growled. "Miron Akim sent my
mother along with Siraj Akim's squad to take out the other wing.
How's it going here?"

Zoshak gestured. "See for yourself."

Merrick peered down at the wing. Actually, there wasn't a lot
to be seen through the wispy white smoke pouring up from the
crack he'd cut through the metal's coating. Briefly, he ran through
his optical enhancers' various settings, but none of them did much
good against the smoke. "Any idea how we'll know when we're deep
enough to cut through the control cables?" he asked.

"When the weapons fall silent," Zoshak said, carefully dribbling
some more acid from his flask into the smoking groove. "We'll
get word—"

"Incoming aft!" one of the Djinn up on the hull snapped a
warning. An instant later he gurgled and collapsed as a barrage
of laser bolts riddled him from somewhere to their rear.

"Watch it!" Merrick shouted, dropping flat onto the wing and
pulling Zoshak down with him. At the other end of the ship a
dozen armored Trofts had appeared and were moving toward them
along the hull, their lasers spitting fire at the intruders.

Frantically, Merrick looked around. But there was literally no
cover anywhere to be had. Nowhere to hide, and only one place
to run. "Get out of here!" he snapped at Zoshak as he swiveled
around to bring his antiarmor laser to bear. "Leave the acid and
take the others down the bridge. I'll cover you."

"Yes, cover me," Zoshak snapped back as he set down the acid
flask and headed at a quick crawl toward the end of the wing and
the bridge waiting there.

Clenching his teeth, Merrick targeted the first three of the
approaching Trofts with his antiarmor laser. If the aliens had been
traveling single file, he might have been able to take all of them.
But they were bunched together, using each other's armored bodies as partial shields.

He could hear Zoshak doing something with the bridge now,

and only then did it occur to him that for the rest of the Djinn to escape someone was going to have to hold the end of the bridge for them. A laser shot grazed across his upper arm, and his nanocomputer took over, rolling him away from the shot as his own laser continued firing. From the far side of the crest he could see other flashes of blue light as his mother joined in the battle, and he sent up a quick prayer for her safety. The Djinn were firing, too, the flashes from their glove lasers fainter in comparison with either the Troft or Cobra weapons, and Merrick wondered if their efforts were doing anything more than distracting the aliens. There was a sudden movement at Merrick's side.

And he jerked reflexively as something long and dark and big went whipping across his line of sight, spinning in a flat arc toward the rear of the ship. He had just enough time to recognize it as their rope bridge before it slammed into the cluster of Trofts, sending their shots wildly in all directions as it wrapped them in a tangle of rope and wood.

"Attack!" Zoshak shouted. He leaped past Merrick onto the hull, his glove lasers blazing at the Trofts, the two remaining Djinn of his team right behind him.

Merrick leaped to his feet, hesitating as he tried to decide whether to join the mad rush or stay here and try to pick off more of the attackers. But the Trofts were pushing their way free of the bridge and starting to fire again, and there was no more time for thinking or planning. Gauging the distance, he bent his knees and jumped.

He had just left the wing when a brilliant laser flash lanced across the space he'd vacated, blasting a cloud of metal splinters from the wing's trailing edge. Merrick bit out a curse as he glanced down at the smoking metal, wondering where that shot had come from. A second later he hit the hull crest, landing two meters in front of Zoshak and the other Djinn and barely four meters away from the approaching Trofts. A half-dozen alien lasers tracked toward him—

Their shots went wild as Merrick fired a full-power burst from his sonic. He fired again, staggering them back, then thrust his right hand forward and activated his arcthrower.

The lightning bolt caught the lead Troft squarely in the torso, throwing him backward into the two directly behind him. Merrick shifted aim and fired the arcthrower again, this time catching one of the Trofts' lasers and shattering it into a burst of shrapnel.

He was lining up on one of the other Trofts when a laser shot caught him in his stomach.

For that first frozen second there was no pain, only the horrifying realization that his luck had finally run out. His knees buckled as the shock swept through him, and he felt himself falling as if in slow motion. He heard a voice shout his name as he landed hard on his knees, and from somewhere behind him he saw a sudden barrage of brilliant blue laser shots flashing across the remaining Trofts, throwing clouds of vaporized metal from their armor and twisting and throwing them into little piles of death.

And then, suddenly, the pain was there, rushing through him like a flash flood in a mountain arroyo. He gasped, gripping his stomach with both hands, feeling himself swaying as his eyes dimmed and he started to fall over.

He was headed face-first toward the hull when a hand came from behind him and grabbed him beneath his left arm in a steadying grip. A second hand took his other arm, and suddenly he was being lifted upright again, swaying a little as the two people made a mad dash along the hull. Dimly through the pain he saw an open hatchway with another Troft helmet just emerging, and then a gray-suited figure leaped over him from behind and a blue laser bolt sent the Troft tumbling out of sight. The figure stopped beside the hatchway, sending a flurry of bolts down into the opening as Merrick's handlers hustled him past. Through his wavering vision he could see the sentry ship's aft wings looming ahead...

With a jolt, he snapped back to consciousness and found himself sitting in the middle of one of the aft wings. Crouching in front of him was Siraj Akim, sorting quickly through a set of small hypos. Behind him, Zoshak was crouching beside the hull end of the wing, more white smoke drifting around him as he poured acid into the metal. "What—?" Merrick croaked.

"Just sit still," his mother's taut voice came from behind him, and only then did he realize that her grip on his upper arms was what was holding him upright. "Siraj Akim is trying to stabilize you."

Merrick turned his head to look toward the forward wings, wincing as he spotted the motionless bodies lying there. "Where are the others?"

"Most gave their lives for Qasama," Siraj said grimly as he carefully stuck the needle into Merrick's side. "I've already ordered the survivors away."

"The Trofts started firing at us with the weapons clusters under these aft wings," Jin explained. "Must have done some quick recalibrating—usually you can't fire on your own ship that way."

"They seem to have managed it just fine," Merrick said, knowing that she was talking mostly to distract him. Or to distract herself.

He focused on Siraj's grim expression as the Djinni selected another hypo. Yet more Djinn deaths on the young man's conscience. He wondered how Siraj was feeling, but his mind didn't seem to be working very well. But at least the pain was fading. "Did we take the ship?" he asked. "I mean the ground troops. Did they get inside?"

"I don't think so," Jin said. "And it's about to be too late. You feel that?"

With an effort, Merrick concentrated what little mind he seemed to have left. "The vibration?" he asked.

"Right," Jin said. "The Trofts are about to—there we go."

Merrick blinked as the cityscape around them suddenly shifted. The sentry ship they were huddled on was lifting off the pavement on its gravity lifts, rising above the level of the surrounding buildings and starting to turn toward the spaceport.

"So once again we've failed," Zoshak said bitterly. "More lives lost for nothing."

"At least we chased them away," Merrick said, a fresh ache flooding through him at Zoshak's words. He tried to think of what they might have done differently, how they might have pulled out the victory that Zoshak and Siraj deserved and the Qasamans so desperately needed. But his mind was drifting. "Sends them a message, anyway."

Zoshak hissed between his teeth. "You'll forgive me if I don't find that message worth the cost."

"You are forgiven, Djinni Zoshak," Siraj said.

Merrick frowned, trying to focus his increasingly bleary eyes on the other. Siraj was actually *smiling*. A grim, vicious smile, but a smile nonetheless. "You all right?" Merrick asked.

"I'm quite well, thank you," Siraj said. "You speak of a message, Merrick Moreau. And you, Djinni Zoshak, speak of cost." Dramatically, he pointed toward the street below. "Behold."

Merrick turned his head. In the center of the market place that their particular sentry ship had been overlooking, a large section of pavement had opened up to reveal a dark, deep pit. Too big a hole for individual soldiers, his sluggish mind realized, but also with no visible ramp for ground vehicles.

Which left only... "Mom?" he croaked.

And caught his breath as a helicopter shot out of the opening. A slender helicopter, lean and deadly-looking as an Arkon's dragonfly, black and gray in the reflected light, clusters of weapons visible beneath its own set of stubby support wings as it climbed rapidly into the sky. Hard on its tail was a second gunship, and a third, and a fourth, and a fifth.

Behind him, Merrick heard his mother gasp. "*SkyJos?*" she said.

"Indeed," Siraj confirmed, and there was no mistaking the satisfaction in his voice. "Trapped uselessly in their underground hangar until *we* drove their unsuspecting guardian away."

The words were barely out of his mouth when the SkyJos opened fire.

The earlier diversionary attack on the sentry ship had been loud. But it was nothing compared to this. Merrick gazed out across at the city, wishing he could close his ears against the hammering as the SkyJos fired lasers and heavy missiles and multiple hailstorms of armor-piercing rounds at their invaders.

The Troft sentry ships didn't have a chance. Caught on the ground, their weaponry designed for repulsing ground-based attacks, they began to disintegrate beneath the pounding. A few of the more distant ones made it off the ground, but by the time they did, other hidden nests around the city, now likewise freed from their enemy guardians, were sending their own fleets of SkyJos to join in the attack.

Away to the north, Merrick could see the first signs of movement from the airfield as some of the larger Troft ships tried to beat the approaching Qasamans into the air. One of the heavy ships succeeded in its attempts, rising above the buildings and picking up speed as it turned toward the nearest group of incoming SkyJos.

An instant later it was caught in a terrifying pillar of fire as the control tower it was passing over disintegrated in a thunderous explosion. The crippled ship veered violently sideways, tried to back up, then crashed to the ground. From the multiple flashes of secondary explosions, Merrick guessed it had probably crashed on top of some of the other Troft ships.

He turned back to Siraj. "You're right," he slurred through suddenly numb lips. "That was one hell of a message."

The last thing he remembered as Siraj's face blurred and then faded into darkness was the sight of a pair of SkyJos coming up behind Siraj, their lowered grab nets fluttering in the breeze.

CHAPTER TWENTY-ONE

The deep-forest village was quiet and dark as the SkyJo settled into the center square. "Where is everyone?" Jin asked as the pilot cut the engines.

"He's waiting," the other said tersely, pointing to one of the larger houses bordering on the square. "You go alone."

Jin unstrapped from her jumpseat, keying her optical enhancers as she did so. There were two men flanking the building's front entrance, standing with the stiffness of military guards. "Understood," she said, turning for a final look at Merrick. His eyes were closed, and even in the dim light she could see that his face was unnaturally pale. But his chest was rising and falling rhythmically, and the stretcher's readouts were showing a cautious stability in his other vital signs.

"He's waiting," the pilot repeated.

"Go ahead," Zoshak said. "Ifrit Akim and I will wait with him. Go and find out what this is all about."

"All right," Jin said, wondering what exactly she was going to tell the two of them when she came back. According to the plan, she and Merrick were to have been brought out here alone, not with a pair of Qasaman hitchhikers in tow. Certainly not with Miron Akim's own son along for the ride.

But there was nothing for it now but to play it through and

hope Akim was able to improvise. Opening the gunship's side door, she stepped out onto the wet grass and started toward the house.

From the air, the village had looked deserted. From ground level, it looked dead. There were no lights showing anywhere that Jin could see, and the only sound aside from the light wind rustling through the trees and bushes was the faint whooshing from the second SkyJo flying high cover above them. Even her infrareds were unable to pick up human heat sources in any of the buildings except the one she was heading for.

Had Miron Akim cleared out the entire village for this?

One of the two door guards stirred as she approached. "He's waiting," he said, leaning over and pushing open the door. "First room on the right."

"Thank you." Stepping between them, Jin walked into the house and turned into the indicated doorway.

And stopped abruptly in her tracks. "Good evening, Jasmine Moreau," Moffren Omnathi said gravely from the depths of an armchair in the center of the room. "How nice to see you again."

It took Jin two tries to find her voice. "And you as well, Advisor Omnathi," she said between frozen lips, her heartbeat thudding suddenly in her chest.

"Yet you seem surprised to see me," Omnathi said calmly. "Almost as if you were expecting someone else."

"Indeed," Jin said as calmly as she could. So it was over. Akim's plan, and her own hopes. Omnathi had found out about it, and it was all over. "Tell me, what have you done with Miron Akim?"

"I?" Omnathi asked, as if surprised she would even think such a thing. "I do nothing to anyone. Surely you know that."

"Of course," Jin said. "My mistake. You merely give the orders. Others carry them out."

"Yes," Omnathi said. It was a simple statement of fact, unencumbered by either embarrassment or pride. "But do not concern yourself," he continued. "As I'm sure Miron Akim himself told you, he is far too valuable to be disciplined."

"I'm relieved to hear that," Jin said. As if she actually believed it. "Do my son and I stand in similar positions?"

"You made an agreement with the Shahni," he reminded her, his voice going a shade darker. "Your nanocomputer for the chance to warn your people of the impending Troft attack. Despite that agreement, you and Miron Akim conspired to send both you and your son away without fulfilling your side of the bargain."

"Yes, I know what was said and done," Jin said, suddenly tired of playing games. "Whatever you're going to do to us, get on with it."

"Please; indulge me," Omnathi said gravely. "I lay out the facts solely to impress upon you the understanding that I know everything there is to know about the path you and Miron Akim have chosen." He paused. "So that you will know that I speak from full understanding when I tell you I agree with that path."

Jin's bewilderment must have shown in her face, because Omnathi actually smiled. "You doubt my sincerity?" he asked. "Or merely my sanity?"

"I'm ... confused," Jin managed. Was this some sort of cruel joke? "If you disagreed with the original deal ...?"

"Why did I not speak up?" Omnathi sighed. "Because despite the firm belief of our people, the Shahni's decisions are not always wise. In this case, they completely failed to understand the realities of our situation. Even if I held your nanocomputer in my hand right now, it would take months to decipher the programming and weeks or months more to construct enough of them for our needs. After that it would be months before we learned how to create the fiber control network and the bone laminae, to say nothing of the necessary techniques for implanting the servos."

"None of which you've been able to do in thirty years of trying," Jin murmured. "Miron Akim told me."

"In fact, it has been far more than thirty years," Omnathi said. "We have been trying to reconstruct your weaponry ever since your people's first visit here six decades ago. Even with your wholehearted assistance, I fear we would still fail in our attempts."

His gaze drifted away from her, his eyes focused on infinity. "No, Jasmine Moreau," he said quietly. "The promise of your nanocomputer, even offered in good faith, is a false hope. The Trofts were handed a terrible defeat tonight, and indeed many of them have fled from our world in disarray. But if this is indeed a war against all humankind, they will not stay away for long. They will return, more cautious and more determined. And we will have no further surprises with which to shake them."

His eyes came back to her. "We can survive for a season. But barring a miracle, ultimate victory cannot and will not be ours. Not alone. Not without aid from your people. If you fail to fulfill your promise to Miron Akim, Qasama will die."

Jin swallowed hard. Never before had she seen a Qasaman leader stripped of his pride and bluster and supreme confidence in himself. It was eerie, and more than a little unnerving.

But as she looked into Omnathi's eyes, she felt her fatigue and uncertainty hardening into a brittle, ice-cold resolve. Behind the cultural arrogance were real, genuine human beings. Human beings worth saving. "I won't fail, Moffren Omnathi," she promised him quietly "Whatever help I can find, I *will* bring back to you."

"Then I will trust you." Omnathi smiled again, but this time the smile was edged with sadness. "For indeed, I have no choice."

Placing his hands on the armrests, he pushed himself carefully to his feet. "Come. Your departure is at hand."

He walked past Jin out into the hallway and turned toward the rear of the house. "Where are the rest of the villagers?" Jin asked as she moved up beside him.

"The women and children have moved to nearby mines or ravines for safety," Omnathi said. "The rest are out in the forest, either hunting wayward Trofts or guarding the transport we have captured for your use."

Jin pursed her lips. "You *do* know, don't you, that I don't know how to fly a Troft ship?"

"That is being taken care of as we speak." Omnathi stopped at a door and gestured to it. "Please; after you."

Jin opened the door and stepped through into a large, brightly lit dining room, to find herself facing an extraordinary sight. Seated at a long dining table was a bedraggled-looking Troft, wearing a standard, unarmored leotard. Behind him stood two Qasamans, a young man and woman, the former wearing a Djinn combat suit, both of them peering unblinkingly at the alien's every move. Off to the side was a third Qasaman, this one a middle-aged man. The latter looked up as Jin and Omnathi entered, but none of the others in the room seemed to even notice them. Omnathi flicked his fingers at the older Qasaman, who nodded and turned back to the Troft. [An attack, it comes from behind,] he said in cattertalk.

The Troft's hands reached to the table in front of him, his fingers darting back and forth across the smooth wooden surface. [A radio challenge, it requires a response,] the Qasaman said.

The Troft swiveled around in his seat and again drummed his fingers, this time on a different part of the table. Like he was punching actual buttons, Jin thought, and operating an actual control board.

Which was, she realized abruptly, exactly what he thought he was doing.

She looked sharply at Omnathi. "The pilot of the transport we have obtained," the other murmured. "He believes himself to be in his control room."

Jin looked at the two young Qasamans, a shiver running up her back. And even as the middle-aged man manipulated his drugged Troft puppet, the two observers were watching his every move, their own drugged minds recording every nuance of his actions.

"You do not approve?" Omnathi asked.

With an effort, Jin pushed the shivers away. "It'll get us home," she said. "That's all that matters."

Out of the corner of her eye, she saw Omnathi nod. "Good," he murmured. "They will be finished soon. Let us go examine your vehicle."

The Troft transport was parked about a hundred meters from the village, nestled into a small clearing that fit it so well that Jin suspected the trees had been cut down specifically for the purpose. "There were nearly a dozen razorarms in the cargo bay when we took the vehicle," Omnathi said as the two of them walked through a sentry line of grim-faced villagers. "We assumed you wouldn't wish to be bothered with their care and feeding during the voyage home and therefore released them back into the woods."

Jin nodded. It might have been smarter to leave the predators aboard in case they ran into an advance ship near Aventine whose crew decided to be suspicious and examine their cargo. But it was too late to do anything about that now. "How big a crew will we have?" she asked as Omnathi led the way through the open hatchway.

"Only the two you saw back there," Omnathi said. "The woman is Rashida Vil, the man is Ghofl Khatir."

"Who's also a Djinni," Jin murmured.

"Obviously," Omnathi said. "Interestingly, he was slated to lead tonight's attack on the sentry ship. The attack you weren't originally scheduled to take part in," he added offhandedly.

Jin swallowed. That had also been part of the deal she'd worked out with Miron Akim, something to give the attack better odds of success. Was there anything about her private conversations, she wondered, that Omnathi didn't know? "What happened?" she asked.

"Nothing mysterious," Omnathi assured her. "Miron Akim learned he was a qualified pilot and so pulled him off the attack so that he could be sent here to prepare for your flight to Aventine."

And put in his own son as second squad leader instead. Jin had wondered about that, especially so soon after Siraj's defeat the previous day. "And the young woman?"

"Rashida Vil is also a qualified pilot, and is furthermore fluent in the Troft language," Omnathi said. "That will be helpful if there are any sentries still in position over Qasama who will need the pilot's pass codes and clearances. As to the rest of your fellow travelers, I presume you already know them."

Jin frowned. Fellow travelers, plural? "Isn't it just my son and me?"

"Hardly," Omnathi said. "You didn't really think Miron Akim would allow you to leave Qasama without an escort, did you?"

Jin grimaced. No, actually, she shouldn't have thought that. "Let me guess," she said. "His son Siraj is coming."

"Correct," Omnathi confirmed. "And as long as Djinni Zoshak is here anyway, he might as well also accompany you."

"There's really no need for you to send them," Jin said. The thought of taking a pair of Qasaman Djinn into the middle of Capitalia... "You know as well as I do that the treatment I received this morning only temporarily shrunk my tumor. If I don't come back to Qasama I'll still have no more than three months to live."

"I have no doubts that you'll return," Omnathi assured her calmly. "If for no other reason than to get your son."

Jin jerked her head around. "We had a deal, Moffren Omnathi," she bit out.

"A deal I was fully prepared to carry out," Omnathi said. "But the situation has changed. Merrick Moreau is far too badly injured to accompany you now. He needs treatment, and he needs it here."

A red haze of fury seemed to drop down in front of Jin's eyes. No wonder Omnathi had been so willing to honor Akim's deal and let her leave. He'd known all along that he had a hostage to her good behavior. "And if during this treatment his nanocomputer just happens to fall out into someone's hands?"

"Did I spend precious minutes of my life explaining my reasoning to you for nothing?" Omnathi countered, his voice going cold. "I have already told you I do not want his nanocomputer. Allow me to make it even clearer: I will not take his nanocomputer. Based on his performance this night, I am far more interested in seeing him healed and fighting again on our side."

Jin glared at him, the red haze slowly fading away. He could be lying, of course. But the logic held true.

And if he *was* lying, her tired brain and eyes would never pick up on it anyway. "He'll fight for you," she said, turning away. "Provided the Shahni allow him to do so."

"I will deal with the Shahni," Omnathi promised grimly. "As Miron Akim said to you once, victory is more important than honor."

He took a deep breath. "Let us return to the SkyJo. You may say your final farewells to your son, and I shall instruct Djinni Zoshak and Ifrit Akim on their new mission." His lip twitched. "Their reactions, I expect, will be most interesting."

"Father?" Fadil Sammon called gently.

For a moment the man lying on the hospital bed made no reaction. Then, to Fadil's relief, Daulo Sammon's eyes opened a bit. "Fadil?" he murmured.

Fadil breathed a quiet sigh of relief. At least his father was lucid this evening. With the array of healing drugs coursing through his veins, that wasn't always the case. "I came to say good-bye, Father," he said. "I'm going off for a while, and I don't know when I'll be back again to see you."

He waited patiently while his father's sluggish mind processed the words. "Where is it you're going?" the elder Sammon asked, frowning. "Back to war?"

"Not exactly," Fadil said, wondering if he should tell his father that the Trofts had left. Probably not, he decided regretfully. The invaders would be back—everyone he'd spoken to agreed on that. Best not to confuse the issue while his father wasn't thinking straight. "But it is related to our defense," he continued. "Anyway, I just wanted to say good-bye, and to tell you that the doctors say you're doing well. Another two or three weeks and you should be completely healed."

Daulo smiled weakly. "Three more weeks, is it?" he murmured. "I must have been hurt more badly than I thought."

Fadil swallowed hard. He'd been hurt, all right. In fact, he'd nearly died in that first failed attack against the Trofts. Even now, there was some serious reconstruction going on within his right shoulder and arm. "There were others hurt worse than you who are also going to be fine," he assured his father. "And before that you'll be well enough for me to take you home." Assuming, he added silently, that the Trofts didn't launch their next attack before then.

"Good." Daulo's eyes flicked upward to the feeding tube attached to his arm. "I do so dislike hospital food."

"I'll get you home as soon as I can," Fadil promised. "Until then, you just rest, do what they tell you, and concentrate on getting well." He looked at the bedside clock. "I need to go now, Father. Farewell."

"And to you, my son," Daulo said. His left arm twitched, and Fadil reached down to take his father's hand. "Whatever you're doing, I know you'll make our family proud."

"I'll do my best," Fadil promised. Giving his father's hand a final squeeze, he turned and walked away.

Daulo's breathing had settled into the steady rhythm of sleep even before Fadil had made it out of earshot.

Miron Akim was waiting in the treatment center's anteroom when Fadil arrived. "You said your farewells?" Akim asked, gesturing Fadil to the chair in front of him.

"To my father, yes," Fadil said, settling gingerly into the chair. This was it, he knew, an unpleasant tingling sensation running up his spine. This was his last chance to turn back. "I was wondering if I might also be permitted to say good-bye to Merrick Moreau and his mother."

Akim shook his head. "Unfortunately, neither is available at the moment."

"Because the Shahni have sent them home?" Fadil asked.

For the first time in their admittedly brief acquaintance Akim actually seemed taken aback. "Why do you say such an outrageous thing?" he asked cautiously.

"Because I've noticed their absence these past few days," Fadil said. "Yet there's no report of their deaths, which would certainly be on public record with so distinguished a pair of warriors."

"Perhaps they've simply been assigned to a different area," Akim suggested.

"Perhaps," Fadil said. "But I note also the absence of Carsh Zoshak and your son Siraj Akim. From that I deduce that Merrick Moreau and his mother didn't simply flee Qasama, but have been sent back to their home for some other purpose."

Akim eyed him in silence for a few heartbeats. "They're off Qasama," he conceded at last. "That's all you need to know." He raised his eyebrows slightly. "It's also far more than you *should* know."

"I understand," Fadil said. "Please forgive any impertinence. I mention it only to remind you that I *am* able to think deeply and logically, and am therefore worthy to participate in this experiment."

"An experiment which may seriously and permanently damage you," Akim reminded him in turn. "I'm required by law to confirm your acceptance of that risk this one final time."

Fadil suppressed a grimace. The drugs and medicines the Qasaman scientists and doctors had so painstakingly developed over the centuries were highly useful, both to individuals and to the society as a whole. But each of those drugs also carried its own set of risks, risks that increased in direct proportion to its power. Fadil's family had historically chosen to err on the side of caution, avoiding all but necessary medical drugs.

But Qasama was at war, and the alien antipersonnel missiles targeted the very radio signals that her defenders needed to coordinate both attack and defense. Somewhere, Fadil knew, there had to be a solution to that problem. But so far none of the techs had been able to come up with one.

It was time to try something more drastic. And since the true experts were far too valuable to risk this way, someone else would have to step up to that duty. Someone who was otherwise expendable to the war effort.

Someone like Fadil Sammon.

"I understand fully the risks inherent in the use of chemicals of mental stimulation," he said, quoting the words of the formal agreement. "I accept those risks, and am prepared to proceed."

"Then proceed you will," Akim said. Standing up, he opened the door to the treatment room proper and gestured.

Fadil stood up, feeling a slight trembling in his arms and legs. The die was cast, and there was no turning back. Whatever happened over the next few hours and days, whether his gamble succeeded or failed, he would willingly bear the cost.

And win or lose, at least the people of Qasama would never again look quite so condescendingly upon villagers. That alone made the risk worthwhile.

Squaring his shoulders, he followed Akim through the doorway.

CHAPTER TWENTY-TWO

"One minute," Khatir called from the pilot's seat.

"Acknowledged," Jin said. It was an unnecessary announcement, really, given that all five of the ship's complement had been gathered here in the transport's command room for the past half hour.

Surreptitiously, she looked around at each of the others, wondering what was going on behind all those dark eyes. Carsh Zoshak had taken the news of his new assignment very well, almost eagerly. But over the course of the past five days he'd grown quieter and more distant. Perhaps he was having second thoughts.

Siraj Akim didn't need to have second thoughts. It had been clear from the beginning that his first thoughts were bad enough. The fact that it was his own father who'd come up with this gamble was probably at the heart of his attitude, and Jin had never quite decided whether Moffren Omnathi signing off on it had made Siraj's discomfiture better or worse. Still, he was polite enough, and followed Jin's orders without question or argument.

Ghofl Khatir, in contrast, had not only started the mission eagerly but had managed to hold on to that cheery outlook. Talkative by nature, he nevertheless seldom spoke to Jin herself unless required to by his duties. Her best guess was that he was mostly excited by the chance to actually fly a starship, even if it was one his own people hadn't designed or built.

And then there was the young woman Rashida Vil. She said little to anyone, maintaining a rigid professionalism at all times that Jin sometimes found almost painful to watch. Perhaps as a female pilot from a male-dominated world she felt she had to continually prove herself and her abilities.

It was a challenge, and an attitude, with which Jin could definitely sympathize.

"Here we go," Khatir said, resettling his hands on the control yoke.

Jin grimaced. Because looming on the horizon was the biggest wild card of all: the leaders and people of the Cobra Worlds. What would they say, she wondered uneasily, when she landed a stolen Troft vehicle full of Qasamans on the Capitalia landing field and asked for help? Would they ignore her? Would they cry treason and try to lock her up? They'd nearly done that the last time she'd come back from Qasama, and she hadn't brought any visitors with her that time.

Or would they actually see the logic and humanity in her plea?

On the control board, the timer ran down and the stars burst into view through the command room viewport. A hundred thousand kilometers directly in front of them, a glorious visual symphony in white and blue and brown, was Jin's home.

It was only as she tore her eyes from the planet itself that she saw the ring of ships floating in a lazy orbital ring above Aventine's equator.

The Troft attack had already begun.

For a long minute no one spoke. Jin stared at the fleet, her heart aching, her stomach wanting to be sick. It was over. Aventine had been invaded, and her mission was over before it had even begun. There would be no help for Qasama from here. The people of the Cobra Worlds were in their own war for survival.

Beside her, Zoshak stirred. "What now?" he asked.

"We go back," Siraj said before Jin could find an answer. "It was a fool's notion to hope for any help from here anyway. We go back, and we fight the invaders with whatever strength we have, until that strength is gone."

"You can't win a war of attrition," Jin told him, trying desperately to think. But her brain was as frozen as her heart. "Neither can we. We have to come up with something else."

"Like what?" Siraj countered. "Unless you're prepared to run that gauntlet—"

"Signal!" Khatir snapped, swinging around to the communications part of his board. "We're being hailed."

"I'll take it," Rashida said, her voice glacially calm. "What do you want me to say?"

Jin pursed her lips. "Let's start by finding out what they want," she told the younger woman as Khatir half turned in his seat and tossed translator earphones to Zoshak and Siraj. "As far as they're concerned we're just the latest in a long line of transports coming from Qasama."

"Should I transmit the clearance codes we used to leave Qasama?" Rashida asked.

"Let's wait until someone asks," Jin said. "There might be different codes for landing on Aventine that we didn't get."

Rashida nodded and keyed the transmitter. [The signal, it is acknowledged,] she said in flawless cattertalk. [Assistance, how may we render it?]

[Your cargo bay, analysis shows it to be empty,] a Troft voice came back. [The predators, why have you none?]

Jin winced. So the Troft ship out there had decided to take the time to give their harmless little transport a deep scan. "Tell them—"

Rashida silenced her with an upraised hand. [The predators, all died en route,] she said. [A disease, it was apparently brought aboard.]

Zoshak nudged Jin's side. "How good are these sensors of theirs?" he murmured. "Will they be able to tell we're not Trofts?"

"I don't know," Jin murmured back. "Probably depends on how much effort they're willing to put into this."

[The message, it is understood,] the Troft replied. There was a short pause. [Jasmine Jin Moreau, is there word from her?]

Jin felt her heart seize up in her chest. So it really *was* over. The ship had scanned them and had spotted the humans. Now, they wouldn't even have the option of returning to Qasama.

And then, suddenly the obvious fact struck her. *How had the Trofts come up with her name?*

She frowned, peering at the display. The only ship close enough for that kind of scan appeared to be a simple freighter, not any kind of warship. More than that, as near as she could tell from the cattertalk curlies on the hull, it was not only a freighter, but a *Tlossie* freighter. A ship from one of the Cobra Worlds' longtime trading partners.

Abruptly, she realized that all four Qasamans were looking expectantly at her. "What kind of signal are they using?" she asked quietly.

Khatir took a quick look at his board. "It looks like a tight beam."

[Jasmine Jin Moreau, is there word from her?] the Troft asked again.

Jin braced herself. [Jasmine Jin Moreau, it is I,] she called toward the microphone.

If the Troft in the other ship was surprised to hear from Jin herself, it didn't show in his voice. [The news from Qasama, what is it?] he asked.

The news from Qasama? What in the Worlds did he mean by that? [The battle, it has been won,] Jin said cautiously.

[Yet the war, it has been lost?]

[The war, it is not yet over,] Jin corrected.

There was a long silence. [Then our mission, it has failed,] the Troft said sadly.

"What mission?" Siraj muttered.

[Your pardon, I crave it,] Jin said. [Your mission, what is its purpose and meaning?]

[The mission, it is of no matter,] the Troft said. [Its failure, that is all I need know.]

Jin felt her mouth fall open as the last piece finally fell into place. [The message, from *you* it came,] she said. [To Qasama, you wished me to go.]

"*They* sent you the message?" Siraj demanded, his eyes wide with disbelief.

"Apparently so," Jin said as it all suddenly made sense. "Disguised to look like it came from someone on Qasama, of course, in case it was intercepted."

"But why?" Zoshak demanded.

Jin lifted a finger and switched back to cattertalk. [Your mission, I understand it now,] she said. [War with Aventine, your demesne-lord does not wish. Yet a stand against the attacking demesnes, he dare not take alone. A victory against them, one must first exist.]

"I'll be damned," Khatir murmured.

[The truth, you speak it,] the Troft said. [A stand, other demesne-lords wish to make. But a stand against a victorious army, one cannot be made.]

[The reality, I understand it,] Jin said grimly. [But hope, do not abandon it.] "Djinn Khatir, what's our fuel situation?"

Again, Khatir studied his displays. "We're down about one-third," he reported.

Jin did a quick calculation. Probably enough, but better to err on the safe side. [Refueling, our transport needs,] she said. [Extra fuel, can you supply it?]

There was a pause. [To return to Qasama, enough exists.]

[The truth, you speak it,] Jin agreed. [But Qasama, we do not yet return there. Extra fuel, can you supply it?]

[This fuel, to what use?]

Jin smiled tightly. [Victory against the attacking demesne-lords, its use will be.]

There was another pause. Jin could feel the eyes of the Qasamans on her; deliberately, she kept her own gaze on the Troft ship on the display. [Your course, you will hold it,] the Troft said at last. [To your side, we will come.]

[Our gratitude, you have it,] Jin said. [Your arrival, we will await it.]

There was a click from the speaker. Jin gestured, and Rashida flicked off their own transmitter. "Is this making of rash promises a general trait of your people?" Khatir asked mildly. "Or is it just you personally?"

"I've made no rash promises," Jin assured him. "To anyone," she added, looking at Siraj Akim. "I promised Miron Akim that I would return with help. And I will." She gestured toward the besieged world hanging in space in the distance. "I simply came to the wrong place to get it."

"I thought Aventine was the capital and most powerful of your worlds," Akim said, frowning.

"It is," Jin said, nodding. "It has one and a quarter million inhabitants, about eighty-five percent of our total population. If the Trofts have any tactical sense at all, this is where they'll throw the bulk of their forces."

"Obviously, they have," Khatir said, waving at the distant ring of ships.

"But there's another world out there," Jin continued. "A world named Caelian, with a little over four thousand colonists. Tactically and strategically speaking, it's a completely insignificant place. I can't imagine any competent military commander putting more than a token force there, if that much."

"And you expect all four thousand to rise to our aid?" Siraj scoffed.

"Not at all," Jin said. "The point is that among those four thousand colonists are seven hundred Cobras."

And suddenly, the atmosphere in the control room was charged with electricity. The Qasamans sat up a little straighter, flicking glances back and forth between them, and Jin could see in their faces a sense of understanding and a freshly renewed hope.

As well as a freshly renewed fear.

She couldn't blame them. They had grown up hating and fearing the Cobra Worlds, the people in general and the Cobras in particular. Now, suddenly, their leaders had ordered that those very Cobras be asked for help.

Would the ultimate result of that plea be Qasama's salvation? Or was it a pact with the devil that would lead to their ruin?

It was a question none of them could answer. Including Jin herself.

Typically, it was Khatir who broke the silence. "So what are we doing here?" he asked. "Let's get this ship fueled, and go find some demon warriors."

"I just hope some of them will be willing to come to Qasama to fight," Siraj added doubtfully.

"I know at least one who will," Jin told him, a sudden pang in her heart. "My husband is there. Along with my daughter."

Siraj snorted. "*One* Cobra? Yes, that will certainly bring us victory."

Zoshak stirred. "If he fights as do Jasmine and Merrick Moreau," he said quietly, "it very well might."

"There will be more," Jin promised.

And she meant it. Whatever it took, she *would* assemble a fighting force to take back with them.

Because the Tlossies were right. They needed a clear-cut human victory if they were to have any hope of rallying support among the other Troft demesnes. From the number of sentry ships encircling Aventine, it was clear that victory wasn't going to be achieved there. Not any time soon.

Perhaps that was only fitting. The war had begun on Qasama. One way or another, it was going to end there.

COBRA
GUARDIAN

CHAPTER ONE

The first indication that it was going to be one of those days was when the cooker burned the leftover pizza Lorne Broom had planned to have for breakfast.

"Oh, for—" he choked off the curse before it could get out past his throat, old habits of propriety kicking in as he glared at the cooker. This was the third time this month the stupid thing had gone gunnybags on him, and with everything else weighing on his shoulders he had precious little patience left for balky appliances.

Or, better even than a curse, he could deal with the balky cooker once and for all. A single, full-power fingertip laser blast into the cooker's core would turn the thing into a conversation-piece paperweight. A shot with his arcthrower would send the cooker beyond paperweight status into a slagged heap that even the revivalist Earth artist Salvador Dali would have been proud of. Even better, a blast from his antiarmor laser—

Lorne took a deep breath, forcing down the surge of frustration. A blast from his antiarmor laser would not only blow a hole through the cooker, but also through the kitchen wall, the wall behind that, and possibly the wall beyond that into the building corridor. At that point, he could say good-bye not only to the cooker, but to his damage deposit as well.

With a sigh, he unloaded the burned pizza and pushed the cooker back into its niche at the back of the counter. The depressing fact was that Cobra salaries had been on a steady downward slide for the past two years, and even with the extra hazard pay he got out here at the edge of Aventine's expansion area, he simply couldn't afford to dump uncooperative appliances. Not when there was still a chance they could be repaired.

Unfortunately, he couldn't afford to dump a ruined meal, either.

He picked away as much of the blackened cheese as he could without giving up on the meal entirely. Then, taking the plate over to the breakfast nook, he keyed his computer for the news feed and sat down to eat.

The news, as usual, was right up there with the quality of his meal. The late-year election season was heating up, and puff ads by incumbents and hopefuls were starting to crowd out the usual selection of business and service commercials. Viminal, the latest addition to the Cobra Worlds, announced that its population had just passed the twenty-two thousand mark, and Governor Conzjuaraz was taking the opportunity to remind Aventinians that there was a world's worth of good land out there going cheap.

And right at the end, almost as an afterthought, came a report that there'd been another spine leopard attack at the edge of a settlement out past Mayring in Willaway Province. Five of the big predators had been involved, killing three settlers and injuring eight others. The local Cobras were already on the hunt in hopes of catching and killing the family-pack before it struck again.

The report was only an hour old, but already two of Aventine's most outspoken politicians had jumped on it with their usual and predictable stances as the news switched over into commentary. Governor Ellen Hoffman had gotten on record first, pointing to the incident as proof that the government needed to budget more money for Cobra recruitment and training. Senior Governor Tomo Treakness was right behind her, sympathizing with the victims while at the same time managing to imply it was partially their fault for moving out into the planet's wilderness areas in the first place instead of filling up the cities and farms the way good sociable people were apparently supposed to. He also made it clear that he

would vigorously oppose pouring more money into the MacDonald and Sun Centers, declaring that the incident proved that an
expansion of the Cobra program wasn't the solution.

By the time Lorne finally turned off the feed in disgust, the
worst taste in his mouth was no longer that of burned pizza.

He loaded the dishes in the washer for later, giving the cooker
a baleful look as he did so and wondering once again how long
he could keep his shaky finances a secret from the rest of his
family. His brother Merrick, who had been assigned to the small
Cobra contingent in Capitalia, was paid even less than Lorne
was, but the Cobra barracks attached to the MacDonald Center
had rooms that went for a quarter of the price of even Lorne's
miniscule apartment. Besides that, Merrick had parents and
grandparents right there in the city with him, whose houses he
could go to for meals on a regular basis. Especially since with
his gourmet skills he could bargain for those meals with the
offer to cook them.

Someday, Lorne vowed to himself, he really should learn how
to cook something.

He was fastening his tunic and heading for the door when his
comm buzzed. He pulled it out, frowning at the ID as he keyed it
on. What in the Worlds was Commandant Yoshio Ishikuma calling
for when Lorne would be there in another fifteen minutes? Keying
it on, he held it to his ear. "Broom."

"You left your apartment yet?" Ishikuma asked.

"Just heading out now," Lorne assured him.

"Well, when you hit the door, break left instead of right," Ishikuma said. "There's an aircar coming in from the Dome to get you."

Lorne felt his stomach close into a hard knot around his breakfast. "What's happened?"

"No idea," Ishikuma said. "But they're not coming with an
armed guard, so whatever you've been doing in your off-hours
you can relax about."

"Like we actually have any off-hours," Lorne said, trying to
sound his usual flippant self even as his stomach tightened another
couple of turns. Had something happened to his father or sister

on Caelian? On that hell-world, death could come in a splintered heartbeat, and from any of a hundred different directions.

Or could someone have found out where Lorne's mother and Merrick had disappeared to?

"Just remember that it could always be worse," Ishikuma said. "You could be on burial duty in Hunter's Crossing."

"Yes, I heard about that," Lorne said grimly. "We sending anyone to help in the hunt?"

"So far, they haven't asked," Ishikuma said. "But it might not matter. If Willaway is getting an uptick in spiny activity, we could see the same thing here by the end of next week. So whatever the fancy desks in Capitalia want with you, close it down fast and get your tail back out here."

"Don't worry," Lorne promised. He pulled open the building's front door and turned left toward the airfield eight blocks away. "By the way, if they're calling me in to tell me they want to shower us with new funding, how much do we want?"

"Chin-deep ought to do it," Ishikuma said. "No need to be greedy."

"Chin-deep it is," Lorne agreed. "See you soon."

"Just watch your back," Ishikuma warned. "These days, every Cobra in the Worlds has a bull's-eye tattooed there."

"Understood," Lorne said. "I'll be back as soon as I can." He keyed off the comm and picked up his pace.

It was definitely going to be one of those days.

The aircar waiting on the field had Directorate markings on it, which meant the vehicle and its driver were attached to the fifteen most powerful people in the Cobra Worlds. Given the violent political polarizations currently swirling around those fifteen people, Lorne expected the driver to present as neutral and nonaligned an attitude as it was possible for a human being to achieve.

Sure enough, the other greeted Lorne with exactly the correct degree of cool courtesy as he ushered him into the passenger section. He quickly and efficiently got the vehicle into the air, and then spent the next two and a half hours saying absolutely nothing.

They put down in the private landing terrace behind the Dome, the two-decades-old governmental building that had been named after the much larger and more dramatic structure in the main governmental center of the distant Dominion of Man. Lorne had always thought the name here to be more than a little pretentious, given that the Dominion held sway over seventy worlds—possibly more than that now—while the Cobra Worlds numbered a paltry and underdeveloped five.

Still, it could have been worse. They could have named the center after one of the previous governor-generals, very few of whom had been worth naming anything significant after. At least, not as Lorne read his family's history.

The driver had called ahead, and there was a young woman with a red-and-white shoulder band waiting when Lorne emerged from the aircar. "Cobra Lorne Broom?" she asked briskly.

"Yes," Lorne confirmed, slightly taken aback by her open face and genuinely pleasant smile. Either her job was secure enough that she didn't have to worry about keeping her head below the political firestorms, or else she hadn't been at the Dome long enough to have learned the driver's studied caution and neutrality.

"Welcome to the Dome," she said, holding out her hand. "I'm Nissa Gendreves, secondary assistant to Governor-General Chintawa."

"Nice to meet you," Lorne said, taking her hand in a brief handshake. The woman had a good, firm grip. "What exactly does a secondary assistant do?"

"All the unpaid, unglamorous, and dirty jobs no one else wants," she said straightforwardly and unapologetically, her friendly smile going a little dry. "Though I think that in this particular case someone must have slipped up." She gestured to a door behind her, flanked by two Cobras in semidress uniforms. "If you'll follow me, the governor-general is waiting."

She led the way through the door into a nicely appointed hallway filled with other governmental types. The older ones—the governors, syndics, and top bureaucrats—mostly moved at sedate walks, as befit their noble status and venerable ages. Those of Nissa's age or slightly older moved much faster on apparently less dignified errands. Most of the latter group, Lorne noted, had assistant or aide shoulder bands of various colors. "What did you mean that someone must have slipped up?" he asked as they headed toward the center of the building.

"I meant that acting as your escort is hardly one of the dirty jobs," Nissa said. "You're something of a celebrity, you know. Or at least your family is."

"Was," Lorne corrected. "Not so much anymore."

"Perhaps, but they certainly were once," Nissa conceded. "I read about your mother when I was a little girl, the first female Cobra and all. Even if the Qasaman mission didn't come out the way everyone hoped, she was still the first woman to step up and take the challenge. That makes her someone special."

"I've always thought so," Lorne murmured, wondering what Nissa would say if he told her that the official history of the Qasaman mission was pretty much a complete and bald-faced fabrication. Wondered what her response would be if he told her that his mother had actually succeeded in every damn thing they'd sent her to Qasama to accomplish, and a whole lot more.

But it wasn't worth the effort. Nissa was young and idealistic, and that sort of revelation would either upset her or simply convince her that Lorne was a biased and untrustworthy observer. Nissa had passed through the Worlds' school system, and as he himself had learned, that system never let truth get in the way of the official line. "So what am I doing here?" he asked instead.

"I really don't know," she said. "But Governor-General Chintawa seemed very anxious to see you."

"So it's just the governor-general who's waiting for me?" Lorne probed gently.

"I don't know—he didn't have me on conference call," Nissa said dryly. "Come on, Cobra Broom. I know your family was well-known for its political machinations, but pumping me for information isn't going to get you anywhere."

"Yes, I can see that," Lorne said, pushing back a fresh flicker of annoyance.

Still, that one, at least, *did* have a certain ring of truth to it.

There was a secretary and another pair of Cobra guards stationed outside Chintawa's private office. The former looked up and silently nodded Nissa toward the door, while the latter moved a step farther apart to indicate their own acceptance of the visitors' right to pass unchallenged. One of the Cobras caught Lorne's eye and gave him a microscopic nod of acknowledgment as Nissa led the way between them and pushed open the door.

Lorne had visited the governor-general's official office once or twice, that large and photogenic chamber where public business, meetings, and interviews took place. He'd never before seen Chintawa's private office, though, and his first impression as he followed Nissa in was that a Willaway windstorm must have swept through overnight. The oversized desk was almost literally covered with scattered stacks of papers, though none of the stacks seemed to be more than a few pages deep. The floor-to-ceiling shelves were crammed with books, awards, and dozens of small mementos Chintawa had collected during his years on the political scene, all arranged haphazardly without any of the calculated symmetry or eye appeal of the similar shelves in the official office. There were no windows, but across from the shelves was a group of nine displays, all of them set to different news channels with the volume down and simul transcriptions crawling across the pictures. Directly across from the desk, where it was the first thing Chintawa would see when he lifted his head from his papers or his computer, was a full-wall montage of scenes from different parts of the five Cobra Worlds.

"Cobra Broom," Chintawa said, smiling as he looked up. "Good of you to come. Please, sit down." He gestured to a chair at the corner of his desk. "Can Nissa get you some refreshment?"

"No, thank you," Lorne said as he crossed to the indicated chair and sat down.

Chintawa nodded to Nissa. "Dismissed."

"Yes, sir." Nissa's eyes flicked once to Lorne, and then she was gone.

"Impressive young lady," Chintawa commented as the door closed behind her with a solid-sounding thunk. "I'm sure you didn't get much of a feel for her on the short walk from the landing terrace, but she really is quite bright."

"Well read, too," Lorne murmured. "She was telling me all about my family history."

"Now, now—you're way too young to go all cynical on me," Chintawa chided mildly. "Anyway, she's young yet. Idealistic. Believes what she reads in school. She'll learn." He leaned back in his chair. "But I didn't ask you here to talk about your family's past. I brought you here to talk about your family's present."

Lorne frowned. "Excuse me?"

"Specifically," Chintawa continued, "I want to know where your mother is."

Lorne felt his heart seize up inside his ceramic-laminated rib cage. Had Chintawa somehow found out about his mother and brother's quiet and incredibly illegal trip to Qasama? "She's somewhere in the wilderness out past Pindar," he said, managing with a supreme effort to keep his voice steady. "Didn't Merrick tell Commandant Dreysler that when he requested temporary leave?"

"Yes, he did," Chintawa said, eyeing Lorne closely. "And at the time I was willing to let it slide."

"What do you mean?" Lorne asked, and immediately cursed himself for doing so. Now he was going to have to hear Chintawa's answer, and he was pretty sure he wasn't going to like it.

He was right. "Please, Broom," Chintawa scoffed. "Jin Moreau Broom, the first woman Cobra, who single-handedly took down a traitorous Qasaman and his Troft allies, suddenly going all to pieces in the Esserling scrubland just because her husband and daughter have gone off on a visit to Caelian?" He snorted. "You forget that as governor-general I have access to *genuine* Cobra Worlds' history."

"We really should see about getting that published someday," Lorne said stiffly. "As to Mom being upset about Dad and Jody going to Caelian, I didn't realize Cobras weren't allowed to be concerned about their loved ones."

"Of course she's allowed to be concerned," Chintawa said. "But going off to commune with nature simply isn't her style."

"People's styles change."

"Not that much they don't," Chintawa said flatly. "More significantly, people worried about their loved ones don't deliberately go incommunicado for days at a time. We've tried both their comms— repeatedly—and get nothing but their voice stacks."

"Maybe they just don't feel like talking to anyone in the Dome."

"Or maybe they aren't out crying in the wilderness at all," Chintawa countered brusquely. "They're with your great-uncle Corwin, aren't they?"

Lorne blinked, the sheer unexpectedness of the question bringing his mad scramble for a good defensible position to a skidding halt. "*What?*" he asked.

"No games," Chintawa said sternly. "I've been keeping track of Corwin Moreau's work over the years. I know that right now he's trying to develop a type of bone laminate that might ease some of the long-term anemia and arthritis problems. The fact that your mother and brother have suddenly disappeared tells me he's reached the point where he's ready to do some field tests with actual Cobras."

"That's ridiculous," Lorne said with as much dignity as he could drum up on the spur of the moment. It *was* ridiculous, actually— Uncle Corwin had been working on-and-off on the Cobra medical problems for most of Lorne's lifetime, and as far as Lorne knew he'd never gotten any traction with any of them.

But Chintawa obviously didn't know that. And in fact, the more Lorne thought about it, the more he realized the governor-general's suspicions made for a much better cover story than even the one he, Merrick, Jody, and their dad had come up with.

"It's not ridiculous, and I frankly don't care what any of them is doing," Chintawa said. "The point is that I need your mother here, and I need her here now."

"What for?"

"Something important and confidential," Chintawa said. "Also something I think will help put your family in a better light than it's been in for the past several years." He smiled faintly. "She's not in trouble, if that's what you're wondering."

If you only knew, Lorne thought grimly. "It would certainly be nice to have the record set at least a little straighter," he said, "though it would probably be terribly confusing to people like Nissa. You say you need her right now?"

"By noon tomorrow, actually," Chintawa said. "If absolutely necessary I could probably postpone the ceremony a couple of days."

Lorne frowned. "Ceremony?"

Chintawa smiled faintly. "You'll know when your mother knows," he said. "Until then, it's my prerogative to be mysterious."

"In that case, it's my prerogative to take my leave," Lorne said, standing up. "If I hear from her, I'll be sure and let her know you're looking for her."

"Just a minute," Chintawa said, his voice darkening as he also stood up. "That's it?"

"What do you want me to say?" Lorne countered. "That I'll bring my mother in whether she wants to be here or not? I can't promise that. If you want to tell me something that'll sweeten the pot, I'll be happy to hear it."

"You want the pot sweetened?" Chintawa rumbled. "Fine. Tell her that if she isn't here, other people will get all the credit and she'll get nothing. *And* they'll get to put their own spin on it, which will leave the Moreau name right where it is: in the historical gutter."

Lorne snorted. "With all due respect, sir, my family stopped caring about who got credit for what a long time ago. And unless you're planning to nominate my mother for sainthood, it's going to take more than anything you can do to put our family name back where it deserves."

"Certainly not if you aren't willing to make some effort of your own," Chintawa ground out. "If you can't see that, why should I waste my time trying to help?"

"I don't know," Lorne said sarcastically. This was probably not the direction his mother or father would take the conversation, and certainly not where Uncle Corwin would go. But he didn't have their verbal finesse, and he simply couldn't think of anything else to try. "Maybe because you see some political gain in it for yourself?"

Chintawa's face darkened like an approaching thunderstorm. "How in the Worlds did you grow up in the Moreau family without learning anything about politics?" he demanded. "It's not a zero-sum game, you know. What's gain for me can also be gain for you."

"And all you need for that gain is to put my mother up on a stage like your private sock puppet?" Lorne suggested.

Chintawa muttered something under his breath. "Get out of here," he ordered. "Just get out."

"As you wish, Governor-General Chintawa," Lorne said formally, starting to breathe again as he stood up. It had actually worked. He'd made Chintawa so mad at him that he didn't even want to see Lorne's mother anymore.

Now if Chintawa would just stay this mad long enough for Lorne to get out of Capitalia and back to DeVegas Province, this whole thing might blow over. Or at least quiet down long enough for his mother and brother to finish up their mysterious errand on Qasama and get back home.

He'd made it halfway to the office door when Chintawa cleared his throat. "And where exactly do you think you're going?"

Lorne stopped but didn't turn around. "I'm going back to my duty station," he said over his shoulder. "As per your orders."

"I've given you no such orders," Chintawa said. "But since you bring it up, let's do that, shall we? You're hereby relieved of all other duties and tasked with the job of finding Cobra Jasmine Moreau Broom and bringing her to the Dome."

Lorne turned around, feeling his mouth drop open. "*What*?"

"You heard me," Chintawa said. The thunderstorm of anger had passed, leaving frozen ground behind it. "Until your mother is standing in front of me, you're not going back to Archway or anywhere else."

"This is ridiculous," Lorne protested. "I have work to do."

"Then you'd better persuade your mother to come in, hadn't you?" Chintawa said. "Otherwise, you'd better get used to living in your parents' house again."

"This is illegal and out of channels. Sir," Lorne bit out. "Barring a declared state of emergency, you can't counteract standing orders and assignments."

"You're welcome to appeal to Commandant Dreysler," Chintawa said. "But I can tell you right now that the orders will be cut before you even reach his office."

For a long moment the two men locked eyes. "Fine," Lorne said stiffly. It was clear that Chintawa had his mind made up. It was also clear that Lorne himself didn't have the faintest idea of what to do now.

But he knew who might. "I'll need a way to get to Uncle Corwin's house," he continued. "Cobra pay doesn't stretch far enough to cover car rentals."

Chintawa reached over and touched a switch on his intercom. "Nissa, come in here, please."

He straightened up again, and the staring contest resumed. Thirty-two seconds later by Lorne's nanocomputer clock, the door opened and Nissa stepped inside. "Yes, sir?" she asked, a slight frown creasing her forehead as her eyes flicked back and forth between the two men.

"Until further notice, you're assigned to Cobra Broom," Chintawa told her. "Check out a car and take him anywhere in or around Capitalia he wants to go. If he wants to leave the city, call Ms. Oomara first and have her clear it with me."

"Yes, sir," Nissa said, her forehead clearing as she apparently decided whatever was happening was none of her business. "Cobra Broom?"

Lorne held his glare another second and a half. Then, turning away from Chintawa, he stalked across the room, past the girl, and out the door.

It was going to be one of those days, all right. And then some.

Corwin Moreau listened silently as Lorne described the morning's events, occasionally nodding in reaction to something his great-nephew said, his fingertips occasionally rubbing gently at the arm of his chair in response to some inner thoughts or musings of his own.

"And so I came here," Lorne finished, looking briefly over at Aunt Thena, who had listened to the tale in the same silence as her husband. "It might not have been very smart, but I couldn't think of anything else to do."

"No, you did fine," Corwin assured him, looking questioningly at Thena. She gave a slight shrug in return. "Is the young lady still waiting out there? We should at least invite her in for lunch."

"I don't know if she's there or not," Lorne said. "Probably not—I told her I'd be here for a while, and she told me she has family a couple of blocks away. Maybe that's why Chintawa gave her the job of carting me around in the first place. He probably figured I'd go to ground here, and she might as well have someplace of her own to wait for me."

"Or else she got the job because he thought you might open up to someone who wasn't a hardened politician," Thena offered. "It's an old trick, and not beneath Chintawa's dignity."

"Certainly not if lying isn't," Lorne growled.

Corwin cocked an eyebrow at him. "What did he lie about?"

"Oh, come on," Lorne scoffed. "This whole secret ceremony thing? How obvious can a lie get?"

"Well, that's the point, isn't it?" Corwin said thoughtfully. "It's such an obviously ridiculous cover story that one has to wonder whether it might actually be true."

Lorne frowned. "Have you heard something?"

"No, not a whisper," Corwin said. "But I'm hardly in the official gossip ring these days."

"Besides being obvious, the story's also pointless," Thena added. "As a Cobra, your mother is still a reservist, and hence subject to immediate call-up by the governor-general for any reason. He can order her to appear at the Dome, or order you to go get her, with no explanation needed."

"Maybe," Lorne said. "But right now it doesn't really matter why he wants her. What we need is a way to stall him off. And I can tell you right now, he didn't look to be in a stalling mood."

"Not if he's willing to pull a Cobra in from frontier duty," Corwin agreed heavily. "Especially right after a major spine leopard attack in the same general region. Any chance he could be persuaded to accept the story that she and Merrick are off on a retreat somewhere?"

"No," Lorne said. "And in fact, he pointed out the logical flaw in it: that they wouldn't go off without leaving some way of contacting them."

"Yes, that was always the weak spot," Corwin said heavily. "I should have come up with something better."

"You didn't have much time," Thena pointed out. "Besides, there was no way to guess that anyone would take more than a passing interest in their absence."

"I suppose," Corwin conceded. "So now what?"

"Well, we can't pretend they're hiding here," Thena said slowly. "If Chintawa is determined enough to get a search warrant, a few patrollers could pop that balloon within half an hour."

"So again, they're somewhere else," Corwin said. "Someplace where Lorne presumably can try to call them."

"Right now?" Lorne asked, pulling out his comm.

"Yes, this would be good," Corwin confirmed, looking at his watch. "You've been here just long enough to have consulted with us, and for us to have decided together that this is worth breaking into her solitude. Go ahead—your mother first."

Lorne nodded and punched in his mother's number. "I presume this is purely for the benefit of anyone who might decide to pull my comm records later?"

"Correct." Corwin hesitated. "It'll also put all the rest of us in a slightly better legal position should the worst-case scenario happen."

Lorne felt his throat tighten. That scenario being if his mother and brother got caught sneaking back onto Aventine from Qasama and were brought up on charges of treason.

At which point, of course, all of Uncle Corwin's caution would go scattering to the four winds, because Lorne was absolutely not going to hunker down behind legal excuses while two of his family stood in the dock. He would be right up there with them, as would his father and sister. And probably Uncle Corwin and Aunt Thena, too.

At which point Chintawa and the Directorate would have to decide whether they really wanted to risk the kind of political fallout that could come of prosecuting the whole family.

Lorne almost hoped they did. He would use the occasion to make sure the true story of his mother's original mission to Qasama got brought up into the open from the shallow grave where Uncle Corwin's political enemies had buried it.

"Hello, this is Jasmine," his mother's voice came in his ear. "I'm not available right now, but if you'd care to leave a message..."

Lorne waited for the greeting to run its course, recorded a short message telling her to call as soon as it was convenient, and keyed off. "Now Merrick?" he asked.

Corwin nodded, and Lorne went through the same charade with his brother's voice stack. "That sound okay?" he asked when he was finished.

"Perfect," Corwin said. "Another half hour, I think, and it'll be time to try again." He squinted toward one of the windows that looked out onto the walkway leading between the front door and the gate at the edge of the grounds. "Meanwhile, let's put our heads together and see if we can come up with a plan."

"We can do that while we eat," Thena said firmly. "If we're all going to end up in jail tonight, we might as well have a good meal first."

Lunch was, Lorne assumed, up to Thena's usual culinary standards. He didn't know for sure because he didn't really taste any of it. His full attention then, and for the rest of the afternoon, was on their conversation and brainstorming.

He continued to call his mother and brother at half-hour intervals, leaving messages that under Uncle Corwin's coaching gradually increased in anxiety and frustration. It would take a preliminary indictment and court order to tap into those messages, he knew, but at this point he wouldn't put anything past Chintawa.

Late in the afternoon the governor-general himself called, looking for a progress report. In complete honesty, Lorne told him that, no, the missing family members weren't at Uncle Corwin's, and that he hadn't been able to get hold of either of them by comm. Chintawa ordered him to keep trying, and hung up.

The three of them were sitting down to dinner when Nissa called to ask Lorne if he would be needing her to drive him anywhere else. Lorne assured her that he would be staying the night, and that he'd be sure to call her if and when he needed to go somewhere. She reminded him that she was always available, should he change his mind, slipped in a subtle reminder that wandering off without her would get both of them in trouble with Chintawa, and wished him a pleasant good evening.

"You'd better watch that girl," Corwin warned after Lorne relayed the conversation. "She may come across as a wide-eyed ingenue standing high above the political mud, but she clearly knows how to find and push a person's buttons."

"What, because she told me she'd get in trouble if I ditched her?" Lorne scoffed.

"Exactly," Corwin said. "Take it from someone who once played on that same field. She's got your profile down cold, and I don't think she'd hesitate to bring the lasers to bear if she was ordered to do so."

They finished dinner, which Lorne again assumed was excellent, and continued talking well past sundown and into the night. A hundred plans were brought up, discussed, and ultimately discarded, and by the time Lorne said his good-nights and headed to the guest room they were no further toward a solution than they were when they'd started.

He slept fitfully, waking up for long stretches at a time. Probably the city noises, he told himself, which he was no longer accustomed to after all the time he'd spent fighting spine leopards at the edges of civilization.

It was still dark, and he'd finally fallen into a deep sleep, when he was jolted awake by the trilling of his comm.

He grabbed the device and keyed it on, his first half-fogged thought that Merrick and his mother were back on Aventine and were returning his calls. "Hello?" he croaked.

"It's Nissa," Nissa's voice came, quivering with tension. "Get dressed—I need to get you back to the Dome right away. I'll be there in five minutes—"

"Wait a second, hold on," Lorne interrupted, his brain snapping fully awake at the simmering panic in her voice. "What's going on?"

"There's no time," she said. "An astronomer at North Bank picked up a fleet of ships—Troft ships, they think—heading eastward towards Capitalia from orbit. And none of the ships register on radar."

Lorne felt his muscles tense as the full implications of that fact blew away the last wisps of sleepiness. "I'll meet you at the gate," he said, and keyed off. Dropping the comm on the bed, he grabbed for his clothes.

He'd been afraid the call was bad news about his mother and brother. It was far worse ... because there was just one type of ship designed not to show up on traffic control's radar.

Warships.

A century ago, the Dominion of Man had set up the Aventine colony, ostensibly as a way to get rid of the Cobra war veterans, but also as a deterrent to the Trofts against launching future attacks on Dominion worlds. Barely twenty-five years later, the colonists' connection to the rest of humanity had been closed, but the deterrent effect of the Cobras' presence had remained.

Until now. It was unbelievable. It was insane. But apparently, it was also true. The Cobras' century-old bluff had been called.

Aventine was under attack.

CHAPTER TWO

"The secret to a contented life," Paul Broom commented sagely as he scraped bits of green spore off his silliweave tunic, "is to find a comfortable morning routine and stick with it."

Jody Broom paused in the process of scraping her own tunic and gave her father one of the disbelieving stares she'd worked so hard to master during her teenage years. "You really want to be saying things like that when I have a razor in my hand?" she asked.

"But I thought this was the life you'd always dreamed about," he said, turning innocent eyes on her. "Out here in the wilds of humanity's frontier, degrees in animal physiology and management firmly in hand, cutting an impressive swath through—" He indicated the tunic in his hand. "Well, through tiny little creatures growing on silicon clothing."

"Oh, this is the life, all right," Jody said sourly, turning back to her work. "It's also been occurring to me more and more lately that I could just as easily have turned my impressive animal management degree into the field of hamster breeding."

"Hamsters? Pheh," her father scoffed. "Where's the fame and glory in that?"

"You ever see a hamster go rogue?" Jody countered. "Or worse, a whole herd of them?"

Paul gave a low whistle. "I had no idea how dangerous—" He

broke off, shifting his scraper to his other hand and flashing a fingertip laser blast across the room. Jody turned in time to see a coin-sized buzzic drop to the floor. "How dangerous livestock that size could be," he continued, his eyes carefully sweeping the room. "I'm grateful now that you didn't choose to go into that line of work. Get down a bit, would you?"

Jody dropped into a low crouch, wincing as her father fired four more laser shots over her head into the wall and ceiling. There were four more thunks, louder ones this time, and she turned to see four freshly killed thumb-sized flycrawlers smoldering on the floor behind her. "I think they're getting bigger," Paul commented.

"Almost big enough to take on my hamster farm," Jody agreed, her throat tightening. "How in the Worlds are bugs that size getting in?"

"The boys must have missed a spot," Paul said, crossing the room and peering down at the insects. "Maybe in one of the upper corners or alongside a window where a vine's taken root and started pulling the plaster apart. You let them get a foothold and start a crack, and that's all they need."

Jody went to her father's side. Already tiny spots of green were starting to appear on the burned insect carcasses as microscopic airborne spores found something to eat and set to work with a vengeance. And once the flycrawlers settled in, she knew, the mice-whiskers would be right behind them, and before long it would take a Cobra to clear them all out.

Luckily for Jody and her two teammates, they had one. "Have I mentioned lately how grateful I am you came along on this trip?" she asked her father.

"Once or twice," he assured her. "I was just trying to think of that poem. 'Big fleas have little fleas upon their backs to bite 'em. And little fleas something something.'"

"'And little fleas have lesser fleas, and so *ad infinitum*,'" Jody quoted. "Except that on Caelian, the whole process seems to work backwards."

There was a double thunk as the airlock door one room over opened and closed, and Jody turned to see Geoff Boulton and

Freylan Sonderby walk into the room. "Okay, the house is all scraped," Geoff announced briskly as he brushed at some dust on his tunic sleeve. "Ready to head out as soon as—" He stopped as he suddenly seemed to notice the odd way Jody and her father were standing. "What is it?" he asked.

Paul gestured silently to the floor. Geoff threw a look at Freylan, and the two young men crossed to Jody's side.

For a moment no one said anything, but simply stood in their semicircle staring at the dead insects as if it was some sort of funereal viewing ritual. Then, Freylan stirred. "It's the southeast corner," he said. "There's a flange up there that I've never thought looked quite right."

"And you didn't do anything about it?" Geoff asked, a dark edge to his voice.

"I thought it was all right," Freylan said with a sigh. "It looked solid enough, just a little oddly shaped."

"What did Governor Uy tell us when we first got here?" Geoff demanded. "Odd shapes, odd fittings, and odd colorations are the first signs of trouble. Blast it all, Freylan." He waved a hand in disgust. "Come on—show me where it is."

"You won't be able to reach it," Freylan said, a sort of kicked-dog look in his eyes as he headed back toward the door. "The step stool isn't tall enough. We'll have to find a ladder we can borrow."

"I can get up there," Paul volunteered. "Let me finish with my tunic and I'll go with you."

"Go ahead," Jody said. "I'll finish your tunic."

"What, go out in my underwear?" Paul asked, sounding vaguely scandalized as he gestured to his silliweave singlet.

"People in Stronghold go outside in their underwear all the time," Jody growled, warning him with her eyes. This wasn't the time for jokes.

Fortunately, he got the message. "We'll be back in a minute," he said. He gestured Freylan ahead of him, and the two men left the room.

"I'll do that," Geoff growled, holding out his hand as Jody picked up her father's tunic. "You've got your own to do."

"I've got it," Jody said firmly, half turning and bumping his arm aside with her shoulder as he tried to take the tunic from her. "You go make sure the packs are ready."

"Are you mad at me for telling Freylan he screwed up?" Geoff demanded. "Damn it all, Jody, this is *Caelian*. You screw up here and you get eaten alive."

"Yes, I remember the lecture," Jody said as she started scraping the bits of green off the tunic. "I also remember that none of us has exactly been the pride of the litter as far as screw-ups are concerned."

"We've been here eleven days," Geoff growled. "Screw-up incidence is supposed to be on a downward curve by now."

"It is," Jody said flatly. "And jumping down Freylan's throat isn't going to flatten the curve any faster."

Geoff hissed between his teeth. "You're sorry you came along on this fiasco, aren't you?"

"I didn't say that."

"But you're *thinking* it."

Jody didn't answer, but kept working at the tunic. There wasn't supposed to be anything organic in the material for the little green spores to eat, but as the wind blew the spores themselves through the Caelian air, it also blew along microscopic bits of their food.

And as her father had pointed out, letting even harmless spores get ahead of them was the first step on the road to disaster.

"I said you were thinking it," Geoff repeated into the silence, a fresh edge of challenge in his voice.

Jody took a deep breath. So he was in the mood for a fight, was he? Fine. She was willing to oblige. "I came along because I thought my training might help in figuring out a solution to this place," she said stiffly. "But that wasn't the reason I was invited, was it?"

A sudden shadow flicked across the anger and frustration in Geoff's face. "What are you talking about?" he asked carefully.

"I'm talking about the *real* reason you asked me to join you and Freylan out here," Jody said. "It wasn't my animal training you wanted at all. It was—"

She broke off at the sound of the double doors opening again, and turned her attention back to the tunic she was supposed to be scraping.

But before she did, she had the slightly guilty pleasure of seeing a look of shame briefly cross Geoff's face.

"That was the spot, all right," Paul announced as he and Freylan came into the room. "It should be all right now."

"At least until the next vine gets a grip," Freylan muttered, still brooding over his failure to catch the chink earlier.

"When it does, we'll deal with it," Paul said calmly. "How are we doing in here?"

"Almost ready," Jody said, giving her father's tunic a final inspection. Geoff, she noted, had quietly slipped into the other room where the packs were stacked. "Yes, it's done," she confirmed, handing it over. "I wonder what you do if you're allergic to this stuff."

"You probably itch a lot," Paul said, giving the tunic a quick once-over of his own and then slipping it on. "Either that, or you get used to walking around naked."

"Not you personally," Freylan added hastily, his cheeks reddening.

Jody turned back to her own unfinished tunic, a smile sneaking onto her face despite her grouchy mood. Freylan could be so adorably awkward sometimes. "I know," she said over her shoulder to him. "But at least you'd still have your skin."

"Speaking of skin," Paul said, stepping smoothly in on top of Freylan's embarrassment, "did you get anything more from that red-tail?"

"Not really," Freylan said, and Jody could hear the relief in his voice at the return to safer scientific ground. "I'm still ninety percent convinced that odor has something to do with it. But there's too much overlap between the red-tail and the groundsniffer for me to figure out what the key might be."

"If it's there at all," Paul warned.

"It's there," Freylan said firmly. "*Something's* there. Otherwise, the spores and other vegetation would attack *all* hair and fur, instead of just everything from five or six millimeters out."

Jody grimaced, running her fingers over the stubble that had once been a lovingly-cared-for head of hair. The very first thing they'd been ordered to do when the *Freedom's Fire* lifted off Aventine en route for Caelian was to shave their heads and body hair. Of all the unpleasant aspects of their brief time here, that was the one she still couldn't get used to.

But it wasn't like there was any choice in the matter. Caelian's rich and aggressive plant life attacked anything with even a trace of organic, carbon-bearing material in it, the skin of living beings the only exception to that rule. And much as she missed her hair, Jody had no wish to wake up every morning with her body covered by little green spores.

In and of themselves, the spores wouldn't have been so bad. They loved to settle on and eat the natural fibers and synthetics that made up most clothing, but that was a slow process and would hardly leave a person running home from the shops clutching rags to her chest, despite the way her father had made it sound.

The problem was that vigorous Caelian plants attracted voracious Caelian animals. The first to come were always the insects, from buzzics to flycrawlers all the way up to some that Jody hadn't seen yet but was told could be mistaken for small birds. The insects would start eating the plants, inevitably moth-chewing some of the clothing material in the process, and eventually a person *would* be running home covered in nothing but rags and insects.

But it got worse. Brushed-off insects attracted carrion eaters, plants and animals both, which attracted larger animals, which attracted still larger animals, which finally attracted the massive, tiger-sized predators who could take on human-sized prey without even blinking.

It was how all planetary ecologies worked, of course. The problem was that on Caelian it worked faster and more violently than on Aventine or any other world humanity had run into over the centuries.

Worse yet, even by Caelian's own harsh standards, the ecology seemed to work harder and faster against humans than against its own members. It was as if the planet itself resented the newcomers who had pushed their way into its private biological war and had mustered all its combined forces in an effort to force them off.

"But at the same time odor can't be the whole story," Freylan went on into Jody's musings, "because artificial odor applications don't do any good, or at least nothing has that's been tried. It has to be some combination of things no one's figured out yet."

"Well, I hope someone does so soon," Paul said, making a face as he worked his shoulders against his tunic. "I don't mind mineral-based houses and furniture, but this clothing is about as uncomfortable as anything I've ever worn in my life."

"I've heard there are supposed to be a couple of companies on Aventine that are working on alternatives," Freylan said. "But with a potential customer base of less than five thousand, I doubt they're working very hard."

Geoff poked his head around the doorway. "We going to talk all morning, or are we going to check on the trap?" he asked crossly. "Come on, come on."

"We're ready," Paul said, meeting the younger man's irritation with the steadfast calm Jody had found annoying when she was growing up and had only gradually learned to admire.

"Ready," Jody confirmed, giving her tunic one last sweep of the razor and slipping it on.

"I'll grab my pack and go get the aircar started," Freylan volunteered, slipping a bit gingerly past Geoff and heading for the door.

"I'll go with you," Paul said, and followed him out.

Geoff looked at Jody, and she could see him wondering if she was going to drag them back to the conversation the others' arrival had interrupted. But Jody's anger had cooled to mere annoyance. She simply returned his gaze in silence, and after a moment he nodded. "Okay, then," he said with forced briskness. "Let's go see if we've finally got ourselves a gigger."

"Yes, let's." Jody gestured toward the door. "After you."

The first colonists on Caelian, knowing from the assessment teams the kind of aggressive ecology they were up against, had envisioned a series of small towns encircled by high walls to protect against the larger predators, with the settlements connected by a network of roads made by clearing, sterilizing, and melt-paving wide pathways through the forest.

It hadn't worked out that way. The ceramic walls had worked

for a few months, but eventually the stubborn airborne spores had managed to get a foothold, and once that happened the rest inevitably followed. Stronghold's replacement wall, this one not of ceramic but stainless steel, worked better, but even with periodic scraping its surface had become badly pitted.

The roads hadn't worked at all. The effects of standard burning lasted a few days at the most, and even sterilizing burns were only good for a few weeks at a time. The fifty-meter-wide clear zone outside Stronghold's wall, plus the larger rectangle adjoining it to the south that acted as the planet's spaceport landing area, were cleared every two weeks. Ground vehicles were still of some use inside Caelian's six remaining towns, but outside those walls aircars were the only practical means of transportation.

The forest beyond Stronghold's clear zone was as teeming with life as anywhere else on the planet, and in theory the team could have worked their traps right there. But Geoff and Freylan had wanted to get a little farther from any effects of human civilization, miniscule though those effects might be, and had opted instead for a hillside about five kilometers northwest of the main gate.

The four of them had spent their first day on Caelian burning off a small section of ground to serve as a landing pad for their rented aircar. Six days later they'd repeated the process. Now, only four days after that, not only had most of the grasses come back, but several small bushes had taken root as well. Jody winced at the teeth-tingling screech of thorns against metal as Geoff set them down on the pad, wondering how much of a bite the fresh scratches were going to take out of the rental's damage deposit.

But at least they'd finally nailed a gigger. As Geoff shut down the aircar's engine, she could hear the small predator's outraged snarling a dozen meters away.

"Sounds like we've got one," Freylan said with a mixture of relief and excitement as he started to open his door.

And stopped as Paul touched his shoulder. "My turn to go out first," the older man said mildly.

"Right," Freylan said, his voice muffled with embarrassment.

Mentally, Jody shook her head. Back on Aventine, when she'd

first been brought aboard the project, she'd noticed Freylan's tendency to get so focused on some part of his work that he totally forgot where he was.

In Capitalia, that could be an embarrassment. On Caelian, it could get you killed.

Paul climbed out of his side of the aircar, closing the door behind him, and for a minute he stood with his back to the vehicle, his head moving slowly back and forth as his enhanced vision and hearing scoped out the section of forest closest to them. Jody held her breath, wondering which variety of Caelian's fauna would decide to check out the intruders this time. The forest had gone quiet, almost as if in anticipation of the drama about to take place...

Abruptly, Paul leaned over, brought his left leg up, and fired a burst from his antiarmor laser into a stand of bushes behind the aircar. There was a piercing scream, and with a crackle of broken branches a screech tiger half leaped, half fell into view between two of the bushes. Paul gave the area another slow sweep, then gestured the all clear.

"Man, those things are big," Geoff muttered, his eyes on the dead screech tiger as he climbed gingerly out of the car.

"Amazingly quiet, too," Paul agreed. "Especially considering their size. I didn't even know it was coming toward us until I picked up its infrared signature."

"I sure hope we find some kind of breakthrough before we have to go that far up the food chain," Freylan said feelingly as he looked at the screech tiger. "I *really* don't want to have to take blood and tissue samples from a live one of those."

"A hearty amen to that," Jody agreed, tearing her eyes away from the dead predator and looking around. The usual midmorning lull in the wind was right on schedule, and the still air around her seemed to press in with a sense of watchful foreboding. "Let's grab the gigger and get out of here before the scavengers pick up the scent."

Their animal trap was simplicity itself, consisting of a rectangular mesh box set up with its floor and sides bunched together and held loosely at ground level beneath a layer of leaves and over a deep hole dug in the ground. The minute an animal put its weight on the mesh, the floor was designed to collapse, dropping the animal into the newly formed box while a spring-loaded lid swung over from concealment to seal off the top. Jody's contribution to the contraption had been the set of cylindrical free-spinning tubes around each of the mesh's main wires, which were designed to send the captured animal's legs straight through to hang uselessly in midair in the hole instead of leaving them inside the box proper where the animal could make full use of its claws to try to escape.

The trap had worked perfectly on the team's first two captures, and as Jody reached the hole and peered down through the mesh top she saw that they were now three for three. The gigger was lying on its belly inside the box, rocking back and forth as it tried to get some kind of purchase with its feet, jabbing uselessly at the sides with the pair of hollow mouth tusks it used to impale and then suck the blood from its victims.

"Ugly little beasts, aren't they?" Geoff commented as he squatted down and started brushing the leaves from the two carrying bars that ran through the top of the cage. "Freylan, you want to get the other end?"

"Hold it," Paul said sharply. "Everyone be quiet."

Jody froze, the other two following suit. In the unmoving air the forest around her was alive with quiet sounds, muted chirps and soft buzzings. She strained her ears, wondering anxiously just how big the predator was that her father had heard sneaking up on them.

And then, somewhere in the distance, she heard a rumbling roar. Not the roar of any of Caelian's predators, but the roar of approaching aircraft. *Big* aircraft. She turned toward her father, frowning, as the sound rapidly intensified.

And suddenly, a pair of large ships shot past to the south, their upper sides visible for just an instant above the trees. The roar cut off suddenly—

"Alert!" Governor Uy's voice crackled abruptly from their aircar's comm. "All Caelians! Troft gunships have landed at Stronghold. We are under—"

The voice cut off. "Dad—?" Jody began.

"Shh," Paul said, a darkness in his voice that Jody had never heard there before. She listened to the sounds of the forest and the sudden thundering of her own pulse.

And then, drifting through the still air, she heard the distant, muffled crack of an explosion. Followed by another, and another, and another.

She looked at Geoff's taut face, and at Freylan's pale one, and at her father's grim one... and slowly, it dawned on her that the unthinkable had happened. The Trofts had invaded Caelian.

The Cobra Worlds were at war.

CHAPTER THREE

Nissa was waiting when Lorne reached the gate at the end of the walkway. "Any ID on the ships yet?" he asked as he dropped into the seat beside her.

"They're Trofts," she said tautly as she pulled back onto the deserted street and shoved her foot against the accelerator, sending the car leaping forward like a scalded leatherwing. "What else do we need to know?"

"Whose demesne they're from, for starters," Lorne said, grabbing at the armrest for support and fastening the restraints across his chest and hips. "It might also be nice to know if anyone's been threatening us or is an unhappy customer or something."

"I don't know anything about that," Nissa said, taking a corner dangerously fast. "Governor-General Chintawa said not to use the comm any more than I had to—he wanted to keep the system open for emergency use."

She had pulled onto Cavendish Boulevard, the main thoroughfare leading into the central part of the city, when the western sky abruptly lit up with the red firefly glows of a hundred distant grav lifts. "Here they come," Lorne said, pointing.

"Oh, God," Nissa breathed, her voice sounding half strangled. "What do we *do*?"

"We keep going," he told her, peering past the girl's head and trying to gauge the ships' speed. Two minutes, he estimated, maybe three, and the armada would be right on top of them. He and Nissa should make it to the government section of the city by then, but probably not to the Dome itself. "Can you get any more speed out of this thing?" he asked.

"I don't think so," Nissa said, leaning forward a little as she presumably pressed harder on the accelerator. There was no change in the car's speed that Lorne could detect. "Where are we going?" she asked.

"The Dome, right?" Lorne countered. "That's where Chintawa told you to bring me."

"Yes, but—" She flashed a look at him. "Aren't *they* going to the Dome, too?"

"They're probably going everywhere in Capitalia," Lorne said grimly, ducking his head a little lower to try to get the best view out her window that he could from his angle. The ships were still coming in, but they were also spreading out, and he saw several of the ones in back drop precipitously out of sight below the skyline as they headed for landing points in the western parts of the city. "Where does this car live?"

"What?" Nissa asked, sounding confused.

"Is it usually parked in the main car park?" Lorne clarified. "Because there's a private tunnel connecting that to the Dome itself. Right?"

"Yes, but I'm only a second assistant," she said. "I can't use it."

"I don't think this is going to be a morning for arguing regulations," Lorne said. "If we can make it to the car park—"

And with a sudden thundering roar, the leading edge of the Troft armada shot past above them.

"Pull over!" Lorne snapped as the car bucked violently in the crosswind of the spacecrafts' slipstreams. An instant later he was thrown against the restraints as Nissa slammed on the brakes, fighting the car to a skidding halt beside the curb.

Just as a tall, shadowy ship settled on its grav lifts into the center of the intersection two blocks directly ahead.

"Out!" Lorne ordered, popping his restraints.

"But—" Nissa protested, pointing at the Troft ship, towering over the shorter buildings around them.

"I said *out*!" Lorne said, reaching over and releasing her restraints himself. Out the windshield he could see another, more compact set of grav lifts glowing their way out of the sky toward them, apparently aiming for a spot directly in front of the big warship. Pushing open his door, he got a grip on Nissa's arm and hauled her out of the car.

"What are you doing?" she gasped, struggling in his grip. "Let me go—"

Ignoring her protests, Lorne pushed her down into a crouched position against the side of the car. "Quiet," he muttered, looking cautiously over the hood. Ahead, the incoming grav lifts he'd seen resolved themselves into a small transport that was settling to the pavement about fifty meters in front of the looming Troft warship.

"Great," he muttered under his breath. A troop carrier, undoubtedly. Another minute, and they would be up to their eyebrows in Troft soldiers. "We have to get to cover," he murmured to Nissa. "Any ideas?"

"The car park's over there," she said. "Up there on the left."

Lorne grimaced. Unfortunately, the structure she was pointing to was right beside the Troft warship, directly beneath one of the stubby wings sticking out from the ship's flank up near the crest.

Wings that seemed curiously lumpy and decidedly non-aerodynamic, now that he focused on them. Frowning, he keyed in his vision enhancers' telescopic setting.

And hissed between his teeth. The wings didn't look aerodynamic because they had absolutely nothing to do with the ship's flight characteristics. They were nothing more or less than the supports for a set of incredibly nasty-looking weapons clusters: pylon-mounted lasers and missile tubes both. "Forget the car park," he told Nissa, looking around them. Most of the nearby buildings were either retail businesses or office space for the myriad of support groups and hangers-on that always collected around governmental seats of power. At this hour, with dawn only now starting to break in the east, all those buildings would be unoccupied and locked down tight.

But the four-story structure directly ahead of them on their right had the look of an apartment building. An upper-class one, too, if the stone facing and fancy balconies were anything to go by. If they could get in there before the soldiers appeared . . .

Too late. Even as he looked back at the transport he saw the side loading hatches swing ponderously down.

Only it wasn't a squad of Troft soldiers who swarmed out onto the deserted street.

It was a pack of spine leopards.

Beside him, Nissa gave a muffled gasp. "Are those—?"

"They sure are," Lorne said grimly.

And suddenly it was more urgent than ever that he and Nissa get off the streets. The spinies looked a little wobbly as they walked around, as if the trip in the transport had left them groggy or disoriented. But that wouldn't last long. The minute they caught human scent out here, they would be on the hunt.

Nissa knew it, too. "You have to kill them," she said urgently, her voice trembling. "Before they get to us."

Lorne gazed at the animals, his heart sinking. There were at least fifteen of the beasts out there, plus however many more might still be out of sight in the transport's hold. Did Nissa really think a single Cobra could take on that many all by himself?

And then his stomach tightened as he finally got it. Of course no single Cobra was up to this kind of challenge. It would take a group of them, working together, to take down that many predators.

Right in the shadow of the Trofts' heavy lasers and missiles.

"You have to kill them," Nissa pleaded again.

"Maybe later," Lorne said, shifting his eyes back to the apartment building. Earlier, before the transport had unloaded its cargo, the distance to the front door had looked reasonable. Now, with spinies roaming the streets, the trip was a lot more problematic.

"What do you mean?" Nissa demanded, her voice starting to shake again. "You can't let them stay out here on the streets. You have to get rid of them."

"Quiet," Lorne bit out, looking around. With the whole area deserted, any sudden movement on his and Nissa's part would instantly draw the attention of both the Trofts and the spinies. Movement was always noticeable, and in this case movement would probably be fatal.

Unless something else started moving first.

"Are the keys still in the car?" he asked, peering in through the window.

"No, I've got them," Nissa said, holding up a closed fist as she started to move toward the car door. "Can they get through the doors or windows?"

"Probably," Lorne said. "Give me the keys, then find a place to duck down and don't move until I tell you."

She turned bewildered eyes on him. "What? You want me to stay out *here*?"

"Until I tell you," Lorne repeated, pushing her gently but firmly a meter back from the car. Prying the keys from her frozen fist, he climbed back into the car, stretching out on his stomach across the front seats. He fitted the keys into the starter and turned it on.

"What are you *doing*?" Nissa called from behind him.

"Hopefully, creating a diversion," Lorne told her, easing his head up to windshield height and turning the steering wheel toward the transport and the milling spinies. "You have anything I can use to hold down the accelerator?"

"Like what?"

"Never mind," Lorne said, prying up the floor mat and rolling it up as tightly as he could. He folded the slightly floppy cylinder over once and wedged it between the lower dashboard and the accelerator. It wouldn't stay in place very long, but with luck it would stay there long enough. Pressing his left hand down on the brake, he shifted the car into gear with his right. Then, setting his right hand against the inner edge of the driver's seat, he shoved hard on the seat, launching himself backward through the open door and simultaneously pulling his left hand off the brake.

He'd hoped to move backward fast enough to make it out of the car before the vehicle picked up too much momentum. But he wasn't quite fast enough. The edge of the doorframe clipped him across his shoulder as the car leaped forward, sending a quick jolt of pain through the shoulder and upper arm and spinning him partway around. An instant later he was clear, the doorframe narrowly missing the side of his head as the car curved away from the curb, and he got his hands under him just in time as he slammed full length onto the hard pavement. The car straightened out of its sharp turn as the steering system's self-alignment kicked in, leaving it rushing more or less in the direction of the Troft transport.

And for the next few seconds, the spinies grouped around the ship would have something more urgent to look at than a couple of distant humans. "Come on," Lorne muttered, pushing himself up and grabbing Nissa's arm. "That building right there," he added, nodding toward the apartment as he pulled her to her feet. "Keep low, and *go*."

She was on the move before he'd even finished the sentence, with no need for the shove he'd planned to give her if she'd needed added encouragement. Lorne gave the car and the spinies one last look, then followed.

They were halfway to their target building when the street lit up with a brilliant flash of blue light. Lorne twisted his head around as the sizzling thunderclap of the high-power laser blast slapped across his ears.

Just in time to see the car he'd sent rolling down the street explode.

Nissa shrieked something unintelligible, her reflexive yelp nearly drowned out by the crackling of flame from the burning car and the creaking thud as it twisted violently around and flipped over onto its side. Putting on a burst of speed, Lorne caught up with the girl, grabbing her around the waist and pulling her along with him, trying to reach safety before the Troft gunners in the ship out there raised their aim.

They were five meters away when the door was abruptly flung open. "Come on!" someone shouted to them. Leaning into his stride, Lorne kicked full power to his leg servos, his skin tingling with heat from the blazing car and crawling with anticipation of the laser blast that would disintegrate him where he stood.

And then they were there, charging through the open door and into an ornately decorated lobby. Lorne caught a glimpse of dozens of people in night-robes and slippers standing tensely around the darkened room—

"Whoa!" a middle-aged man directly in front of them gasped, holding up his hands.

Lorne tried to stop, but he had too little time and too much momentum. With his arm still around Nissa's waist he crashed full tilt into the older man, sending all three of them sprawling onto the thick carpet.

"Sorry," Lorne said, scrambling to his feet and throwing a quick look over his shoulder. "Someone close that door. Lock it if you can."

"You think a *lock's* going to keep them out?" someone demanded in a sort of moaning snarl.

"Just do it," Lorne ordered. He watched long enough to make sure it was being done, then turned back and offered a hand each to Nissa and the man. "You okay?" he asked.

"I think so," Nissa said in a shaky voice as she took Lorne's hand and let him help her to her feet.

"I'm fine," the middle-aged man seconded, ignoring the proffered hand and getting up on his own. "Didn't expect you to be coming in so fast."

"Didn't expect to find someone in our way," Lorne said. "Sorry."

"It's okay," the man said, lowering his voice. "I'm just glad you got here at all."

Lorne frowned. "Oh?"

The other glanced around and lowered his voice still more. "My name's Poole," he said. "I'm an assistant to Senior Governor Tomo Treakness."

Lorne felt his stomach tighten. Treakness, the single loudest and most virulent anti-Cobra voice in the entire Cobra Worlds Directorate. "I guess I need to work on my aim," he said.

Poole frowned. "What?"

"Never mind," Lorne said, feeling a flicker of embarrassment. No matter how Treakness treated the Cobras, a comment like that was uncalled for. "Is the governor aware of what's happened?"

Poole frowned a little harder. "What do you mean?"

"I mean does he know about that," Lorne said patiently, waving a hand in the direction of the Troft warships and the spine leopards.

"Of course he knows," Poole said. "Why do you think you're here?"

It was Lorne's turn to frown. "What?"

"That's why Governor-General Chintawa called you," Poole said, as if it was obvious. "You've been assigned to escort Governor Treakness."

"Escort him where?"

"Where else?" Poole glanced at Nissa, then looked back at Lorne. "Out of the city."

Treakness's apartment, as befit the senior governor's exalted rank, was on the top floor, with a northern exposure that presumably gave him a panoramic view of the city center, Dome, and the distant mountains.

At the moment, though, it was clear that his view was nowhere near the top of the governor's considerations. "About time," he snapped as he opened the door and stepped aside, gesturing the three of them inside with short, imperious movements. "What did you do, Poole, sit them down and discuss the weather?"

"No, sir, of course not," Poole said hastily as he ducked his head in deference. "I brought them up as soon as they arrived."

"So the delay is *your* fault?" Treakness demanded, shifting his eyes to Lorne. "Or hers?"

"We got here as fast as anyone could have," Lorne said, returning the governor's glare. "But of course, at the time we were under the impression that we were urgently needed for serious duty."

Treakness's eyes narrowed. "Meaning?"

"Meaning we've just been invaded, and this is hardly the time for anyone to run whimpering away with his tail between his legs," Lorne said. "Particularly senior governmental officials."

"I agree," Treakness said icily. "If you see anyone doing that, you're authorized to shoot him down."

"Really," Lorne said. "Do you want a running start? Or do you want it right here?"

Treakness threw a look at Poole. "I *did* tell them," the other said. "Just like you told me. I told them we were leaving the city."

Treakness hissed between his teeth. "You are useless, Poole. You know that?" He turned back to Lorne. "Yes, we're leaving the city. No, we aren't running."

"Well, that's clear," Lorne said sarcastically.

"You don't need an explanation, Cobra Broom," Treakness ground out. "All you need to do is follow orders."

"Great—except I don't really have any, do I?" Lorne countered. "I haven't heard word one about any of this from Chintawa."

"And you're not going to any time soon, either," Treakness said heavily. "The whole comm system's down, either destroyed or jammed."

"Cobra Broom!" Nissa snapped.

Lorne turned. She was standing by one of the windows, gazing down at the street below, a look of horror on her face. "The other Cobras. They're here."

Lorne felt his throat tighten. "Hell," he muttered, hurrying to her side.

There were Cobras down there, all right. Five of them, all wearing the semidress uniforms of the Dome security force, working together in deadly efficiency as they lasered, stunned, and otherwise methodically worked their way through the spine leopards the Trofts had turned loose on the streets. Already five of the spinies were down, and Lorne's memory flickered with the all-too-familiar acrid odor of burned flesh and muscle and bone.

"We have to warn them," Nissa breathed.

"About what?" Treakness asked as he and Poole took up positions at the other side of the window. "They seem to be doing all right."

"You don't get it," Lorne said darkly, his mind swirling with useless plans. The comms were being jammed, which probably meant the field radios were also useless, even if Lorne had had one with him. A warning flash through the window from his own laser? That would do nothing but distract and confuse them.

And going down there would only get him killed along with them.

"Don't get what?" Treakness demanded.

"There!" Poole said, jabbing a rigid finger. "Look!"

Lorne lifted his eyes from the carnage going on below them. All across the city, a dozen or more of the tall Troft warships could be seen across the skyline, the whole scene faintly lit by the reddish light from the east. Poole was pointing at one of the ships that had taken up position due west of the governmental center.

And as Lorne watched, the reddish sheen on its hull was suddenly joined by a flicker of sharper blue light from somewhere beneath it.

"They're using the spinies to draw out the Cobras," Lorne said, his voice distant in his ears. "And then they're killing them."

The words were barely out of his mouth when the ground below them and the buildings to either side lit up with another, eye-searing blue flash.

And when he looked down again, he saw the smoldering bodies of his fellow Cobras sprawled on the pavement.

For a long minute no one spoke. Then, Poole took a shuddering breath. "Oh, God," he said, very quietly.

With an effort, Lorne turned away from the grisly sight. Across the city to the northeast, another of the Troft ships was flickering with blue light. "Governor, how many Cobras are in the city?" he asked. "Any idea?"

"There are a little over three thousand on Aventine," Treakness said. For once, Lorne noted almost absently, there wasn't a single trace of arrogance or self-importance in the man's voice. "But of course most of them are in the outer provinces. There can't be more than—I don't know. Maybe two or three hundred in Capitalia proper." He hunched his shoulders.

"They didn't let them kill all the spine leopards first," Nissa said quietly, still gazing down through the window.

"What?" Poole asked.

"They didn't let the Cobras kill all of them," she told him, pointing. "There are still five of them alive out there."

"Of course not," Treakness said bitterly. "After all, once they've suckered the Cobras into the open there'll still be the patroller corps to deal with. Broom, we've got to get out of here."

Lorne felt a sudden flash of anger, as bitter and lethal-edged as the Troft lasers. How *dare* this stupid, pompous fool just casually brush aside the deaths of his comrades down there—men Treakness himself had probably passed at doorways in the Dome's halls a hundred times—as if nothing had happened? "Is that all you can say, Governor?" he snarled, curling his hands into fists and taking a step toward the other.

Treakness held his ground, meeting Lorne's eyes without flinching. "Yes, I know what just happened," he said quietly. "But we can't help them now. Under the circumstances, I don't think we ever could have. What we *can* do is try to make their sacrifice mean something."

"Like what?" Lorne demanded.

"We have a mission," Treakness said. "An urgent errand that Governor-General Chintawa has ordered us to do." He nodded microscopically toward the window. "There were fifteen spine leopards out there, ready to kill anyone who stepped outside. Now, there are only five. If we're going to go, this is the time to do it."

Lorne took a deep breath, forcing back the anger and the heartache. Treakness was still a fool. But he was also right. "You say we're leaving the city," he said. "Where are we going?"

"There's a Troft freighter waiting at Creeksedge Spaceport," he said. "A Tlossie freighter, to be exact."

"And?"

"And the Tlossies are on our side," Treakness said. "Or at least, they're not against us. The point is, the ship's master has agreed to take me to his demesne-lord to plead our case for assistance."

Lorne felt the first stirrings of hope. The Tlos'khin'fahi Demesne had been one of the Cobra Worlds' best trading partners over the past several decades. If they could be persuaded to come into this—whatever the hell *this* was—it could make all the difference between defeat and victory.

Unfortunately, the invading Trofts undoubtedly knew that, too. "What if the invaders don't let him leave with you aboard?"

"I think they will," Treakness said. "This particular shipmaster happens to be the demesne-lord's second heir. There's a fairly rigid protocol between demesnes on such matters." His lip twitched. "Especially since if we do it right they won't know we're aboard."

Lorne grimaced. "Which I presume means they don't want to fly over here and pick us up."

"Even if they were willing, we can't risk it," Treakness said. "We'll just have to go to him."

"What's our timing?"

Treakness seemed to brace himself. "Ingidi-inhiliziyo—that's the heir—has given us until tomorrow daybreak," he said. "Otherwise, he says he'll have to lift without us."

"Terrific," Lorne muttered under his breath. Creeksedge was only about twenty kilometers away as the leatherwing flew. Under normal conditions, a reasonably healthy person could probably walk it in four hours.

But conditions here were far from normal. And they weren't likely to get any better anytime soon, either.

He turned and looked out the window, his eyes drifting across the city skyline, his stomach tightening into a hard knot. Forest territory, plains, streams or small lakes—those he understood. He'd lived with that kind of terrain for the past three years, and he could travel those places with the confidence of knowing where the dangers lurked and the knowledge of how to evade or neutralize them.

But this was a city occupied by enemy soldiers and warships. He didn't have the faintest idea how to function here.

"Governor, we're wasting time," Poole murmured urgently.

Treakness ignored him. "Broom?" he asked.

Lorne looked at Nissa and Poole. Both of them were watching him, their faces rigid with fear and helplessness.

And slowly, it occurred to him that whatever uncertainties he was feeling, the other three people in the room had it far worse. They were political creatures, adept at conference room maneuvering and backstage deals, but at their core they were just civilians.

Lorne might not know the techniques of urban evasion and combat, but at least he knew how to fight.

"Like Mr. Poole said, we're wasting time," he said, putting as much confidence into his voice as he could.

"That we are," Treakness said, managing to sound relieved and annoyed at the same time. "Took you long enough. Poole, go get my bags from the bedroom."

"Whoa, whoa," Lorne said as Poole started to leave the room. "What kind of bags? What's in them?"

"The things I need for a trip to the Tlossie demesne world, of course," Treakness said. "Clothing, credentials, papers—"

"Forget 'em," Lorne interrupted. "Everything except the credentials—you can take those."

"What do you mean, forget them?" Treakness said, sounding annoyed again. "You want me to have to explain to a demesne-lord in his own audience hall that I've been wearing the same clothes for the past week?"

"I'd worry more about how you're going to explain to the Trofts right here in Capitalia why you're packed for a long trip," Lorne countered. "You can take your credentials and any food bars or bottled water you have. That's it."

"Fine," Treakness bit out. "Poole, go to the kitchen—there's an emergency bag in the cabinet above the cooker and some bottles of water in the cooler."

"Better split everything into four packs," Lorne added as Poole made for the kitchen. "Nissa, go help him."

"Yes, sir," Nissa said, and followed Poole out of the room.

Leaving Lorne and Treakness alone. "We're bringing her, too?" Treakness asked quietly.

"You were thinking of leaving her here alone?"

"Frankly, yes," Treakness said evenly. "Troft history indicates they don't mistreat their conquered peoples, at least as long as the conquered peoples behave themselves. She could stay here in my apartment—there's plenty of food—and try to ride it out. And you know as well as I do that a party of three will be easier to sneak past Troft sentries than a party of four."

"Why not just make it a party of two, then?" Lorne challenged. "Leave Nissa someone to talk to while she's hunkered down here."

"Poole comes with me," Treakness said firmly. "Bad enough that you won't let me take proper ceremonial clothing. I am *not* traveling without an assistant. Period."

"Fine," Lorne said with a shrug. "In that case, neither am I."

"Nissa Gendreves isn't your assistant."

"She is now," Lorne said. "If you don't like it, try to remember that this mess is at least partially your fault. If you'd headed directly to Creeksedge the minute North Bank picked up the incoming ships, you could have had your feet up in the Tlossie freighter before the first invaders even landed."

"Believe me, I'd rather have done it that way," Treakness said. "But there was a small fly in the batter." His glare sharpened a few degrees. "You."

Lorne frowned. "What's that supposed to mean?"

"You're the son of Jasmine Moreau," Treakness told him. "For whatever ridiculous reason, the Tlossies seem to have been impressed with the Moreau name over the years."

"Have they, now," Lorne said, permitting himself a small smile. "You'll have to send them a copy of the official report on my mother's mission. I'm sure that'll cool any ardor they feel for us."

"I'm not going to argue politics with you, Broom," Treakness growled. "This isn't the time for it. The bottom line is that, for whatever reason, you're high up in the Tlossies' estimation, and Chintawa insisted that you accompany me to their demesne-lord. So we waited for you." He jerked a hand toward the window. "You see the result."

Lorne grimaced. If Chintawa had just said something to Nissa when he'd called her . . . but that was water over the rim now. "Well, we'll just have to do the best we can," he said.

"I suppose we will," Treakness said with just a hint of sarcasm in his voice. "You have a plan?"

"I have the start of one," Lorne said. "This building have an east entrance?"

Treakness nodded. "It opens into the service street."

"That's where we go out, then," Lorne said. "It's out of sight of the warship, and with luck the spinies won't have gotten back there yet. We'll head south for a couple of blocks, by which time we should have some idea of how well they've got the city covered. Hopefully, at that point or shortly thereafter we'll be able to turn west and head toward Creeksedge."

"And the spine leopards?" Treakness asked. "I presume this ship isn't the only one that's released them out into the streets."

"We'll deal with them as necessary," Lorne said. "If the Trofts didn't grab family groups, they should split up as soon as they realize the city's open and start marking off individual territories for themselves. If there *are* any family groups, unfortunately, they'll probably stick together, at least for now." He gestured toward the east. "And of course, once we're at full daylight, I'll be able to use my lasers out in the open without it being as obvious as it would be right now. Something the Trofts might not have thought about when they planned their attack for dawn."

There was the sound of footsteps, and he turned as Nissa and Poole returned from the kitchen, four belt bags in hand. "We divided up the food and water," Poole said, offering one of his bags to Treakness. "Oh, and we also divided the medical kit from the emergency bag, too. I hope that's all right."

"Of course it's all right," Treakness growled, snatching the belt bag from the other's hand. "Just because Cobra Broom said to take just the food didn't mean you were supposed to turn off your brain."

Poole winced. "Sorry," he muttered.

Lorne suppressed the retort that wanted so badly to come out. If this wasn't the time to talk politics, it also wasn't the time to lecture Treakness about courtesy toward subordinates. "Here's the plan," he said, looking at each of them in turn. "Governor Treakness will take point when we hit the street—he lives here, so he presumably knows this neighborhood best. Nissa, you'll walk behind him to his left; Poole, you'll walk to her right; I'll bring up the rear a little to Poole's right where I can see what's coming from ahead but will also be able to take on anything that comes up from behind. Everyone is to walk as quietly as you can, and no talking unless it's absolutely necessary—I'll need to have my audio enhancers going in order to keep track of what's going on around us. We'll start by heading south, but our ultimate route will depend on the positioning of the Troft ships, the deployment of their troops, and what the spinies decide to do. Got it?"

"Got it," Treakness said for all of them.

"Good," Lorne said. "And from now on, everyone is to call me *Lorne*, not *Cobra Broom*." He took a deep breath. "Okay. Let's go."

CHAPTER FOUR

The explosions from the direction of Stronghold had faded away into the forest chatterings when Paul called them all back into the aircar for a council of war.

It was, Jody remembered distantly as she closed her door, her parents' favorite term over the years to describe formal family discussions. Never in her life had she imagined that she would ever take part in real council of actual war.

If the expressions on Geoff's and Freylan's faces were any indication, they were thinking the same thing.

"First things first," Paul said when the last door had been sealed. "What we've just heard is real. It wasn't a mistake, a joke, or a misinterpretation. Caelian has been invaded."

"But why?" Geoff asked, his voice barely above a moan. "It doesn't make sense."

"Well, it obviously makes sense to the Troft demesnes involved," Paul pointed out. "Otherwise, they wouldn't have done it. But that's not something we're going to figure out now. Nor should we waste a lot of time on it. Our first task is to consider what we're going to do with the situation we've been handed."

"We have to get out of here," Geoff said tightly. "We have to—well, we have to get *out*, that's all."

"And go where?" Paul asked. "Running away from something is useless in and of itself, Geoff. You have to run *to* something."

334

"There's Aerie," Freylan suggested hesitantly. "It's only fifty kilometers away. Or we could try Essbend. That's one-thirty."

Geoff snorted. "And what, you think the Trofts might have missed them?"

"It's possible," Freylan countered. "At less than five hundred people each, they're certainly small enough. Anyway, what would it hurt to try?"

"Well, for starters, it'll burn a bunch of fuel," Geoff growled. "Not to mention time."

"Actually, I think Freylan's right," Paul said. "Though it's probably more a matter of the Trofts not bothering with the other towns than it is of them having missed seeing them. Unfortunately, wherever we go, it can't be by aircar. As of right now, all travel is strictly on foot."

Geoff stared at him in disbelief. Freylan's face actually paled. "What are you talking about?" Geoff demanded. "I was kidding about the fuel—we've got practically a full tank."

"And any invasion force worth its pay will be watching closely for enemy aircraft," Paul told him. "*All* enemy aircraft, military or civilian. We get above treetop level, and chances are they'll be right on top of us."

"So we don't go that high," Freylan suggested. "There must be ways to maneuver through the forest instead of going over it."

Geoff hissed contemptuously. "Have you *looked* out there lately?"

"Unfortunately, Geoff's right," Paul said. "Unless we can fly this thing sideways, we're not getting through any of that."

"Well, we're sure not taking a fifty-kilometer walk," Jody said firmly. "Not through a Caelian forest."

"Agreed," Paul said. "And since those explosions were likely the comm towers being destroyed, we're not going to be calling anyone for help, either."

"Wait a second," Geoff said. "How do you know those were the comm towers?"

"I don't," Paul said. "But it's a fair enough assumption. Trofts don't go in for wholesale slaughter, and there was barely enough time for the town to even notice them, let alone launch some kind of attack that the Trofts might have been reacting to. Given the timing, the first explosion was almost certainly the primary tower, from which it follows that the others were probably the secondary ones."

"The timing?" Geoff asked, sounding bewildered.

"There was a fifteen-second gap between the cutoff of Uy's transmission and the sound of the first explosion," Freylan murmured. "Three seconds per kilometer for the sound to get here. Didn't you ever count seconds after a lightning flash?"

"Right," Paul said. "Which is also why I said earlier that you were probably right about Aerie and Essbend and the other towns not being attacked. The only reason I can think of to destroy the comm system instead of temporarily jamming it is to permanently keep Stronghold from talking to possible allies. No reason to waste perfectly good explosives on the towers if those allies are also pinned down."

"So our job is to hang tough and see if the other towns got Uy's message and are able to do something about it?" Jody asked.

"That's one option." Her father cocked an eyebrow. "The other would be to see whether we can do something about it ourselves."

Geoff's eyes widened. "You're joking. *Us?*"

"Why not?" Paul countered calmly. "Most of their attention's going to be focused on Stronghold, not out here."

Geoff shook his head disbelievingly. "You're not joking, you're insane. Look, I know you Cobras are supposed to be real hotshots at this sort of thing, but come *on.*"

"It can't hurt to go back and poke around a little," Jody offered, trying hard to match her father's outward composure. Her skin was crawling at the thought of deliberately walking into enemy territory, but there was no way she was going to let Geoff and Freylan know that. "Anyway, if we get caught, as long as we don't make threatening moves the Trofts will probably just put us in the town with everyone else."

Freylan whistled softly. "Insanity must run in your family."

"Very possibly," Paul conceded. "I'm open to other suggestions."

"Well, *I'm* not going," Geoff said flatly. "You three want to play hero, go right ahead. But I didn't sign up for any suicide missions."

For a moment the aircar was silent. Then Freylan stirred. "That's fine," he said. "You can stay here. Just make sure you cook that gigger all the way through or you might end up with parasites."

Geoff frowned at him. "What are you talking about? There's a full survival kit back there with a couple dozen ration bars."

"Thirty, actually," Freylan said. "But we're going to be on the move, and won't have time for hunting or cooking. Certainly not that close to the Trofts." He waved a hand around them. "You, on the other hand, will have the time *and* the distance *and* the trap. Perfect conditions for living off the land."

"You can't be serious," Geoff protested. "You want me to *leave the aircar*? Alone?"

"Why not?" Freylan said coolly. "We're going to."

"But not alone," Geoff said, his voice taking on an edge of pleading. "You can't expect me to—" He shot a hooded look at Jody. "Jody, tell him."

"I'm sorry, but he's right," Jody said, working hard to keep a straight face. Despite the desperate danger they were in, watching Geoff the glib manipulator being verbally outmaneuvered by his quieter, more socially awkward friend and co-worker was just too funny. "Or you could come with us. That way you won't be alone."

"*And* you won't have to cook," Freylan added.

Geoff shot him a glare. "Yeah, I get it," he growled. "Cute. Both of you."

"So it's agreed," Paul said. "We stick together, and go see what's happening with Stronghold." He lifted a finger. "And in case you're working on your worst-case scenarios, let me set your minds at ease. No matter what the situation is back there, I'm not going to ask any of you to do any fighting."

"Yeah, thanks," Geoff muttered. "That makes it sound *so* much better."

"What do you want us to do?" Freylan asked.

"You three get the survival bag out and start sorting everything into smaller, carry-size packs," Paul instructed. "There may be some fold-up backpacks in there you can use. I'll go and see if I can scope out the best route."

"I'll come with you," Jody volunteered. "If we're not going to take samples from that gigger, we need to either release it or kill it. I'm not leaving it in the cage to starve to death."

"Better just kill it," Freylan suggested. "You don't want it turning on you when you open the lid."

"And it's not like the forest is likely to run out of the damn things," Geoff added sourly.

The wind was picking up again as Jody and her father left the aircar and made their way south up the hillside. "Clever of them to come during the midmorning lull," Paul commented as they walked. "The spores stop flying, ribbon vines stop flowing and twisting around where they might snag landing gear and get into opening hatches, and the major predators stop moving around until the wind starts covering their movements again. Perfect time to land—"

He spun around and Jody felt a sudden jolt of mild disorientation as she caught the edge of his sonic blast. A trio of striped saberclaws burst through the tall grass and bushes, staggering toward them, and there were three quick thunderclaps as Paul sent an arcthrower blast into each of them. "—and consolidate their position," he finished, turning his head back and forth in a quick sweep of the area. "Whoever this is, they've done their homework."

"But why?" Jody protested, blinking hard to shake away the last of the sonic's effects. "Why would anyone invade Caelian? What in the Worlds could they possibly want here?"

"I don't know," Paul said grimly. "But my guess is that if they're *here*, they're everywhere else, too."

Jody swallowed. "You mean Aventine."

"And Palatine and probably Esquiline and Viminal, too." He looked sideways at her. "I wouldn't worry about Lorne, though," he added. "The Trofts can't possibly have enough troops to occupy the entire planet. As long as he stays out in the expansion region, he should be okay."

"Unless Chintawa had time to call everyone back to the cities," Jody said.

"Not if the Trofts were as fast there as they were here," Paul pointed out. "But either way, Lorne's fate is out of our hands, and you need to set it aside. Our concern right now—our *only* concern—is our own survival."

They reached the top of the hill, which turned out to be already occupied by a stand of hookgrass. Paul used his fingertip lasers to burn a path through it, and a moment later they were standing at the crest gazing away to the south.

It was a stunning view, a panorama of multiple shades of green highlighted with swathes of light blue, red, and yellow. The original assessment teams had been astonished at its beauty during their first survey flights over the forests, and Jody herself had had her breath taken away as she watched on the *Freedom's Fire*'s viewscreens during their arrival.

Now, after less than two weeks on the ground, she couldn't even see the beauty anymore. All she could see was how the forest provided the perfect habitat for huge insects, painful or poisonous plants, and deadly predators.

"We'll start by following that ridge," her father said, pointing to a low, mostly treeless crest meandering its way through the greenery. "We'll be open to view from above, but we won't have as many trees for the arboreal predators to jump at us from."

"The Trofts ought to be too busy for a while to organize overflights, anyway," Jody said, trying to visualize the map of the region. "I think that'll take us most of the way to the river. I wonder if the survival kit includes an inflatable boat."

Paul grunted. "I wouldn't trust it even if it did," he said. "Way too many things with sharp teeth infesting the waterways here. Let's go deal with that gigger and get moving. We're going to be pushing our available daylight as it is."

They retraced their steps back to the aircar, where Geoff and Freylan were busily sorting out the survival pack's contents, and continued past to the gigger still rocking back and forth inside its prison. "I presume you'd like to keep the trap itself intact?" Paul asked as they gazed down at the growling predator.

"If possible," Jody said, frowning. The gigger was growling up a storm, complete with a set of subsonics she could feel right through the ground.

"Okay." Paul lifted his hands, aiming his fingertip lasers at the predator's head—

"Wait," Jody said suddenly.

Her father paused, his thumbs resting on his trigger fingers. "Trouble?"

"I'm not sure," Jody said, gazing down at the gigger. "You remember when we first got here, a screech tiger moved in and you had to shoot it? I'm not absolutely sure, but I don't think the gigger was growling during that time."

Slowly, Paul lowered his hands. "Interesting," he said. "Walk me through it."

Jody huffed. "I've hardly even got it myself."

"Then walk both of us through it."

Jody chewed her lip. "Okay. Assume I'm right about the gigger's moment of silence. It could just mean that he heard or smelled the screech tiger coming and wanted to keep a low profile. Except that from everything I've read on Caelian ecology the predators here don't usually eat other predators."

"Though it's a rare animal indeed that'll turn down a free lunch," Paul pointed out. "If the gigger realized he now fell into that category, it would be all the more reason to shut up when he knew something bigger was in the area."

"Maybe," Jody conceded. "In which case, this whole train of thought has already stopped in the station."

"Or?" Paul prompted.

"Or it could be something more complicated," Jody said slowly. "If the gigger is announcing his presence and claiming his territory... only then he stops when something bigger with a better claim to that territory comes along..." She shook her head. "I don't know, Dad. There's something going on here—I'm sure of it. But I don't have any kind of real grip on it yet."

For a moment they stood silently, gazing down at the rumbling gigger. "Well, when you run out of theory, it's time for an experiment. You feel up to carrying a double load of survival equipment?"

"Probably," Jody said, frowning at him. "Why?"

He gestured down at the cage. "If we each take a double load, it'll free up Geoff and Freylan to carry our new friend here. A little five-kilometer stroll through the forest would be the perfect way to observe his growling habits in the wild."

"Ooh, I don't think they'll go for that," Jody said doubtfully. "That trap is heavier than it looks. Especially with a full-grown gigger inside."

"Let's ask them," Paul suggested. "Maybe they'll surprise you."

To Jody's surprise, they did. "Interesting," Geoff said, frowning thoughtfully as he stuffed food bars and water purification tablets into one of the backpacks. "I don't think anyone's gone that direction before."

"And why would they?" Freylan agreed as he finished with one of his two backpacks and started on the second. "I don't think there's any known ecology where that kind of interspecies territorial hierarchy exists, at least not the kind you're suggesting. Land and mate wars usually only take place between members of the same species."

"It might explain why Caelian has so little predator-on-predator killing, too," Geoff said. "Damn. Wouldn't it be a real kick if the solution to this mess was nothing more complicated than everyone carrying around a recording of screech tiger screeches?"

"'Course, your population will be totally deaf within three weeks," Freylan said dryly. "But there should be a way to engineer active-cancellation earplugs to filter out most of the sound."

"So you don't mind dragging him along?" Jody asked, still not quite believing they were going for this so enthusiastically.

"No problem," Geoff assured her. "Freylan, you think you can rig up something so that we can carry the bars on our shoulders instead of having to actually hold them the whole way?"

"No problem," Freylan assured him. "We can probably even use the spare straps from the survival kit to rig cross-shoulder harnesses so the guy in back can see over the cage." He gave Jody a tentative smile. "Great idea, Jody."

"Well, let's not award ourselves any prizes yet," Jody warned. "It could easily just be a gigger trying not to attract attention."

"Which is fine, too," Geoff said. "If and when he shuts up it'll mean we need to be extra careful to watch for something big to come at us. Okay, so Freylan and I will rig the cage and carry the gigger, while—"

"Snouts," Freylan said.

They all looked at him. "What?" Jody asked.

"That's his new name," Freylan said. "Snouts."

Jody looked questioningly at Geoff. The other just shrugged. "He used to name his lab equipment back at school, too," he said. "Don't worry, it's harmless. So like I was saying, Freylan and I will carry Snouts, and you, Jody will carry all the packs."

"She'll carry two of them," Paul corrected. "I'll carry the others."

"Sorry, but you're the sole defense of this little expedition," Geoff said, shaking his head. "That means you need to be free and unencumbered at all times."

"I think you're underestimating my abilities," Paul said mildly. "Besides, with a little luck, I'll be able to hear or see any trouble coming long before I need to use any of my combat reflexes."

Geoff snorted. "If we had any luck, we wouldn't be sitting in the middle of a Troft invasion."

"No, he's right, Dad," Jody said reluctantly, eyeing the four bulging backpacks. "I guess we shouldn't have wasted time dividing up the kit."

"Not at all," Geoff soothed. "It'll be easier to distribute the weight around your shoulders and hips this way."

Jody narrowed her eyes slightly at him. "You're enjoying this, aren't you?" she challenged.

"As much as I've enjoyed anything in the past ten minutes, pretty much," he agreed. He smiled, the old confident Geoff smile that had won the group so much of their corporate funding over the past few months. "If it helps any," he added, "and should the need arise, I'll also be available to do all the cooking."

"Oh, yeah," Jody said, nodding. "You're enjoying this."

"Probably not for long," Freylan said, reaching to the seat beside him and picking up a pair of stun sticks. "Here—you should probably carry one of these. Geoff, you want the other one?"

"Just a minute," Paul said as Jody gingerly took the two weapons and started to hand one to Geoff. "Do any of you know how to use one of those?"

"We all took the intro course aboard the *Freedom's Fire*," Jody reminded him.

"Yes, I sat in on that," Paul said. "Let me rephrase: has any of you ever actually *used* anything like those?"

"I had a fencing unit in high school," Jody offered.

"Did the foils generate current in the half-megavolt range?" Paul asked pointedly.

"Well, no," Jody conceded.

"Then your answer would be no," Paul told her. "Either of you?"

"No," Geoff said as Freylan shook his head.

"Then they stay in the bag," Paul said firmly. "Unless you've had actual training—and that shipboard lecture doesn't qualify— they'll be more of a danger to you than to anything you're likely to meet out there."

"Yes, but—" Geoff began.

"They stay in the packs," Paul said firmly. "Trust me. Some of the animals here are big enough to take a jolt that would kill you outright."

"Maybe we should just leave them here, then," Freylan suggested. "They're pretty heavy for something we can't use."

"No, let's take them," Paul said. "They may be useful in setting up a perimeter wherever we wind up spending the night. Just make sure they're locked in the off position before you put them back in the bags."

"They are," Jody confirmed as she handed the weapons back to Freylan. "Anyway, don't worry about the weight," she added. "*I'll* be the one carrying them, remember?"

"So let's grab everything and get going," Paul said, opening his door. "Time to hit the trail."

"Just no hiking songs," Jody warned. "I've heard you sing, and this planet hates us enough as it is."

CHAPTER FIVE

At Lorne's direction, Treakness led the group down a back stairway, out of sight of the Troft warship, which would hopefully also allow them to bypass the nervous residents Lorne and Nissa had left in the lobby.

They reached the back door to find that a smaller group was likewise milling around the smaller area there. But everyone seemed preoccupied with his or her own thoughts and concerns, and none of them challenged the intentions of four people foolish enough to venture out into the streets of a freshly occupied city. Certainly none of them asked to come along. Lorne opened the door a crack, confirmed that nothing was moving nearby, and the group slipped out into the early morning gloom.

By this time, Lorne knew, Capitalia would normally be starting to come to life. Traffic would be picking up as merchants arrived at their stores for pre-opening checks, restaurateurs began preparing the day's dishes, and early-rising office workers got a jump on the traffic and headed in to tackle the work waiting on their desks.

But not today. Today, the rising sun might as well have been looking down on a ghost town.

Or at least a ghost neighborhood. Over the thudding of the group's footsteps in his enhanced hearing Lorne could pick out the confused-sounding rumbles of multiple spine leopards as they

344

tried to figure out the unfamiliar surroundings they'd been unceremoniously dumped into. Behind the sounds of the animals he could hear muffled metallic whirrings and clanks as the Trofts in their warships finished locking down their landing gear, tested the gimbals on their wing-mounted weapons, and probably prepared their troop deployment.

"Where is everyone?" Nissa shouted.

Lorne jumped, cursing, as he quickly dialed back his audios. "Sorry," Nissa said, her voice this time sounding more like the murmur the question had actually been.

"Where do you think they are?" Treakness growled before Lorne could answer. "You expect them to all rush outside to see the pretty fireworks?"

"I was asking about the Trofts, sir," Nissa countered stiffly. "Shouldn't they be moving troops into the Dome or the patroller stations or something?"

"Don't worry, that'll happen soon enough," Lorne said. "My guess is that they're waiting for the spinies to sort themselves out into territories, maybe draw a few more Cobras or patrollers into the open—"

And with his audios off, he was caught completely off guard by the spine leopard that appeared suddenly from behind an underdrop trash container across the street and charged.

Reflexively, Lorne took a long step to his right, perpendicular to the spiny's path, putting some distance between himself and the others. A flick of his eye set a target lock on the predator's head, and he shifted his weight onto his right foot. He would let it close about half the remaining distance, he decided, then swing his left leg up and nail it with an antiarmor laser shot. Maybe a quick burst with his sonic a step or two before that, just to slow it down—

"Lorne!" Nissa gasped.

—and in that frozen second he belatedly remembered where he was and who he was with. Not out in the Aventinian wilderness with his fellow Cobras, but in a city with a trio of helpless civilians. Civilians who couldn't fight, couldn't get out of the way, and probably didn't even have enough sense to duck.

And the spine leopard was charging directly toward them.

Lorne cursed under his breath, leaping back again to put himself between the civilians and the predator, realizing in that same instant that he couldn't use his planned response. An audible sonic, a visible flash, and he would have every Troft in range converging on this street.

Which left him only one option.

The spiny had made it two more steps, with maybe six more and a short leap to go, by the time Lorne had his original head shot cancelled and a new targeting lock on the front of the animal's neck where it met the lower jaw. Then, bracing himself, he squatted down and fell backwards, doing a controlled roll from hips to shoulder blades onto his back. He heard Nissa gasp something else as the spine leopard, sensing wounded prey, shifted direction slightly and bore straight down on him. As the predator shoved itself off the pavement into what it surely expected to be a killing leap, Lorne triggered his antiarmor laser. His leg servos, responding to the spiny's position and Lorne's own programmed target lock, swung his left leg up to meet the incoming threat.

And as Lorne's heel connected solidly with the attacker's throat, the laser finally fired, burning instantly through muscle and throat and brain.

The spine leopard's momentum kept it moving, caroming off Lorne's foot and flying over his body. But the creature was dead long before it thudded to the pavement.

"What the *hell* was that?" Treakness demanded as Lorne rolled back up onto his feet.

"It's called saving your lives," Lorne said stiffly. Going over to the dead spine leopard, he scooped it up in his arms, hearing the faint sound of his arm servos as they took the predator's weight. "You might say thank you."

"*Thank* you," Treakness growled. "What I *meant* was why didn't you just shoot the damn thing instead of playing patty-cake with it?"

Poole cleared his throat. "I think he was trying not to let the Trofts see the flash—"

"Shut up, Poole," Treakness cut him off. He was still glaring, but

Lorne could see the anger starting to fade as he realized his aide was right. "Fine, so you're brave and strong *and* clever. Now what?"

"First, we find a place to stash the evidence," Lorne said, looking around. The closest stashing place was the trash container where the animal had been hiding. "Wait here," he said, and crossed the street to the bin.

He'd hoped he would be able to dump the carcass inside, but the overhead conduit that carried the building's trash out to the bin fit too snugly for him to slip the animal through. He had to settle for shoving the animal behind the bin, pushing it as far out of sight as he could.

The others were looking nervously around when he rejoined them. "Come on, come on," Treakness muttered. "Another two blocks and we'll hit Palisade Park. Mostly low buildings around it, so we should be able to see all of the nearby Troft ships from there."

"Sounds good," Lorne said, glancing around at the five- and six-story structures rising up around them. "Again, no talking unless absolutely necessary, and keep those footsteps *quiet*."

They had made it halfway down the next block when Lorne began to pick up the distant hum of motors and the dull thuds of thick metal hitting pavement. They had covered another quarter block when the rumble of heavy-duty engines—a lot of them—began.

They had reached the next street, and Lorne was peering carefully around the corner building, when the rumble of engines became a line of boxy vehicles lumbering past along Cavendish Boulevard a block away, each heavily armored and sporting a swivel gun on its roof.

"What is it?" Treakness murmured.

Grimacing, Lorne stepped back and gestured for him to look. Treakness eased his head around the corner, watched for a few seconds, then drew back again. "So much for getting to the park," he said tightly.

"The Trofts?" Poole asked anxiously.

"No, the Ghirdel Pastry Express truck," Treakness snarled. "Use your *brain*, Poole."

"Enough of that," Lorne ordered. "Everyone be quiet a minute."

The others froze. Lorne keyed up his audios again, trying to hear beyond the roar of the traffic rolling past a block away. As far as he could tell, that particular convoy was the only one in the immediate area. "It just seems to be that one bunch," he said, lowering the audios. "Any idea where they might be going?"

"That seems like way too much firepower just to take down the Five Points patroller station," Treakness said thoughtfully. "I'm guessing they're sending those personnel carriers to some central place, probably Five Points, where they'll set up a command base and send the rest of the vehicles out in ones or twos to block and control the rest of the major intersections." He gave Lorne a look of strained patience. "Yes, I *have* studied a bit of military theory, thank you."

"But if they block all the intersections, how are we going to get past them?" Nissa asked nervously.

"That's the question, all right," Treakness agreed. "Hopefully, our brave and clever Cobra escort will come up with something brave and clever."

"Hold it," Lorne said, holding up a hand as he caught a flicker of grav-lift red reflecting from the side of one of the buildings to the east. Reflections were always tricky, but whatever it was definitely appeared to be moving in their direction. "Someone's coming," he said, looking around for the entrance to the building beside them. It was about twenty meters back along the street, beneath a small sign that read WEI KEI'S. "We need to get to cover."

The door was locked, but his fingertip lasers made quick work of the mechanism. The four of them slipped inside and Lorne pulled the door mostly closed again behind them.

As he did so, he saw one of the Trofts' transports settle into the intersection one block north. He stood motionless, the door still open a crack, and watched as the side hatches opened and another group of spine leopards strode out onto the street.

"What is it?" Treakness's voice came from behind him.

Lorne eased the door closed. "More spine leopards," he said.

"Terrific," Treakness growled. "Now what?"

Lorne looked around. They were standing in a narrow exit hallway stretching between the door and an unlit dining room, with a kitchen area visible through a wide doorway to their right. Obviously, Wei Kei's was a restaurant. "I need to find a way up to the top floor," he said. "See if I can spot a clear route west."

"Good idea," Treakness said, peering over at the kitchen. "We'll stay here. Poole, go check out that kitchen and see if you can find us something to eat."

Poole's eyes went a little wide. "Uh—sir, do you think we should do that?"

"This is a restaurant, Poole," Treakness said brusquely. "I'm a senior governor, this is an emergency situation, and I'm hungry. Go get me something to eat."

Poole swallowed visibly. "Yes, sir," he said, and hurried through the doorway into the kitchen.

Nissa touched Lorne's arm. "May I come with you?" she asked, her voice strained. "An extra pair of eyes might be useful."

"Yes, take her," Treakness seconded. "Don't be too long."

"It won't be safe for her," Lorne said between clenched teeth. Apparently, Treakness didn't want witnesses while he raided the restaurant's kitchen. "I'll have to go back outside to get to the main building entrance, and there's a new crop of spinies that's just arrived out there. I may have to do some quick dodging to get around them."

"We don't have to go outside," Nissa said. "There's an inside entrance, too, near the front of the restaurant. I've seen it the couple of times that I've eaten here."

"We'll check it out." Lorne eyed Treakness. "If anyone comes down from the apartments while we're gone, your job is to keep them calm."

"I know what my job is," Treakness said coolly. "You just remember what *yours* is."

The stairway Nissa had mentioned wasn't exactly a true inside stairway, but ran from the street parallel to the restaurant's southern edge. But there was another access door just inside the street entrance that opened up into that corner of the dining room. Again, it was locked, and again Lorne's lasers took care of that. Pulling open the door, they slipped into the stairway and headed up.

The stairway was fairly narrow, covered with sturdy but inexpensive carpeting, lined by undecorated walls. There were four apartments on each floor, each taking up one corner of the building, with a second stairway and a small elevator at the far end of each of the long landings. The landings themselves were deserted, but a quick tweaking of Lorne's audios at each stop picked up the sounds of people moving around inside the apartments.

"Which one do we want?" Nissa asked as they arrived at the top floor.

"This one," Lorne said, nodding toward the southwest apartment. Stepping to the door, he knocked.

For a moment there was no response. Lorne knocked again, then keyed in his audios. Someone was definitely in there, several someones, all of them trying very hard to be quiet. "Hey!" he called. "We need to look out your windows."

There was another short silence. Then, Lorne heard stealthy footsteps approaching. "Who is it?" a nervous voice called through the door.

"It's Nissa Gendreves from Governor-General Chintawa's office," Nissa called back before Lorne could answer. "It's urgent that we come in."

There was one final pause, and then Lorne heard the clicking as the longlock was disengaged. The door opened a crack and a tense, unshaven face peered out. "I'm Nissa Gendreves," Nissa repeated. "This is Lorne Broom."

"What do you want?" the man asked suspiciously, looking back and forth between them. "What the hell's going on out there?"

"That's what we're trying to find out," Lorne told him. "A quick look out your windows, and then we'll be gone."

"I don't think I've seen you before," the man said, his eyes narrowing as he studied Lorne's face. "Who do you work for?"

"He's with Senior Governor Treakness," Nissa said, stepping forward past Lorne and giving the door a gentle but firm push. The man grimaced, but backed out of the way, and Nissa walked past him into the apartment. Lorne followed, staying close behind her. "You're one of Syndic Priesly's aides, right?" Nissa added over her shoulder.

"Yes," the man said as he closed the door behind them. "Kovas Brander. Why didn't anyone tell us this was going to happen?"

"Because nobody knew," Nissa said as the three of them strode past a pair of bedroom doors and into the living room. A tense-looking woman was sitting on a narrow couch, clutching two silent, wide-eyed young children to her sides. "It's all right," Nissa added, nodding to them. "We're with Governor-General Chintawa's office."

"Yes, I heard," the woman said nervously. "Do you know what's going on?"

"So far, only that Capitalia's been invaded and is on its way to being fully occupied," Lorne told her as he and Nissa crossed to the windows and eased back the curtains.

Lorne had expected to see armed Troft soldiers spilling out of the armored vehicles they'd seen earlier, lasers held high as they roamed the streets of their newly conquered city. The aliens out there *were* definitely soldiers, garbed in visored helmets and heavily armored versions of the same leotards the species usually wore, with heavy laser rifles slung over their shoulders.

But they weren't exactly roaming, and the five-meter-long cylinders they were hauling out of the troop carriers didn't look like weapons. Frowning, Lorne focused on two of them as they lugged their burden over to the building on the southwest side of the intersection he and Nissa were looking down onto. The Trofts set the cylinder upright against the building's corner, and as Lorne keyed in his infrareds he spotted the subtle yellow flashes as the cylinder was molecularly welded to the building.

And then, to his astonishment, the Trofts began to unroll the cylinder into a fine mesh, working their way northward across the street.

"What in the *Worlds*?" Nissa breathed.

Lorne didn't answer, frowning in confusion as the Trofts reached the other side of the street, pulled the mesh as tight as they could, and again welded it to the corner of the building there. A quick slash from a plasma torch cut the rest of the roll free, and the two aliens picked it up and headed north toward the next open space.

"They're fencing off the street," Brander said disbelievingly from beside Lorne.

"He's right," Nissa confirmed. Pressing the side of her ear to the glass, she looked as straight down as she could. "They're putting one up on this side, too."

"But that's crazy," Brander protested. "I mean, hell, you can cut the stuff with a torch—I just saw them do it. How do they think it's going to keep us in?"

Lorne focused on the fence the Trofts had just created. Five meters tall, the same height as the fences around most of the major wilderness towns.

And then, he got it. "You're missing the point," he said, stepping around Nissa and moving to the far southwest corner of the room. From his new vantage point he could see a few blocks down the side street the Trofts had just blocked off, far enough to see a similar double barricade being erected around the major avenue three blocks away. "They're not trying to keep us *in*. They're trying to keep the spine leopards *out*."

"The *what*?" Brander asked.

"You're right," Nissa said, her voice suddenly taut. "Oh, God."

"What spine leopards?" Brander demanded.

"They're bringing in spine leopards," Nissa told him. "We've already seen two transports letting groups of them out onto the streets."

"And it looks like there are more on the way," Lorne said, nodding toward a pair of distant transports as they disappeared beneath the city's skyline.

Brander cursed under his breath. "Where are the damn Cobras?" he demanded. "Isn't that why we've got them, to handle things like this?"

Lorne turned toward him, a sudden surge of anger tightening his stomach—"They *are* handling it," Nissa said, throwing Lorne a quick warning look. "Or they were. We saw five of them out in the street, taking out that first group. They were doing fine until the Trofts killed them."

"And they didn't fight back?" Brander demanded. "Well, *hell*. What are we paying them for anyway?"

"Brander, go see to your family," Lorne ordered, jerking his head toward the woman and children. "Nissa, I need you over here, please."

Brander made as if to speak, took a second look at Lorne's expression, and seemed to think better of it. Turning, he walked back across the room.

"I'm sorry," Nissa said quietly as she stepped to Lorne's side.

"Yeah," Lorne growled back. Of course she was sorry now, now when it was too late to do anything. Where had her sorry been back when people like Treakness were demanding the Cobra program be gutted to save a few *klae* from the budget?

For that matter, where had the people of the Cobra Worlds been when Treakness had first won his seat by making loud promises to support those cutbacks? Were the people who'd voted for him and his allies even now staring out their windows at the Troft soldiers and vehicles, cursing the Cobras just like Brander had for not saving them?

He took a deep breath, striving for some of his father's and brother's inborn calm. The past was the past, and so were its mistakes and conceits. Holding onto it would just siphon off mental energy that he desperately needed elsewhere. "Stand here and look due west," he told Nissa, motioning her to the corner of the window. "You see how the street three blocks away is also being fenced in?"

"Yes," she said. "You think they're crosshatching the city?"

"I don't think so," Lorne said. "Why bother fencing both sides of the same street if they're just doing a crosshatch?"

"Corridors, then?" Nissa suggested. "Maybe they're setting up patrol routes that their soldiers can use without worrying about spine leopard attacks."

"If that's the plan, they're in for a rude awakening," Lorne said. "Like Brander said, that mesh may keep spinies out, but you can cut it with a torch. We do that, and they'll be in the same boat we are."

"Humans of Aventine," a computerized voice called faintly from somewhere below them. "Humans of Aventine, awake and listen."

"Do these open?" Lorne called to Brander, running his fingers along the window's edges as he searched in vain for a catch.

"Yeah, I'll get it," Brander said, bounding up from the couch and hurrying over. He did something, and the window swung open a few centimeters.

"Humans of Aventine," the Troft voice came again, much louder and clearer this time. Lorne nudged up his audios as the voice ended, and caught three distinct and distant echoes. Apparently, the Trofts were delivering the same message simultaneously across the whole city. "Humans of Aventine, awake and listen."

"We *are* awake, you son of a chicken," Brander muttered. "Get on with it."

"Humans of Aventine, in payment for the crimes of your government, you are now under the rule and authority of the Trof'te Assemblage. If you cooperate without resistance, you will not be harmed, and will be permitted to continue your daily lives.

"Your first orders are the following: For the next three hours you are to remain inside your residences or other interior locations; when the three hours have ended, you will have permission to emerge, but only into the fenced zones which we are currently building. All humans traveling outside those zones will be subject to immediate death.

"Also at the end of those three hours, your chief leaders will meet us in the assembly center known as the Dome, where detailed instructions will be delivered to them. Any of the chief leaders who fails to attend will also be subject to immediate death."

Lorne looked sideways at Nissa, and found her looking back at him. Would the invaders even know who all the governors and syndics were? Probably. Everything else that had happened, from the coordinated predawn invasion to the efficient fencing work, indicated that they knew what they were doing. They would spot Treakness's absence, all right, and they would certainly call Chintawa on it.

Hopefully, the governor-general could work up a plausible story for them. If not, their already tight timetable was likely to get a lot tighter.

"One final order," the loudspeaker below boomed. "Any human who hides or assists an armed patroller or a *koubrah*-soldier will be punished. Any human who exposes the existence and location of an armed patroller or *koubrah*-soldier will be rewarded."

The loudspeaker fell silent . . . and Lorne felt a shiver run up the back of his neck. A day ago, back in the expansion region, he would have dismissed any such carrot/stick ploy as a pathetic waste of time. He knew the people out there, and there was no way they would turn on him or the rest of the men who risked their lives on a daily basis to protect them.

But he was in the city now, surrounded by people with Brander's same attitude of contempt or indifference toward those guardians. What would *they* do with the handful of Cobras still among them? How big would the promised rewards and threatened punishments have to get before the betrayals started?

Or would the carrots and sticks not even be necessary? Would the people turn in the Cobras simply out of spite for their perceived failure in preventing the invasion in the first place?

He could feel Nissa's eyes on him. Deliberately, he didn't look back at her. "Sounds like that's it for now," he said, forcing his voice to remain calm. "Come on, we'd better get back downstairs."

"Wait a minute," Nissa said slowly.

Lorne turned, to find that he'd been wrong about her looking at him. In fact, she was frowning out at the cityscape below. "What is it?" he asked.

"This doesn't make any sense," she said, pointing down the side street. "That's Broadway over there, the one they're fencing off. It's mostly shopping, with the Gregorius Omni a block north and the Wickstra Performing Arts Center four blocks south."

"Okay," Lorne said, pulling up his own somewhat hazy memories of the central city's layout. "So?"

"So most of the residences in this area are *between* here and there," Nissa said. "In fact, almost all of them are, since there aren't even many of these store-and-apartment setups on Broadway. Nearly everything there above the shopping levels is office space."

"Again, so?" Lorne said, still not seeing where she was going with all this.

"So all those apartments and homes are outside the fences," Nissa said. "How are the people in there supposed to get to the fenced-in areas the Trofts are setting up?"

"Oh, hell," Lorne said as it finally clicked. "You're right, they *aren't* going to get there. Not without help." He hissed contemptuously. "Brilliant. Carrots, sticks, *and* bludgeons."

"What do you mean?" Brander asked, frowning.

"He means they're expecting the Cobras to go in and get the people out," Nissa murmured.

"Thereby giving the Trofts yet another free shot at them," Lorne said. "If the spinies don't get them first."

He took one final look at the fence construction going on along the street, then took Nissa's arm. "Come on," he said. "We need a consultation."

The restaurant had filled up in the time they'd been upstairs. There were upwards of twenty people in the dining room, a few still in nightdress and robes but the majority properly dressed. They were mostly clumped together in small groups, as had been the case back in the lobby of Treakness's apartment building, whispering nervously among themselves as they gazed out the windows at the construction going on outside.

All eyes turned to Lorne and Nissa as they came though the door, and for a moment the whispering went silent. But Lorne merely nodded a wordless acknowledgment to them and headed across the room toward the rear corner table where Treakness and Poole had taken up residence. A moment later, as it became clear that the newcomers had no fresh information to share, the whispering resumed.

"You enjoy your snack?" Lorne asked as he and Nissa sat down in the table's two empty seats.

"It was adequate," Treakness said coolly. "I presume you heard the announcement. How did things look from up there?"

"About like they do from down here," Lorne said. "The Trofts are busy fencing off this street and Broadway. Probably others, too, but Broadway was as far as we could see."

"Wait a minute," Poole said, frowning. "*Just* this one and Broadway?"

"*And* others they already said they couldn't see," Treakness growled. "Pay attention."

"No, no, that's not what I meant," Poole said, fumbling the words. "I meant what about the streets *between* here and Broadway?"

Treakness rolled his eyes. "They already said—"

"What Poole means," Lorne cut him off, "is whether the people living on those other streets are being thrown to the wolves. The answer is, yes, they are."

Treakness's lips compressed into a thin line. "I see," he said grimly. "So in other words, the Trofts are letting us choose between hundreds of civilian casualties and sending our remaining Cobras back out into the open."

"That about sums it up," Lorne agreed. "So what do we do?"

Treakness hissed thoughtfully. "Well, for the next three hours, at least, we do nothing," he said. "We're pretty well stuck here until the Trofts' quarantine period is up. After that..." He shrugged. "I suppose that particular decision will be landing in Chintawa's lap. Lucky him."

"Shouldn't we at least alert him as to what's going on out here?" Lorne asked. "And while we're at it, we should also find out what's happening back at the Dome. It might be nice to have some idea about the tactical landscape once we *are* able to move."

"My, aren't we enjoying our military jargon," Treakness said with an edge of sarcasm. "Unfortunately, the Trofts have jammed the comm system. Until they unjam it—if they ever do—the tactical landscape is going to be a discover-as-we-go proposition."

Poole stirred uneasily. "This isn't good," he murmured. "I don't think we can afford to just sit here for three hours."

"Good point," Treakness said. "Maybe we should try jogging in place."

"Please stop that," Nissa said suddenly.

"Stop what?" Treakness asked, frowning at her.

"Stop treating Poole that way," Nissa said. "I know you're frightened. We're all frightened. It doesn't help for you to keep picking on him."

"You think that my ignoring stupidity will be an asset in getting us through this?" Treakness countered.

"Your disagreeing with something doesn't make it stupid," Nissa said stubbornly. "And in fact, I agree with him. I don't think we can afford to just give up the next three hours."

Treakness looked at Lorne. "Well?" he challenged.

"If you're looking for support, look somewhere else," Lorne said. "I agree with them."

Treakness lifted his hands, palms upward. "Strength, resolve, and unanimity. How wonderful for us all. But unless you also have a cloak of invisibility, none of that will get us a single meter outside that door."

"There must be a way," Nissa insisted. "Maybe we can building-hop. You know: go in the front door, through the building, and out the back."

"And how exactly will that get us across Cavendish Boulevard?" Treakness asked, waving at the activity taking place outside the restaurant's windows. "You think that if we walk nonchalantly enough, the Trofts won't notice us?"

"What about the storm drain system?" Lorne asked. "That runs under the streets, right?"

"Yes, it does," Treakness said. "Do you have any idea how the system is laid out?"

Lorne grimaced. "No," he conceded.

"I do," a voice said from behind Lorne.

Lorne turned around, startled. While the four of them had been talking—reasonably quietly, or so he'd thought—all other conversation in the restaurant had once again ceased.

And to his uneasy surprise, he found that the whole crowd was silently watching them.

He focused on the man who'd just spoken. He was middle-aged and bulky, with a lined face and a rigid expression. "I beg your pardon?" Treakness asked.

"I said I know the drainage system," the man told him. "Been working down there for most of the past twenty years."

"You could show us how to get through it?" Treakness asked.

"I *could*, sure," the man said, eyeing Lorne. "The question is, *should* I?"

Lorne frowned. "Meaning...?"

"Meaning he wants payment," Treakness said calmly. "A reasonable enough request. How much?"

"See, it's not so much quick cash as a long-term investment that

I really need," the man said, still looking at Lorne. "Boils down to who pays better. You, or the Trofts."

"What, that thing about rewards and punishments?" Treakness scoffed. "You really think you can trust anything they say?"

"Yeah, actually, I can," the man said, finally turning his eyes away from Lorne and looking at Treakness. "See, I've read my history, Governor Treakness. I've read about the Troft occupation of Silvern and Adirondack during the Dominion-Troft war. Seems to me that when they promised something to the people there, they delivered on it."

"I wouldn't put a lot of weight on that if I were you," Lorne warned. "There are hundreds of Troft demesnes in the Assemblage, each with its own way of doing things. Just because the group that attacked the Dominion played by those rules doesn't mean this bunch will."

"I think it's worth the risk," he said. "Especially since they can get me something that maybe you can't."

"And what would that be?" Treakness asked.

The man looked behind him. "You folks mind?" he asked, raising his voice. "This here's a private conversation."

For a moment, no one moved. Then, a white-haired, leathery-skinned man in the middle of the group snorted and turned away, heading toward one of the tables by the windows. As if on signal, the others followed suit, moving back and re-forming themselves into their conversational clusters closer to the windows.

The man watched until they had all moved out of earshot. Then, grabbing a chair from one of the nearby tables, he pulled it over, nudging it in between Poole and Nissa. "Let's start with what exactly *you* want," he said as he sat down. "Then I'll tell you what *I* want."

"Actually, let's start with your name," Treakness said, pulling a small comboard from his jacket pocket. "No offense, but I want to make sure you can do what you claim you can."

The man gave him a twisted smile. "Aaron Koshevski," he said. "Address, apartment two-oh-one right above you. Occupation, mechanical and structural maintenance engineer."

Treakness nodded and started punching in the data. As he did so, Lorne looked back at the other people in the dining room, wondering what they were making of all this. But they seemed to have already lost interest, their attention back on the Troft soldiers working on their fencing project.

"All right, Mr. Koshevski," Treakness said, setting his comboard down on the table. "You do indeed appear to be who you say you are. What we want is to head west, obviously without interference from the Trofts. How can you help us do that?"

"How _far_ west?" Koshevski countered. "Creeksedge Spaceport? Crystal Lake? The corner of Twenty-Eight and Panora? I need some idea of where exactly we're going."

"To the lake," Treakness said without hesitation. "Though I'm obviously not expecting the drainage system to get us that whole distance."

"You got that one right, anyway," Koshevski said with a grunt, his eyes narrowing with concentration.

Lorne looked at Nissa, noted her compete lack of expression, and adjusted his own face accordingly. Of course they weren't going to Crystal Lake—that area with its expensive houses and rolling parklands was a good thirty kilometers past the spaceport. But Treakness obviously had no intention of giving a total stranger their actual destination. Especially a total stranger who'd already hinted that he might prefer making a deal with the Trofts.

"Okay, here's what I can do," Koshevski said. "I can get you about nine kilometers west through the system, to somewhere around Ridgeline Street. Past that point, with the lower water table and better drainage, they put in smaller conduits that you won't be able to get through."

"Nine kilometers will be a good start," Treakness said, nodding. "What do you want in return?"

Koshevski pursed his lips. "My brother's family lives in an apartment building on West Twenty-Third, between Toyo and Mitterly," he said. "It's a residential area, not very fancy, about four kilometers southwest of here. From the way you were talking earlier, I'm guessing their block's going to end up in one of the unfenced zones."

He folded his arms across his chest. "Here's the deal. You get them to one of the safe areas, and I get you to Ridgeline Street."

"Can we get close to their building through the drainage system?" Treakness asked.

"I can get you practically to the front door," Koshevski said. "But Danny's wife has Jarvvi's Disease and won't be able to get through the conduits. You'll have to get them to the safe zones at street level."

"Fair enough," Treakness said. "Very well, you have a deal."

"Uh . . . sir?" Poole spoke up hesitantly. "Are you sure—?"

He broke off at an almost casual glare from his boss. "We'll want to leave as soon as possible," Treakness said. "How do we get in?"

"There's an access point right out there," Koshevski said, jabbing a thumb toward the rear of the restaurant. "Mid-block, about fifty meters north."

"Any special tools necessary for opening it?"

Koshevski shook his head. "All it takes is muscle." He looked Lorne up and down. "You got muscle?"

"We have muscle," Treakness confirmed, pushing back his chair and standing up. "Let's go."

The others followed suit, and as Lorne stood up he glanced one last time around the dining room.

And felt a shiver run up his spine. He'd been wrong earlier about everyone's attention being on the Trofts outside. One of them, the white-haired man who'd led the group retreat earlier at Koshevski's insistence, was sitting alone at one of the tables.

Watching them.

The man's gaze flicked to Lorne, and for a moment they locked eyes. Then, casually, the other turned away, as if there was nothing of interest there, that he'd just happened to be looking in that direction.

"Coming?" Treakness asked.

Lorne gazed at the white-haired man for another moment. Then, taking a deep breath, he turned away. "Yes," he told Treakness. Whether the other man had recognized Treakness, or whatever else his interest in the group might be, there was nothing Lorne could do about it now. At least the other had been too far away to eavesdrop on the critical parts of their conversation.

"Good," Koshevski said, taking Lorne's arm and pointing down the corridor toward the rear door. "After you."

There was a lone spine leopard wandering the street when Lorne eased the rear door open and stepped outside. The predator turned at the sound of the door, or possibly at the scent of fresh prey, and for a moment it eyed the rash human who had invaded its territory. But either it wasn't yet hungry, or else it hadn't finished staking out that part of the block as its territory. With a sniff and a brief flaring of its foreleg spines, it turned and walked away. "Clear," Lorne murmured over his shoulder, stepping aside and giving the rest of the street a quick look. No one was visible, human or Troft. "Where's this access point?"

"Right there," Koshevski said, pointing toward a round metal cover set flush into the street midway down the block, colored and textured to match the pavement around it. "Gripper holes in the edge—just grab them and pull straight up."

Lorne nodded and headed off down the walkway at a quick jog. He reached the cover, got his fingers into the gripper holes, and pulled. The cover was heavier than it looked, but his finger locks and arm servos were more than up to the task, and with a little effort he levered it up.

Treakness and the others were there by the time the way was clear. "You first," Treakness murmured, gesturing Koshevski down into the dank-smelling hole.

Koshevski nodded. Sitting down on the edge of the hole, he found one of the two sets of embedded rungs with his feet and started down. Treakness was right behind him, followed by Poole, followed by Nissa. Balancing the cover on its edge, Lorne stepped into the opening and worked his way a couple of rungs downward. Then, spreading his legs and balancing himself, he picked up the cover and lowered it back into place, plunging them all into nearly total darkness. Keying in his opticals, he got his hands on the rungs and started down.

He'd gone only a few steps when, warned by the sound of footsteps and rustling cloth, he was able to key down the enhancers just as Treakness turned on the flashlight from his pack.

A minute later he arrived at the bottom, and found himself in a small chamber with meter-and-a-half-diameter cylindrical conduits leading off horizontally in four directions. "We go this way," Koshevski murmured, taking the flashlight from Treakness and shining it down the southward conduit.

"Why can't we just go west?" Treakness asked.

"Could, but won't," Koshevski said. "My brother is on West Twenty-Third, remember? Follow me. And be quiet—sound travels real good in here."

Bending over, he stepped into the conduit and headed off, the light bobbing drunkenly as he walked along the curved surface. Treakness followed, his hands splayed awkwardly to both sides for balance. Poole was again close behind him. Nissa paused long enough to give Lorne a strained smile, then followed.

Grimacing, Lorne watched them go, feeling a sudden twinge of claustrophobia as he eyed the narrow opening. But it was better than facing Troft lasers. Bending at the waist and the knees, he eased his way into the conduit. If this worked, he reminded himself firmly, they were going to gain almost half the distance to the spaceport and get a significant jump on the Trofts' efforts to lock down the city.

If it *didn't* work, this was going to be a very uncomfortable place to get caught in an ambush.

But there was nothing to do now but see it through. Keying up his audios as much as he dared, keeping a wary eye on their rear, he hurried to catch up.

CHAPTER SIX

It was five kilometers back to Stronghold as the aircar flew. By foot, Jody knew, it would be seven or eight. On Aventine, even the longer trip would be no more than a brisk two-hour walk. With a good nine hours remaining until sundown, she had wondered earlier what her father had meant with his comment about pushing their available daylight.

Within the first fifty meters of their journey, she'd figured it out.

The spores and other tiny plants that rode the Caelian wind were bad enough inside Stronghold. Here, away from the protection of the town's high wall, they were far worse. They whipped across her face and hands, tickling her ears and neck, and generally making a nuisance of themselves.

There were larger versions as well, versions that seldom made it into Stronghold. Some of those had tiny hooks designed to catch on something—anything—that would provide an opportunity for growth. They could actually sting if one of the hooks managed to snag a particularly sensitive section of skin, reminding Jody of her first experience on an Aventinian beach, when a rising wind had whipped sand across her face.

And of course, the eddy currents created by the trees and landscape meant that the whole spectrum of airborne plants could come from any direction, not just that of the prevailing wind.

364

The insects were out in force, too, following right behind the spores. In theory, since the spores didn't attach to living skin, the insects didn't have any reason to land on Jody's face or hands and try to take a bite. In actual practice, a lot of them did anyway. Others, the clumsier ones no doubt, simply lumbered into her, bouncing off and continuing on their way. The majority, content with merely swarming around the intruders, added their own layer of distraction and irritation.

Jody had known about all that from their previous times outside the town, and had mentally prepared herself for it. What she hadn't expected was the ferocity of Caelian's larger forms of plant life.

Stronghold was kept largely devoid of native plants, except for the handful that had been cultivated or were in the process of becoming so. She'd seen some of those, and of course she'd also seen the vegetation that had covered their testing area landing site before she and the others had burned it off.

It somehow had never occurred to her that perhaps Geoff and Freylan had chosen that spot precisely because of its lack of the nastier forms of Caelian plant life.

But all those forms were here now, splashed across the ridge that her father had chosen as their path. There were plants that tried to tangle her feet, and others that grabbed onto her trouser legs with tiny or not-so-tiny hooks, barbs, and thorns and tried to either trip her or shred the silliweave material. Other varieties exuded poisons or skin irritants or adhesives, the latter rather like Aventine's native gluevines, only worse. And even the innocuous plants did their bit to conceal tangled tree roots, ground insect mounds, or more dangerous plants.

In view of all that, it was probably remarkable that the group made it a full hundred meters before they had their first accident.

It happened to be Freylan, though in retrospect Jody realized it could have been any of them. Carrying the rear poles of the gigger's cage, he got his foot caught in a tangle of vines and sprawled facefirst on the ground. That by itself wouldn't have been so bad, but his left hand unfortunately hit the low hill of one of Caelian's antlike insect forms. This species was fortunately not poisonous or even biting, but enough of them got up his sleeve before he could disengage that he had to strip off his entire outfit in order to get clear of them.

Jody dutifully faced away from the situation, which was why she missed the additional drama of her father lasering a pair of orctangs that tried to take advantage of the party's preoccupation and creep up on them.

They got Freylan put back together and continued on, only to run into a patch of blue lettros fifty meters later lurking beneath a stand of solotropes. Paul was able to burn away just enough of the patch's end for them to get around it, but barely ten meters further on they hit a line of blue treacle that went all the way down the ridge on both sides. That meant there was no going around it, which meant Paul had to not only cut their way through the plants themselves but then use his arcthrower to systematically flash-burn a path through the adhesive that the lasered plants leaked all over the ground. That single patch took over half an hour to pass.

Midway through the operation they were attacked by two whisperlings that Paul had to kill. At the far edge of the patch, just as they were starting to pick up some speed again, he had to fend off two hooded clovens. Through all of it, Snouts never stopped growling once.

The next incident was Jody's, involving a nest of micewhiskers that she managed to kick as she was trying to avoid a patch of hookgrass, and left her with a bruise on her forehead and some madly itching scratches on her cheek. Her father and Geoff took the brunt of the next one, when a branch Paul was cutting fell the wrong way and sent some tendrils of poison shink whipping across both their faces. The resulting inflamed scratches not only itched, but hurt as well.

Still, the animal attacks were the most serious threat. Fortunately, Paul was mostly able to hear or see them coming in plenty of time to thwart them.

The sun was nearing the western horizon, and Jody estimated they'd covered about six of the seven or eight kilometers back to Stronghold, when one of the attacks finally got through.

❖   ❖   ❖

With one final sizzle of charged vegetation, the last bit of poison shink blocking their path blackened and curled away. "Okay," Paul said, peering forward at the immediate terrain ahead, then lifting his head to survey the multiple arches of tree branches stretching out above them.

Jody looked up, too, eyeing the brilliant greenery distrustfully. Many of the trees they'd passed beneath during that long afternoon had featured lower branches that were dead and leafless and had thus provided little cover for anything larger than a nest of split-tails.

Not so this bunch. This bunch had apparently choked out all competing large vegetation, with the result that their branches had more or less free access to the region's daily quota of sunlight. That, along with the spiral arrangement of the branches, meant that it was worthwhile for nearly all of those branches to sprout leaves to catch that sunlight.

Which meant pretty much anything could be hiding up there.

Jody didn't like the look of the path. Not a bit. But they had little choice. A brief reconnoiter had showed a huge patch of green treacle to their left, and an equally large expanse of impassible marshland to their right. The only other option was to backtrack and find another route, and with the forest having grown steadily denser as they traveled there was a good chance they would find themselves in a similar situation somewhere else down the line anyway.

The others had clearly, and probably just as reluctantly, come to the same conclusion. "Are we going, or aren't we?" Geoff, at the cage's rear, growled as the seconds ticked past without anyone moving. "Come on, I don't want to be out in the open when the sun goes down and the predator night shift starts."

"Good point," Freylan agreed reluctantly. He took a deep breath. "Okay—"

"Hold it," Paul said suddenly. "Listen."

Jody frowned, straining her ears. What had he heard?

"Uh-oh," Freylan said quietly, twisting half around to look over his shoulder at the cage.

And Jody felt her breath catch in her throat as she suddenly got it. For the first time in hours, Snouts had gone silent.

"You three wait here," Paul said, starting to ease forward past Freylan. "I'll check it out."

"Hold it," Geoff said. "All things being equal, if something decides to jump us I'd rather be up there with you than back here alone."

"I agree," Freylan seconded.

Paul's lip twitched, but he reluctantly nodded. "If it'll make you feel better," he said. "But stay a couple of paces back, and don't crowd me."

They set off, Paul in the lead, followed closely by Freylan, the swaying cage, and Geoff. Jody walked at Geoff's left, keeping her eyes moving and making especially sure to keep an eye behind them. During the past half hour an odd haze had begin to take over her mind, no doubt brought on by a day's worth of fear, fatigue, and adrenaline overload.

And they still had a good kilometer or two to go. At this point, she wasn't at all sure she was going to make it.

"Jody, you have those stun sticks handy?" Geoff murmured in her ear.

"Handy enough," Jody said, frowning at him. "Why?"

"Why do you think?" Geoff muttered. "Let me have one."

"Dad said you weren't supposed to," Jody reminded him.

"I don't care what he said," Geoff bit out. "Hand it over. Now."

Jody threw a quick glance forward. Her father, his attention on the area ahead and above them, didn't seem to have heard the exchange.

And suddenly she realized that she would rather like to have a weapon handy, too. Sliding open the fastener on one of the two packs hanging across her chest, she pulled out the two stun sticks and handed one to Geoff. "Be careful with it," she muttered.

"Don't worry," he said. Shifting it across to his right hand, he clicked off the safety catch and rested his thumb on the activation switch. Swallowing hard, wondering what her father would say if he caught them with the weapons, Jody did the same.

They'd gone ten more paces when the entire grove exploded in ululating howls and a dozen snarling, wolflike animals leaped from the branches above them.

Reflexively, Jody dropped into a crouch, turning half around as two of the animals hit the ground three meters away and charged toward her. Vaguely, she heard herself screaming at them in turn as she frantically tried to activate her stun stick.

But somehow, her madly searching thumb couldn't seem to find the switch. The nearest of the predators had opened its jaws wide, giving her a horrifying glimpse of sharp teeth and a bright red mouth.

Abruptly a brilliant flash of blue light slashed across the animal's flank. The creature twitched violently in midstride, then nose-dived onto the matted ribbon vines. Its partner dodged to the side, opened its own jaws, then also fell as a second antiarmor laser shot took it out.

And then, Jody's scrabbling thumb found the stun stick's activation button, and the sizzle of half a megavolt of electricity joined the cacophony of howling filling the grove. Something moved at the corner of her eye, and she swung around, trying to bring up the stun stick to intercept it.

She didn't make it. The creature slammed into her, its jaws stretching toward her throat, its body shoving her arm and the stun stick violently to the side. The impact turned her whole body into instant jelly, and her suddenly hazy brain realized she was being slammed to the ground. Her head hit the ground hard...

The darkness evaporated, and she found herself lying on her back in the grass. Freylan was kneeling over her, his arm stretched out rigidly, whipping the crackling stun stick in his hand back and forth in a hundred-eighty-degree arc, yelling defiantly at the pack of animals still filling the grove with their howls. Jody tried to roll away or get up and help, but her body inexplicably refused to move.

And then, someone shot past above Freylan's head, and Jody rolled her eyes to the side and saw that it was her father. He landed in front of the snarling animals, sending servo-powered kicks at the nearest ones while his fingertip lasers flashed death at those out of kicking range. Two of the animals leaped at him from behind, but before they could make contact he threw himself into a low leap over the ones in front of him. He hit the grass and rolled, and as the two animals leaped again, his antiarmor laser flashed twice, sending their charred bodies to thud against the ground. The rest of the pack turned to the attack, only to find themselves in the middle of a three-prong laser barrage.

A few seconds later, the last of them was dead.

The sizzling of Freylan's stun stick, audible now that the howling had stopped, also went silent, and she looked up to see Freylan lower the weapon to his side, his whole body shaking with reaction. He took a careful breath, gave one final look around the grove, then looked down at Jody. "You all right?" he asked.

"I do' know," Jody said. The words came out embarrassingly slurred, her mouth as numb as the rest of her. "Wha' ha'n'ed?"

"We were attacked by a pack of—I don't know what; call them tree wolves," Freylan said. "Your dad did a spinning sonic blast to try to slow them down, but I guess when one of them slammed into you, it bumped you and the stun stick over into Geoff."

Jody grimaced. Or tried to, anyway—she had no idea whether her facial muscles were even responding. "An' the curren' go' all th'ee o' us," she muttered.

"Yeah," Freylan said. He looked somewhere to his left, his face hardening. "With Geoff taking the brunt of it."

Jody felt a sudden flash of horror roll through her useless body as she remembered her father's warning that the stun sticks could deliver a lethal jolt. "Is he a' right?" she breathed.

"I don't know," Freylan said grimly. "He's still breathing, though."

"No thanks to you," Jody's father's voice came from the direction Freylan was looking, an uncharacteristic anger in his voice that made Jody wince. "*Or* to him. What in the *Worlds* did you two think you were doing?"

"I'm sorry," Jody said. Her mouth was starting to come back now, and with an effort she managed to turn her head.

Geoff was lying on his back on the ground, his eyes closed, his face pale. Paul was kneeling over him, busy pulling the cap off a hypo, the survival kit's medical pack laid open on the ground beside him. "Yeah," Paul rumbled. "Sorry."

"We were afraid," Jody said, knowing even as she said them how lame the words sounded. That was an excuse, not a reason, and her parents had never much liked excuses. "We thought that if...no. We weren't really thinking at all, were we?"

"No, you weren't," Paul ground out as he slipped the needle into Geoff's arm and pressed the plunger. "There's a reason why you need training to use a weapon. *Any* weapon." He held his fingers against Geoff's neck for a few seconds, then looked up at Jody. "But I think he'll be okay," he added, the anger starting to fade from his voice. His eyes flicked to Freylan. "How about you, Freylan?"

"I'm all right," Freylan said. He looked back down at Jody, as if suddenly realizing how close he was still kneeling to her, and got stiffly to his feet.

Only then did Jody see the blood-stained slashes in the side of his silliweave tunic.

"Freylan!" she gasped, struggling to get her body working again.

"Don't worry, it's okay," Freylan hastened to assure her. "They hurt, but they don't feel very deep."

"What happened?" Jody demanded, running her eyes over the rest of his outfit. There didn't seem to be any damage anywhere else.

"Nothing serious," Freylan said. "When the first tree wolves attacked, your father had to get out of their way so that he could set up his counterattack." He shrugged. "One of them got through before he could do that."

And then, suddenly, Jody understood.

She turned to her father again, her eyes tracing out the tension lines in his face and throat, the repressed anger still simmering there. Only it wasn't her and Geoff he was primarily angry at.

It was himself.

Jody closed her eyes, a wave of frustration and sympathy flowing through her. From the very beginning of the Dominion's Cobra project a hundred years ago, the men who volunteered to become their elite soldiers were carefully screened, not just for mental and emotional stability, but also for the kind of outward-centered personalities that would permit the downplaying of their personal desires and the elevation of the lives and safety of the civilians they would be fighting for. That screening had gotten tighter and more sophisticated over the years, but the goal was still the same:

to create warriors who were able and willing to give their lives if necessary for their people and their worlds.

Only the military planners who'd created the Cobras' equipment hadn't seen it quite that way. The combat reflexes programmed into their nanocomputers weren't designed so that Cobras could throw themselves into self-sacrificing lunges into enemy fire in defense of the small and helpless. They were designed to get the Cobra himself out of harm's way, therefore permitting him to survive long enough to launch his own counterattacks against the enemy.

Even if it meant abandoning one of the small and helpless to take the brunt of the attack alone.

Freylan clearly understood that. But not everyone did. Jody had heard heartbreaking stories from her brothers and their friends about incidents in the Aventinian frontier, incidents where Cobras had lived and civilians had died. Every one of those stories had been told with a catch in the Cobra's voice, and usually a stiff drink in the Cobra's hand.

It wasn't a problem that was going to go away, either. The Dominion had given the Cobra Worlds the equipment necessary to reproduce the Cobra equipment, but not the ability to reprogram the nanocomputers.

There was a groan from Jody's side. "Geoff?" she called, trying again to get up. She halfway succeeded this time, rolling part of the way up onto her side. "You okay?"

"Thin' so," he said, his voice as slurred as Jody's had been a minute ago. "Kind o' nu'. Thin' it's gettin' better—startin' t' hurt now."

"Oh, good," Jody said.

"Just lie there for a few more minutes," Paul said, collecting the medical pack and standing up. "Your turn, Freylan. Let me help you with that tunic."

"It wa' 'y faul', Co'a Broo'," Geoff called as Paul stepped over to Freylan and the two of them started easing off Freylan's bloodied tunic. "I m-mean m-my fault. Not Jody's."

"I appreciate knowing that," Paul said. "I hope *you* appreciate now that stun sticks aren't toys." He flashed a look at Jody. "Both of you."

"Trust me," Jody said fervently, trying to sit up. Once again, she was halfway successful. "What's the plan?"

"There's no point in trying to get any farther tonight," Paul told her, peering at Freylan's gashes and selecting an anti-infection salve from the kit. "After I get Freylan fixed up, I'll see what I can put together in the way of a shelter."

Jody looked around at all the predator corpses scattered around them, corpses the scavenger insects and carrion animals were already flocking to. "You think it'll be safe here?"

"As safe as anywhere else," Paul said. "If this pack of tree wolves permanently held this territory, we can hope it'll take any other predators at least until tomorrow to realize they're gone and move in."

"Unless they share the area with a nocturnal batch," Freylan warned, wincing as Paul applied the salve.

"In which case, again, we're in no more danger here than a hundred meters down the road," Paul said. "Let me get some sealant and bandages on this, and then the three of you can rest while I build us a shelter."

Jody expected the shelter to be something simple, perhaps a hedge of uprooted thorn bushes with a few well-placed treacles gluing it all together.

She was wrong.

By the time she was able to fully sit up, her father had burned off a three-by-four-meter area about ten meters upwind of the scattering of dead tree wolves. By the time she was able to stand up and hobble around, he'd begun lasering down some of the smaller trees, cutting them into sections, and lugging them to the cleared area. By the time her fine-muscle control had recovered to the point where she was able to start assembling the survival pack's silliweave tent, he'd put together a waist-high barrier enclosing the campsite on three sides.

And by the time Geoff had also recovered from his encounter with the stun stick, the sun was going down and the tent was nestled snugly inside a chest-high barrier that would give pause to even the most determined predator.

Clearly, her father had had a lot more frustration to work out than she'd realized.

"The last step will be to string the extra support wire across the entrance once you're settled down in there," Paul said as Jody and the others finished collecting the rest of the equipment and supplies. "I can tie in the stun sticks and rig a pressure switch so that anything that hits the wires hard enough will get a good jolt. That and the barricade should keep anything serious from getting through from the sides."

"And the top cover and support poles should be springy enough to bounce off anything that leaps in from the top," Freylan said. "At least, that's what the manual said is supposed to happen."

"We'll probably get a chance to see how that works," Paul said grimly. "Make sure you've done any business you need to do out here, then get inside."

"What about Snouts?" Freylan asked, nodding toward the gigger snarling quietly in its cage. "We just going to leave him out here?"

"You want him in there with us?" Geoff countered.

"He was a good early-warning system for the tree wolves," Freylan said doggedly. "He might do the same for the nighttime predators, too."

"Only if they run the same territorial game the daytime ones do," Geoff said.

"It's still worth a try," Paul decided. "You two put him next to the tent, and I'll string the wire so that he'll be inside the perimeter. Just make sure to position him where his tusks can't poke through the tent and hit something."

Jody watched as the two young men maneuvered the cage into position, then stood aside and let them slip through the tent flap. "You want any help with that?" she asked as her father started unspooling the wire.

"No, I'm all right," Paul assured her. "Go on in and get settled. Make sure you leave me enough room just inside the flap where I can get out if there's trouble."

"I will." Jody took a step toward him and lowered her voice. "It wasn't your fault, you know, that the wolf got through to Freylan."

"Yes, I know," Paul said, a hint of his earlier frustration briefly touching his voice. "You know it, too. Does that knowledge make you feel any better?"

Jody grimaced. "Not really."

"It doesn't for us, either." He sighed. "I don't know, Jody. Maybe people like Treakness are right. Maybe it's time for the Cobras to fade gracefully into the sunset."

Jody peered at him in the gathering gloom, a knot forming in her stomach. This didn't sound like her calm, cool-headed father. "Not sure the middle of a Troft invasion is the right time to hand in your resignation," she warned.

"Fine, so we don't fade away, but instead go out in a blaze of glory," he said. "Same end result."

"That's nonsense," Jody insisted. "The Cobras are the best—"

"The Cobras are a hundred-year-old tactical concept, Jody," he interrupted quietly. "Surely there must be better and more practical weapons available by now. Combat suits, exoskeletons, remote drones—something."

"Okay, so you're old," Jody said. "Not all military doctrines go out of style, you know. There's this little something called *concentration of firepower* that I believe has been around since, oh, the invention of reliable firearms. It might go back to the longbow, too. Not sure about that."

Paul shook his head. "Hardly the same thing."

"There's also the old, time-tested doctrine of never trusting conclusions, strategic or otherwise, that you reach when you're tired," Jody continued. "So finish with your wire and stun sticks and get some sleep. If you really want to walk to the scrap center, tomorrow will be soon enough."

Paul snorted. "You sound like your mother," he said. "Except the scrap center part."

"Probably because if you head there she logically has to go with you," Jody said, her mind flicking briefly to her mother and brother on Qasama, wondering what the problem was that her mother's old friend Daulo Sammon had called them there to solve. Something incredibly thorny, no doubt.

But at least they weren't in the middle of a Troft invasion. "But the principle still holds," she added. "Namely, listen to the women in your family."

"A principle that I believe predates even concentration of fire-power," Paul said, some of his usual dry humor finally peeking through.

"Absolutely," Jody said, starting to breathe a little easier. "And while you mull that over, toss me the end of that wire. The sooner we get this thing strung, the sooner we can both get some sleep."

CHAPTER SEVEN

Traveling through the drainage conduit wasn't nearly as bad as Lorne had expected it to be. Once he got past that first touch of claustrophobia in the narrow confines, he was able to configure his back and knee servos to take most of the strain off his muscles and joints as he walked.

Unfortunately, the trip wasn't nearly so easy for the others. The hunched-over, bent-knee postures they had to adopt quickly changed from awkward to uncomfortable to agonizing. By the time the group had covered their first half kilometer they were having to pause every few minutes to stretch aching backs and knees. The conduit's interior was also somewhat slimy, making footing treacherous, and as knees and backs began to give way, the number of slips and tumbles increased dramatically. Eventually, all of them except Koshevski and Lorne were forced to walk with their hands pressed against the ceramic at both sides, their palms walking across the repulsive surface in an effort to maintain their balance.

They had been underground for three hours, and had covered a little under three of the four kilometers to Koshevski's brother's apartment building, when they heard the faint sound of the Troft loudspeakers wafting down from overhead. Lorne keyed up his audios, and despite the confusing echoes in the conduits he was able to get most of the message.

"Well?" Treakness asked when the voice from above had faded away.

"They've finished the fencing and people are now being allowed outside," Lorne relayed. "And they again reminded everyone that there's a bounty on patrollers and Cobras."

"That it?" Koshevski asked, an odd expression on his face.

Lorne looked at him...and it occurred to him that, working in the conduits all these years, the bulky maintenance engineer had probably learned how to sift through the confusing echoes and decipher what was being said in the streets above. "They're also now specifying the bounty," he said evenly. "Anyone fingering a Cobra gets a transfer into one of the safe zones for themselves and their family, plus a week's worth of food. Anyone who assists a Cobra gets transferred the other direction, *out* of the safe zone."

"Yeah, that's what he said, all right," Koshevski said, a grim smile twitching briefly across his face. "Thought you might try to pull a fast one and skip that part."

"Why would he?" Treakness asked, eyeing Koshevski. "It's not like anyone here would ever think of betraying him. Right?"

"Of course not," Koshevski said. "We ready to get moving again?"

Treakness inclined his head. "After you."

Another hour had passed, and they were nearing Toyo Avenue, when the faint sound of another Troft announcement came distantly from above them. "What did they say?" Treakness asked when the loudspeakers fell silent.

"I couldn't tell," Lorne said, shaking his head. "It was too faint for me to get anything."

"We're between access points," Koshevski said, looking around. "I didn't get any of it, either."

"He sounded mad, though," Nissa murmured uneasily.

Lorne thought back. Now that she mentioned it, there *did* seem to have been a harder edge to that particular communiqué.

"You're imagining things," Treakness said brusquely. "We're almost there, right?"

"That's our exit, right there," Koshevski said, pointing to a faint sheen of diffuse light about fifty meters ahead. "We should probably let your Cobra go up first, of course."

"Of course," Treakness said.

Three minutes later, Lorne was climbing back up to street level, wincing a little as he was finally able to stretch his back and knees fully straight again. He reached the top of the shaft, pausing there for a moment with his audios at full power. But if there was anything moving up there, he couldn't hear it. "Seems clear," he whispered down to the others. "Stay there while I take a look." Bracing his feet on the rungs on the opposite sides of the shaft, he got his hands beneath one edge of the cover and eased it upward.

He found himself looking down a narrow street lined with medium-sized apartment buildings, a double row of neatly trimmed trees, and a handful of parked cars. He could hear the murmur of people in the distance, but they were too far away for him to pick anything out of the sound and from his vantage point he couldn't see them. Easing the cover back down, he turned himself around to the other side and again lifted the cover.

And nearly lost his balance as a spine leopard snout jabbed suddenly through the opening squarely in his face.

"Whoa!" Lorne jerked back from the snapping teeth, reflexively dropping the cover onto the predator's snout and pinning the creature in place.

The spine leopard was still struggling to free itself when Lorne's fingertip lasers, cutting zigzag paths through bone and flesh and brain, finally destroyed enough of the predator's decentralized nervous system to kill it.

"What the hell is going on up there?" Treakness called tautly.

Lorne took a deep breath and flicked a fingernail sharply against the spine leopard's nose, just to make sure. "I found the block patrol," he called back.

"Trofts?"

"Spine leopard." Setting his feet again, Lorne lifted the cover and peered out. "It's clear—come on up." Sliding the cover over onto the pavement beside him, he climbed the rest of the way out of the shaft.

Koshevski was the next one out. "It's that one over there," he said, pointing to the building to the left of the one directly across the street from them.

Lorne glanced both ways down the still-deserted street. Apparently, the spine leopard he'd killed had had this block to himself. "Go," he told Koshevski. "Get the door open, then stay there and keep it open for the others."

Koshevski nodded and took off, running as fast as his bulk would allow. By the time he reached the door and started pounding on it, Treakness was also out of the shaft and following after him. Poole had joined the group, and Nissa was nearly there, when the door was finally flung open and they all piled inside. Lorne slid the cover back into place over the shaft, then scooped up the dead spiny's carcass and sprinted to the apartment building.

Koshevski was still holding the door as ordered, his eyes wide as he watched Lorne approach with his burden. "What the hell are you doing?" he asked.

"Can't leave it out there for the Trofts to trip over," Lorne explained as he slipped past the other into the relative safety inside. "Is there a trash bin or shed or something where I can dump it?"

"Yeah, there's a bin out back," Koshevski said, pointing down the hallway.

"Thanks," Lorne said. "Go tell your brother to get his family ready to go. Which apartment is it?"

"Four-oh-two," Koshevski said, heading for the stairs. "The door'll be open for you."

"Right," Lorne said, turning around carefully in the cramped space. "I'll be up in a minute."

"I'll go with you," Poole volunteered, ducking gingerly past the spiny's snout and stepping out in front of Lorne. "I can get the doors and lids and stuff."

"Poole—" Treakness began threateningly.

"I'll be all right," Poole said quickly. "I mean, if it's all right with you."

Treakness grimaced, but then nodded. "Be quick about it," he growled. Turning, he headed up the stairs. Nissa gave Poole a quizzical look of her own and followed.

"Thank you, sir," Poole called after them. "I'll get the door," he added to Lorne, and hurried down the corridor.

Lorne caught up with him at the rear door. "Thanks," he said as Poole unfastened the lock. "Push it open, but stay inside, just in case. I'll go first."

"Yeah, just a second," Poole said, leaving the door closed and peering down at the dead spine leopard in Lorne's arms. "I'd like a quick look here, if you don't mind."

"Sure," Lorne said, frowning. "First one you've seen up close?"

"No, not really," Poole said absently as he began probing the fur between the animal's shoulders with his fingers. "I was just wondering..."

He trailed off, his face suddenly tightening. "What?" Lorne asked.

Poole took a deep breath. "Did it occur to you to wonder," he asked, "how the Trofts managed to sneak onto Aventine for the hours or days it would take to collect all the spine leopards they've been dumping in Capitalia this morning?"

"I—" Lorne paused. With all the more immediate problems to deal with, he suddenly realized he *hadn't* gotten around to wondering that. "So how did they?"

"They didn't." Poole touched the section of fur he'd been studying. "The skin under the fur here is heavily calloused, over a region fifteen or twenty centimeters square. I'm no expert, but it seems to me these are the kind of calluses an animal could only build up if something with sharp claws routinely hung onto the skin there."

Lorne stared at him. "Are you suggesting...?"

"I'm not *suggesting*, Cobra Broom," Poole said bitterly. "I'm *saying* it. This spine leopard came from Qasama.

"The Qasamans and Trofts have made an alliance."

Lorne looked down again at the carcass in his arms, his head spinning. No—that couldn't be right. Qasaman paranoia coupled with their awareness of how the Trofts had tried to manipulate their world thirty-two years ago would surely make such an alliance impossible.

Or would it? Even a culture as heavily steeped in its own past as the Qasamans' could change. Could a new generation of Shahni have decided to break with their traditions, to work with the distrusted Trofts in order to strike back at the hated Cobra Worlds?

Was that the crisis situation the mysterious message from Daulo Sammon to their family had been referring to?

Was that alliance the crisis situation that his mother and brother had flown right into the middle of?

"Broom?"

Lorne started. "Sorry," he apologized. "I was just wondering if that's really possible."

"Looks pretty possible from where I'm standing," Poole said heavily. "And if it is, we're in worse trouble than we thought. As Koshevski said, Dominion history says that Troft soldiers don't go in for random killing. We have no idea whether the Qasamans will be that restrained." He hissed out a sigh and stepped back to the door. "Let's dump this thing and get upstairs. Governor Treakness needs to hear about this as soon as possible."

"And no one else?" Lorne suggested.

"Absolutely no one else."

The trash bin behind the building was only half full, leaving plenty of room for the dead spiny. "So how long have you been with Treakness, anyway?" Lorne asked as he slid the carcass through the opening into the bin.

"Not long," Poole said. "Don't know how much longer I'll be with him, either. He's . . . difficult sometimes."

"Or some might say criminally abusive," Lorne said bluntly. "I'm surprised you didn't walk out your first day on the job."

"Governor Treakness has his own way of doing things," Poole said diplomatically. "You just have to understand him." He shrugged. "And as you know, sometimes you have to put up with something you don't like in order to get something you want."

Lorne cocked an eyebrow at him. "Are you talking about Treakness? Or about you?"

"Maybe a little bit of both." Poole lowered the lid on the bin. "Come on, we need to get back."

Koshevski had said he would leave the apartment door open. What Lorne hadn't counted on was that every other door on the fourth floor would also be open, and that every resident from behind those doors would be standing in the hallway, gazing at the visitors in silent pleading. "What's going on?" he asked as he and Poole eased gingerly through the silent throng to the doorway of 402 where Nissa was waiting, her face troubled as she surveyed the crowd.

"The word spread," she said quietly. "They're asking if we'll take all of them across to the Trofts' safe zone, too."

Lorne winced. "What does the boss say?"

"Governor Treakness is against the idea." She smiled wanly at Lorne's expression. "Don't worry, they've all already recognized him." Her smile faded. "Which is another problem. That Troft announcement a few minutes ago, the one we couldn't understand? It said that Governor Treakness had missed the meeting at the Dome and announced a bounty for his capture."

"Terrific," Lorne growled. "Same one they've put on the Cobras?"

"Better, actually," Nissa said. "Two weeks' worth of free food instead of just one."

"That's stupid," Poole murmured. His face had gone rigid as he, too, eyed the silent crowd. "Cobras are far more dangerous to them than politicians."

"Your boss might think otherwise," Lorne said.

"Especially when that boss has important work to do," Treakness's voice called from inside the apartment. "You three, stop jabbering and get in here."

They found Treakness standing in the middle of the living room talking quietly with Koshevski and a somewhat younger man with a distinct family resemblance. Seated on a chair to one side was a woman with a lined, strained face and the slight trembling in her legs that was the sign of Jarvvi's Disease. Three teenagers—two girls and a boy—stood behind her. All four were listening closely to the conversation, their faces taut and nervous. "This is Mr. Koshevski the Younger and his family." Treakness introduced them briefly as Lorne and the others came up. "They're packed and ready to go."

"What about the people out there?" Lorne asked.

"What about them?" Treakness asked. "The deal was for Mr. Koshevski's family."

"I'm not talking about the deal," Lorne said. "I'm talking about basic humanity."

Treakness shook his head. "Sorry, but humanity doesn't enter into any of this."

"Maybe not to you it doesn't," Lorne said, feeling the first stirrings of anger. "But it does to me. I'm a guardian of the people of Aventine—the oath I took specifically used that word."

"So did mine," Treakness agreed. "We also took an oath to obey orders given to us by our superiors, in this case Governor-General Chintawa himself."

"But we can help them," Lorne said.

"We can help them more by completing our mission," Treakness said firmly. "We can't do that unless we can get out of here without attracting Troft attention." He waved a hand in dismissal. "Discussion closed. Now, the nearest fenced street appears to be three blocks to the north. If we go with Ms. Gendreves's building-hopping idea, that means we'll have three streets to cross—"

"The discussion is *not* closed," Lorne interrupted. "We can't just walk away and leave them here."

For a moment Treakness eyed him coolly. "Fine, I'm listening," he said at last. "But tell me first where you propose to draw the line."

"What do you mean?"

"I mean do we take just the people on this floor?" Treakness asked. "Or do we open the invitation to everyone in the building? And if the whole building, why not the whole neighborhood?"

"If they can be ready in the next five minutes, why not?" Lorne countered.

"I'll tell you why not," Treakness said. "Because there will be Troft soldiers walking the safe-zone fences, and probably some sort of air surveillance. Even if we avoid the actual streets by going through buildings, odds are we'll be spotted before we reach the fence."

"So they spot us," Lorne said impatiently. "So what?"

"So remember why they created all these spine leopard-infested areas in the first place," Treakness said. "Do you really think the Troft who spots a crowd that size will assume all those people simultaneously decided to make a break for it on their own?"

Lorne frowned. "I don't understand."

"He's saying *one* family might be crazy enough to do something like this without a Cobra escort," Poole said quietly. "But not five or six or ten of them."

"*I'll* decide what I'm saying, if you don't mind," Treakness growled, glaring briefly at his aide. "But in this case, Broom, he's right. If the Trofts spot the kind of train you're talking about, they're going to damn well know there's a Cobra in there with them. And if the train attracts a spine leopard and you have to kill it, they'll even know which one of us you are."

Lorne grimaced. He was right, of course. On all of it. "I suppose," he said reluctantly.

"Glad you agree," Treakness said acidly. "Now, let's focus on the topic at hand: getting Mr. Koshevski's family out so we can get back on our way."

"That way ultimately being to Crystal Lake," Koshevski put in, tapping his brother on the arm, "which we still haven't quite figured out. I can get him to Ridgeline, but I'm stuck on how to get him past that. You have any ideas?"

"There's a bunch of warehousing and light industry just west of there," the younger Koshevski said doubtfully. "Plenty of cover. But *getting* them that far will be tricky..."

Lorne moved away from the discussion, his mind still snarled in frustration, and crossed to the room's wide, north-facing window. Directly below him was the street they'd just come in from, lined on the other side by apartment buildings. Through the small gaps between the buildings, he could see that the block was a narrow one, and that the buildings there went straight through to face onto the next street. One more street after that, according to Treakness, and they would reach one of the buildings facing into the Trofts' fenced-in safety zone.

Even that short a journey through spiny territory would be dangerous for a group of civilians. With a Cobra along, though, it would be nearly as safe as a walk through Calay Park.

But surely the Trofts knew that, he realized suddenly. In fact, wouldn't their automatic assumption be that *any* group, of *any* size, would only venture out under Cobra protection?

In which case, Treakness's argument for limiting the break to

Koshevski's family was exactly backwards. A smaller group would merely make it easier for the Trofts to intercept and corral them, and probably ferret out Treakness's identity along with it. What they actually needed was as large a group as feasible, a mob that Treakness could more easily lose himself in.

And if they could throw a little extra confusion and chaos into the mix...

He leaned close to the window and looked as far as he could to both sides. Due west, seven or eight blocks away, was another of the Trofts' narrow warships, towering over the buildings immediately around it. To the northeast, another of the ships was visible, this one probably ten blocks away. The first ship was pointing south, the second east, but with their main weaponry mounted on swivels on the fore and aft wings, the alignment of the ships themselves was mostly irrelevant. Any trouble here, and both ships' arsenals would be locked onto him in seconds.

Or rather, they would be if he was four stories up, the way he was right now. At street level, the weapons would be blocked by the neighborhood's other buildings.

Would the Trofts be willing to destroy one or more of those buildings just to get at a Cobra they knew was lurking behind it? Lorne had no way of knowing for sure, but at this point it was probably a fair assumption that they wouldn't. The invasion was less than half a day old, and as far as he knew the Cobras hadn't yet started making a nuisance of themselves. The Trofts could probably afford to wait for easier pickings, and save the escalation to scorched-ground level until they needed it.

Still, with a little careful nudging, Lorne could probably persuade them to add the extra confusion of gunfire to the plan that was rapidly forming in his mind.

The only trick then would be living through it.

The conversation behind him had switched to Sunset Avenue and roadside culverts when he took a deep breath and turned around to face them. "I can do it," he announced.

The discussion broke off in mid-sentence. "You can do what?" Treakness asked suspiciously.

Lorne looked over the governor's shoulder and gestured to Nissa. "Tell the people out there they have five minutes to get ready," he said. "One backpack or less per person, and light enough that they can run with it for three blocks if they have to."

"Gendreves, don't move," Treakness ordered. "Broom, in case you've forgotten, we've already decided we're not taking a crowd."

"No, *you* decided we weren't taking a crowd," Lorne said. "And you were wrong. Nissa told me the Trofts are looking for you. You really think you'll be able to lose yourself in a group of ten people?"

"They have to spot us first," Treakness countered. "A group of forty will make that discovery inevitable."

"They're going to spot us no matter how many of us there are," Lorne said. "The trick is going to be to create so much confusion that we can slip into whatever group of civilians is on the other side of the fence before they can rope us all in and take us somewhere for a detailed look."

"And you think you can create that much confusion?"

"Yes," Lorne said flatly. "One way or another, I'll get us through."

"You'd bet your life on that?"

"I fully intend to."

For a long moment Treakness studied him. "I'll take that bet." He turned and nodded to Nissa. "Go ahead and tell them." He held up his hand, fingers splayed. "*Five* minutes."

Four minutes and thirty seconds later, Lorne, Treakness, and Poole were standing just inside the door they'd entered half an hour earlier, a long line of nervous civilians behind them. "What's your plan?" Treakness murmured as they peered outside.

"We start by getting across this street," Lorne said, leaning forward to look up and down the street. "Should be safe enough—I've killed the spiny who'd staked out this particular territory, and none of the others should have noticed it's empty and moved in yet. We'll head straight across to that apartment building over there, burn off the lock if necessary, and go through. Since the buildings over there face directly onto the next street, we won't have to worry about getting past any spine leopards that might be lurking in a back area or courtyard."

"But they'll be waiting for us in the street itself?"

"Probably," Lorne conceded. "And the next street will be even worse. From the level of crowd noise I heard when we first arrived, I'm guessing there are a lot of people out in the streets inside the Troft barriers."

Treakness grunted. "Yes, I heard it, too. They're probably mobbing the stores, panic-buying food and other supplies."

"The point is that a high concentration of potential prey always draws large numbers of spinies," Lorne said. "That's because it shrinks the viable territories—"

"The technical reasons aren't important," Treakness cut him off. "The point, it seems to me, is that next to the fence is also where the Trofts are most likely to see you kill one of them."

"True," Lorne said. "But I think I can turn that attention away from you and the others and give you a chance to melt into the rest of the crowds across the fence."

"By drawing all that attention onto you?" Poole asked.

"Hopefully, not for long." Lorne looked over his shoulder. "Nissa?" he called.

"We're ready," her voice called faintly back.

"Okay," Lorne called, grimacing as he turned to the door again. He hadn't wanted to put Nissa in the rear of the group this way, but Treakness had insisted that one of their party be back there to guard against stragglers, stating that if they were going to do this they were going to do it right. Since Lorne and Treakness needed to be in front to lead, and since Treakness had made it clear he didn't trust Poole not to botch the job, the task had fallen to Nissa.

At least Koshevski and his brother would be back there with her to help in case of trouble. Both men had insisted on taking that much of the risk on themselves. "Everyone stay close together," Lorne called. "Here we go." Pulling open the door, he strode out into the late morning sunlight, Treakness and Poole right behind him.

He'd expected the group to get across the street without difficulty, and he was right. What he hadn't anticipated was that some of the target building's residents had spotted the exit from the storm drain system, including the obvious fact that Lorne was a Cobra, and that the word had spread quickly enough for them all to be prepared to join in the mass escape.

"Was this part of the plan, too?" Treakness grumbled to Lorne after the group waiting in the lower lobby area had made their request.

"You're the one who suggested we bring the whole neighborhood," Lorne reminded him. "Anybody been keeping tabs on the street to the north?"

"I have," one of the residents spoke up. "There are at least two spine leopards out there."

"One of them killed and ate a squintal from one of the trees," someone else offered. "Will that make it less hungry?"

"A little," Lorne said. "Not enough. Is the building straight across another apartment building?"

"No, that one's all commercial," the first person said. "A two-story restaurant downstairs, a couple of attorneys' offices upstairs. There's an apartment building just to the west of it, but its street door is usually locked."

"That won't be a problem," Treakness said.

"But we could get in faster and more conveniently if I didn't have to burn it," Lorne said, thinking hard. "Okay. I'm going to need a large piece of paper, or several small ones, and a big marker. And a second- or third-floor apartment that faces that building."

"I've got all of that in my place," a young woman spoke up. "I'll take you up."

"What do you want the rest of us to do?" Treakness asked.

"Just stay here," Lorne told him. "I'll be back in a minute."

The woman's apartment was small and crammed full of travel souvenirs and mementos from all over Aventine. "I teach a children's art class," she explained as she pulled a roll of banner paper and a marker from one of the shelves. "They like to draw murals. Are you stationed here in Capitalia?"

"DeVegas Province," Lorne told her as he opened the marker and began to write on the paper in large letters.

"Ah—Archway," she said, nodding. "I visited there once. The Braided Falls area to the north is beautiful."

"They're hoping to turn that into a resort someday," Lorne said. "Do you know how the next couple of blocks to the north are laid out? Supposedly, we've got just one more street to go before we hit one of the Trofts' safe zones."

"That's right," the woman said. "I was up on the roof earlier for a look. Twentieth Street is all fenced off with some kind of tall mesh."

"That's the safe zone, all right," Lorne said. "Tell me all about it."

"I'll make you a sketch," the woman said, tearing another small sheet off the roll and picking up a pen.

By the time Lorne finished writing his message she was done. "Okay, we're here," she said, pointing to a square bordering one of the streets. "That apartment building, plus the one next to it and the two behind it, are part of a four-building complex with this play/gathering area in the middle."

"What does the gathering area look like?" Lorne asked. "Grass and play structures?"

"Over here, yes," the woman said, touching the western part of the open area. "This side has trees and a walking garden."

Lorne grimaced. Which undoubtedly was hosting a spine leopard or two at the moment. "Okay, so we get through the garden and past or through the next building north," he said. "What's this big building across the street?"

"That's Hendrezon's of Westport," the woman said. "It's the biggest store in the area—covers that whole half block, right through to Twentieth."

Which meant that going in from their side of the building would lead the refugee group straight into the fenced-in safe zone. "And it has a door on this side?"

"It has three of them," the woman said, adding their locations to her sketch. "Though under the circumstances, the ones on this side are probably locked."

"As Governor Treakness said, locks are the least of our problems," Lorne said. "Okay, looks like we've got a plan." He gestured to his own paper. "What do you think? Will it be legible from across the street?"

"'Need to get through,'" the woman read aloud. "'Please unlock front door.' Should be clear enough. *If* someone sees it."

"Someone will," Lorne promised, gathering up the paper. "Go open that window over there, will you?"

The woman complied, and Lorne stepped up beside her, centering himself in the open section and handing her one end of his banner. Keying his opticals to a medium telescopic setting, he focused on one of the other building's windows and fired a low-power burst from his sonic.

The window he was watching didn't even quiver. He notched up the power setting and tried again. Still nothing. "What are you doing?" the woman asked.

"Trying to get their attention," Lorne told her. He notched up the weapon and fired again.

This time, he saw the glass vibrate a little. He keyed the sonic up one final notch and lowered his opticals' enhancement back to normal. "Help me watch the windows," he told the woman. "Let me know when you spot someone." Trying to watch the whole side of the building at once, he fired three short bursts.

Nothing happened. He fired the triple burst again, then again, then again. Vibrating windows were a fairly subtle signal, he knew, but they were perfectly noticeable to anyone paying even a modicum of attention to their surroundings. Certainly anyone who'd spent any time in the expansion regions would know that vibrating windows were often an indication that Cobras were tackling spine leopards nearby.

"There!" the woman said suddenly. "Top floor, second in from the right."

Lorne found the window. An old man was standing there, peering down at the street. A moment later, a younger man joined him, also scanning the area below. Lorne gave another triple burst with his sonic, and this time the young man looked up. His body seemed to twitch, and he tapped the back of his hand against the older man's arm and pointed at Lorne's sign.

The other looked up, too, and for a long moment both of them just stood there, staring. Lorne pointed at the sign, then lifted his hands in silent question.

392 Timothy Zahn

The younger man said something inaudible, his eyes still on the sign. The older answered, glancing at his friend and then looking back at the sign. The younger man said something else—

"They're going to betray you," the woman beside Lorne said suddenly. "They're talking about it right now."

Lorne frowned. "What makes you say that? Do you know them?"

"No, but I know that look," she said. "They heard the Trofts' offer, and they're going for it. They're just trying to figure out how to collect."

CHAPTER EIGHT

Lorne stared across the street at the two men, a cold feeling knotting itself into the pit of his stomach. If they'd been in DeVegas Province he would have told the woman she was imagining things. The people out there would never betray their guardians, no matter how much the Trofts offered them.

But they were in the city now. Here, Cobras weren't associated with safety, but with dress uniforms and governmental pomp and ceremony. And no one here had ever seen a spine leopard, much less had any idea of how to deal with it.

No, he realized, the Trofts had figured the psychology of the situation perfectly. For way too many people, the chance to escape deadly danger at the cost of someone they didn't even know would be an easy decision to make. Especially when they could rationalize it by telling themselves they were doing it for their children, or spouse, or parents.

"What are you going to do?" the woman asked.

"Not much I can do except keep going," Lorne told her. "I was already planning to make as much noise and chaos as I could anyway, to try to get you all through the store and into the crowds on the other side before the Trofts could identify you and gather you together for a closer look. Now, I'll just have to make sure that wherever I finish up at the end of that is far enough away that it'll be hard for anyone in our group to point me out."

"Sounds dangerous."

Lorne shrugged. "The original plan wasn't going to be a whole lot safer."

Across the street, the two men finished their conversation. The younger caught Lorne's eye, pointed to the message in the window, and gave a thumbs-up. He touched the older man's arm, and together they left their window.

"I guess we're on," Lorne said, gathering up the banner and folding it up.

"You're still going to go through with it?" the woman asked.

"It's either that, or we give up and settle down here," he pointed out. "Let's take another look at that map of yours."

They stepped over to her schematic of the street. "Okay, so this is Hendrezon's," Lorne said, indicating the long building. "How tall is it?"

"Four stories," the woman said.

"What about the buildings on either side?"

"The one to the east is—let's see—I think it's five stories," she said. "The one across Mitterly Street to the west is four, the same as Hendrezon's."

"What about the two to the west of that?" Lorne asked.

"The first is also four stories, and the next one is three," she said slowly. "I think. Yes, it's three."

"Are all three of the buildings on that block connected to each other?"

"No, there are service alleys separating them," she said. "Not very wide, maybe one normal street lane each."

"And the other side of that third building runs up to Ellis Avenue," Lorne said slowly, trying to visualize the area and fit the terrain into the modified plan forming in his mind. It would be tight, but it should work. "We'd better get downstairs now, before they wonder if we got lost." He turned and headed for the door.

"Wait a second," the woman said, crossing in front of him and angling over to a free-standing wardrobe beside the kitchen nook. "They say Trofts aren't very good at picking out human faces," she continued as she flipped through the clothes inside, "but even they can remember someone's clothes." She pulled out a long, brown coat and held it out to Lorne. "Here—put this on. Once you get away, you can slip it off and melt into the crowd."

"Thanks," Lorne said, frowning as he took the coat. "How do I get it back to you?"

"You don't, genius," she growled. "You kick it under a parked car and get the blazes out of there."

"Ah," Lorne said, eyeing her closely. "You sure you want to do this? If the Trofts catch you helping me, they're going to kick you right back into the spine leopard zone again."

"Let them," the woman said firmly. "No, I mean that. You Cobras are our best chance of getting them off our planet. Whatever we can do to help you, that's what we need to do. And whatever *you* need to do, you do that, too. Okay?"

"Okay," Lorne said, slipping on the coat. The bulk of his belt bag made the garment too tight around his waist to seal, and he had to settle for sealing it only from neck to stomach.

He looked back at the woman, feeling a fresh sense of determination. Whether or not those two men across the way were planning to betray him, there were still people in Capitalia worth fighting for. "Thanks," he said.

"Thank me by staying alive," she countered. "And by getting us out of this."

The crowd in the downstairs hallway had grown considerably in the time that Lorne and the woman had been away, the word of the mass escape apparently having spread to the entire building. The murmur of conversation stopped as Lorne appeared, the people melting away to either side as he headed toward the far end.

Treakness and Poole were waiting by the door when he arrived. "There are a couple of men inside the door over there," Treakness said, eyeing Lorne's new coat. "Looks like they're set to open it for us."

"Good," Lorne said. "Here's how it'll work. I'll lead us to about the middle of the street, then stop there and watch our flanks while you take everyone the rest of the way."

"What if a spine leopard attacks before we reach the middle?" Poole asked.

"Then he'll stop a little earlier," Treakness said acidly. "Sounds good." He turned to the crowd. "We're heading out," he called. "Here are the rules. You will not spread out—no more than three people abreast. You will walk—*walk*—as quickly as you can without stepping on the person in front of you. You will stay close together, and no matter what happens you will *not* run. Running leads to chaos and panic, and we will not put up with either."

"And keep as quiet as you can," Lorne added. "I need to be able to hear trouble coming."

"Right," Treakness said. "Everyone understand?"

There was a general murmur of agreement. Treakness turned back to Lorne and gave him a sharp nod. "Go."

Taking a deep breath, Lorne pulled the door open and once again headed into the sunlight.

He'd hoped to make it halfway across the street before stopping. He had in fact covered no more than half that distance when the spine leopard attacked.

It came from above, from the branches of one of the neatly trimmed trees lining both sides of the street. Unfortunately for it, Lorne had caught the quiet rustling of leaves as it prepared for its attack, and was already pivoting up onto his right foot as the animal leaped into sight. There was no time for a proper target lock, but he had his leg up in time to slash an antiarmor laser blast across the spiny's flank as it arrowed toward the line of people behind him.

The creature was already dead when it slammed limply into a man and woman a few meters behind Lorne, tumbling all of them onto the pavement.

"It's all right," Lorne barked over the bubbling of reflexive screams as the two would-be victims scrambled madly to get back up on their feet and away from the predator. "Don't worry—it's dead. Everyone keep calm and keep moving."

To his mild surprise, they obeyed. There were a few muffled sobs of released tension, but for the most part the long line of people continued quickly and silently on their way. A hint of movement on the other side of the column caught Lorne's eye, and he made a quick rolling leap over the crowd. But it turned out to be merely a large squintal loping across the street on its way from one tree to another. Lorne stayed on that side, alert for more trouble, until Nissa and the Koshevski brothers appeared, bringing up the end of the line. Lorne fell into step behind them, and a few seconds later they were all safely inside their target building.

The two men were still holding the door open. "Thanks for your help," Lorne said, nodding to them. As he did so, he activated his opticals' infrared, creating a patterned red haze across their faces. "Nice to know there are still people you can rely on."

"No problem," the younger man said. His infrared pattern changed subtly, indicating an increase in heat output that might have been merely the result of the extra blood flow to his facial muscles as he spoke.

But there was no such innocent explanation possible for the rush of heat into the older man's face. His heartbeat had suddenly increased, the irrefutable mark of either exertion or emotion. And given that he was just standing there, it clearly wasn't exertion.

The woman had been right, Lorne realized with a sinking feeling. The two men were indeed planning to betray him.

Unless, maybe, he preempted that treachery by offering them the most important part of the Trofts' bribe himself. "We're heading over to the safe zone," he continued, nodding toward the people crowded into the hallway. "You two want to tag along?"

"Yes," the older man said without hesitation. "Thank you."

The younger man gave him a startled look, and his lip twitched. "Yeah," he said, with considerably less enthusiasm. "Sure."

"Good," Lorne said. "You've got five minutes to get anything you want to take with you."

The hallway here was narrower and more tightly packed than the last one had been, but again the crowd managed to move aside enough to let Lorne pass. "That went well," he commented to Treakness as he arrived at the governor's side.

"If you liked that, you're going to love this," the governor said sourly, gesturing through the door toward the gathering area beyond it. "There are at least two spine leopards back there."

"Probably even more than that," Lorne agreed, keeping his voice calm as he peered out the door's window. There were several trees back there, a couple of stands of bushes, a reed-and-flower patch big enough for a couple of spinies to hide behind, plus several benches and a children's play apparatus. "I'm guessing a family's moved in there. I'll need a few minutes to clear them out."

"You need any help?" Poole asked.

"Like what?" Treakness growled. "You offering to be bait?"

Poole grimaced. "No."

"Just wait here," Lorne told them. "Keep everyone calm and ready to go."

Dealing with spine leopard families came with both pluses and minuses. The big minuses were that there could be up to ten of the predators in a comparatively small area, and that they would move against their prey with the kind of close coordination that a similarly sized group of individual spinies never achieved. The chief plus was that the pattern those coordinated attacks normally took was straightforward and well known.

In this case there were eight of them, stalking him from the trees, bushes, and benches. They attacked in the standard twos and threes, and as Lorne gradually but steadily wore down their numbers, the stalking time between attacks increased, requiring him to make a turn or two through the gathering area in order to persuade them to move out of their concealment.

The whole thing took nearly ten minutes. In the end, Lorne got them all.

He was standing in the middle of the gathering area, breathing heavily as he scanned the treetops with his infrareds just to be sure, when the glow of grav lifts drifted into sight from behind the line of buildings to the east.

He dropped into a crouch beside a bench, keying in his tele-scopics. The incoming aircraft was a civilian-style transport, the same type as the ones the Trofts were using to bring in their spine leopards. But this particular transport wasn't showing any of the brisk determination he'd seen in others that morning as they went about their tasks. On the contrary, it was just wandering lazily across the sky, as if it had nothing in particular to do.

Or as if it was looking for the source of noises that might have caught the attention of the Trofts two streets away. Like, perhaps, the screams of dying spine leopards.

Grimacing, keeping an eye on the hovering transport, Lorne hurried back to the apartment building.

"Interesting technique," Treakness commented as Lorne rejoined him inside. "Very different from the robot spine leopard and Troft battles they run trainees through at the Sun and MacDonald Centers."

"You should try seeing the full range of those tests sometime," Lorne said. "We need to get going. There's a transport wandering around that's clearly looking for something."

Treakness's lip twitched. "Did they spot you?"

"I don't think so," Lorne said. "If they had, there should be more than just one of them up there. I'm thinking someone in the safe zone either heard the dying spine leopards or caught a reflection of one of my laser shots."

"Understood," Treakness said. "I notice there's a good-sized gap between the buildings over there. Did you see whether it went all the way through to the street?"

"I never looked in that direction, but one way or another we'll get through," Lorne assured him. "It'll be risky, running straight out into the street that way. But it'll be faster than going through the building, and speed is what we need right now."

"Agreed," Treakness said. "Same marching plan as the last street?"

"With one difference," Lorne said. "As soon as you're all through, maybe a little before that, I'm going to head off and try to draw the Trofts' attention away from you."

"How?" Poole asked.

"Just as safely as I can," Lorne said. "Regardless, we're going to be split up. I suggest that once we're inside the safe zone we plan to meet up six blocks to the west, on the northeast corner."

"Six *blocks*?" Treakness demanded, his eyes widening.

"We need the rendezvous to be far enough away from the chaos I'm hoping to create," Lorne explained. "We'll touch that corner on the hour and the half hour until we link up again."

"But who's going to protect us while you're off making noise or whatever?" Treakness protested.

"You'll just have to make sure you stay out of trouble," Lorne said impatiently.

Treakness clamped his mouth shut. "Fine," he ground out. "Anything else?"

"Just pass the word on to Nissa for me," Lorne hesitated. "And if any of us hasn't made it to the rendezvous in two hours, the others need to go on without him or her."

"Understood," Treakness said grimly. "Well, if we're going to go, let's go."

"Right," Lorne said. "Good luck."

Pulling open the door, he headed across the gathering area at a dead run, quickly crossing it and ducking into the narrow passageway between the two buildings on the far side. At the other end of the walkway, he saw now, their exit was blocked by a short wrought-iron fence. He target-locked the tops and bottoms of four of the vertical bars as he ran, and at five paces away he fired eight quick bursts from his fingertip lasers. Three of the bars snapped and fell to the ground, the fourth managing to hang on until the impact of Lorne's shoulder broke it free.

On the far side of the fence a pair of two-meter-tall blueleaf bushes decorated the buildings' corners. Between them, Lorne could see the street, and beyond that the stonework façade of the Hendrezon's storefront. Bracing himself, he raced between the bushes and out into the street.

And squarely into the path of two spine leopards.

There was no time for subtlety. Lorne leaped aside out of the predators' paths, target-locking both as he hit the pavement and rolled over on his shoulder. As the animals landed and started to spin back toward him he fired a pair of laser shots that dropped them both.

He rolled back to his feet, doing a quick three-sixty as he did so. There were three more of the predators to the east, but they were over a block away, out of position to attack the refugees now streaming across the street. To the west, two more spine leopards appeared as they charged around the corner of the Hendrezon's building where they'd probably been hungrily eyeing the human prey passing so tantalizingly close on the far side of the Trofts' fence. A quick double target lock, two more antiarmor blasts, and both predators were dead.

"Broom!" Treakness shouted from the front of the line of refugees, now running openly as they crossed the street behind him. "The door!"

Lorne had forgotten that the door on this side would probably be locked against the spine leopard threat. Turning toward the door, he swung his leg around and blasted the lock. "Get them in and through," he shouted back to Treakness. He gave the street one final visual sweep, then raised his eyes to the sky above him.

The transport that had been wandering around up there wasn't wandering anymore. It was arrowing straight toward him, weaving between the buildings as it dropped toward the street like a hawk zeroing in on a large rodent.

Lorne had no way of knowing whether or not the Trofts had added extra armor plate to the spacecraft, though at this distance it was doubtful whether a Cobra antiarmor laser would be powerful enough to penetrate even an unarmored hull. But the transport was a civilian design, and Lorne had seen plenty of such vehicles over the years. Keying in his telescopics, he located and target-locked the transport's nose sensor array and poured a full second of laser fire into it. Without waiting to see the crew's reaction, he turned and made for the Hendrezon's storefront, sprinting past the line of running refugees. Five meters from the building, he bent his knees in midstride, and shoved off the pavement as hard as his servos could manage.

He hadn't done a wall jump like that since his first week in basic training. But the maneuver was part of his collection of programmed reflexes, and as he flew facefirst into the patterned stone, his computer took over, extending his arms to first absorb the impact and then curving his fingers into talons and locking them solidly into handholds on the uneven stone. Before he was even completely settled he pulled convulsively down with his arms, shoving himself farther up along the wall, his hooked fingers again scrabbling for and then finding grips. Three more repetitions, and he made it to the roof.

He headed across at a dead run, dodging the various vents and protrusions, counting on his reflexes to handle any problems with the uneven surface as he focused his main attention outward. The transport that he'd fired on was still in sight but was no longer trying to close the distance between them. Off to the north, two more sets of grav lifts had appeared, both sets heading his way at high speed.

And off to the west and northeast, the two warships that were within firing range of him loomed ominously over the buildings around them. Lorne felt his skin tingling as he ran, wondering if their heavy lasers and missile launchers were even now being swiveled to target him.

If they were, their commanders had apparently not yet been given permission to fire. Lorne reached the northern end of the roof and skidded to a halt, dropping down onto one knee and peering cautiously over the edge.

He'd speculated earlier that the safe zone between the Trofts' fences would be crowded with people trying to stock up on food and other necessities. But he'd had no idea that it would be *this* crowded. The street scene below looked like a parade route, except that the street itself was as packed as the walkways on either side. Parked in the center of each of the three intersections Lorne could see one of the armored vehicles he'd seen driving briskly down the street just before he and the others had taken to the underground drainage conduits. Each of the trucks had four or five Trofts perched on top, monitoring the activity of the crowds swirling along below them. Other Trofts stood sentry along various sections of the fence, the laser rifles held prominently across their chests guaranteeing that the mob would keep a respectful distance.

And every eye behind every one of those helmet visors was turned upward toward Lorne.

"Well, you wanted them all looking at you," he muttered under his breath. Throwing targeting locks on each of the five Trofts on the vehicle in the intersection to the west, he pushed back from the edge of the roof and headed in that direction at a quick zigzag run. A few laser bolts sizzled past him from the street, but he was far enough in from the edge that they did nothing but blow some chips from the stonework.

The big ships still waited silently. Either they were hoping the ground troops could capture this particular Cobra alive, or else they were simply waiting for an easier shot.

If it was the latter, Lorne reflected grimly, they were about to get their chance. The edge of the building and the wide street beyond were coming up fast. Eyeing the chasm, using his opticals' target-lock system to measure the distance, he made a final adjustment to his stride, and as he reached the end of the Hendrezon's building he jumped.

And an instant later he was soaring across the street in a flat arc, the absolutely best and easiest target any Troft gunner could ever hope for.

He had gambled that the Trofts wouldn't be ready for this stunt, and it was quickly clear that he'd been right. He was already past the midpoint of his jump before any of the Trofts below even recovered enough to start firing at him, and none of those shots came very close to their intended target. Either the invaders were unaware of the full range of Cobra abilities, or else they had badly underestimated the depths of Cobra audacity and recklessness.

For five of the Trofts, it was probably the last lesson they ever learned. Lorne was nearly to the other roof, the laser fire from below still running wide of its target, when he tucked his left leg behind him and sent five quick antiarmor bursts slashing across the Trofts he'd targeted half a minute ago from the rooftop's northern edge. There was a faint scream from somewhere, rage or pain or death.

Then he was safely across, his knees bending as his servos absorbed the impact of his landing. He dropped into a partial crouch, then straightened both knees and body as he shoved off into a resumption of his zigzag run.

He'd gone five steps when the whole sky lit up in front of him.

Reflexively, he squeezed his eyes shut against the brilliant flash of blue, his arms flailing momentarily for balance as a blast of heat and a tornado wind slammed sideways across him, nearly knocking him off his feet. His nanocomputer took over, ducking him away from the heat and then twisting him back into his zigzag pattern. The warship's laser fired again, this shot coming close enough for Lorne to smell the acrid scent of ozone. He kept his eyes shut, using his opticals to find safe footing. He dodged around a pro-truding vent, turned again in time to avoid another shot. Ahead, the edge of the roof was rushing toward him, and he could see the five-meter gap of the service alley that separated him from the next building over. It was a much shorter distance, and therefore an even simpler jump, than the one he'd already performed in getting across Mitterly Street from the Hendrezon's building roof.

Only this time, he knew, that trick wouldn't work. The instant his feet left the rooftop he would once again be on a ballistic path which would allow no zigzagging or dodging or any of the maneuvering that was currently keeping him alive.

The Trofts hadn't been ready the last time he'd pulled that stunt. This time, they would be.

And it was becoming apparent that the Trofts had done the same calculation and come to the same conclusion. The massive ship-mounted laser ahead that had been firing uselessly at him had gone silent, its gunners waiting in anticipation of the moment when Lorne would have to either jump or else come to a sitting-duck halt at the edge of the roof. Whichever he chose, it would then take only a single clean shot to end it all.

Reaching the end of the roof, Lorne jumped.

But not up and over as he had the last time, with the goal of bridging the gap and landing on the next rooftop. Instead, he leaped *downward*, aiming for the side of the other building.

For the second time in two minutes, the Trofts were caught completely by surprise. Lorne's body was in the middle of its rotation when the ship-mounted laser slashed its fiery death over his head, squarely through the space where he would have been if he'd tried to jump the gap. A second shot slashed through the edge of the roof, vaporizing a groove through the tile and stone and steel and raining a shower of debris along the wall toward him.

But Lorne was no longer there. His nanocomputer had once again taken over, turning him just enough in midair so that he hit the far wall feetfirst. His knees took the impact, the friction of his feet against the wall fractionally slowing him down and starting to flip him over. Before he could simply bounce off the wall and fall straight down, his knees straightened again, sending him back toward the side of his original building in a heels-over-head flip that again brought him to a feetfirst impact on the other wall, a few meters lower than the point where he'd started. Again his knees bent and straightened, again slowing him down and sending him back across the alley. One more bounce-and-flip, and he reached the ground, his knees bending one final time as he hit the service alley pavement—

—Dead center into a group of three very startled spine leopards.

Fortunately, Lorne had no intention of staying long enough for them to recover from their surprise. His knees straightened convulsively as he launched himself into a rolling leap over the Trofts' fence into the safe zone beyond.

This time, he nearly bowled over a knot of spectators who had been in view of his building-hop and were still standing there, wide-eyed, as he landed in their midst. "Sorry," he apologized as he bumped hard into two of them before he could catch his balance, staggering them backwards into another group. He craned his neck over the crowds, trying to see whether or not Treakness and the other refugees had made it through the Hendrezon's building yet and were coming out onto the street.

"Hey!" someone shouted.

Lorne turned. But the man wasn't shouting to him. Instead, he was facing the Troft armored vehicle and soldiers half a block away, waving his hand urgently over the mass of people. "Hey! He's over here. Damn it, he's over—"

He was cut off in mid sentence as another man stepped forward and backhanded him hard across the face. "Shut up, you fool," the second man snarled as the first spun around with the impact and fell heavily onto the pavement. "You want them shooting at us?"

He jabbed a finger at Lorne. "You—get out of here," he bit out. "You hear me? *Go*. We've got enough trouble as it is."

But I can help you! Lorne wanted to say.

The words died in his throat . . . because the man was right. Lorne *couldn't* help them, at least not with the help they wanted. He couldn't get them food or shelter or safety. All he could do was run around and make trouble, and probably get someone killed.

He looked at the other people around him. On every one of those faces were expressions of fear or despair, anger or even hatred. Not a single person was looking at Lorne with respect, trust, or hope.

"I understand," he said quietly. "Good luck."

Without waiting for a reply, he ducked between two of them and threaded his way through the crowds that were doing their panicked best to hurry away from the burst of combat that had unexpectedly brought fire and death into their captivity.

Midway down the block, he slipped off the coat the woman had given him and tossed it against the side of the nearest building.

He let the crowd carry him another block, wondering what he should do. The arrangement with Treakness had been to rendezvous six blocks west of Hendrezon's, but now that Lorne was actually experiencing the barely controlled chaos he was wondering if the governor and the others were ever going to be able to make it that far on their own.

But going back to get them entailed its own set of risks. It had been several minutes since the exchange of laser fire, and the crowd was starting to settle down, but the general movement in Lorne's vicinity was still away from the site of the brief battle. Turning around would mean going upstream against the flow, posing additional risk to the civilians he would be pushing past, but also possibly attracting Troft attention. Worse, if any of the people who'd had a clear look at him were still in that area, he might even find himself being pointed out to the invaders.

The thought of being killed by aliens who had invaded his world was bad enough. The thought of being betrayed to those aliens by his own people was far worse.

He was still trying to figure out what to do when a hand abruptly grabbed his arm.

Reflexively, he twisted around, trying to break the grip. But instead of letting go, the hand tugged back, yanking him nearly off his feet and spinning him all the way around.

He found himself staring into the angry eyes of a medium-tall, heavyset man. "You stupid idiot," the man snarled, just barely loud enough for Lorne to hear. "What the *hell* do you think you're doing?"

"Who are you?" Lorne demanded. Or tried to demand, anyway. The words came out sounding more like a nervous plea than an order.

"Name's Emile," the man said. He glanced around, then gave Lorne's arm another tug, this one lifting him a couple of centimeters clear of the pavement, and started pulling him through the crowd toward the side of the street. "Come on. We need to talk."

CHAPTER NINE

With a start, Jody woke up from her nightmare—the third, by her slightly foggy count, of the long night.

For a minute or two she lay still, her brain trying to work through the horrifying images of the dream, her mouth working moisture into an unusually bad taste, her eyes gazing upward at the blackness of the tent roof above her, her ears sifting through the eerie and dangerous sounds of the Caelian night.

She had counted the muted growls of three different animals, the buzzing of probably five different types of insects, and the slow breathing of Geoff and Freylan beside her when she suddenly realized that there was one sound that she should have been hearing but wasn't.

Her father's breathing wasn't there.

She pushed off the cover of her sleep sack and sat up, being careful not to jostle the others. Her father, who had been sleeping beside her against the tent's door, was gone.

"Great," she muttered under her breath as she slid out of the sack and rolled up onto her knees. She stepped over her father's empty sleep sack to the tent's flap, opened it a few centimeters, and peered out.

The forest was nearly as dark as the inside of the tent, the brilliant starscape visible from the middle of Stronghold almost completely blocked off by the trees rising around them.

But there was enough light filtering in through the vegetation to show that the trip wire barrier her father had set up was still in place, as were the two stun sticks he'd hooked to them to give any intruder a good jolt. The small clearing in front of the tent also had enough light for her to see that her father wasn't out there, either.

She frowned. Had he heard the inconvenient midnight call, as her brother Lorne used to call it when they were children? But there were trees all over the place out there that he could use for that. Surely he wouldn't have chosen one that took him out of sight of the tent.

Steeling herself, she slipped outside into the narrow area between the tent and the trip wires, being very careful not to touch the latter. "Dad?" she called softly.

There was no answer. But as the sound of her voice faded away, it seemed to her that there was a noticeable dip in the volume of growls, chirps, and scurryings around her. The creatures of the Caelian night had been made freshly aware of her presence among them. Setting her teeth, trying to watch everywhere at once, she slowly bent down and disengaged one of the stun sticks from the barrier. Holding it well away from her body, she straightened up again—

"That's probably not a good idea," a calm voice said from behind her.

If she'd been fully awake, Jody reflected, she probably would have jumped straight over the trip-wire barrier in front of her from a standing start, and with half a meter's clearance. But with her brain and body still half numb with interrupted sleep, she didn't even twitch. Raising the stun stick higher, she turned toward the voice.

The man was perched on top of one of the sections of the log-and-sapling wall Jody's father had built around the tent yesterday when he'd been working off his frustration. She couldn't see much of the stranger's face in the dim light, but from his voice and overall silhouette she guessed he was young, probably in his mid-twenties.

And from the way he was sitting, with all of his weight on his rear and right leg and his left leg free to move in any direction, she guessed he was probably a Cobra. "Why not?" she asked, hefting the stun stick a little. "You don't think I know how to use it?"

"Pretty rollin' sure you don't," he said unapologetically. "You're Capitalia born and bred. Not much call for that kind of weapon back in civilization."

"What makes you think I'm from Capitalia?" Jody countered.

"One: your accent," he said, holding up fingers. "Two: the way you moved when you bent over to pick up the stun stick."

"Really," Jody said, impressed in spite of herself. "All that just from the way I picked up something?"

"Yeah," he said, and she caught a faint flicker of reflected starlight from his teeth as he grinned. "And number three: your father told us. Jody Broom, right?"

"Jody *Moreau* Broom," she corrected. "I imagine a good Cobra like you remembers that name."

"What makes you think I'm a Cobra?" he countered in turn. "Not everyone out here is, you know."

"One: because you're not looking around right now," she said. "That means you're relying on your hearing to let you know if anything's sneaking up on us, and only Cobra audios are up to that kind of work. Two: you sit like a Cobra, with your antiarmor laser available for a quick shot. And three: my father wouldn't have left us under the care of anyone else. Where is he, by the way?"

The man touched his fingertips to his forehead in a mock salute. "Touché, I think the term is," he said, sliding off the barrier and walking around to the front. "He's gone off to Stronghold to confer with Harli. Harli Uy, that is, the governor's son."

"He's gone *into* Stronghold?"

"No, just near it," the man corrected. "As far as I know, no one's gotten into or out of the town since the Trofts landed."

Jody looked around, taking in the darkness around her. Caelian's daytime horrors were bad enough, and the nighttime collection was even worse.

But she couldn't just sit here behind logs and stun sticks and Cobra guards while her father was out there in who knew what kind of danger. "I'd like to see him," she said. "Can I get someone to take me there?"

"Sure," the Cobra said. "You can get me. He said when he left that you'd probably wake up eventually and want to join the party. Name's Kemp, by the way."

"Nice to meet you, Kemp," Jody said, wondering uneasily just what kind of party he was talking about. Surely they weren't tackling the invading Trofts already, were they? "How far away is this party?"

"About a kilometer," Kemp said. "Nice evening stroll. Smitty? Can you watch things here?"

"No problem," a second voice called back from one of the trees at the edge of the small clearing. Jody peered in that direction, and was just able to make out the silhouette of another man sitting in the low branches. "You want me to call Tammling to give you a hand?"

"No, I can handle it," Kemp said. "Just keep an eye on the other two."

Jody looked at the tent. "Maybe we should bring them with us," she suggested.

"Might as well let them sleep," Kemp said. "Your father said they'd had a hard day, and there's not much of anything they can do, anyway. Really not much *we* can do, either, until the rest of the group shows up."

"So who *are* you?" Jody asked. "I mean, if you're not from Stronghold, where *are* you from?"

"We're the Aerie contingent," Kemp said. "We're assuming Essbend caught Governor Uy's interrupted warning and is also on the way here, but with the comm system down there's no way to know for sure. Harli was planning on giving them until tomorrow to show up."

"Wait a second," Jody said, feeling her eyes widen. Aerie was fifty kilometers away. "You walked all the way from *Aerie*?"

"Oh, no, we came on spookers," Kemp said. "Grav-lift cycles we use for fast travel through the forest."

"That would have been nice to have," Jody murmured, thinking about their long walk through the woods yesterday.

Kemp snorted. "You'd have run them into a tree inside the first minute," he said. "They're nothing for amateurs to fool around with." He gestured toward the stun stick still in Jody's hand. "Speaking of which, you should probably leave that here."

"That's okay," Jody said, putting the safety back on and clipping the weapon to her belt. "You said it's a party, and this is the closest thing I've got to a party outfit."

"Not a good idea," Kemp said firmly. "If you want a weapon, the group's probably got a spare shotgun or rifle."

"Never used one of those before," Jody said. "At least I've got a little experience with this."

"Yeah, I can guess," Kemp said dubiously. "Fine—whatever. Come on—Wonderland awaits."

"Wonderland?"

"Everything on Caelian outside the towns, which is pretty much most of it," Kemp explained. "You probably have a different name for it in Capitalia."

"People have lots of names for it," Jody admitted. "I like *Wonderland* better. So what's the plan? I lead, and you hang back a little on my right where you can protect us both?"

"Actually, I prefer hanging a little to your left," Kemp said. "Otherwise, yes, that's the marching order. You're a fast learner."

"Caelian's a good teacher," Jody said dryly. "We ready?"

Kemp gestured. "After you."

Kemp had been joking, Jody knew, about the trip to Stronghold being a nice evening stroll. For one thing, it was the dead of the night, not evening. For another, it had taken Jody's group most of the previous day to get through the first six kilometers of their journey, and that had been in broad daylight. Covering the final kilometer would probably take most—if not all—of the rest of the night. If, the morose thought occurred to her, they made it at all.

Only Kemp *hadn't* been joking.

It was, very literally, the difference between night and day. Jody's father had picked his way carefully along their trail, checking every stand of trees and patch of bushes for stinging insects, watching the plants themselves for thorns and adhesives and other surprises, and above all keeping a wary eye and ear out for predators of all shapes and sizes.

Kemp didn't do that. Any of it. He strode through the forest like he owned it, apparently in complete unconcern, his fingers nudging at the small of Jody's back in silent encouragement every time she tried to slow down the pace. Occasionally he would touch one of her shoulders or the other, pressing with his fingertips until she'd veered far enough to avoid some unseen obstacle, then easing off until the next course change.

And every few seconds the forest would vibrate with a deep boom from his sonic, or would light up with the flash of his fingertip lasers or arcthrower as he drove off, burned, or killed yet another attacking predator or startled a spine-equipped herbivore.

"You're good at this," she commented once as he deftly took out a saberclaw with two laser shots.

"Like you said, Caelian's a good teacher," he said. "Quiet, now—I have to listen."

They'd gone another hundred meters when Jody began to see a hint of blue flickers ahead of them. The flickers grew brighter, then became half-seen flashes through the foliage, and finally resolved into a group of perhaps a dozen men standing silently together beside a thick tree bole.

Jody peered uncertainly at them, trying to figure out if her father was somewhere in the group. But before she could come to any conclusions, one of the men near the middle stirred and turned around. "I thought that was probably you," Paul said heavily. "I wish sometimes you were more for sleeping in."

"Never can unless I'm in my own bed," Jody said, frowning as she stepped up to him. She could feel the sense of unwelcomeness around her, almost as thick as the darkness. "Is there a problem? I mean, aside from the obvious? Kemp said you'd invited me to this party."

"That was before I had a full grasp of the situation," Paul said. One of the other men half turned and fired his laser at something, and in the brief flash Jody saw that her father's face was as tense as his voice. "Maybe it would be best if Kemp took you back to the camp."

"Only if you *and* Kemp are looking for extra trouble," Jody warned, a creepy feeling settling in on the back of her neck. She'd never seen such a dark mood in her father before. "Tell me what's happened. Maybe there's something I can do to help."

"We appreciate the offer, Ms. Broom," the man her father had been talking to spoke up. "But this is war. No place for civilians."

"This is Harli Uy, Jody," Paul said, gesturing to the other man. "Currently in command of the Cobra forces on Caelian."

"Honored to meet you, Cobra Uy," Jody said, ducking her head politely. "May I respectfully point out that your father thought I could handle myself well enough to allow me to come to Caelian. Let me repeat: whatever's going on, I'd like to help."

"And what exactly is this help you're offering?" Harli asked.

"I don't know yet," Jody said evenly. "Tell me what you need, and I'll tell you what I can do." She hesitated, but this was no time for modesty. "For whatever it's worth, my family has a long history of being underestimated."

Harli snorted. "That's the Moreau side of the family talking, no doubt."

"Actually, she gets it from both sides," Paul said. "But she's right about one thing: you never know what someone can bring to the table until you ask. Besides, it's not like we have anything in particular to lose by postponing the test a few minutes. Why not give her the basics of the situation?"

Harli snorted again. "Fine," he growled, beckoning to one of the other men. "Matigo? Make it the quick version."

Reluctantly, Jody thought, the man he'd called stepped forward and dropped into a crouch. "Down here," he said brusquely, gesturing Jody to join him. "Can you see?"

"Just a second," Jody said, getting down beside him and pulling out her flashlight. She turned it to its faintest setting and switched it on. "Ready. What am I looking at?"

"Nothing, yet," Matigo growled as he brushed away the leaves and other ground cover with his hand, leaving a more or less clear patch of dirt in the center of Jody's faint glow. "Here's Stronghold," he said, drawing a quick circle with his finger. "Clear zone around here; landing field here." He added another narrow ring around the first circle, then a rectangle on the south side. "The two Troft ships are here"—he drew a short line in the dirt on the rectangle, paralleling the edge of the circle—"and here"—he added a second line on the opposite side of the circle, again lengthwise. "They're good-sized, probably thirty meters tall and sixty or seventy long, though only thirteen or fourteen meters wide."

"Makes for a narrow frontal target," someone murmured.

"If they were fighting in space, which they're not," Matigo retorted. "Weapons seem to be concentrated in pivoting clusters on two pairs of small wings near the top of each ship, fore and aft and starboard and port. Looks like heavy lasers and missiles both, though we haven't seen them in action yet." He paused. "At least, *we* haven't."

Jody swallowed as she caught his meaning. "But the people inside Stronghold have?"

"We think so," Paul said grimly. "Matigo spotted a lot of burns and fresh fire-grooves in the buildings and grounds inside the wall. There's also a fair amount of new scoring on the top of the wall itself."

"I didn't think Trofts went in for mass killing," Jody said.

"Maybe we were wrong about that," Matigo said.

"Or possibly the Cobras in the city mounted some sort of counterattack shortly after the Trofts landed," Paul said. "If so, it doesn't look like they got very far before they were pushed back."

"And at this point we have no way of learning any of those details, either," Harli added. "With the comm system down and our handful of short-range radio frequencies being blocked, we can't communicate with anyone inside the wall."

Jody nodded. No wonder her father had sounded so grim. "So what's this test you mentioned?"

"We need a look at their weapons' capabilities," Paul explained. "The lasers in particular. We need to see their general power output, recovery cycle time, targeting arrangements, and anything else we can dig out."

"How are you going to get all that?" Jody asked.

"How do you think?" Matigo growled. "We're going to shoot at them and try to get them to shoot back."

Jody felt her stomach tighten. "You're not serious."

"Yes, we're serious; and no, of course it's not what you're thinking," Harli said. "You think Caelian's got Cobras to waste on suicide work?"

"They're going to send some men into a few of the trees," Paul explained. "They'll fire antiarmor shots at the weapons clusters from behind the boles."

"What about return fire?" Jody asked.

"We're talking steelwood trees here," Harli said. "Big, thick, heavy ones, too. There are ways of taking them down, but laser fire isn't one of them."

Jody grimaced. Unless, of course, the Trofts' weapons were accurate enough to fire straight back at the attacking lasers, in which case, some of the Cobras were about to become instant amputees. But that probably wasn't something she should bring up. Especially since they'd all probably already thought of it on their own. "You think it's a good idea to let the Trofts know there are Cobras out here?" she asked instead.

"What, you think maybe they haven't noticed?" Matigo asked sarcastically. His head snapped around, and he fired a double fingertip laser burst at something in one of the nearby tree branches. "Unless they're blind, they know we're here."

"Yes, but—" Jody stopped at her father's touch on her arm.

"All right, then," Harli said briskly. "Cobras, to your stations."

The group broke up, all the men except her father heading off in Stronghold's general direction. Jody watched them go, her hands clenched painfully. "It'll be all right," Paul told her quietly. "I've seen them. *You've* seen them. They know what they're doing."

"Against the Caelian forest, sure," Jody said. "But against Trofts?"

Paul exhaled quietly. "Come on," he said, taking her arm. "I need to help with the observation."

The spot Harli had chosen for the test was at the northwest edge of Stronghold's fifty-meter-wide clear zone, about three hundred meters from the northernmost of the two enemy positions. By the time Jody and her father reached the stand of trees that Harli and four of the others had settled behind, Jody could hear the sound of rustling leaves as the Cobras who would be taking the brunt of the risk worked their respective ways up into their chosen firing positions.

And as Jody peeked out between the trees she got her first clear look at the Troft warship.

It was every bit as big and imposing as Kemp's description had suggested, looming silent and dark over the town, its hull gleaming faintly in the starlight, its stubby wings with their collections of weapons pods reminding her of fists stretched out over the townspeople in a twisted parody of a blessing.

It was probably an image that the Trofts hoped would inspire fear and despair. But to Jody's surprise, the predominant emotion stirring inside her was anger. Anger that these aliens would invade her worlds. Anger that they would frighten and kill her people.

And whether Harli or Matigo or any of the Cobras believed it or not, she was damn well going to help them throw the invaders out. Somehow.

"Everyone set?" Harli asked quietly.

There was no answer. But Harli nodded twice, and Jody realized that all the Cobras were simply responding in voices too soft for her to hear, with their audio enhancers turned up to hear them. "Acknowledged," Harli said. "On one. Three, two, *one*."

And abruptly the landscape blazed with a barrage of painfully bright laser fire as a half dozen Cobras opened fire on the Troft ship, the bursts focused on the wings.

Jody winced back, squinting at the sudden assault on night-accustomed eyes. The attack seemed to go on forever, though it was probably only a few seconds.

The Cobras were still firing when the Trofts finally replied.

The answering fire came in a single, massive salvo that flashed across the open air as abruptly as the Cobras' own fire had begun, and suddenly the forest was filled with the stuttering crackle of blasted tree trunks and the secondary sizzle as hundreds of splinters and wood fragments rained down through the leaves around them. Both barrages ended, and for a pair of heartbeats the forest was dark and silent once again.

And then, without warning, a single flash lit up the night sky.

Only this one wasn't from the Cobras or the nearby Troft ship. This one came from the other Troft ship, the one a kilometer away to the south.

And it wasn't splinters and burned wood that hit the ground this time. This time, it was a human body.

His name, Jody learned, had been Buckley.

No one said much as two of the Cobras moved the badly burned body deeper into the forest, away from the Troft ship, and wrapped it in one of the silliweave shelters. Matigo muttered something over and over under his breath as they worked, but whether it was a prayer or a curse Jody couldn't tell. Nor did she feel any inclination to ask.

Harli didn't say any more than any of the others. But the glimpses of his face that Jody caught in the reflected light of the group's sporadic but never-ending antipredator fire sent shivers up her back.

Finally, with the body as protected from scavengers as they could make it, Harli called the group together. "All right," he said, his voice glacially calm. "Either the old legends were wrong about the Trofts not engaging in unnecessary killing, or else this bunch doesn't play by those rules. So be it. They've made their point, that with the geometry of their ship placement a simple frontal assault won't work. Our next attack will just have to be clever."

Beside Jody, Paul cleared his throat. "You assume the killing wasn't necessary," he said. "What if the Trofts thought it was?"

"You trying to excuse them?" Matigo demanded.

"I'm trying to understand them," Paul corrected. "That's what this test was supposed to gain us, right? Information?"

"If you think—" Matigo began.

Harli stopped him with a gesture. "Explain," he said.

"Suppose our barrage did more damage than we thought," Paul said. "Something that really worried them. In that case, they would have to do something to discourage us from trying it again. The northern ship couldn't get to the attackers through the tree boles, so they had to use the southern ship's weapons, which had clear shots of everyone. In fact, in that scenario, killing only one of us could actually be considered restrained."

Someone swore. "Restrained. Right."

"He's right, Broom," Kemp seconded. "We'd already finished firing."

"But the Trofts didn't know that," Paul pointed out. "As far as they knew, we might just be taking a breather before launching another attack."

"It's an interesting theory," Harli said. "So what exactly is this damage we supposedly did to their ship?"

"I don't know," Paul admitted. "I didn't see anything that should have worried them very much. But just because I didn't see anything doesn't mean it wasn't there."

"Spotters?" Harli invited, looking around the circle. "Anyone?"

"We were burning something off the wing," one of the others spoke up. "I could see bits of smoke where the shots were hitting. But it didn't look like the hullmetal was even getting scratched."

"Yeah, I didn't see anything, either," another man spoke up. "Though I suppose it's possible we warped the missile tubes a little."

"They still looked pretty straight to me," a third man said doubtfully. "And I was specifically watching for that."

"Anyone else?" Harli asked.

No one spoke up. "So," Harli said. "The smoke was probably just us burning off some kind of anti-radar coating. Hardly important unless they're expecting a space battle sometime in the near future."

"Sure as hell not worth killing for," Matigo growled. "So what's next? We got a plan?"

"Maybe," Harli said slowly, scratching his chin. "They may have already made a big mistake. Anyone else notice how close that ship is parked to the edge of the clear zone?"

There was a chorus of affirmative murmurs. "That could be our ticket in," Harli continued. "Wonderland's already starting to reclaim the land, and you might also have noticed there are a couple of access doors on the corners of the bow. If we can hang on out here and give the vegetation a few days to grow, we may be able to sneak up on them."

"That assumes they can't fire that close to their ship," Paul pointed out.

"Rotating weapons systems are always restrained so that they can't accidentally fire on their own ship or vehicle," someone said.

"I agree that you'd want to avoid misfires," Paul said. "But a blanket statement like that makes me nervous. Especially when none of us has had a great deal of experience with such things."

"When you get the Trofts to hand over the technical specs of their ships, let me know," Harli said. "Until then, we'll just have to give it a shot and see what happens."

"Maybe not," Jody spoke up.

"Look, kid—" Matigo growled.

"What do you mean?" Paul asked.

"Let's see what they can do," Jody said, her mind racing as she tried to work through the details of the plan that had only now come to her. "We send something poking around one of those doors and see what they do about it."

"And how do we do that?" Harli asked. "You have some special rapport with Caelian's animals?"

"Not really," Jody said. "But I do have some rapport with their dining preferences."

In the faint starlight, she saw Harli's eyes narrow. "Continue," he said.

"First of all, we'll need some bait," Jody said, sifting rapidly through the mental encyclopedia of Caelian's flora and fauna that she'd crammed into her brain on the trip over from Aventine. "A fleeceback, maybe—they're easy to catch and will go practically anywhere for midlia fruit."

"Midlia fruit?" Matigo echoed, sounding puzzled.

"She means tardrops," Harli told him.

"Right—that's what I meant," Jody said, feeling her face warming. "We collect some tardrops, crack them open and throw them against the hull near one of the doors—I'm assuming you can throw things that far—then turn our captured fleeceback loose."

Harli threw a frown at Matigo. "Are you expecting the Trofts to panic when they see a fleeceback charging their ship?" he asked.

"Not at all," Jody said. "As I said before, the fleeceback is just the bait. Once it's busy licking tardrop husk off the door, we send a gigger in after it."

"And you're expecting the Trofts to panic when they see a *gigger* charging at their ship?" Harli said again, his patience starting to show signs of coming apart.

"Not the gigger itself, no," Jody said. "But when they see what we've attached to the gigger's mouth tusks, maybe." Reaching to her belt, she unhooked the stun stick. "This."

Harli stared at the weapon, his forehead furrowed in thought. Then, slowly, his forehead cleared, and to Jody's astonishment he actually smiled. It was a thin smile, cold and not particularly friendly. But it was a smile. "Nice," he said. "We rig the stun stick to go off when the gigger hits the hull with it."

"Making for a nice high-voltage light show," Matigo added. Unlike Harli, he wasn't smiling. But at least his tone wasn't as hostile as it usually was. "And there's no place on a fleeceback to tie the thing, which is why you're talking a three-stage operation. Cute."

"Might even work," Harli said. He gestured to Matigo. "Take a couple of men and go hunt us down a fleeceback. I saw a couple of tardrop bushes back a ways—pick up some of the fruit while you're at it. Tracker, you're in charge of finding us a gigger."

"That won't be necessary," Jody said. "We have a caged one back at our camp."

"You have a caged *gigger*?" Harli asked, sounding stunned.

"She's right," Kemp confirmed. "I saw it."

Harli held up his hands. "I'm not even going to ask. Fine. Kemp, take Tracker and go get it. The rest of us will head around the rim and look for a good staging area."

He gestured. "We're burning darkness, gentlemen. Let's get to it."

CHAPTER TEN

The plumbing supply store Emile half led, half dragged Lorne into wasn't as crowded as the street, but there were still plenty of people milling around inside, busily cleaning the place out of supplies. Some of Capitalia's residents, apparently, were taking the long view of the Troft occupation. Still holding onto Lorne's arm, Emile maneuvered them through the shoppers and into an unoccupied office in the back.

"All right," the bulky man said when he'd closed the door behind them. "You obviously didn't get the memo, so let me lay it out for you. We are not, repeat, *not* to attack, antagonize, or otherwise disturb the Trofts. Got that?"

Lorne stared at him. "You're joking."

"Do I *look* like I'm joking?" Emile countered, pointing both index fingers at his scowling face. "That's straight from Governor-General Chintawa and the Directorate. Everyone in government service is to stand down and wait for further instructions."

"Including the Cobras?"

"*Especially* the Cobras," Emile growled. "Whatever the hell you thought you were doing up there, I hope you had fun, because that was your last hurrah."

"Until when?" Lorne asked.

"Like I said, until further instructions," Emile said.

Lorne stared at him, a hazy numbness settling across his mind. So they were giving up? The whole planet was just giving up?

Or was this some sort of Troft trick? "You have any proof of this order?" he asked.

Emile snorted. "What, you want an official government document with time-stamp fibers?"

"That would be nice," Lorne said. "Let's start with where you got your information. Better yet, let's start with some proof of who you are."

Scowling, Emile lifted his left hand and fired a low-power laser blast from his little finger into the floor. "Emile Chun-Wei, Dome Security, Cobra contingent," he said formally. "And you're Lorne Broom, current assignment DeVegas Province." He gave Lorne a tight smile. "Don't look so surprised. *No one* gets into the Dome without being properly logged in. Not even an off-the-record visitor to the governor-general." The smile turned sour. "Not even when he's the son of the infamous Jin Moreau."

"Her name is *Jasmine* Moreau Broom," Lorne said stiffly. "Only family and friends get to call her Jin."

"Whatever," Emile growled. "The point is that while you were stomping around the sewers this morning, the rest of us Cobras were setting up talking posts all across the city." He smiled again, or maybe it was more of a smirk. "And yes, we know all about you and Governor Treakness making for Crystal Lake."

Lorne grimaced. "The white-haired man back in Wei Kei's," he said, nodding. "Yes, I assumed at the time he wasn't close enough to overhear us. But of course, I also assumed a Cobra would have come over and offered to help."

"Those assumptions will get you every time," Emile said. "Interesting thing about it is that Chintawa hasn't said anything about Treakness being on any special missions."

Lorne felt his throat tighten. Treakness had told him Chintawa had authorized this mission. But he'd never heard it from Chintawa himself. Was it possible Treakness had made the whole thing up? "Maybe Chintawa was worried that word of the mission would leak out," he said, keeping his voice casual. "You mentioned talking posts. What are they?"

Emile rolled his eyes. "They're a set of top-floor windows where we sit with lights and tap out Dida code to each other," he said with exaggerated patience. "Surely your brother or father told you about Dida code."

"They may have mentioned it," Lorne conceded, feeling like an idiot. Of course he'd heard of Dida code. It was a semi-secret system of dots and dashes that Cobras on Aventinian big-city duty were taught at the beginning of their tenure, a fallback method for maintaining short- and medium-distance communication if the comm system ever failed.

Lorne's father presumably knew Dida, as did Lorne's brother Merrick, who'd been assigned to Capitalia two years ago. In fact, now that Lorne thought about it, he realized that Dida was probably what Merrick had been talking about way back then when he grumbled about the complexities of city duty. Lorne himself, with his own life and career still wrapped up in the expansion regions, had actually forgotten the system even existed. "Well, then, there's your answer," he told Emile. "Chintawa was afraid the Trofts would tap into your light show, so he didn't say anything."

"The Trofts don't know Dida code," Emile scoffed. But his tone nevertheless sounded a little less truculent.

"Doesn't mean they can't record what you send and decipher the messages later," Lorne pointed out.

"I suppose," Emile said. "Kinda moot now, though. Where's Treakness?"

"Why?" Lorne asked cautiously.

"Why do you think?" Emile growled. "So we can take him back to the Dome and get the Trofts off our backs about our missing governor."

Lorne stared at him. "You mean you're just going to hand him over to them?"

"Of course," Emile said. "Face it, Broom, there's nothing he can do flailing around out here on his own. The Trofts want him, and they're going to keep giving the whole city grief until they get him."

"Since when do we cave in to grief?" Lorne demanded. "What happened to the oaths we took as Cobras?"

"You mean our oath to defend the people of Aventine?" Emile

countered. "The people who are going to be dumped on just because some cowardly politician feels like running instead of sticking around to face the music like everyone else? *Those* people?"

"Treakness isn't running," Lorne insisted. "He's on a mission."

"Again, who says?" Emile asked.

"Chintawa sent one of his aides to get me before the Trofts landed," Lorne said stubbornly. "Why would he do that if Treakness just made up this whole thing?"

"How should *I* know?" Emile asked impatiently. "He could have had a hundred reasons for wanting you in the Dome when the balloon went up. You seriously think Treakness isn't smart enough to spot an opportunity when it falls into his lap and grab it with both hands? Come on, kid, use your head. He's using you, pure and simple. Now, where is he?"

Lorne took a deep breath. "You're right, I don't know for sure what's going on," he said. "But I don't believe that Governor Treakness is lying to me. I also promised I'd do everything in my power to get him out of the city where he needs to go."

Emile shook his head. "You still don't get it, do you? You can't *get* him out. That's the point." He waved his hand. "You see this safe zone? It's an island. A completely enclosed chunk of civilization in the middle of a spiny-infested city. The rest of the safe zones are exactly the same: a few fenced-in streets centered around one or two of their sentry ships, completely isolated from all the others. Even if you had a car, you couldn't drive from one to another."

"What about the cars outside the safe zones?" Lorne suggested. "I could get Treakness out there and grab one of those."

"And you don't think the Trofts will notice you driving around?" Emile scoffed. "You think that just because they've seeded the area with a few spinies that they're ignoring those areas? Hardly. They have armored troop carriers driving around the spiny zones, *plus* a line of fresh transports coming in from orbit all the time that have orders to survey the territory on their way down, *plus* a bunch of observation drones flying around the city and countryside watching for unauthorized movement."

"Then I guess we'll just have to walk," Lorne said through clenched teeth.

"Oh, right—that'll work," Emile said sarcastically. "Just be sure the spinies leave enough of Treakness for the Trofts to identify afterward. Come on, we're wasting time."

"You're right, we are," Lorne agreed, bracing himself. "I'm leaving. You can help me or stay out of my way."

Emile barked a short laugh. "You really think—?"

And dropped to the floor like a heavy sack as the high-voltage current from Lorne's stunner arced through him.

For a long moment Lorne gazed down at the unconscious Cobra, his heart thudding painfully in his chest. If Emile was right—if Treakness had lied to Lorne about his mission and his instructions coming from Governor-General Chintawa . . .

But it was too late to worry about that now. Way too late. Taking a couple of deep breaths, he slipped out of the room.

He'd told Treakness he would rendezvous with the group six blocks west of the Hendrezon's building. Given the faster time Lorne had been making as he ran along the rooftops, he expected to be the first one to arrive. To his mild surprise, he reached the corner to find Poole and the elder Koshevski already waiting, the latter looking darkly around, the former with his arms crossed over his chest, his fingers tapping nervously against his rib cage.

"There you are," Poole said, sagging with relief as Lorne slipped through the crowd and came up to them. "I was afraid you'd been—I mean, after you left us, and then we got here—"

"Yeah, all of two minutes ago," Koshevski interrupted, eyeing Lorne. "Got to say, though, that was a damn good show."

"Glad you liked it," Lorne said, looking around. "Where are the others?"

"They stopped at one of the health stores down the block," Poole said, jerking his head back in the direction they'd come from. "Nissa thought some—" he lowered his voice conspiratorially "—some disguise materials were probably called for."

"Good idea," Lorne agreed, turning to Koshevski. "What's happening with your brother and his family?"

"They've got some friends down the street," Koshevski said. "They should be able to stay with them, at least for a while."

"What about you?" Lorne asked.

Koshevski shrugged. "I'll probably stick around. There's nothing back at my place I can't get here. Been wanting to spend more time with my nieces and nephew anyway." His lip twitched. "But first we've got to get you to Ridgeline."

Lorne frowned. After the man in the crowd who'd tried to sell him to the Trofts, and Emile's flat-out refusal to lift a finger to help them, he'd sort of expected Koshevski to bail on them, too. "You're still up for that?"

"A deal's a deal," Koshevski said with another shrug. "There's an access point behind an arbor bench a block over that we should be able to use without being spotted. Soon as the others get here, we'll head over and you can take a look."

"Sounds good." Lorne nodded toward an exotic foods shop across the street. "Let's go look around in there while we wait. We're a bit conspicuous just standing around."

Most of the more popular foodstuffs had already been cleared off the shelves, with only a few of the more acquired-taste items remaining. Lorne kept an eye on the rendezvous corner as they browsed, and when he spotted Nissa and Treakness approaching he bought a package of cured Esquiline trihorn meat and ushered the others back outside.

The two groups reached the corner at the same time. "I see you're still alive," Treakness greeted Lorne shortly. "Good."

"Thanks for your concern," Lorne said stiffly. "You're looking interesting yourself."

Treakness snorted. "I look like a fool," he said bluntly, patting gingerly at the streaks of color Nissa had run through his hair. "Hair coloring, cheekbone highlighting, and whatever this stuff is she's got all over my face."

"It's tan-effect," Nissa said. "It darkens your skin."

"And it itches like crazy," Treakness growled. "We have a plan?"

"Access point's half a block that way," Koshevski said, nodding in that direction. "We're ready when you are."

"Excellent," Treakness said. Apparently, the thought that Koshevski might quit now that he'd gotten what he wanted had never occurred to him. "Lead on."

The access point was as Koshevski had described, tucked away behind the bench and spread of miniature trees that formed the small pedestrian arbor area, and just inside the Trofts' fence. "This should do nicely," Treakness said, looking around as the group gathered together around the cover. "Whenever you're ready, Broom."

"In a second," Lorne said, keying in his enhancers and giving the sky above them a quick but careful scan. "I'm told the Trofts have observation drones flying over the city."

"Where'd you hear that?" Koshevski asked.

"From someone who should know," Lorne said. If the Trofts had any drones up there at the moment, though, they were too high for him to spot. "Get ready," he said, getting a grip on the access cover. "Koshevski, you're first."

A minute later, with their sequential disappearance having apparently gone unnoticed by the milling crowds, Lorne carefully settled the cover back into place above his head and made the dark descent into the drainage system. "Everyone okay?" he asked quietly when he reached the bottom.

"Everyone except my back," Treakness said sourly. "It's already aching in anticipation. You people don't really *walk* these conduits all the time, do you?"

"No, we have rolling platforms and kneepads," Koshevski said. "But that stuff is all kept in the substations, and there aren't any anywhere along our way."

"Of course there aren't," Treakness growled. "Fine. Let's get on with it."

"I need a quick word with Governor Treakness first," Lorne said. "The rest of you go on ahead. We'll catch up."

"Okay, but don't get too far behind," Koshevski warned. "There are a couple of tricky spots a few blocks ahead."

"We won't be that long," Lorne said. "Get going."

He and Treakness stood together in silence until the sound of the others' footsteps had faded away into the faint murmur of the crowds going by overhead. "So?" Treakness asked.

"The man who told me about the Trofts' observation drones was another Cobra," Lorne told him. "He also said—"

"You met another Cobra up there?" Treakness interrupted. "Why in hell's name didn't you invite him to join us? We can use all the help we can get."

"I *did* invite him," Lorne said. "He said Governor-General Chintawa never said a thing about this special mission of yours. To anyone."

For a long moment Treakness didn't answer. Lorne keyed in his light-amps, to find that the governor's expression was as unreadable as his silence. "In other words, he thinks I lied to you," Treakness said at last. "What do *you* think?"

"I'd like to think I can trust you," Lorne said. "But to be honest, I'm not sure I can. I've been thinking about this thing, and parts of it just don't add up."

"Such as?"

"For starters, if this mission is really so vital, why am I the only Cobra on the job?" Lorne asked. "There were other Cobras in your neighborhood—we saw them get slaughtered by the Trofts right after I arrived. And as you said, we could certainly use more help. So why weren't they brought in?"

"Probably because by the time Chintawa was ready to start calling them the Trofts had the comm system shut down," Treakness said.

"He got through to me just fine," Lorne pointed out.

"Because you were the first one on his list," Treakness said. "Or rather, Ms. Gendreves was, with instructions to go get you. By the time he finished talking to the Tlossies at Creeksedge and a few other people, the Trofts had crashed the system."

"Which was apparently replaced fairly quickly by a Dida-code flash setup," Lorne said. "So even if he couldn't get more Cobras to us at the beginning, he could have sent some after us."

"Yes, he could," Treakness agreed. "And no, I don't know why he didn't. All I can suggest is that he was afraid letting more people into the secret than he had to would increase the risk of word leaking out to the Trofts."

Which was essentially the same excuse that Lorne himself had offered to Emile. It didn't sound nearly as convincing coming out of Treakness's mouth. "That's one theory," he said. "You also told me Chintawa insisted I accompany you, which is supposedly why you waited until I showed up before heading to Creeksedge. But if the Tlossies are really on our side, why didn't you ask them to send a shuttle to pick up both of us? If the invaders aren't bothering their freighter, they probably wouldn't have shot down one of their shuttles, either."

"An interesting question," Treakness said. "Let me ask you one in return. Would you be performing this same cross-examination if, say, you'd been asked to escort Governor Ellen Hoffman to Creeksedge instead of me?"

"Under the same circumstances?" Lorne asked. "Of course."

"Really?" Treakness asked. "Because I'm sure you're as familiar with Governor Hoffman's pro-Cobra stance as you are with my own somewhat less enthusiastic position."

"That has nothing to do with the case," Lorne said.

"I think it does," Treakness said. "In your mind, my position on the Cobras automatically colors every other perception you have of me, including your opinion of my integrity and my honesty. So I ask again: would you automatically assume Hoffman would lie to save her own skin, the way you're thinking I would?"

"I'm not accusing you of lying," Lorne insisted. But down deep, he realized he couldn't dismiss Treakness's accusations nearly that easily.

Because the governor was right. If it were Ellen Hoffman standing here, he would indeed have been more inclined to accept her story about a secret mission. He certainly would have been more willing to risk his life for her.

And then, Lorne felt his breath catch in his throat as a horrible suspicion flooded in on him. "Poole," he murmured.

"What?" Treakness asked, frowning.

"Poole," Lorne said, activating his infrared and gazing intently at the heat pattern of Treakness's face. If the governor lied now, he should be able to spot it. "It suddenly occurred to me why he's here."

Treakness's heat pattern darkened, subtly but noticeably. "What are you talking about?" he demanded.

"I'm talking about you and traveler's insurance," Lorne said. "That's the real reason he's with us, isn't it?"

Treakness's pattern darkened even more. "I have no idea what you're talking about," he said stiffly.

"I think you do," Lorne said, the sheer arrogance of the man turning his stomach. "You know how most Cobras feel about you and your policies. You know that any of us would accept an order to protect you, but that not many of us would put much enthusiasm into the job."

He waved down the conduit. "So you invited Poole along, a nice convenient innocent bystander, to guarantee I'd put some real effort into getting you out." He felt his eyes narrow as another thought occurred to him. "Is that why Nissa's along, too? Did Chintawa send her to get me instead of asking the Tlossies to pick us up so that I'd have one more innocent bystander to play guardian to?"

"The Tlossies wouldn't leave the spaceport," Treakness said, some of the fresh heat fading from his face. "As to the rest, you can believe whatever you want as long as you obey your orders."

Lorne snorted. "So that's the bottom line?"

"Obeying orders?" Treakness asked. "Yes. And if you're worth the Cobra name, you'll do the same."

With a supreme effort, Lorne choked back his anger and contempt. "As you wish, Governor," he said, pitching his voice parade-ground formal. "Don't worry, I'll get you to the spaceport."

Lorne moved a step closer to the other. "But understand that this isn't over," he added softly. "Once this is all over, however long it takes, I *will* petition the Directorate for a full investigation of everything that's happened here today."

"That's your right as a citizen of Aventine," Treakness said, his own voice going as neutral as Lorne's. "Was there anything else?"

The man was cool, all right. Way too cool for Lorne's taste. "No, I think we're done," he said. "For now."

"Then I suggest we catch up with the others," Treakness said, gesturing toward the conduit. "It would be rather embarrassing to admit at the trial that you lost half our party while you were busy browbeating me with worthless questions."

"I suppose it would," Lorne agreed, gesturing in turn. "After you."

If any of the party had hoped this leg of their underground journey would be easier than the previous one, they were quickly disillusioned. The conduits on the west side of Capitalia were every bit as cramped, slimy, and uncomfortable as the ones closer to the central city. That meant there were just as many slips as before, and the same number of stops along the way to relieve the strain on backs and knees.

Still, Lorne noticed there was less groaning and fewer under-the-breath complaints than there had been earlier. Possibly the brief above-ground break had given everyone's joints and muscles sufficient recovery time to ease the discomfort.

Or maybe it was the thought of armed Trofts and hungry spine leopards roaming the landscape above that had given them all a new perspective on the advantages of this mode of travel.

But the trip was still long and slow, and within the first hour they began to encounter additional complications as they reached a more modern section of the drainage system where many of the larger conduits had given way to smaller ones. Koshevski never got lost in the maze, but as the percentage of passable conduits steadily decreased, he was forced to lead them through extra turns and sometimes long detours in order to keep them moving westward.

It was three hours past sundown by Lorne's nanocomputer clock when Koshevski finally came to a halt in a T-junction chamber. "End of the line," he murmured, gesturing to his right and left. "The only passable routes that are left lead northeast and straight south, neither of which will get you any closer to Crystal Lake or any facility or resource that might help you get there."

"So where exactly are we?" Treakness asked. "What's around us right now?"

"Okay, this is Duell Street," Koshevski said, pointing straight up.

"It's a residential area two blocks west of Ridgeline. About three blocks north is Estes Park, five or six blocks south and a couple east is the Indus Entertainment Center, and about seven blocks west you hit the edge of the Vandalio Industrial Park."

"What do they make there?" Poole asked.

"Vandalio is mostly light industry," Treakness told him. "Electronics and small consumer appliances."

"Right," Koshevski said. "If you need a drill or laser torch, that would be a good place to look."

"What about the spaceport?" Treakness asked. "Where's that, exactly?"

"It's ten, maybe eleven kilometers west and a little north of the industrial park," Koshevski said, pointing at the blank wall beside him where another westward conduit should have been. "You don't want to go there, though."

"Why not?" Nissa asked.

"Because the first thing a smart invasion force does is secure the local transportation centers," Koshevski said. "Here, that means Creeksedge."

"Understood," Treakness agreed, nodding. "We'll be sure to give the place a wide berth."

"Yeah, good luck with that," Koshevski said. "Good luck with the rest of it, too. I'm sorry I can't do more, but this really is as far as I can get you."

"No apologies needed," Treakness assured him, offering his hand. "We're most grateful for your help. Thank you."

"You're welcome," Koshevski said. He shook Treakness's hand briefly, then did the same with the others. "You going to be all right if I just leave you here?"

"We'll be fine," Treakness said. "You just worry about getting back to your family."

"No problem," Koshevski promised. "Again, good luck."

With that, he slipped past them and headed back down the conduit, the faint glow from his flashlight just bright enough to show the footing ahead. A minute later, the bobbing light vanished around a turn.

"So what *are* we going to do?" Poole asked hesitantly.

"Well, we're *not* giving the spaceport a wide berth, if that's what you were wondering," Treakness growled. "Broom? You're up. What's the plan?"

"First thing we need is a look outside," Lorne said, taking hold of the rungs and starting up the shaft. "Wait here, and be quiet."

He reached the top of the shaft, and for a minute pressed his ear to the cover, his audios at full power. Nothing. Balancing his feet on the rungs, he eased the cover up a few centimeters and looked out.

Somewhere along the way they'd moved from Capitalia's central section, with its taller buildings and denser population, into one of the more spread-out suburban areas. Lining both sides of the street, set back behind trees, walkways, and softly glowing street-lights, were rows of single-family houses, each surrounded by a modest lawn of blueblade or curly-grass.

None of the houses showed any lights, and Lorne's first thought was that the residents had already fled to one of the safe zones. But his infrareds showed that all the houses were indeed inhabited, most of them by several people. Apparently, the occupants had decided to leave their lights off as a way of keeping a low profile.

It wasn't hard to figure out why. Lorne could see a half-dozen spine leopards from where he stood, moving about like shadows among the houses and shrubbery as they hunted for prey. Three blocks to the north, probably settled into the middle of the park Koshevski had mentioned, one of the Trofts' tall sentry ships towered over the neighborhood.

And drifting across the night sky were a handful of small grav lifts. Not transports—they were too small for that—which meant they were probably the observation drones Emile had told him about.

For a moment Lorne watched them meandering their lazy circles, a sour taste in his mouth. Through the long walk through the drainage system he'd come up with a plan for getting Treakness and the others at least to the vicinity of the spaceport, though if the Trofts had the whole place locked down, getting them the rest of the way to the waiting freighter might prove to be tricky.

But even the first part of Lorne's plan assumed that the Troft drones were only watching for moving cars and other powered equipment. If they were programmed to watch for *all* movement, pedestrian as well as vehicular, they probably wouldn't even get as far as the industrial park, let alone all the way to Creeksedge.

What he needed was a technical readout or spec sheet for those drones. Would the Tlossies at the spaceport have such data, or at least an idea of the invaders' capabilities?

Probably. But with the comm system still down, he had no way of putting that question to them. Even if the system was back in service, he couldn't trust it not to have Troft eavesdropping computers monitoring all of the planet's conversations.

Somewhere in the distance, a hint of a deep throbbing sound caught his attention. He keyed up his audios, and the sound resolved into the soft, throaty growl of a heavy engine. Some Troft vehicle, obviously, probably one of the armored troop carriers he'd seen back in the safe zone.

And as Lorne listened to the approaching vehicle, it occurred to him that he might not have to bother the Tlossies with this one after all.

Lowering the cover back in place, he climbed quickly down to the others. "Well?" Treakness asked.

"I'm going to have to go out for a while," Lorne told him. "All of you need to stay put until I get back." Reversing direction, he started back up again.

"Wait a minute," Treakness said. "Going out where?"

"If I'm lucky, I'll be back in an hour," Lorne told him. "But it could be two, or possibly three."

"What if you don't come back at all?" Treakness demanded harshly. "How will we know if you've been killed?"

"Just listen for laser fire and screaming Trofts," Lorne said impatiently. "That's usually a good clue. Just keep quiet—this is going to be tricky enough as it is."

He reached the top of the shaft and again carefully lifted the cover. The rumble of the troop carrier was definitely getting closer, and he could now see the faint sheen of headlights flicking across the landscape to the south as the vehicle approached. If it was heading back toward the ship three blocks north, it ought to be turning onto Lorne's street any time now...

And then, the headlights sharpened, and a large vehicle rolled into sight two blocks away. Lorne got just a glimpse of the vehicle's dark bulk before it finished its turn and the glare of the headlights washed out any hope of seeing anything more behind them.

But the brief look was enough to show him that it was indeed one of the armored carriers. More importantly, it had also showed the top of the vehicle's silhouette to be smooth, with no sign of Troft soldiers sitting on top as they had been back in the safe zone.

Which made perfect sense, of course. No sane soldier, no matter how good his body armor, would voluntarily expose himself to spine leopard attacks. Not when he could ride in safety and comfort inside an armored vehicle.

Quickly, Lorne lowered the cover back into place. The Trofts inside the carrier weren't likely to notice something as subtle as an askew drainage system cover, but there was no need to take that risk. Again pressing his ear against the metal plate, Lorne listened as the vehicle drew steadily nearer.

And as the leading edge passed over him, he pushed up on the cover, extended the little finger of his right hand through the opening, and fired his arcthrower.

The world around Lorne lit up briefly as the high-voltage arc slammed into the underside of the carrier. He fired again and again, aiming at the general area where the engine rumbling seemed to be loudest, trying to hit a vulnerable spot.

He was starting to wonder if the carrier even *had* any vulnerable spots when the engine abruptly died and the vehicle rolled to a halt.

Lorne took a deep breath, easing the cover all the way up and looking around. Most of the carrier had already passed him by, but the vehicle was long enough that its bulk still completely covered him. Equally important, the vehicle's designers had given it nearly half a meter of ground clearance, probably with the curbs and medians of a modern city in mind. There was plenty of room for Lorne to slide out of the shaft and get a grip on whatever convenient handholds the vehicle's underside presented him with.

Only to his surprise and consternation, there weren't any.

Frowning, he keyed his light-amps up a notch and looked again. No mistake: the long expanse of metal stretched out overhead was as solid as a family promise. There were a few small bulges and depressions, but no hooks, grilles, intakes, or knobs. Nothing that even servo-assisted fingers could get a solid hold on.

Something caught the corner of his eye, and he turned to see a new set of headlights coming toward him from the north. Apparently, the Trofts in the stalled vehicle had called for assistance, and that assistance was on its way.

Lorne slipped back down into the shaft, pulling the cover into place above him, and climbed down three steps. Again straddling the rungs, he got a grip on the topmost rung on one side with his left hand, pointed his right little finger at the spot where the curved metal joined the shaft, and fired his laser.

The shaft lit up with blue light, the metal sizzling as it disintegrated under the laser's heat. Droplets of metal scattered across his hands, and Lorne winced against the pinpricks of pain. A few seconds later the laser finished its work, and he shifted its aim to the other end of the rung. More sizzling, more tiny burns, and the rung came free in his hand. Tucking it under his arm, he got to work on the next rung down.

Half a minute later, with both rungs free, he again eased the cover off and looked out. The second vehicle had come alongside the stalled carrier, and Lorne could hear snatches of cattertalk over the rumbling of the newcomer's engine as the Trofts discussed both the unexpected engine trouble and the question of how best to get the disabled vehicle back to the ship. Sliding out onto the pavement, Lorne set the cover back in place over the shaft and rolled onto his back. He was taking a risk, he knew—if the Trofts decided to examine the dead carrier's engine out here, they would surely realize that it was no mere malfunction, but deliberate sabotage. If any of them then took the obvious step of looking underneath the carrier, this whole thing would come to an abrupt and violent end.

But chances were that none of them would want to linger in spiny-infested territory any longer than they had to. Listening to the ongoing conversation with half an ear, he set one of the rungs against the underside of the carrier and set to work.

By the time the conversation ended and the second vehicle began maneuvering itself into pushing position behind the first, he had both rungs spot-welded to the featureless metal at the right locations to serve as hand- and footholds. A minute later, as he pulled himself up as close to the undercarriage as he could, there was a sudden lurch and the stalled vehicle was once again in motion. Gazing out at his truncated view of the pavement, walkways, and lower parts of trees, streetlights, and houses, Lorne wondered if this plan was really as insane as it seemed, or whether it was even more so.

Two minutes later, they were there.

Lorne hadn't had a chance earlier to see any of the Troft ships unload its complement of ground vehicles, but he'd assumed that they were housed on the lowest level and simply rolled out once the proper hatches were opened. He was, he now discovered, half right. As they approached the ship, he saw a long ramp swing down from the narrow end, leading up to a hatchway that wasn't in the ship's lowest section, but instead was a good two or three decks above it. The two vehicles angled up onto the ramp, the second carrier's engine straining with the double load, and Lorne could see the faint glow of standard dark-orange Troft nighttime lighting coming from the wide opening ahead. The two vehicles reached the top of the ramp and leveled out, traveling perhaps another twenty meters through some sort of equipment bay before grinding to a final halt. There was another subtle change in the engine tone, and Lorne watched as the second carrier reversed direction and backed out and down the ramp, apparently heading out to continue the rest of the stalled carrier's patrol. As the engine sounds faded away, Lorne could hear the faint straining of other, quieter motors as the ramp was pulled back up again into closed position. The last hint of city light faded away into the gloomy orange, and with a hiss of pressure locks the ramp sealed itself into place.

And Lorne was alone. Inside an enemy ship.

Surrounded by enemy soldiers.

CHAPTER ELEVEN

Carefully, he took a deep breath. *I planned this*, he reminded himself. *This was my idea, and it's working perfectly.*

So far.

Above him, he heard a pair of dull thuds as the carrier's rear doors were opened and felt the slight rocking as the Trofts inside climbed out, their conversation revolving around the annoying engine trouble that had forced them to cut short their patrol. There were also several contemptuous comments about the lack of fighting spirit among Aventine's humans. Lorne watched their armored feet as the soldiers made their way across a floor crammed with machinery and other vehicles. They disappeared through a heavy door and headed one by one up a stairway. There was the sound of a hatch closing.

And then, silence.

Disengaging from his hand- and footholds, Lorne eased himself down onto his back on the deck, keying his audios to full power. The cold metal beneath him was an excellent conductor of sound, and he could hear a whole range of soft noises coming from deep inside the ship, everything from the hum of engines and ventilation fans to murmurs of distant conversation. But the vehicle bay itself appeared to be deserted. Fingertip lasers at the ready, he eased out from under the carrier and got to his feet.

The bay, as he'd already noted, was crammed with equipment and vehicles, including several one-man floatcycles, two more troop carriers like the one he'd disabled, and an even more heavily armored vehicle that was probably the Troft version of a compact urban battle tank. There were also racks of extra guns, wheels, and other large replacement parts. At the far end of the bay, across from the hatch and ramp, was a doorway leading into what appeared to be a long, well-equipped machine shop. Also at the far end of the bay, near the entrance to the shop, were a pair of doors on opposite sides. The one on the left was the one all of the departing Troft soldiers had taken on their way out, with the other door directly across the bay from it.

Lorne looked around the bay again. Everything here was ground vehicles, with no sign of the observation drones that he'd seen flying over the city. Assuming that they were based from these sentry ships, they must operate from a different deck.

He turned back to the hatchways on the bay's two sides, keying in his telescopics and light-amps to try to read the markings on them. Unfortunately, all they said were DECK 6-A and DECK 6-B, with no indication as to the rooms or departments they connected to.

Still, the soldiers had taken the left exit, presumably heading to their quarters or to check in with a duty officer. Either way, that was definitely not a direction Lorne wanted to go. Mentally crossing his fingers, he headed to the right.

Pressing his ear to the door again gained him nothing but another set of faint sounds. He pushed open the heavy door, a much quieter operation than he'd feared it would be, and found himself looking into a narrow staircase that switchbacked its way both up and down. Stepping onto the landing, he looked up.

The stairs weren't solid, but were made of the same weight-saving metal gridwork used in the Cobra Worlds' own modest collection of starships. The interference between the sections of mesh kept Lorne from seeing more than about two floors up or down, but that plus his hearing was enough to show that the stairway was as deserted as the vehicle bay. On the assumption that flying equipment like observation drones would be located higher in the ship than ground vehicles, he started up, his ears straining, his fingertip lasers ready.

And his heart pounding painfully hard in his chest. It was nerve-wracking enough to be wandering around a warship full of enemy soldiers. It was even more ominous when those soldiers inexplicably seemed to have vanished. Could they really all have retired to their quarters or wardrooms for the night? *All* of them?

He was midway up the first flight of steps when it occurred to him that, yes, they really *could* have done that. The dawn landing had required everyone to be up early, and the invasion had been followed by a busy day of fence-building, negotiating, and spiny-unloading. Trofts could push themselves as hard as humans when they had to, but heavy physical labor took as much of a toll on them as it did on anyone else.

And it wasn't as if they were facing any serious resistance out there. From the comments Lorne had overheard, it was clear that Emile had been telling the truth about Chintawa and the Director-ate having essentially capitulated. The government was cooperating with the invaders, the Cobras and patrollers had been ordered to stand down, and the average citizens were either cowering in their homes or scrambling to grab extra food and supplies with no inter-est or energy to spare for making trouble. Why *not* simply give the bulk of the invasion force the night off to rest, safe inside their warships, and leave the dull task of monitoring the night to the roving carrier patrols, the flying drones, and the spine leopards? In their position, a human commander would probably do the same.

He reached the first landing and eased the door open a crack. Beyond was a long corridor, again bathed in the nighttime orange, that seemed to stretch the entire width of the ship. There were several doors leading off in both directions, but none of them were open and he could hear no sounds of activity nearby. Closing the door again, he continued up.

He'd made it another half flight of steps, and was nearly to the midway landing, when the door one deck above him opened with a soft clang. A pair of Trofts, talking together in low voices, strode onto the landing and started down.

Frantically, Lorne reversed direction, heading back down toward the landing and the door below. But before he'd taken more than a couple of steps he knew he'd never make it in time, certainly not silently, certainly not without the approaching Trofts spotting his movement through the grillwork of the steps. The only way he was going to avoid being caught was to hide.

And in a bare stairwell, there was only one possible place to do that.

Pressing against the guardrail, he crouched motionlessly as he watched the Trofts come down the section of stairway above and to his right, heading toward the landing he'd just retreated from. He waited until they were two steps from the landing, then leaped up to the underside of their part of the stairway. His reaching fingers slipped into the grillwork they had just passed, getting a firm grip on the mesh. He pulled his body up beneath the stairs and swung his legs up and wedged his feet against the supports on either side of the steps. Pressing as close as he could to the underside of the steps, he froze.

The Trofts, their attention focused on their footing and conversation, never saw a thing. As Lorne held his breath, they made the turn around the landing and started down the steps beside him, the winglike radiator membranes on the backs of their arms brushing past barely half a meter from Lorne's own shoulder. He watched as they passed the vehicle bay door and continued one deck farther down before leaving the stairway and heading though the door back into the main part of the ship.

Lorne waited until the faint reverberations of the closing door had faded away and silence again filled the stairwell. Then, with a sigh of relief, he released his feet from their perch, got them back on the guardrail, and let himself back onto the other section of switchback. Wiping some of the sweat off his forehead, he continued on up to the door from which the two Trofts had entered the stairway.

The corridor beyond the door looked a lot like the one Lorne had seen one deck lower. With one difference: midway along this one was an open door. Notching up his audios, Lorne picked up the sound of low voices and the hum of machinery coming from that direction. He glanced up and down the stairway one final time and slipped into the corridor. Moving silently to the open door, he eased an eye around the jamb.

The room was a long one, nearly as long as the vehicle bay downstairs, though about a quarter of the way back it was cut into two sections by a thick transparent glass or plastic partition. On Lorne's side, in the smaller part, were three sets of curved monitor banks, each with twenty displays, each bank also including a full panel of controls. One of the panels was positioned straight back from the door, with the other two angled off to either side. The two Trofts he'd heard were sitting at the central and right-hand banks. Between them was a rolling heat cart on which sat a pot of simmering light-brown liquid that gave off a warm, spicy aroma.

In the larger part of the room, beyond the partition, were a pair of repair and fueling stations and two racks of two-meter-long, armored, dartlike machines equipped with floatwings and oversized sensor arrays.

Lorne took a deep breath. Perfect. Now if he could just get a good look at the monitor displays and figure out what exactly the observation drones were set to look for, he could start finding a way out of this place.

He was starting to ramp up his telescopics when, behind him, he heard the sound of the stairwell door starting to open.

There was no time to think, and only one place to go. Slipping around the doorjamb into the monitor room, he took a long step to his left and dropped into a crouch beside the couch of the unoccupied console, pulling the couch as much in front of him as he could.

The footsteps were coming closer. Lorne froze in place, hoping that the newcomer would continue on past and go off somewhere else on his errand.

With a rustle of radiator membranes, a Troft carrying a covered tray walked into the room.

The Troft tech at the central console swiveled around. [The time, it is overripe,] he said in cattertalk as he impatiently beckoned the newcomer toward him. [The view, was it sufficiently rewarding?]

[The meal, it was the only view I saw,] the newcomer countered stiffly. [The boredom out there, it is intense.]

[The boredom in here, it is likewise,] the tech at the other console said, also turning to face the newcomer. [The humans, they are hardly the danger we were warned of.]

[The other humans, perhaps it is they to whom the legends refer,] the newcomer suggested as the three Trofts busied themselves with the contents of the tray, which seemed to consist of some sort of small snack cakes. [Our strength, we waste it here.]

Keeping half an eye on them, Lorne rose a little higher from behind the couch and keyed in his telescopics.

The views on the monitors seemed to be of three types. One group, consisting of only a handful of displays, were set at a relatively low altitude and were stationary. Another, slightly larger group were ground-level and moving. The third group, which included the majority, were high-altitude and also moving. Another group of monitors were black, possibly the readouts from sensors that were only useful in space or atmospheric travel.

The first set of images, Lorne realized after a moment, were giving the view from the upper parts of the ship itself, probably from the weapons cluster wings, guarding the approaches to the Trofts' mobile fortress. The second group were more obvious: they were coming from the transport patrols as they wended their way through the ship's assigned territory. The third set were from the drones.

Lorne studied that last group, trying to figure out exactly what he was seeing. He could see the landscape stretching out across the displays, complete with houses, streets, trees, streetlights, industrial buildings, and some of the streams that fed into Crystal Lake to the west. The views seemed to overlap for a complete medium-altitude coverage, and on some of them he could see a bright mark or two that he tentatively identified as the roving Troft carriers.

And that was it. There were no individual heat signatures, no small-scale movement readings, not even any overall location patterns or flow data. Nothing that would give the invaders any hint that four humans were making a surreptitious journey across their freshly conquered land.

[—replace, and my post, I will return to it.]

Lorne snapped his attention back to the Troft conversation, and the sudden realization that he'd pushed his luck too far. The Troft who had brought in the tray had shifted his footing, and while his attention was still on the two at their consoles it was clear he was about to turn back to the door.

At which point he would be looking straight at Lorne.

Kill them! the frantic thought shot across Lorne's mind, the words as startling as they were appalling. Never in his life had he been angry enough or frightened enough to even consider killing someone, not even an alien.

But even as the fear of discovery flooded through him, the cold logic of the situation came in right on top of it. Even if none of the Trofts managed to cry out before they died, killing them would send bodies flying or falling all over the place, and he'd already noted how well these metal decks conducted sound. Even if no one heard and came running, someone would eventually come to relieve these posts, and the resulting outcry and manhunt would eliminate any chance of getting Treakness to the spaceport. Lorne's only hope was to escape from the room and from the ship without being seen, and the only way to do that now would be to create a distraction.

His eyes fell on the rolling heat cart and the pot of simmering brown liquid.

There was no time to come up with anything better. Aiming his torso toward the pot, he activated his sonic.

The Troft with the tray had finished his conversation and had turned nearly to face Lorne when the pot shattered.

The three Trofts screeched in unison as they scrambled to get out of the way of the shards of glass and the hot brown liquid flying everywhere. With the aliens' full attention now turned in that direction, Lorne slipped out of the room, and a few seconds later was back in the relative safety of the stairway.

Earlier that day, outside Treakness's apartment building, he'd noted that the Troft ships had small ground-level doors at the bow. If he could get down there without being caught, maybe he could exit through one of them.

Of course, at that point he would still be in view of the weapon cluster cameras. But with the Trofts in the monitor room busy cleaning up the shattered pot, he could hopefully get clear before they were in any condition to take notice of his departure.

But even with the aliens' obvious contempt for the people they'd just conquered, they weren't being stupid about it. As Lorne pressed his ear to the lowest stairway door, he heard at least four different voices chatting casually to each other. The Trofts might not have sentries standing guard in the middle of spiny territory, but they were cautious enough to have those soldiers in position to act should something out there require it. Unless Lorne was willing to take on the whole bunch of them, he wasn't getting out this way. Grimacing, he retraced his steps up the stairway and returned to the vehicle bay.

The room was still deserted, whoever was in charge having apparently decided that repairs on the damaged carrier could wait until morning. Keeping an ear cocked for the sound of unexpected arrivals, Lorne made his way through the equipment and vehicles to the end where he'd entered. If he could find the controls to lower the ramp, he might still have time to get away before the Trofts upstairs finished their cleanup duty.

He'd found the board and was trying to figure out the controls when there was the sudden whine of motors and the ramp began lowering all by itself. The cool outside air flooded over him, and as it did the whine of the ramp's motors was joined by the rumble of a larger, heavier engine.

One of the Troft carriers was coming home.

Once again, there was no time to think it through. The ramp had already swiveled a third of the way down. A few more seconds, and the carrier would be on its way up. Half a minute after that, there would be Trofts stomping all around the bay. Lorne either had to hide, or he had to find a way to take advantage of the narrow window he'd been given.

And as he stepped to the edge of the hatchway, it suddenly occurred to him that the window was narrower than he'd first realized. The carrier's headlights aimed mostly forward and down, he'd noted earlier, and as long as the vehicle was on the street, the top of the ramp was mostly out of their range.

But the minute those front wheels hit the ramp and angled up, the headlights would be aimed squarely into the bay. If Lorne wasn't out of sight by then, he would be nailed like a gan fly against a white wall.

Clenching his teeth, wondering distantly if warfare was always this reckless and unplanned, he crouched down inside the bay with his back to the edge of the ramp, and as the far end of the ramp thudded onto the street, he frog-hopped a meter out onto the near end, then gave a second hop backwards that took him off the edge of the ramp into empty space. As he started to fall, he grabbed the edge with both hands, holding on just long enough for his body to rotate around the pivot points and swing underneath the ramp. At the inwardmost part of the swing, he let go and dropped to the pavement five meters below. His knee and ankle servos absorbed the impact, and for the moment he was safe.

But only for the moment. Right now he was out of sight of both the carrier's driver and the ship-mounted cameras, but as soon as the carrier reached the bay and the ramp swung up again he would be right back to the fly/wall predicament. His only hope was to take off right now and assume the Trofts in the monitor room would be focusing so much of their attention on the incoming vehicle that they wouldn't pay attention to any other movement.

It wasn't a good plan, and he knew it. The Trofts up there might be bored, but it was pretty unlikely they would be so inattentive that they could fail to see a human running madly away from the vicinity of their ship. But it was all he had, and waiting until the carrier was gone and the ramp was back in place would be even worse.

He was bracing himself for an all-or-nothing sprint when he heard a soft sound behind him.

And as his nanocomputer took over his servos and threw him to the side a spine leopard leaped past, its extended leg spines coming close enough to brush through the hair at the side of his head.

Reflexively, Lorne swiveled around on his hip, bringing his antiarmor laser to bear as he flicked a target lock onto the predator's head. The spine leopard braked to a halt and spun around, its eyes glittering eerily in the shadow of the ramp angling down above it. Its jaws opened halfway, and it lowered itself in preparation for another try.

And with a sudden rush of adrenaline, Lorne realized that maybe he had his ticket out of here.

He froze in place, half sitting and half lying as he waited for the spiny to make its move. The predator, perhaps sensing something was wrong, also hesitated, its eyes boring into Lorne's. Then, opening its jaws the rest of the way, it leaped.

Lorne waited until it was nearly to him before triggering his antiarmor laser. His leg swung up and there was a brief flash of blue just as the spiny slammed into his foot, the impact shoving Lorne half a meter backward along the pavement. The animal dropped with a thud to the ground, and as it did so Lorne heard the engine noise from the carrier above him change pitch as the vehicle finished its climb and rolled into the equipment bay. Jumping back to his feet, Lorne grabbed the dead spiny's front legs, being careful not to impale his hands on the spines, and flung the carcass across his shoulders like a heavy backpack.

And as the ramp began to swing up again, he bent over at the waist, crouched down as far as he could, and took off.

The first fifty meters were the hardest. He ran it in a terrified cold sweat, his feet trying to match the lope of a running spine leopard, his brain screaming the fact that his imitation wasn't even close, his back crawling with anticipation of the heavy laser that would surely cut through any second now, wiping him out of existence before any of his senses could even register the attack.

But the attack didn't come. He reached the side of the street and ran up onto the nearest lawn, crossing it and darting between two of the houses. Reaching the rear, he leaped over a fence the way a spiny would and no non-Cobra could hope to accomplish. He passed through another row of houses and loped onto and across the next street, angling a little to cut behind a row of trees that would momentarily shield him from the Troft cameras and lasers. Once behind the trees, he changed direction again, staying in their shadow as he angled toward the next row of houses.

Only then, as the fear-induced sweat began to dry, did he finally begin slowing his pace a little to something less frenetic. Whether the Trofts had missed the reflection of his brief laser flash in the glare of the carrier's headlights, or whether they'd seen it and attributed the flicker to something else, it was clear that they'd been completely taken in by Lorne's sheep's-clothing ruse.

The tension had almost faded, and Lorne was starting to congratulate himself on his cleverness and his luck, when two spine leopards appeared out of nowhere and jumped him.

He managed to discourage them without using his lasers, dodging their attacks and throwing servo-powered punches and kicks in return until they both gave up and left in search of easier prey. He wasn't so lucky with the next attack, though, and was forced to use his fingertip lasers and even a short arcthrower burst to finally put the spine leopards down. Again, while it seemed impossible that the Trofts hadn't spotted the brief battle, there wasn't any obvious response.

He'd made it halfway through another block of darkened houses when it belatedly occurred to him that the lack of *obvious* response didn't necessarily mean the lack of response.

Ahead was a sculpted bush. He dropped down beside it, freezing in place and keying his opticals and audios to full power. In the near distance he could hear the sounds of a pair of Troft transports, much softer than he'd usually heard them, as if they had been put on some kind of stealth mode. It was hard to tell, but they seemed to be coming up on both sides of him, working their way toward the area where he'd last fired his arcthrower.

He tilted his head back and studied the sky above him. One of the observation drones was hovering nearly overhead, while two more were moving into the area from opposite directions.

"Damn," he muttered under his breath. His plan had been to

make his way to the industrial park Koshevski had mentioned and try to cobble together something that he could use to protect Treakness and the others from spine leopard attacks during the long walk the rest of the way to the spaceport.

But it was clear the Trofts knew or at least suspected a Cobra was working the neighborhood. The drones up there might not be programmed to watch for movement, but they clearly knew laser and arcthrower blasts when they saw them. And if there was one thing certain, Lorne would never make it to the industrial park without having to use at least one of those weapons again. Whatever he was going to put together, he was going to have to do it right here in this neighborhood, with whatever resources he could find.

Or rather, not in *this* neighborhood, but whichever neighborhood he could find to escape to. Mentally marking the locations of the two approaching carriers, he slipped away from the concealing bush and turned back toward the Troft sentry ship.

The dead spine leopard he'd used as camouflage was right where he'd dropped it during that first predator attack. Slinging it on his back again, he headed north, moving as casually as he could. The dead spine leopard's residual heat profile should help protect him from whatever infrared sensors the Trofts in the carriers were using, but rapid, panicky movement was even more eye-catching than heat profiles, and the last thing he could afford right now was to catch any of the Trofts' eyes.

Fortunately, the two carriers were still well to the south of him as the Trofts apparently worked on bracketing his last known position. Possibly they assumed he had gone to ground at their approach, and Lorne winced at the thought of the house-to-house search that was probably next on their agenda. Briefly, he wondered why they weren't bringing in reinforcements, a question that was answered a moment later as he got a glimpse of the sentry ship through the houses and saw the vehicle ramp starting down again. Grimacing, concentrating on looking inconspicuous, he kept going.

He was six blocks north of the ship, with no sign of alien forces gathering around him, before he finally began to breathe easy again. He gave it one more block, and then turned eastward back toward the central city. According to Koshevski, the accessible part of the drainage conduit system angled northeast. Lorne had to find an access point into that section and get back to the others before they concluded he'd been taken and Treakness decided to do something stupid.

And once he'd done all *that*, he still had to figure out how to get them across the rest of the spine leopard territory to the spaceport.

He was passing one of the darkened houses when he spotted exactly what he needed.

He was still two blocks away from the group huddled in the underground chamber when he began to hear their worried whispered conversation. He was a block away when he was able to see them with his light-amplifiers.

They didn't see or hear him until he was ten meters away and turned his flashlight on his own face.

To their credit, the loudest reaction he heard was a gasped curse. "What the *hell* are you doing coming in from there?" Treakness demanded as Lorne reached the end of the conduit and joined the others in the narrow chamber. "I thought you were going to come back that way." He jabbed a finger upwards.

"Change of plans," Lorne said. "We need to head north. And keep your voices down—the Trofts are on the move out there."

"Looking for you, I assume?"

"More or less," Lorne said. "The good news is that the observation drones aren't keyed to look for individuals on foot. Not all that surprising, I guess, since any kind of motion sensors would keep getting triggered by the roving spinies."

"Aren't their infrareds good enough to distinguish between spine leopards and humans?" Nissa asked, frowning.

"You can't get fine-tuned infrared profiles from a grav-lift craft that small," Poole said. "The grav lifts cause too much interference with the readings. You can distinguish a human or large animal from, say, a car engine, but not two animals of about the same size."

"Been spending our weekends with the Dome's tech manuals, have we?" Treakness asked acidly.

Poole ducked his head. "Sorry, sir."

"But he's right, isn't he?" Nissa asked.

"*Yes*, he's right," Treakness growled. "Fine, so they can't pick us up from the air. But that won't stop them from picking us up on the ground. You have an answer for that one, Broom?"

"Actually, from what I saw the Trofts should only be a minor problem," Lorne said, studying the other's face with his infrareds. Poole's unsolicited comment had sparked way more heat in Treakness than Lorne had expected, even from him. He hoped the governor wasn't starting to come apart. "They seem to be relying on the spine leopards to do most of the patrolling in this part of the city, which means they have only token forces of their own on the streets."

"If that hasn't changed now that they know you're out there," Treakness pointed out.

"True," Lorne conceded. "But I'm expecting them to concentrate on the neighborhood where I killed a couple of spinies, which we won't be going anywhere near. The spinies are going to be the big problem, and I'm pretty sure the Trofts know it. If I use my lasers, the drones will spot it in an instant and send the troops straight to wherever we are. If I *don't* use my weapons, the spinies will eventually nail us."

"I trust you have a solution to that problem?" Treakness asked.

"I think so, yes," Lorne said. He bent over at the waist and headed back into the conduit. "Come and take a look."

Traveling this part of the drainage system was every bit as unpleasant and backbreaking as all the earlier parts had been. But for Lorne, at least, it was worth all the trouble just to see Treakness's expression when the governor raised his head through the access point opening and got his first look at what Lorne had brought for them. "What in the name of hell is *that*?" he demanded.

"It's a garden shed," Lorne said, gesturing toward the squat, three-meter-square structure he'd borrowed from one of the homes down the block. "I know you don't see any of them in the city, but I'm sure you use things like this at your country estate—"

"I *know* what it is," Treakness growled. "What are you expecting us to do with it?"

"Walk to the spaceport, of course," Lorne said, beckoning. "If you'd step out of there, please, and let the others come up?"

"What, inside *that*?" Treakness demanded, making no attempt to move out of the others' way. "Don't be ridiculous—it's nothing but stamped sheet metal. It won't even stop a target slug, let alone a Troft laser."

"Technically, it's sheet metal over a ceramic grid foundation," Lorne corrected, giving the sky overhead a quick look. So far the drones still seemed to be concentrating on the area to the southwest where he'd given the Trofts the slip. "And as I told you before, if we pick our route properly the Trofts should never even notice us."

"So then why the—? Oh," Treakness interrupted himself, finally climbing the rest of the way out of the shaft. "It's supposed to keep the spine leopards away from us."

"Exactly," Lorne said as Nissa popped into view behind the governor. "And we're wasting time."

"Ah—a portable bunker," Poole said approvingly as he climbed out of the shaft behind Nissa. "And all the metal will even help diffuse our heat signatures for any roving Troft patrols. Very nice."

"Only if the spine leopards aren't able to bite through it," Treakness warned, tapping his fingertips against the metal. "This isn't very thick, you know."

"It doesn't have to be," Lorne assured him. "The first time a spiny starts nosing around I set the shed down onto its ceramic supports—you can see they stretch a few centimeters below the metal—and run a little current from my arcthrower into the appropriate spot. The spiny gets enough of a shock to discourage further investigation, but the Trofts don't see any of the big flashes their drones are looking for."

"Maybe," Treakness said doubtfully. "Too bad we can't give it a field test first."

"We can," Lorne said, "and I have. Twice, in fact, on the way over here. Everyone inside, please. We still have a long way to go."

After everything that had gone before, the walk to the spaceport ended up being refreshingly anticlimactic. The shed weighed over

eighty kilos, a daunting challenge for human muscles but a casual
load for Cobra servos and laminated bones. Lorne held the structure
up by its center, keeping it high enough for general ground clearance
but low enough that a roving spine leopard wouldn't be able to poke
its snout underneath for a quick bite. Nissa walked directly in front
of him, peering through one of the under-eave ventilation slits where
she could murmur warnings about curbs, bushes, houses, and other
obstructions. Treakness and Poole walked at Lorne's right and left,
watching for trouble through other slots and making sure they kept
clear of the Troft sentry ships dotting the area.

Several times along the way Lorne had to set the shed down
and deliver a mild shock to a persistent spine leopard. Twice during the trip they ended up sitting in one spot for several minutes
while he drove off an entire family group that refused to take no
for an answer.

But that was the worst of it. The sporadic Troft patrols themselves caused no trouble at all, since the rumble of their carriers'
engines always announced their imminent appearance. That gave
Lorne plenty of time to get the shed to an innocent-looking landing
place beside someone's house or driveway, where it looked perfectly
at home to anyone who didn't know the area.

Once, as the sound of the carrier began to fade away, Lorne
noticed the twitch of a curtain in the house beside their mobile
bunker, and his mind flashed back to the hostile crowd he'd had to
face in the Twentieth Street safe zone. But either the homeowner
didn't grasp the significance of the shed that had magically appeared
beside his house in the middle of the night, or else he wasn't yet
ready to betray his people to the occupiers.

Still, for the next two kilometers Lorne paid extra attention to
the stray noises around them.

Two hours before dawn, they arrived at the Creeksedge Spaceport.

Lorne had expected it to be bad. It was worse.

"God," Nissa murmured as the four of them crouched beside one
of the squat guidance beacons a kilometer from the spaceport's edge.

"And then some," Poole said soberly.

Lorne nodded in silent agreement as he gazed across the open ground. At the edges of the field, marking the four points of the compass, the invaders had placed four warships, bigger ones than the sentry ships they'd sent to guard Capitalia's intersections. Clustered around them like chicks around a mother hen were a dozen or more of the smaller transports that they'd used to bring in all the Qasaman spine leopards. In and amidst it all were dozens of Troft soldiers, some walking guard patrols, others driving carts laden with supplies into the spaceport's terminal and storage buildings or running hoses from the big fueling stations out to some of the transports.

"An interesting challenge," Treakness said calmly. "I trust you have a plan, Broom?"

Lorne grimaced, keying up his opticals a little as he gave the area a second, more careful look. Aside from the close-in foot patrols, there were also several of the armored carriers that had been set up in guard positions outside the cluster of ships, their roof-mounted swivel guns pointed outward. Still farther out, other carriers were tracing an outer sentry circle that, judging from the fresh ruts he could see in the ground, were coming no more than halfway to the beacon where their group was huddled.

But while the roving patrols weren't coming anywhere near their current position, Lorne noticed suddenly, they were coming right to the edge of the line of posts marking the banks of Tyler's Creek. "Which one is the Tlossie freighter?" he asked Treakness. "Do we know?"

"It should be that one right there," the governor said, pointing. "The one with the blue running lights."

Lorne grimaced. The transport was the ship currently nearest them, probably by the Tlossies' deliberate design. And that would have been very handy if the refugees could head directly there. Unfortunately, it was a quarter of the field away from the creek's closest approach, with two of the invaders' own ships between them.

But they would just have to deal with that. "Okay, here's the plan," he said. "We go back, head south, and get into Tyler's Creek. We'll head along it—"

"Wait a minute," Treakness interrupted him. "Did you say we get *into* the creek?"

"Afraid so," Lorne said. "The cut's pretty deep along there, but I doubt there's enough room on the edge above the water level for us to stay out of the big ships' sensor range. And unfortunately, the creek's the only way we're going to get in close enough without being spotted."

"But that water is *cold*," Treakness protested. "We'll die of hypothermia before we even get that far."

"It's not *that* cold," Lorne growled.

"Actually, lowering our body temperatures a bit will make us harder to identify," Poole murmured helpfully.

Treakness turned to him—

"I'm open to other suggestions," Lorne put in before the governor could get out whatever retort he was planning. "I just don't think there are any."

For a minute Treakness glared in silence across the distance, the light from the roving troop carriers glinting off his eyes. "We'll still need a way to attract the Tlossies' attention," he said at last. "They may possibly be willing to come out a ways and pick us up, but they're definitely not going to park by the creek and wait."

"I've got a couple of ideas," Lorne assured him. "With luck, we won't have to impose too far on their diplomatic immunity."

"Glad to hear it," Treakness said grimly. "Because I'm not at all sure how far that immunity extends." He exhaled a hissing sigh. "No point in putting it off, I suppose. I think the Chino Park picnic area will probably be the best place to get into the creek."

"Sounds good," Lorne said. "Let's get to it."

CHAPTER TWELVE

Fleecebacks, as Jody had already noted, were easy enough to catch. For Cobras, apparently, they were even easier, because the team that had been sent out to find one returned only minutes after Harli finally decided on the site for the test's staging area.

"I hope Freylan won't have a problem sending Snouts on a suicide mission," Paul commented to Jody as they sat on the ground a bit apart from the others.

"I'm sure he won't," Jody assured him. "It's not like they've had a long and rewarding relationship together. Remember, Freylan's the guy who used to name his lab equipment."

"Right." Paul paused. "This is a good plan, Jody," he continued. "I just wanted you to know that."

"Thanks," Jody said dryly. "But you'd better save the accolades until we see if it works."

"Success or failure doesn't change the quality of the plan," Paul said. "It only defines whether a good plan is also a *successful* good plan."

"Right. Important distinction."

"Actually, it is," Paul said, lowering his voice. "Harli's plan, for example, didn't work as well as we'd all hoped it would. But it was still a good plan, which is what made it worth trying."

Jody looked over at the other Cobras. Harli's back was to them,

457

and she could see no sign that he'd heard her father's comment. But she knew he probably had. "What's your definition of not working?" she asked quietly. "Because Buckley got killed?"

"That's part of it," her father said. "But mostly it didn't work because we didn't really learn anything."

"What do you mean?" Jody asked, frowning. "They shot back. We must have gotten *something* out of that."

"We saw the power levels they used against us, but we don't know if that was their full power or not," Paul said. "We saw their targeting capabilities, but they waited long enough to begin firing back that we don't know if the lasers were sensor-locked or manually aimed." He grimaced. "And as we've already discussed, we don't know whether Buckley's death was because our attack got too close to something important, or whether it was simply the Trofts sending a message."

"Yes, I see," Jody murmured, peering through the trees. A bit of Stronghold's wall was visible, a sliver of dull metallic sheen in the starlight. "Maybe *we* didn't learn anything, but if Matigo is right about the Cobras in the town launching an attack earlier, someone in *there* must have some better data on the Trofts' weapons."

"Which, even if true, is irrelevant," Harli spoke up, his back still to them. "We can't talk to them, they can't talk to us, and if the Trofts are smart they'll keep it that way." He half turned. "They're coming."

Jody tensed. "The Trofts?"

"Kemp and the others," Paul told her. He cocked his head. "And it sounds like Freylan and Geoff are with them."

He was right. Half a minute later, with soft footsteps through the leaves on the part of the Cobras and much louder ones on the part of Geoff and Freylan, the group arrived.

"Good morning, gentlemen," Paul said, nodding greetings at Jody's teammates. "I'm a bit surprised to see you here."

"We're a little surprised to be here," Geoff agreed, looking around. "A bit surprised at the company, too. You guys really made it all the way from Aerie? That's amazing."

"We're good at what we do," Harli said, stepping forward and peering into the cage swinging from the two Aventinians' shoulders. "Apparently, so are you. Most caged giggers I've seen tear themselves apart trying to break out. This one looks completely intact."

"Actually, the cage is Jody's—Ms. Broom's—design," Geoff told him.

"I see." Harli looked at Jody. "Did you also have a plan for rigging the stun stick to its mouth tusks?"

"Wait a minute," Freylan said before Jody could answer. "Stun stick? Kemp didn't say anything about a stun stick."

"We have to use Snouts against the Trofts," Jody said, wincing. She'd assured her father that Freylan wasn't attached to the animal, but seeing the intensity in his face she suddenly wasn't so sure about that. "I'm sorry."

"Never mind the gigger," Freylan said. "I'm talking about you. You and stun sticks don't exactly work well together."

"Don't worry. Jody's just going to describe the positioning," Paul told him. "We'll let one of the Caelians do the actual attachment."

"Oh," Freylan said, and to Jody's surprise the intensity and concern faded from his face. Apparently, he really *hadn't* been worried about Snouts. "I—yeah. Okay."

Paul looked at Jody, and even in the faint light she could swear she saw an amused smile tugging at his mouth. "I believe Cobra Uy asked you a question, Jody?" he said.

It took Jody a second to backtrack her memory that far. "I was thinking we could fasten it between the tusks, pointing forward, then rig it so that it would go off on impact. It would then fire when the tusks hit the fleeceback, which would presumably be right beside the ship. If everything goes right, that should kick up a show the Trofts won't be able to ignore."

"Things going right doesn't seem to be the pattern tonight," Harli growled. "But it sounds reasonable. You won't need a trigger, though—stun sticks have an on-contact activation setting."

"Really?" Jody said, feeling heat rise in her cheeks. "I guess I skipped that page in the manual."

"Not that we had much time for reading," Freylan put in.

"One reason we don't like visitors playing with Caelian gadgets," Harli said. "Any volunteers for belling the cat?"

"I'll do it," Kemp said, producing a small coil of tie wire as he stepped to the side of the cage. "Lower it down a bit, please. Not too much—I don't want its feet touching the ground. Ms. Broom?"

Jody handed him her stun stick, then took a long step back to watch.

She'd dealt with giggers and their rotten dispositions a couple of times during their brief stay on Caelian, and fully expected the operation to be, at the very least, noisy and, at the very most, to draw a little of Kemp's blood. Fortunately, neither prediction came true. Kemp snapped a hand into the cage and got a grip on the back of Snouts's head, transferred the animal's neck into an armlock that pinned the struggling predator firmly in place, then braided the stun stick into position with the tie wire.

"Looks good," Harli said, nodding as he leaned in for a closer look. "Spotters, get to your positions. Remember that we want to see not only if the Trofts can hit a target right beside their hull, but also which lasers they use and what kinds of adjustments, if any, it looks like they have to make. Kemp, you stay with the gigger—release it on my signal. Tracker, Matigo, you're on fruit and fleeceback delivery. The rest of you, make a rearguard circle—I don't want something sneaking up on us while we're busy looking the other way. One minute."

Paul took Jody's arm. "Come on—you're with me," he said, and headed off to the right. Geoff and Freylan, Jody noted, were close behind.

Exactly one minute later, as they all watched through the trees, there was a sudden swishing of leaves and three small, dark objects arced through the darkness. Jody listened hard, and a couple of seconds later she heard the faint multiple thud as the tardrops splattered against the Troft ship. A few seconds later, with another flurry of movement and crinkled leaves, the fleeceback appeared. Sniffling audibly, it made a zigzag line toward the aroma Jody assumed was now wafting across the open ground of the clear zone.

"If nothing else, they might at least get some scratches on their nice clean spaceship," Geoff murmured.

Jody nodded, her fingertips tingling with memory. Despite the encyclopedia's warning that "fleeceback" was more sarcastic than descriptive, the first time she'd encountered one she'd nevertheless given in to the urge to touch the feathery soft-looking fur. The multiple finger prickings she'd received from something more akin to steel wool than the actual thing had dismayed her, amused Geoff, and worried Freylan.

The fleeceback had apparently spotted the dripping fruit now, and the zigzags changed into a straight-in run. So far, there was no visible response from the Trofts. The fleeceback trotted to a halt, gave a quick look around for trouble, then settled in to licking up the thick juice.

And with a final crackling of leaves, Kemp released Snouts.

Jody had never seen a gigger hunt before, though she knew that the encyclopedia listed the species as one of the least subtle predators on Caelian. Once again, the book proved correct. Snouts took off across the clear zone, arrowing straight for the fleeceback without the slightest attempt at silence or cover. Jody held her breath as it lowered its tusks and rammed into the fleeceback's side—

The lower front of the Troft ship exploded into a flickering crackle of blue-white light as the stun stick went off, pouring four hundred thousand volts of stored power into the fleeceback and the metal hull beyond. Through the flash and sizzle Jody saw Snouts jerk with surprise and pain as its own body caught the edge of the current flow.

The stun stick was still spitting out its fire when the forest lit up with the brilliant flash and thundercrack of a Troft heavy laser.

Jody still had her eyes squeezed tightly shut, the afterimage throbbing through her brain, when she felt her father's hand around her wrist. "Come on," he murmured in her ear. "Time to go."

"So that's that," Harli said, his voice dark and bitter. "They can fire right at the edge of their ship. Which means we're out of luck."

"Not necessarily," Paul said. "The Trofts had plenty of time to see the parade coming at them and figure out we were up to something. It may still be that their lasers are normally geared to avoid the hull, and that they had to do some kind of manual override to hit the gigger."

"So what?" Matigo countered. "Even if you're right about an override, it obviously only took them a few seconds to work it. That's not nearly long enough for us to get through that door."

"Unless we can figure out a way to make that work for us," Kemp suggested thoughtfully.

"Meaning?" Harli asked.

"I was just thinking that if they can fire on a gigger beside the door, maybe they can fire on the door itself," Kemp said. "If so, maybe we can trick them into blasting it open for us."

"Right," someone scoffed. "How stupid do you think they are?"

"Stupidity isn't the issue," Paul said. "The middle of a battle is a loud, tense, nerve-wracking thing, the kind of place where people can easily make mistakes."

"That may be how it is in the simulation room," Matigo said. "Not so sure about the real thing."

"The real thing is even worse," Paul told him firmly. "Trust me. I've heard my wife talk about the small battles she was in on Qasama. At times like that people tend to react without thinking. The trick is to get them to react the way you want them to."

"Maybe people are like that," Matigo said. "Trofts might be a little cooler under fire."

"That's possible," Paul conceded. "Jin never fought actual Troft soldiers, only armed merchantmen. But my guess is even Troft soldiers get rattled if you shake them hard enough."

"Which we don't know how to do," Matigo said.

"No, *we* don't," Harli agreed darkly. "But Stronghold took them on. Maybe they do." He swore viciously. "Damn it, we have *got* to find out what went down yesterday."

Jody took a careful breath. "Someone's going to have to go in there," she said. "Someone who can find out what happened and get that information back out here to you."

"How?" Matigo retorted. "Have someone write messages on paper aircars and send them over the wall?"

"I was thinking more about sending the data out via Dida code," Jody told him. "All that takes is a flashlight and a clear view over the wall."

"What's Dida code?" Geoff asked.

"It's a secret blink-code system that civilians like you two aren't supposed to know about," Paul said, an edge to his voice. "Thanks so much, Jody, for bringing that up."

"You're welcome," Jody said tartly. "So what's wrong with the idea?"

"Because like most games, Dida takes two to play," her father said patiently. "Unless I'm mistaken, I'm the only one here who ever served patroller duty in an Aventinian city. Cobra Uy?"

"You're right," Harli said. "As far as I know, every Cobra on Caelian came here directly from the academy, without even interning in the Aventinian expansion regions first." He cocked his head to the side. "But we're fast learners."

"I doubt you're fast enough," Paul said heavily. "Dida was deliberately designed to be as obtuse and hard to decipher as possible. When I served in Capitalia it took us two weeks to learn the system. I doubt you could learn it any faster."

"Fine, so it takes two weeks," Harli said. "I don't think the Trofts are going anywhere."

Jody braced herself. This was going to be awkward. "Or, even simpler, you could just send me in," she said. "I already know it."

It was, she reflected, probably just as well that she couldn't see her father's expression. "You *what*?" he asked, sounding as stunned as Jody had ever heard him. "How?"

"How do you think?" she said. "Back when Merrick was learning the system he needed someone to practice with." She lifted her hands, palms upward. "He was lousy at it. I was good at it. What can I say?"

"What can you *say*?" Paul echoed, his famous patience teetering on the edge. "What were you *thinking*? What was *he* thinking?"

"Yes, I know," Jody said, her own far-less-than-famous patience even closer to the crumbling point. "If it helps, we both feel terrible about it. The point is that I've got the skill, and we need it, and the thought of a D-class felony charge doesn't seem all that important out here with saberclaws and Trofts trying to kill us."

For a long minute no one spoke. Then, Paul stirred. "You have your flashlight?"

"Right here," Jody said, pulling it out.

"Lowest setting," her father ordered. "Tell me you honor and respect me, that I'm thirty point two times as experienced as you are, and that you'll never break a twenty-second-degree, hullmetal-clad rule again."

Swallowing, Jody keyed the flashlight for touch operation and set to work.

The Dida code was every bit as complex as Paul had told Harli, and Jody had nearly forgotten how long it took to send anything with any detail to it. Three minutes later, she finally finished. "That it?" her father asked.

"Yes," Jody said, refraining from pointing out that he already knew that. The close-off was, after all, an important part of any coded message.

"How'd she do?" Freylan asked. "Did she get it right?"

"Letter-perfect, actually," Paul told him. "She even got the numbers right, which is the trickiest part of the code." He looked at Harli. "I think we're in business. How do you want to work this?"

"Well, there's no point in trying to sneak in," Harli said. Jody couldn't see his expression, but his voice suddenly sounded a lot more respectful than it ever had before, at least when he was talking to her. "With the clear zone, and the way the two ships are positioned, there aren't any blind spots where she could even get to the wall without being spotted."

"Let alone over it," Paul agreed.

"Right," Harli said. "So it seems to me that the best approach is for her to have been outside the city when the Trofts landed—which the city records will show she genuinely was—and only now is coming back."

"She was out taking samples," Geoff suggested. "I mean, that's what we were doing anyway."

"You mean *we* were out taking samples," Freylan said firmly.

"Yeah, I said that," Geoff said, sounding puzzled.

"I mean we, as in all three of us are going back in together," Freylan said.

"Out of the question," Harli said firmly before Geoff could answer. "You two are staying here with us."

"And letting Jody go in alone?" Freylan shook his head. "No."
He leveled a finger at Geoff. "*You*, of all people, ought to be telling
them that. You're the one who—"

"May I have a moment alone with my colleague?" Jody jumped
in, grabbing Freylan's arm. "Thank you. Come on, Freylan."

"But—"

"Come *on*," Jody said, pulling him outside the circle. "The rest
of you, a little privacy, please?"

"Make it fast," Harli growled.

Jody nodded and kept going, pulling Freylan as far away from
the others and the safety of their weapons as she dared. "Look,
Freylan, I appreciate your concern," she murmured. "But they're right.
You're safer out here with them than you are in there with me."

"All the more reason for someone to go in with you," Freylan
said stubbornly. "If Geoff isn't going to volunteer, it's up to me."

"I appreciate the offer," Jody said. "But you're making it for the
wrong reason."

"What reason is that?"

"You're being all brave and noble because you think I'm not
here because of my degrees in animal physiology and management," she said. "You think Geoff invited me to join the team for
some other reason entirely."

Freylan sighed. "So you know," he said heavily. "I'm sorry. I
should have stood up to him right from the beginning. But"—he
waved a hand helplessly—"he can talk me into anything. He can
talk *anyone* into anything. That's how we got our funding in the
first place."

"Which is why he's so valuable to the team," Jody said. "But you
still don't get it. His reason for inviting me isn't what you think."

"Of course it is," Freylan said, and Jody could hear the embarrassment in his voice. "I was *there*, Jody. I saw how he looked at
your picture on the registry. His eyes just—you know—kind of . . .
you know."

In the darkness, Jody didn't even bother to suppress her sudden smile. Freylan was so *earnest* sometimes. Like a big, earnest,
awkward dog. "He wasn't looking at my picture, Freylan," she said

gently. "He was looking at my family affiliations, which are on that same registry page. *That's* what he was drooling over, not my face or my body or anything else."

She could sense Freylan's frown in the darkness. "I don't get it."

Jody sighed. Big, earnest, awkward, and innocent. "He saw that my father and brothers were all Cobras," she said. "He figured that if he got me to Caelian, one of them would probably volunteer to come along, thereby saving the team the expense of hiring someone to guard us while we were out in the wilderness collecting our samples."

Freylan seemed to digest that. "You mean he didn't—?"

"Of course not," Jody said, putting a little additional steel into her voice. "And if I'd even suspected he wanted me along for any sort of recreational purposes, I'd have turned him down flat."

"But—" Freylan shook his head. "And all this time I thought... he's crazy, you know."

"He's driven by thoughts of fame and fortune," Jody said dryly. "When a person like Geoff gets that taste in his mouth, everything else pretty much goes by the boards."

"I see." Freylan straightened up. "Thank you for clearing that up. I guess I've misjudged him." He hesitated. "And you, too. I'm sorry."

"No apology needed," Jody assured him. "Meanwhile, we *are* keeping everyone else waiting."

"Right." Freylan gestured. "After you."

They returned to the group. "Everything settled?" Paul asked, his tone suggesting that he'd probably heard more than Jody would have liked.

"Yes," Freylan said firmly. "We're both going."

Jody felt her jaw drop. "Freylan, I just got done explaining—"

"I'm not going because I feel obligated on behalf of the team to protect you," Freylan said. "If the Trofts bother to look at the records, they'll see that *four* of us left in that aircar. We might be able to explain splitting into groups of two, but we're never going to convince them that three of us stayed together and sent one back alone."

"He has a point," Harli said reluctantly. "The first rule of Caelian travel is to never do it alone."

"So I go with you," Freylan concluded. "Meanwhile, your father will be here with the rest of the Cobras, where he can assist wherever they need him. If they need to trap more animals for an attack on the ships, they'll have Geoff here, too."

Jody glared through the darkness at him. But his logic was unassailable, and he knew it. So did everyone else.

And even if all he could do was give her moral support, she had to admit such support would be more than welcome. "I give up," she said with a sigh. "So do we head out tonight or wait until morning?"

"Both," Harli said. "You leave from here right now, but you don't head back to Stronghold until morning. You can't plausibly leave from where you landed and pretend you didn't know the Trofts had invaded. Your site was way too close for that."

"True," Paul agreed. "Not only did we see them come in, but we also heard the explosions when they demolished the comm towers."

"And you'd be hard pressed to explain why you came strolling back to a city you knew had been occupied by an enemy force," Harli said. "So we're going to spend the rest of the night getting you and the aircar as far out into Wonderland as we can, so that you can innocently blunder into an occupied city all shocked and stunned by the situation."

"What if they spot us lifting the aircar out of the forest?" Freylan asked.

"They won't, because we're not going to," Harli told him. "We're going to turn the thing up on its side, strap five or six of our spookers to it, and haul it out through the woods."

Jody blinked. "Oh."

"Unless there are objections," Harli continued, in a tone that said there had better not be, "let's get to it. The six of you on transport duty, get to your spookers. The rest of you, gather around. We've got some thinking to do."

Jody had never ridden any kind of grav cycle before, not even the sporty little ones she'd seen scooting around Capitalia's streets. The Caelian spookers, which were at least twice those scooters' size and rigged with clusters of spines and rim guards to keep away opportunistic predators, were intimidating to the point of borderline panic.

But given that the other option was to walk the Caelian gauntlet, Jody didn't argue.

At least Kemp seemed to be a competent enough driver. She rode behind him on his spooker, holding tightly to the grip bar in front of her, torn between the urge to look over his shoulder and see what dangers might be lying ahead of them, and the equally powerful urge to just press her forehead against his back, keep her eyes shut, and not know.

From the glimpses she got of Freylan, hunched over behind Tracker, he wasn't doing much better than she was.

Jody hadn't expected six Cobras to have any trouble turning an aircar up on its side, and they didn't. Fifteen minutes after reaching the camp, they were off again.

It was nearly dawn by the time they reached the spot Kemp had chosen. "That's the Jakjo River," he said, pointing down the slope as the other Cobras unfastened the aircar and turned it upright again. "The place has a crazy ecology, probably because there's something in the water that supports a rollin' big number of pantra shrubs and kokkok vines. Perfect place for visiting animal researchers."

"Sounds good," Jody agreed, feeling her pulse thudding in her throat. Up to this point most of her attention had been focused on the dangers of Caelian itself. Now, suddenly, the full magnitude of the job she'd volunteered for was looming in front of her. "Are you and the others heading back to Stronghold?"

"Right," Kemp said. "Just as soon—" He broke off, swiveling around and snapping his leg up to send a laser shot into a saber-claw that had just been starting its leap. "As soon as you're in the air," he finished. "Oh, and once you're inside, make sure you put everything back in place. The Trofts'll find it pretty strange if they check out the aircar and find all the loose gear piled up along one side."

"We'll do that," Jody promised.

Kemp peered closely at her. "You ready for this?"

"No idea," Jody said honestly. "But whether I am or not, I'm doing it." She reached down and squeezed his hand. "Thanks for everything."

"No problem," Kemp said, squeezing rather shyly back. "Watch yourselves, okay?"

"You, too," Jody said. "Tell Cobra Harli that when I have something to report I'll try to find a place where I can signal due west."

"We'll watch for you," Kemp promised. "Good luck."

The trip through the forest by spooker had been a long, tedious, dangerous affair. The flight over the forest by aircar was considerably faster, and a whole lot safer. Within a few minutes, it seemed, Jody was able to see the sheen of Stronghold's wall in the sunlight now peeking over the forest to the east. "You ready?" she asked Freylan.

"Yes," he said, his voice shaking slightly. "You want me to do the talking?"

"No, that's okay," Jody said. It was probably a toss-up as to which of them was more nervous, but he *sounded* more nervous, and that could make all the difference. "I'll handle it."

The laser burn marks her father had told them about weren't visible right away, certainly not until after the Troft ships themselves came into view. But as Jody headed down toward their rental house she finally spotted them: small, crisply-defined black grooves in various places on the ground and several of the houses, all of them angling back toward one or the other of the warships' wing-mounted weapons.

She was searching the wall for signs of the scoring Paul had also mentioned when a two-meter-long, dartlike device suddenly appeared by her side mirror. "Whoa!" she gasped, jerking in reaction. She started to twitch the aircar away from the thing—

"Careful—there's one over here, too," Freylan warned.

Jody leaned forward and looked past him. The Trofts had the aircar flanked, all right. "Any idea what they want?"

As if in answer, the machine on Freylan's side edged over and nudged the aircar to the left. Jody tweaked her own controls that direction in response, then repeated the adjustment twice more as the dart continued its nudging. By the time it finally pulled back to its original escort position she was pointed at a spot just inside the wall and right by the northernmost Troft ship.

And as she headed for the ground Jody saw a group of armed Trofts emerge from one of the buildings beside her new landing site. They formed a semicircle around the open area, their heads and lasers pointed toward her. Keeping one eye on the lasers, Jody put the aircar down squarely in the middle of their semicircle.

"What's going on?" she called toward them as she and Freylan opened their doors and climbed out. Now that they were closer, she could see that, along with being armed, the Trofts were also wearing helmets and armored leotards. "What's wrong," she called again. "Did some screech tigers get in?"

"Identify yourselves," a flat translator-type voice came from somewhere in the group.

"I'm Jody Broom," Jody said. "This is Freylan Sonderby. Didn't we fill out the paperwork right?"

"Empty your pockets," the Troft ordered. "Everything on the ground. Now."

Grimacing, Jody obeyed, making a small pile of her comm, pen and notebook, aircar keys, multitool, wallet, and flashlight. Beside her, Freylan was doing the same. "What's going on?" she asked again as she straightened up.

Two of the Trofts left the group, their weapons leveled, and strode toward Jody and Freylan. "You will come with us," one of them said.

"Why?" Jody asked. The flat translator voices, she could tell now, were emanating from round pins that each of the aliens had fastened to his left shoulder. "Come on, this is crazy. What's going on, anyway?"

One of the two Trofts marched straight up to her and pressed the muzzle of his laser against her chest. "You foolish humans," he intoned. "Do you think we are foolish, too?"

Jody heard a sharp intake of air, and out of the corner of her eye she saw Freylan stir, then freeze as the second Troft also jabbed his laser into his new prisoner's chest. "I don't understand," she said, a sinking feeling in the pit of her stomach.

"Did you think we would not see that you were outside the wall with the *koubrah*-soldiers?" the Troft demanded. "Now you return to the settlement as spies."

"That's crazy," Jody insisted, knowing it was hopeless but also knowing she had to try. "We've been up by the Jakjo River since yesterday morning."

"You will learn now the fate of all enemies of the Drim'hco'plai Demesne." The Troft jabbed her again with his laser muzzle. "Turn around, and walk."

CHAPTER THIRTEEN

The water in Tyler's Creek was swift, noisy, and every bit as cold as Treakness had warned it would be. Before the group had gone even fifty meters Lorne's feet and legs were numb, and before they'd gone fifty meters more his whole body was starting to shiver violently enough that he was making little splashes in the water. The other three weren't doing any better.

In fact, as Lorne studied them, he realized they were doing considerably worse. Their breathing was shaky as they waded through the water, and their infrared signatures were slowly but steadily fading as they lost body heat. The water only came up to their waists, which meant that their torsos should be out of the direct effects of the chill, but that small advantage was effectively nullified as, one by one, they lost their footing in the current pushing against them from behind and fell full length into the creek. Before they'd made it even halfway, all four of them were soaked to the skin.

They were still a good hundred meters from Lorne's exit point when Nissa had finally had enough.

"It's no good," she gasped, her teeth chattering violently as she staggered like a drunk against Lorne's side. "The governor—this is killing him. It's going to stop his heart. We can't do this."

Lorne looked at Treakness. The older man was staggering as

badly as Nissa was, his infrared signature ominously low. He was losing heat fast, and whether he had heart problems or not was no longer the point. "You're right," Lorne conceded, trying desperately to think. He'd started this trip with a plan, and his cold-numbed brain still remembered what that plan was. But at this point, with his synapses frozen together like window frost patterns, he couldn't begin to come up with a rational alternative. Maybe if they climbed up onto the slope of the cut, staying out of the water but below the level of the landing field, they could crawl their way to the exit point without being seen.

But even if they did that, wouldn't their soaked clothes be just as cold in the air as in the water? Lorne tried to reason it out, but he couldn't seem to come up with the right answer.

"No," Treakness murmured.

Lorne frowned, focusing on the governor, wondering if he was imagining things. Treakness was still barely in control of his legs, and was clutching onto Poole for support as the two of them stumbled together through the water. But even through the shivering and the chattering teeth Lorne could see the determination in the man's face. "We go on," Treakness told him. "We have to. If we don't—" Another violent shiver ran through him, and as his hands slipped from their deadened grip on Poole's shoulder he fell to his knees in the creek, his head bowed with fatigue and cold.

Lorne felt his own frozen lips curl back in a silent snarl. Nissa was right—this was insanity. But Treakness was also right—if they quit now, they might as well just turn themselves in to the Trofts.

And if a Cobra-hating governor had the strength of will to go on, Lorne was damned if he would be the one to call a halt.

"We go on," he told Nissa. Wading over to Treakness, he pulled the kneeling governor back up onto his feet. Then, stepping between him and Poole, he got an arm around each man's waist and locked his elbow servos to keep them upright. "Nissa?" he called, nodding her toward him. "Behind me—arms around my neck."

For a moment she just stared blankly at him. Then, she seemed to get it. Sloshing up behind him, she raised her arms and dropped them limply across his shoulders. Lorne turned his head to his left, pinning her left arm to his shoulder. Hardly an ideal situation, but it was the best he could come up with. "Okay," he said. "Let's go."

"Lorne?"

Lorne blinked, some of the fog that had wrapped itself around his brain clearing away. He was still supporting Treakness's and Poole's sagging bodies, but Nissa was no longer hanging onto his neck from behind him. Instead, she had somehow gotten in front of him and was slapping his cheek. "Lorne!" she repeated. "We're here. Lorne?"

Lorne blinked at her . . . and then, through his mental sluggishness he heard the rumble of an approaching Troft armored carrier.

Abruptly the rest of the fog vanished. "Yeah, I'm on it," he said. "Here—hold him," he added, shrugging his shoulder and shoving Poole into Nissa's arms. Shifting his other hand from Treakness's waist to his arm, he slogged over to the spaceport edge of the creek and started climbing the bank.

He had gotten one arm up onto the grass and was hanging there, shivering and gasping for breath, when the headlights from the carrier flared like twin suns squarely in his face. There was a sudden surge of its engines as the vehicle leaped forward, the glare intensifying to a painful level. Lorne turned his face away, his eyes squeezed tightly shut, and a few seconds later the engine's surge abruptly dropped back to a rumbling idle as the carrier braked to a halt. There was a sound of metal doors being flung open—

"Over here," Lorne gasped, not trying to suppress any of the trembling in his voice. His brain still wasn't working at full power, but he remembered enough about his plan to know that the more helpless the Trofts thought he and the others were, the better. "Please—he's dying. Please."

"Identify yourselves," a flat translator voice demanded.

"Carl DeVille," Lorne said. The carrier's headlights were still blazing into his face, but with his opticals he could see that the vehicle had stopped only seven or eight meters away from him. Two of the Trofts were striding in his direction, their weapons pointed at him, while two more stood back beside the carrier in covering positions. Behind them, he saw, the rear of the vehicle was still disgorging alien soldiers. "I'm an aide to Senior Governor Tomo Treakness," he continued. "I've got the governor here with me. Please—the cold—he's going to die if we don't get him out of the water."

One of the approaching Trofts lifted a hand to cover something on his shoulder, and Lorne keyed up his audios in hopes of catching whatever the Troft was saying to his superiors. But between the distance, the blockage of the Troft's faceplate, and the background noises of the carrier and the creek he couldn't hear anything.

Only then did it occur to him that if the Trofts wanted the missing governor dead and not captured, Lorne had just effectively abetted in the man's murder.

But even before that horrible thought was fully formed the Troft lowered his hand, slung his laser rifle over his shoulder, and squatted down at the edge of the creek a meter to Lorne's left. He spotted Treakness, hanging limply half in and half out of the water, then nimbly hopped down into the creek. Wrapping his arms around the governor's waist, he pulled him free of Lorne's grip and started up the slope. By the time he was halfway to the top, two more of the aliens had joined him, and together they pulled Treakness up onto the bank. The first Troft slid back down into the creek and repeated the operation with Poole.

They were pulling Nissa up onto the bank when a pair of armored hands closed around Lorne's forearms and pulled him the rest of the way up onto the grass. His rescuers turned him over onto his stomach, maintaining their grip on his arms, as a third moved toward them, the glint of wrist shackles in his hand.

And in that instant, Lorne made his move.

He heaved upward against the hands holding his arms, pulling himself off the ground and up into a kneeling position. Swinging his arms around and forward, he wrenched them out of the startled Trofts' grips, then continued the swinging motion up and back and slammed the backs of his fists into the sides of the Trofts' helmets. As their grips vanished and they toppled sideways away from him, he curved his right hand, little finger pointed at the soldier with the wrist shackles, and fired his stunner.

The Troft twitched violently as the current slammed through him, and fell flat on his back. Six meters behind him, the group of Trofts who'd taken up backup positions swung their lasers around toward Lorne, only to stagger back as a double blast from the Cobra's sonic rocked them off balance. To Lorne's left, the three aliens who had pulled the rest of the shivering humans from the creek made a desperate scramble for their own weapons, then fell to the ground as three more lightning bolts from Lorne's stunner took them out. Surging all the way up onto his feet, Lorne charged into the group of sonic-staggered aliens, his stunner and servo-enhanced hands systematically laying them out.

The driver had thrown the carrier into reverse and was trying frantically to get out of there when Lorne ran behind the vehicle, ducked inside through the still-open rear doors, and nailed him with a final stunner blast.

The carrier was still moving backwards. Lorne ran forward to the cab, hauled the unconscious driver out of his seat, then dropped onto it himself. The controls were laid out differently from those of other Troft vehicles he'd seen, but they were easy enough to figure out. Bringing the carrier to a halt, he reversed direction and drove back to where he'd left the others, turning the vehicle sharply in toward the landing field as he stopped. Climbing out of the seat, he ran back to the rear and jumped out.

Treakness, Poole, and Nissa were still sitting on the ground, huddled together for warmth, looking around in confusion and disbelief at the unconscious Trofts scattered all around them. "Up, up, up," Lorne ordered, grabbing Treakness's and Poole's forearms and hauling them up onto their feet. "Move it, before they decide to start shooting."

"We're up," Treakness said, his voice slurred but his eyes starting to come back to full awareness. Weakly, he twisted his arm free of Lorne's grip and took hold of Poole's and Nissa's. "Go get it started," he told Lorne, staggering a little as he pulled the others toward the carrier. "Go on—we're coming."

"I'll be right there," Lorne said. Stepping over to the nearest group of unconscious Trofts, he loaded two of them over his shoulders,

jogged past Treakness and the others to the carrier, and dumped
the two aliens inside the back. By the time the three shivering
humans reached the vehicle he had added four more to the pile.

"What are you doing that for?" Treakness huffed as Lorne pulled
him inside and sat him down beside one of the crew couches.

"Insurance," Lorne said as he hauled Poole and Nissa inside and
closed the doors behind them. "I'm hoping they'll be less likely
to shoot at us if some of their own people are aboard. Everyone
sit down and hold onto one of the benches." He pulled off one of
the unconscious Trofts' helmets and headed forward toward the
carrier's cab, jamming the helmet over his own head as he did so.

[—report, it will be submitted at once,] a stern Troft voice
ordered into Lorne's ear. [The prisoners' status, it is what?]

[The prisoners, they have broken free,] Lorne called back in cattertalk, putting an edge of urgency into his voice. The driver was
still lying limply on the floor; hauling him up, Lorne maneuvered
them both onto the driver's seat, positioning the Troft so that he
was between Lorne and any laser fire that might come through
the windshield or side windows. [The remaining soldiers, they are
attempting to subdue,] he added, and jammed his foot down hard
on the accelerator.

The carrier leaped forward with considerably more acceleration
than Lorne had expected. [The soldiers, they cannot hold them,]
he continued into his borrowed helmet's microphone, letting his
earlier urgency edge toward panic. A small part of his still sluggish mind wondered if Troft solders ever actually panicked, but
he also knew that putting too much calmness into his masquerade
wouldn't get him what he needed.

[The soldiers, they are to shoot to kill,] the controller's voice
said grimly. [Group Leader Paeyrdosi, you will respond.]

[Group Leader Paeyrdosi, he is down,] Lorne said, turning the
carrier toward a group of storage and fuel outbuildings a hundred
meters to the right of one of the big Troft warships. Behind the
outbuildings he could see one of the invaders' transports; behind
it, though not visible from his position, should be the Tlossie
freighter that was their goal. If he could keep the charade and

the Trofts' uncertainty going for two or three more minutes, they might just make it.

But even in the dark, foggy hour before dawn the Trofts weren't *that* gullible. [To me, who is this who speaks?] the voice in Lorne's ear demanded. [One of the humans, are you he?]

Lorne grimaced. [Understanding, I have not,] he gave it a final try. [The prisoners, this vehicle they now command. The vehicle, they have ordered—]

"Yes, one of the humans I am," Treakness's voice cut in.

Lorne twisted his head around. Treakness, holding tightly onto one of the benches beside Poole and Nissa as the carrier bounced along the landing field, had appropriated another of the Troft helmets and had it over his head. "This is Senior Governor Tomo Treakness," he continued, the words coming out proud and stern despite his still shaking voice. "I'm in control of this vehicle and this spaceport. Do as I say, or suffer a level of death and destruction the likes of which your demesne-lords have never dreamed of."

[This destruction, you yourself will unleash it?] the Troft scoffed.

"This destruction, it is already prepared," Treakness ground out. "Did your demesne-lords really think that the people foresighted enough to create Cobra warriors wouldn't know that a day of invasion would someday come to us? The entire Creeksedge area has been carefully mined with explosives, many of them directly beneath your warships, all of them now armed and with operators standing ready to ignite them."

The Troft snarled something Lorne couldn't translate. [A bluff, you make it,] the alien accused.

"You can believe that if you choose," Treakness said. "And I certainly wouldn't order the destruction of our own facility unless absolutely necessary. But even leaving that aside, you can't deny that we have several of your soldiers with us inside this vehicle. Their lives, at least, rest on your balance pin."

[Foolishness, you speak it,] the Troft said contemptuously. [The suppressor's crew, their lives you think so valuable that concessions, you expect us to make them?]

"Well-trained soldiers are a valuable commodity," Treakness

said. "A wise commander doesn't simply discard them for no reason. Especially since all I want in exchange for their lives is to borrow that transport we're heading toward, the one just past the fueling station."

[The planet, you cannot be permitted to leave it,] the Troft insisted.

"I have no intention of leaving Aventine," Treakness said stiffly. "My government-in-exile will dedicate itself to continuing the fight until every last one of you has been thrown off our world."

There was a brief silence. Lorne kept going, pushing the carrier for all it was worth, trying to watch everywhere at once. A small part of his mind wondered if the Tlossie freighter might have given up and left Aventine while they were nearly killing themselves wading through the creek, and wondered what he and the others would do if that were the case.

[The transport, you may go to it,] the Troft said suddenly.

"And you'll keep your people strictly away," Treakness warned. "Remember, we'll be able to see it the whole rest of the way. If anyone approaches it—*anyone*—I'll order the destruction to begin."

[The transport, no one will approach it,] the Troft promised. [In peace, you may board it and your departure, you may make it.]

Out of the corner of his eye, Lorne saw Treakness step from the rear into the carrier's cab and crouch down beside him, the helmet he'd been wearing no longer over his head. "What do you think?" he asked quietly.

"I don't like it," Lorne said, shaking his head. "They gave in way too easy."

"Agreed," Treakness said. "Fortunately, whatever they're planning to do once we're inside the transport is irrelevant. When you reach it, just circle around it and head for the Tlossie freighter."

"What if the Trofts decide to take us out before then?"

"How?" Treakness countered, waving a hand around them. "The armor on this thing is damn thick, probably thick enough to take a few shots from even ship-based lasers."

"Except for the windshield."

"Which is already at too low an angle for all but maybe one

of the ships to hit it." Treakness pointed at the unconscious Troft sharing the driver's seat with Lorne. "Besides, you've cleverly set it up so that killing you would mean killing him, too. If Trofts hesitate to kill conquered peoples without reason, they certainly ought to hesitate even more before killing one of their own. Not until they're desperate."

"I hope you're right." The cluster of outbuildings was looming ahead on their left, and Lorne turned slightly to the right to give them an extra wide berth. He didn't really think the Troft commander would have a group of soldiers lurking among the buildings ready to leap onto the captured carrier and try to force their way inside, but he had no interest in finding out the hard way. "I still think they've got something in the works," he added. Out of the corner of his eye he saw a brilliant flicker of blue light out the side window—

And with a blast of billowing blue-yellow fire, the cluster of outbuildings exploded.

The carrier caught the full brunt of the shock wave, skidding violently sideways for a few meters before toppling over onto its right side. Lorne, wedged in place between the seat and the unconscious Troft's rigid body armor, stayed in place just long enough for him to grab the edge of the seat before he and his living shield came loose and tumbled out to fall the full width of the carrier. The Troft fell straight down, landing with a sickening thud on his shoulder and back, while Lorne was able to hang onto the seat long enough to turn himself vertical and land instead on his feet.

For a moment he crouched there, his brain spinning with the aftereffects of the explosion. Behind him in the carrier's main section, Poole and Nissa were struggling to extricate themselves from the limp Troft bodies that had been thrown all around them when the vehicle was pushed over. Straight above him, through the driver's side window, he could see yellow flame and roiling clouds of smoke from the burning fuel station and other buildings.

And at his feet, twitching like an injured insect, was Treakness. Blood running down the side of his head.

"Poole!" Lorne snapped as he dropped down beside the governor, his fingers probing gently at the blood flow. The cut didn't seem too wide, but he could feel the skin around it starting to swell. He must have hit his head when the carrier was blown over. "Poole!" he called again. "Nissa! Damn it, somebody get over here."

"What is it?" Nissa asked, her voice shaky as she worked her way to her feet. "What happened?"

"The governor's hurt," Lorne gritted out, pulling open his belt bag and hunting through it for his share of the group's medical supplies. "Looks like he hit his head."

"They *fired* on us?" Nissa said incredulously.

"On the fueling station," Lorne corrected tightly. "Probably figured the soldiers we were holding were armored and we weren't. Worth the gamble." He found a package of compression bandages and tore off the wrapping. "Here—lift his head for me."

"No, don't," Poole said as he came up unsteadily behind Nissa. "It's dangerous to move a head-injury patient unless you know what you're doing."

"You want to just leave him here?" Lorne demanded, glaring at him.

"The Trofts will take care of him," Poole said. "They want the governors and syndics as hostages or figureheads, not corpses."

"I don't care what the Trofts want," Lorne bit out. "If he doesn't get on that Tlossie freighter, the rest of us might as well not go, either."

"Leave me."

Lorne looked down. Treakness's eyes were open, gazing up at Lorne and the others with determination. "Hold still," Lorne ordered, unfolding the bandage and easing it into place over the wound as best he could without moving Treakness's head. "Don't worry, we'll get you out of here."

"Are you deaf?" Treakness continued. "I said *go*. Take Poole and Ms. Gendreves and get *out*."

"You don't understand," Lorne said, looking around for something they could use to immobilize his head in case Treakness had also suffered neck injuries. The benches fastened to the floor—the wall, now—were pretty narrow, but they were the best he was going to get. He started to stand up.

And stopped as Treakness reached up and grabbed his arm in a weak but determined grip. "I gave you an order, Cobra Broom," he wheezed out. "The Trofts could be here any time. Leave me and go."

"He's right," Poole said quietly. "We have to go."

Lorne twisted around to look at him. In the few seconds he'd been concentrating on Treakness, the nervous, mousy Poole they'd all spent the day with had vanished. In his place was a new Poole, a Poole who wore a quiet confidence and professionalism that Lorne hadn't even guessed might be lurking beneath the surface.

He turned back to Treakness. "What the hell is going on?" he asked quietly.

"I lied to you, Broom," Treakness said. He let go of Lorne's arm and touched the bandage on his head, wincing as his fingers brushed the injured skin. "Poole's the one who has to get on that Tlossie freighter, not me." A faint smile touched his lips. "I'm just the camouflage."

"I'll explain later," Poole added, his eyes aching as he gazed down at Treakness. "The question is whether we can get to the Tlossies before the other Trofts get here."

"I don't know," Lorne said. "Look, I don't care what you say. *Either* of you. We can't just leave him here."

"I'll stay with him," Nissa volunteered, her voice shaking.

"No," Treakness said. "If you're caught..." He gestured weakly toward her. "You're the new camouflage, Nissa Gendreves. As the highest-ranking Dome official still known to be free, I hereby grant you full authority of negotiation and treaty. You're the Cobra Worlds' representative to the universe at large." He shifted his pointing finger toward Lorne. "Remember that," he added. "If you're caught, she's the one you were trying to get off Aventine. Not Poole. Her." His finger flicked toward the carrier's rear doors. "Now go," he said. "If I'm to die, don't let me die having failed in my last attempt to serve my world."

Lorne felt his throat tighten. He still had no idea what was going on, but Treakness was right. Whatever was at stake here, if they stayed they would lose by default. "Promise to be a rotten prisoner for them," he told Treakness, and got to his feet. "You two, come on."

The rear doors hadn't been damaged or even bent out of true by the carrier's crash. Lorne popped them without trouble, letting in a cloud of acrid black smoke as the lower door dropped to the ground with a thud. "Close your eyes," he ordered Poole and Nissa as he squeezed his own eyes shut and keyed in his opticals. Grabbing them around their waists, he headed out.

The smoke was even more intense outside, burning into his nose and lungs, and the angry crackle of the flames drowned out every other sound around him. Clutching his companions close to his sides, he led the group around the rear of the carrier and toward its front. The air was churning violently as the fire sucked in air from everywhere around it, and Lorne could feel the heat of the flames prickling at his skin. So far the carrier was blocking the worst of the heat, but that protection was about to end. Through the smoke, his infrareds could pick out the transport fifty meters ahead, the vehicle Treakness had theoretically bargained away from the Trofts.

He could also see the shadowy figures of Troft soldiers hurrying toward it, moving under cover of the smoke to prepare an ambush for the arrogant humans should they somehow manage to survive the crash and the fire.

Lorne grimaced, the smoke burning his lungs now starting to seep in around his tightly closed eyelids. In theory, the Trofts may very well have outsmarted themselves, with the smoke from their fire hiding their quarry from unaided eyes and the fire itself blanketing even their infrared signatures. In actual practice, though, the path in front of them was a horrendously daunting one. They would need to get away from the fire without succumbing to either the heat or the smoke, then get past the transport and the ambush the Trofts were setting up, and finally cover however much open ground remained before they reached the Tlossie freighter. If, indeed, the freighter was even still there.

He was still crouched by the front of the carrier, still trying to find a way to get his charges through all of that, when something large lifted into view above the Troft transport.

It was the Tlossie freighter.

And it was leaving.

Lorne's heart seemed to seize up. *No!* he shouted silently toward it. *We're here! Come back!*

And then, even as he stared helplessly at the departing freighter, it came around in a sharp right turn and headed straight toward the three humans hunched beside the downed carrier.

Lorne stiffened, the heat and smoke abruptly forgotten in a rush of hope and apprehension. The Tlossies were coming to them, all right—there was no reason for them to pass so close to the fire otherwise. But diplomatic immunity or not, they surely weren't going to be so brazen as to land under the invaders' guns. Did they have a plan? Or were they expecting their would-be passengers to come up with one?

Lorne was staring at the incoming craft, trying to come up with something, when the freighter's starboard bow hatchway ramp flipped down and what appeared to be a weighted cargo net rolled out.

The Tlossies had a plan, all right. The question was, would it work?

"Get ready," he shouted over the roaring of the fire, his opticals counting down the distance to the fluttering net, his brain whirring with the logistics. Nissa, the lighter of the two, would have to go first. "Nissa, I'm going to throw you into the air toward a hanging net," he told the young woman. "When I shout *open*, you open your eyes so that you can see to grab it. Got that?"

"What do—?" Nissa began, breaking off in a fit of coughing.

"I said *got that*?" Lorne snapped, his own lungs feeling like they were rapidly becoming coated with tar.

Still coughing, she nodded.

"Poole, you'll be next," Lorne said, letting go of Poole's waist and getting a two-handed grip on Nissa's belt and left leg. "Same deal. Ready?"

"Ready," Poole said.

The freighter and net were still coming. Lorne braced himself, tightening his grip on Nissa as he gauged the distance. Nearly in position...

And with a surge of servo-powered strength, he hurled her upward.

She might have gasped something, but with the roar of the fire he couldn't be sure. Turning to Poole, he got the same grip on his belt and leg as he watched Nissa hit the top of her arc and start down again. "Open!" he shouted.

There was no way to tell if she had actually opened her eyes or, if she had, whether she could even see the net sweeping toward her amid all the smoke. Lorne held his breath as the mesh slammed into her, slapping her out of her ballistic path. Her hands scrambled wildly for purchase, and then her fingers slipped into the net and she was hanging on for dear life, her body bouncing wildly in the wind. An instant later Poole was flying through the air after her, and half a second later he also had grabbed solidly onto the mesh.

And as the freighter and net shot past overhead, Lorne turned and charged after them, driving his leg servos as hard and as fast as he could. Five seconds later he'd closed the gap enough to make a leap of his own for the netting. He caught the edge of the mesh, wincing as the full blast of heat from the fire burned momentarily into his skin. The freighter cut sharply to the left and angled up toward the sky, and as he again squeezed his eyes tight against the sudden roar of wind he felt the vibration of the net being reeled in. He held on tightly, watching Nissa and Poole, wondering if either of them would lose their grip as they were buffeted around and wondering what he could do if that happened.

But they didn't, and he didn't, and a handful of long, terrifying, agonizing seconds later they were hauled up onto the ramp and through the hatchway into a large airlock vestibule. As they sprawled on the deck, the hatchway closed behind them, and they were safely aboard.

"Lorne?" Nissa breathed, her reddened, squinting eyes staring at something behind him. Blinking some moisture into his own smoke-burned eyes, Lorne turned to look.

Behind them stood a semicircle of silent Trofts, each armed with a hand-and-a-half laser.

All of them leveled and pointed at the three humans.

[Your hands, you will raise them,] the Troft in the middle ordered sternly.

"I don't think that will be necessary," Poole said calmly. "It certainly won't be very effective."

For a moment the Troft eyed him. Then, gesturing to the others, he raised the muzzle of his laser to point at the ceiling. [The *koubrah*-soldier, you are he?] he asked Poole.

"No, *this* is the Cobra," Poole said, pointing to Lorne. "Cobra Lorne Moreau Broom, as your shipmaster requested."

[The *koubrah*-soldier Lorne Moreau Broom, you are he?] a new voice asked.

Lorne turned around again. Another Troft had stepped into the vestibule from the door leading forward toward the freighter's bridge and control areas. The newcomer was clothed in the same style of leotard as the others, but wrapped around his abdomen was the distinctive red sash of an heir of the Tlossie demesne-lord. [Lorne Moreau Broom, I am he,] Lorne confirmed in his best cattertalk as he climbed to his feet. The task was harder than he'd expected, and he had to use his servos to keep from dropping back to the deck halfway up. Clearly, the ordeal of fire and water had drained him more than he'd realized. [My deep and humble thanks for this rescue, to whom do I owe it?] he asked.

The Troft inclined his head. [The language of the Trof'te, you speak it well,] he said approvingly. [Ingidi-inhiliziyo, second heir of the Tlos'khin'fahi Demesne, I am he.] He gave a sort of clicking laugh. [*Warrior*, instead you may call me,] he added. [My full and proper name, it is difficult for humans to pronounce.]

Lorne bowed, his servos once again keeping him from falling onto his face. [Graciousness, it is yours,] he said.

Warrior's gaze brushed past Poole and settled on Nissa. [Three passengers, there were to be,] he said. [But males, they were all to be.]

"There was a last-minute alteration in the plan," Poole said, his voice low and strained. Unlike Lorne, he and Nissa weren't even trying to stand up. "Senior Governor Treakness was unable to join us." He gestured to Nissa. "This is Nissa Gendreves, assistant to Governor-General Chintawa. In Governor Treakness's absence, he's given her full diplomatic authorization."

COBRA GUARDIAN 487

[Authorization, we know not for what,] Lorne put in. [This mystery, will you not explain it?]

Warrior gestured at Poole. [The explanation, Dr. Glas Croi will provide it.]

Lorne frowned at Poole. "Who?"

"Me," Poole said gravely. "I'm sorry, Broom, but I couldn't let you know my true identity. Neither of you," he added, nodding to Nissa. "We couldn't take the risk that the invaders would capture us and figure out who I was. That's why Governor Treakness and I came up with the plan for me to play the part of a kicked-around aide. We hoped that if we were caught they would concentrate on him and ignore me."

"How clever of you," Lorne growled. "It never occurred to you that it might be useful if the man who was supposed to be guarding you knew exactly who he was guarding?"

"It did, and we decided against it," Croi said evenly. "My life, in and of itself, wasn't important. What was important was that we delay my identification long enough for Ingidi-inhiliziyo and this freighter to get safely off Aventine."

Lorne looked at Warrior. "I thought you had diplomatic immunity."

[To a point only, my safety lies there,] Warrior said.

"And still does," Croi said. "Tell me, Broom, how long did it take the surgeons to turn you into a Cobra?"

Lorne frowned at the sudden change of subject. "What?"

"Your Cobra surgery," Croi repeated. "How long?"

"Same as everyone else's," Lorne said. "Two weeks."

"How much of that was actually spent on the operating table?"

"I don't really remember," Lorne said. "Something like ten hours a day for eleven of those fourteen days. Call it a hundred-ten hours, I guess."

"Actually, it's a hundred and twelve," Croi said. "How would you like to have had it all done in five days, and only forty hours on the table?"

"Not possible," Lorne said flatly. "They're tricky operations. Even experienced surgeons like those at the academy hospital can only work so fast."

"Agreed," Croi said. "But that assumes human beings doing the surgery."

Beside Lorne, Nissa inhaled sharply. "Isis," she breathed.

"What?" Lorne asked, frowning again.

"It was a reference in one of Governor-General Chintawa's reports," she said, staring wide-eyed at Croi. "It's an acronym for Integrated Structural Implantation System."

Lorne looked back at Croi, a strange feeling in the pit of his stomach. "What exactly are you saying?"

"What I'm saying is that we're sitting on a huge technological breakthrough," Croi said quietly. He gestured past the circle of Trofts toward the freighter's stern. "Back there, tucked away in a hundred packing crates, is our brand-new prototype, Isis.

"The world's first fully automated Cobra factory."

CHAPTER FOURTEEN

For a long moment no one spoke. Lorne looked at Croi, then at Nissa, then at Warrior, then back at Croi. "You're not serious," he said at last.

"Deadly serious," Croi assured him grimly. "And you see now why it was vital that we get it off Aventine before the invaders caught wind of it. All of our Cobra equipment and weaponry, with no fail-safes or self-destructs in place, just waiting for someone to come along and take it apart until they learn everything about it and every single way to defeat you."

"Right," Lorne said, looking back at the circle of armed Trofts and putting a targeting lock on each of the aliens' foreheads. A probably useless gesture—an heir's ship would be teeming with Tlossie soldiers—but if this whole thing fell apart he would have to at least try. "No, we wouldn't want the Trofts getting hold of the stuff, would we?"

Croi snorted. "Relax, Broom. The reason Isis is aboard this ship is that Ingidi-inhiliziyo helped develop it."

"He *what*?" Lorne demanded. "Who authorized *that*?"

"I said *relax*," Croi said, starting to sound annoyed. "He hasn't been allowed to see or study any of the actual equipment. He just helped me create the robotics systems that Isis uses to implant it."

"He helped *you*," Lorne said catching the pronoun's significance. "So you're a robotics expert, too?"

489

"Hardly, though I do dabble a little," Croi said. "I'm actually a surgeon by training, which meant our areas of expertise intersected quite well."

"Handy when that happens," Lorne said, eyeing Warrior. [Your robotics expertise, it impresses me.]

[Surprises you, it in fact does,] Warrior corrected calmly. [Yet surprised, you should not be. A useless parasite, an heir is not one.]

[The truth, so it would seem,] Lorne said, turning back to Croi. "So that's the *what*. Let's hear the *why*."

"You mean why create Isis in the first place?" Croi asked. "Actually—and you're going to laugh—it was Governor Treakness's idea."

Lorne raised his eyebrows. "*Treakness*?"

"Governor Tomo Treakness of the loud rants against the whole Cobra project," Croi confirmed. "Now suggesting a new project costing even more money, at least at the outset. Ironic, isn't it?"

"I imagine he feels a bit differently about the Cobras now," Lorne murmured.

"Knowing the governor, I wouldn't bet on it," Croi said. "Regardless, Isis was an idea he and Governor Ellen Hoffman cooked up between them a few months ago. The prototype was supposed to be unveiled with all due pomp and ceremony sometime in the next day or two, then shipped out to Donyang Province for its trial run. The ultimate goal was to scatter these things all around the expansion areas and new worlds, where they would not only save costs but would also shift the center of Cobra operations completely away from Capitalia and putting them where most of the actual needs are."

"And where most of the recruits are coming from, anyway," Lorne said, a stray memory suddenly clicking. "Was that the ceremony Chintawa wanted my mother to come into town for?"

"Exactly," Croi said, nodding. "You know how politicians think: the woman who redefined the Cobra profile thirty years ago, on hand to offer a send-off to the next stage of Cobra redefinition, and all that."

Lorne grimaced. Except that no one in the Dome had allowed his mother's redefinition of the Cobra profile to stick, and moreover had actively concealed what she'd actually done for the Cobra Worlds. She would have been little more than a figurehead at Chintawa's big show, someone to extol and ignore at the same time. "Well, we're for sure not going to Donyang now," he said. "So what's the new plan?"

Croi's cheek twitched. "There's currently a lack of agreement on that point," he said. "Ingidi-inhiliziyo wants to head straight back to his demesne and bury Isis as fast and as deeply as possible."

"Really," Lorne said, flicking a target lock onto Warrior as well.

"Yes, really," Croi said. "And before you start leaping to paranoid conclusions again, Cobra gear won't work on Tlossies. Their bone structure, the way their ligaments work and are attached, even the available body cavities—just trust me, they can't use the gear. Neither can any other Trofts."

[Yet as a way to destroy the Tlos'khin'fahi Demesne, it would serve well,] Warrior put in grimly. Behind him, the door leading to the control areas opened and another Troft strode quickly in and stepped to Warrior's side.

"What do you mean?" Lorne asked.

Warrior didn't answer, his full attention clearly on the newcomer murmuring in his ear. Lorne notched up his audios— [is here,] he caught the tail end of the Troft's words. [In person, do you wish to speak?]

[In person, I will,] Warrior agreed, his voice tight. Without even a glance at the three humans, he and the other Troft turned and walked quickly from the vestibule.

Lorne looked back at the ring of silent Troft soldiers, their weapons still pointed at the ceiling, then turned back to Croi. "Fine," he said. "I'll ask *you*, then. What did Warrior mean about someone using Isis to destroy the Tlossies?"

"Because its very existence is proof they collaborated with us," Croi said, frowning for a moment at the door where Warrior had disappeared. "In the past, their trading relationship with us has been a pretty good thing, for both sides. At the moment, though, all the political pressure is going the other direction."

"So I noticed," Lorne said. "Okay, Warrior wants to bury the project. What do *you* want to do with it?"

"Use it, of course," Croi said. "I think we should take Isis to Esquiline or Viminal, make a whole bunch of Cobras as fast as we can, then bring them back here to Aventine."

Nissa stirred. "You assume the Trofts haven't already landed on those worlds," she said, her voice limp with fatigue.

"You also assume you'll be able to convince enough psychologically qualified people to go under your robotic knife, knowing they're going to be thrown immediately into a war," Lorne added. "That may be harder than you think."

"The Dominion of Man had no trouble finding recruits a hundred years ago in *their* war with the Trofts," Croi pointed out.

Lorne shook his head. "Unfair comparison," he said. "The Dominion of Man had seventy worlds to draw from. We have five. *And* that still ignores Nissa's point that if the invaders have any brains at all they already have troops on *all* our worlds."

"I guess that's just something we're going to have to risk, isn't it?" Croi growled. "You have a better idea?"

A wave of sudden tiredness washed over Lorne's mind. "I can't even think five minutes ahead right now," he conceded.

Croi took a deep breath. "You're right, of course," he said. He took another breath and gestured to the soldiers. "Is there some place we can go and rest for a while? Maybe clean up a little, too?"

One of the Trofts gestured toward the door leading aft. [A place, it has been prepared for you,] he said. [Though the place, it was designed for three males.]

Lorne looked at Nissa. "It's all right," she said. "We'll manage." Gathering herself, she climbed to her feet.

"Fine," Croi said, doing likewise. He started to stumble, nodded his thanks as Lorne reached out a hand and steadied him.

They had all turned toward the aft door when Lorne heard the forward door open behind them. He looked over his shoulder to see the Troft who'd brought Warrior his mysterious message reenter the vestibule, his radiator membranes quivering with tension. [Your presence, Cobra Broom, the heir requests it,] he said.

A shiver ran up Lorne's back. Had the invaders spotted the surreptitious passenger pickup at Creeksedge and sent word ahead to stop the Tlossies? "Go ahead," he told Croi and Nissa. "I'll be there in a minute."

The Troft led him through a prep room, a narrow monitor and engineering station, and through a final door onto the bridge. Warrior was standing in the center of the room, gazing at a wraparound display showing the full three-hundred-sixty-degree view around them.

Lorne looked over his shoulder as he crossed the room to Warrior's side, grimacing as he spotted the ring of ships running a slow orbit above Aventine's equator. Not only did the invaders already have massive firepower on the ground, but they had extra backup waiting in the sky. Even if Croi was able to find enough recruits on Esquiline or Viminal, he would have the devil's own time getting them back onto Aventinian soil again.

[The approaching ship, do you see it?] Warrior asked.

Lorne shifted his attention forward. There was a flashing red ring superimposed on the image of a transport approaching from deep space. [The ship, I do,] Lorne confirmed. [The invaders, it is one of theirs?]

[The invaders, it is one of theirs,] Warrior confirmed. [Yet its occupants, Trofts they are not. Its occupants, humans they are.]

Lorne felt a sudden leap of hope. Had someone on Palatine or one of the smaller worlds managed to defeat the invaders, or at least push them back long enough to steal one of their transports?

And then, like a splash of cold water, the more likely explanation hit him. [Qasamans, they are?] he asked.

[Qasamans, they would appear to be,] Warrior confirmed.

Lorne took a deep breath. Croi had called it, all right, back when the two of them were dumping the dead spine leopard at Koshevski's brother's building. The invading Trofts and Qasamans had struck a deal, and the Qasamans were here to gloat. Or possibly to survey their new real estate. [Avoid them, we must,] he told Warrior urgently. [Your passengers, they must not identify us.]

[My passengers, they will not,] Warrior assured him. [Our sensors, far more advanced they are.]

Which made sense, Lorne realized. An heir's ship would have

upgrades on pretty much everything, including the sensor array.
[Avoid them, we must still do it,] he said.

[Speak with them, I must.] Warrior threw Lorne a stern look.
[Silence, you will maintain it.]

[Silence, I will maintain it,] Lorne promised.

Warrior gestured to one of the Trofts, and a green circle appeared
around the red-circled transport. Apparently, Warrior had decided
to use a tight beam for his hail.

The seconds ticked by. Lorne looked around the other sections
of the wraparound, noting the dozen or more transports moving
inward toward Aventine. The second wave of Troft soldiers?

[The signal, it is acknowledged,] a voice came from the speaker.
A woman's voice, Lorne decided, assuming Warrior had been right
about the occupants being humans. Her cattertalk was far crisper
and better enunciated than his, too, he noted with grudging admiration. [Assistance, how may we render it?]

[Your cargo bay, analysis shows it to be empty,] Warrior replied.
[The predators, why have you none?]

Lorne grimaced. So it wasn't soldiers the transports were bringing in, but more spine leopards. Terrific.

[The predators, all died en route,] the woman in the transport
said. [A disease, it was apparently brought aboard.]

[The message, it is understood.] Warrior hesitated, flashing
an unreadable look at Lorne. [Jasmine Jin Moreau, is there word
from her?]

Lorne felt his breath catch in his throat. *How in space had Warrior known that his mother had gone to Qasama?* He started to ask
that question, stopped as Warrior lifted a warning hand. [Jasmine
Jin Moreau, is there word from her?] he repeated.

And then, to Lorne's utter astonishment, a familiar, achingly
missed voice came on. [Jasmine Jin Moreau, it is I.]

Again, Warrior lifted a warning hand. But this time, Lorne didn't
have to be reminded to keep quiet. Whatever was going on over
there, he had no intention of letting the occupants know that Jin
Broom's son was listening in on the conversation. [The news from
Qasama, what is it?] Warrior asked.

[The battle, it has been won,] Jin said, her voice cautious.

[Yet the war, it has been lost?] Warrior asked.

[The war, it is not yet over,] Jin corrected.

For a moment Warrior didn't speak. Lorne studied his face, sifting through his limited knowledge of Troft facial expressions and trying to figure out what the other was thinking and feeling. He was disturbed, certainly. That much was clear. But disturbed about what?

Warrior's radiator membranes fluttered. [Then our mission, it has failed,] he said, his voice tight and sad.

[Your pardon, I crave it,] Jin said. [Your mission, what is its purpose and meaning?]

Warrior looked at Lorne. [The mission, it is of no matter,] he said. [Its failure, that is all I need know.]

[The message, from *you* it came,] Jin said, her tone changing as if with a sudden revelation. [To Qasama, you wished me to go.]

Lorne felt a jolt run through him as the whole thing suddenly fell into place. The mysterious and unsigned note that had sent Jin and Merrick to Qasama in the first place—the collaboration with Treakness—Warrior taking the risk of staying put on Aventine through the initial stage of the invasion in hopes of getting Croi and Isis off the planet. "You knew this was coming," he murmured, just loud enough for Warrior to hear. "You knew we were about to be invaded."

The other didn't reply. But the fluttering of his radiator membranes was all the answer Lorne needed.

[Your mission, I understand it now,] Jin's voice came again. [War with Aventine, your demesne-lord does not wish. Yet a stand against the attacking demesnes, he dare not take alone. A victory against them, one must first exist.]

[The truth, you speak it,] Warrior said. [A stand, other demesne-lords wish to make. But a stand against a victorious army, one cannot be made.]

[The reality, I understand it,] Jin said, her voice grim. [But hope, do not abandon it.]

Warrior looked at Lorne. [Understand, do you now?] he murmured.

Lorne inclined his head, hoping that would be taken as an assent. Certainly he understood what Warrior was attempting to imply about the situation and the Tlossies' involvement in it.

But there was another, darker possibility that made just as snug a fit around Lorne's limited collection of facts: the possibility that the Tlossies were in fact in league with the invaders. That they'd waited for Croi and Lorne, not to heroically smuggle them off Aventine, but so that they could deliver both Isis and its co-creator in a single, neatly-wrapped package. That they'd deliberately sent Jin and Merrick into a trap on Qasama, and that Lorne's mother was even now a prisoner on that transport.

But Lorne wasn't going to bring up any of those possibilities. Not until he had a better idea what part the Tlossies were playing in this drama. Certainly not here on the freighter's bridge, on ground of Warrior's choosing.

[Refueling, our transport needs,] Jin said into Lorne's musings. [Extra fuel, can you supply it?]

Warrior's membranes fluttered again. [To return to Qasama, enough exists,] he pointed out warily.

[The truth, you speak it,] Jin agreed. [But Qasama, we do not yet return there. Extra fuel, can you supply it?]

[This fuel, to what use?] Warrior asked.

[Victory against the attacking demesne-lords, its use will be,] Jin said, and in his mind's eye Lorne could see a dark, tight smile on her face.

Warrior gestured, and the green circle around the distant transport began fluttering as the Troft at the communications board muted the transmitter. [Her purpose, what is it?] he asked Lorne.

[Her purpose, you heard it,] Lorne said, gesturing toward the comm board. [Victory against the invaders, she intends.]

[Such a purpose, she cannot possibly carry it out,] Warrior protested.

[Such a purpose, perhaps she cannot,] Lorne agreed. [But such a purpose, perhaps she can. My mother, others also have underestimated.]

Warrior looked back at the display . . . and as he gazed at the

Troft's profile, Lorne suddenly realized how ridiculous his earlier suspicions had been. Of course the Tlossies weren't in league with the invaders. If they were, why go to all the trouble of running from Creeksedge instead of simply letting Lorne and Croi come aboard, gassing them in the airlock vestibule, and handing them over to their allies right there and then?

And why send Jin and Merrick to Qasama at all, where something unknown but obviously extremely interesting had apparently taken place?

Because his mother wasn't a prisoner aboard that transport, Lorne knew now. Even if the Qasamans had somehow been able to capture and restrain her, there was no way they could restrain her voice. Lorne had been analyzing his family's speech patterns all his life, and the tension level he'd heard in her voice had dropped when she figured out that Warrior was on the Cobra Worlds' side. That wouldn't have happened if she was a prisoner.

Warrior himself, though, was still staring at the transport's image, his expression still uncertain. Perhaps he was thinking through the stories of the young Jin Moreau's exploits on Qasama thirty years ago. Perhaps he was contemplating the ramifications of the older Jin Moreau Broom's presence aboard an enemy transport with a group of Qasamans.

Perhaps he simply knew he had no other choice but to hold onto hope.

He gestured again, and the green circle steadied. [Your course, you will hold it,] he told the transport. [To your side, we will come.]

[Our gratitude, you have it,] Jin said. [Your arrival, we will await it.]

Warrior gestured one final time, and the green transmission circle vanished. [The transport, journey to it,] he ordered. [A fuel download, prepare it.]

There were a pair of acknowledgments from two of the Trofts on the bridge. For a moment Warrior continued to gaze at the display, then turned again to Lorne. [Jasmine Jin Moreau Broom, to where does she intend to go?] he asked.

[The question, shall I ask it?] Lorne offered.

Warrior looked again at the display. [The question, you shall not ask it,] he said firmly. [Your presence here, she would question. The Isis, it must remain secret.]

[Wisdom, you speak it,] Lorne conceded. Sitting here while his mother's ship refueled alongside, knowing he was bare meters away from her without being able to find out what was going on, was going to kill him.

But while she was probably not the Qasamans' prisoner, he still had no idea of her actual status with them. Letting them know who and what was aboard the Tlossie freighter could be a very bad idea. Certainly not one they could afford to risk. [The question, if I may not ask, then the question, I cannot answer.]

[A new question, I then ask,] Warrior said. [Isis, what shall be done with it?]

Lorne grimaced. Terrific. The two people who actually knew the full capabilities of the damn thing had deadlocked, so they were bringing in an amateur to flip the coin for them.

And then, even as he wondered which one of them he least wanted mad at him, a sudden thought flashed through the fatigue coating his brain like the sludge in Capitalia's drainage tunnels. [To hide Isis, you wish it,] he told Warrior. [To employ Isis, Dr. Croi wishes it. Both ways, perhaps we can have them.]

For a moment Warrior eyed him. Then, with one final flutter, his radiator membranes settled back onto his upper arms. [Your statement, it intrigues me,] he said. [More, I would hear.]

"The tanks are nearly full," Ghofl Khatir reported from the transport's helm, craning his neck to look at his readouts one final time before swiveling around to face Jin. "A few more minutes, and we can be on our way."

"To Caelian," Carsh Zoshak muttered under his breath.

"Yes, to Caelian," Jin confirmed, eyeing him. "Have you a different option to suggest?"

The young Qasaman's lip twitched. "Nothing that would be better," he conceded. "It's just that I've been thinking about what you said about there being seven hundred Cobras on Caelian out of a total population of a little more than four thousand. One in six is an incredibly high number."

"I already explained that," Jin reminded him. "The planet is immensely and actively hostile toward the humans who live there. They need all those Cobras in order to survive."

"Yes, I remember," Zoshak said. "It also occurs to me that if the Cobras are that vital to the inhabitants' day-to-day lives, how do you intend to persuade any of them to come to Qasama with us?"

Jin grimaced. That was the crucial question, all right. Unfortunately, she still didn't have an answer to it. "We'll find a way," she said. "Certainly not all of them will come. Probably not even most of them. But enough will."

"Enough for what?" Siraj Akim put in. "Enough to actually throw back the next wave of Trofts who land on our world? Or merely enough to die alongside us in a blaze of glory?"

"I'm not particularly interested in death with glory, Siraj Akim," Jin said firmly. "For any of us: Cobra, Djinni, or civilian. My goals are life, victory, and freedom."

Beside Khatir, seated at the helm's second position, Rashida Vil stirred. "Tell us more about this Caelian," she said. "You speak of active attacks. How active are they?"

"The environmental pressure is pretty much constant," Jin told her, wincing. Up to now, with the Troft attack on Qasama, the discovery of her brain tumor, her son Merrick's wounding, and then this risky voyage to Aventine, she'd mostly succeeded in pushing Caelian to the back of her mind.

Now, though, all her thoughts and fears about what might be happening to her husband and daughter were coming back full force. "There are lots of predators, small, medium, and large," she told Rashida, "plus lots of herbivores with sharp spikes, poisoned tongues and quills, and other defenses. Organic plant life floats through the air and takes root on pretty much everything, which in turn draws insects and then the smaller predators."

Siraj snorted. "Sounds worse even than Qasaman village life."

"It does indeed," Rashida agreed soberly. "And I find myself agreeing with Carsh Zoshak's concerns. What can we say that will

induce these Cobras to abandon their people to such attacks in
order to help us?"

"That's not actually the proper question," Khatir said, running
his fingers through his—unusual for a Qasaman—red hair. "The
proper question is what can we offer them in trade."

"Are you suggesting we *buy* their assistance?" Siraj growled.

Khatir shrugged. "Be realistic, Siraj Akim. No one does anything
except for a price."

"*We* do," Siraj insisted, slapping his chest in emphasis. "We serve
the Shahni and the people of Qasama with no hope or expecta-
tion of any reward."

"Of course you expect something," Rashida said. "The price
you've been paid—all three of you—is the right to call yourselves
Djinn of Qasama."

"That's not the same thing," Siraj insisted.

"Actually, it is," Jin said. "Honor may not be a form of wealth,
but it's a reward and a price just the same."

"Is that the price your leaders paid for you, too?" Siraj asked,
a slight sneer in his voice.

"As a matter of fact, yes, it was," Jin said calmly. "We are very similar, Siraj Akim. More similar perhaps than you would like to admit."

Zoshak chuckled. "Now you're just being insulting," he said.

Abruptly, Siraj stood up. "Do you make humor at my expense?"
he demanded.

The whole room seemed to freeze in place. Jin stared at Siraj,
not moving, hardly daring to breathe. Both he and Zoshak were
dressed in their Djinn combat suits, snug outfits of treated krissjaw
hide stiffened by fiber meshwork, with strength-enhancing servos at
the joints that keyed directly off the wearer's own nervous-system
electrical impulses. Neither of them was wearing his helmet or the
gloves that contained the Qasamans' version of Cobra fingertip lasers,
but even without those weapons the suits made them into awesome
fighting machines, in some ways even superior to Cobras. If they
came to blows, it could be an extremely dangerous confrontation.

In the old days, Jin knew, clashes of honor on Qasama had
taken the form of duels, some styles leading to death, others only

wounding the loser's pride. With the cultural changes that had taken place over the past few decades, she had no idea what the current style of ritualized combat was. She was also not at all anxious to find out.

Fortunately, for now at least, she wouldn't have to. "My apologies, Ifrit Akim," Zoshak said formally. "No offense was intended."

For a moment Siraj continued to glare. Then, perhaps suddenly remembering that there were two non-Djinn outsiders present, both of them women, he let his shoulders relax. "Accepted, Djinni Zoshak," he said just as formally as he resumed his seat.

"So that's settled," Khatir said cheerfully into the lingering tension. "Excellent. According to the navigation data in the ship's computer, it should take no more than thirty-two hours to get to Caelian. Since we don't know whether the Cobras on Caelian will be willing to trade in the coin of honor and glory, I suggest we all spend those hours making lists of what we and the Shahni might offer for their assistance."

"What *we* might offer for their assistance," Siraj corrected firmly. "The Shahni are not here, and we cannot bind them to any agreements." He raised his eyebrows. "Cannot, and *will* not."

"No, of course not," Khatir said hastily. "I was merely suggesting that as the highest-ranking Djinni aboard you might be able to make tentative agreements, subject of course to later consideration and approval."

"We are warriors of the Shahni, Ghofl Khatir, not the Shahni themselves," Siraj ground out. "I will make no promise, and no bargain, that I personally cannot keep." He shifted his glare to Jin. "If that's not enough for the Cobras of Caelian, then we shall shake the dust of that world from our feet and return home."

"They'll come," Jin promised, a lump rising into her throat. "Enough of them will."

Siraj growled something under his breath. "I hope so, if only for the sake of my father," he said darkly. "*He* certainly believed in you." He shifted his gaze to the display, and the Troft freighter starting to move away from them. "But we shall see. We shall see."

✧   ✧   ✧

The quarters Warrior had assigned his guests appeared to be a standard crew room, hastily and incompletely modified to accommodate human physiology. At one end of the room was a three-tiered bunk bed, at the other a compact shower/toilet/sink combination, with the walls between them occupied by a fold-down game table and a set of three lockers.

By the time Lorne dragged himself wearily through the door, Nissa had finished her shower and was fast asleep on the top bunk, dressed in one of a set of robes that the Trofts had left for them. Croi, in the midst of a cloud of steam behind the frosted glass, was busily scrubbing himself down.

Wearily, Lorne dropped onto the lowest bunk and pried off his shoes. He was sorely tempted to just roll over onto his side, close his eyes, and forget his own shower until after he'd gotten some desperately needed sleep. But he was filthy, his whole body ached with the day's activities, and a soothing shower would go a long way toward making him feel like a civilized human being again.

Besides, if he went to sleep now, it would probably be hours before he woke up. Croi had a right to hear about the decision Lorne and Warrior had come to sooner than then.

And he had a right to hear about it from Lorne.

Lorne had fallen into a light doze, still sitting up, when he was jarred awake by the gentle slapping of Croi's hand on his shoulder. "Broom?" the other said. "Shower's free."

Lorne blinked his eyes open, wincing at the sandlike grit beneath the lids. "Thanks," he said. "But we need to talk first."

"Not long, I hope," Croi said, sitting down on the edge of the bed beside him. "What are we talking about?"

Lorne hesitated, searching for the best way to say this. But he was too tired to even try to be diplomatic. "Warrior and I have decided where to take Isis," he said.

Croi's eyes narrowed. "*You* decided?"

"Yes," Lorne said. "We're taking it to Caelian."

Croi's jaw dropped. *"Caelian?"*

"Think about it," Lorne urged. "He wants it hidden? Fine—there are a hundred places on Caelian where we could put it where any invaders would literally kill themselves trying to get to it. You want to use it? Also fine—the people there are rough and tough, and heading to Aventine to fight a war would probably seem like a vacation compared to their life there."

"I don't know," Croi said, rubbing the bridge of his nose thoughtfully. But at least he wasn't yelling. "I'm not involved with the Cobra screening process myself, but the people who are say that the average Caelianite is borderline crazy."

"Because they prefer to stay put in their homes instead of moving to Viminal?"

"That's probably part of it," Croi said. "The point is that we may have trouble finding three hundred men who can pass the screening test."

"So open it up to women, too," Lorne suggested.

Something behind Croi's eyes seemed to suddenly turn to stone. "You're not serious."

"Why not?" Lorne countered. "You want to win this war and throw the Trofts off Aventine? Or are you more interested in playing by someone else's idea of what the proper rules of life ought to be?"

Croi snorted. "Look who's talking about playing by someone else's rules. Is that what this whole thing is about to you? Some bizarre way to justify your mother and your family?"

Lorne stared at him. "Are you even *listening* to yourself? Do you really think I had a plan involving stuff I didn't even know about until an hour ago?"

"It hardly matters what I think anymore, does it?" Croi shot back. "You and Ingidi-inhiliziyo have made your deal. The rest of us either can like it or live with it."

"Pretty much, yes," Lorne said, suddenly tired of this conversation. "And while you're deciding which you're going to do, I suggest you get some sleep. The whole thing will look a lot more reasonable in the morning."

"Which will be just about the time we'll be getting there, won't it?" Croi growled. "What is it, thirty hours to Caelian at a freighter's top speed?"

"From here, about thirty-one," Lorne said, standing up and starting to pull off his clothes. "I'm going to take a shower. Don't wait up."

Croi's only answer was another snort as he pulled his feet up onto the bunk, stretched out on his side, and pointedly rolled over to turn his back to Lorne and the universe at large. With a sigh, Lorne finished undressing, adding his torn, filthy, smoky clothing to the pile beside the door.

He was about to step into the shower when something made him turn around. Croi was still turned to the wall, but Nissa was lying facing out into the room. Her eyes were closed, and her breathing was slow and regular, but as Lorne keyed in his infrareds he saw that her heat signature was too high for that of a sleeping person.

Had she woken up during his argument with Croi? If so, how much had she heard? And what had she made of it all?

But his brain was too foggy to even consider such questions. Closing the shower door behind him, he turned on the water. His only goal right now was to clean himself off, get dressed, and climb up into the remaining bunk.

And to stay awake until he got there.

CHAPTER FIFTEEN

Given the way the Troft at the reception point had snarled at them, Jody spent the entire walk across Stronghold expecting to find an execution block waiting for her and Freylan at the other end. It was therefore with a mixture of relief and embarrassment that she discovered they were simply being escorted to the three-story Government Building near the center of town, where they were taken straight up to the governor's residence on the top floor.

They found Governor Uy standing in the living room, gazing out one of the north-facing windows, his hands clasped tightly behind his back. "Ms. Broom; Mr. Sonderby," he greeted them, looking surprised as he strode across the room toward them. "So that *was* your aircar I saw put down a few minutes ago. I was hoping it was."

"Yes, sir," Jody said as their Troft guard backed out of the apartment and closed the door. "We're very sorry for the intrusion."

"Don't be, my dear, dear young people," Uy said feelingly as he reached them.

And to Jody's astonishment he pulled both her and Freylan close to him, wrapping them in a tight group hug.

Which wasn't at all what it seemed. "Cameras and microphones in the living and dining room; microphones everywhere else," the governor whispered as he pressed their heads close to his. "Don't say anything you don't want them to hear. Understood?"

505

Jody nodded, a tiny movement in Uy's crushing embrace, and felt Freylan do likewise. Uy held the hug another second, then released them and stepped back. "You must be famished," he went on. "And badly in need of sleep, too, I warrant. An entire night spent out in Wonderland. My wife Elssa's in the other room—shall I ask her to fix you some food? Or would you prefer a place to rest first?"

"Both sound good," Jody said. "But before that, maybe you can tell us what in the Worlds happened here. I mean, we take off yesterday to get some samples, and come back to find armed Trofts in the streets."

"If it was a shock to you, I can assure you it was no less so to us," Uy said, gesturing to a conversation circle at the west end of the room. "The fact of the matter is that we appear to have been invaded."

"Incredible," Jody said as they all sat down, she and Freylan on one of the couches, Uy in an armchair facing them. "But that would certainly explain the laser slash marks we saw as we were coming in. They came in shooting?"

"Not exactly," Uy said. "I think they more or less expected us to simply and calmly accept their presence without making any trouble."

"And you didn't?" Freylan suggested.

Uy's throat tightened. "Not at all," he confirmed. "We were afraid that if we waited until they'd settled in and disembarked their troops it would put the civilians in greater danger than if we attacked before that happened. So we did. The Cobras targeted those little wings where most of the weapons seemed to be clustered and opened fire."

Jody winced. "Only even Cobra antiarmor lasers didn't do any good against them."

"No, they didn't," Uy said, his voice going bitter. "And then they fired back. We lost eighteen Cobras in that first salvo."

"Sending a message," Freylan murmured, his voice thoughtful. "The way they did last night."

Uy looked sharply at him, but Jody lifted a calming hand. It wasn't like the Trofts listening in didn't know all about last night's events, after all.

As Uy himself also quickly realized. "Yes, I woke up in time to catch the end of that show," he said. He hesitated, and Jody saw him brace himself. "You said they sent the same kind of message?"

"Their return fire killed a Cobra named Buckley," Jody said. "I think he was the only one."

"Buckley," Uy mused, and she saw him relax fractionally at the news that the Troft's violent response hadn't taken his own son. "Inevitable, I suppose, that it was him. You didn't know the man, but Joe was one of those who courted death on nearly a daily basis, yet always came cheerfully back for more."

"I'm sorry," Jody said, quietly. "So that brings the total to sixteen?"

"Oh, it brings it much higher than that," Uy said sourly. "We'd learned our lesson on that one, all right, but the day's seminars were hardly over. A few minutes after we gave up our assault, a ramp lowered from partway up the bow of each of the ships and a half dozen floatcycles came buzzing out and headed over the wall toward the gate. We took out three of them before the ship's lasers opened fire again. We lost five more on that one."

"I spotted what looked like the wreckage of a house at the south end of town," Freylan said. "Bad marksmanship on the Trofts' part? Or were some Cobras using it as a base?"

"Very perceptive," Uy said, nodding. "Yes, once the soldiers on the floatcycles got the gate open, the ship ramps went down all the way and a group of armored trucks came out and rolled into town. Six of the Cobras figured they would have a clear line of sight from the old Wymack place and decided to try a concentration of firepower on the windshield of the first truck in line."

"Did it work?" Jody asked.

Uy shrugged. "Better than anything else we'd tried, which isn't saying much. The volley stopped the tank, though the spotters said the windshield instantly blackened where the lasers hit, which blocked most of the blast and limited the damage. The Trofts' helmet faceplates work the same way, incidentally, which makes fingertip lasers useless against them. A close-in antiarmor shot will overwhelm that particular defense, though. We found that out later."

"Also the hard way, I expect," Freylan murmured.

"Very much so," Uy said. "As I said, the attack stopped the truck, though the spotters think the driver was still alive when they hauled him out and took him back to the ship. But before the Cobras could shift aim to the next truck in line, the northern ship decided to up the ante and fired a missile into the house. The blast not only killed all six Cobras, but also two civilians in the house next door."

Jody winced. "And after the trucks came in and started unloading soldiers, I take it you took a crack at them, too?"

"Of course," Uy said. "We had slightly better luck here. Hardly surprising, I suppose, since one-on-one ground warfare was what Cobras were originally designed for. Turns out their stunners work just fine straight through Troft armor, though you have to get within two or three meters for that kind of shot. The sonics and arcthrowers are good for a couple of meters more, and antiarmor lasers can nail them at about ten meters—twelve or thirteen if you aim for the faceplates. All told, we took out probably fifteen of them."

"At a cost of...?" Jody asked carefully.

Uy exhaled. "Fifteen more Cobras and five civilians. After that, the Trofts declared something they called martial stasis and ordered everyone to stay indoors under penalty of immediate execution."

Jody felt a shiver run up her back. Stronghold's original Cobra contingent had only numbered about a hundred and twenty. In a single day of facing down the Trofts—possibly even in just a few hours—they'd lost over a third of them. "What about food and water?" she asked. "Are the Trofts supplying those to the people?"

Uy shook his head. "They're apparently assuming we all have our own supplies—which we do, of course—and that we can make do until they decide the resistance has ended and that we can start coming out and shopping again."

For a moment no one spoke. "I didn't see any of the trucks you mentioned on our way in," Freylan said. "Did they pull them back into the ships?"

"I doubt it," Uy said. "I obviously haven't gotten any word from our spotters since we were all sent to our rooms, but my guess is that they're just hidden or camouflaged enough to make them hard to spot." He smiled tightly. "They know enough about Caelian to know there are a lot more Cobras here than the ones they've got pinned down in Stronghold. They aren't going to want to make it too easy for any fresh attackers to sniff them out."

And even Stronghold's remaining Cobras were probably not nearly as pinned down as the Trofts might think, Jody knew. But she knew better than to say that out loud.

"What I *do* know is that the Trofts have also instituted foot patrols," Uy continued. "I see them passing by as they roam the streets. We've had a couple of incidents nearby where they've fired shots, but whether they were shooting into the buildings or at someone outside I couldn't tell. I don't even know if anyone was killed or wounded. I've asked the soldiers outside to allow me to speak with one of their senior officers, but so far there's been no response."

He took a deep breath, his eyes locking on Jody's face. "So," he said, and stopped.

Jody grimaced. She knew what he wanted to ask: whether his son was all right, how many Cobras there were out there, and what they were planning.

And they both knew that she couldn't say a thing, about any of it.

"I have another question," Freylan spoke up. "You said the big ramp opened to let the floatcycles and trucks out. I also noticed two smaller hatchways on either side of the main ramp—horizontal ones, maybe three meters long and one high. Any idea what those are for?"

"You have sharp eyes," Uy complimented him. "Those are the access hatches for a bunch of dart-shaped flying things like the two they sent out to meet you a few minutes ago. Sensor drones, probably, since the first thing they did after the ships landed was to pop those hatches and send out a dozen of the things."

"A dozen from each ship, or a dozen between them?" Freylan asked.

"Six from each ship," Uy said. "More specifically, three from each of the hatches."

"Are they still out there?" Jody asked, her stomach tightening.

If the Trofts had drones watching every move her father and the rest of the Cobras made...

"No, and they probably won't be sending more out any time soon," Uy said. "That was the other minor success of the day: we managed to nail seven of the drones—three that were hovering over Stronghold during our first attack, and another four when they were returning to their ships. As far as I know they didn't send any of them out again until the two that escorted you in."

His throat tightened. "All of that cost us another two Cobras."

"I'm sorry," Jody said quietly.

"As are we all," Uy said. "One other thing which may interest you. A couple of our spotters told me that, given the ship-mounted lasers' firing pattern, they think the weapons are automatically aimed but manually fired."

"Really," Jody said. "Yes, that *is* interesting. Do they have any ideas as to why the Trofts would set it up that way?"

"I assume it has to do with avoiding misfires," Uy said. "Or possibly sensor-locked fire controls are too easy to confuse or manipulate. I just thought it was curious, and that maybe you would, too."

"Yes, indeed," Jody said. And with that, she decided, she had enough to fill a preliminary report. Time to check in with her father on the other side of the wall. "I appreciate the information—I can't tell you how concerned Freylan and I were when we saw all those laser burns."

"I can imagine," Uy said, giving her a strained smile. "But enough talk. Can I now interest you in some food?"

"Yes, please," Jody said. She stood up.

And abruptly swayed, her knees buckling under her and sending her toppling toward the floor.

Both men lunged toward her. Uy was closer and got there first, catching her in a cradling embrace before she could hit the rug, pulling her in close to his chest. "Ms. Broom?" he asked anxiously.

Jody leaned in close to him. "West-facing bedroom," she whispered. "Any cameras?"

She felt the governor twitch as he realized that her collapse had been a fake. "No cameras," he whispered back. "At least one microphone."

"Sorry," she said aloud, breathing heavily into his neck as she pushed herself weakly away from him. "Sorry. That was embarrassing."

"Don't worry about it," Uy said, easing her around into a sitting position on the floor. Freylan had his own grip on her arm now, helping her down. "Are you feeling ill? Do you need to lie down?"

"I'm okay," Jody assured both of them. "But I think maybe I'd better lie down for a while. I guess I was more tired than I realized."

"Caelian can take a lot out of a person," Uy said. "Come on, let's get you to the guest room. Mr. Sonderby?"

The men each took an arm and helped Jody to her feet. Then, walking her like a toddler, they took her out of the living room, down a short hallway, and into a small but cheerfully furnished bedroom.

"Can I get you anything else?" Uy asked as they sat her down on the edge of the bed.

"No, this will be wonderful," Jody assured him. "Maybe Freylan can take you up on that offer of food."

"Actually, I think I'm too tired to eat yet, too," Freylan said. "It's not like either of us got much sleep out on the river."

"I suppose not," Jody said, putting a warning finger to her lips. He nodded, touching his ear to show he understood. "Maybe the governor could find someplace for you to lie down, too."

"I was thinking I could just stay here with you," he suggested. "I mean, not *with* you," he added, his face reddening. "I could sleep in that chair over there."

Jody frowned. *Trouble?* she mouthed silently.

You might need me, he mouthed back.

She hesitated, then nodded. "As long as you don't snore, sure, help yourself."

"I'll leave you two alone, then," Uy said, backing toward the door. "Whenever you're ready for food, just let me know." With a final nod at each of them, he left the room, closing the door behind him.

Now what? Freylan mouthed.

I need to find something to signal with, Jody mouthed back, looking around the room. The Trofts had taken her flashlight, and a quick check of the lamps showed that they were the multilevel type that would be useless for Dida signaling. Uy undoubtedly had a flashlight out there somewhere, but getting to it with Troft cameras watching could be tricky. "I meant what I said about the snoring," she said aloud as she went to the nightstand and pulled open the drawer. There was a pen and a pad of note paper inside, along with a small box of tissues, a small reader, and a set of book chips. No light. She started to close the drawer—

"You know, this bed really *is* big enough for two," Freylan said, coming up suddenly behind her and grabbing her hand. As she frowned at him, he reached into the drawer and pulled out the notepad. "I mean, I could sleep on one side and you could sleep on the other," he went on, stepping back and holding up the pad so that Jody was looking at its surface. He rotated it ninety degrees, turning the edge to her, then rotated it back up again. He repeated the operation, raising his eyebrows questioningly.

Jody smiled tightly, inclining her head to him. Providing her father and the other Cobras were paying attention, it should work. "Fine," she said, taking the pad from him and walking around the end of the bed toward the window. "Just be sure you *stay* on that side."

"I will," he promised, sitting down on the bed with a slight but audible creak from the frame.

Jody reached the other side of the bed and sat down facing the window. One of the trees beyond the wall had an odd look, and with a shiver she realized it was one of the ones that the Troft ship had blasted last night in an effort to kill the Cobra holding on behind it. Holding the pad up in front of her chest, she flipped it over and back five times. *Dit dit dit dit dit. Calling—anyone there?*

She repeated the signal, and again, and again, systematically checking out all the different trees she could see from her vantage point. Nothing. Were all Cobras positioned off to the side where they couldn't see her? Or could she be too far inside the window for even a Cobra to spot the flashing white of the paper?

And then, from one of the trees just to the left of the blasted one, she spotted a small, flickering light. *Dit dah dit dah dit dah. Received and understood—stand by.*

Taking a deep breath, she set the pad flat against her chest and waited. Two minutes later, the light began to flash again. *Dit dit dah dit dit dah. Ready—proceed.*

Squaring her shoulders, hoping her fatigued brain remembered everything Uy had told them, she began her report.

Paul finished his report, and for a minute the rest of the Cobras in the circle were silent. "Seems pretty obvious to me," Harli said at last. "The doorways at the base of the ship are easiest to get to, which means they're the ones that'll be the most heavily guarded. These upper ones, the big ramp and the little drone ports, are the ones they're not expecting trouble from. Ergo, those are our best bet."

"Except that all three are way too high for us to get to," Matigo pointed out. "Unless you know a way to rewire the spookers for more altitude?"

"No, but I wasn't really planning on a frontal assault," Harli said. "I was thinking more along the lines of delivering a package or two. Tracker, what's the explosives situation?"

"We've got enough to make a good-sized crater," Tracker confirmed. "'Course, we're first gonna have to find a way to make the Trofts open up and say ah."

"I assume you're suggesting we throw a bomb in through one of the ports?" Paul asked.

"Exactly," Harli said, nodding. "If Dad's right about the lasers being fired manually, it should work. Actually, I should have figured that one out on my own—auto-fire is way too easy to manipulate. If we toss in a few mining explosives, there's a good chance they'll get in before the gunners spot the threat and take them out."

"We can't just use them as is, though," Tracker warned. "Right now, everything's got hard-wire triggers. We'll have to put together some timers or else rig up something wireless to set them off."

"That's okay—we've got time to work that out," Harli said. "Go grab everyone who's got explosives experience and get them working on delivery packages. Let's be optimistic and make four, one for each of the ports. Kemp, Matigo, you grab your spookers and head toward Essbend. They should have been here by now—maybe they missed that last message Dad was able to send out."

"Or they may be tied up with something else," Matigo suggested.

"In that case, untie them and tell them to gear their rears on over here," Harli said grimly. "They can leave a squad to guard the town, but everyone else is with us. We're going to need everyone we can get if we're going to take these bastards down."

"Got it." Matigo gestured to Kemp, and together they strode off into the woods.

Harli eyed Paul. "You got a brave little girl there, Broom," he said, almost grudgingly. "Don't worry—when the time comes, we'll get her back out."

"I know," Paul confirmed, feeling a familiar tightness in his chest. It was a tightness that had been with him almost continually during his long years of service to Aventine. It was the tightness that came of knowing that someone he cared about was in continual, deadly danger.

He'd mostly come to terms with that feeling as far as his two Cobra sons went. He'd never counted on having to feel that way about his daughter. Or his wife.

Caelian and Qasama, the two most dangerous places in the known universe. And he'd sent members of his family to each of them.

With an effort, he pushed away the dark thoughts. Dark thoughts in the face of danger were a good way to get yourself killed. "What do you want me to tell her?" he asked.

"Tell her—" Harli broke off as he sent a flurry of fingertip laser fire at a group of doremis that had just launched themselves from low-hanging tree branches toward the two Cobras. "Tell her we'll contact her tomorrow morning," he said as the birds thudded into the carpet of dead leaves at their feet. "Let's make it right at nine-twenty. By then we should have the bombs ready and either have Essbend's group here or at least on the way."

"Right." Paul turned and started to climb back up his signaling tree.

"And if she can," Harli added, his voice sounding a little embarrassed, "have her tell my father that we're all right."

"I will," Paul promised.

And as he resumed his climb, he wondered distantly if Harli was also feeling that same tightness in his chest.

Jody had fallen into a light doze on the bed when she was startled awake by Freylan's hand tapping against her cheek. She opened her eyes, and was opening her mouth to speak when he touched a finger to her lips. Frowning at the unexpected intimacy, she reached up and started to push the finger aside.

And then the reality of their situation came roaring back through the fog, and she nodded both understanding and her thanks. *What is it?* she mouthed.

He pointed to the window. *Your dad's signaling.*

Jody sat up, blinking her eyes to focus again. *Dit dit dit dit dit*, she could see the small light flashing from the tree.

She picked up the pad. *Dit dit dah dit dit dah*, she sent.

Three minutes later, with a quiet sigh, she again laid the pad aside. *What is it?* Freylan mouthed.

More instructions tomorrow at nine-twenty, she told him. *Hang loose until then. Harli Uy's best to his father.*

Freylan grimaced. *Hang loose.*

Jody nodded. Like they were really going to relax here in the middle of an occupied city. *You hungry?*

Still more tired than hungry, he told her.

Me too. Pulling her feet up, she lay back down on the bed. Fifteen minutes, she promised herself, and then she would get up and go find food.

It was after noon when Governor Uy finally came in and woke them up with the news that lunch was ready. A few minutes later Jody dragged herself out of the room and headed toward the dining room, an equally bleary Freylan beside her.

It was, she decided, going to be a long, long day.

CHAPTER SIXTEEN

The next twenty-six hours were a flurry of work and preparation, with the added complication of continually having to shoot, stun, or beat back Caelian's assortment of deadly wildlife. For Paul, who'd already gone through one mostly sleepless night, the list of the day's activities promised to be an uphill climb.

Fortunately, Harli was a good enough leader to know better than to push his men too hard, especially with a Caelian Cobra's need for extra alertness. Despite his long to-do list, he made sure each member of the group got at least two four-hour sleep periods sometime during that long day and night. Paul, who knew nothing about explosives and was clearly considered by most of the others to be useless as a guard, got somewhat more.

Aside from the sleep and meal breaks, though, the group worked around the clock. By nine-fifteen the next morning, everything was ready.

Except that the Essbend Cobras still hadn't arrived.

"What the *hell* is keeping them?" Harli fumed as he glared westward, as if sheer force of will would enable him to see through a hundred thirty kilometers of wilderness to Caelian's second largest settlement.

"So do we wait?" Matigo asked.

Harli's jaw tightened. "No," he said. "Everyone's ready, and delay

516

just gives the Trofts more time to spot the teams." He lifted a finger suddenly. "You know, come to think of it, maybe we can use this to our advantage. Broom?"

"Ready," Paul said.

"Okay," Harli said slowly, eyes narrowed in thought. "Send this to your daughter..."

With the remnants of her long day and short night having made for an early bedtime, Jody had woken up an hour before dawn, with a fresh plan of action for the day. Her father had told her during that last contact that he would be sending her information that she was in turn to leak to the listening Trofts. Jody had spent much of the previous day wondering how exactly she would do that without it *looking* like she was deliberately feeding it to them.

Now, with ten straight hours of sleep having finally cleared the dust and cobwebs from her brain, she'd figured out a plan. After all, an information slip would seem much more reasonable if the aliens thought *she* thought the governor's residence was no longer being monitored.

And so, with the rest of the household still asleep, she set about examining every square centimeter of the residence's public areas, searching for, finding, and destroying every hidden camera and buried microphone that the invaders had surreptitiously planted.

All of them...except one.

By the time Uy and his wife Elssa emerged from their room, she was able to report her success and give them a carefully edited version of what she and her father had discussed earlier from her guest room vantage point.

By the time the morning's message finally came through, Uy, Elssa, Freylan, and—hopefully—the listening Trofts were all ready and eager to hear it.

"It turns out your son didn't tell us everything when we were with him two nights ago," she told the group assembled in the living room. "The Cobras from Essbend hadn't shown up yet because they were working on something special to use against the Trofts. Apparently, they've finished it and are now on their way."

"Are we talking about a plan, or a device, or what?" Elssa asked. "I'm worried about the people of Stronghold."

"The biggest worry they have is regaining their freedom," Uy reminded her firmly. "Whatever Essbend's come up with, it's worth the risk to try it."

"Dad didn't say what exactly it is, Mrs. Uy," Jody said. "But from everything else we've seen on Caelian, I'm willing to bet it's going to be spectacular."

"I wonder which of the ships they'll target," Freylan mused, craning his neck to look out the window at the Troft warship looming against the forest backdrop to the north. "Be just our luck if they take out the south one and we don't get to watch."

"Well, you've got a fifty-fifty chance," Jody reminded him as she stood up. "Enjoy. Me, I need to get back in case they need to send us something else. I just wanted you all to have a heads-up."

"We appreciate that," Uy said, the crinkly lines around his eyes telling Jody that he was fully aware of the part he and the others were playing in her disinformation scheme. "Let me know if there's anything else they need me to do."

"I will," Jody said, and left the room.

And that was that, she thought, permitting herself a small smile as she once again settled herself and her notepad by the guest room window. If the Trofts had even a shred of military competence, not to mention a flicker of curiosity, they would be readying one or more of their drones to take to the air and head toward Essbend for a look at the Cobras' mysterious superweapon.

And when they did, they would be in for a surprise. Hopefully, a very loud, very violent surprise.

"That's it," Lorne said, nodding ahead at the dark planetary curve stretching out across much of the Tlossie freighter's wraparound display. "That's Caelian."

[A place of lush greenery, it is,] Warrior commented from beside him. [A peaceful place, it appears from the sky.]

[A peaceful appearance, it is a lie,] Lorne told him, gazing at the thin blur of atmosphere at the edge of the dark disk, a queasy feeling in the pit of his stomach. There were reasons why people didn't usually come out of hyperspace this close to a planetary body, chief among them the fact that doing it wrong could easily get you killed. Apparently, Warrior had decided he would rather take those risks than give any enemy ships or probes in the area the time and distance for a long, lingering look at them.

Either he had a great deal of confidence in his crew, or else he had a reckless streak that Lorne hadn't previously been aware of. Or possibly both.

[A landing site, you will now provide one.]

"Working on it," Lorne told him, shifting his eyes from the main display to the false-color sensor image and trying to figure out just where over Caelian they were. If that was the edge of Southway they were coming up on, then the Whitebank River should be about eight hundred kilometers to the east. They could look along the river until they found the heat signature of Essbend, tucked between the water and the Banded Hills. After that, it would be a simple matter of going due east another hundred thirty kilometers until they found Stronghold.

[A radio challenge, it is given,] the Troft at the comm board reported. [Our identity, it is demanded.]

[Our identity, transmit it,] Warrior said calmly.

[Our identity, it is transmitted.]

Lorne took a deep breath. So the invaders *had* sent a force to Caelian. He had hoped fervently that they wouldn't bother.

Still, they *were* aboard an heir-ship of the Tlossie demesne. The invaders had honored that immunity once. They would surely do so again.

[A second craft, it has arrived at the planet,] the Troft at the sensors spoke up suddenly. [A radio challenge, the planet has also sent one.]

[The new craft, identify and locate it,] Warrior ordered. His voice was still calm, but Lorne could see that his radiator membranes were fluttering slightly against his arms.

[The craft, a medium-range transport it is,] the Troft reported. [Its location, at *var* by *yei* by *sist* it is.]

Lorne felt his stomach tighten. That vector put it slightly above and almost directly behind their own freighter. If someone was trying to box them in against the planet, he was doing a damn good job of it.

[Our immediate departure, the planetary authority demands,] the Troft at the comm board reported. [Our presence, it will not permit.]

[Our identity, again transmit it,] Warrior said. [Our business and presence, they must not be interfered with.]

[Our immediate departure, the authority insists upon it,] the Troft repeated. His radiator membranes were starting to flutter now, as well. [A landing, he will use force to prevent one.]

[Armaments, does this vessel possess them?] Lorne asked carefully.

[Armaments, it does not possess them,] Warrior said, an edge of anger coloring his voice. [A bluff, the authority makes one. An heir of the Tlos'khin'fahi Demesne, he will not attack him.]

[Our departure, the authority demands it,] the Troft at the comm said tensely. His membranes had now risen halfway up from his arms. [Our final warning, he states this is it.]

[Our course, continue it,] Warrior ordered. [A bluff, he makes one.]

[The order, I obey it.]

[If a bluff, he does not make one?] Lorne asked carefully.

[A bluff, he makes one,] Warrior said firmly. [A watch, you will keep it. A lesson, you will learn it.]

Or else he has a reckless streak, the thought ran through Lorne's mind again. Grimacing, he hunched his shoulders and settled in to watch.

Paul was staring with full telescopics at his assigned drone hatchway on the southern warship, waiting for the first sign that it was about to open, when the whole image suddenly spun and veered crazily. Jerking as a flash of vertigo slapped across his brain, he hastily keyed his opticals back to normal sight.

Just in time to see the southern Troft warship lift ponderously from the landing field. Leaning forward as large ships tended to do, it threw power to its grav lifts and rose into the sky, heading westward.

"What the *hell*?" Harli breathed from Paul's side.

"Looks like Jody convinced them, all right," Paul said grimly. "Only instead of sending out their drones, they decided to go check out Essbend for themselves."

"Well, *damn*," Harli said, turning around to gaze at the departing warship as it headed off into the distance.

"So what now?" Paul asked.

For a long moment Harli didn't answer. Paul watched as the Troft warship continued to climb and faded into the morning haze. "They want to play it that way?" Harli said. "Fine—we can play it that way, too. Everyone grab your bombs and come with me."

Without waiting for a response, he set off into the forest at a fast jog. "Where are we going?" Paul asked, hurrying to catch up.

Harli flashed him a tight grin. "Maybe the Trofts haven't thought about this part of it," he said, "but they've just taken fifty percent of their heavy firepower out of the picture."

He turned to face front again, his grin turning into a snarl. "Let's see if we can do something about the other fifty percent."

[The atmosphere, a ship has cleared it,] the Troft at the sensor board reported. [A course to our vessel, it has set one.]

[The type of craft, identify it,] Warrior ordered.

[A Drim'hco'plai Class II city sentry warship, it is one,] the Troft said. [The Aventine city sentries, of the same type it is.]

[Orders, I request them,] the helmsman spoke up.

[Our course, continue it,] Warrior said. [Our identity, again transmit it.]

[The warship's weapons, he has activated them,] the sensor Troft said, his membranes fully extended now.

[Orders, I request them,] the helmsman repeated more urgently. [Evasion, shall I initiate it?]

[Evasion, you shall not initiate it,] Warrior said.

Behind Lorne, the bridge door slid open, and he turned as Croi and Nissa hurried in. "What's going on?" Croi demanded, his eyes flicking over the displays. "Someone out there said we were under attack."

"Right now, we're just under observation," Lorne told them. "But the other is definitely waiting in the wings."

"Anything I can do?" Croi asked.

"I doubt it," Lorne said. "Surgeons are usually more useful after a fight than during it."

"Funny," Croi muttered. "I *can* fight, you know."

"So go get your biggest scalpel," Lorne said. "Something the size of a sword, if you have one."

"Broom—"

"If you haven't, I suggest you both go back to our quarters and wait," Lorne cut him off. "And if you hear laser fire, you'd better get all the rest of your scalpels ready."

"New blip," Khatir snapped, hunching over the transport's helm display. "Big one, coming up from the surface."

"Identification?" Jin asked.

"It's too far away for good resolution," Khatir said. "But from its overall size and shape, it could be one of the same kind of sentry ship we faced in the streets of Sollas."

Jin's hands curled into fists. She'd hoped against hope that the invaders would consider Caelian so useless and insignificant that they wouldn't even bother sending a force to occupy it.

And not only had they sent a force, they'd sent enough of one that they could spare a warship from their ground operation to come up here and check out an unexpected and uninvited intruder.

Or rather, *two* uninvited intruders. "Rashida Vil, can you confirm yet whether or not the freighter up there is the Tlossie who refueled us at Aventine?"

"What do you want me to say?" the young woman asked stiffly, throwing Jin a dark look. "We're too far away to see the hull markings, and we never had a transmitted ID signal from them."

"But who else could they be?" Siraj put in brusquely. "They're the only ones who knew who we were. They're the only ones who could have guessed where we were going." He shook his head. "The mission is over, Jasmine Moreau. I say we leave right now, before that warship gets within firing range."

"And return to Qasama empty-handed?" Jin asked. "That will hardly bring us honor."

"Better to arrive empty-handed than with no hands at all," Siraj countered. "If we linger, they'll take us all."

"We need allies," Jin insisted.

"There are none," Rashida said, her tone dark. "Your hope has failed, Jasmine Moreau. There are no friends for Qasama anywhere out here. There are only enemies."

"So you agree with Siraj Akim." Jin turned to Zoshak. "Carsh Zoshak?" she invited.

"I must also agree," Zoshak said. Unlike Siraj and Rashida, he sounded more disappointed than angry or bitter. "The freighter must have followed us here, coming out of hyperspace ahead of us so as to be able to give the alert to the other invaders. Why else would they be here?"

"I don't know," Jin said. "But the Tlossies aren't *other* invaders. They're not part of the group who've attacked our worlds."

"Yet here they are," Siraj pointed out, gesturing toward the forward display. "If they're not the invaders' allies, answer Carsh Zoshak's question. Why are they here?"

"Why did they allow us to escape Aventine instead of betraying us right then and there?" Jin countered. "Here, we still have a chance to escape. At Aventine, surrounded by warships, we would have had none at all."

"Perhaps they wished to see where we'd go next," Rashida suggested.

"According to Siraj Akim's reasoning, they already knew where we were going," Jin reminded her. "You can't have it both ways."

"We may not get it either way," Khatir put in, his voice suddenly odd. "The rising warship isn't heading toward us. It's heading toward the freighter."

"That's good, isn't it?" Rashida asked, looking at her own set of displays.

"Good for us," Khatir agreed. "Not so good for the Tlossies."

Siraj sniffed. "A meeting of allies."

"To what end?" Zoshak asked. "They can speak together just as well by comm."

"He's right," Jin said grimly. "The invaders are going in because they want a closer look at the freighter."

"As I said, not so good for the Tlossies," Khatir said. "Jasmine Moreau, do you wish me to go around them and try for the surface?"

Jin braced herself. "No," she said. "Transmit the clearance codes we got from the transport's pilot back at Qasama. Tell the warship that the Tlossies are with us."

Siraj's mouth dropped open. *"What?"*

"They risked their lives to help us back at Aventine," Jin said. "It's our turn now to help them."

"And if the Tlossies aren't as they appear?" Siraj demanded. "If they're allies of the invaders and are merely playing games with us?"

"They're not our enemies," Jin insisted. "They sent Merrick and me to Qasama to help you. They refueled us and got us away from Aventine. And they've been our trading partners for decades."

"Do you truly believe they're our friends?" Zoshak asked.

Jin looked him straight in the eye. "Yes."

Zoshak exhaled heavily. "Then I say we do it," he said. "Jasmine Moreau is our ally, Siraj Akim, and so far her instincts have proved to be good. I say we trust those instincts one more time."

"I too am willing," Rashida said.

Siraj snorted. "You're a woman."

"I'm translator and second pilot," Rashida said stiffly. "My opinion has a right to be heard and weighed."

Siraj glared at her a moment, then shifted the glare to Khatir. "And you, Ghofl Khatir?"

Khatir shrugged. "My opinion hardly matters," he pointed out. "You're the senior Djinni aboard. The decision is yours."

"But whatever you decide, it must be quick," Jin added.

Siraj locked eyes with her, his lips compressed into a thin, pale line. "What would you say to them?" he asked.

"We tell them we're from the Qasaman contingent," Jin said, thinking quickly. "Just in case the clearance codes are different between the different invasion groups. The Tlossies are a potential ally, and we were ordered to bring them here for a closer look at Caelian."

"Why would they want a look at a living death trap?" Siraj scoffed.

"Because there may be useful plants and animals down there," Khatir offered. "Or possibly mineral wealth."

"We'll go with the plants," Jin decided. "Especially their potential pharmaceutical uses. The Tlossies do a lot with that sort of thing."

Siraj gave a curt nod and shifted his eyes to Rashida. "Go ahead," he ordered her. "Be convincing."

Rashida turned around and keyed her board. [Your attention, we request it,] she said in cattertalk.

Jin listened with half an ear, watching the displays and trying to figure out what they would do if the invaders didn't go for their story. At the moment, the warship was far enough in, and their own transport far enough out, that they could duck back into hyperspace reasonably safely and get out of the system.

But that would mean abandoning the freighter to face the warship alone. Worse, by identifying themselves as the Tlossies' escort, Rashida had now effectively linked the two ships together. If the Qasamans made a run for it, or did anything else guilty-looking, that same level of guilt would automatically shift over to the freighter.

[—your course, you will hold it,] the Troft voice ordered, the words snapping Jin out of her thoughts. [Your orders, we will examine them.]

"Uh-oh," Khatir murmured.

Rashida turned around. "Jasmine Moreau?" she asked tightly. "What do I say?"

"What do I do?" Khatir added.

And suddenly, all eyes were on Jin. "Hold your course," she told them, her mouth going dry. "Just hold your course. I'll think of something."

"Fire in three!" Harli shouted, his voice from half a kilometer away perfectly clear in Paul's enhanced hearing. "Audios down!"

Obediently, Paul keyed them back . . . and exactly three seconds later, the forest was rocked by a violent triple explosion. The echoes of the blast faded away.

And with a softer but even more horrendous crunching noise, the three huge steelwood trees that Harli's men had mined tilted over and fell, slamming with a rolling crunch against the top of the Troft warship.

The ship was big and massive. But so were the trees, and the ship's design had given it a dangerously narrow base...and as Paul watched in awe the ship tilted sideways and ponderously toppled over to slam into the city's outer wall. For a moment it balanced there, squeezed like the center of a sandwich between stainless steel wall below and Caelian steelwood tree above.

But the wall had never been designed for this kind of abuse. The rustling of branches from the fallen trees was still audible when the wall gave an abrupt screech of its own and collapsed beneath the warship's weight. With a final crunch of buildings and vehicles, the Troft ship came to rest on its side.

"Attack!" Paul heard Harli's distant shout. "All Cobras, attack!"

"We have no choice," Siraj said, his voice tight. "Do you hear me, Jasmine Moreau? We must leave. *Now*."

"Ghofl Khatir?" Jin asked, her eyes flicking back and forth between the approaching warship's image and the rapidly decreasing distance indicator on the nav display.

"He may be right," Khatir said. "There's no way for us to know the range of its weapons."

"We will when they start firing," Siraj bit out. "You saw their power on Qasama, Jasmine Moreau. You know what they can do."

Jin grimaced. She knew, all right. And here they were, sitting in a transport designed for hauling people and cargo, with no extra armor anywhere on it.

Siraj was right. Staying here until they were blown out of the sky wouldn't gain either them or the Tlossies anything. All they could do was try to balance the line, to draw the warship as far from the freighter as they could before they ran, and hope the Tlossies would take the hint also and run for it.

"Wait a minute," Rashida said suddenly. "Ghofl Khatir? Am I reading this correctly?"

"You are," Khatir confirmed, sounding as puzzled as she did. "They're veering off. Hard. Heading . . . yes—heading back to the surface." He frowned at Jin. "Could they have been frightened off by something?"

"Are there any other spacecraft in the region?" Siraj asked.

"Nothing I can see," Khatir said.

"Unbelievable," Siraj murmured. "Why would they just leave that way?"

"They must have been called back," Jin said. "There must be some trouble in Stronghold that they need the warship there to deal with."

"God help those people," Zoshak murmured. "But if we still want to land, this is our chance."

Jin looked at Siraj. He hesitated, then nodded. "Take us in," he ordered. "Try to catch up with the freighter on the way. I'd very much like to know what he wants here, and I'd prefer to know it *before* we land."

"Acknowledged," Khatir said, and Jin felt herself being pressed back into her seat as he ran full power to the drive.

Jin took a deep breath. A brief respite at best, but maybe it would be enough. If they could get to the surface and into some kind of cover before the warship finished its other business and came back to look for them—

Her thoughts froze, a sudden chill running through her. *Before it finishes its business* . . . and whatever that business was, it almost certainly involved the killing or wounding of some of Stronghold's citizens. Human beings just like her.

And yet, until that moment not a single thought of their welfare had even crossed her mind.

A queasy feeling settled into her stomach. Was this what it was like to be a soldier? To become so focused on your own private corner of a battle or war that you had no attention left to spare for anyone else?

"We're gaining on them," Khatir announced. "Either that or they're deliberately holding back to let us catch—"

And then, without warning, the command room flared with a sudden blaze of light and the entire transport was jerked violently sideways.

Jin gasped as the scream of the depressurization alarm split the air, her mind flashing back to that horrible moment when the shuttle carrying her on her first trip to Qasama had also blazed with light and fury and tangled metal, and everyone except Jin herself had died a sudden, violent death. Her vision clouded over...

"Jasmine Moreau! Jasmine Moreau!"

Jin snapped her eyes open. Zoshak and Siraj were hunched over her, the latter anxiously and gingerly slapping at her cheek. "What happened?" she croaked.

"The warship apparently had second thoughts about us," Siraj said grimly. "Possibly they were bothered by our sudden change in velocity toward the freighter."

"They're coming back?" Jin asked, her heart seizing up as she checked her nanocomputer's clock.

But as best she could tell, she'd been unconscious for over ten minutes. If the warship had decided to come after them, it should surely have been here by now.

"No, they're still returning to the surface," Siraj said. "But they decided to take a parting shot at us."

Jin focused on the wall behind him. That whole side of the command room had turned the mottled, lumpy gray of emergency hull sealant. "Is it holding?" she asked.

"So far," Siraj said, glancing over his shoulder at the sealant. "But Ghofl Khatir says we've also taken some damage to the drive and grav lifts."

"How bad?"

"We'll make it to ground all right," Khatir said grimly from the helm. "But I don't know how close we'll make it to any of the towns."

Jin winced. On the ground, in the Caelian wilderness. This just got better and better. "Have you talked to the Tlossies?" she asked. "Is there anything they can do?"

"Yes, and yes," Zoshak said. "They're going to accompany us down, and then land with us whenever we have to."

"I told you they were our friends," Jin said, frowning at the two men still standing over her. All four Qasamans, she noticed belatedly, seemed to have come through the attack just fine. "What happened to me?" she asked.

Zoshak and Siraj exchanged looks. "We're not sure," Zoshak said. "You may have hyperventilated, or possibly something struck you. We didn't see anything, but we *were* all preoccupied with other matters at the time."

Jin felt a tightening in her chest. "Or else it's my brain tumor starting to cause trouble again. Is that what you're thinking?"

A shadow crossed Zoshak's face. "That was our other thought," he conceded. "I don't know what specific treatment the doctors gave you before we left, but I do know that all such techniques are only temporary. It may be that the weakness and blackouts you experienced on Qasama are beginning to come back."

"Is there anything we can get you?" Siraj asked.

Jin closed her eyes. Back on Qasama, Siraj's father Miron Akim had told her that she still had three months before the tumor in her brain killed her. Plenty of time, he'd assured her, for her and the others to gather whatever Cobras were willing to come to Qasama and return for her surgery.

Maybe he'd been wrong.

With an effort, she swallowed back the sudden fear. If he'd been wrong, then she was going to die, and there was nothing she or anyone else out here could do about it. At least she'd be able to see Paul and Jody one last time.

Provided, of course, that they made it to the surface alive. "Yes, there is," she told Siraj. "You can tell Ghofl Khatir and Rashida Vil to get us down in one piece. After everything we've been through, dying in a crash-landing would be just plain embarrassing."

Almost unwillingly, she thought, Siraj smiled. "That it would," he agreed. "Sit back and rest, Jasmine Moreau. We'll take it from here."

CHAPTER SEVENTEEN

With a horrible, incredible, utterly awesome crash, the Troft ship north of Stronghold toppled over onto the wall. It paused there for a second or two, then crunched through the stainless steel, smashing two homes and an aircar that happened to be directly beneath it, and slammed into the ground, one of the weapons wings on that side digging itself halfway into the plowed dirt of one of the town's vegetable gardens.

"Holy cats," Freylan muttered into the sudden silence.

"And you were afraid we were going to miss the show," Jody said, staring in disbelief at the downed warship. She'd read about how heavy steelwood was, but she would never have believed that three trees' worth of it could do *that*. Through the partially open window, she heard a distant shout.

And suddenly the forest beyond the ruined wall exploded with movement and the flashes of laser fire.

Harli's Cobras were attacking.

Instantly, Governor Uy was on his feet, charging to the window and throwing it wide open. "Cobras! Attack!" he shouted to the town below. "All Cobras—"

There was a flash of light, and with a choked-off gasp he fell backward and collapsed to the floor.

"Rom!" his wife Elssa gasped, jumping up from her chair and hurrying to her husband's side.

Jody got there first, knocking the older woman to the floor before she could reach the window. "No—keep down," Jody snapped as she helped Elssa back up onto her hands and knees. The window frame was flashing now with reflected laser fire, the town below them roaring with shouts and screams and the sound of breaking glass and heat-shattered building material. "Where's your medical kit?" Jody shouted over the din.

"Kitchen—cabinet beside the cooker," Elssa said as she crawled the rest of the way to Uy's side.

"Freylan?" Jody called.

"I'm on it," Freylan said, already running stooped-over toward the kitchen.

Jody looked down at Uy. His breathing was rapid and shallow, his face twisted with pain. Over his left lung, there was a small, char-edged hole in his jacket.

"What's happening out there?" Elssa asked, tears running down her face as she carefully lifted her husband's head off the floor. "Jody? What's happening?"

Jody's first thought was that the woman should be focusing her priorities on her husband, not her town. But a second later she understood: Elssa's son Harli was in the middle of the hell out there. "I'll check," she said, and crawled to the window. Bracing herself, she eased up beside it and looked out.

It was like a scene from a war movie, the whole thing strangely unreal while at the same time feeling genuinely, dangerously real. Below her, laser fire filled the streets, blasting chunks from buildings and shattering glass. The screaming she'd heard a moment ago was mostly gone now, replaced by shouts and grunts and the sounds of destruction. Across the city, the downed Troft ship's upper wings were spitting out rapid laser fire of their own, and Jody's throat tightened at the thought of her father and Harli and the other Cobras out there. The chaos seemed to rise over her like the edge of a wilderness dust storm, numbing her eyes and brain. A sudden impulse swept through her, an overwhelming urge to duck away from the fire and destruction and throw herself flat on the floor where she would be safe, or at least have the illusion of safety.

"What's happening?" Elssa asked again, her voice pleading.

Jody clenched her teeth hard enough to hurt, hard enough even to stop their fear-driven chattering, and with a supreme effort stayed by the window. *I'm a Moreau, and a Broom*, she reminded herself, *and I will damn it all not act like a terrified child*. Not in front of Uy and his wife; absolutely not in front of Freylan. *I'm also a scientist*, she added, *trained in observation. So get your mind in gear, kiddo, and observe*. Unclenching her jaw, transferring her internal tension instead into a death grip on the window sill, she once again peered outside.

The battle was still going strong, possibly even more devastating now in its noise and fury. But this time, as she forced herself to methodically scan the areas she could see, she noticed something she'd missed the first time.

All across the town, small groups of Trofts were heading north toward the damaged ship. The groups she could see had formed themselves into tight knots, their weapons turned outward from the centers as they fired continuously in all directions.

And with that, the seeming chaos blew away, exactly like the dust storm she'd just been comparing it to.

Because there was no chaos out there. Nor was there some horrible mass slaughter. The rapid-fire laser bolts were nothing more than cover fire, laid down by the Troft soldiers as they tried to retreat to their damaged warship.

She lifted her eyes to the ship itself. Its own heavy fire was the same thing, she saw: a desperate attempt to blanket the area around it with death to keep the Cobras from getting close enough to do any further damage.

"Jody?" Elssa asked.

"The Trofts are retreating toward the ship," Jody told her, daring to raise her head a little higher. A movement between two of the buildings caught her eye, and she saw one of the armored trucks similarly heading north. "Soldiers and vehicles both. Lot of firing going on, but I don't think they're actually hitting much."

She turned, her throat tightening as she realized what she'd just said. Uy, at least, had most definitely been hit. "How's he doing?"

she asked, dropping back to her hands and knees and crawling over to them.

"I don't know," Elssa said tightly. She had moved around behind her husband and now had his head cradled on her lap. "His breathing is terrible, but he doesn't seem to be losing much blood."

Jody nodded. One of the few advantages of taking laser fire instead of a projectile shot was that laser wounds tended to cauterize, usually preventing the victim from bleeding out.

Unless, of course, all of the bleeding was going on inside. In that case, Uy was in just as much trouble as if he was bleeding into his shirt. Probably even more.

There was a movement at the corner of her eye, and Freylan skidded to a halt on his knees beside her, the emergency kit clutched in his hand. "Got it," he panted. "What do we do first?"

"Anti-shock," Elssa said, taking the kit from him and pulling it open. "Here—inject it into his thigh," she said, handing him a hypo.

Freylan grimaced, but took the hypo and pulled off the cap. "Internal wound sealant," Elssa continued, pulling out another hypo. "Jody, can you tear away his jacket?"

They had given Uy both hypos plus one containing a sedative and painkiller, and Elssa had the ventilator strapped over her husband's nose and mouth when a sudden peal of thunder roared across the city, rattling the windows. "Jody?" Elssa gasped.

"I'll check," Jody said, handing Freylan the hand pump half of the ventilator and scrambling back up onto her hands and knees. She moved over to the window and cautiously looked outside.

The second Troft warship had returned.

It was impossible, she knew, for a chunk of metal to look angry. Even so, for those first couple of heartbeats she could swear that the warship looked furious. It was hovering on its grav lifts directly above the downed ship like an avenging phoenix hawk standing over its fallen mate. Its own lasers had joined the massive firestorm, all four clusters spitting out a wide swath of destruction around the ship and the ground troops now clustered around it. This time, the circle of death not only carved through the forest but also across the northern end of the town itself. "The other ship's back," she told the others. "They're firing. A lot."

"Get away from the window," Freylan said, his voice tight. "And get back here. We need you."

The laser firestorm had slowed to mostly sporadic shots by the time they'd done everything they could for Uy. "It sounds like it might be safe enough out there to go get a doctor," Jody said, peering into Uy's sleeping face. His breathing was still labored, but it seemed reasonably stable. "Where's the nearest one?"

"Dr. MacClave's office is two blocks east," Elssa said hesitantly. "But I don't know if you should. Even if the Troft soldiers aren't back yet, the ship will still be able to see you between the buildings. I don't like sending you out into that."

"It'll be all right," Jody assured her, taking a deep breath and handing the ventilator pump to Freylan. "I'll be back as soon as I can."

"No, you won't," Freylan said, and to Jody's surprise he handed the pump back to her. "Mrs. Uy needs to stay here with her husband. You're the only one who can talk to the Cobras out there. That leaves me. I'll go."

But the Trofts might think you're a Cobra! "But—" Jody began.

She stopped. Jody, as a woman, the Trofts might question. Freylan, as a man, they might shoot down on sight. He knew all of that, of course.

But he was right. There was no one who could go but him. "Be careful," she said instead.

"Trust me," Freylan said, giving her a forced smile as he got to his feet. "Two blocks east, you said?"

Elssa nodded. "Thank you," she said quietly.

"No problem," he said. "We'll be back as quick as we can." Nodding at Jody, he hurried from the room.

"He's brave," Elssa murmured, cradling her husband's head.

"Yes, he is," Jody said, staring at the spot from where Freylan had disappeared. Freylan Sonderby, the quiet, awkward, earnest one. Who would have thought he had that kind of strength under the surface?

"So are you," Elssa added.

Jody grimaced. *Right*, she thought sourly. *Like a big, fearsome fluffy rabbit I am*. "He'll be all right," she said. "So will Harli."

Elssa didn't answer. But then, Jody didn't believe it, either.

Sighing quietly, she fixed her eyes on Governor Uy's face and settled into a steady rhythm with the ventilator pump.

The transport had made it past the Whitebank River and was heading toward Stronghold when its damaged grav lifts finally gave up. Once again, as the ship slammed its violent, noisy way through the treetops, Jin had a terrifying flashback to that first crash landing on Qasama.

But once again, the present didn't repeat the past. Between them, Khatir and Rashida managed to bring the transport down with a minimum of buffeting and a maximum of intact hull.

"Any idea where we are?" Jin asked as they unstrapped from their seats.

"About seventy kilometers past the river and the village you said was there," Khatir said. "If your numbers are correct, that should put us about fifty kilometers from Stronghold."

Jin grimaced. Fifty kilometers, on foot, through the Caelian wilderness. That was not a pleasant thing to contemplate.

Unless perhaps they could hitch a ride with the Tlossies? But letting the freighter get too close to the invaders would also not be a good idea. Briefly, Jin wondered how good the enemy's sensors might be, and realized she didn't have the faintest idea.

But the Tlossies might. "Any idea where the freighter put down?" she asked.

"Sure—it's right behind us," Khatir said dryly. "We cut a pretty deep swathe through the trees on our way down."

"Shall I call them?" Rashida offered, turning to the comm board.

"No, we'd better just go back there and talk to them," Jin said. "We may be close enough to Stronghold for the invaders to pick up radio transmissions." She gestured to Siraj. "The three of you will want full gear, gloves and helmets both. Knowing Caelian, chances are there'll be something nasty waiting just outside the hatch."

Five minutes later, they were ready. "Okay," Jin said, taking a deep breath. "I'll go first. Rashida Vil, you might as well stay inside until we've talked to the Tlossies."

"Fine," Siraj said, slipping deftly in front of Jin. "Except that *I* will go first."

"Siraj Akim—"

"I'm senior Djinni, and you are ill," he cut her off. "There will be no argument."

Turning to face the hatch, he keyed the release and the hatch slid open as the ramp swung down to the ground. He stepped out, pausing at the top of the ramp to look around.

And abruptly spun a quarter turn to his left, his glove lasers spitting a double burst even as he twisted over hard at the waist. A large, tawny creature shot past, crashing with a heavy thud onto the ground at the other side of the ramp. "It's all right," Siraj called back inside. "I think I—"

He broke off, staggering as a burst of deep sound resonated through the open hatchway. A second later a figure dropped onto the ramp from the roof, batted Siraj's arms aside as he tried to bring his glove lasers around, and sent a second, more potent sonic burst rattling straight through the opening into the freighter.

But Jin's nanocomputer had already evaluated the danger and thrown her onto her back on the deck, her palms pressed hard against her ears to minimize the weapon's effects. As the sound washed mostly harmlessly past her, she rolled her torso toward the open hatch, and as a second figure dropped off the transport's roof to join the first, she fired her own sonic.

Both figures staggered back, their arms waving madly as they fought for balance. Jin continued her roll onto her stomach, then shoved off the deck and bounced herself back up onto her feet. Three quick steps and she was on the ramp, grabbing one of the staggering men and locking her arms around his torso, pinning his arms to his sides. "Hold it!" she shouted.

"Identify yourself!" a voice ordered from somewhere in the forest around them.

"I'm a citizen of Aventine," Jin called back. "What in the name of hell do you think you're doing?"

There was a short pause. Then, with a soft rustle of leaves, a young man stepped out into the narrow clearing that the transport's violent passage through the trees had created. "Who's in there with you, citizen of Aventine?" he called.

Jin keyed her opticals for a closer look at his face. He still looked wary, but at least his hands and fingertip lasers were at his sides instead of pointed at Jin and Siraj.

Though of course there were probably other Cobras out there whose weapons *were* trained on her. "They're allies," she told the young man. "You attack everyone who comes to Caelian?"

"Everyone who comes here in Troft spaceships, yes," the young man said stiffly. "In case you didn't know, we're at war here. You have a name?"

"Jasmine Broom," Jin said. "You?"

The man's face seemed to tighten, and she saw the telltale twitch as he activated his own opticals. "Jasmine *Moreau* Broom?" he asked carefully.

"Yes," Jin said. "And you?"

"My name's Kemp," the other said. "I believe I've met your husband and daughter."

Jin felt her heart leap inside her. "They're all right?" she asked.

He hesitated, just a fraction of a second too long. "Last I knew, yes," he said.

"What's happened?" Jin demanded, her pulse starting to pound in her throat. "Something's happened. What is it?"

Kemp's lip twitched. "Who are these supposed allies you've brought with you?"

And then, to Jin's utter amazement, a familiar voice called distantly from the direction of the Tlossie freighter. "One of them is her son, Cobra Lorne Moreau Broom," Lorne shouted. "The lady asked you a question, Kemp."

Jin twisted her head to look in that direction, a flash of dizziness briefly touching her as the landscape rushed past in her telescopic vision. Lorne was pressed against the freighter's bow, his fingertip lasers pointed warningly across the distance at Kemp.

And in that brief moment of distraction, the man she was holding turned suddenly in her grip, forcing enough slack to slip partially out of her hold. He grabbed her arm and bent it up, completing his escape. Still clutching her arm, he spun back around toward her, bringing up his free hand and angling his torso once again toward her.

Only to topple backward and slam hard onto the ramp as the still kneeling Siraj slapped his legs out from under him.

"Enough!" Jin bellowed, a fresh wave of dizziness rolling over her. With a supreme effort, she fought it back. This was no time to look weak. "All of you, just *stop* it! You want to fight the Trofts, or each other?"

For a stunned moment no one moved or spoke, and Jin could feel their eyes boring into her. "Speaking as Jin Moreau's son, gentlemen," Lorne called, his voice deadly serious, "and as one who's heard that tone many times before, I can tell you right now that you ignore it at your peril."

Jin focused on Kemp. For another moment he stood as still as the trees around him. And then, to her surprise, he actually chuckled. "Point taken, Cobra Broom," he called. Lifting a hand, he gave a signal.

And with a general crunching of leaves, a semicircle of over twenty Cobras emerged warily from the forest. "We've now met your number one ally, Cobra Jasmine Broom," Kemp said. "Would you care to introduce the rest of your team?"

Jin braced herself. "I've brought four representatives of the planet Qasama," she said. "They seek your help, and offer theirs in return." She shot at look at the Troft freighter. "I believe we also have possible allies in a group of Trofts from the Tlos'khin'fahi Demesne."

One of the Cobras spat. "You expect us to trust *Trofts*?"

"The Tlossies have been our trading partners for over a generation," Jin reminded him.

"Maybe *you* trade with them," the Cobra countered. "You and Stronghold. We don't get much drop-in traffic out in Essbend."

"Well, you're making up for that today," Lorne put in. His voice was clear and even, Jin noted, but in her enhanced vision she could see the wariness in his own eyes as he gazed at Siraj in his scaled gray Djinn combat suit. "Not only do we have Qasamans and Tlossies, but we also have a representative from the Dome, as well as one of the surgeons who probably helped many of you become Cobras back on Aventine."

"Who?" one of the other Cobras asked suspiciously.

"Dr. Glas Croi," Lorne said. He paused, and Jin heard a murmur ripple through the Caelians. They knew that name, all right. "And for the record," Lorne continued, "the commander of this freighter isn't just some Troft merchant. He's Ingidi-inhiliziyo, second heir to the Tlossie demesne-lord."

Jin waited, expecting another murmur of amazement. But there was only silence. Apparently, these men weren't nearly as impressed by Troft demesne-heirs as they were by Cobra surgeons.

Fortunately, they were impressed enough. "It's pretty rollin' clear that this is going to take some time to sort out," Kemp said, giving another hand signal. "But we can't do it out here in the open. Your, uh, landing"—his eyes flicked pointedly to the transport's crumpled bow—"drove away a lot of the predators, but they're starting to come back."

"No point in doing it here anyway," one of the older Cobras added. "Harli's waiting for us at Stronghold."

"And whatever you have to say, you'd just have to repeat it to him anyway," Kemp agreed. He locked eyes with Jin. "You trust these people?"

"I already have," Jin said firmly. "With my life. More importantly, with my son's life."

"Okay," Kemp said. He still didn't look particularly happy about the situation, but it was clear he knew that any further decisions rested with someone higher up the command structure than he was. "We'll bring in the spookers and load up. I hope you haven't got much you need to take—it's going to be tricky enough riding double with all our stuff as it is."

"We'll manage," Jin promised.

"But we can't just leave the freighter here out in the open," Lorne called, pointing at the vehicle behind him. "We need someplace to hide it in case the invaders spotted us coming in. A deep river or lake will do—Warrior says a few days' immersion in water won't hurt it any. Any ideas?"

Kemp looked around the group. "Gish? You're the expert on this part of Wonderland."

"There's the Octagon Cave complex," one of the Cobras said. "That would probably be proof against at least a casual sensor scan. You sure you want to let them out of our sight?"

"Don't worry, it won't be all of them," Lorne told him. "Warrior— that's Ingidi-inhiliziyo's more pronounceable name—has already told me he wants to be in on any discussions we might have."

"Oh, *does* he?" Gish growled.

"Yes, he does," Lorne said calmly. "And I think Nissa and Dr. Croi should come with us, too."

"At least Dr. Croi," Kemp agreed. "No offense, Broom, but his opinion regarding your Troft pals is going to carry a lot more weight here than yours."

"No offense taken," Lorne said. "If you'll send someone back here with the coordinates to those caves, I'll get the others ready to travel."

CHAPTER EIGHTEEN

For Lorne, the spooker ride turned out to be far and away the most terrifying part of his entire wartime experience so far. His Caelian driver, a Cobra named Fourdalay who was clearly a lunatic, pushed the cranked-up, spike-covered grav cycle like he was trying to burn out all of its thrusters in one massive overload.

Or possibly his death wish involved something more spectacular. A thundering high-speed crash, say, followed by a massive fireball. The way he shaved the tolerances between the corners of the spooker and Caelian's never-ending assortment of trees, thorn bushes, and rock outcroppings—that could very well have been his plan. Clutching the grip bar, Lorne decided that even facing down two Troft warships on the rooftops of Aventine hadn't been this frightening.

His only comfort, and it wasn't much of one, was that all the rest of the Cobras were driving with exactly the same degree of recklessness.

The ordeal seemed to last forever. But finally, Fourdalay eased back on the throttle, and a couple of minutes later they glided to a smooth halt beside a pair of other men. There was a brief, quiet conversation between them and Kemp that Lorne didn't even bother to eavesdrop on, and with clear reluctance the visitors were passed through and escorted a dozen meters farther to where Governor Uy's son Harli was waiting for them.

Lorne had expected Harli to be just as suspicious of the new-comers as Kemp and his crowd had been, or even more so. To his surprise, once the initial shock had faded away, the Cobras' leader welcomed them all with at least a measure of guarded civility. It was only later that it occurred to Lorne that perhaps Harli's brief acquaintance with Paul and Jody may have paved the way for him to trust Jin's judgment as to the trustworthiness of both the Qasamans and the Tlossies.

And a few minutes later, after the Essbend contingent had been sent to one of the equipment caches to unload their gear, and sentries had been posted against the ever-present predator threat, Harli sat them all down in a circle and the debriefing began.

The stories were many and varied, and even with obvious time-editing going on, it took nearly an hour for the Qasaman, Aventin-ian, and Caelian accounts to be laid out before the entire group.

Lorne didn't say much during that hour. Croi had made it clear before they left the freighter that he, not Lorne or Nissa, would tell their part of the story. He'd made it even more clear that none of them was to even hint at the existence of the precious cargo aboard the freighter that Warrior's crew had now hidden away in Gish's cave complex. Despite Jin's assurances, it was obvious he didn't trust the Qasamans any farther than he could spit them.

The Qasamans. Lorne studied them as Siraj Akim presented their part of the story to the rest of the gathering in fairly decent Anglic. The head of the three Djinn didn't trust any of them, and wasn't particularly happy to be here, an attitude abundantly clear from the tightness Lorne could see in his cheek and throat muscles. But he spoke calmly and fearlessly enough as he described the attack on Qasama and the reason he and the others had traveled with Lorne's mother to the Cobra Worlds.

His grasp of Anglic puzzled Lorne until he realized that the Djinn had probably been created as an answer to the Cobras, with the intent of fighting them toe-to-toe whenever the expected Cobra Worlds' invasion of Qasama began. Under that scenario, one of a Djinni's jobs would certainly be to learn the invaders' language.

The second Djinni, Carsh Zoshak, seemed a bit more comfortable

with the group as a whole. Reading between the lines of his part
of the story, Lorne guessed that his greater acceptance was tied
to the additional time he'd spent fighting alongside both Jin and
Merrick back on Qasama. As with Harli, familiarity with members
of the Broom family seemed to create a higher level of trust in
their judgment.

Lorne did notice, though, that neither Siraj nor Zoshak seemed
to be allowing Jin to add much to their rendition. More than once,
he wondered if she'd been ordered to stay out of the discussion,
just as he and Nissa had been ordered by Croi to do likewise.

The Qasaman woman, Rashida Vil, seemed nearly as nervous
about the group as Siraj. But in addition, Lorne had the impression
that she was trying very hard to make herself invisible, possibly
trying to press herself into the massive tree trunk she was sitting
against. She'd contributed virtually nothing to the conversation,
and then only to answer direct questions posed to her by Harli
or one of the other Caelians. Considering that she was not only
the Qasaman's second pilot but also their primary Troft translator, Lorne could only assume that she'd received the same order
of silence that his mother had.

The surprising one of the bunch was the third Djinni, Ghofl
Khatir, who in contrast to the other Qasamans seemed completely
at ease with his surroundings. Possibly more at ease, in fact, than
even the Caelian Cobras. He had settled himself at the side of the
circle beside Croi and Warrior, tossing in occasional comments
wherever appropriate and smiling genially at everyone around
him whenever he wasn't talking. Croi and Warrior, for their part,
seemed to regard Khatir like a black-sheep distant cousin who'd
unexpectedly showed up at a family reunion and whom no one
could quite figure out what to do with.

But the Qasamans weren't the real problem, at least not from
Lorne's point of view. True, their government had once sworn
eternal hatred against the Cobra Worlds, but that was all in the
distant past. His mother had vouched for this particular group,
and that was good enough for him.

What was bothering him was what his mother *wasn't* saying.

Because there was something she was holding deep inside her. Something tense and unpleasant. Lorne had always been able to detect one of his siblings' illnesses, usually before even the sibling was aware of it, and he could clearly see the signs of stress in his mother. He could see the extra tension around her eyes, well beyond even what their current situation warranted. He could hear the slight hesitation in her voice during her rare comments, her careful weighing of every word as if she was afraid she would slip and say something she shouldn't. He could see it in the way she'd been gripping her husband's hand ever since they'd all sat down together.

Even more significantly, he could see it in the Qasamans' faces. Though they were clearly trying to hide it, all four of them were paying close attention to her, their eyes flicking over to her for a quick evaluation every few seconds. Zoshak in particular seemed to be not quite settled on his patch of ground, as if he was expecting he might have to leap to her side at a second's notice.

Was there something important that she and the Qasamans were holding back? Something of the same caliber as the Aventinians' own Isis secret?

Or was it something more personal? She'd told them briefly about the injuries Merrick had suffered in the Qasamans' final attack on the invaders' occupation force. Had she been wounded, too, perhaps internally where it didn't show?

He didn't dare ask, not here in the middle of a war council. But he would find an opportunity to do so. And soon.

"Well," Harli commented when the last report was finished and the last question answered. "I guess I never really believed that Caelian was the focus of this whole Troft invasion. But I would never have believed how damn serious they were about the whole thing, either." He eyed Jin thoughtfully. "Though the reason why Warrior and his buddies would send you to Qasama still eludes me."

"Perhaps *because* you wouldn't otherwise have believed that the Qasamans had also been attacked," Jin suggested. "If Siraj Akim and the others had shown up here alone, would you have listened to them?"

Harli made a face. "Probably not," he conceded, looking over at Siraj. "I'm still not sure what you think we can do for you, but right now that's kind of a side issue. Our first job is to figure out how we're going to get these damn Trofts off Caelian." He threw a hooded look at Warrior. "No offense," he added.

[Offense, I do not take it,] the Tlossie assured him.

"So what exactly is the situation over there?" Lorne asked. "You said the one ship had fallen onto the town's outer wall?"

"Was pushed over onto it, yes," Harli said. "A good-sized section was crushed, which is going to be another rollin' problem pretty quick down the road. Anyway, the second ship has set up shop right behind it, and they've put a cordon of armored trucks and troops around both of them. Your sister's currently got the best vantage point of any of us, and her guess is that they're trying to take off the downed ship's grav lifts and reposition them so that they can get the thing stood upright again."

"They can't just turn the grav lifts around in place?" Croi asked.

"Apparently not," Paul told him.

[Such equipment, it is not usually moveable,] Warrior put in. [A situation like this, one does not often encounter it.]

"Warrior agrees," Paul translated. "They're going to have to physically take the grav lifts off."

Harli snorted. "Pretty stupid design for a warship, if you ask me."

"You wouldn't think that if you'd seen how they took over the streets of Capitalia," Lorne said grimly. "They're exactly the right design for dropping into the middle of city intersections as mobile command posts."

"Well, they don't make much sense *here*," Harli said. "The point is that right now we've got the advantage, but only until they get that first ship back up again. Any ideas?"

"There's a hatch on the upper hull near the stern," Jin said. "Any chance the Cobras in Stronghold can get to it?"

"Maybe, but it would be damn costly," Harli said. "Like I said, they've put out a ring of armored trucks and soldiers, including the part that's sticking into Stronghold. I don't doubt the other ship has most of its weapons tasked for defense, too."

"More than that, we've already lost over a third of Stronghold's Cobras," Kemp added. "Sending the rest in an open attack against a target everyone knows is obvious would be a pretty sure form of suicide."

"He's right," Harli said. "I won't order it except as an absolute last resort. Even then only if you can convince me it has a real chance of success."

"Why do you ask about that particular hatch?" a Cobra named Matigo asked. "Is it more vulnerable than any of the others?"

"I don't know," Jin said. "But that's the one I got a look at, and I know how the catches and seals are positioned. I also got a quick look at the room below it. If we can get a small group of Cobras inside they should be able to take that area and hold it."

A ripple ran though the group. "You saw *inside* one of their ships?" Kemp asked.

"Briefly, yes," Jin said. "Unfortunately, we didn't have the time or the manpower necessary to do anything more."

"Pity," Harli said. "But like I say, the downed ship is being watched like a sticker's nest, which is why I want us to find a way to hit the other one. If the Trofts have any brains at all, they won't be expecting our attack there."

"What about Caelian itself?" Siraj spoke up. "Even from our few hours here we've seen how dangerous and persistent its wildlife can be. Can we allow that wildlife to deal with the invaders?"

"Personally, I think it would be a rollin' kick to sit back and watch how badly a bunch of inexperienced Trofts do against Wonderland," Harli said. "Unfortunately, we can't afford the time. The floating organics and insects have started being trouble for them, but so far the big predators haven't seemed interested."

"Speaking of which, you're all going to need to shave your heads if you don't want your hair turning green," Matigo warned, gesturing toward the newcomers. "You'll have to learn how to scrape your clothes, too."

"That can wait," Harli said. "But the predator idea is still worth pursuing, even if only as a distraction. We've got a few men in the woods right now, collecting plants that should attract some of the bigger animals. That other friend of Jody's, Geoff Boulton, is helping fine-tune the selection."

"The problem being that we've already pulled that trick once," Paul put in. "Having now seen it, the Trofts will undoubtedly be watching for us to try it again."

"Those bow hatches will be tricky anyway," Lorne told him. "They've got troops sitting just inside waiting to shoot at anything non-Troft that barges in."

"What, *you* got to see inside one of their ships, too?" Matigo asked.

"I didn't see the guard spots themselves," Lorne said. "I was inside one of the stairways that run along the sides of the ship in that area. But I could hear the troops through the door."

"Wait a second," Paul said, frowning. "You got *inside* one of their ships?"

"For a few minutes, yes," Lorne said. "I hitched a ride underneath one of their armored trucks."

"You didn't tell us anything about that," Croi said, staring in disbelief at him. "No wonder the Trofts were so serious about hunting you down afterward."

"Oh, I don't think they ever knew I was there," Lorne assured him. "I only went in to try and find out how sophisticated their drones were."

"How sophisticated were they?" Paul asked.

"Near as I could tell, they were only running visual and large-engine heat signatures," Lorne said. "That means they shouldn't be able to distinguish us from any of the large predators out here. The shipboard sensors are probably better, though."

"They are," Harli said grimly. "Trust me. Did you happen to find a way to disable those trucks while you were hitching that ride, by the way?"

"A few arcthrower shots into the engine from underneath seemed to do the trick," Lorne said. "But I suspect the topside armor is more resilient."

"The soldiers themselves are tricky, too," Jin said. "The armor is pretty thick, and those faceplates blacken if you fire a fingertip laser at them, which blocks the shot. But sonics can still stun them, and antiarmors and arcthrowers still work, too. The lower-power stunner that most of you have will also get through the armor, though you have to be pretty close to use it."

"If we ever decide we just want to wound them, we'll let you know," Harli said sourly. He shifted his attention to the three gray-suited Qasamans. "What about you? Any special weapons in those—what did you say they were? krissjaw hide?—those krissjaw-hide suits?"

"We have small lasers in the gloves," Siraj said, indicating the slender tube running beneath the little finger of each of his glove. "They are similar to yours."

"Only more powerful," Jin added. "Theirs *can* punch straight through the Troft faceplates and kill them."

"We also have a version of your sonic stunner," Siraj continued, "though from what I've seen it is less versatile than yours. As far as I know, it was never directly used on the Trofts during their invasion of Qasama, so I do not know how effective it would be against them."

"Each of us also carries three small gas canisters with a quick-acting sleeping gas," Zoshak said, tapping his belt. "The same gas as was used in the Lodestar Hospital," he added, looking at Jin.

"How quick-acting was it?" Paul asked.

"Very," Jin confirmed. "As far as I know, the Trofts in the building went down without ever firing a shot." She grimaced. "Unfortunately, it affects humans just as fast as it does Trofts."

"We have special filters permanently implanted in our nostrils to protect us," Zoshak said. "Unfortunately, we have nothing similar to offer you."

"Well, gas is a moot point until we're inside the ship, anyway," Paul said. "What about the Trofts' ground tactics? You have any insights to offer?"

"They're about what you'd expect," Jin told him. "They use their heavy weapons freely in fending off attacks and supporting their troops, but they do still seem reluctant to engage in mass kill-ings, at least of civilians. The troops themselves sometimes have a tendency to bunch up, which helps protect the ones in back who then shoot over the shoulders of the ones in front. One way to take down that kind of formation is to first hit them with a sonic, then jump or run into the middle of the group and start taking them out with arcthrowers, antiarmors, or fists and feet."

"Is that last one theory, or did you actually do it?" Kemp asked.

"She actually did it," Zoshak said, an edge to his voice. "On top of one of those ships, in fact."

Kemp inclined his head. "I'm impressed," he said, and to Lorne's ears he sounded like he genuinely meant it.

"My grandfather was Jonny Moreau," Jin reminded him. "We've been fighting Trofts off and on for a long time."

"So it sounds like our best bet is to put the Djinn in near the front of any attack, where their glove lasers can nail the first line of soldiers," Paul said thoughtfully. "Supported by a full line of Cobras, of course."

"Maybe some of them up in trees where they can bring their antiarmors more fully into the fight," Jin added.

"Good idea," Paul said, nodding. "Possibly with some flash-bang or smoke grenades going off, too, if we can rig up something like that."

"None of which will make a shred of difference once they open up with those shipboard lasers," Harli said heavily. "We're going to need some way to either shield ourselves from them or else get them tied up shooting in some other direction."

"Why not just blind them?" Lorne suggested. "The cameras are right there on the wings along with the weapons. They ought to be easy enough to take out."

"How do you know about the cameras?" Matigo asked, frowning.

"I told you—I was in the ship's monitor room," Lorne said. "From the images I could see on the displays, it was pretty clear that's where the cameras were."

"I'll be damned," Harli murmured. "You were right, Broom. They didn't kill Buckley just to send a message. They really *were* reacting to a real, genuine threat."

"When was this?" Jin asked.

"When we were trying to evaluate their targeting capabilities by shooting at the weapons clusters," Paul said.

"You know, in that case we may just have a plan here," Harli said, the first hint of cautious excitement slipping into his voice. "We disable the cameras, and then hit them as hard and as fast as we can."

"I don't know," Matigo said doubtfully. "They're not going to just sit around being blind, you know. They have to have some backup system available."

"Of course they do," Harli said with a tight smile. "They've got those flying drones." He leveled a finger at Matigo. "Only the minute they open the hatches to send them out, we'll lob in a few bombs. Maybe some of the Qasamans' gas canisters, too."

"Won't do any good," Lorne told him. "The monitor room is part of the drone bay, but it's separated from that end by a big divider, glass or plastic, I'm not sure which. A bomb going off inside the hatch might damage a drone or two, but it'll be a pretty isolated effect. And gas won't do any good at all."

Harli swore under his breath. "But damn it all, the thing's a *hatch*," he growled. "A hatch they're going to just open up for us. There has to be a way to turn that to our advantage."

"Of course there is," Siraj said.

Everyone looked at him. "And?" Harli prompted.

"A bomb or a canister will not work," Siraj said calmly. "We must therefore send a man."

"That's a nice thought," Harli said. "Unfortunately, our spookers won't go that high, and it's too far for even Cobras to jump."

"Not so fast," Paul said, looking up at the trees towering over them. "What if we started the jump from halfway up a tree?"

"Too unstable a launch position," Matigo said. "Besides, any tree close enough to have a clear shot at the hatch will be visible from the ground. We'd never get high enough before we were spotted and shot."

"A tree is not necessary," Siraj said. "We—the Djinn—can throw him."

"You can *throw* him?" Harli echoed incredulously. "How strong are those suits of yours, anyway?"

"They're plenty strong," Jin said, frowning intently at Siraj. "But not *that* strong." She lifted a finger. "Unless their human payload does his full share of the work."

"Correct," Siraj said, nodding. "The two on the ground will throw the third upward. As he is being thrown, he will straighten his own leg servos to push off the others' hands."

"Adding in another pair of servos' worth of boost," Paul said, nodding slowly. "Tricky, but it might work."

"More than just tricky," Harli warned. "That sort of stunt takes serious timing to pull off, and as far as I know nothing like that is programmed into our nanocomputers."

"No, but we've got time to practice," Lorne said. "I assume we won't want to move until nightfall anyway."

"What, you saying *you're* going to go?" Harli shook his head. "Sorry. Matigo or Tracker can do it."

"Carsh Zoshak will do it," Siraj said firmly. "He has trained for such maneuvers."

"Good—I'll be happy to have the company," Lorne said. "But I'm the one who's actually been inside one of those things. Whoever else goes, I have to go, too."

Harli glared at him. Lorne returned his gaze calmly and evenly, waiting the other out, knowing he really didn't have any choice in the matter. "Speaking for ourselves," Siraj said into the taut silence, "we have fought alongside one son of Jasmine Moreau." He nodded gravely at Lorne. "We would welcome the chance to fight alongside another."

There was another brief silence. Then, Harli gave a noisy sigh. "Fine," he said. "Kemp, get some men together and take the Djinn and Broom somewhere where they can practice. Devole's Canyon, maybe. The rest of you, we've got a lot of work to do. And someone get Boulton back here—we'll want to pick his brain on all this."

"Right," Kemp said briskly, getting to his feet. "Broom? Djinn?"

The Qasamans stood up and followed Kemp as he headed back through the trees toward the spot where the Caelians had left their spookers. Bracing himself, Lorne stood up, too, and turned to his parents. "Gotta go," he said as casually as he could.

"We know," his mother said. Her face was pinched, and he could see a fresh layer of fear in her eyes. But she nevertheless forced a smile. "Be careful."

"I will." Lorne nodded at his father. "Keep an eye on her, okay? This place isn't exactly safe."

"I will," Paul promised, and Lorne could see him give Jin's hand an extra squeeze. "Have we mentioned lately how proud we are of you?"

"Thanks," Lorne said. "But it's not like I've got a choice. I'm a Moreau and a Broom. I've got a lot to live up to."

"You've already lived up to it," Paul assured him. "And you'll be adding even more to that legacy tonight." He gestured. "Now get going. You've got a busy day ahead of you."

Governor Uy shook his head. "They're insane," he murmured. "You realize that, don't you?"

"Probably," Jody agreed, keeping her voice down despite the fact that she'd long since destroyed all the Troft microphones in the governor's bedroom. "My family is, anyway. I can't speak for yours."

"Oh, no, Harli's as mad as they come," Uy assured her, a weak smile touching his lips. The smile disappeared into a fit of coughing, his face contorting in pain with each convulsion.

Jody winced, frustration simmering like bile in her stomach. The doctor had stabilized Uy as best she could. But it was going to require the equipment at the town's medical center to properly deal with his injury, and the center was within laser shot of the sentry ring the Trofts had thrown around their downed ship. Uy had flatly forbidden any of them to even approach the place, let alone try to get him there.

Jody didn't like it any better than any of the others did. But she could understand his reasoning. With the mood the Trofts were probably in right now, walking into their sights would not be a good idea.

But it meant that all she and Elssa could do was try to keep him comfortable, give him pain medication when he needed it, and watch him suffer.

And hope that Harli's plan actually worked.

The coughing ran its course, and for another minute Uy lay back against his pillows, refilling his lungs with short, panting breaths. "Well, mad or not, it sounds at least possible," he said when he had finally recovered enough to speak. "Did he say what he wanted me and the Stronghold Cobras to do?"

"I think his exact words were that you were to rest, recover, and stay out of the line of fire," Jody said. "He also sent his love."

"Yes," Uy murmured, and Jody again felt her stomach tightening as she saw in his face the recognition that this might be his son's last night alive.

Just as it might be the last night for Jody's own mother, father, and brother. Three of the four people she held most dear in all the universe could be taken from her before Caelian's next dawn.

At least they had preparations to help keep their minds off the danger ahead. Jody had nothing.

"Well, that's me," Uy said. "What about our Cobras? Does he want them to provide diversion or flanking or anything else?"

"I'm sure he'd love for them to do that," Jody said. "But since we're all stuck in our houses and can't properly communicate with them, he's decided he can't really give them any instructions."

"They won't need any," Uy said. "They'll know when to take action."

"Yes, he thought they might," Jody said. "I guess we'll just have to leave it to them to decide what to do."

"They'll do their job," Uy said. He paused, and Jody could see him making a conscious effort to push his fears away. "They'll be all right," he added quietly. "Your family will. They've survived Aventine's expansion regions, not to mention everything Caelian's been able to throw at them. They'll make it."

"I know," Jody said, forcing a smile she didn't feel. "So will Harli."

"I know," Uy said.

Jody took a deep breath. "Right," she said. "Meanwhile, it's time for your medicine."

She turned to the table beside the bed, blinking back tears. They were liars, of course. Both of them.

She just wasn't as good at it as he was.

CHAPTER NINETEEN

Night had fallen on Stronghold, and two hours of darkness had crawled slowly past. The sky was cloudless above the trees, the stars of Caelian blazing down on the town and the forest arrayed against it.

And all was finally ready.

Jin stood with Kemp and Matigo and the rest of the Cobras that Harli had dubbed the spearhead team, gazing through the trees at the ring of outward-facing floodlights the Trofts had set in front of their sentry line. Whether the lights were supposed to blind potential attackers or merely keep them from sneaking up on the ships unnoticed, Jin didn't know. All she knew was that she and her family were about to go into deadly danger.

Would any of them survive this night? There was no way to know. Even Jody, in the relative safety of Stronghold, wasn't immune to the fire and hell about to burst on the region like a volcanic eruption. Governor Uy's wounding earlier that morning clearly showed that much. By the time the Caelian wilderness was again dark and silent, everyone she held dear might be dead.

And there was nothing she could do to prevent it, except do her best.

She felt her throat tighten. She'd done her best back on Qasama, too. But that hadn't been enough to keep her eldest son Merrick from being critically wounded.

For a moment her thoughts flicked to him across the light-years. Was he recovering now under the care of the Qasaman doctors and their vast pharmacopoeia of healing drugs? Had he suffered a relapse, and was even now barely clinging to life?

Or had he already lost that final battle?

There was no way to know. There was also nothing to be gained by thinking that way. Nothing she could do, not even doing her best in the impending battle, could help him now. All she could do was hope they could win this battle, and that they could persuade some of the Caelian Cobras to return to Qasama with them. Only then would she finally be able to see Merrick again, and to learn what his fate had been.

Something brushed her arm, and she looked down to see a delicate insect with a wingspan the size of her fist nibbling away at her sleeve. With a grimace, she shook it off, encouraging its departure with a flick of her fingers. For the battle Harli had sent someone back to Aerie to get the Cobras' official operation suits, ceremoniously presented to them on graduation from the academy and stored away ever since their arrival on Caelian. The outfits were more comfortable and far better suited for combat than anything else available, but the fact that they were partially made of organic fibers meant that the Cobras were going to have to put up with all the annoyances of Caelian ecology while they fought against the Trofts.

It was only minor comfort to know that the Trofts were also having to deal with the floating spores and organics and the wide range of fauna ready, eager, and willing to come in for dinner.

"Gunners, ready," Harli's distant voice came in Jin's enhanced hearing, just barely audible over Caelian's night noises. "Fire in three; audios down."

Taking a deep breath, Jin keyed off her audios...and two heartbeats later the forest exploded with a crashing volley of shotgun fire. A heartbeat later came a second volley, this one slightly more spread out than the first, and then a third, this one easily discernable as six separate shots.

And as the thunder faded away, the night returned to relative silence. "Broom?" Kemp murmured from behind her.

Jin leaned a little to the side, giving herself a view of the standing warship's forward starboard wing through the tree branches. The berries Tracker and his team had just fired up into the weapons cluster showed up clearly on her telescopics, the sticky husks dotting the lasers and missile tubes, the viscous juice slowly and reluctantly moving across the metal.

"Here they come," someone murmured. "I can hear them."

Jin notched up her audios...and even as she caught the feathery rush of batting wings a swarm of mothlike insects burst into view. They flew to the weapons cluster, jostling each other as they vied for the sweet roseberry juice, creating a wide, dense cloud of wings and bodies in front of the Trofts' cameras.

A laser flared through the swarm, the intensity of the light jolting through Jin's enhanced vision like a slap across the face. Another shot blazed out, vaporizing another handful of moths, and then two more shots snapped out in rapid succession. Peripherally, Jin could see that all the other weapons clusters on the two ships were also firing blindly now as they attempted to drive the insects away.

But the moths' brains were far too small to realize that their fellows were being slaughtered by the bucketful, and they wouldn't have cared even if they had realized it. As each shot opened a pathway through the cloud it was instantly filled as moths on the periphery crowded in toward the alluring smell of the berries.

With a few handfuls of berries, and help from the relentless Caelian ecology, the Trofts inside the ship were now blind.

Jin took a deep breath. "Get ready," she said. "It won't be long now."

"There!" Jody said, jabbing a finger at the warship wings as she handed Uy's night binoculars to Freylan. "You can see the fluffers clouding in."

"Yeah, I see them," Freylan confirmed, pressing the binoculars to his eyes. "They must have used roseberries—there's nothing else that drives those things that crazy."

"Way to go, Geoff," Jody murmured, wincing as the ships' lasers suddenly flashed to life, blazing through the swarming insects. If the Trofts were able to kill enough of the fluffers or just drive them away...

Freylan snorted. "Like *that's* going to do any good," he said contemptuously. He handed the binoculars back to Jody and reached to the table beside them for the flare pistol Uy had found in his emergency kit. "Let me know when."

Jody nodded, her throat tight as she watched the Troft lasers still trying to drive the fluffers away. Any minute now...

Twenty meters up his assigned tree, holding tightly to the branches, Paul watched the Trofts' useless light show as they tried to drive the moths away from their monitor cameras. Any minute now...

"Perimeter team: fire," Harli's voice drifted over the mad fluttering of insect wings.

And all around the area, the ground and trees came alive with Cobra antiarmor laser fire.

Paul was right in there with them, pressing his left leg close to the tree trunk as he targeted and blasted the four floodlights of the Troft perimeter nearest his position. He had finished knocking out the last of them when a flurry of return fire slammed into his tree, blowing splinters and chunks of charred wood across his sight.

Instantly, he swung his leg back behind the trunk and let go his grip, dropping below the hail of laser fire to the next set of handholds he'd prepared. Glancing around the trunk, he targeted three of the Troft soldiers who were firing at his tree and again swung his leg around into position. Three quick shots, and then he pulled the leg back and dropped again. This time he was in position and scouting his next target when the return fire began hammering at the spot he'd just vacated.

Again he peered around the tree, ignoring the splinters raining down as he took stock of the situation. The duck-shoot phase, as Harli had dubbed it, was unfortunately over. The remaining ground troops were abandoning their exposed positions behind the ring of shattered floodlights and were scurrying as fast as they could for the cover of the armored trucks. The trucks themselves were rolling forward, coming to their troops' support—

There was a brilliant triple flash, and one entire side of the tree just above Paul vaporized as one of the trucks fired a cluster shot into the wood. Grimacing, Paul dropped another three meters, then shoved himself sideways off his branches and leaped to the next tree over.

Just in time. The truck's commander had decided Paul's first tree was definitely serving as enemy cover and was methodically firing shot after shot into it with the clear intent of bringing it down.

From somewhere to Paul's left another shotgun blast thundered across the crackling of wood and the hissing of laser fire. Having blinded the warships, the gunners were now trying to do the same to the trucks by sending roseberries into their windshields.

Only this time the shotguns' blasts were followed by the multiple crackle of small but deadly explosions.

Paul winced. Jin and the Qasamans had warned them about the small, self-homing antipersonnel missiles the Trofts had used against riflemen in Sollas, but he'd hoped that this group of Trofts had assumed they would be facing only Cobras and had therefore not bothered to deploy that particular weapon. Unfortunately, it was clear now that they had, and he could only hope the gunners were following Harli's orders to get clear of their positions the second they fired.

He looked around the tree again, keying in his opticals and studying the ground soldiers carefully. Most were carrying the standard hand-and-a-half laser rifles, but crouched beside one of the trucks he could see a soldier holding something considerably bigger. Flicking a target lock onto the weapon, Paul curved his leg around the tree and fired.

And instantly dropped down again, this time all the way to the ground, as another pair of trucks fired a withering hail of laser fire at him. Still, even as the tree shattered above him, he was able to take some satisfaction in the distant sound of a muffled explosion. One antipersonnel missile launcher, apparently, eliminated.

Only now he had some serious problems of his own. Someone had tagged this tree as being the hiding place of the Cobra who'd taken out their missile-tube operator, and that someone seemed to be taking it personally. Even as Paul huddled down behind the trunk, trying to squeeze himself into the smallest possible target, he could hear and feel the tree being literally taken apart above him. And not just the tree—the rapid fire was flanking the trunk on both sides, preventing him from going either direction. If the Trofts kept this up, sooner or later they would get him.

"Broom!" a voice called urgently from above and to his right.

Paul looked up. One of the Caelian Cobras was clinging to a tree about ten meters away, looking across at him. "Back it up ten meters," the Cobra called, jerking his head that direction. Shifting his attention back toward the battle line, he lifted his left leg and began some rapid fire of his own.

Paul tensed, waiting for the inevitable burst of killing enemy fire. But even as the laser blasts against his own tree faltered and started to shift to this new target, the Cobra hunched up, pressed his right leg and hand against the tree trunk, and shoved himself violently backwards away from the tree. As he soared through the branches he spun halfway around, turning a full hundred eighty degrees just as he reached another tree four meters behind him. He struck it off-center, catching the trunk with his right hand and pivoting around that grip to swing around to safety behind it. He took a second to settle himself, then repeated the hunch-and-shove maneuver, ending up behind a tree three meters farther back. "Broom!" he snapped.

With a start, Paul realized that he was still behind his smashed tree, and that the Trofts had shifted their attack over to the tree where the other Cobra had been twenty seconds earlier. Staying low, he backed away from his own tree, retreating to the one ten meters back that he'd been directed to.

The other Cobra was already there, crouched behind the tree and some associated bushes, when Paul slipped around to safety on the other side. "Thanks," he murmured.

"No problem," the other said. "You okay?"

Quickly, Paul took inventory. His leg was throbbing with a couple of minor burns, and there were probably a dozen wood splinters digging through his clothing in various places. Nothing serious.

"Okay enough to get back in the game," he told the other. "We might want to try a different neighborhood, though."

"There's an empty spot over there," the Cobra said grimly, pointing to their left. "I'm pretty sure Yates and Colchak are both down."

Paul grimaced. "Okay," he said. "I'll take point."

They had made it about five meters when once again Paul heard Harli's voice lift above the noise of battle. "Kangaroos—go!"

"Kangaroos—"

Even before Harli finished giving the order, Zoshak was off, sprinting along the hardened, leaf-free path Lorne and the Qasamans had painstakingly cleared during the hour before sundown.

Lorne watched him go, his hands feeling unnaturally sweaty as he shifted his attention back and forth between Zoshak and the other two Djinn standing ready at the far end of the path. He'd learned the maneuver well enough, at least according to them, and in fact had nailed their last five practice throws perfectly.

But that had been out in the Caelian forest, in the middle of the afternoon and far removed from any Trofts with lasers. If this jump turned out to be the one Lorne botched, he was going to come tumbling down into the middle of an armed camp.

But there was no time to worry about that now. Zoshak reached the other two Qasamans and leaped up and forward toward them. Siraj and Khatir caught his feet in their gloved hands and hurled him upward and forward through the few light branches still between him and the clear zone. He arched upward across the night sky, heading toward the drone hatchway that was even now folding down from the side of the ship.

And now it was Lorne's turn.

He took off down the path, watching his footing, watching the two waiting Qasamans, adjusting his stride, trying to remember everything he'd learned, trying to forget the armed Trofts he would be flying helplessly over. He reached the jump-off point and leaped, tucking himself and bending his knees as he flew toward them. The Qasamans caught his feet, and as they shoved him up he also shoved himself downward with the full strength of his leg servos.

And with a brief slapping of branches across his face he found himself soaring high over the clear zone.

Over the battlefield.

It was like nothing Lorne had ever seen before, and even the brief glimpse was enough to turn his stomach. The blazing sizzle of blue laser light was everywhere, brilliant eye-hurting flashes from the armored trucks' swivel guns, somewhat dimmer ones from the Cobras lurking among the trees. The sound of splintering wood and shattered rock filled the night air, punctuated by gunshots, small explosions, and the grunts and screams of the injured and dying. Scattered across the clear zone, briefly lit by every laser flash that shot past, were the unmoving bodies of dead Trofts.

Resolutely, he tore his eyes away from the carnage, shifting them back to the ship now rushing toward him. Ahead, Zoshak finished his own journey by slamming into the hullmetal just above the drone hatch, the combat suit servos in his outstretched arms and legs absorbing the impact. Smoothly, almost gracefully, he slid neatly down the hull and disappeared through the opening.

It was only then that Lorne realized to his horror that his own jump was going to be short.

He tensed, keying his opticals for a quick range check. But there was no mistake. Instead of hitting the opening, or even hitting the hull above it as Zoshak had just done, he was going to hit below the open hatch.

There was only one chance. Stretching his arms as far as he could above his head, he curled his fingers into hooks and locked the servos into place.

He made it, but just barely. His fingers caught the edge of the hatch, his legs swinging around to slam shins-first against the hull below.

For a second the vibration of the impact threatened to slide the hooked fingers loose and send him tumbling to the ground below. He tried to get his thumbs up underneath, but the metal was too thick for them to reach. In desperation, he pulled himself up and jammed the top of his head against the underside of the hatch, wedging his fingers tightly in place and finally stopping their drift toward the edge. He gave himself another second to dampen out the motion, then reset his grip and pulled himself up onto the hatch, catching a hint of reflected laser light from inside as he rolled onto his side and slid sideways through the opening. Bouncing off the drone that had been moving up toward the opening when it was so rudely interrupted, he tumbled onto the bay deck.

To find himself in the middle of yet another battle zone.

Fortunately, so far the battle was only going one direction. Crouched on the deck beside a tall rack of drones, Zoshak was firing a barrage from his glove lasers, shooting through the glass partition at the Troft techs scrambling madly to get off their couches and into cover behind the consoles. He'd already nailed one of the aliens, and as Lorne scrambled back to his feet another one twitched and toppled limply to the ground.

"No visor blackening here," Zoshak called, his voice grimly pleased as he continued to fire.

"No need for it inside," Lorne called back, eyeing the tiny slagged holes in the glass where the Djinni's lasers had punched through the barrier. "Watch your fire—I'm going to see if I can get us through it."

He was halfway to the barrier, wincing a little as Zoshak's fire shot past him on both sides, when the door at the far end of the monitor room swung open and a half-dozen armored Troft soldiers appeared, charging through the doorway in two-by-two formation. Their lasers swiveled around as they spotted the intruders beyond the glass—

"Cover!" Lorne shouted back over his shoulder. He leaped up into the air, his left leg swinging around in a quick arc as he raked the soldiers with laser fire.

The blast caught the first two across their faceplates, and as their shots sizzled through the barrier and burned past Lorne's head they jerked back and fell. But as Lorne finished his sweep and swung his leg back to trace another arc across the ones next in line he realized that he'd made a fatal mistake. This second, lower sweep of his laser was catching the Trofts across their chests instead of their faceplates, and with the small but significant attenuation created by the glass he was shooting through even his antiarmor laser wasn't quite powerful enough for quick-kill shots through the aliens' armor.

And as the aliens staggered back, their torso armor spraying out smoke and bits of metal and ceramic, their lasers were now tracking toward him.

Desperately, he tried to bring his laser around for another pass. But the momentum was going the wrong way, and he was still flying through the air with no way to take cover. When those lasers finally lined up on him, he knew, he would be dead.

And then suddenly Zoshak was leaping across Lorne's line of sight, flying forward in a sideways arc like a Cobra executing the kind of wall jump Lorne had used to get off the rooftops back in Capitalia. The Djinni's feet hit the barrier with a resonating thud.

And to Lorne's astonishment, a jagged oval of glass popped out of the barrier and tumbled into the monitor room. "Take them!" Zoshak snapped, dropping flat on the deck out of Lorne's line of fire.

And with a section of the barrier out of the way, Lorne's laser *was* now capable of punching through the aliens' armor with a single shot.

The four remaining soldiers knew it, too. They were already on the move, giving up their chance to catch Lorne with a killing shot as they dove for cover behind the center console.

But Lorne's lasers weren't a Cobra's only weapons. Even as Lorne landed again on the deck, he raised his right hand, little finger pointed forward, and fired his arcthrower. With an ear-splitting thunderclap the lightning bolt flashed through the hole in the barrier and into the center console.

And with a thunderclap almost as loud as that of the arcthrower itself, the delicate electronics and control systems inside flash-vaporized, shattering the displays and blowing the cabinet apart.

The soldiers pressed against it never even had a chance. The blast slammed them backwards, staggering them once more out into the open.

They were once again trying to bring their weapons to bear when Lorne's antiarmor laser ended the battle for good.

"Well done," Zoshak said, jumping back to his feet.

"You, too," Lorne said, eyeing the hole in the glass. It was way too small to get through, which meant they were either going to have to see if their sonics could shatter it or else break through it with brute strength. Gingerly, he got a grip on one edge.

And watched, wide-eyed, as Zoshak casually kicked the area directly beneath the hole, breaking it free and leaving an opening that they *could* get through. "After you," the Djinni said, gesturing.

"How did you *do* that?" Lorne asked as he ducked down and slipped gingerly through into the monitor section.

"It was your laser shot," Zoshak said, sounding surprised that Lorne would even have to ask. "I noticed that as you shot at the Trofts you were also carving a circle in the glass, weakening it. I simply supplied the force necessary to break it free."

Lorne felt his cheeks warming. He'd noticed the effect Zoshak's own lasers were having on the glass, but the fact that he was doing exactly the same thing had missed him completely. "And that?" he asked, gesturing at the lower section.

"I used my glove lasers to weaken it while you were dealing with the soldiers," Zoshak said. "To the stairway?"

"To the stairway," Lorne confirmed. He crossed the room, stepping gingerly over the smoldering alien corpses, and eased his head out the door.

For the moment, the corridor was deserted. But he doubted the Trofts would leave it that way for very long. The stairway to the right was marginally closer; slipping outside, he headed that direction. If they could get down the stairway to the guardroom at the bottom, Zoshak should be able to lob one of his gas canisters in and take out the whole squad without any further fuss or bother. He reached the door and opened it a crack.

And flung it wide open as he caught a glimpse of two Troft soldiers a meter away charging across the landing toward him.

He gave them a quick burst from his sonic as he leaped forward, and as they staggered back he grabbed their lasers and wrenched the weapons away from them. "Above!" Zoshak shouted.

Lorne had just enough time to look up and see the crowd of

armored figures clattering down the grillwork stairway toward him before Zoshak grabbed his arm and yanked hard, throwing him back through the door into the corridor. "Wait here!" the Qasaman shouted.

He was pulling one of the gas canisters from his belt as he grabbed the edge of the door and slammed it shut in Lorne's face.

"Damn!" Lorne snarled. Zoshak was alone in there, even with that fancy Qasaman gas...

But it was too late to argue the point. Even if he thought he could hold his breath long enough to help Zoshak take out all those Trofts, opening the door now would let the gas dissipate out here into the corridor. Without that edge, taking on that number of enemy soldiers would probably get them both killed.

But if Zoshak thought Lorne was just going to stand here waiting for permission to rejoin the fight, he was badly mistaken. Throwing a final glare at the door, sending up a quick prayer for the Qasaman's safety, he turned and headed back toward the monitor room.

The lasers were still flashing, and the cold feeling that her younger son was dead was starting to settle into Jin's heart, when the standing warship's portside door abruptly swung open. "There!" she called loudly. "The door's open! It's open!" She started to stand up for a better look.

And was yanked back down again. "Easy," Kemp murmured. "I'm sure Harli heard you just fine. Don't make yourself a target, too."

Jin winced. He was right, of course.

But hunched close to the ground this way, she didn't have a clear view of that open door. There was no way to see if Lorne and Zoshak were both in there waiting for the spearhead team.

Or whether it was only Zoshak who was still alive.

"Damn," one of the other Cobras muttered.

Jin's heart skipped a beat. "What is it?"

"They've spotted the open door," the Cobra said tensely. "They're heading back toward it."

Jin stood straight up, shaking off Kemp's hand on her arm. Three groups of Troft soldiers were on the move, abandoning the relative safety of the armored trucks and running toward the warship, pouring laser fire through the open doorway as they went.

The other Cobras had spotted the sudden activity, too. All around Jin, the blue laser flashes intensified, their focus shifting from the trucks and the soldiers still huddled beside them to the groups converging on the open door.

But the Trofts were too far away for good shots, and many of the Cobras' lines of sight were blocked by the trucks, and the trucks themselves were stepping up their own fire in reply.

And as Jin watched helplessly, she saw that the desperate counterattack would fail. The Trofts would make it back to the ship, or enough of them would.

And whoever was waiting by the door, if her son was still alive, he wouldn't be alive much longer.

"It's open!" Freylan announced excitedly. "They did it. They got the ship's door open."

"I see," Jody said, a hard lump in her throat as she peered across the town. Yes, Lorne and the Qasaman who'd pulled off that human birdman stunt had indeed done it, fighting their way down to the bow door and getting it open.

But unless the Cobra assault force could get across the battlefield to it, the whole thing would be for nothing. And there were still a lot of soldiers, trucks, and gunfire between the edge of the forest and the warship.

And then, she saw something that froze her heart. Three groups of Troft soldiers had left the battle line and were charging back toward the open door, firing at it as accurately as they could while still running at top speed. "Freylan?" she asked.

"I see them," he said grimly. "Damn it all—I was hoping they wouldn't spot it so quickly."

"Can the Cobras out there stop them?"

"I don't know," Freylan said, sweeping the edge of the forest slowly with the binoculars. "I don't think so."

Jody took a deep breath. "In that case," she said, "it's time."

Picking up the flare pistol from her lap, she pointed it out the window in the direction of the Troft ship and fired.

The flare ignited, its red glow barely even registering amid the stuttering laser fire. Jody watched the running Trofts, waiting for something to happen.

But nothing did. Down in the town part of the invaders' sentry ring, one of the Trofts took a shot at the flare, the beam slicing through the sky beside it but missing both the parachute and the flare itself. From somewhere below came a high-pitched bellow, like a human voice trying to imitate the roar of a screech tiger.

And suddenly, the town exploded with laser fire. Some of it came from the houses and buildings, targeting the ring of Trofts inside the wall. Another group came from positions on top of the wall itself, that group cutting across the aliens racing toward the open warship door.

The Stronghold Cobras had joined the battle.

CHAPTER TWENTY

The distant screech echoed across the battlefield, and Paul had just enough time to wonder what it was when a fresh barrage of laser fire exploded from the top of Stronghold's wall.

And as he watched from his new treetop firing post he saw the Trofts racing for the warship stagger and twitch and fall.

One of the other Cobras nearby gave a war whoop. "Way to *roll*, Shingas," he called even as he sent another pair of laser bolts at the nearest Troft truck. The truck replied by swiveling its gun toward him and firing back.

Targeting the gun barrel, Paul fired a pair of shots of his own. The trucks were still holding up well against the Cobras' onslaught, but someone in Paul's group of fighters had come up with the idea that if they could hit the gun barrels hard enough and often enough the metal might warp enough to ruin the lasers' alignment and render them useless.

So far the plan didn't seem to have yielded much in the way of results. But Paul had nothing better to offer. The truck was still firing at the other Cobra, shredding the other's tree, its gun barrel still presenting a perfect target to Paul's own position. Targeting it again, he sent two more bolts into the metal.

And gasped as an unexpected shot from somewhere else blazed across his sight and sliced a line of pain across his exposed left leg.

He didn't remember falling from his perch, but what seemed like an instant later he found himself sprawled on the ground at the base of the tree, his eyes squeezed shut against a rain of charred wood and smoking branches, his entire leg throbbing. He groped a shaking hand toward it—

"Don't touch," a gruff voice said from above him.

Paul opened his eyes to slits. One of the other Cobras was kneeling over him, his body partially blocking the rain of debris, his face set in stone as he dug through his medical pack. "Never even saw it," Paul heard himself murmur, the small part of his brain that was still functioning amid the agony vaguely surprised at how calm his voice sounded.

"They had a backup truck all set," the Cobra said grimly. "Sent the first one out as bait, and then tried picking us off when we shot at it."

"And I fell for it." Fell for the trick, then fell out of the tree. Somehow, that struck him as incredibly funny. "How bad is it?"

"Bad enough," the Cobra said. "I've given you something for the pain and infection, but we're going to have to wrap it."

Paul nodded. The pain was starting to fade away, a strange light-headedness moving in like a fogbank to take its place. "I'll do it," he said. "They need you out there." He reached to his throbbing leg.

To find that one entire side of it was missing. The Troft laser blast had burned out a line of skin and muscle and tendon that reached nearly all the way down to the ceramic-laminated bones.

"Get *away* from that," the Cobra ordered, slapping Paul's hand away from the injury. "Doesn't matter anyway. We're dead—we're all dead."

"No, we're not," Paul insisted through the gathering haze. "We can still do this."

"How?" the other demanded. "We've got nothing that can stop those damn trucks."

And as if on deliberate cue, a sudden thundering crash came from beyond the line of trees. "What the—?" the Cobra said, hopping to his feet and staring through the trees into the clear zone. Clenching his teeth, ignoring the remnants of pain in his leg, Paul forced himself up on his elbows and craned his neck to see over the low bushes in front of him.

One of the Troft trucks, either the one he'd been shooting at or the one that had shot at him, was spread out on the ground, its wheels splayed outward, its swivel gun bent uselessly, its entire roof caved in. Mashed across the crushed roof, having clearly descended at a very high rate of speed, was a mass of wrecked and unrecognizable machinery.

And then, even through the haze of the drug, Paul got it. Lifting his eyes, he peered up at the warship and the still-open drone hatch.

Just in time to see another drone float carefully out of the opening. It drifted away from the ship and moved slowly across the battlefield as if taking stock of the situation. Then, turning its nose downward, it dove at full speed toward the ground and slammed squarely into the top of a truck a hundred meters away.

And despite the pain and the knowledge that he would never walk properly again, Paul smiled. "What was that," he said to the other Cobra, "about having nothing that can stop the damn trucks?"

The last image on Lorne's monitor was that of an armored truck's roof rushing toward him. Then, abruptly, the monitor scrambled and went dark. A second later, through the hatch opening, he heard the distant boom of another Troft vehicle biting the dust.

Two trucks down. No idea, actually, of how many more to go.

But then, he didn't have to take out *all* of them. The eagle's-eye look he'd gotten of the battlefield with that second drone had shown that there were only three of the vehicles in position to attack the spearhead force preparing to cross the clear zone to the door Zoshak had opened for them. Those three—those two, now, actually—were the only ones he absolutely had to neutralize.

Assuming, of course, that Zoshak had in fact managed to get the door open. Both of Lorne's drones had necessarily had to start their attacks from a serious height, and he hadn't yet had a chance to float one of them lower to check out the door in person. But he'd seen a sample of Zoshak's work, and he had no reason to believe the Qasaman hadn't fully completed his job.

Time for Lorne to do likewise.

The display winked: the third drone was ready to launch. Keying over the control stick, Lorne activated the grav lifts and released the drone's rack restraints. Sooner or later, he knew, the Trofts still inside the ship with him would tumble to what he was doing and send someone in here to stop him.

Hopefully, he would finish clearing the way for his mother and her team before that happened.

One guard truck down. Two more to go. Concentrating on not banging the drone against the bay wall, he maneuvered the slender machine up and out through the hatchway.

Jin watched as a drone came for the third and final truck blocking their path to the ship. The Trofts inside the vehicle had figured out what was happening and were taking frantic steps to avoid it. The soldiers who'd earlier taken refuge inside it came boiling out through the rear doors, firing their lasers skyward as Lorne or Zoshak or whoever buzzed the drone high above their heads. The truck itself, meanwhile, had abandoned its post and was driving around in a sort of high-speed evasive course which, considering the situation, was nearly as useless as it was ludicrous.

But the soldiers weren't trained for that kind of straight-up shooting, and were moreover now within range of the Cobras in both the woods and the town. Even as they jerked and died the drone did its now familiar swan dive straight down into the desperately running truck. There was one final teeth-tingling grinding of metal on metal, and the truck slammed to a halt.

And with the final barrier down, the way was now open.

"That's it," Kemp snapped. "Let's go." He lunged up out of cover and sprinted at full speed across the clear zone toward the open warship door.

Jin had intended to be right behind him. But even as she straightened and started to run, she found herself in fourth place among the other twelve Cobras.

Mentally, she shook her head. She really *was* getting old.

And yet, even as she tried to emulate Kemp's evasive, broken-vector running style, she felt a surge of exhilaration run through her. *This is how it should have been on her first trip to Qasama: not a lone Cobra facing danger, but a whole team of them working together to defeat an enemy. This was what she'd volunteered to become all those years ago. This, ultimately, was what she'd been created to do.*

There was a close-in flash of laser light, and the Cobra running beside her gave a gasping choke and sprawled facefirst onto the ground.

Jin redoubled her pace, the adrenaline still pumping through her veins but the budding thrill of battle abruptly gone like dust in the wind. Ahead, Kemp had reached the warship door, and without even pausing to check for lurking danger he sprinted inside. Jin watched closely as the other Cobras ahead of her followed, waiting tensely for the sudden volley of laser fire from inside that would mean the open door had been a trap.

But no such enemy fire came. She reached the door, and with a final leaping step was temporarily safe. "Watch it," someone warned.

Jin keyed in her opticals, her own eyes still recovering from the dazzling display of laser fire outside. She was in a narrow room about seven meters long and three wide, with long benches along both sides and weapons racks on the walls above them, some of the clips still holding lasers and other weapons. The half-dozen Trofts who had apparently been manning the place were sprawled on the deck, dead or unconscious, Jin didn't know which. As she quickly picked her way through the bodies, she saw Zoshak and Kemp at the far end of the room, conversing in low voices beside a half-open door with a stairway visible beyond it.

"Do we seal up?" someone called from behind Jin, and she turned to see that the last member of their team had joined them inside.

Or rather, the last surviving member of the team. Four of the original thirteen, she saw, were no longer with them.

"No, leave it open," Kemp told him. "Some of the others might get a chance to join us. You stay here and watch—if the Trofts make a try for it instead, seal it up."

"The control box is on the wall to the right of the door," Zoshak added, pointing. "The red control should seal the door."

"The rest of you, we're heading up," Kemp said. "There are"—he grimaced as his eyes flicked over the group—"nine of us, so we'll run groups of three. Spread out, kill any Troft you run into—"

"Unless he surrenders," Jin put in. "We might want some of them kept alive for questioning."

"Unless he surrenders," Kemp confirmed, not looking especially happy about it but apparently accepting her logic. "Jasmine, Zoshak, you're with me. We'll take the top deck—the rest of you, group up and each take one of the lower decks."

"What about Lorne?" Jin asked.

"From the way those drones were hawk-diving out of the sky out there, I'd guess he's in the drone control room," Kemp said. "That was Deck Four, Zoshak?"

"Yes, sixth door on the left," Zoshak confirmed. "Shall we go to assist him?"

"No, I want us to go find that upper hatch, the one Jasmine says she got a look into on Qasama," Kemp said. "Olwen, take two men up to Deck Four—give Lorne some backup. And everyone keep an eye out for anything that might be a fire-control room. If we can get control of those wing-mounted weapons, we'll be able to end this thing right here and now."

After the firestorm of laser bolts they'd had to fight through outside the ship, Jin had expected to face much the same level of resistance inside. To her surprise, not only was the stairway deserted, but so was the Deck One corridor when they arrived there a cautious minute later. "Where is everyone?" she murmured.

"Probably in there," Kemp said, nodding at the rows of closed doors lining the corridor. "I'm betting they started out the evening with most of their actual soldiers outside, and that Zoshak and Lorne have already taken care of a lot of the ones that weren't. Now that a whole bunch of us are in here, too, their only chance is to go to ground."

"This is the deck we want," Zoshak said firmly. "This is where all the important command centers are located."

"How do you know?" Kemp asked, frowning as he cocked his head to the side. "I don't hear anything."

"The room identification plaques," Zoshak said, stepping to the nearest door and pointing to a small discolored patch beside the nearest door. "They have all been removed." He tried the handle. "And the doors themselves are of course locked."

"Good call, Carsh Zoshak," Jin said approvingly. "So. Door to door?"

"Door to door," Kemp confirmed. "But let's see first if we can figure out which ones have actual Trofts cowering behind them. I'll take left; you take right."

Jin nodded and stepped to the nearest door on the right. Pressing her ear against it, she keyed in her audio enhancers.

The faint background noises of the ship leaped suddenly into sharp focus. Consciously, she pushed aside the various generator, pump, and relay noises and tried to sort out the sounds of breathing, conversation, or flapping radiator membranes.

Nothing. Keying down her audios, she headed down the corridor toward the next door in line.

She had made it halfway when a sudden new sound cut through the background noise: a sharp, multiple snapping noise, coming from at least two directions. "Kemp?" she whispered.

"I hear them," Kemp said grimly. "Damn."

"What is it?" Zoshak demanded.

"High-energy capacitors discharging," Kemp told him. "Sounds like they've got the big lasers going again. The fluffers must have finished off the roseberries and cleared out."

And with the big weapons' targeting systems clear, the Cobras in both the town and the forest were now in deadly danger. "We have to shut them down," she said.

"No argument." Kemp waved a hand down the corridor. "Any guesses as to where they're firing them from?"

"No, but you and Carsh Zoshak are going to find out," Jin said, peering down the corridor. Midway to the other end was another corridor that bisected theirs. At the aft end of that corridor, if she was visualizing things correctly, would be the ready room attached to the topside hatch. "I'll go on top and see what I can do about them from outside."

"What?" Kemp demanded. "Wait a minute—"

"If you get control of the weapons, fire a burst high over the forest or town," Jin called over her shoulder as she ran toward the corridor. "Good luck, and watch yourselves."

The cross-corridor, thankfully, was also deserted. Jin headed aft, keeping her audios high enough to hear incautious footsteps. The corridor ended in yet another unmarked door; bracing herself, Jin tried the handle.

It was unlocked. Readying her sonic, she pushed it open a crack and looked inside.

The room was small and as deserted as the corridors. On its walls were more of the weapons racks she'd seen in the guard-room downstairs, except that these racks were all empty. Along with removing the room ID plaques, the techs up here had also taken the time to raid the local armory before locking themselves in their rooms.

In the center of the ceiling, at the top of a narrow stairway, was the hatch.

Seconds later she was up on top of the hull crest, the wind whipping across her face and tugging at her green-flecked operation suit, her eyes and ears filling once again with the light and noise of the battle still raging on far below.

And as she stood there, getting her bearings, one of the wing lasers flared, flashing brilliance across the landscape as it blazed death and destruction somewhere inside the forest.

She took a deep breath. Kemp and Zoshak might find the weapons control room in time. Having located it, they might figure out how to break in and fight their way through the Trofts inside without getting themselves killed.

But the odds were that they wouldn't. Not until a lot more Cobras out there had died.

Which meant it was up to her. Somehow, she had to come up with a way to disable the weapons from up here.

And she'd better come up with it fast.

Jody's experience with battles up to now had consisted of detailed descriptions in books, many of them accompanied by neat lines and arrows. Compared to that, the real-life battle raging across the town and clear zone around her was utter chaos.

Nevertheless, as near as she could tell, it had looked like the Cobras were going to pull it off. Certainly once her mother's group made it inside the warship, she had dared to hope that it was almost over.

But that was before the big wing-mounted lasers had unexpectedly sprung to life. Now, watching helplessly as the weapons blazed death and destruction across the human forces, slicing through trees and houses, her hopes were suddenly hanging by a thread.

"They'll make it," Freylan said, his hands gripping the binoculars tightly as he pressed them to his face. He'd taken over binocular duty a few minutes ago, when the violence and death had unexpectedly hit Jody's gag reflex and she couldn't bear to watch it close-up anymore. "They're probably just having to fight their way through a few leftover soldiers. They'll make it, and they'll get those lasers shut down."

"I know," Jody murmured. But she knew no such thing, and neither did he. The Trofts wouldn't have just a few leftover soldiers in there—the ones inside the ship would undoubtedly be their best. That was certainly how Jody would have arranged things, anyway. There was no guarantee that the Cobras would be able to fight through those soldiers and find their way to the weapons control room. Certainly not without taking serious casualties.

And Jody's mother was a fifty-two-year-old Cobra with arthritis and a bad knee. If any of the attack team was going to die, it would probably be her.

"Whoa!" Freylan said suddenly, leaning toward the window. "What the . . . ? Jody, your mother's up on top of the ship!"

"What?" Jody snatched the binoculars from him and pressed them to her eyes. To her utter amazement, she found that he was right.

Her first reaction was a sigh of relief that Jin hadn't been killed fighting her way inside. But midway through the sigh, the realization of what her mother was doing up there suddenly flooded in on her. "Oh, no," she breathed. Shoving the binoculars back into Freylan's hands, she dashed toward the living room doorway, banging her knee against the couch in her haste. "Get away from the window," she snapped.

"What are you doing?" Freylan asked as he hastily climbed out of his chair and pressed himself against the wall.

"I have to let Dad know," she said, finding the light switch. "She's going to try to knock out the lasers from up there."

"By *herself*?"

"You see anyone else up there?" Jody shot back, her brain working furiously to compose a message she could send quickly. "Close your eyes or lose your night vision."

Squeezing her own eyes tightly shut, she began flipping the switch, on-off, on-off in Dida code. *Mom on top of ship—trying for lasers. Assist?*

"Tell him to contact Lorne," Freylan said suddenly. "If he hasn't used up all those drones yet, maybe he can throw some of them into the weapons clusters."

Jody nodded. "Right."

It was only as she was starting her third repeat of the message that it occurred to her that there might no longer be anyone out there capable of reading it.

"Broom? *Broom!*"

With a start, Paul snapped back to consciousness. A foggy, dreamy sort of consciousness, but consciousness just the same. "What is it?" he asked, his voice sounding oddly slurred.

"We got a message," the Cobra said as he grabbed Paul's chest under his arms and pulled him up into a sitting position. "There— the governor's residence."

"I see it," Paul said, blinking a couple of times to clear his vision and his brain. *Dit dah dah dah dit dah dit dit . . .*

"Well?"

"She says Jin's on top of the warship," Paul said, struggling to push himself higher. "I need to tell Lorne to fly his drones into the clusters." He took a deep breath.

And broke into a sudden fit of coughing.

"S'okay," the other Cobra said, lowering him to the ground again. "I got it."

He got Paul settled, then stood upright behind one of the trees and filled his lungs. "Lorne Broom," he bellowed. "Cobra skipper nest! Drones hoverbird feeding! Move it!"

"What was that?" one of the Cobras, a rough-looking man named Olwen, said suddenly.

"What was what?" Lorne asked, staring at his displays with a sinking heart as he waited for the ready light to come on. There were still two of those armored trucks out there, not counting whatever was still operational inside Stronghold, and he'd figured on taking them out with his last two drones.

Only now the game had suddenly changed. From the intensity of the laser fire outside, it was clear that the Trofts had the ship's main weapons clusters operational again.

"I heard someone call your name," Olwen said, ducking though the hole in the barrier and hurrying toward the open drone hatch. "Yes," he added, raising his voice as he crooked his ear toward the open drone hatch. "He's saying 'Lorne Broom . . . Cobra skipper nest . . . drones hoverbird feeding . . . move it.'"

Lorne stared at him. *"What?"*

"Skipper nests are at the very tops of trees," one of the other Cobras said. "Sounds like Kemp or one of the others made it up on top of the ship."

"And hoverbirds come up underneath hanging flowers to feed," the other Cobra added.

"I'm guessing that means they want you to ram the drones into the weapons clusters," Olwen concluded.

"Right," Lorne said, grimacing. Great plan.

Only there were four weapons clusters, and he only had two drones.

But he could at least take down two of them. "Let's give it a try," he said. "Olwen, stand clear."

Olwen nodded and took a couple of steps to the side. The forward starboard cluster first, Lorne decided as he popped the second-to-last drone from its rack and sent it drifting toward the hatchway. Not only was that the closest group, it was also the one with the widest field of fire into the area where most of Harli's

Cobras were positioned. Resettling his grip on the control stick, he flew the drone past Olwen and out through the opening.

He'd gotten it maybe four meters outside the ship when the starboard lasers flared, and the indicators went crazy as the drone was shattered to scrap. The monitor blanked, the indicators went solid red, and even from the far side of the barrier Lorne had no difficulty hearing its remains crash to the ground.

"Well, *damn* it," one of the other Cobras muttered.

"Yeah," Lorne said. There were still four weapons clusters, and he only had one drone left. "Any ideas?"

There was a moment of silence. Then, through the barrier he heard Olwen snort. "Matter of fact, yeah, maybe I do," the Cobra said. "How good are you with that control stick?"

Lorne shrugged. "I nailed six out of six trucks, and three of them were trying to run. That good enough?"

"Should be, yeah," Olwen said. "Hang on."

He turned to the opening, and Lorne saw him fill his lungs. "Twist and whist!" he shouted. "Twist and whist, on the half-gigger!"

Frowning, Lorne looked at the other Cobras. They looked every bit as puzzled as he felt.

And then, their expressions cleared and understanding appeared. Still frowning, Lorne notched up his hearing a little, wondering what kind of response Olwen would get from below.

Apparently, they had understood the reference down there, too. "Twist and whist on the half-gigger," Harli's voice came drifting up to them. "Twist and whist on mark."

"We're on," Olwen announced, hurrying back through the barrier. "How fast can you get that last drone in the air?"

"It's running startup now," Lorne said. "Another ninety seconds."

"Good," Olwen said. "Here's what you're going to do..."

For a minute Jin crouched on the warship's crest, listening to the battle below as she tried to come up with a plan.

The list of options wasn't very long. Her fingertip lasers would be useless against the weapons clusters—they were far too heavily armored. Her antiarmor laser might make some headway at close range, but only if she could sit there and continue to pour fire into the things.

Only she couldn't do that. Back on Qasama, the Trofts had shown they could adjust the aiming of each cluster to fire above the other wing on its side. Once she climbed out onto any one of the wings, she would have minutes at the most before the Trofts at the controls were able to remove the safeties that prevented accidental misfires of that sort, target her, and fry her right where she sat.

She frowned suddenly, her ears pricking up. Had someone down there just called Lorne's name? She notched up her audios, her heart pounding suddenly in her throat, wondering if they were calling for a medic for him.

But it was just a group of strange words, probably some kind of code message being sent to him inside the drone control room. Keying her audios back down, she turned back to the immediate problem at hand.

Or tried to turn back to it. Her brain felt sluggish, the way it had at critical times back on Qasama. More evidence, if she'd needed it, that her brain tumor was starting to reassert itself.

But the tumor would kill her in weeks or months. The Trofts would kill her tonight, and everyone else with her, if she didn't get back on top of this. Shaking her head to try to clear it, she focused again on the options.

Her lasers were out. Her sonics were obviously out. Using her servos to physically rip the weapons out of the cluster was even more obviously out.

Which left her arcthrower.

Grimacing, she squatted down on the crest beside the aft-portside wing, keying her telescopics and peering forward at the bow-portside wing. There was at least one missile tube in there among the lasers, she knew, and while the missiles waiting inside were well protected from laser fire from below, she doubted its designers had anticipated that it would have to withstand a high-voltage current hitting it at this range.

The problem was that in order to do that she would have to

climb out onto the wing, lean over the edge, and fire her arcthrower straight down the missile tube at point-blank range.

She swallowed hard. There was no way it could work, she knew in the cold depths of her mind. The Trofts monitoring the weapons would spot her as she moved onto the wing, and either her target cluster's own lasers would get her while she was leaning over, or else the forward ones would shoot back and nail her before she got even that far.

But she had to try. Even if all she accomplished was to demonstrate the technique to the Cobras who would come after her, and to warn them of the risks, she still had to try. Taking a deep breath, still maintaining a low stance, she eased toward the aft wing.

And then, over the crest of the hull, she saw the diffuse reflected light of a sudden barrage of laser fire. She had just enough time to wonder what they were shooting at when the ones on her side of the ship also erupted in a massive firestorm. Not into the forest or town, but straight across the landscape.

She was staring at the blazing fury of the attack, wondering what in the Worlds was going on, when an object shot into view across the warship's bow, twisting and turning and jinking across her line of sight, staying about a quarter second ahead of the laser fire.

It was one of the drones, the kind that Lorne had dropped on several of the trucks earlier to clear the path for her team. Jin watched, waiting for it to do the same sort of nosedive, wondering which truck was in for it this time.

Or maybe he had something else in mind, she thought with a surge of hope. Maybe he was trying to get the drone clear so that he could drive it into one of the weapons clusters. If he could do that, maybe she wouldn't have to give up her life after all.

But the drone seemed to be making no attempt to attack the clusters. For that matter, it didn't seem to be doing anything at all. It just flew back and forth, staying ahead of the lasers, as if Lorne was daring the Troft gunners to take it down.

And then, through her foggy mind, Jin suddenly got it. This

particular drone wasn't an attack, the way the Troft gunners obviously assumed.

This one was a diversion.

And even as Jin belatedly came to that realization, another group of laser bolts abruptly lit up the night sky.

But this fire wasn't coming from any of the ship's weapons. It was coming from the swivel guns of four of the trucks Lorne had earlier disabled and the Trofts had subsequently abandoned.

And all four of the lasers were firing at the forward weapons cluster on Jin's side.

The drone was instantly forgotten as the Troft gunners shifted their aim to the unexpected attack from below. But the trucks had been built to withstand such intense attacks, and even as all four trucks became enveloped by clouds of vaporized armor plating, their guns continued to fire. Jin held her breath...

And with a thunderous explosion, the weapons cluster erupted in a blaze of fire as its missile pack ignited. The blast sent debris shooting past Jin as the shock wave slammed into her, threatening to throw her off of her perch. She ducked lower, steadying herself, as the fireball faded away. Daring to hope, she peered through the spreading cloud of smoke.

To find that the attack had succeeded. The cluster was completely gone.

So was the wing the cluster had been attached to.

The mate to the wing that Jin was about to climb out onto.

There was nothing to be gained by thinking about it. Turning her eyes away from the jagged stump where the forward wing had once been, Jin jumped onto the aft wing beside her and dropped flat onto her belly. The warship's assault on the trucks had faltered, she noticed, the Trofts in fire control no doubt reeling from the unexpected loss of a full quarter of their weaponry. Jin had to do this now, before they got their mental balance back and spotted her up here.

If she died, she died. At least it would be quick.

Pulling herself forward, she leaned over the leading edge of the wing and aimed her little finger straight into one of the missile tubes. Taking a deep breath, she fired her arcthrower.

She never even heard the explosion that shattered the cluster and hurled her upward across the sky.

The four lasers lanced up from the ground beyond the wall, converging on the weapons beneath the warship's forward wing. The ship responded with an intense barrage of its own, and for a half-dozen agonizing seconds the duel raged on. Jody watched, holding her breath.

And then, with a brilliant flash, the forward cluster exploded, sending flaming debris flying in all directions and hurling the crumpled wing itself high into the air. It arced up and back down, and as the echoes of the explosion faded she distinctly heard the muffled thud as it landed somewhere inside Stronghold. "One down," she said with grim satisfaction. "Three more to go."

"Maybe just two," Freylan said. "If your mother can—oh, God."

"What is it?" Jody asked tensely.

"It's your mom," Freylan said, his voice rigid with horror. "She's on the aft wing. She's *on* the wing."

"*What?*" Jody gasped, her breath catching in her throat. "But didn't she see that—?"

"Of course she saw," Freylan said. "She's going to do it anyway."

"No," Jody breathed, her stomach churning as she watched the distant figure hunch forward on the small wing. "She can't."

But of course she could. And she would. Because there was danger, and war. And because Jin Moreau Broom was first and foremost a Cobra.

A Cobra.

It was a small chance. But it was the only one Jody had. Leaping to the window, she flung it all the way open. "Cobras!" she shouted as loudly as she could, knowing that there were still Trofts inside Stronghold's wall who might shoot at her and not giving a damn. "Cobra on the ship wing—needs assist and rescue!"

She was filling her lungs to repeat the message when the wing exploded.

"*No!*" she screamed, all of her pain and fear and rage compressed into that single word. The fireball was dissipating—

"There!" Freylan snapped. "There—way up there!"

Jody's eyes darted back and forth across the starry sky, her heart thudding in her throat.

And then, suddenly, she saw her mother, arcing high overhead, a piece of the wing soaring along beneath her as if flying in formation. She was tumbling slowly head over heels, her arms and legs splayed out limply, unconscious or injured.

Or dead.

Time seemed to stretch out. Helplessly, hopelessly, Jody watched as her mother reached the top of her arc and almost lazily curved over and started down again. She was still tumbling slowly, and a small, detached part of Jody's mind wondered how she would be turned when she hit the ground. Not that it probably even mattered. An impact from that height would probably kill her no matter how she landed. If she wasn't dead already.

She was picking up speed now, and Jody saw that she would land just inside the wall a little ways to the west, in an open area where Jody would be able to see her all the way to the end. If, that is, Jody had the courage to stay with her mother the whole way. Would she have that courage, or would she turn away, abandoning her mother to die alone, with no one even watching? A movement to her left caught her eye, and she shifted her eyes that direction—

To see a figure jump up onto the wall from somewhere outside and launch himself upward in a powerful Cobra leap aiming straight for Jody's mother.

Jody had barely enough time to tense up as the two arcing paths approached each other. The two figures intersected—

"He's got her," Freylan crowed. "He's got her!"

Jody nodded, not daring to speak, not daring to breathe. The Cobra's own upward arc had been flattened as he caught the falling body, and now both of them were falling back to earth. Jody watched, her hands tightened into fists, knowing that Cobra leg servos could absorb a lot of the force of the impending impact, but also knowing how easy it would be for her mother's rescuer to lose his balance and slam both of them facefirst onto the ground. Almost there...

And then they were down, the Cobra's knees bending hard with the impact, his legs simultaneously pumping as he tried to get his feet moving to catch up with his horizontal momentum.

But there was too much to be made up, and his legs were already busy trying to slow their descent, and as Jody watched she knew he wasn't going to make it. His body staggered off-balance and he started to pitch forward.

And then, suddenly, two more Cobras appeared out of nowhere, sprinting up behind the staggering figure and grabbing both him and Jin's limp body into their arms, locking the four of them together as they all ran, first stabilizing their group momentum, then braking to a fast but controlled halt.

"She's okay," Freylan said, his voice weak with relief as he handed Jody the binoculars. "I saw her blink, Jody. She's okay."

Jody pressed the binoculars to her eyes, almost afraid to hope. But he was right. Though her mother's face was flushed and burned, her eyelids were fluttering with slowly returning consciousness.

It was only then, as Jody let her eyes drift with relief and gratitude from her mother's face, that she saw that the arms still cradling Jin were clad in gloves and sleeves of scaled gray.

It wasn't one of the Cobras who had answered Jody's frantic call for help, who had raced across the battle zone, risking his own life, and leaped up from the wall to save the life of her mother.

It was one of the Qasamans.

Jody was still trying to wrap her mind around that when the forest once again lit up with laser fire.

She snapped her eyes back to the warship. The lasers from its remaining two weapons clusters were firing, all right.

But they were firing high above the forest, away from any of the Cobras.

[Soldiers of the Drim'hco'plai Demesne, I speak to them,] an amplified voice rolled across the suddenly quiet battlefield. [Our surrender, we have given it. Your surrender, you must also give it.]

"What's he saying?" Freylan asked.

Jody took a deep breath. "He's saying it's over," she said. "We've won."

For a moment Freylan seemed to ponder that. "No," he said quietly. "We may have won. But it's not over. Not by a long shot."

CHAPTER TWENTY-ONE

It took the rest of the night to collect the wounded and get them under the care of Stronghold's medical personnel; to gather, disarm, and contain the Troft prisoners; and to gather and seal the dead for proper burial.

To Lorne's way of thinking, there were far too many in all three categories.

The sun was rising over the eastern forest when the word came that Harli Uy had summoned him to the Government Building for a final council of war.

The main conference room was already crowded when Lorne arrived. Harli was there, seated in the chair at the head where his father would normally be. Occupying the three chairs on either side of him were six other Caelian Cobras: Matigo, Olwen, Kemp, Tracker, and two more from the Stronghold contingent whom Lorne didn't know. Beside them to Harli's right were Lorne's parents and sister, with an empty chair between his mother and Jody that was obviously being saved for him. Facing them on the opposite side were the four Qasamans and Warrior, the Troft looking joltingly out of place among the humans. Lined up around the walls were more Cobras and a few of Stronghold's ordinary citizens, plus Croi and Nissa, who were hovering nervously behind Warrior. Behind Jody, Lorne noticed as he sat down, were Freylan and Geoff, both of them looking even more lost than Croi and Nissa did.

Lorne was apparently the last of the invited group to arrive. Even as he took his seat, Harli stirred and rose from his. "Thank you all for coming," he said, nodding first at those around the table and then acknowledging the people lining the walls. "I know you're all dead tired, and I also know there's still a lot of work to do, so I'll make this as brief as possible." He gestured to the four Qasamans. "Some of you know, others of you may not, that we have four representatives from the planet Qasama among us."

From the complete lack of reaction at Harli's announcement, Lorne concluded that everyone in the room had indeed already heard that particular news. Probably everyone in Stronghold knew it by now. "And all four of them were highly instrumental in kicking the Trofts' collective butt," he added.

"Thank you, Broom, I *was* getting to that," Harli said, throwing a brief glower at Lorne. "As Cobra Lorne Broom says, they were indispensable members of our attack force. In fact, I'd go further. Without them, we would almost certainly have lost the battle. We would absolutely have lost a great many more Cobras."

Lorne glanced around, noting all the nodding heads. The people of Stronghold knew that, too.

"What you probably *don't* know," Harli continued, "is that Ifrit Siraj Akim and his people came to Caelian looking for help. Apparently the Trofts—*some* of the Trofts," he corrected, nodding a tacit apology to Warrior, "have decided they don't like sharing this part of space with us humans. Just as Caelian and Aventine have been attacked, so also was Qasama. Ifrit Akim has therefore come here looking for help."

He looked around the room again. "Specifically, he's looking for Cobras willing to go back to Qasama with them and fight."

Lorne had expected that one to generate at least a murmur, whether of disbelief, disapproval, or dismay. The silence that instead filled the room was far more ominous.

Matigo broke the silence first. "What does your father say?" he asked.

"The governor's still in emergency surgery," Harli said. "I didn't have time to brief him on their request before he went under."

Matigo nodded and shifted his attention to the Qasamans. "How many Cobras would you need?"

"As many as are willing to come," Siraj said. "As many as you can spare."

"And therein lies the problem," Harli said heavily. "As of three days ago, before the Trofts landed, we had around seven hundred Cobras on Caelian. Even with that we were barely holding our own." He waved a hand. "As of right now, we're down over three hundred from that number, including the dead and wounded. We also have a major part of the Stronghold wall to rebuild, nearly two hundred Troft prisoners to manage, plus all the rest of Caelian's challenges to deal with."

"In other words," Siraj said, his eyes boring into Harli's, "your answer is no."

"That's not fair," Jody spoke up fiercely. "We wouldn't even be sitting here if it wasn't for them. You said that yourself. You can't just say thank you and send them away."

"What do you suggest?" Harli countered. "You've seen what we have to deal with on Caelian. How many Cobras of our current four hundred do *you* think we can spare?"

"That's the wrong question," Jin said, her voice less agitated than her daughter's but no less firm. "It's not a matter of what the cost will be of sending Cobras to Qasama. The real question is what the cost will be if you don't."

"Seems to me that if we're going to send our Cobras anywhere it ought to be to Aventine," one of the men along the wall muttered, his eyes hard as he stared at the four Qasamans. "*They* haven't been running around for fifty years swearing to destroy us."

"The situation on Qasama has changed," Siraj said evenly. "The Shahni are willing to let go of the insults of the past."

The man by the wall snorted. "Big of them," he growled.

"The Qasamans are a proud people," Jin said. "They would never ask help from someone they considered enemies. The fact that they sent Ifrit Akim here is proof that the old animosities are gone, or at least faded enough for us to try to make a new start."

"Wait a minute," Nissa spoke up from behind Warrior. "Why

are we even talking about more fighting? Warrior said that once we had a victory against the invaders the Tlossies and some of the other demesnes would be willing to help us."

Warrior's radiator membranes fluttered. [A victory, this is not a sufficient one,] he said.

"What did he say?" Harli asked.

"He said this wasn't a sufficient victory," Paul spoke up. "Unfortunately, he's right."

Matigo sent a hard look at the Troft. "In whose opinion?" he growled.

"In everyone's," Paul told him. Matigo turned to him— "Yes, I was there, too," Paul continued before the other could speak. "I saw what it cost." He waved at his heavily bandaged left leg. "I paid some of that cost myself, you know."

"The problem is that Caelian's too unimportant for anyone to care about," Harli said. "Is that what you're saying?"

"That, and the battle itself was too small for the Tlossies or anyone else to consider it genuinely significant," Paul said. "I'm sorry, but that's just how it is. A small group of humans taking down two ships' worth of Trofts could easily be considered a fluke. Especially since you had a fair amount of help from Caelian's own flora and fauna."

"What it boils down to is that there are only two places where a significant victory will be enough to get the Tlossies moving," Jin said. "Aventine and Qasama." She looked at Warrior. "Am I right?"

[A victory on either, it would be significant,] the Troft agreed.

"Well, Aventine's out," Lorne said. "Not only would we never get in past all the ships the invaders have in orbit, but the people and government there are pretty much useless."

"How *dare* you?" Nissa snapped. "Just because Governor-General Chintawa didn't go running out into the street with a gun you think he's *useless*?"

"No, I'm saying he's useless because he ordered the Cobras to stand down without even trying to fight," Lorne countered. "He also called the governors and syndics together so that he could call for a nice, neat surrender."

"He was buying time," Nissa retorted. "Buying *us* time, so that we could get off Aventine with—"

"I have a question," Croi spoke up suddenly from beside her. "Cobra Uy, you say you don't have enough Cobras to send to Qasama. What if we could get you some more?"

Matigo snorted. "As long as we're wishing, how about getting us a Dominion of Man naval squadron?"

"I'm serious," Croi insisted. "What if I could get you some fresh Cobras? Would you have enough then to send some of yours to Qasama?"

"How many extras are we talking about?" Harli asked.

"I can get you three hundred," Croi said.

"And how fast can you get them here?"

Croi hesitated, his eyes flicking around the room. "About five days."

"Five *days*?" Matigo echoed as a stunned murmur broke out among the observers.

"Relax, everyone," Harli said, raising his voice over the excited chatter. "He's talking about Viminal, which also means he's talking through his ear. Sorry to break this to you, Dr. Croi, but if the invaders bothered to hit Caelian, they certainly didn't forget about Viminal."

"I'm not talking about Viminal," Croi said, looking around the room again. "I just can't—here with all these people—"

And in that moment, the fog of fatigue around Lorne's mind seemed to part . . . and suddenly he knew what he had to do. "He's talking about Isis," he spoke up. "It's an automated—"

"Broom, shut your mouth!" Nissa snapped, stepping up to her side of the table.

"It's an automated Cobra factory currently aboard—"

"*Damn* you, Broom, shut *up*!" Nissa snarled, her face rigid with anger as she jabbed a finger at the men standing behind the Broom family. "You—Cobras—shut him up!"

"Hold," Harli said, his voice icy cold as he held up a restraining hand, his eyes locked on Lorne's. "I want to hear this."

"No," Nissa ground out. "Cobra Uy, if this man says another

word—if you *listen* to another word—I swear I'll have you and everyone else in this room up on charges."

"On whose authority?" Paul asked mildly.

"On the authority given me by Senior Governor Tomo Treakness," she said, turning her glare on him. "Dr. Croi heard him, and so did Cobra Broom. He granted me full authority of negotiation and treaty, and named me the Cobra Worlds' representative to the universe at large."

"I don't think this is exactly what he had in mind," Croi said hesitantly.

"I don't care what he may or may not have had in mind," Nissa retorted. "What he *said* was that I have full Dome authority. I'm exercising that authority now."

For a long moment the room was silent. Then, Harli stirred. "Your authority and orders are noted," he said quietly. "I still want to hear it."

"Cobra Uy—"

"And if you persist in interrupting," he added, still quietly, "I'll have you removed from this room." He turned back to Lorne. "Cobra Broom?"

Lorne took a deep breath, his mind flashing back to the family dinner—was it only three weeks ago?—where they'd all discussed the ramifications of the urgent note his mother had received to go to Qasama. Even then, he remembered, the risk of treason charges had been mentioned. Somehow, he'd never really expected it to come down to that.

Apparently, it had.

"Isis is an experimental program," he said, keeping his attention fixed on Harli. Even out of the corner of his eye he could see the fury on Nissa's face. "It's a robotic system for creating Cobras, bypassing the human surgeons. I gather it's pretty much self-contained, and I'm told it'll shorten the time necessary for equipment implantation from two weeks to five days."

Harli looked at Croi. "Has it been tested?"

"It has," Croi said. "The prototype"—he glanced at Nissa, looked hurriedly away—"is in the cargo hold of Ingidi-inhiliziyo's freighter."

"And you say it has enough equipment to make three hundred Cobras?"

"Yes." Croi hunched his shoulders. "Fewer if there's some breakage, of course."

Matigo whistled softly. "Damn, but three hundred new Cobras would be nice to have."

"I'm sure they would." Lorne braced himself. "But I'm afraid you'll have to wait for the next one." He looked at Siraj. "This one's going to Qasama."

"What?" Matigo demanded, his voice barely audible over the sudden uproar from the room.

"It has to," Lorne insisted, raising his own voice as he tried to be heard. "Listen to me. Please—*listen* to me."

"Quiet," Uy ordered.

The governor's son hadn't even raised his voice, Lorne noted. But within a couple of seconds the room was quiet again. "Continue, Broom," he said into the rigid silence.

"We can't win this war by ourselves," Lorne said, keeping his voice as steady as he could. "That should be obvious to everyone in this room. The Cobra Worlds haven't got the numbers, the weapons, or the industrial capability. No matter how many Cobras we have, if we try to go head to head with the invaders, we *will* eventually lose." He gestured toward Warrior. "The only way to win will be to persuade the Tlossies and some of the other local demesnes onto our side."

"Who've already said they won't come aboard without a major victory," Jin murmured.

"Exactly," Lorne said. "As was already stated, it has to be Aventine, or Qasama."

"So take this Cobra factory to Aventine," Matigo said.

Lorne shook his head. "We already covered that," he said. "Aventine is out."

"Because the people won't fight?" Nissa demanded bitterly.

"Because they aren't ready for war," Lorne told her. "They don't have the weapons or the soldiers." He grimaced. "And from what little I saw, they don't really have the mind-set."

"But the Qasamans have all of that," Jin said. "And they have more." She looked at Harli. "Lorne's right, Cobra Uy. Humanity has just one chance to pull this off. That chance is Qasama."

"Let's suppose you're right," Harli said slowly. "Let's suppose you take this Isis thing to Qasama, and you win. What then?"

"What do you mean?" Jin asked, frowning.

"I mean the Qasamans will have Cobras," Harli said flatly, his eyes shifting to Siraj. "And new, milder tone or not, I don't think we can trust them not to turn around and send those Cobras straight back at us once this is over."

"I have already said the Shahni no longer see your worlds that way," Siraj reminded him.

"I understand," Harli said. "And for whatever it's worth, I think you're being sincere about that. The problem is that you're making promises for your government, and I frankly don't think you have the authority to do that."

Beside him, Khatir stirred. "No, he doesn't," he agreed. Reaching into his pocket, he pulled out a small, ornate disk and laid it quietly on the table in front of him. "But I do."

Siraj leaned forward for a closer look at the disk, his eyes widening. Lorne keyed in his infrareds, and there was no mistaking the utter surprise flowing across the other's face. "You're an *ambassador*?" he asked, looking with astonishment at Khatir.

"Yes," Khatir said. "Though only for the purposes of this mission, of course." He looked at Siraj and Zoshak. "That was why I was removed from that final battle in Sollas," he added. "I needed as much instruction as possible in the demands and parameters of my new position."

"I thought you came merely to serve as our pilot," Zoshak said, sounding as confused as Siraj.

Khatir shrugged. "Certainly I'm that as well," he said. "But Rashida Vil is far better qualified than I. No, *this* was my ultimate purpose in coming on this mission."

"Even though you don't even like us?" Jin murmured.

"My personal preferences are of no matter," Khatir said evenly. "But since you mention that, allow me to state that much of my animosity toward you in Sollas was based on my doubts about your abilities." He looked at Harli. "Having now seen you in true combat, those doubts have been put to rest."

"Mighty generous of you," Harli said dryly. He gestured at the disk. "I take it that's the sign of your diplomatic authority?"

"It is an ambassadorial signet," Siraj confirmed. He still looked flabbergasted, but his infrared pattern indicated he was starting to get back on balance again. "Such tokens are old and revered, and are given only to the highest of the Shahni's negotiators."

"And as such, I place the future of our peoples in your hands," Khatir said, visibly bracing himself. "Do you wish a full treaty of friendship with the Shahni? Do you wish merely a pact of nonaggression? Whatever your desire, you need only place it in writing, and I will sign it."

"I appreciate the offer," Harli said hesitantly. "Unfortunately, *I* don't have that kind of authority. Neither does my father."

"But there's someone here who does," Croi spoke up suddenly. "As Ms. Gendreves has already stated, she has full power of negotiation and treaty."

Nissa snorted. "Please," she said disdainfully. "If you think I'm going to hand these people Cobra capabilities in exchange for a worthless piece of paper, you're sadly mistaken."

"Why?" Jin asked. "Fine, so assume that Ghofl Khatir is lying, and that any treaty he signs is worthless. Even with Cobras, how could Qasama ever be a threat to the Cobra Worlds? *Why* would they be a threat? They don't need our land or resources—they have more than enough of their own."

"What about revenge?" Nissa countered.

"They don't even have space-flight capability," Jin argued. "How exactly would they go about invading us?"

"When this war is over, our full attention will be turned toward the rebuilding of our world," Khatir added. "Besides, revenge is for fools."

"The driving force behind the Qasamans' animosity hasn't been revenge," Jin continued. "It's been the fear of another incursion by us. If we have a nonaggression treaty, and they don't have to worry about that, whatever's left of those feelings are going to go away."

"Unless you're suggesting that *our* side of the treaty would be the worthless half," Lorne put in pointedly.

Nissa shook her head. "No," she said flatly.

"What if the Qasamans sweeten the deal?" Jody spoke up suddenly. "What if they offer us a peace treaty *plus* something we can't get anywhere else?"

Nissa snorted. "Such as?"

Jody leveled a finger across the table. "Look at their combat suits," she said. "*There aren't any organics on them.*"

And for the first time since the meeting started, a genuinely stunned silence filled the room. "That's impossible," Kemp said. "They must have scraped them."

"We have done nothing of the sort," Siraj said, frowning curiously as he gazed at his arm, turning it around to look at it from all directions.

"You people have been looking for something that'll keep the organics, spores, and insects off you for decades," Jody went on. "Well, somehow, the Qasamans have come up with one."

"Actually, it may be even better than that," Lorne added as a stray thought suddenly rose from his memory. "Out in Devole's Canyon, when we were practicing for our attack, the giggers and screech tigers were just as annoying and persistent as they apparently always are. But I don't think anything smaller even came near them."

"He is correct," Siraj confirmed. "I noticed that also, but it seemed of only minor importance at the time."

"What exactly is that material?" Freylan asked, leaving his place by the wall and circling around the end of the table to the Qasamans' side.

"Treated krissjaw hide," Siraj told him, pulling one of his gloves from his belt and handing it to Freylan for examination.

"We've tried treated predator hides," Matigo said. "They don't do a bit of good."

"Maybe it's something unique in the treatment process," Freylan suggested, kneading the material of the glove as he studied it. "Or something *inside* the material. What are all these fibrous things?"

"They are stiffeners," Siraj said. "They give extra strength to the material when the servos are operating, becoming rigid when a small current runs through them."

"I'll be damned," Geoff said softly.

Lorne turned in his chair to look at him. "What do you mean?"

"It's the current," Geoff said, his voice chagrinned, embarrassed, and excited all at the same time. "Why the hell didn't anyone see that before? The current in the Djinn combat suits—it creates the same kind of low-level electric field produced by the skin, muscles, and nervous systems of living creatures."

"Thereby fooling the organics and spores into thinking it's living animal tissue," Harli said, some of Geoff's excitement starting to creep into his voice. "You might be right. You rollin' well might be right."

"So what kept the predators away?" Kemp asked.

"Who cares?" Geoff said. "I mean, yes, that's important, and we'll need to figure that out. But the point is that with those suits, you've got ninety percent of the Caelian problem licked."

"More than that," Freylan added. "Remember, these things are at heart combat suits. They've got sonics and lasers built right into them. More than enough to handle giggers and probably even screech tigers." He held up the glove toward Harli, then waved it around the room. "Don't you see? With enough of these suits *Caelian won't need Cobras anymore.*"

"At least not the numbers you need now," Jin said. "But the point's well taken." She looked at Khatir. "Ghofl Khatir?"

"Add it to the treaty," Khatir said without hesitation. "As many suits as you need, once the war has concluded, plus peace between our worlds in exchange for the Isis facility."

Siraj leaned over and murmured something to him. "A correction," Khatir said. "The main combat suit delivery will still need to wait until after the war, but I am informed that there are two spare suits currently aboard our transport. You may have those immediately."

Jin turned to Nissa. "Well, Ms. Gendreves?"

"I don't care if they offer to cover every Cobra Worlds citizen with gold," Nissa said icily. "I will not sign any treaty with these people."

"That's all right," Paul spoke up unexpectedly. "I'll sign it."

Nissa drew back, her eyes running up and down him. "*You?* You have no authority to speak for the Dome."

Paul folded his arms across his chest. "Prove it."

For the first time, Nissa seemed actually at a loss for words. "You can't just sign for the governor-general," she insisted after a few seconds.

"The Dome could renounce it," Harli agreed quietly. "Probably would, in fact."

"Fine," Paul said. "But in the meantime, the Qasamans will have their Cobras." He looked at Khatir. "And with luck, we'll have our victory."

"This is insane," Nissa snapped. "Cobra Uy, I demand you stop this travesty at once."

For a long moment, Harli gazed at Paul's face. Then, slowly and deliberately, he sent the same gaze around the room. He gave a small nod, and finally looked back at Nissa. "I'm sorry, Ms. Gendreves," he said. "But I have no evidence that Cobra Paul Broom doesn't have the authority he claims. I therefore can't interfere with him."

Nissa actually sputtered. "This is lunacy!" she snarled. She spun to glare at Paul. "This is *treason*."

"This is war," Harli said bluntly. "We do what we have to."

Nissa shot a look of her own around the room. Then, slowly, she straightened to her full height. "Fine," she said, her voice back under control. "You do your little treaty. I can't stop you. *But*."

She leveled a finger at Paul. "If you do," she continued, her voice deadly, "I state right now, in front of all these witnesses, that you have committed high treason. And I *will* have you arrested and brought up on those charges."

"Understood," Paul said. "Understand in turn that if you're able to find a court at the Dome to file those charges with, it'll mean we've won the war. In that case, I'll consider any punishment I receive to be a small price to pay."

For a moment Nissa held his gaze. Then, without a word, she turned and stalked out of the room.

Paul took a deep breath. "Cobra Uy?" he asked. "Do you have someone trained in writing up official documents?"

"I'll get him on it right away," Harli promised. "In the meantime, Matigo, perhaps you'd be good enough to gather a team to escort Warrior back to his ship and bring it here to Stronghold." He gave Khatir a strained smile. "I'd like to at least see this Isis thing before we all commit treason with it."

Twelve hours later, they were once again in space.

Lorne was sitting alone in the Troft freighter's cramped dining area, gazing out at the stars, when he heard soft footsteps approaching from behind him. From their rhythm . . . "Hi, Mom," he said, not turning around. "Dad gone to sleep yet?"

"Yes, just now," she said, coming over and sitting down beside him. "How are you doing?"

Lorne huffed. "How do I even answer that?" he asked. "Five days ago, I was standing in front of Governor-General Chintawa, listening to him rant and rave and demand that I drag you to Capitalia for some big overblown politically-charged ceremony. Since then I've fought my way through one war zone, fought my way through *another* war zone, and am on my way to a third. My father's had his leg nearly blown off, and I've found out that my brother's also been badly wounded and that my mother has a brain tumor. Oh, and almost single-handedly, my sister's solved the Caelian problem."

He turned to look at her, forcing a small smile. "There's also the minor point that my entire family's been branded as traitors," he added. "You tell me. How *should* I be doing?"

"You should be looking at the half-full side of the glass," Jin told him soberly. "Two war zones, yes, and you survived both of them. So did the rest of your family."

"I suppose," Lorne said, a knot forming in his stomach. "You really think the Qasamans can regrow all that muscle and skin on Dad's leg?"

Jin shrugged. "Carsh Zoshak is pretty sure they can. They've also told me they can remove my tumor just fine."

Lorne grimaced. "Not exactly high-confidence ways of phrasing it."

"Life is uncertain," Jin said. "As for the treason part, let's just see what happens. As Dr. Croi pointed out, Governor Treakness's last-minute blessing on Nissa Gendreves was hardly intended to cover the situation we all found ourselves in."

"But we *did* still give top-secret Worlds technology to the Qasamans."

"With the tacit agreement of Harli Uy and the rest of the Caelian hierarchy," his mother reminded him. "Under the circumstances, I rather think they'll be on our side in any future political confrontations with the Dome."

"Certainly after Jody's had a few weeks to work her charm on them." Lorne shook his head. "I still can't figure out how I'm supposed to feel about leaving her there alone."

"What alone?" Jin scoffed. "She's got Geoff, Freylan, and a whole planetful of Caelians who have this crazy notion that they owe a debt of gratitude to the Broom family. She's also got Rashida Vil."

Lorne felt his mouth drop open. "*Rashida* got left there, too?"

"You didn't know that?" Jin frowned. "No, of course you didn't—you were helping get your father aboard when that was decided. No, Harli needed someone to translate between him and the prisoners until Warrior can send back to his demesne-lord to arrange to have them taken off. Since we don't need a pilot anymore, Siraj Akim ordered Rashida to stay on Caelian for the duration."

Lorne grimaced. "You sure he didn't just decide to leave a hostage as a guarantee of Qasama's good behavior?"

"There may have been some of that," she conceded. "It's a very Qasaman way of thinking. You might as well start getting used to it. As for Jody, would you really rather we had brought her with us into yet another war zone?"

"I know, that sounds ridiculous," Lorne said. "That's why I'm having trouble knowing how to feel about it."

"Well, if I were you, I'd put that one out of my mind right now," Jin said firmly. "You saw her face—she wasn't about to leave Freylan and Geoff to experiment on those Djinn combat suits without her. It would have taken all of us *plus* Harli's Cobras to drag her out of there."

She reached over and patted his knee. "And I'd put all the rest of it out of my mind, too," she added. "You're hungry, you're tired, and you're suffering the emotional roller coaster that comes of being in the middle of combat. Trust me—I've been there. Food, and then sleep, are the order of the day."

"Okay." Lorne hesitated. "Mom...do we really have a chance?"

"To win this war?" Jin shook her head. "I don't know, Lorne. What I *do* know is that when you stood there in that meeting and said the Qasamans were the most well-equipped of all of us, you were speaking truer words than even you knew. They have soldiers, they have weapons, they have whole underground cities."

"Cities, huh?" Lorne said, his mind flashing back to all the backbreaking hours of travel through Aventine's drainage conduits.

"Whole cities," Jin confirmed. "*And* they've got Djinn."

Lorne swallowed. "And now they've got Cobras. *If* they can get them deployed fast enough."

"I think they can," Jin said. "The Qasamans probably already know which of their people have the personalities to be Cobras, which will cut out most of our usual two-week screening process. Isis will cut the two weeks of implantation to five days, and their accelerated-learning drugs will probably cut the usual nine-week training regimen by at least two thirds. Maybe more."

"*If* that stuff really works."

"Oh, it works just fine," Jin assured him. "Ghofl Khatir and Rashida Vil learned to fly that Troft transport in a single evening. There'll probably be side effects, but it'll work."

She squeezed his knee. "And those Cobras are going to make a huge difference."

"Three hundred of them?" Lorne asked skeptically. "To defend a whole planet?"

"Yes indeed." Jin smiled tightly. "Because the invaders will be coming back prepared to deal with the people and weapons and Djinn. But they won't be ready for Cobras."

"Maybe," Lorne said. "I just hope it'll be enough."

"So do I," Jin said. "I guess we'll both find out."

COBRA
GAMBLE

CHAPTER ONE

The Troft demesne-ship was dark and mostly silent, only the soft rumble of the engines playing about the background, when Jin Moreau Broom suddenly awoke.

For a minute she lay unmoving in her bunk, wondering what had awakened her. She could hear the steady breathing of her husband Paul on the other side of the tiny cabin, the terrible injury that had torn away most of the flesh on his left leg apparently not interfering with his own slumber. Or maybe it was the massive load of painkillers flowing through his bloodstream that was the source of his untroubled sleep. Jin keyed in her optical enhancers, confirmed that she and Paul were the only two people in the room, then raised the level on her audios.

Paul's breathing and the rumble of the engines grew louder. Trying to shut them out of her consciousness, Jin listened.

There it was: footsteps coming from somewhere below her. Irregular footsteps, continually changing in both rhythm and intensity.

Frowning, she keyed her audios back down and checked her nanocomputer's clock circuit. It was three-ten in the morning, an unlikely time for a shift change. Not really the time for any other serious activity, either.

So who was running around at this hour?

She keyed in her infrareds again, studying her husband's face.

He was deeply asleep, with little chance he would wake up soon and need her. Slipping out of bed, she dressed and left the cabin.

They'd lifted from Caelian less than twenty-four hours ago, but Jin had made a point of memorizing the ship's deck plans as soon as she and Paul were settled into their cabin. From the direction of the sounds, she tentatively concluded they were coming from the engine core area. Working from her memory of the plans, she found the nearest stairway and headed down.

The engine core was a long cylinder at the lowest part of the ship, bracketed by a pair of narrow, four-meter-high access corridors that doubled as heat-flow mixers. Jin arrived at the catwalk grid running above the starboard corridor and looked down.

In the narrow passageway below her were two of the Qasaman Djinn warriors, Carsh Zoshak and his commander Siraj Akim. Both men were dressed in their powered combat suits, complete with gloves and soft helmets. As Jin watched, Siraj leaped upward, twisting sideways and firing a short burst from the laser that ran along his left forearm to his glove's little finger, targeting a bundle of empty ration cans that had been placed against the far wall. At the same time, Zoshak dived to the floor beneath him, sliding for a meter on his stomach and firing a burst of his own into a similar package at the opposite end of the passageway. As he slid to a halt he rolled over onto his back, kicked his legs up over his head in a somersault, and ended up facing the opposite direction just as Siraj landed back on the floor in front of him. Over the engine hum Jin heard a triple tongue cluck, and Siraj dropped flat onto the floor in time to get clear as Zoshak fired another shot over his back.

"One of these days," a soft voice murmured from Jin's left, "*one* of them is going to miss."

Jin turned. Her younger son Lorne was sitting on a thick heat-exchange return pipe, gazing at the activity below them. "I would hope they've cranked their lasers down to some kind of practice mode," she said.

"I'd hope that, too," Lorne agreed. "But from the damage they're doing to those cans, I'd say they're still set high enough to hurt. A lot."

Jin grimaced. Knowing the Qasamans, Lorne was probably right. "How long have they been here?"

"I don't know," Lorne said. "They were already hard at it ten minutes ago when I arrived." He gestured. "They also haven't started repeating themselves yet."

"*We* certainly have more than ten minutes' worth of drills," Jin pointed out. "I can't see Djinni training being any less rigorous than ours was."

"Probably not," Lorne murmured. "I wonder what they're going to do when they get to combine the two regimens."

Jin looked sideways at her son. "You having second thoughts about this?"

Lorne sighed. "I don't know, Mom. Nissa Gendreves was right, you know. Technically, what we're doing *is* treason."

"No *technically* about it," Jin agreed soberly. If there was any single secret the Dome politicians back on Aventine would fight to the death for, it was the Cobra technology.

And now she, her son, and her husband were on their way to Qasama to hand over that technology to people they barely knew.

People, moreover, who'd once sworn to destroy the Cobra Worlds.

And not just any Cobra technology, either. Dr. Glas Croi's fancy Integrated Structural Implantation System represented a giant leap forward in the hundred-year-old Cobra program. With the help of the Troft who called himself *Warrior*—more properly Ingidi-inhiliziyo—Croi had developed Isis to be a fully automated, fully computerized system for implanting bone laminae, servos, and weapons.

In more basic terms, a self-contained Cobra factory.

Governor General Chintawa had intended to announce the Isis project with all due pomp and ceremony and then set up the prototype in Aventine's expansion regions, where the need for Cobras was the greatest. Instead, he'd ended up scrambling desperately to get the equipment off Aventine before the Troft invaders could discover it. Croi's mission had been to get it to Caelian, where it could be hidden away from prying Troft eyes and hands.

Instead, Jin and Paul had talked them into giving the whole thing to the Qasamans.

"Maybe it won't be as bad as we're thinking," Lorne said hesitantly into her thoughts. "Dr. Croi said that when Warrior was collaborating on Isis he wasn't allowed to study the Cobra equipment itself. Maybe the gear's sealed somehow."

"Warrior was working with Isis under strictly controlled conditions," Jin reminded him. "He was also kept at a distance while the tests were being done. So were the rest of the Tlossies. But the Qasamans will be right there in the middle of it."

"I meant that maybe the nanocomputers and laminae depositors will be fail-safed so that the Qasamans observing the operation won't be able to get hold of them," Lorne said.

Jin shook her head. "If Moffren Omnathi and the Shahni want to get hold of the raw components, they will."

"I suppose," Lorne conceded. "From what I've heard of the Shahni, they'll haul one of their own people right off the assembly line and dissect him if they have to."

Jin felt her throat tighten. Barely two weeks ago, the Shahni had in fact been planning to do essentially that very thing to Jin herself. For all their ingenuity in mimicking Cobra capabilities with their Djinni combat suits, the Qasamans had hit a roadblock when they tried to duplicate the nanocomputer and preprogrammed reflexes that were the core of the whole Cobra project.

They'd wanted Jin's nanocomputer. She'd made a counter-offer: she and her elder son Merrick would instead go back to Aventine and bring them more Cobras.

But that was before Merrick had been seriously wounded in the Qasamans' final and successful bid to reclaim their capital city of Sollas and drive the invaders at least temporarily from their world. So badly wounded that it had been impossible for him to accompany Jin back to the Cobra Worlds.

Omnathi had promised that the Qasamans would work to heal her son. He'd further pledged that they would leave Merrick's implanted Cobra equipment strictly alone.

But while Omnathi was a highly-regarded senior advisor to the Shahni, he wasn't an actual member of that elite group. Some of those leaders appreciated the work Jin and Merrick had done to help defend their world. But others bitterly resented the fact that the Troft invasion had forced them to work with representatives from the hated Cobra Worlds.

And Jin had no idea which side of that argument was the stronger. Would she arrive at Qasama to find that Merrick had been stripped of his equipment?

Would she arrive to find him dead?

A flicker of pain shot through her head. She fought it back, trying not to let it show in her face. *The great, legendary Moreau family*, she thought with a touch of bitterness. Merrick's fate was unknown, Jin's husband Paul was lying in their cabin with his leg mostly blown away, and Jin herself stood here with a brain tumor that was inoperable by all Cobra Worlds standards.

Not only was the future of a half dozen worlds hanging by a thread, so were the lives of nearly everyone she loved.

"You okay?" Lorne asked.

"I'm fine," Jin assured him, trying to sound nonchalant.

It was a waste of effort. As a boy, Lorne had had an uncanny ability to sense pain or sickness in his family and close friends, and that skill had only improved with age. "Right," he said darkly. "Your head again?"

"It's all right—it's passed."

"Right," Lorne said again, hopping off his seat on the pipe. "Come on—I'm taking you back to your cabin."

He was reaching for her arm when, with a suddenness that nearly triggered Jin's programmed evasion reflexes, Zoshak leaped upward and caught the section of catwalk grid beside Jin. He steadied himself, then let go with one hand and fired his glove laser in four carefully aimed bursts at the corner screws that connected his section of mesh to the support rails. Shifting his grip, he pushed up the now released section of catwalk, deftly swung his legs up and through the opening, and landed on top of the next section over. "If you'll permit me, Lorne Moreau," he said as he straightened up, "I would be honored to escort Jin Moreau back to her quarters."

"I appreciate the offer, Carsh Zoshak," Lorne said, inclining his head. "But I wouldn't want to take you away from your practice."

"For the moment, my part of the practice is over," Zoshak said. "Ifrit Siraj Akim humbly requests that your part begin."

Lorne frowned. "*My* part?"

"We seek your advice on narrow-space maneuvering and combat," Siraj called up from the deck below. "We have several techniques of our own, and would like to show them to you and hear your thoughts. After that, perhaps we could see some of *your* techniques."

Lorne looked at Jin. "Mom?"

"It's fine with me," Jin said. "Actually, all three of you could get busy with that. I can make it back to my quarters on my own."

Lorne shook his head. "No," he said firmly.

"Agreed," Zoshak said, just as firmly. "And I would request the honor of escorting our ally back to her place of rest."

Jin felt her stomach tighten. Allies. The Shahni, at least by proxy, had indeed made promises of alliance and cooperation. Harli Uy, temporarily sitting in for his wounded father as governor of Caelian, had accepted those promises and given some reciprocal promises of his own, going so far as to back up his side of the deal by sending two of his own precious Cobras and an equally rare linguist to travel to Qasama with them.

But Harli had no authorization whatsoever to make such a deal. On the contrary, the single genuinely official voice who'd spoken on the matter had vehemently disavowed the entire transaction.

If her family lived through this, Jin thought morosely, they would very likely spend the rest of their lives in an Aventine prison. Or be executed.

But she already had way too many things to worry about to add that one to her list. "Very well," she said, nodding to Zoshak. "I accept with thanks. Lorne, I'll see you later. And don't hurt each other, all right? It's going to take a while to get Isis up and running, and we're going to need all of you in good fighting trim until then."

"Don't worry, we'll play nice," Lorne said. He looked at Zoshak, still standing on the catwalk, and made a small gesture downward.

For a moment Zoshak frowned. Then his face cleared, and he gave Lorne a short nod. Lorne nodded back.

Without warning, Lorne leaned forward like he was going to fall on his face and shoved himself off into a low dive straight toward Zoshak.

But even as his feet pushed off the floor Zoshak was also in motion, dropping into a crouch and snatching up the section of grid that he'd cut free. Lorne reached the opening, caught the supporting side rails with both hands, and turned his flat leap into a roll-and-drop through toward the deck below. As he fell he spun a hundred-eighty degrees and landed on his feet a meter away from Siraj.

"Impressive," Zoshak called down as he returned the section of catwalk to its proper place. "We look forward to seeing what you can teach us."

"As I'm looking forward to learning your tricks," Lorne called back up. "Hurry back."

"I shall." Zoshak straightened up and offered his arm to Jin. "Shall we go?"

"Thank you," Jin said, nodding at the catwalk and curling her hands into fingertip-laser firing position. "But first we need to tack that down. Warrior won't be happy if one of his crewers bumps it loose and falls through. I'll do these two corners—you take the other two."

CHAPTER TWO

It was an hour after sundown, and the stars were blazing down through the canopy of trees above them, when the fourteen men from the Qasaman village of Milika arrived at their chosen hunting spot.

"There," Gama Yithtra murmured, pointing toward the north. "Do you hear them?"

"Yes," Merrick Moreau Broom murmured back as he keyed in his optical enhancers. The trees were thick in that direction, but he was able to catch glimpses of the grav lifts' glow through the branches. From the high infrared output, he guessed the Trofts had been at this for at least three hours. "Sounds like four of them, all spotters. I don't hear a transport."

"Don't worry, it's here," Yithtra said. "Marslo Charak saw it late in the afternoon, about two kilometers west." He turned to Merrick, his lips twisting in a smirk. "It would seem that your worlds are about to receive yet another dose of your own chosen medicine."

Merrick didn't answer. The second Troft invasion of Qasama was well underway, with all the alien ships that had fled two weeks ago already returned, with probably more on the way. The scattered reports that had come in from the rest of the Great Arc indicated that the invaders were unhurriedly and systematically blasting the capital city of Sollas to rubble, and had put the Qasamans' other four main cities and three smaller ones under siege. So far the Trofts seemed to be mostly ignoring the villages, but Merrick knew it was only a matter of time before the sky out here would also fill up with alien warships.

Yet in the midst of all that, Yithtra somehow always managed to find time to get in a dig about what the Trofts were probably doing to Aventine and the other Cobra Worlds with the razorarms they were harvesting from Qasama's forests.

Earlier that day, Merrick had tried explaining to Yithtra why the Cobra Worlds had seeded Qasama with the predators two generations ago, that it had been an attempt to free the Qasamans from the subtle grip of the semi-sentient native birds called mojos. But Yithtra hadn't seemed interested in hearing the Cobra Worlds' side of the story, and Merrick had given up the effort.

Fortunately, not everyone in Milika was so antagonistic toward their offworld visitor. Most were at least neutral toward him, while a few had apparently heard reports from friends or relatives about the battles in Sollas that Merrick and his mother had taken part in. Those few treated Merrick with a degree of actual respect.

And even some of the neutral ones were starting to get tired of Yithtra's verbal barbs. "Seems to me there's plenty of medicine to go around," an older Qasaman named Balis Kinstra growled. "Can we perhaps keep our minds on the job, Gama Yithtra?"

"My mind *is* on the job," Yithtra said calmly. "Teams of two: spread out and find the freighter. You, Balis Kinstra, since you're such a friend of demon warriors, will pair with Merrick Moreau. Runners meet back here in thirty minutes with reports."

There were murmurs of acknowledgement, and the Qasamans paired up and slipped away into the woods.

"I must apologize for Gama Yithtra," Kinstra said as the others' footsteps faded into the forest. "He doesn't speak for all of us."

"I know that," Merrick assured him. "And to be honest, he has a point."

"Point or not, this is not the place for such debates."

Kinstra gestured around them. "You're the one most experienced with these invaders. What are your thoughts?"

Merrick looked around them. During the Trofts' first incursion onto Qasama, the aliens had simply sent out spotter aircraft equipped with infrareds and motion sensors to locate their target razorarms, which were then neutralized with small tranquilizer gas bombs. When the spotters decided they had enough for a pick-up, a freighter would put down in a convenient clearing and armed parties would go out to collect the sleeping predators.

The parties had been careful to steer clear of the villages scattered through the forest. But they'd quickly learned that avoiding the villages didn't necessarily mean avoiding the villagers. The rural Qasamans were just as outraged by the invasion as their city counterparts, and while there were few actual soldiers among them there were plenty of expert hunters.

It wasn't long before the Trofts discovered the flaw in their harvesting technique: there simply weren't all that many clearings large enough for even a small freighter to put down in. That meant the harvesting parties had to locate a suitable landing spot before they sent out their spotter ships. All the Qasamans had to do was study the search pattern and figure out which clearing the Trofts were planning to use, then be waiting in force when the freighter put down.

The Trofts had lost a couple of harvesting parties before they caught on. Their next approach had been to create their own clearings, blasting the trees with lasers and occasionally with missiles from above so that the villagers wouldn't know in advance where they would be landing.

The Qasaman response had been to track the razorarms, concentrating on the larger family groups that the Trofts preferred, and scatter their own hunters around the most likely target zones. Often they guessed wrong, but there were enough times when they guessed right. And of course, once the trees started falling, any team within earshot knew exactly where the evening's entertainment was going to be held.

The harvesting had stopped, along with all other Troft activity, when the Sollas forces drove the invaders off the planet. But with this second incursion the razorarm raids had resumed. The aliens' latest tactic was to not land the freighters at all, but to simply hover over their latest prize and rappel a team of soldiers down to roll the sleeping animal onto a lift pad and winch it up.

Unfortunately for them, hovering freighters made wonderful targets, and the five days of calm between invasions had given the Qasaman military enough time to get a few heavy weapons into the villagers' hands. Two of the village teams south of Milika had succeeded in severely damaging Troft freighters with mortar fire a couple of days ago, and there were rumors that a team still farther south had destroyed one completely.

The Troft response had been to again halt the hunts, and for the past two nights the spotters and freighters had stayed close to the forces besieging the cities. But tonight they were back.

Merrick was looking forward to seeing what new wrinkle they'd come up with.

"For starters, I'm guessing they're finished with the hover-and-rappel approach," he told Kinstra. "That one cost them way too much."

"Agreed," Kinstra said. He paused, and with his enhanced vision Merrick saw the man's nose wrinkle. "You smell that?"

Merrick took a cautious sniff. The air was brimming with the usual mix of Qasaman woodland aromas. "Is there something different?" he asked.

"I don't know," Kinstra said, sniffing harder. "It just smells odd. Like . . . springtime."

Merrick frowned. "Come again?"

"I know that sounds strange," Kinstra said. "But it just smells somehow like it's springtime."

"Okay," Merrick said, sniffing the air again. Like that would help. He'd been on Qasama barely three weeks, and was just now starting to figure out which aromas came from cooking or perfumes and which were from the local flora and fauna. Even the spine leopards the Cobra Worlds had seeded here, the predators the Qasamans called razorarms, smelled slightly different than they did on Aventine. Probably a result of their altered diet.

There was a sudden quiet rustle from the trees behind them. Merrick spun around, his arms snapping up and his hands curling into fingertip-laser firing positions. Sure enough, there was a razorarm back there, striding through the undergrowth.

But it wasn't heading toward Merrick and Kinstra. In fact, it didn't seem to even notice the two humans. It was angling somewhere off to Merrick's right, its ears twitching, the mojo clinging onto its back fluttering its wings for balance. The predator and its avian symbiont passed by and disappeared again into the forest.

"That's odd," Kinstra murmured. "I've never seen a razorarm do *that*. They always at least *look* at a hunter. So does the mojo."

"Assessing the threat versus snack benefits," Merrick agreed, frowning after the departed razorarm. It had been a long time since he'd been on duty out in Aventine's frontier region, but there was something about the way the razorarm had moved that had seemed vaguely familiar.

And then, abruptly, he got it. The razorarm's disinterest, the spring-like smell, the predator heading directly into the gentle wind— "It's pheromones," he told Kinstra. "The Trofts are using razorarm mating pheromones. In the spring, when it's mating season—"

"Yes, yes, I understand," Kinstra interrupted hastily. The Qasamans had a long list of topics that were taboo for casual, non-family conversation, and reproductive issues were near the top of that file. "Clever. They send up spotter aircraft to distract our attention while luring the razorarms to an entirely different location."

"Clever and elegant both," Merrick agreed. "Certainly compared to some of the other stuff they've been pulling lately." He gestured after the animal. "I'll go after it, see if I can find the pickup spot. You wait here until the runners get back and follow me."

"No time," Kinstra said. "It's thirty minutes until the runners return, and then they'll have to go back and collect their huntmates. If the invaders are smart, they'll have gathered their quota and left by then."

Unfortunately, he was probably right. The Trofts had certainly had enough experience with the Qasaman attack teams to have figured out their typical response profile. "You'd better stay here anyway," he said. "Gama Yithtra may return early, and he'll be highly annoyed if he misses the party."

"Gama Yithtra's wounded feelings aren't our concern," Kinstra said tartly. "We go together." He gestured in the direction the razorarm had gone. "And this talk wastes time."

Merrick hesitated, then nodded. "All right," he said. "Quickly, and quietly."

Kinstra slung his rifle over his shoulder. "Lead the way."

Quickly was easy. The forest floor was deeply dark at night, but Merrick's optical enhancements were more than able to compensate. He circled the various trees and bushes with ease, dodging the more subtle obstacles nearly as effortlessly. Kinstra, running two meters behind him, would be making sure he precisely hit each of the Cobra's footprints.

Quietly was more problematic. If there was a way to move silently through knee-high branches and a bed of dead leaves, Merrick had never learned it.

But that was all right. The Trofts would be expecting to hear the sound of large creatures traveling through the undergrowth.

And then, suddenly, they had arrived. Through the trees, Merrick spotted a curved wall of dark metal in the middle of a clearing, with silent figures moving restlessly back and forth in front of it.

He slowed to a halt, signaling for Kinstra do the same. "There," he whispered, pointing.

"I see them," Kinstra whispered back as he unslung his rifle from his shoulder. "We need to get closer."

Merrick considered suggesting the other stay back while he scouted, decided it would be a waste of breath, and nodded. "Quietly."

A minute later, they had reached the last line of big trees at the edge of the clearing. They took up position behind two of the largest and Merrick cautiously peered out.

The freighter was a bit smaller than some he'd seen the Trofts use. But it looked more than capable of the task of hauling predators across the forty-five light-years separating Qasama and Aventine. There were four Trofts on guard duty, their laser rifles held ready, a compact missile launcher squatting on the ground in front of them like a short cylindrical guard dog. Four more of the aliens were off to the side, maneuvering a sleeping razorarm onto a cart for transport through the open hatchway behind them.

Kinstra leaned close. "Launcher."

Merrick nodded. The Trofts' tiny antipersonnel missiles had proved to be one of the invaders' most devastating weapons. Their primary targets were always Qasamans' radio transmitters, after which they were designed to home in on the sounds of gunfire and the heat signatures of large lasers. Daulo Sammon, Merrick's mother's old friend from her first covert visit to this world some three decades ago, had been severely wounded by one of those missiles during the Qasamans' first counterattack back in Sollas.

Throughout the twelve days of Merrick's own recovery the Qasaman doctors had pumped him full of their exotic rapid-healing drugs, one side effect of which had been to leave his memories of his convalescence extremely hazy. Still, he could distinctly remember several occasions where he'd asked about Daulo. What he couldn't remember was whether he'd ever gotten a straight answer back.

With an effort, he shook away the thought. His recovery was still incomplete, and while his current regimen of drugs didn't make him go all loopy the way the last batch had, they did have a tendency to encourage mental wandering.

He focused again on the enemy encampment. The missile launcher was definitely the first thing on their to-do list. Merrick keyed a target-lock onto the launcher's base, where the weapon's sensor/guidance array was located, then turned to the roving soldier patrol. They were wearing full armor, but at this range a shot from the antiarmor laser running down Merrick's left leg should cut through the aliens' neck protection with ease and rack up a couple of quick kills.

Four guards, plus the launcher. Five shots in all. With the task of aiming and firing controlled by Merrick's nanocomputer, he could probably get off that many blasts before the Trofts even had time to react. He targeted the nearest soldier, moved on to the second.

And paused. For no particular reason, a story about his great-grandfather Jonny Moreau floated up from his memory. How the legendary First Cobra and revered Cobra Worlds statesman, when faced by a ship full of Trofts, had chosen to merely neutralize instead of kill.

Of course, that situation had been entirely different. Jonny had been alone and hoping to make a deal with his captors. Merrick was in the midst of an invasion, facing attackers who were currently running a grinding machine across Qasama's capital city and probably killing untold numbers of citizens in the process.

Merrick had already killed in this war. He'd taken more lives than he'd ever dreamed would fall by his hand. But all of those enemies had been already shooting at him or other humans, or had been in the process of taking civilian hostages whom Merrick was committed to rescuing. These particular Trofts weren't doing any such thing.

But they *were* collecting predators to use against Merrick's own people. Wasn't that just as bad?

He grimaced, his sudden indecision both unexpected and disconcerting. Was he rethinking the whole concept of this war and his place in it?

Or was this simply a reaction to his own near-death on the battlefield? Was he shying away from killing in the hope that by doing so he might himself survive?

"Merrick Moreau?" Kinstra prompted.

Abruptly, Merrick came to a decision. Releasing the target locks on the Troft guards, he instead locked onto their weapons. The ultimate purpose of these counterattacks was to discourage the razorarm hunts and drive the Trofts from the forests. He could do that just as well by chasing them back to the cities, where they would be the Qasaman military's problem.

"Merrick Moreau?" Kinstra repeated, more urgently this time.

"Ready," Merrick said. "Keep your head down." Moving out of the relative safety of the tree, he rolled onto his right side, giving his left leg the freedom of movement the nanocomputer would need to handle the fire pattern Merrick had set for it. He took a deep breath, and triggered his laser.

The brilliant beam slashed through the darkness of the night, a multiple stuttering of light cutting through leaves and undergrowth and flash-vaporizing the metal, ceramic, and plastic of the launcher and the Trofts' lasers. The last of the five shots blazed out and Merrick pushed himself up off the ground for a quick assessment.

And dropped instantly back down as the launcher erupted in a blistering staccato fire of its own, its antipersonnel missiles screaming through the forest and blasting huge chunks of wood from the trees above Merrick's head.

Reflexively, he reached out a hand to grab Kinstra and pull him down. But the Qasaman was already there, pressed against the matted covering of dead leaves, his mouth moving as he shouted something. Merrick adjusted his auditory enhancers, trying to filter out the cracks of the explosives. "—posed to kill them!" he caught Kinstra's last words.

"We're supposed to *stop* them," Merrick called back. A new crunching sound penetrated his hearing, and he looked up to see the tree he'd been hiding behind starting to lean sideways as the Troft missiles tore apart its trunk half a meter above Merrick's eyes. "Come on," Merrick called, getting a grip on Kinstra's arm. The tree above them leaned farther and farther, then ponderously toppled over, crashing through the other trees and bushes beside it.

And as it slammed into the forest floor, its impact raising a blinding cloud of leaves and dust, Merrick pulled Kinstra up onto his elbows and knees and headed away as fast as they could crawl.

They'd made about twenty meters when the missile launcher finally fell silent. Even as both men turned carefully around, they spotted the glow of the repulsorlifts flickering through the trees as the freighter headed hastily into the night sky.

A thin layer of clouds had covered up the stars by the time the team once again passed through the gate into the village of Milika.

It was, for Merrick, an odd homecoming. When he'd first been brought back here eight days ago to complete his recovery, the village's lights had glowed cheerfully long into the night. But not anymore. Since the second wave of Trofts had arrived, Milika and the other forest villages had returned to the rhythms of humanity's past, to the time when activity was governed by the sun. Now, the town began to close down when the sun reached the treetops, the vendors bidding farewell to their final customers of the day and hurriedly closing up their shops. By the time the first stars appeared, the open areas of Milika were all but deserted, the people busy with their evening meals and quiet indoor activities as the village was slowly swallowed by the darkening forest.

It was a little silly, in Merrick's opinion, given that the Trofts' infrared detectors were perfectly capable of picking out the heat signatures of several hundred humans from the relative coolness of the forest around them. If they came looking for villages, they could certainly find them.

The Qasamans had to know that, too. Perhaps the darkness and silence were a matter of token defiance, something to help the villagers keep their focus, to keep their animosity toward the invaders fresh in their minds.

The team began to split up as they trudged through the village, each of the men and teens heading to their individual homes where anxious family members awaited them. Kinstra was the last to leave, murmuring a final farewell as he walked up the steps to his home.

And Merrick was alone.

He'd never had trouble with solitude before. Solitude was time to observe the world around him, and to think in the quietness.

But the world now wrapped around him was hardly conducive toward peaceful contemplation. And all of his thoughts were edged with fear and darkness.

What was happening in the cities? More importantly, what was happening to the people he'd left behind there? Daulo Sammon, badly injured, whose fate he still didn't know. The Djinni warrior Carsh Zoshak, who in a few short days of combat had grown from a suspicious and reluctant fellow soldier to a trusted comrade and true friend.

But worst of all were the haunting questions of what was happening to Merrick's family.

He looked up at the clouds drifting by overhead. Had his mother made it safely back to Aventine? Or had she been intercepted by the Trofts and captured or killed?

Merrick's younger brother Lorne was also on Aventine, most likely smack in the middle of whatever the Trofts were doing there. Merrick's father and sister were probably in even worse shape, stuck on the hell-world Caelian.

Were any of them looking up at their own stars right now? Were they thinking about Merrick, and wondering if he was dead?

"So you return."

Merrick lowered his eyes from the sky and his contemplation. Davi Krites, the doctor who Senior Advisor Moffren Omnathi had sent from Sollas to monitor Merrick's recovery, was standing at the entrance to the courtyard of the Sammon family home. His arms were folded across his chest, and Merrick didn't need his Cobra opticals to see the annoyance in the other's face and stance. "Did you think I wouldn't?" he asked as he walked up to the doctor.

"We could hear the sound of the missile attack from here, you know," Krites said grimly. "I fully expected the others to bring you back in pieces."

"It wasn't that bad," Merrick assured him. "Probably sounded worse than it was."

"I'm sure you know best," Krites said, running a critical eye over Merrick's body. "At least you're not bleeding. Not externally, at any rate."

"I really am fine," Merrick said. "If you're concerned, you can haul me in for an exam right now. I promise I won't argue."

"Tempting," Krites said. "But you'd just fall asleep on my table. Morning will be soon enough. Besides, Master Sammon wants to see you."

Merrick felt his stomach tighten. Fadil Sammon, Daulo's son, had been wide awake earlier this afternoon, and for longer than usual. Merrick had hoped the young Qasaman would be asleep by now. "I'll go at once," he said.

He started past Krites, stopped as the doctor caught his arm. "He'll want to know about his father," the other warned.

"I know," Merrick said. "I'll just have to tell him again that there's no news."

"I don't like to see him agitated," Krites said, still gripping Merrick's arm. "Can't you give him some hope?"

"You mean lie to him?"

"You're not Qasaman," Krites reminded him. "You grew up in a different culture. Your reactions and facial nuances are different from ours. You might be able to get away with it."

"I'll take it under advisement." Merrick gestured to Krites's hand on his arm. "May I?"

Reluctantly, Krites let go. Nodding a farewell, Merrick crossed the courtyard and went into the house.

Fadil's suite was at one end of the north wing, with the size and lavish decoration that befit the son of an important village leader. The furniture in the gathering area was made of carved wood and tanned krissjaw hide, dyed with subtle and shimmering stains. There were layered paintings on the walls and sculptured plant holders with flowing greenery scattered around the room. Embedded gemstones in the ceiling gave the illusion of the night sky, and night breezes flowed in through wide, open windows.

All of which made the stark metal medical bed resting in the center of the darkened room a disconcerting visual shock.

"Merrick Moreau?"

"Yes," Merrick confirmed, keying in his opticals as he started across the room. Fadil had turned his head to look toward his visitor, and even in Merrick's artificially enhanced view the young Qasaman's eyes looked unpleasantly bright. "How may I serve you?"

It took Merrick eight steps to get to the bed. Fadil watched him the whole way in silence, then turned away. "No news," he said quietly.

"No," Merrick said. So much for lying to the other. The powerful mind-enhancing drugs that Fadil had taken back in Sollas still saturated his brain, giving him powers of observation and analysis well beyond those of normal human beings. The effect was usually temporary, Krites had told Merrick, but sometimes could be permanent.

There was no such uncertainty about the drugs' side effects. The paralysis that had engulfed Fadil's body below his neck barely an hour after the mind-enhancement procedure *was* permanent.

Fadil's contribution to the war effort had made him a quadriplegic. Forever.

"What's happening in Sollas?" Fadil asked.

Merrick wasn't even tempted to lie. "According to the last report, the Troft ships spent most of the day blowing up more of the western and northeastern parts of the city," he said. "They've probably stopped now—so far their pattern's been to break off the demolition work at nightfall."

"They want to see what it is they're destroying," Fadil murmured. "They don't want to risk missing something when they have only infrared and light-amplification to see by."

"Probably," Merrick said. "It still seems like they're taking an awfully long time to destroy a single city."

"Because they're not really interested in Sollas itself," Fadil told him. "Their goal is to destroy the subcity—all of its levels, all of its chambers. The part that's aboveground is merely in the way."

Merrick nodded. That last part was sadly obvious. What *wasn't* obvious was whether or not the Shahni and the Djinn would be able to mount any sort of defense or counterattack before Sollas and all the rest of the cities had been turned to rubble and dead bodies.

"And you've heard nothing about my father?" Fadil asked into Merrick's thoughts.

"No," Merrick said. Fadil had already concluded that, of course, from his reading of Merrick's face and body language. But even so, he asked the question.

As he always did, every time he saw Merrick. Always at least twice. Sometimes three or four times.

For a moment Fadil was silent. "Perhaps tomorrow there'll be news," he said at last. "I'm told the invaders launched a missile attack on you tonight. Were there casualties?"

"None," Merrick said. "And it wasn't exactly an attack. I blew up the guidance section of one of their antipersonnel launchers, and the thing went berserk. Probably programmed to shift to a random, rapid-fire spread within a defined arc to try to drive away whoever's attacking them."

"Thus giving themselves time to regroup for counterattack or escape."

"In this case the latter," Merrick said. "They were in the air before the rest of the team even caught up with us."

"Did they leave with razorarms?"

"I don't know," Merrick said. "But if they did get any, I'm guessing they didn't get the number they were hoping for. I think we can claim at least half a victory on this one."

"Indeed," Fadil said. "Now tell me: why are you still alive?"

Merrick felt an unpleasant tingle run up his back. Gama Yithtra, after the rest of the team had belatedly arrived, had been furious that Merrick and Kinstra had taken on the Trofts all by themselves. Was Fadil suggesting that Yithtra might actually have ordered some kind of lethal action against them for that? "I don't understand," he said carefully.

"You said the launcher fired a random pattern," Fadil said. "How is it none of the missiles struck you?"

Merrick frowned, thinking back. "Because we were flat on the ground," he said slowly, "and all the shots were over our heads."

"Does that seem odd to you?"

"Yes, now that you mention it," Merrick agreed. "I didn't even notice at the time."

"Of course not." In the darkness, Merrick saw Fadil's bitter-edged smile. "You still have your arms and legs."

Merrick felt a fresh ache in his heart. "Fadil Sammon—"

"No, Merrick Moreau, don't speak," Fadil interrupted quietly. "That was unfair and cruel. My apologies. The decision that put me in this situation was mine and mine alone. And many others have suffered far worse."

He gave a small nod toward the window. "And through it all, I did my part for the people of Qasama. My gamble and sacrifice were not for nothing."

"I know," Merrick said, wishing he knew what that meant. Whatever Fadil had taken the mind-enhancing drugs for, it had apparently been secret enough that neither Merrick nor anyone else in Milika had heard anything about it.

"No you don't," Fadil said, a touch of wry humor peeking through the depression. "But that's all right. Someday, if we win, all Qasama will know. And if we lose, no one will be left to care."

"We're going to win," Merrick said firmly. "I know my mother. One way or another, she'll get Aventine to send the Cobras we need. The next time we throw the Trofts off Qasama, it'll be for good."

"Perhaps." Fadil nodded again, this time toward Merrick. "You'd best get to bed. Though the invaders' missiles may not have harmed you, I doubt you made it through the mission unscathed."

Merrick shrugged. "I'm mostly unscathed."

But once again, Fadil was right. Merrick could feel fresh aches and pains in a couple of places where his not-entirely healed muscles and skin had taken fresh damage. Dr. Krites would undoubtedly find more small injuries in the morning when he did a complete exam, and Dr. Krites would be very unhappy about it.

But that was tomorrow's trouble. Merrick had already had enough for today.

"You'd better get some sleep yourself," he told Fadil, backing toward the door. "Maybe there'll be news in the morning."

"Perhaps," Fadil said. "Good-night, Merrick Moreau. May God watch over you."

"And you, Fadil Sammon."

And with that, Merrick escaped from the room. And from the pitiful creature that Fadil Sammon had become.

After all the stress of the night's attack Merrick had looked forward to sleeping at least a little later than usual into the morning.

He didn't. The sun was barely up when he was jolted awake by the sound of heavy grav lifts. Rolling out of his bed, wincing at the fresh strains in his muscles, he slipped over to the window and eased aside the curtain.

To find a Troft warship like the ones he and the Djinn had fought in Sollas settling onto the road that led to the main Milika gate.

CHAPTER THREE

They were ten minutes from Qasama when Dr. Glas Croi, who'd hardly showed his face since the departure from Caelian, finally appeared in the dining area where Paul, his wife and son, and Carsh Zoshak were finishing up their lunch.

Paul's leg had been feeling better that morning, enough so that he'd taken only half of his prescribed painkiller dosage. He felt well enough, in fact, that Croi actually looked worse than Paul felt.

Jin noticed it, too. "Dr. Croi," she said, gesturing him toward the empty seat beside Lorne. "Are you all right?"

"What?" Croi asked, blinking like someone still trying to pry sleep-goo out of his eyes. "Oh. Hello, Cobra Broom." He frowned. "I guess that's Cobra Brooms all around, isn't it?"

"Except for me," Zoshak said, lifting his hand a few centimeters. "Though perhaps someday soon I shall be Cobra Zoshak."

It seemed to Paul that Croi's jaw tightened slightly. "Yes. Perhaps."

Lorne had picked up on it, too. "Something wrong?" he asked.

Furtively, Croi's eyes flicked to Zoshak, flicked away again. "I don't know yet," he said. "I hope not."

Lorne glanced at his father. "Meaning?"

Croi's jaw tightened again. "It's just that Isis was never meant to be taken off Aventine," he said reluctantly. "It was certainly never meant to be a secret installation."

"We could throw a blanket over it," Lorne suggested.

"This isn't a joke," Croi bit out, glaring at him. "It turns out there's a substantial and highly distinctive radio leakage signal that comes from the assembly coordination computer."

Paul felt Jin stir in the chair beside him. "Distinctive how?" she asked.

"Distinctive enough to show it's coming from a manufacturing computer," Croi said.

"Surely there are other manufacturing computers on Qasama," Paul said, frowning. His wife's reaction had been small, but still stronger than it should have been.

"You're missing the point," Jin said. "The Trofts monitor all radio usage here. Their antipersonnel missiles automatically target any transmissions within range."

"We believe they also had some of their shipboard missiles programmed for larger-scale attacks," Zoshak said. "Jin Moreau is right, Dr. Croi. Any radio signal on Qasama, distinctive or otherwise, will be an invitation to death."

"So we'll just have to make sure it's well shielded," Paul said, a lump forming in his throat. No wonder Jin had reacted to Croi's news. Lugging Isis all the way here just to have it blown up would pretty much end it for all of them. "How do we do that?"

"Well, that's the question, isn't it?" Croi said heavily. "And the answer is, I don't know." He waved a hand vaguely aft. "Ingidi-inhiliziyo and I have spent the past five days working on it. The problem we keep coming up with is that even if we shield the main computer, there's still leakage around the cable connections and from the intersect planes. I have a bad feeling that if the invaders return before we've finished equipping the new Cobras we're going to have serious trouble on our hands."

"I see," Jin said. She turned to Zoshak. "Djinni Zoshak? May I?"

Paul looked at the young Qasaman warrior. His expression was tight, but he nodded. "Under the circumstances," he said, "I think it acceptable that you tell them."

"Perhaps we should consult Ifrit Akim first," Jin suggested.

"No need," Zoshak said, more firmly. "We're allies now." He gestured. "Go ahead."

Jin nodded and looked back at Croi. "There shouldn't be any problem with leakage," she said. "The Qasamans have underground chambers deep beneath their cities. Between the steel, ceramic, and native rock, there should be enough material to block any signals from getting out."

"Really," Croi said, his voice a mixture of relief and chagrin. "You couldn't have told me all this five days ago?"

"I didn't know what you were working on," Jin reminded him. "Besides, the subcities are as much a military secret as Isis."

Croi took a deep breath. "Yes, of course. My apologies."

There was a ping from the intercom system. [Jasmine Jin Moreau Broom, she will come immediately to the bridge,] a tight Troft voice called.

Jin and Paul exchanged looks. "That doesn't sound good," Paul said as Jin got to her feet.

"No, it didn't," Jin agreed. "I'll be back as soon as I can."

"If you think you're going anywhere without us, you're nuts," Lorne said, tapping Zoshak's arm and standing up. He looked at Croi and crooked a finger. "You, too, Doc—come on."

"But they only asked for her," Croi objected.

"I must have heard it wrong." Lorne looked at Paul. "You staying here?"

"Not a chance," Paul said firmly, getting a grip on the arms of his chair and using his arm servos to lever himself upright. "Go—I'm right behind you."

Jin had already disappeared through the forward door, with Zoshak close behind her. Lorne looked in that direction, then turned and rounded the table to his father's side.

"I said you should go ahead," Paul repeated, trying to fend him off.

"I must have heard that wrong, too," Lorne said.

He evaded his father's brushing movements with ease and moved up beside him, wrapping his arm around the older man's waist. Paul tried to push the arm away, but Lorne had locked the servos and the arm wasn't going anywhere. "Just relax and let me take the weight."

"I thought we taught you to respect your elders' wishes," Paul grumbled as they headed toward the door. Still, he had to admit this was a lot easier than trying to limp around on his own.

"Stop having silly wishes and I will," Lorne said. "Easy now, and watch the door jamb."

Jin and Zoshak were standing behind the helm console when Paul and Lorne reached the bridge. Between them, Paul could see the Troft at the helm, and the fluttering arch currently being formed by his upper-arm radiator membranes. Something was wrong, all right. "What have we got?" he asked, glancing around at the other Trofts at their stations. All of them were showing the same degree of stress as the helmsman.

[The Drim'hco'plai invaders, they have returned,] a Troft voice came from the side of the room.

Paul looked toward the voice. The ship's master, Ingidi-inhiliziyo—*Warrior* to all the humans aboard except Croi, who could actually pronounce the alien's name—was standing by the communications board, resplendent in the red heir-sash that identified him as the second in line to the Tlos'khin'fahi demesne-lord. Unlike the other Trofts on the bridge, his radiator membranes weren't fluttering, but were barely extended from his arms.

But then, a Troft of his rank and position was supposed to stay calmer than his crew. "How seriously have they returned?" Paul asked.

[A siege, they have mounted one at all Qasaman cities.] Warrior said. [Our presence, they demand an explanation of it.]

A hollow feeling formed at the pit of Paul's stomach. He'd assumed the invaders would run home with their tails tucked, where they would regroup, restrategize, and collect fresh ships and soldiers before taking another crack at the Qasamans.

Yet here they were, already well into a fresh campaign. Clearly, they were more determined than he'd realized.

And with that, everything he and Jin and the others had discussed and thought about and planned over the past five days was gone. With the invaders already back and settled into siege mode, there was no way Ingidi-inhiliziyo could get his ship close enough to Sollas to offload the Isis equipment and hide it in the depths of the hidden subcity.

That was bad enough. But for Paul and Jin personally, it was even worse.

Because the Qasamans' best medical facilities were in the cities. A siege of those cities meant that Paul's ravaged leg would not, in fact, be healed. Not any time soon.

Nor would the tumor that was slowly killing his beloved wife be removed.

"Maybe there's still a way," Lorne murmured hesitantly from his side. "It's possible Warrior can play the demesne-heir card and get us permission to land at least somewhere near Sollas. If the subcity extends outside the city wall, maybe we can get some of Isis into it without the invaders noticing."

[The cities, permission to land there we may not have,] Warrior said. [Such instruction, it has already been achieved.]

"But you're a demesne heir," Lorne pressed. "Can't you do *something*?"

"It would serve no purpose for us to land there, Lorne Moreau," Zoshak said quietly, his eyes on one of the helm displays. "Sollas is gone."

Jin caught her breath. *"What?"*

[The truth, show it to them,] Warrior ordered.

[The order, I obey it.] The helm officer touched a switch, and a section of the wraparound display changed from a view of the stars around the ship to a close-up of the planet ahead.

Paul felt his lips curl back from his teeth. Zoshak was exaggerating, but not by much. Probably a third of the city was still there, mostly the southern and eastern sections, snugged up inside their outer wall.

But the northern third was completely gone. The buildings there had been turned to rubble, the ground beneath them gouged out at least three or four stories deep. The third of the city in the middle was in transition, many of the buildings already down and the excavation below them just starting.

"They're trying to destroy the subcity," Jin murmured. "That's where their defeat came from the last time. They want to make sure that doesn't happen again."

"Terrific," Croi said grimly. "What do we do now?"

"We figure out something else," Lorne told him. "That's a big planet down there. There has to be some other place you can set up shop."

Croi snorted. "Where? We need power, Cobra Broom, power and buildings and people. We can't just drop Isis in the middle of nowhere."

Paul looked at Jin, a sudden thought stirring inside him. A bit of family history his wife and son seemed to have forgotten... "How many buildings would you need?" he asked.

"I don't know," Croi said, turning puzzled eyes on him. "Someplace to set up the Isis machinery, plus a prep area, plus a postoperative recovery area. Three at least, or I suppose one really big building might do."

"You have an idea?" Lorne asked.

"I think so," Paul told him. "Remember, Jin, on your first visit to Qasama you saw a mine that Daulo Sammon's family was operating inside Milika. Do you know if it's still there?"

"No, I don't." She looked at Zoshak. "Carsh Zoshak?"

"Yes, it's there," the Qasaman said, his tone oddly hesitant. "It may work."

"Except...?" Lorne prompted.

Zoshak's lip twitched. "The people there are villagers," he said reluctantly. "Not..."

"Not city dwellers?" Jin asked.

Zoshak's lip twitched again. "Not soldiers," he said. "It may be difficult to find the proper subjects for the Isis transformation."

Paul looked at Jin. Over the years she'd talked about the political and philosophical divide between the Qasaman cities and villages, those conversations usually in the context of some policy the government geniuses at Dome were trying to inflict on Aventine's own rural and expansion regions.

She'd always hoped the antagonism would fade with time. Apparently, it hadn't.

"Don't worry, we'll find the right people," he told Zoshak. "I doubt the villagers are any less patriotic than the city dwellers. There'll be plenty of volunteers."

"Perhaps we should call Siraj Akim," Jin suggested. "He's the senior here. He might have other ideas."

[A response, the invaders await it,] Warrior spoke up. [Instruction, I await it.]

Zoshak took a deep breath. "Ifrit Akim's presence is not required," he said. "The idea is sound. We'll use it."

He turned to Warrior. "We go southwest of Sollas approximately twelve hundred kilometers," he said. "Follow the Great Arc to Azras. Milika is in the forest approximately thirty kilometers northwest of Azras."

"You could tell them you're here looking for plants with possible pharmaceutical value," Jin suggested.

"Isn't that the story you spun the Trofts at Caelian?" Lorne asked. "I seem to remember it not working out so great."

[A reason, it is still a logical one,] Warrior assured him, gesturing to one of the other Trofts. [The response, you will give it.]

[The order, I obey it.]

The Troft murmured the story into his microphone, and for a moment the bridge was silent. Paul gazed at the image of the ruined city far below, feeling his leg throbbing with fatigue and sympathetic pain. How many Qasamans, he wondered, had been killed in the invaders' demolition? Was the destruction a genuine and reasoned reaction to the Qasamans' hidden subcity arsenal, and a military desire to eliminate that threat? Or was it driven by a desire for revenge over the invaders' earlier defeat?

The Troft at the radio had made his request, and the conversation had now switched over to some kind of oddly poetic give-and-take bargaining or posturing that Paul had never heard before between Trofts. He continued to study the image of the devastated Qasaman capital, his mind drifting away from the conversation.

Three months. That was what the Qasaman doctors had told Jin. Three months to get that tumor out of her brain before it killed her.

She'd accepted that diagnosis calmly, reminding Paul whenever he brought up the subject that if they couldn't beat back the invaders within that timeframe that they weren't likely to ever do so.

Plenty of time, she continually reassured him, for her to go under the knife and be healed.

Only what if the doctors had been wrong? What if it was only two months, or one and a half? She'd already used up two weeks of that time flying from Qasama to Aventine to Caelian and now back to Qasama. What if there was only a single month left?

Even worse, what if the doctors were right about three months before the tumor killed her, but that there was only a month or two before the point of no return on an operation? Jin had always had a bad tendency to run medical things right up to the last minute. What if she pushed this one to the edge, only to discover that the edge had already been crossed?

[Warrior, an infrared scan of the ships, may I have it?] Lorne asked suddenly.

[The purpose of a scan, what is it?] Warrior asked.

[The invaders' ships, I wish to know if they have been recently moved,] Lorne said. [Future movement, I wish to estimate its likelihood.]

With an effort, Paul dragged his attention back from a bleak future to the equally bleak present. "What for?" he asked.

Lorne pointed to the display. "You see that warship on the far left? It can't be more than fifty meters from the edge of the forest. Once we have a few more Cobras, I'm thinking we could sneak up or even rush it, take over, then use its lasers and missiles to blast all the others. But that only works if it's likely to stay put for the next few weeks."

"Hence, the IR scan," Paul said, nodding. "You want to see how cold the grav lifts and drive are."

Lorne nodded back. "Exactly."

[The floatators and drives, they are inactive and cold,] Warrior said. [But the plan, it will not succeed.]

"Sure it will," Lorne said. "All we have to do is—"

[The plan, why will it not work?] Paul asked.

[Encrypted ally-identification systems, all Trof'te warships have them,] Warrior explained.

"Yeah, of course they do," Lorne said sourly. "Damn."

"What's an ally-identification system?" Croi asked.

"Probably like an IFF," Paul told him. "That's short for *Identify Friend or Foe*. It's a set of transponders designed to keep an army's warships from accidentally firing on each other."

"You sure they actually have something like that?" Lorne asked. "You saw how easily we got the armored trucks to fire on their ships on Caelian."

[The ally-identification system, ground vehicles do not have it,] Warrior said. [The risk of enemy capture and deciphering, it is too great. But the ally-identification system, all air combat vehicles and sensor drones will carry it.]

[Certainty, you have it?] Lorne persisted.

[Certainty, I have it,] Warrior said, starting to sound annoyed. [The ally-identification system, I saw it when Harli Uy and I toured the Drim'hco'plai warship.]

"Give it a rest, Lorne," Paul advised. "I'm sure he knows what he's talking about."

"Fine," Lorne growled. "It still might be worth taking that ship."

"Let's get safely down first," Paul said. "Then we can discuss strategy."

There was a ping from one of the consoles, and cattertalk script appeared on the display. [Official clearance, we have been given it,] Warrior announced.

"We're going to Milika?" Paul asked him.

"We're going *close* to Milika," Lorne said, giving his father an odd look. "He already said that."

"Oh," Paul said with a flush of embarrassment. That must have happened while he was contemplating his and his wife's medical situations. "Yes. Right."

"You okay?" Lorne asked, still giving him that look.

"Of course," Paul told him. "I got distracted, that's all. How close—?"

"Is your leg hurting?" Jin put in. "Maybe you should go lie down."

"I said I just got distracted," Paul said, more firmly this time. "Is there a problem with Milika?"

[A problem, it has not been specified,] Warrior said. [The village, we must not approach it.]

"Which I just said sounds a little ominous," Lorne said, "and asked if there was any way to get a look at the place."

[The attempt, we will make it.] Warrior gestured to one of the other Trofts, and the image of Sollas suddenly disappeared into a dizzying flurry of forest. Hastily, Paul averted his eyes as a surge of vertigo threatened to overwhelm him. [The added distance, it may make seeing difficult,] Warrior added. Out of the corner of his eye Paul saw the image steady...

"No," Jin breathed.

Paul snapped his eyes back to the display. For that first second all he saw was a hazy image of tangled Qasaman forest with an equally hazy walled village in the center.

And then, belatedly, he spotted what had sparked his wife's reaction. There was a Troft warship squatting in the middle of the road outside the main gate, its stubby weapon-laden wings poised like hawk talons over the village.

For a long moment no one spoke. Then, Croi stirred. "So that's it," he said, an edge of bitterness in his voice. "We have a traitor aboard."

Warrior's radiator membranes fluttered. [Your words, explain them.]

"Isn't it obvious?" Croi snarled. "Someone leaked the news that we were going to Milika." He turned and looked pointedly at Zoshak. "Someone who knew how to privately contact the invaders."

"You mean one of the people who helped us wreck one Troft warship on Caelian and capture the other one?" Lorne asked scornfully.

"If we hadn't won on Caelian we wouldn't have brought Isis to Qasama, would we?" Croi countered.

"They didn't know about Isis until after we won the battle," Lorne said.

"So they say." Croi's eyes narrowed. "So *you* say. You whose family is awfully cozy with the Qasamans."

"Enough," Paul put in. "With all due respect, Dr. Croi, you're being an idiot. Look at the infrared display—that ship's gravs are stone-cold. It's been sitting there for hours."

Still glowering, Croi looked at the sensor control board. Warrior pointed silently to the proper display, and there was another moment of silence. "Fine," Croi growled, turning away again. "Whatever. In that case, what in hell *are* they doing there?"

"It's Merrick," Jin said, her voice so quiet Paul barely heard her. "He's there."

"You sure?" Lorne asked, frowning up at the display. "How do you know?"

"I just do," Jin said, her voice filling with dread. "It's the logical place for Moffren Omnathi to send him for his convalescence. Somehow, the Trofts found out he was there." She exhaled in a painful-sounding huff. "And to get him . . . they're going to destroy Milika."

"No," Paul said as firmly as he could with his own heart suddenly racing. She was probably right about Merrick being there. With Jin having left, he was the only Cobra on Qasama, and the invaders would be seriously motivated to find and neutralize him.

But there was still a ray of hope that Jin apparently hadn't yet grasped. "I just said they've been there for hours," he reminded her. "If they were going to destroy the village, they would surely already have started."

"He's right," Zoshak said. "We still have time."

"Time for what?" Croi asked glumly. "Milika was our last chance. Now it's gone."

"Not for long," Zoshak said evenly. "First, we unload and secure Isis. Then we—"

"*Secure* it?" Croi cut him off. "Secure it where? In the middle of the *forest*?"

"Yes." Zoshak turned to Warrior. "Thirty kilometers west and south of the village is a clearing. It should be large enough for you to land. Can you take us there?"

Warrior's arm membranes fluttered. [The clearing, we are familiar with it.]

"Wait a second," Croi objected. "I was *joking*."

"This isn't a joke," Zoshak assured him. "Thirty years ago, after Jin Moreau's first visit to Qasama, the Shahni calculated that that clearing was where her team had intended to land."

"Except that we were shot down," Jin murmured. "But you're right, that *was* our planned drop zone."

"And so the Shahni prepared for the next expected incursion," Zoshak said. "There's a military watch station buried beneath the forest floor in sight of the clearing."

"It's *buried*?" Croi said, a fresh hope stirring in his voice. "How deep?"

"Not deeply enough, I'm afraid," Zoshak told him. "Besides which, it's almost certainly too small, and the generators are unlikely to still be functional. The station was abandoned over ten years ago."

"But it should be a good place to stash the gear while we find out what's going on in Milika," Paul said. "Warrior?"

[Your analysis, I agree with it.] Warrior gestured to the helm. [The clearing, we will go there.]

[The order, I obey it,] the other Troft said.

Lorne took a step closer to his father. "Okay, we stash the gear," he said quietly. "But then what? If they've really got Merrick pinned down in there—and if they know they've got him pinned—they aren't going to be inclined to just give up and go away."

"Do not fear, Lorne Moreau," Zoshak said, a dark edge to his voice. "We've taken down Troft warships before. If necessary, we can do it again."

Paul felt a fresh throbbing in his injured leg. They'd taken down Troft warships on Caelian, all right. Two of them, in fact.

But it had taken nearly the planet's entire contingent of Cobras to do it. And even then, victory had come at a terrible cost.

But Zoshak was right. That was Paul's son down there in danger. Whatever it took, they would get him out.

CHAPTER FOUR

The evacuation warning was so subtle that at first Daulo Sammon didn't even notice it. He was still lying in his recovery room bed, wondering what the gentle warbling meant, when a doctor hurried in, his mouth moving but no sound coming out. "What is it?" Daulo asked. His own voice sounded odd, deep and strangely distant. "Speak up. Speak *up*."

The doctor came to a halt beside the bed, his hand reaching up to touch something in Daulo's right ear.

And suddenly the warbling exploded into a howling roar.

"Ahh!" Daulo gasped, grabbing for his ears.

The doctor was faster, doing something else with his ear that brought the howl down to something much more manageable. "Apologies," the man said, his voice carrying easily over the din. "Your hearing hasn't fully recovered. That's an evacuation order. We need to leave here at once."

Daulo frowned. Then, suddenly, it all flooded back in on him. That first, failed counterattack against the invading Troft forces—his own severe wounding—doctors and drugs and foggy images of faces and noise and fury—

"*Come*," the doctor snapped.

With another jolt, Daulo realized that the tubes connecting him to the feeders and other devices by his bedside had been removed from his arm. "Where are we going?" he asked as the doctor swung his legs off the bed and slid wraparound shoes over his feet.

"To a departure area," the other said, steadying Daulo with one hand as he pulled over a wheelchair with the other. "We're leaving the city."

"Now?" Daulo looked at the dangling tubes as he settled into the chair. "But I'm not healed yet." A sudden, horrible thought blew away some of the cobwebs still filling his brain. If this was as good as he was ever going to get—"*Am* I?"

"I don't know," the doctor said, and Daulo had to grab for the armrests as the chair suddenly took off toward the door. "It all depends."

"On what?"

"On how long the Trofts let us live," the doctor said grimly. "Hang on."

Daulo had expected the corridor outside to be buzzing with activity as doctors and attendants wheeled out the sick and injured. But to his surprise, the two of them were the only ones in sight. Thankfully, the alarm that had been rattling his room was also barely audible out here. "Where is everyone?" he asked, grabbing for the armrests again as the doctor took a corner way too fast.

"All those who remain should already be gathering at the staging area," the doctor panted. "But there was someone who wished first to say farewell to you."

Whether from the fresher air, the lack of medicine being pumped into his body, or the sheer adrenaline-driven fear caused by the doctor's reckless driving, Daulo's head had mostly cleared by the time they reached their destination. It turned out to be a medium-sized conference room equipped with a table, a dozen chairs, and a line of blank monitor screens. Seated at the table were three older men, while six younger men dressed in the gray Djinni combat suits stood silently at the ready around the room's edges.

The three older men looked up, and with a jolt Daulo realized he knew two of them. One was Moffren Omnathi, special advisor to the Shahni and a legend among the Qasamans. The other was Miron Akim, who with the rank of Marid was overall commander of the planet's entire Djinni combat force.

"Daulo Sammon," Omnathi said gravely as the doctor wheeled Daulo's chair up to the table. "My apologies for bringing you here instead of letting you go directly to your departure area."

"No apologies needed, Your Excellency," Daulo said, making the gesture of respect and throwing a furtive glance at the unknown man. From the look on his face, it was clear he wasn't happy with this interruption to their meeting. "But what is this departure area business? Why is everyone leaving in such a hurry?"

"The invaders are destroying Sollas," Omnathi said, "and that destruction is nearing this area."

Daulo winced. No wonder the doctor had been in such a hurry. "Then you're right, we'd best get moving," he said, glancing down at his robe and recovery jumpsuit. "It would be very embarrassing to die looking like this."

"No fears of that," Omnathi assured him. "Some of the earlier refugees were met with violence, but the later groups have been allowed to leave unharmed." He gestured at Daulo's clothing. "And more suitable travel clothing is waiting at the departure area. The doctor will help you change before you go."

"Thank you, Your Excellency, that will be very helpful," Daulo said, a small relief trickling into the simmering darkness of fear and uncertainty. At least they weren't going to be shot the moment they reached the outside air. "My apologies for the impertinence, but may I ask why exactly I'm here?"

"Marid Miron Akim and I wished to say a final farewell," Omnathi said. "You and your family have served Qasama well, and we wanted you to know how grateful we were for that service. May God watch over you, and may you win through to see your village again."

"Thank you, Your Excellency," Daulo said, again making the sign of respect. "To both Your Excellencies," he added, this time including Miron Akim in the gesture. "But if we're all leaving the city together, it would seem to me that your farewells are premature." He frowned as a thought occurred to him. "Or *won't* we be traveling together?"

"Our paths will lead—" Omnathi's lip twitched "—along different roads. When you and the remaining civilians from this sector depart from the subcity, the invaders will learn the location of one more hidden passageway. With that knowledge, they'll undoubtedly enter to explore for data or useful items that may have been left behind. We will remain behind to make one final assault upon them."

Daulo looked at the six gray-suited men standing silently against the walls. "What, *six* of you against the entire force of invaders?"

"Seven," Akim corrected calmly. "Though I'm a civilian, as Marid-commander I also count myself among the Djinn."

"My apologies, Marid Akim," Daulo said. "But I fail to see how one extra Djinni will tip the military balance. In fact, I can't see how you can accomplish anything but a waste of all your lives."

"Your impertinence is not welcome, villager," the third man said brusquely. "These men are warriors of Qasama. They'll attack the invaders because it's their duty to do so."

"Their duty is to die uselessly?" Daulo countered.

The man's eyes narrowed. "You've said your farewells, villager. Now leave."

There was something in his tone and manner that told Daulo the smart thing to do would be to close his mouth and obey. But just as he had thirty years earlier, when Jin Moreau came to Milika and asked for his help, he ignored the quiet warning. "Not until I understand why you're doing this," he said firmly. "I've faced the invaders' weapons. You may be able to kill a few of them, but you can't prevent them from ultimately winning through. Is there something in here of military value that can't be removed or destroyed?"

"No, nothing," Akim said.

"Then why not just leave with us?" Daulo pressed. "Out in the forest, you can regroup and choose a better time to resume the fight."

"You will be silent, and you *will* leave," the third man repeated, and this time there was no mistaking the authoritative anger in his tone. "Or I will order you to stay and fight alongside them."

Daulo snorted. "And who are you who presumes to order me *and* the Djinn?"

The man drew himself up. "I am Shahni Dariuz Haafiz."

Daulo felt his tongue freeze against the roof of his mouth, a sudden swell of horrified panic washing over him. Dressed in civilian clothing, bereft of the elaborate robes of office, he hadn't been as instantly recognizable as he would normally have been. "My most sincere apologies, Your Excellency," Daulo managed, bowing over in his wheelchair and hastily making the sign of respect.

"Your apologies are tardy and not accepted," Haafiz growled. "Now leave us as you were ordered."

Daulo straightened up. The doctor was starting to pull the wheelchair back from the table, and once again the smart thing to do would be to simply go.

But there was something in Omnathi's expression... "Forgive the further impertinence, Your Excellency," Daulo said, grabbing the wheels and bringing the chair to an abrupt halt. "But I still fail to see why these men are to be needlessly sacrificed."

"Your impertinence is not forgiven," Haafiz bit out. "Nor is your understanding required or sought. Your only task is to obey the orders you've been given."

"The Djinn cannot simply leave with you and the others, Daulo Sammon," Omnathi said. "Their combat suits will instantly identify them to the invaders. If they try to leave, they'll be cut down instantly." He looked at Haafiz. "And their lives will be even more uselessly sacrificed."

Daulo stared at Omnathi, then at Akim and Haafiz. Were all three of them blind? "Then why not have them simply remove the combat suits?" he asked.

"Impossible," Haafiz said. "Without their combat suits, they are nothing."

Akim and Omnathi, Daulo noticed suddenly, were watching him closely. "Your forgiveness, Your Excellency, but that's simply not true," he said firmly. "Without their combat suits—without any weapons at all—they're still warriors of Qasama. As you yourself said only moments ago." He looked into the eyes of the young man standing behind Akim. "And as such they're too valuable to our world to be needlessly thrown away."

Haafiz sniffed contemptuously. "Are you of the Shahni now, Daulo Sammon?" he demanded. "Do you now make the law for Qasama?"

Daulo grimaced, looking around the room. The six Djinn stood stiff and proud, their expressions those of men ready and willing to die for their world and their people.

But as he looked deeper into their eyes, he could also see that they, too, saw no honor in dying in a useless ambush that would serve no genuine purpose.

And they were young. So young. No older than Daulo's own son Fadil.

What had happened to Fadil? With a flush of surprise and shame, Daulo realized he hadn't even thought to ask.

But this wasn't the time for that. There were other young lives balanced on the edge here. Somehow, he had to find a way to save them from this madness.

He looked at Akim as a sudden flash of inspiration struck him. "Of course I'm not of the Shahni," he said. "I'm a citizen of Qasama, wounded while defending this city, who desperately needs help escaping."

One of the Djinn stirred but said nothing. Akim's expression remained unreadable. "Are you asking for our help?" he asked.

"This is ridiculous," Haafiz snapped before Daulo could answer. "Doctor, remove Daulo Sammon and take him to the departure area. You, Marid Akim, will deploy your Djinn as ordered."

"That may not be possible, Your Excellency," Akim said, his eyes still on Daulo. "Daulo Sammon is one of the leaders of his village. The provisions of the war act clearly state that warriors must assist such leaders wherever possible."

"When it does not interfere with other duties," Haafiz said. "Don't quote the law to me, Marid Akim. I *wrote* the law."

Daulo had a second flicker of inspiration— "And if I come under that provision," he said, "it would seem to me that a Shahni of Qasama would be even more firmly under Djinni protection."

"I don't need their protection," Haafiz spat. "I've given them their orders, and they *will* obey them."

Abruptly, he stood up and leveled a finger at the young Djinni behind Akim. "You—Djinni Ghushtre—by order of the Shahni you're hereby promoted to Ifrit and given command of this unit.

Escort Marid Miron Akim and Senior Advisor Moffren Omnathi to the staging area and prepare them and your Djinn for combat."

"Wait a moment," Daulo said, frowning as he focused on the deep age lines crisscrossing Omnathi's face. "Advisor *Omnathi* is to be part of the attack? Why?"

"Djinni, you've been given an order by a Shahni of Qasama," Haafiz said, ignoring Daulo's question. "You will carry it out."

Ghushtre hesitated, his eyes flicking uncertainly to the back of Akim's head— "What about me?" Daulo put in, trying one last time. "I'm a village leader. What about you, Shahni Haafiz?" He waved a hand behind him. "For that matter, what about the rest of the civilians at the departure area? They're city dwellers—once outside the wall they'll be helpless. Where will they go? How will they find food and shelter? They need an escort of trained warriors."

"We need no such escort," Haafiz scoffed, his eyes still on Ghushtre. "Travel supplies are available at the departure area, and there are straight and clear roads to Purma and the towns and villages around it."

"There are still the dangers of the forest," Daulo pressed. "*And* those of the invaders."

"Ifrit Ghushtre, I give you one final chance," Haafiz said, again ignoring Daulo. "Obey my order, or be executed where you stand for treason."

"There will be no executions," Akim said firmly. "Nor will there be any such charges against my Djinn. I am the Marid, and decisions of discipline are mine. All honor or shame is ultimately gathered to me."

Haafiz glared down at him. "And your decision, Marid of the Djinn?" he demanded.

Akim's eyes flicked down to Daulo's wheelchair. "Daulo Sammon, are you able to walk?"

"For short distances, yes," Daulo said. "But my strength and stamina aren't yet fully returned. I don't know how far I can go before they give way."

Akim grunted. "For now, stay in the wheelchair—you should be able to cross most of the city in it. Djinn, your first priority is to escort Shahni Haafiz and Village Leader Daulo Sammon to safety. Accordingly, you are ordered to remove your combat suits—"

"Miron Akim, I warn you—" Haafiz began.

"—and report to the departure area," Akim said, his voice deathly calm. "Collect what food and water is available and assure that the civilians and medical personnel are prepared for travel. Moffren Omnathi and I will follow in a moment with Shahni Haafiz."

"Marid Akim—"

"You have your orders, Djinn," Akim said. "Carry them out."

There were twenty civilians, including five women and three children, waiting in a tense atmosphere when Daulo, the doctor, and the six Djinn arrived at the departure point. Accompanying the group were two other doctors and three medical attendants. As Omnathi had said, there were plenty of changes of clothing available, and within two minutes the Djinn had stripped off their combat suits and transformed themselves into six more civilians.

Daulo had also changed into more appropriate travel clothing, and was helping one of the Djinni load water bottles into the small carrier bag beneath his wheelchair, when Akim, Omnathi, and Haafiz arrived. Akim looked tense, Omnathi seemed oddly calm, and Haafiz looked like an afternoon thunderstorm looming on the horizon waiting to explode in all its fury.

But at least he wasn't threatening anyone. At least not at the moment. In fact, he didn't seem inclined to say anything at all.

Ten minutes later, with two of the civilian-clothed Djinn in the lead and Haafiz glowering right behind them, the group filed up a long ramp and through a door out into the open sunshine.

Into a ruined city.

Daulo looked around, his heart sinking, as the doctor wheeled him along the silent streets. Omnathi had said the invaders were destroying Sollas, but Daulo had had no idea how deep and thorough that destruction had been.

The southern part of the city, the part their group was traveling through, was still relatively intact, though there were numerous cracks and ridges in the pavement. But as they passed the wide avenues leading northwest, Daulo could see mounds of rubble to the north where buildings had once stood. Further north, beyond the rubble, were places where there was nothing but gaping holes, the devastation half concealed by a haze of dust or smoke.

Occasionally, he heard one of the others in their group murmur something to a companion, most of the comments edged with sadness or shaking with anger. But mostly the only sounds were the shuffling of feet through gravel, the creaking of the wheelchair as it moved across the uneven terrain, and the crackle and thud of the distant and ongoing destruction.

Aside from themselves, the only living beings in view were the invaders.

From the way Omnathi had talked, Daulo had expected the Trofts to be standing right at the exit as the refugees emerged onto the street, stopping each in turn and checking them for weapons, contraband of whatever sort, and Djinni combat suits. To his mild surprise, the aliens instead kept a cautious distance, watching warily but never approaching closer than fifty meters as the little clump of humans made their way along the deserted streets.

From a tactical point of view it seemed dangerously careless. It also made Daulo wonder what the whole fuss back in the conference room had been about.

The refugees had covered about half the distance to the city's southwest gate when he found out. As the group rounded a corner, they abruptly found themselves surrounded by a double ring of Trofts. The aliens in the inner circle gave a single order.

"Humans: halt."

The Trofts then proceeded to do a quick search of everyone, including taking brief but thorough looks beneath the men's robes and tunics. The outer ring stayed well back, their lasers trained on the humans, until the search was over. Then, as silently as they'd descended on the refugees, the aliens withdrew, returning to doorways, alleys, and the other places where they'd apparently been standing their unobtrusive watch.

The group had made it another two blocks before an odd thought suddenly struck Daulo.

Why was Haafiz still with them?

He stared at the back of the Shahni's head, frowning as his chair bumped its way down the street. One of the Trofts' first objectives in their invasion had been the Palace, with the clear intent of capturing or neutralizing Qasaman leaders.

Yet now, with one of those Shahni standing a meter away, they'd failed to take him. Could the aliens really be so careless or gullible that a simple change of clothing could deceive them?

"Clever, wouldn't you say?" Omnathi murmured from beside the bouncing wheelchair.

Daulo looked up, startled. "Excuse me?"

"The invaders' tactic of waiting until we were well away from the exit passage before searching us," Omnathi said, nodding behind them. "By letting us first get out of sight of the subcity exit, they were able to avoid the risk of a coordinated attack from that exit or others nearby."

Daulo thought about that. "Unless they happened to pick a spot for their search that was in view of another exit, one they knew nothing about."

"At which point such an attack would have given them the location of another exit," Omnathi said. "All warfare involves risks. The goal is to balance potential losses with potential gains."

"I see," Daulo said. Jin Moreau, he remembered from all those years ago, had also been able to think that way. So had he, once, at least to a limited degree.

Right now, though, that gift seemed to have deserted him. Probably it was the medication still flowing through his not-yet-healed body.

Maybe that was why he couldn't figure out why the Trofts hadn't plucked Haafiz from the midst of the group.

"Tell me, Daulo Sammon," Omnathi said into his thoughts. "When we leave the city, where would you recommend we go?"

Daulo felt his eyes widen with surprise. "You're asking *me*, Your Excellency?"

"I am," Omnathi said, and Daulo was startled by the sudden dark edge to his voice. "Our friend up there, he whom we will not name in public, may think nothing of a brisk walk to the next town down the road. He might even make it all the way to Purma before the supplies run out. Unfortunately, for some of us that isn't a practical solution."

Belatedly, Daulo noticed the slight limp in Omnathi's step. How old *was* the man, anyway? Somewhere in his eighties, certainly, possibly even in his early nineties. A long, wearying trek to the next major town or minor city along the Great Arc was out of the question.

There were, of course, a number of smaller towns along the road that would be much easier to reach. But given the quiet and apparent lifelessness of the Sollas neighborhoods around them, Daulo suspected that all of those towns were already filled to capacity with earlier refugees.

"The problem is that all the towns along the main road will probably have all the newcomers they can handle," Omnathi continued, echoing Daulo's own unspoken musings. "In addition, the invaders will most likely maintain a presence there, certainly in the larger towns. I'd prefer to avoid any additional scrutiny."

"Understood," Daulo said. "I suppose that leaves only the outlying villages. But travel through the forest carries its own set of risks."

"True," Omnathi said. "Though the forests are safer than they were even ten years ago. So you think one of the forest villages would be our best hope?"

Daulo frowned. Had he said that? "They'll certainly be less crowded," he said cautiously. "Though I'm not sure how many of us a single village could take. Even this close to Sollas, most of them are pretty small."

Omnathi was silent for a few more steps. "Do you know anything about a village called Windloom?"

"Yes, I think so," Daulo said, searching his memory. "It's about thirty kilometers northwest of Sollas. Decent-sized place—maybe nine hundred residents—on the bank of the Westfork River."

"That sounds correct," Omnathi confirmed. "I gather you've visited the place?"

"A few times, but the most recent was several years ago," Daulo told him. "They support a small artists' community which makes metal and carved wood jewelry and trinkets, mostly for sale to the citizens of Sollas. At one time they bought some of the more exotic metals from our mines."

"Do you think they'd accept strangers into their midst?" Omnathi asked. "Especially city dwellers?"

"No," the doctor pushing Daulo's wheelchair said.

Daulo twisted his head around to look up at the other. "Your pardon?" Omnathi asked.

"If you're thinking of dragging us all into the forest, the answer is no," the doctor said firmly. "We have women and injured men who need the kind of medical facilities that can only be found in a town. A *real* town, not some dirtback village." He looked down at Daulo. "So does this one, for that matter."

"The nearest sizeable town is Tazreel," Omnathi said. "Nearly forty kilometers away. Windloom's closer."

"Tazreel has proper medical facilities," the doctor countered. "*And* it lies along a wide, well-maintained road that predators have learned to avoid. There's also a way station about halfway from Sollas where we can rest for the night."

"And the invaders?" Omnathi asked. "They'll be certain to be watching all such towns and way stations."

"I seriously doubt the invaders will have the resources to examine each individual refugee," the doctor said. "Besides," he continued, lowering his voice, "you wouldn't need to stay in Tazreel for long. You could commandeer a vehicle there and go to Purma or anywhere else you wished."

"*If* there are still any vehicles left, and *if* there's still fuel to run them," Omnathi said.

The doctor sniffed. "It's still better than a village."

"Perhaps," Omnathi said. "At any rate, you must do whatever you feel is best for your charges."

The doctor's mouth dropped open. "*My* charges? But you're—"

"Your charges," Omnathi said firmly. "I hereby place you in command of this group of refugees. As for my companions and me, we shall attempt to join up with Daulo Sammon's friends in Windloom."

The doctor looked down at Daulo, then back up at Omnathi.

"If that's your decision, I will obey," he said. "But I strongly advise against it." He gestured a hand up and down Omnathi's body. "Especially for a man of your years. One never knows when immediate medical care will be required."

"Perhaps it would be more proper for a man of my years to graciously step aside and allow what medical care still exists to be given to the young," Omnathi said. "But I appreciate your concern." He gestured ahead. "For now, though, I suggest we concentrate on getting safely through the city."

From somewhere to the north came a muffled *crack* and the stuttering rumble of yet another building coming down. "A point well taken," the doctor said grimly. "Watch your step there."

Fifteen minutes later, they reached the southwest gate.

There were more Trofts standing guard there, and Daulo felt himself tensing as the little clump of refugees approached. But to his relief, the aliens merely stood by watchfully as the humans filed between the vehicle barriers that had been set up.

Daulo half turned in his chair as they passed through the gate, moved by some obscure impulse to have one final look at the once-proud capital of his world.

One way or another, he doubted he would ever come here again.

The sun was low in the sky by the time the group reached Bay Grove Road, with no more than two hours before dusk and perhaps two and a half before full dark. There, Daulo's doctor made one last effort to persuade Omnathi to continue on with them to Tazreel. Once again, Omnathi quietly but firmly declined.

"Now what?" Haafiz demanded in a low voice as they watched the rest of the refugees disappear around a bend in the road.

"Daulo Sammon?" Omnathi invited.

"What?" Haafiz cut in before Daulo could answer. "You're putting *him* in charge?"

"I am," Omnathi said calmly. "Daulo Sammon has been to this village. More than that, he's the only one among us with extensive forest experience." He turned to Daulo and raised his eyebrows. "Daulo Sammon?"

Daulo grimaced, running his eyes over the group. Six young Djinn, warrior-trained but unarmed. Two old men, plus one more—Akim—who had prematurely aged after years of dosing himself with enhancement drugs. And Daulo himself, still recovering from near-fatal injuries. With the daylight rapidly diminishing, the plan looked a lot less feasible than it had in the bright sunlight inside the Sollas wall.

But it was the forest or the Trofts. Under the circumstances, razorarms and baelcras were still the better bet. "It's still almost twenty kilometers to Windloom," he said. "There's no way we're going to make it that far before dark."

"I don't suppose there are any way stations as there are on the *real* road," Haafiz growled.

Daulo shook his head. "There weren't the last time I was there."

"But there's a large flood-control culvert under the road about five kilometers ahead," Akim said. "It's large enough to accommodate all of us, and we should be able to get there while we still have enough light to put together some sort of barriers at the ends to discourage predators."

"A *culvert*?" Haafiz echoed, sounding outraged. "You expect me to spend the night in a *culvert*?"

"Not at all, Your Excellency," Akim said courteously. "You're welcome to remain outside in the forest instead."

Haafiz glared at him. "There will be payment for this day, Miron Akim," he said, his tone dark. "And for you as well, Moffren Omnathi." With an effort, he straightened up. "If this is our path, let us get on with it."

"Very well, Your Excellency." Akim half turned and gestured to one of the Djinn. "Kavad, you'll be first on wheelchair duty. The rest of you, screen formation."

"And watch for danger," Omnathi added as they all set off together. "In every and all directions."

They headed off, Akim and Omnathi in the lead, a glowering Haafiz a few steps behind them, Daulo and Kavad bringing up the rear. The rest of the Djinn formed a sort of moving circle around them, their eyes continually sweeping the landscape.

And as they reached the edge of the forest and continued on beneath the canopy of branches and leaves, Daulo found himself wondering if this really had been his suggestion, the way Omnathi had said.

And wondered, too, how exactly Akim knew about a culvert five kilometers up a lonely forest road.

CHAPTER FIVE

Jin had wanted Warrior to fly the demesne ship over Milika as they headed out into the forest, arguing that they needed to get a better look at what the Trofts were doing in and around the village.

But Siraj had argued that such a move might be seen as provocative or at least suspicious, and that the last thing they could afford was to spark a reaction from one of the invaders' warships. Warrior had agreed, and had ordered his pilot to give Milika a casual but wide berth as they headed to the drop point.

From Zoshak's description of the clearing, and Warrior's response to that description, Jin had already concluded that it was the same place where she and Merrick had been dropped on their clandestine arrival two and a half weeks ago. That conclusion turned out to be correct. The demesne ship was considerably larger than the freighter she and Merrick had traveled in, but Warrior's pilot managed to squeeze it into the available space with only a single stand of crushed bushes at one end.

Having seen firsthand the extensive subcity the Qasamans had created beneath Sollas, Jin had expected Zoshak's watch station to be a similarly extensive system of rooms and corridors and defenses, though of course on a much smaller scale. It was a slight disappointment to find that the station consisted of a single large room with living facilities at one end, an empty weapons rack at the other, and a set of blank monitors in the center.

But of course, the station *was* thirty years old. The Qasamans had probably been new at this whole rabbit burrow thing back then.

The watch station entrance was a simple trapdoor leading to a narrow fold-down stairway, the station itself wasn't exactly spacious, and the Isis gear consisted of a hundred good-sized crates. But Jennifer McCollom, the amateur linguist that Harli Uy had sent along with the expedition, turned out to be a master of packing. With her diminutive frame darting around everywhere, directing the Cobras and Djinn as she just barely managed not to get trampled underfoot, they were able to fit everything inside.

And then, to Jin's surprise and dismay, Warrior announced it was time for him to leave.

[Two hours on Qasama, the Tua'lanek'zia demesne has limited our stay,] he explained as his crew resealed the ship's cargo compartments. [Our departure, we must take it immediately.]

"I don't remember hearing anything about a time limit," Lorne said. His tone was respectful enough, but Jin could hear the suspicion lurking behind the words.

[The limit, it was not imposed by the Balin'ckha'spmi demesne upon our arrival,] Warrior explained. [The limit, it was given later. The unloading, you were performing it at the time.]

"Wait a second," Lorne said, frowning. "You just said it was the Balin demesne who we talked to, and that the Tua demesne is kicking you out. But on our way in you said it was *Drim* invaders who'd returned. Just how many demesnes have we got on Qasama, anyway?"

[Three demesnes at the least, they are represented here,] Warrior said. [The demesne that rules, its identity I cannot say.]

"But you must have *some* idea who's—" Lorne began.

"However the order came, you'd better obey it before your time limit runs out," Paul interrupted, shifting the arm he had resting for support on Jin's shoulder. "Thank you for getting us here."

[Your future, it lies now in your own hands.] Warrior's arm membranes fluttered. [That future, do not allow it to slip and fall to destruction.]

"We won't," Paul promised. "And you'll speak to your demesne-lord about sending ships back to Caelian and taking off the Drim prisoners?"

[The request, I will make it,] Warrior said. [Good fortune, I wish it for you.]

Ten minutes later, with the Cobras and Djinn gathered together at the clearing's edge, the demesne ship lifted on its gravs and rose swiftly into the darkening sky. "And with that," Paul murmured, "we're back where we started: humanity standing alone against the Trofts."

"Large bunches of Trofts, from the sound of it," Lorne said sourly. "Why did you cut me off back there? There have to be some interesting politics going on between the different groups of invaders. We might have gotten Warrior to tell us more about it."

"If he knew more of the situation, would he not have spoken of it in more detail during the voyage?" Siraj asked.

"Not necessarily," Lorne said. "We already know Warrior has at least one agenda of his own going, namely for us to kick the invaders hard enough that the Tlossies and some of the other demesnes can come in and hopefully stare them down. Warrior may have other cards he's not showing."

"In which case, more questioning wouldn't have gotten us anywhere anyway," Paul said. "More importantly, Warrior's new two-hour limit was about up. He had to get moving before the invaders—*any* of them—decided to come out here and shoo him off Qasama."

"I suppose," Lorne conceded reluctantly. "So what now? We head to Milika and find out what's going on?"

"Two of us will, anyway," Everette Beach, one of the two Caelian Cobras, put in. "Either Wendell or me to drive the spooker and Siraj, Zoshak, or Khatir along as native guide."

Jin looked up at the sky. No more than another hour until nightfall, she estimated. Predator-wise, nighttime travel on Qasama was more dangerous than doing so in the daytime, though it wasn't nearly as bad as it once was. "Not much time left before dark," she warned.

"Which will be perfect," Siraj said. "By the time we reach Milika the larger nocturnal predators will be out and about, which will help diffuse the attention of the invaders' infrared scans."

"So let's make it a party of four," Lorne suggested. "We've got two spookers, and two of you to drive them. That way I can go, too."

"No," Paul said before Beach could answer. "Let's keep it at two."

"But—" Lorne began.

"That leaves one spooker here in case there's an emergency," his father continued calmly. "Besides, it's only an assumption that the invaders won't wonder what Warrior and the Tlossies wanted out here. We need to keep as much of a force here as possible in case someone decides to come out and take a look."

"Agreed," Beach said before Lorne could say anything else. "You care which of us goes?"

"Not really," Paul said. "Jin? You have a preference?"

Jin eyed the two Caelians. Everette Beach was a big man, a couple of years younger than her own fifty-two, with a lot of gray sprinkling his brown hair and a seemingly permanent half-grin on his face. Wendell McCollom, who also happened to be Jennifer's husband, was even bigger, though he usually maintained a more serious air than his colleague. Possibly something that had rubbed off from his wife, who was apparently the closest thing Caelian had to an expert on matters Qasaman and Troft. Both men, Jin suspected, had probably been formidable fighters in their youthful days, even before they became Cobras. "Everette will go," she decided. "I'm also thinking Carsh Zoshak should be the one to accompany him. He's been inside Milika, and therefore knows both the area and the village layout."

"Your reasoning is sound," Siraj said, nodding. "Djinni Zoshak? Retrieve your outer clothing and two survival bags and meet Cobra Beach at the spookers."

Fifteen minutes later, dressed in Qasaman clothing and equipped with survival bags, the two men zoomed out of the clearing on their battered grav-lift cycle and disappeared into the forest.

"I'll take the first watch," Wendell volunteered. "The rest of you can head downstairs and get something to eat."

"I should probably stay with you," Jin offered. "I know the local predators. You don't."

"Don't worry about it," Wendell assured her. "Anything with teeth or claws gets too close, I'll just kill it. Once I've got a collection, you can come and tell me which is which."

Jin grimaced. Still, the razorarms were the most dangerous predators out here, and with mojos riding herd on them they should steer clear of human scent. "Just don't let them get too close," she warned. "And use your sonic whenever possible. Laser shots will start being more and more visible as the sun goes down."

"Thank you; I *had* figured that one out," Wendell said dryly. "One of you can relieve me in a couple of hours. Oh, and make sure Jennifer eats too, will you? She sometimes gets so busy she forgets."

"We'll force-feed her if we have to," Paul promised. "See you in two hours."

Jin, Lorne, and Wendell had unanimously decided that Paul and his damaged leg weren't fit to stand guard. They had thus taken it with varying degrees of consternation when he calmly pulled rank as senior Cobra present and added himself to the sentry rotation anyway.

He was midway through the third watch shift, shivering with the unexpected nighttime chill and wondering whether perhaps he should have just let the others give him a night off, when he heard the sound of an approaching vehicle.

He had levered himself into an upright position and had his thumbs resting lightly on the triggers of his fingertip lasers when the spooker floated into view between the trees and coasted to a halt.

"Over here," Paul called softly as Zoshak and Beach started to dismount. Beach nodded and kicked the spooker forward, crossing the clearing and bringing the grav-lift cycle to a second halt beside Paul. "I wasn't expecting you back until morning," Paul said, notching up his light-amps. There was a hard set to both men's faces. "Do they have Milika blocked off?"

"No, we reached the village just fine," Beach said grimly. "We also heard the Trofts' demands, which they seem to be blasting over a loudspeaker once an hour."

"They want your son, Paul Broom," Zoshak said quietly. "He's to surrender himself to them by dawn or they'll begin destroying the village."

"I see," Paul said, dimly surprised at how calm he sounded. Jin had called it, all right. The Trofts had come to Milika for the express purpose of smoking Merrick out.

And now his earnest, conscientious son was being forced into the most horrible choice any human being could ever face: whether or not to offer himself in exchange for the lives of innocent people.

"The villagers are Qasamans, Cobra Broom, and they're at war," Zoshak said. "They know the risks and the sacrifices required. They won't give him up."

"Are you sure about that?" Paul countered, trying hard to think. What was Merrick going to do? What *could* he do? "Remember, Merrick's a demon warrior. Everyone in Milika probably grew up hating them."

"Perhaps," Zoshak said. The ghost of a smile touched his lips. "But by now they surely hate the invaders far more."

"Don't forget that ship's been sitting there for hours," Beach reminded him. "I think Zoshak's right—if they were going to turn him over to the Trofts, they'd have done it by now."

Except that so far all the Trofts were doing was threatening, and threats by themselves were pretty easy to stand up to. Would that shoulder-to-shoulder human solidarity survive mass death and destruction when the deadline passed and the threats turned into violent action?

And even if the village didn't hand him over, what then? Would they all fight to the death as Milika was leveled around them?

And if *that* happened, what would happen to the mine where Dr. Croi was hoping to set up his Cobra factory?

Merrick was Paul's son, and dearer to him than his own life. But there were bigger things at stake here. If it cost Merrick's life to get the Trofts to leave Milika, that might very well be what he would have to do.

Unless...

"I need to talk to him," Paul said. "Can you get me there?"

"It won't be comfortable," Beach warned, eyeing Paul's bandaged leg. "And I doubt we can get you inside. The ship's sitting in front of the gate, and the entire top of the wall is within their view."

"I just need to get close enough to see and be seen," Paul said. "If I can get his attention we can use Dida code to communicate."

"Okay," Beach said, sounding doubtful. "Is Wendell in the bunker?"

"Why?"

Beach frowned slightly. "Because we're going to need the second spooker and someone to drive it," he said.

"I'll go get him," Zoshak volunteered, hopping off the spooker.

"That's all right," Paul said quickly. "Don't wake him. We can manage with one."

"How you figure that?" Beach asked, his frown deepening. "You and Zoshak going to ride double?"

"We leave Djinni Zoshak here and you take me," Paul said. "I assume your stabilization computer's got an inertial track memory, so we should be able to find Milika again without him."

"Or you and I could go alone," Zoshak offered. Like Beach, there was something in the Qasaman's voice that indicated he'd figured out something was going on, even if he didn't yet know what that something was. "I'm sure I could do an adequate job of driving the vehicle."

"And if he can't, I can," Paul said. "I've driven regular grav-lift cycles before. Whatever extra juice spookers have, I can handle it."

"Uh-huh." Deliberately, Beach folded his arms across his chest. "Okay, let's have it."

"Have what?" Paul asked.

"Whatever it is you're cooking up," Beach said flatly. "Come on, give."

"I agree," Zoshak seconded.

Paul sighed. "We need to get Isis into Milika," he said. "We can't do that while the Trofts are there. They aren't leaving without a Cobra." He braced himself. "So we'll give them one."

Beach's eyes narrowed. "You?"

"Me," Paul confirmed.

Beach looked at Zoshak, back at Paul. "And how exactly do you plan to explain to the Trofts how a young, fit Cobra inside the Milika wall managed to transmogrify himself into an older, half-crippled Cobra *outside* the wall?"

"I don't know yet," Paul said. "And I won't until I talk to Merrick and find out what exactly the Trofts know." He gestured. "So am I getting on that spooker with you? Or do I have to knock you off it and head out on my own?"

"I'd like to see you try," Beach said absently, gazing hard into Paul's face. "Okay, I'll go this far. I'll take you to Milika, but I want a decent plan on the table before you do anything. There's no point in losing both you *and* Merrick to the Trofts. And I still think I should wake Wendell and make this a foursome."

"There's no time," Paul said. "Besides, if we wake him, we'll probably also wake Jin and Lorne."

"Which we probably should," Beach pointed out. "They deserve to know what's going on."

"They'll find out soon enough," Paul said. "And if they find out now, they'll want to argue about it. As I said, we haven't got time."

"You should at least say good-bye," Beach persisted.

"You don't understand," Zoshak asked quietly. "The choice we would set before Jin Moreau would be that of giving the life of her husband or the life of her son. Do you really wish to force that decision upon her?"

Beach's lip twitched. "Yeah, I see your point," he conceded. "Fine. Go ahead and hop on." He shook his head. "Though it occurs to me that if I'm going to have to face her with this after it's over, maybe *I* should be the one the Trofts take."

"Don't worry about it," Paul said as he maneuvered himself carefully onto the spooker. "With two of us against a Troft warship, there's a good chance we'll both be killed anyway."

"Yeah, that's looking on the bright side," Beach said dryly. "Zoshak, mind the store. Broom, you just focus on hanging on."

From the southern edge of Milika the booming translator voice drifted over the village with the same message it had been delivering since the warship first appeared outside the gate.

"To the *koubrah*-soldier of Milika: you will surrender to this vessel by sunrise. If you do not surrender, the village will be destroyed and the people within the wall will be killed."

Merrick listened as the message repeated the usual three times. Then, the loudspeaker fell silent, and the normal forest noises once again began to drift across Milika.

"Only two and a half more hours before sunrise," Dr. Krites commented from Fadil's bedside.

"Yes, I know," Merrick said. Either Krites or Fadil, before the latter had fallen asleep, had made sure to remind him of the approaching deadline roughly every hour since he'd sought refuge and counsel here a little after midnight.

"Knowledge is silver," Krites said tartly. "Wisdom is gold. What do you plan to do?"

Merrick stared at the darkened buildings and homes stretched out beneath the window. It was a question he'd been struggling with ever since the ship had first appeared outside Milika at yesterday's dawn.

On one hand, the answer was simple. He couldn't just sit here while the Trofts destroyed the village, or even started that process. With the first actual laser blast or missile he would have no choice but to leave the Sammon house and march toward the warship with his hands held high in surrender. Certainly that was the reaction the Trofts were counting on.

But the more he dug below the surface of that supposedly simple answer, the more he realized things weren't nearly that straightforward. If the Trofts wanted to kill him, then they would kill him, and there was little Merrick could do except hope that his death would buy Milika a release from this siege.

But what if the Trofts wanted to take him alive? As the hours shrank toward the deadline, that possibility seemed more and more likely. Especially after Fadil had pointed out that the aliens could have forced Merrick's death long ago by simply opening fire on the village and forcing him into a suicidal counterattack.

So what *did* the Trofts want him for? There was only one reason Merrick had been able to come up with, and the very thought of it made his skin crawl.

The invaders had been defeated once by a coalition consisting of hundreds of Qasaman Djinn and two Aventinian Cobras. They'd presumably captured enough Djinn combat suits along the way to know how they operated, and to counter future attacks.

But that was the Djinn. So far, the Trofts hadn't been able to crack the full range of Cobra weapons and capabilities. Remedying that deficiency was very likely the goal of this current operation.

They were hoping to take Merrick so that they could dissect him. Possibly while he was still alive.

Merrick couldn't let them to that, of course. Personal dread aside, he had no intention of giving the invaders a head start in fighting whatever troops his mother succeeded in bringing back.

Fortunately—or as fortunately as it got—he had ultimate veto over that particular scenario. Once the warship opened fire on Milika he could ensure that he ended up in the midst of their attack. With his speed, strength, and reflexes, he should be able to arrange a quick and mostly painless death for himself.

And yet...

He raised his eyes from the darkened village to the stars twinkling against the cloudless sky. Merrick's great-grandfather Jonny Moreau had also been taken alive during his war against the Trofts a century ago. He, too, had realized that the enemy planned to use him to glean information about Cobra abilities and equipment.

But instead of simply sacrificing himself to keep that from happening, Jonny had found a way to turn his captors' plan against them.

Shouldn't Merrick at least try to find a similar solution before he gave up?

There was an urgent knock on the door. "Enter," Krites called softly.

The door swung open to reveal one of the Sammon family servants. "Your pardon," the man panted, glancing at Fadil's closed eyes and then turning to Merrick. "I have an urgent message for Merrick Moreau. One of the wall guards has sighted a small light in the kundur trees to the east."

Merrick frowned. And this had had to do with him how? "Okay," he said cautiously. "And?"

"He speaks of the kundur grove to the east," Fadil said. Merrick jumped—he'd thought Fadil was still asleep. "A light shining into Milika from there would be invisible to the invaders' warship."

"The light gives five short flashes, then a pause," the servant added. "Then five more flashes, then another pause."

Merrick caught his breath. That was Dida code. Five flashes—*dit dit dit dit dit*—was the signal for *calling—anyone there?*

His mother had returned. And she had indeed brought more Cobras with her.

"I need a spot where I can see the light," he told the servant as he scrambled to his feet, a sudden surge of hope blasting away the fatigue hovering at the edges of his brain. "Someplace where I also won't be seen from the ship."

"The meditation dome above the library should work," Fadil said. "Sharmal will take you there."

"Yes, Master Sammon," the servant said. "If you'll follow me, Merrick Moreau?"

Three minutes later, Merrick was in the dome, a small flashlight in hand, his light-amps at full power as he quickly but methodically scanned the area the servant had identified as the kundur tree grove.

There it was, back against one of the tree trunks, between two leafy branches where not even a glint of reflection would be visible to the warship's cameras and sensors. *Dit dit dit dit dit. Dit dit dit dit dit.*

Merrick keyed his flashlight to touch mode and pointed it at the tree. *Dit dit dah dit dit dah*, he sent. *Ready—proceed.*

There was a short pause, and then the other light changed to a new pattern of flashes. *Identify.*

Merrick smiled tightly. Like there was anyone else on Qasama who knew Dida code. *Merrick Moreau Broom*, he tapped out. *Identify.*

Paul Broom.

Merrick's smile vanished. His *father*? *Here*?

But that was impossible. Jin Moreau Broom had gone to Aventine, not Caelian. This had to be some kind of trick by the Trofts, perhaps something designed to flush him out of hiding and then keep him in one place long enough for them to sneak an assault team into the village to nail him.

But how could the invaders have learned Dida code?

Merrick cranked up his opticals to full power, trying to pierce the gloom and rustling leaves. But whoever was back there was too well concealed. All he could see was a shadowy, indistinct form that could be anyone.

Muttering a curse under his breath, he keyed his light again. Whatever was going on, he was not going to let his father's name spook him. *Prove it*, he challenged.

You're an excellent cook, the reply came. *Especially when mixing drogfowl cacciatore with conversations of treason. Situation?*

Merrick felt some of the tension in his chest ease. Not only were his culinary skills his most closely guarded secret, but the figure behind the light out there had even described the meal the family had had the night this whole thing had first started. Impossible or not, that was definitely his father out there. *Trofts demanding surrender by sunrise*, he sent back. *No clean exit available. Suggestions?*

One hour; north wall, his father signaled. *Use Sammon family mine explosives to create exit hole in base. Grav-lift cycle will be waiting beside wall; evasive ride into forest. When pursuit has been lost, go to Shaga.*

Merrick nodded to himself. Shaga was the next village south along the road, about ten kilometers away. *What about you?*

I'll leave the cycle by the wall and retreat to safety. Once the Trofts have left, I'll travel to Shaga and rendezvous with you there.

Merrick pursed his lips. The plan was definitely on the dicey side, especially the dual questions of whether Fadil's people could come up with enough explosives fast enough to make the required exit and what the villagers were going to say about having a section of their wall blown to gravel.

But it was probably the best plan they were going to come up with, given the time and resources they had available. *Acknowledged*, he sent reluctantly. *One hour?*

One hour, his father confirmed. There was just the slightest hesitation. *Good luck, Merrick. I love you.*

I love you too, Dad.

The other light flicked the close-off signal. Merrick sent the proper countersign, then headed down the meditation dome's spiral stairway.

Time to see how fast Fadil could get his people moving.

Fadil's eyes were closed as Merrick related the conversation and described what he and his father needed. The eyes remained closed after Merrick had finished, and Fadil himself remained silent long enough that Merrick wondered if he'd fallen asleep again.

He was just about to check when Fadil's lips puckered. "No," he said, finally opening his eyes.

Merrick stared at him, his heart sinking. After everything else they'd gone through, a flat refusal to help was the last response he'd expected. "Is it about the wall?" he asked. "Because if it is, I make a vow right now that I'll come back to Milika personally and repair it."

"It's not the wall," Fadil said, his voice thoughtful. "It's the plan. There's something wrong with the plan."

Merrick looked at Krites, back again at Fadil. "I agree that it could be tricky to get the grav-lift cycle to the wall without the invaders seeing it," he said. "But—"

"No, that shouldn't be a problem," Fadil said. "Not at the northern wall. There are several wooded approaches that would provide sufficient cover. Tell me, did your father explain why he wanted you to break through the wall?"

"I assume so that I can get out of Milika without getting vaporized," Merrick said.

"Yet there are guards even now walking the top of the wall," Fadil pointed out. "If you joined the patrol as one of them, you could simply drop through one of the many gaps in the wall's upper extension. You'd be beyond easy reach of the invaders' lasers before anyone aboard the warship could react to your action."

Merrick felt a chill run up his back. Fadil was right. With razorarm attacks no longer a problem in the Qasaman forest, the metal mesh extension that had been long ago erected atop Milika's wall had fallen into neglect and disrepair. Merrick had seen the gaps Fadil was talking about, including a couple in the vicinity where his father had called for the blast. "But if the explosion isn't to get me out, what's it for? A diversion?"

"Are you certain it was your father behind the signal light?" Krites asked.

"I am," Merrick said firmly. "He knew things that only he would know. Including the code he used to speak to me."

"Then the answer is clear," Fadil said. "The explosion isn't a diversion, nor is it intended to let you escape. Its purpose is to *prevent* your escape."

Merrick blinked. *"What?"*

"Consider," Fadil continued. "Where will you be when the explosion takes place? Somewhere under protection several meters away at the least. How long after the explosion will it take the debris to cease falling and for you to make your way across the rubble and out into the forest?"

Merrick felt his stomach tighten. Now, of course, it was obvious. Painfully obvious. "He has no intention of letting me hop on any grav-lift cycle and get out of here, does he?" he said, hearing the dark edge in his voice. "He just wants me to draw the Trofts' attention to that part of the wall so that *he* can tear out of here like a bat out of hell and try to draw them away."

"So I would read the plan," Fadil said. "Your father, Merrick Moreau, honors himself and you."

"He is indeed an honorable man," Merrick said, taking a step back toward the door. "Thank you, Fadil Sammon, for your insights. I'll take my leave of you now."

"What will you do?" Fadil asked.

"What I have to," Merrick told him. "If I don't return, please accept my gratitude for all that you, the Sammon family, and the village of Milika have done for me."

"I trust you remember that your body is still not at full capability and function," Krites warned. "Especially considering the internal injuries you reopened in the forest two days ago. If you start bleeding internally again, you could die."

"I'll remember," Merrick assured him. "Thank you, too, Doctor

Krites, for your assistance and care." He took a deep breath. "Farewell, Fadil Sammon."

"Farewell, Merrick Moreau," Fadil replied gravely. "May God go with you."

Paul had said he would be waiting by the wall with the grav-lift cycle in an hour. Merrick's nanocomputer clock circuit showed ten minutes to that deadline as he joined the other guards walking the Milika wall and headed casually toward his chosen gap in the metal mesh.

He tried to watch everywhere at once as he walked, his heart thudding painfully in his chest. There had been no way to physically rehearse what was about to happen, but he'd run the whole operation over and over in his mind as best he could, throwing in all the variants, possible problems, and potential obstacles that he could come up with.

Time now to find out how closely his imagination and planning matched reality.

The clock showed two minutes left as he approached his planned drop zone. A casual glance over the side of the wall showed that his father was already in position, seated on an unexpectedly large and intimidating grav-lift cycle about ten meters from where the explosion was supposed to happen, and about three from the gap Merrick was heading for.

The clock had just passed one minute to zero when Merrick reached the gap. Without breaking stride, he half turned and dropped himself through it.

He landed with a crunch of broken bushes, a controlled bending of knees to absorb the impact, and a look of startled consternation on his father's face. *"Merrick?"* Paul breathed. "You were supposed to—"

"Hi, Dad," Merrick said. "Nice try."

And with a flick of a target lock and a pair of bursts from his fingertip lasers, he neatly cut the wires leading to both of the cycle's left-hand stabilizer sensors. "Merrick—no!" Paul snapped.

But he was too late. The big machine lurched beneath him, its left side canting twenty degrees downward as the grav lifts on that side lost the sensors' feedback.

And as Paul scrambled for a grip on his now badly angled mount, Merrick heard the sounds of the warship's gravs as they revved to full power. "It's okay, Dad—I've got it covered," he said. He took a step toward the forest, then hesitated. "If this doesn't work, say good-bye to Mom and Lorne and Jody for me, will you?"

"I will," Paul said. There was a deep sadness in his voice, and Merrick could hear the almost-echo of words still unformed, words that were still only thoughts and emotions deep within his father's soul.

Words that would never be anything more than those feelings. From the other side of the village came the sibilant hissing of displaced tree branches as the warship lifted from the ground. "Stay safe, Dad," Merrick said quickly, and sprinted away from the wall. The reflected glint of the warship's grav lifts was just hitting the outer ring of trees as he slipped between them and headed into the forest.

And the race was on.

Merrick never knew afterward just how far from Milika he got during the chase. He wove back and forth between the trees and bushes, his light-amps at full power as he looked for the fastest route, his programmed reflexes working hard to maintain his balance on the treacherous footing. Swarms of insects and small groups of birds burst from concealment at various places along his path, and small animals scurried madly to get out of his way. Even the larger predators seemed to realize this was a phenomenon that should be steered clear of and crouched motionless as they watched him sprint past.

All the while, the Troft warship stayed right on top of him, or just behind him, the hum of its gravs audible over the crash of his feet through the dead leaves, the gravs themselves occasionally glowing briefly through the canopy of leafy branches above him. It never opened fire, and none of Merrick's tricks ever lost it for more than a few seconds. The Trofts simply stayed up there, pacing his mad run, waiting for their quarry to finally exhaust his strength.

On that count, at least, they were going to be in for a surprise. New Cobra recruits invariably tried to do this kind of long-range running on their own power, which inevitably led to muscle fatigue and exhaustion. Experienced Cobras like Merrick knew how to let their leg servos do all the work. He could probably run halfway to Sollas without serious problem.

The other possibility, that the ship wasn't trying to run him to ground but was instead subtly herding him toward a particular spot, never even occurred to him. Not until it was too late.

Not until he hit the trap.

It was a simple trap, really: a wall of thick, sturdy netting, laid flat against the ground beneath the leaves and spring-loaded to snap up in front of him at his approach. Almost before his eyes even registered the obstacle, certainly before his programmed reflexes could stop his forward momentum, he hit the wall, yanking the netting out of its frame and wrapping it securely around him.

All three of his lasers flashed, but the bits of netting vaporized were small and insignificant. He tried pressing outward with his arms, but the mesh was highly elastic and merely stretched without tearing. His legs could also stretch out the mesh, and for a few seconds he managed to keep going. But the netting was self-adhering, and his scissoring legs merely tangled it against itself, and a few steps later he found himself sprawled face-first onto the ground.

He was firing his lasers again, trying to maneuver his hands enough to cut an actual tear in the material, when the world faded away into blackness.

The sky to the east was still dark with pre-dawn gloom as Jin walked tiredly through the gate into Milika.

The first news was good. Paul was standing near a few silent villagers, clearly alive and no worse off than he'd been when he slipped away from their encampment a few hours ago.

But Merrick wasn't with him. And the expression of guilt and grief and pain on his face was all she needed to know that the worst had indeed happened.

But something deep inside her still needed to make sure. "He's gone," she said as she came up to him.

Paul nodded heavily. "I'm sorry, Jin," he said. "I tried to stop him."

Jin took a deep breath. He had indeed tried. She knew him well enough to know that he'd done his very best to protect their son.

And yet, if he'd succeeded, she would have gained her son and lost her husband. Or she might have lost them both.

She'd been furious when Zoshak told her about Paul's unilateral decision on what to do about Merrick's situation. But the anger had long since evaporated. All that was left now was weariness and sorrow.

And, to her own private shame, a small nugget of guilty gratitude that he'd taken the decision on his own shoulders instead of giving half of it to her.

A woman should never be forced to choose between the lives of her son and her husband.

"It's all right," she said, reaching up to rest her hand on his cheek. "Merrick's smart and clever, and he has his great-grandfather's genes. He'll get through this."

"I know," Paul said.

He didn't, of course, Jin knew. But then, neither did she.

Many of the families on Qasama and Caelian had lost loved ones to the Troft invasion. It was probably inevitable, she knew, that sooner or later her family would be one of them.

All she could do now was try her damnedest to make sure that Merrick's sacrifice—that *all* of their sacrifices—weren't wasted.

"Did you talk to Fadil Sammon?" she asked, giving Paul's cheek one final caress and then lowering her hand back to her side.

"Yes, and it's all set," he said. "The foreman has three crews below ground right now, clearing out the mining equipment and checking the ventilation, safety, and power systems. By the time we get Isis here, it should be ready for us to move right in."

"Good." Jin took a deep breath, pushing the pain as far back as she could. It wasn't far, but it would hopefully be enough to allow her to function. "Let's see what progress the Djinn have made in organizing a vehicle caravan." She glanced around, spotted Siraj and Zoshak talking to the gate guards while a circle of villagers stood quietly around them. Ghofl Khatir, the third Djinni, was nowhere to be seen. "Do you know what happened to Djinn Khatir?" she asked.

"He's talking to Fadil Sammon," Paul said. "Some high-level conference, I gather, from the way both of them looked when I left."

Jin nodded. She'd wondered why Fadil hadn't been down here to meet her and the others as they arrived. "Is Fadil doing all right?" she asked.

"Actually, no," Paul said, a fresh edge of grimness to his voice. "But we can talk about that later. Right now, we have to get Isis here and get Dr. Croi started putting the pieces together."

"While we meanwhile dig up some recruits," Jin said. "I just hope we can find enough of them."

"I don't think that's going to be a problem," Paul assured her. "From what little I've seen of Milika, I think Siraj Akim and the others should have plenty of volunteers to choose from."

"Assuming he can find whatever qualities the Shahni consider necessary for good Qasaman warriors." Jin looked toward the east, where the sun would soon be coming up, and where the Troft invaders had long since settled in across the Qasaman landscape. "He'd just better find them fast," she added. "Even starting right now, it's ten days minimum before we can get any new Cobras into the field. That's ten more days the invaders will have to work on consolidating their positions and wrecking Qasama's infrastructure."

"We'll make it," Paul said firmly. "Whatever we have to do, we'll make it."

CHAPTER SIX

The sound of hammering and power tools from the northern edge of the Caelian capital of Stronghold had begun right at sunup, jarring Jody Broom out of an already troubled sleep. By the time she finished her morning routine, including the tedious but vital job of scraping the spores and other floating organics off her silliweave clothing, the hammer-and-tongs were going full force.

The door to the rented house's other bedroom was closed, which meant at least one of her two business partners, Geoff Boulton and Freylan Sanderby, was still trying to sleep through the racket. Probably Geoff, she made a private bet with herself. For all of his outgoing energy and easy social enthusiasm, he'd never been much of a morning person. Freylan, the shy introspective one of their research team, was much more likely to have risen at dawn, quietly eager to get back to work on the two combat suits the Qasaman Djinn had given them.

Besides which, Freylan was a light sleeper. There was no way he was still zonked out in there.

Jody had expected to find him outside on the house's small veranda, surrounded by the equipment Geoff had begged or borrowed, working on the puzzle of how exactly the electronics in the Djinni outfits were able to resist the floating organics that attached themselves to all non-living surfaces. But he was nowhere to be seen.

Unfortunately, with the planetary communications system still down, there was no way for her to call him, or even to call someone else to ask about him. At this hour, she decided, her best bet would be to check in with the men at the wrecked wall and see if any of them had seen him. Readjusting the stiff silicon-based fabric across her shoulders, she headed toward the noise.

Caelian's original settlers had quickly learned that the trouble with the floating organics wasn't the tiny spores per se. It was, rather, the tiny insects that eagerly descended on any and all bits of such entrenched vegetation, eating both the spores and bits of whatever carbon-based clothing or building material the spores happened to be attached to at the time. Tiny insects attracted larger insects, which attracted small birds and reptiles, all the way up the food chain to the larger predators that could take on human beings with impunity.

There was nothing anyone had ever been able to do about the spores except try to keep them from finding something edible to attach to. The big predators, though, were another story. They could be shot and killed by projectile weapons and laser fire, which explained Caelian's relatively large contingent of Cobras and its heavily armed non-Cobra populace. Alternatively, the predators could be kept out of the settlements entirely, which explained the tall stainless-steel wall that had been erected around Stronghold.

Only the wall wasn't very stainless anymore. In fact, for about seventy meters of its length along the northern part of the city, it wasn't even a wall. The Troft warship that had fallen sideways squarely on top of it had seen to that.

Since it was the Troft invasion that had brought that warship into proximity to the wall in the first place, it was only fair that it should be the Troft prisoners who'd been tasked with the job of cleaning up the mess.

They were doing a good job of it, Jody saw as she arrived at the downed warship. Or if not a good job, at least a busy and noisy one. The aliens were moving in and out of the wreckage, all two hundred of them, hammering at the ship's lower hull, lugging sections of grav-lift panels, or using pry bars and cutting torches on the weapons pods on the stubby wings. Standing watchful vigilance over the operation were twenty Cobras, some standing above the crowd on the intact sections of wall, others forming a barrier between the prisoners and the rest of the city.

"You're up early."

Jody turned. Harli Uy, Cobra commander and son of Caelian's governor, was walking briskly up behind her. "So are you," she said, eyeing the fatigue lines and blotches in his face. "Only *I* got a decent night's sleep."

He grunted as he came to a halt beside her. "So did I," he said. "As decent a night's sleep as any of us gets these days, anyway."

"That bad, huh?"

"We're doing okay," Harli assured her. "We're just spread a little thin, that's all."

"We knew that was going to happen," Jody reminded him. Now that he was closer, she could see the extra tension that was simmering beneath the tiredness. "How's your father?"

Harli gave a microscopic hunch of his shoulders. "Recovering."

"And?" Jody prompted.

"And what?"

"And what does he think about our agreement with the Qasamans?"

"He's dealing with it." Harli waved at the working Trofts. "So you here for the circus, or the Biblical epic?"

Jody frowned. "The *what*?"

"The Biblical epic," Harli said. "Someone was saying yesterday the whole thing reminded him of Israelite slaves building pyramids back on Earth in some big screen epic."

"Yes, I guess I can see that," Jody agreed, looking closely at Harli's face. "He doesn't like the agreement, does he?"

Harli huffed out a sigh. "No, he's not very happy with it," he conceded. "*Or* with me." His lip twitched. "And to be honest, I'm starting to agree with him."

"He's worried about the Qasamans having Isis?"

"He's more annoyed that we *don't* have it." Harli gestured at two of the Cobras standing on the wall. "I mean, look at them.

They're just standing there, doing absolutely nothing except ride herd on a bunch of prisoners. Meanwhile, Stronghold is running low on food, and the other towns are having to stay inside their own walls because they haven't got enough Cobras to escort anyone heading outside."

And without the ability to send out hunting parties, Jody knew, those other towns would also soon be running short of food. "Maybe we should lock them up in the ships," she suggested. "Or maybe just that one," she added, pointing to the second Troft warship, the one still standing upright beside the sideways one. "At least that would eliminate a lot of the guard duty."

"Then who would do all the work to get the other ship out of there and start repairing the wall?" Harli countered. "Besides, there's no way to know what's still aboard that ship. They could have a hundred of those big hand lasers hidden behind the walls for all we know. Worse, they might find a way to wire around the power and control cables we cut and reactivate what's left of their wing-based weapons."

Weapons that had devastated sections of Stronghold and killed or injured three hundred Cobras, including Jody's own father. Not to mention nearly getting her mother killed outright. "You're right," she acknowledged. "Sorry—I didn't think it through."

"Don't worry about it," Harli said. "We've been working through all the options longer than you have, that's all. The idea actually surfaced almost a week ago, right after your parents and the rest of the crowd headed off for Qasama." He hesitated. "We also considered the idea of just dumping them out in the forest somewhere and letting Wonderland deal with them."

Jody felt a shiver run through her. *Wonderland*—Caelian slang for everything on the planet not under direct human control. Out in the forest, without weapons or defenses, the aliens would be dead within days. Probably within hours. "You might as well just shoot them."

"Which would be completely unethical," Harli agreed grimly. "I know. But ethics don't feed the bulldog, as my grandfather used to say. Doesn't get us any more Cobras, either."

"If sending Isis to Qasama wins us the war, it'll be worth it," Jody reminded him.

"*If*," Harli said. "And if it doesn't kill all of us first."

For a minute they stood together in silence, watching the Trofts work. Most of the aliens she could see had their upper-arm membranes fully extended, the equivalent of heavy sweating for humans. Their overseers were working them hard, all right. Occasionally, Jody caught a flicker of light as one of the Cobras on guard duty fired his antiarmor laser, probably at some predator nosing around the work zone. "What did you mean, the circus?" she asked.

Harli turned a frown onto her. "What?"

"You asked me if I was here for the circus or the Biblical epic," she said. "What circus?"

"Oh. Right." He gestured to her and started walking again toward the gap in the wall. "I just got the word—I was heading to see it myself. This way."

They passed the line of sentries, maneuvered carefully over the crushed wall with its torn and twisted edges and past the equally hazardous wreckage of the downed warship. Some of the Trofts gave them baleful looks as they threaded their way through the work parties, but most of the prisoners ignored them entirely.

And as they approached the last two parties, Jody finally saw what Harli had been referring to.

Standing fifty meters off to the side, his gray combat suit in sharp contrast with the Cobras' muted white silliweave outfits, was Freylan.

Jody rolled her eyes. Freylan knew better than this. Even with all those Cobras on hand to watch for trouble, he really should have known better than this.

He was fighting with a section of support beam twice his size, trying to get it up onto his shoulder, when Jody and Harli reached him. "Freylan, what in the Worlds do you think you're doing?" Jody demanded.

"Oh—hi, Jody," Freylan said, puffing with exertion as he got the beam up high enough to rest on his shoulder. "Hi, Harli. You two are up early."

"All the best shows start early here," Harli said, craning his neck as he looked up at the end of the beam towering over them. "The lady asked you a question."

"What?" Freylan frowned, then his face cleared. "Oh. You mean what am I doing?" He gestured to the beam. "I'm trying out the suit. Wanted to see how much strength the servos have, how the power curve plays out—you know. Try it out."

"You couldn't have done this back at the house?" Jody asked.

"Yeah, I suppose," Freylan said with a shrug. "But I figured as long as I was going to be lifting stuff, why not lift stuff that needed lifting anyway?"

"Except that out here we have to protect you," Harli reminded him. "I don't suppose that occurred to you."

"No, you don't," Freylan said brightly. "Organics don't stick to the suit, remember? And the giggers and screech tigers seem to be avoiding the area—"

"I was thinking about them," Harli said patiently, nodding back toward the toiling Trofts.

Freylan's eyes flicked over Harli's shoulder. "Oh," he said, sounding a little deflated. "You don't think they'd—? But there are Cobras all around them. They wouldn't try anything."

"Who knows what they might try?" Jody said, trying to keep her tone gentle. It wasn't Freylan's fault that the universe and its inhabitants didn't always behave according to his idea of logic and rationality. "Harli's right. You need to move your experiments indoors."

"Okay." Making a face, Freylan carefully eased the beam off his shoulder and lowered it back to the ground. "But you can see how strong these suits—"

"Quiet," Harli snapped, twisting his head around toward the broken wall.

Jody froze in place, her eyes darting back and forth as she searched for signs of trouble. But the Trofts were still working, the Cobra guards were still at their posts. There was nothing she could see that might have caught Harli's attention.

And then, even as Harli hissed out a curse, she spotted one of the Cobras on the distant wall with his hands cupped around his mouth. Clearly, he was calling something that only Cobra enhanced hearing could pick up. She opened her mouth to ask Harli what the problem was—

"*Damn.*" Harli spun halfway around, his head jerking back and forth as he looked around them. "Where's that woman gotten to? The Qasaman woman—Rashida Vil. Either of you see her? Quick!"

Jody felt her breath catch in her throat. Rashida Vil had been the main pilot on the Qasaman team's trip to ask for the Cobra Worlds' help in fighting off the Troft invaders. Siraj Akim had decided that she should stay behind on Caelian, where her Troft language skills would be useful in helping the Caelians work with their prisoners.

"I think she's in there," Freylan offered, pointing to the more intact of the two warships. "I saw her a few minutes ago with a couple of techs—"

He was still in mid-sentence when Harli took off at a dead run toward the ship.

"What is it?" Jody called after him. But there was no answer. "What were they doing?" she asked, grabbing Freylan's arm. "Could you tell? Who was she with?"

"Just a couple of the city's techs," Freylan said, confusion and apprehension stuttering his words. "You don't think—because she's a pilot—?"

"Stay here," Jody ordered him, and took off after Harli.

Harli was long gone by the time Jody reached the ship. But one of the other Cobras, a man named Kemp, was on guard in the troop guard room just inside the door. "What's going on?" Jody panted as she charged in. "Where's Harli?"

"Communications room," Kemp told her, his voice grim. "Deck One—top of the ship. Traffic Control's spotted a Troft ship on its way in."

Jody felt her pounding heart try to seize up inside her. "One of *these*?" she asked, gesturing at the mass of the warship around them.

"Harli doesn't think it's a warship," Kemp said. "Too small. More likely a courier here to check on the situation."

Jody winced. A courier wouldn't be as bad as a full-fledged warship. But it would be bad enough. "We can't let it see what happened here."

"No kidding," Kemp growled. "He's up there trying to see if that Vil woman can wave them off."

Jody nodded. "I'll see if I can help."

The warship had nine decks, which meant eight flights of narrow stairs between her and the comm room. Coming on top of that hundred-meter sprint, Jody's legs felt like rubber by the time she finally emerged from the stairway onto Deck One. Following the sound of voices, she stumbled her way down the corridor to the comm room.

There were three people already there. Rashida was seated at the main console, with Harli and another man standing stiffly behind her. Harli looked back as Jody came in, a warning finger at his lips.

Jody nodded. Like she had extra breath to spare for questions right now anyway.

[The proposed landing area, it is not on our schedule,] a Troft voice was coming from the speaker. [The primary attack site, it is elsewhere on the planet.]

[The primary attack site, it is secure,] Rashida replied in fluent, flawless cattertalk. [The site, you may visit it afterward. But the scouting party, it is in danger. The soldiers, they must be first retrieved.]

Frowning, Jody beckoned to Harli. He hesitated, then silently crossed to her. "What?" he whispered.

"Kemp said you were going to try to wave them away," Jody whispered back. "But she's inviting them down?"

Harli's eyes narrowed. "Is *that* what she's saying?"

"You don't understand cattertalk?"

"Not a word. What's she saying?"

Jody focused on the conversation again. "It sounds like she's telling them there's a scouting party somewhere else on Caelian that needs to be picked up," she said. "She's insisting they do that before they swing by here."

Some of the tension smoothed out of Harli's face. "No, okay, that's good," he said. "She convinced me there was no way they were just going to go home without a look, so I told her to try to stall them. A little side trip into Wonderland ought to do the trick."

At the console, Rashida looked back at Jody, her face tense, her eyes desperate. "I hope you've got a Plan B," Jody warned. "Because it doesn't look like they're going for it."

"Hell," Harli muttered, turning back to Rashida. She shifted her eyes to him and gave a small shake of her head.

"Plan B?" Jody prompted.

"Yeah, yeah, hold on a second," Harli said, his eyes darting around the room as if searching for inspiration. "Okay. If they insist on coming down, tell them fine, come ahead. Then shut down the comm."

Rashida nodded and turned back to her board. [The primary attack site, you may come to it,] she said.

[The instruction, I obey it.]

Rashida touched a switch, and a row of lights went out. "I'm sorry," she said, turning to Harli again. "He insisted."

"That's all right," Harli said, pulling out his field radio. "No—wait a second," he said, stepping back to Rashida's side and running his eyes over the board. "I remember there being some kind of external loudspeaker system that keys in here somewhere. Find it for me, will you?—it'll be a lot faster than using the radios."

Rashida peered at the board, pointed to a set of controls. "There."

"Turn it on," Harli ordered. "How long before they get within eyeshot?"

"Not long," she said, keying the controls and handing him a slender mike. "Five or ten minutes."

"Terrific." Pursing his lips, Harli lifted the mike. "This is Harli," he announced. "We're about to get some company. All Cobras, find yourselves some spots where you'll be out of sight but still able to control the prisoners. Renny, Bill—make it clear to Captain Eubujak that if his people step out of line we *will* shoot to kill."

He covered the mike and gestured at Rashida. "Where did you tell them to land?"

"On the rectangle to the south of the village," she said. "I told them we were doing repairs on a downed ship, and that there was no room for them to land anywhere nearby."

"Good." Harli raised the mike again. "They should be putting down in the landing area," he continued. "Smitty, grab a team from town and get into attack position down there. If and when we get them to open the hatch, you take them out. There's no time for questions—they'll be here in five minutes. Play it by ear and do the best you can. And keep in mind that once they're down we do *not* want them leaving again."

He keyed off the mike and tossed it back to Rashida, his eyes again darting around the room. "Is there any way to see what's happening down there?" he asked.

"There's the drone control room," Jody offered. "Deck Four. That's where—"

"Yes, I know," Harli interrupted. "Except that all the wing cameras on that side of the ship are gone. Plus half the controls got slagged when your brother and Carsh Zoshak ran amok through the place."

"Right," Jody said, wincing with embarrassment. She should have remembered that.

"I was hoping there were some extra cameras somewhere tied in up here," he continued. "But I don't see anything." He snapped his fingers. "But the drone hatchways should still be open. Get down there and see if everyone's doing what I told them to."

"What do I do if they aren't?" Jody asked, backing toward the door.

"Pretend you're their mother and yell at them," Harli growled. "Just get them out of sight."

Jody grimaced. "Right."

The Stronghold techs had finished their checks of Deck Four a couple of days earlier, and the entire area was quiet, dark, and deserted. Fortunately, there was enough light coming in through the open drone hatches for Jody to pick her way across the battle debris and through the damaged barrier to the portside drone hatch. The rectangular opening was a little above her head; getting a grip on the lower edge, she pulled herself up and looked out.

Wherever the Cobras had found to disappear to, they'd done a terrific job of it. The Trofts were still laboring away, but she couldn't see a single white silliweave tunic anywhere among or around them.

No white tunics, but there was still one gray one. Freylan had obeyed the general order to hide, but he'd done it by crouching behind a clump of pankling bushes between Jody and the Troft work groups.

Which left him nicely hidden from the latter, but completely visible from overhead.

Jody ground her teeth. But then, Harli hadn't actually said where the company was coming from. She raised her eyes from Freylan and gave the sky a quick look, wondering if she still had time to shoo Freylan to a better hiding place.

But no. She could see the incoming ship now, a small silvery dot glinting in the sunlight as it approached across the western sky. It was still too far away for Jody to make out any details, but it surely had telescopic cameras already trained on Stronghold and the damaged warships.

Which meant that any movement on Freylan's part would be instantly visible. Awkward and risky though it might be, at this point Freylan would probably do better to just stay put and hope the drab color of his combat suit would keep him from being noticed. Suppressing a curse, Jody looked back down at the ground.

And blinked in surprise. The Troft prisoners had obviously spotted the incoming ship as well. But instead of continuing their work, they'd dropped their tools and were waving.

Not just normal waving, either. They were putting their whole arms into it, swinging them over their heads like parade floatmasters trying to be seen from the back row.

Jody chewed at her lip, indecision tearing at her. Should she stop them? Or, rather, should she order them to stop, which might or might not be the same thing?

Or was it perfectly natural for Drim'hco'plai soldiers on the ground to salute a group of fellow soldiers flying over their heads? Worse, was it *required* that they do so? Without knowing more about the demesne's cultural rules, there was no way to know. If it was a form of military etiquette, ordering them to stop would be a dead giveaway to the courier that something was wrong.

But if it *wasn't* something they were supposed to do, wouldn't that be equally likely to arouse suspicion? Feeling sweat popping out on her forehead, Jody stared down at the gesticulating Trofts, trying to figure out what she could do.

And then, abruptly, she caught her breath. The waving arms...

She took a deep breath and stuck her head as far out of the hatch as she could. "Cobras!" she shouted. "Stop them! They're signaling the ship. *They're signaling the ship!*"

For a long, horrible moment nothing happened. The Trofts continued their waving and the Cobras remained out of sight. Could they not have heard her? Or had they simply decided that Harli's orders superseded hers? A movement from beneath her caught her eye, and she looked down to see Freylan rise from his inadequate concealment, take a couple of quick steps forward with his right arm cocked over his shoulder, and then throw something as hard as he could toward the prisoners. The object arced across the group and disappeared somewhere into the mass of upstretched arms.

Jody frowned. What in the Worlds had he thrown? A rock?

And then, abruptly, the Trofts at the point of impact collapsed to the ground, their falling bodies jostling against those nearest to them. Before their off-balance neighbors could recover, they too staggered and disappeared beneath the sea of waving hands. For a few seconds the effect rippled outward, dropping the aliens as if a silent grenade had been tossed into their midst. Below Jody, Freylan was again in motion, throwing a second object into a different part of the group. Again, the Trofts at the impact point began to stagger and fall.

An instant later, all hell broke loose.

Ten of the Trofts on the edge of the group closest to Freylan abruptly turned and charged away from the latest rippling mass collapse, forming themselves into a close-packed sweeping wedge as they ran. They were maybe ten meters from the rest of the prisoners when the Troft in the lead gave a hand signal, and the whole wedge shifted direction.

Heading directly toward Freylan.

Jody gasped. "Freylan!" she shouted out the drone hatch. "Get inside! Quick!"

But it was too late. Freylan was midway through his third throw, his body twisted and off balance, his feet out of position for any sort of movement, let alone a mad dash anywhere. Jody saw him twitch violently as he spotted the wedge of Trofts charging toward him, and he tried desperately to get himself back into balance. There was some sort of guttural shout from down there, but she couldn't tell whether it came from Freylan or from the Trofts. Freylan's knees gave a sudden, hopeless twitch, which the powered Djinni suit transformed into a two-meter leap.

Only it was his final mistake... because instead of taking him sideways or back toward the warship or anywhere else useful, the reflexive leap had instead sent him soaring straight upward. He would hit the ground again, Jody estimated, just in time to land right in front of the charging Trofts.

At which point they would have the choice of simply knocking him over and continuing on toward the forest, or of pausing long enough to beat him to death.

Clenching her hands around the edge of the drone hatchway, Jody watched helplessly as Freylan hit the top of his arc and started back down.

And jerked in surprise as a multiple burst of laser fire flashed across the landscape beneath him.

She'd completely forgotten about Kemp, standing his quiet guard down at the warship's entrance. Apparently, so had the Trofts. The bolts slashed across the line of charging aliens, dropping them into sprawling, smoking heaps on the ground. The fire cut off as Freylan hit the ground, once again blocking Kemp's line of fire.

He was starting to straighten up when the last two surviving Trofts slammed full-tilt into him, hurling him three meters backward to slam onto the ground.

Jody gasped with sympathetic pain. But even before the aliens had recovered their balance two final laser blasts dropped them to the ground with the others.

Jody took a deep, painful breath... and only then did it occur to her to look back up into the sky.

The Troft ship was considerably closer, close enough now that she could see it was definitely the size of a freighter or courier. But it was no longer coming toward Stronghold. It had instead veered ninety degrees toward the south and was hauling its gravs for all they were worth. They'd gotten the look they'd come for, all right.

And Caelian was suddenly in very big trouble.

"They were forming letters," Jody told the small group that had gathered around Governor Romulo Uy's hospital bed. "Tracing them out, actually, like a child might trace out an up-down-across to make a capital A." She demonstrated. "Each Troft had one letter, repeating it over and over, the whole mass of them tracing out the complete message."

"Only the letters were being traced out horizontally instead of vertically," Harli added. "Visible and obvious from above, but not from ground level." He looked at Jody. "Semi-obvious from above, anyway," he amended. "That was a good call."

Governor Uy gave a sound that was half groan and half grunt. "Don't know as I necessarily agree," he said. "That little battle has now put us in serious jeopardy. The enemy knows beyond a doubt that their invasion failed."

"They would have known that anyway," Harli pointed out. "If Jody and Freylan hadn't garbled the message, it would have given them that and probably a lot more."

"Or they might not even have noticed it was a message," Uy countered. "Or even if they had, they might have thought it was a joke."

"That seems unlikely," Harli said, his tone respectful but giving no ground. "Captain Eubujak certainly thought it would get through."

"Could you tell what it was, Jody?" Kemp asked.

"I didn't get very much," Jody admitted. "The first word was definitely *danger*, and I think the next four were *defeated Cobra numbers diminished*. Two of the ones in the middle, near where Freylan threw the first of his gas canisters, looked like *drone hatch*. But that's all I got."

"He was probably warning them how we got into their ship during the battle," Kemp suggested. "Good thing that little tidbit got erased. We might need to use that back door on the next ship."

Uy grunted again. "It would have been nice if the Qasamans had told us they'd left sleep-gas canisters with their combat suits." His eyes locked on Jody. "Or was that supposed to be a surprise?"

"The canisters are part of the suits," Jody said. "It probably never even occurred to them to mention them."

"And *your* excuse?"

"No excuse, Governor," Jody said, fighting against a surge of annoyance at the injured man. Despite what he obviously thought, none of any of this was her fault. "That wasn't the thrust of our work on the suits, so it also never occurred to us to mention them."

"And we *did* know about them," Harli put in firmly. "I'm mildly surprised that Freylan remembered the things and was able to use them. But I'm glad he did."

For a moment he and his father locked eyes, and Jody had the uncomfortable sense of the silent argument going on between them.

The governor blinked first. "I suppose," he acknowledged, shifting his eyes to one of the other Cobras standing around the hospital room. "Gaber, I assume you've had a talk with Captain Eubujak about this little stunt?"

"For all the good it did," Gaber said ruefully. "All he'll say is that escape is the right and privilege of every prisoner of war, and more or less dared us to punish him for it."

"You ask him what the message was?" Kemp asked.

"I did, and he wouldn't tell me." A hint of a smile touched Gaber's lips. "I did get the impression that he's rather astonished we figured out there *was* a message, let alone figured it out fast enough to do something about it. He did admit that the frontal assault on Freylan was mainly to force us to show the courier that we still had Cobras at our disposal."

"They would have guessed that anyway," Harli said. "This way, at least it cost Eubujak another ten of his troops."

"For whatever that's worth," Uy said. "So to summarize: they know we defeated their initial attack, that we wrecked one of their ships in the process, that we took nearly half of the Troft forces prisoner and killed the rest, and that we still have Cobras. That about cover it?"

"I think so," Harli said. "The next question is what we do now."

"Starting with how long we're going to have to come up with a plan," Gaber said. "It's, what, about five days to Qasama from here?"

"Qasama?" Harli growled. "They can get all the ships they want from Aventine."

"Oh, hell," Gaber muttered. "I hadn't thought about that. They could have a new force here in two days."

"I don't think so," Jody said. "Lorne and Rashida both said that the demesne markings on the warships at Aventine were different from the ones here."

"So?" Gaber asked. "They're allies, aren't they?"

"They may be allies, but they're still Trofts," Jody said. "The ones I've worked with have been extremely competitive, to the point where they'll waste ridiculous amounts of time and money rather than let even a business partner know about a weakness that they can exploit. A Drim courier ship isn't about to tell even an ally that the invasion team muffed it. They're going to go to the nearest Drim force, and according to Rashida that force is on Qasama."

"Unless the Drim have ships on Palatine or Esquiline," Gaber pointed out grimly.

"It doesn't matter," Harli cut in. "If they get help from any of the Cobra Worlds we're dead, period—there's no way we can be ready for them in two or three days. So let's assume Jody is right, and they have to go to Qasama. In that case, what's our timing look like?"

Jody curled her hands into fists. She was hardly an expert on Trofts, especially not on Troft military matters. But with Jennifer McCollom gone to Qasama, and given the rest of the Caelians' self-absorbed isolation, she was probably the best they had. "Let's assume the courier takes five days to get to Qasama," she said slowly, thinking it through. "That's about top speed for our freighters, so it's probably a fair guess. Warships, with all their extra mass and cross-section, will almost certainly be slower—six or seven at least. It may also take a day or two for the Drim commander on the scene to digest the report and decide what he wants to do."

"Or maybe not," Uy said. "Let's go with your eleven-day estimate. In fact, let's err on the safe side and say ten."

"Terrific," Kemp murmured. "Ten days to prepare for another invasion."

"We'll find a way to do it," Uy said. "Because we really don't have a choice." He looked over at his clock. "I want everyone back here in two hours, along with the city council and anybody from Essbend or Aerie who are still here. At that time, you're each to have at least two ideas to bring to the table. Understood?"

An affirmative murmur swept the room. "Good." Uy looked at Jody. "That goes for you, too, Ms. Broom. You *and* your two friends. Two ideas each, and they'd better be good."

"Yes, sir," Jody murmured.

"So get to it," Uy said, looking around the room. "I want answers, gentlemen, and I want them today."

CHAPTER SEVEN

The under-road culvert was exactly where Miron Akim had said it would be, five kilometers up the road to Windloom. It was also as roomy as he'd said, and as easily rigged to be defensible against nocturnal predators.

He hadn't, however, said anything about its comfort, or lack of same. It wasn't long after they'd settled in for the night that Daulo realized why that part had been left out of the discussion.

Even Akim was apparently not all that impressed with the accommodations. During one of Daulo's frequent awakenings, this particular one a little after midnight, he saw Akim slip through the makeshift barrier at one end of the culvert and head out into the night, in the opposite direction from the clump of trees that Omnathi had earlier designated as the group's latrine. For a few minutes Daulo kept his eyes pried open, wondering whether Akim was searching for better padding for his sleeping blanket or whether he was giving up entirely on the culvert and had decided to take his chances with the predators.

But idle curiosity was no match for fatigue. Even with his aching muscles and back, the rigors of the day's events soon forced Daulo's eyelids closed again. The next time he awoke, the culvert and its occupants were once again silent and still.

He was still exhausted when the diffuse sunlight of morning

awakened him for the final time. The rest of the group was already up, he saw as he carefully levered himself into a seating position, wincing at each movement and muscle twinge. Akim was passing out ration bars and water bottles, the six Djinn were busily repacking the equipment for travel, and Shahni Haafiz was scowling as he bit pieces off his breakfast.

Daulo had made it to his feet and was working himself into his wheelchair when Akim came over. "Good morning, Daulo Sammon," he said as he offered Daulo a ration bar and water bottle. "Did you sleep well?"

"Not especially, Marid Akim," Daulo confessed. "I'm afraid Sollas's hospital beds have spoiled me. Culverts just don't seem all that comfortable anymore."

Akim chuckled. "Yes; the soft decadence of a convalescent's life. Don't worry—I'm sure you'll readapt to real life soon enough."

"We can make a contest of it, you and I," Daulo offered. "I noticed you also needed to get up once or twice during the night to stretch your muscles."

Akim's eyes narrowed slightly. "You saw me leave?" he asked, an odd tone to his voice. "When?"

"It was a little after midnight," Daulo said, wondering if he should have lied, or perhaps said that it might have been just a dream. Too late now. "You said something to the Djinni standing guard at the western opening, then slipped out."

"And the second time?"

Daulo frowned. "The second time?"

"You said I left once or twice," Akim reminded him. "When was the second time?"

Daulo frowned. *Had* he said Akim had left twice? He must have. So what exactly had he meant by that? "I think I woke up again a little before dawn and saw you come in," he said slowly, trying to sort through the images, dreams, and half-dreams from the long night. "I just assumed you were coming back from another walk, that you hadn't been gone that whole time. Should I have not said anything?"

For a moment Akim gazed into his eyes, perhaps trying to discern whether or not Daulo was leaving anything out. Then, his lip twitched. "No, that's all right," he said. "But keep this between us, and don't tell any of the others." He looked significantly over at the glowering Haafiz. "*Any* of the others."

"I won't," Daulo promised.

"Good." Akim gestured at the food and water in Daulo's hands. "Then eat up, and prepare yourself for travel. We still have a good fifteen kilometers to go before we reach safety."

The road to Windloom and the villages beyond had been reasonably well maintained. But it was hardly up to the standards of the Great Arc's major roads, and Daulo's wheelchair bounced and bucked on the uneven surface as the group made their way along it. Occasionally they hit a patch that was rougher than usual, or else pockmarked with pits and potholes, which the wheelchair simply couldn't navigate. At those spots Daulo was obliged to get up and hobble across with the assistance of one of the Djinn while a second carried the chair.

But at least the forest predators seemed to be leaving them alone. That was something to be grateful for.

They'd been traveling for three hours, and Daulo was wondering if he should just give up on the chair for a while and see how far he could get on foot when he spotted the shadowy figures silently pacing them through the forest on both sides.

His first panicked thought was that they'd hit a pack of razorarms or some other predators. But the figures seemed to be maintaining their distance, making no effort to either leave or move closer. He kept watching, and a minute later one of them crossed a better-lit section of the woods, and Daulo saw to his relief that it was just a man. A group of villagers, then.

But if they had come out to escort the newcomers into Windloom, why were they skulking out in the woods instead of joining the refugees on the road? And if they were out here for logging or hunting, why were they bothering to pace the visitors at all?

Daulo was still turning the question over in his mind when Akim cleared his throat. "The village should be just around the next bend in the road," he told the rest of the travelers. "You can expect us to be challenged at the gate and our belongings searched."

"*Searched?*" Haafiz demanded, his eyes widening with outrage. "On whose authority do villagers search a Shahni of Qasama?"

"It's not because you're a Shahni," Akim said hastily. "It's merely the fact that we're city dwellers."

"City dwellers whom they dislike?" Haafiz growled, turning his glare onto Daulo. "Is that it, villager? They hate us?"

Wincing, Daulo searched frantically for a diplomatic response. Fortunately, Akim was already on it. "It's not hatred, Your Excellency, but distrust," he said. "With the fall of Sollas they fear a flood of refugees who will severely overtax their resources. More than that, they fear those refugees may bring in weapons or illegal substances that will pose a threat to their people."

Haafiz snorted. "More likely they hope to find medicines or food they can steal."

"That could also be the case," Akim conceded. "In addition, there are rumors that some city dwellers have made devil's bargains with the invaders. They thus also fear the infiltration of spies and saboteurs."

"Ridiculous," Haafiz bit out. "No Qasaman would make such a bargain." His eyes narrowed as he turned his glare onto Omnathi. "Unless you speak of the bargain made with the demon warriors Jin Moreau and her son. *That* pact may prove even more of a disaster for the Qasaman people than the alien invasion itself."

"Yet the Shahni *did* approve the sending of Jin Moreau back to her people for aid," Omnathi pointed out calmly.

"At *your* instigation," Haafiz retorted. "Even then, you had authorization from only three. The rest of us weren't even consulted."

"I had the approval of all who were present," Omnathi said. "That's the law."

"No, that's an excuse." Haafiz flicked his hand in an ancient gesture of challenge that Daulo had never seen anyone use in real life. "And rest assured that I shall deal with those Shahni once the invaders have been pushed forever off Qasama."

"There was no time for further consultation, Your Excellency," Omnathi said. "You in particular were in another part of the sub-city, and all efforts to find you failed."

"So you say," Haafiz said. "We shall see. If those three Shahni survive this war, I'll gladly take the judgment seat at their trial for treason." He raised his eyebrows. "As I'll also gladly sit in judgment at *your* trial on those same charges."

Daulo stared at them, a fresh wave of disbelief washing over him. Moffren Omnathi, venerated hero of Qasama, under suspicion of *treason*? How could anyone, especially one of the Shahni, even think such a thing?

"The future is in its own hands," Akim said. "And if I may say so, Shahni Haafiz, this is neither the time nor the place for such discussions. Windloom and sanctuary lie directly ahead of us. We should continue on."

"*You* may continue on," Haafiz said. "But my part of this journey is at an end."

For the first time since they'd left the Sollas subcity Akim actually seemed taken aback. "What?" he asked.

"I'm leaving." Haafiz gestured around him at the silent Djinn. "The Djinn will accompany me back to the main road. We go to Tazreel and from there to Purma."

"You can't be serious, Your Excellency," Akim said. "We've been over this."

"And I've reconsidered," Haafiz said. "Whatever this haven is that you spoke of, it's now abundantly clear that it's too far out of the main stream of activity to be of any use to me."

"But the cities aren't safe for you," Akim persisted.

"Nowhere on Qasama is safe," Haafiz said. "At least in Purma I'll be able to lead my people."

"You can't," Akim insisted.

Haafiz's eyes narrowed. "Are you now of the Shahni, that you presume to dictate another Shahni's choice of path? Or do you merely presume to circumvent Shahni rule as does Moffren Omnathi?"

Akim flashed Omnathi a look. "But you agreed to come here, Your Excellency."

"I agreed to allow you to offer the protection of the Djinn to an injured village leader," Haafiz countered. "Daulo Sammon is now as safe as it's possible for him to be on Qasama. I now choose to move on."

"But you also must be protected," Akim insisted. "Back in the Great Arc is where the invaders are the strongest."

"Back in the Great Arc is also where any Shahni still alive and free will have gathered," Haafiz countered. "There are rendezvous and communication points in Purma that have been established for this situation. With no ground communications and no radio, I must physically travel there to learn whether others have survived or whether I alone now lead the Qasaman people."

"Let me instead send my Djinn," Akim offered. "They can assess the situation and return with that news."

"While I meanwhile sit uselessly in the middle of the forest?" Haafiz shook his head. "No."

"At least come to Windloom long enough for some proper food and rest," Omnathi said. "I'm certain that Daulo Sammon, as a fellow villager, will use his full influence to make sure you aren't searched or otherwise mistreated."

"Of course," Daulo said, wondering if Omnathi realized how little influence he was likely to have here. Unless some of the metalwork artists he'd dealt with all those years ago had managed to become Windloom's leaders, he would be lucky if anyone here even remembered him.

"Then it's settled," Akim said. "We'll go to Windloom, rest, and take some refreshment. Then, if you still want to go to Purma, you and the Djinn can go with proper equipment and provisions."

Haafiz studied Akim's face. "Very well," he said at last. "An hour, no more, and I leave. Agreed?"

"Agreed," Akim said.

With a loud sniff, Haafiz strode away, passing Akim and Omnathi as he continued down the road. Akim flicked an unreadable look at Daulo, then turned and hurried to catch up.

Daulo's memories of Windloom were several years old. But like Milika, the village hadn't changed appreciably in that time. The outer wall looked just the way he remembered it, though he was pretty sure the gate's hinges had been replaced recently. Most of the buildings clustered together inside the wall had the look of comfortable permanence about them, the same look he'd seen in many of these older Qasaman settlements.

But while the village itself had remained largely unchanged, the villagers had not. The last time Daulo had been here the people had been cautiously welcoming, the typical attitude of people living not far from a major city whose inhabitants looked down on them even while they were buying their goods. Now, though, there was no friendliness in the men at the gate. They were cold and aloof, their questions brusque and suspicious. And all of them carried rifles or sidearms.

As Daulo had privately predicted, he had no influence whatsoever with the guards. But Omnathi's name seemed to carry some weight, and he was able to convince them that Shahni Haafiz should be exempt from any search. The others of the group weren't so lucky, or perhaps weren't so intimidating, and went through the full procedure. Even Daulo's wheelchair was taken away for closer examination, leaving him once again hobbling with Djinni assistance.

Fortunately, he didn't have to hobble very far. Two of the guards escorted them to a house near the gate, where one of them set out food and water while the other headed off with Akim through the narrow streets to meet with the village's leaders.

Daulo was working his way through a second dried meat ring, watching Omnathi and Haafiz studiously not speaking to each other and feeling extremely uncomfortable about it, when Akim and one of the village leaders returned.

And they weren't alone. Flanking them were four more armed men.

"Finally," Haafiz growled, glowering briefly at Akim and then turning his attention to the villagers. "Have you prepared the provisions for my journey to Purma?"

"I regret, Your Excellency, that there will be no such journey," Akim said, his voice tight. "Not for you or anyone else."

"What?" Haafiz demanded. "Marid Akim—"

"Because this was found beneath Daulo Sammon's wheelchair, attached to the front of the carrier bag." Akim held out a slender cylinder about thirteen centimeters long and three in diameter. "It's a radio."

Daulo felt his stomach tighten, peripherally aware that all eyes had turned toward him. Everyone in the room, probably everyone in Windloom, knew that the invaders' weapons were keyed to home in on Qasaman radio transmissions. Even through the hazy memories of his recovery in the subcity he had a vivid image of men coming through the hospital collecting all radio transmitters and other wireless equipment and emphasizing that the use of such instruments could bring death and destruction down on them all. "That isn't mine," he said, striving to keep his voice calm. "It's not even my wheelchair—it was assigned to me in Sollas."

"It doesn't look like any radio I've ever seen," Haafiz said, his eyes flicking between the cylinder and Daulo.

"It's a Djinni field radio," Akim told him. "One of those that were being experimented on in hopes of making them undetectable to the invaders."

"Were the experiments successful?" Haafiz asked.

Akim snorted. "Would we be talking about letting you walk all the way to Purma if they'd been successful?" he countered. "More significant even than the radio, though, is the name of one of the men who worked on that project." He raised his eyebrows slightly. "Fadil Sammon, son of Daulo Sammon."

Daulo felt his mouth drop open. *Fadil*, on a secret high-tech project?

But that was impossible. Fadil was intelligent enough, and dealing with the radios they used in the family mine had given him a working knowledge of the theory and hardware involved. But he didn't have nearly the expertise that Akim would have needed for such work.

Omnathi wasn't buying it, either. "Your logic is tenuous," he rumbled. "Daulo Sammon has been in the Sollas subcity since the first attack, while Fadil Sammon is . . . elsewhere. How could the son have delivered a radio to the father?"

"I don't know," Akim said. "The more intriguing question for me is *why* he would send it to him."

And suddenly, with a rush of fear and horror, the answer slapped
Daulo hard across the face. The only way Fadil could have become
smart enough to join such a high-level project— "You son of a
venomous snake," he snarled, his eyes boring into Akim's face.
"What poisons did you pump into his blood?"

"I gave him precisely what he asked for," Akim said, his voice and
expression carved from midwinter ice. "And it was at *his* request.
He volunteered himself to be part of the project."

"You lie," Daulo bit out, an agony of fire filling his lungs. He'd
heard whispers about these secret drugs, chemicals that could
temporarily enhance creativity and intelligence to an astonishing
degree. But their aftereffects were the stuff of fever nightmares.
"What did you do to him? Where is he?"

"Your son's condition and location are not the point, Daulo
Sammon," Akim said. "The point is whether—"

"God damn you all to hell!" Daulo exploded, leaping to his feet
and sending his chair crashing to the floor behind him. *"Where
is my son?"*

"He's at your home in Milika," Akim said. He hadn't even twitched
at Daulo's outburst. "I'm afraid he's been paralyzed. I'm sorry."

For a long moment Daulo just stared at him, feeling the blood
drain from his face and the strength fade from his legs and body
as his mind tried to wrap itself around Akim's words. His son,
paralyzed? "No," he whispered. "Please, God. No."

"I'm sorry," Akim said again.

"We mourn your loss," Omnathi said in a voice that reeked of
suspicion and impatience and had not a drop of genuine mourning
that Daulo could detect. "Now sit down."

One of the Djinn stepped behind Daulo and set his chair up
again. Slowly, Daulo sank back into it. "Because the point, Daulo
Sammon," Omnathi continued, "is not what the drugs have done
to your son, but what your son may have done to Qasama."

Daulo shook his head tiredly. "I have no idea what you're talking about."

"He's talking about the radio," Akim said. "Why it's here, and
whether you've used it to communicate with the invaders.

"And whether you or your son has committed treason."

The word took several heartbeats to register through the frozen turmoil in Daulo's brain. Then, like the flash of a cutting torch, it abruptly sliced though the swirling emotions. "What did you say?" he demanded. "*Treason*? You can't possibly believe that."

"My beliefs are irrelevant," Akim said. "It will be the facts that ultimately define reality."

Daulo stared at him, then looked at Omnathi. They were serious. God above, they were actually serious. "This is insane," he said, hearing the quaver in his voice but unable to suppress it. "I was nearly killed defending my world and my people. My son is now trapped in a living death for doing likewise. How can you possibly think such things about us?"

"How can this radio have come into your possession?" Omnathi countered. "There are facts here which must be brought into the light."

Daulo raised his head a little higher. "Then assemble your facts, Advisor Omnathi," he said. "I don't fear the truth. Bring your facts into the light, and allow me to face them."

"*After* you've set me on my way to Purma," Haafiz said, standing up. "If there's treason here, there's even more reason for me to quickly make my way elsewhere."

"Elsewhere, certainly," Akim said. "But not to Purma. Without knowing what Daulo Sammon may or may not have told the invaders, we cannot risk you traveling to any place we've spoken of during our journey. The invaders may be even now setting a trap for you there."

"Did you mention Windloom in his hearing?" the village leader put in. "If so, you can't stay here, either."

"Agreed," Akim said. "But we shouldn't need to go far. I'm told there's a quarantine cabin half a kilometer into the forest to the west."

"That's correct," the villager said doubtfully. "But it hasn't been used in years. I can't make any promises for its comfort or even its structural soundness."

"Whatever its condition, we'll make it do," Akim assured him. "Can you provide us with two weeks' worth of food and water?"

"Two *weeks*?" Haafiz echoed. "We're speaking of a summary trial, Marid Akim, not something long and involved. I can't be away from Qasama that long."

"This *is* Qasama," the villager said, an edge to his voice.

"I mean the *real* Qasama," Haafiz retorted, not even wasting a glare on the man. "The Qasama the invaders are conquering and destroying. The Qasama that's *worth* conquering and destroying."

"I understand your wish to return to the main theater of war, Your Excellency," Akim said hastily. "But I'm afraid the delay can't be avoided. We need to bring Fadil Sammon here to testify as to his part in this, and even for Djinn a journey to Milika through forested lands will take at least a week in each direction."

"And thus you rob me even of knowledge," Haafiz growled.

Akim frowned. "I don't understand."

"If you send the Djinn to fetch Fadil Sammon, they can't also go to Purma to learn what the invaders are doing," Haafiz reminded him.

"Ah," Akim said, looking sideways at Omnathi. "Yes, I see. But again, I'm afraid it can't be helped. Before we can make any moves against the invaders we need to learn the extent of the Sammon family's actions against us."

Haafiz hissed between his teeth. "Very well. For the moment, we'll go to this quarantine cabin." He leveled a finger at Akim. "But only for the moment. *I* will decide later just how long my exile will last."

"Of course," Akim said.

"And while we await the son's arrival," Haafiz added, turning to Daulo, "you'll begin your examination of the father. The sooner we determine the extent of his treason, the sooner I'll be able to get back to Purma and locate the remaining Shahni."

He waved a hand at the villager. "Go," he ordered. "Prepare our provisions."

A hint of a scowl touched the other's lips. But he merely nodded, made the sign of respect, and left.

There was an old, overgrown, barely visible path leading away from the clearing around Windloom westward toward the quarantine cabin. It looked way too narrow and plant-choked for the wheelchair, and as the group approached it Daulo found himself wincing at the prospect of trying to drag himself the entire half kilometer on foot.

Fortunately, Akim had already thought it through and come up with a solution. As they reached the path he gave a murmured order, and four of the Djinn took hold of the corners of Daulo's wheelchair, lifting both him and the chair off the ground. With the other two Djinn in the lead, they headed into the forest.

The path was bumpy, with hidden obstacles that threatened to trip up the wheelchair carriers with every step. Daulo was nearly pitched out at least a dozen times along the way, and it was with a sense of relief that he finally spotted the roof of the cabin ahead between the trees.

He'd relaxed too soon. Two steps later, the two Djinn in the lead abruptly turned left, leaving the path and turning southward. Daulo's carriers, and of course Daulo himself, did likewise.

Daulo tensed, a hundred horrible and ominous scenarios flashing through his mind. But whatever was happening, it was quickly clear that he wasn't the only one who hadn't been told of this additional change of plans. "What's this?" Haafiz demanded, stopping in confusion as Akim and Omnathi veered off alongside the Djinn. "Marid Akim? What's going on? Where are you taking us?"

"To the secret haven I told you about back in Sollas," Akim said. "It's a place that was long prepared for just such a situation."

"A place the details of which you were extremely vague about," Haafiz said.

"Be patient, Your Excellency," Akim said. "Your questions will all be answered soon."

They'd been walking for fifteen minutes, and the Djinn carrying Daulo's wheelchair were starting to stagger with their burden, when they reached their destination.

Though for a minute Daulo didn't realize that. The small clearing that had been created by a pair of toppled trees wasn't at all remarkable. It was only as the Djinn set Daulo and his wheelchair down that the ground between the trees magically opened up to reveal the top of a three-meter-diameter shaft leading downward.

"Its designation is Reserve Command Post Sollas Three," Akim said as a pair of young men in gray Djinni combat suits stepped out of the shaft, their hands in laser-firing positions as they eyed the newcomers. "There are thirty such bases scattered around the rural and forested areas of Qasama, designed to serve as regrouping points in case of an overwhelming attack."

"I was never told of these places," Haafiz said, his voice dark with suspicion. "Why were the Shahni not told?"

"As you pointed out earlier, the Shahni have their own emergency gathering places," Akim reminded him. "As we of the military haven't been told where those are, so you of the Shahni haven't been told of these."

"We are the rulers," Haafiz retorted. "We're to know *everything* that happens on our world."

"The high command evidently thought otherwise." Akim gestured to the two Djinn still waiting at the shaft. "Ifrit Narayan? Come near and report."

One of the Djinn lowered his hands, jumped easily over the fallen trees, and strode forward. "We are twenty-eight strong, Marid Akim," he said, making the sign of respect first to Akim and then, almost as an afterthought, to Haafiz. "Two other Ifrits, twenty-five Djinn."

Akim expelled his breath in a huffing sigh. "I'd hoped for more."

"As had we," Narayan conceded heavily. "The invasion has cost many lives."

"Indeed," Akim said. "We can hope that the other posts have had better fortune. Equipment status?"

"Thirteen of us were forced to leave our combat suits behind," Narayan said. "They've been replaced from the stores, with thirty-seven suits remaining." He ran his eyes briefly over the six Djinn in the group. "I'll need to check the available sizes, but I believe we'll be able to refit your escort. As to other equipment, we have full stores."

"Good," Akim said. "Once everyone is below, and Shahni Haafiz and Daulo Sammon are settled, I'll want to meet with you and the other Ifrits. An urgent mission has come up that we need to discuss."

"Yes, Marid." Narayan raised his arm and whistled.

From the woods around them a dozen combat-suited Djinn slipped into view. "Escort Shahni Haafiz and the others below," Narayan ordered. "Daulo Sammon is injured, and will need to be carried in his wheelchair."

Three minutes later, after a slightly nerve-wracking descent down a way-too-steep stairway, they were inside the post.

Daulo had expected to find a place built along the same lines as the Sollas subcity, and he was mostly correct. It was smaller than that vast labyrinth, of course, and cramped to the point of being claustrophobic in places. But it had been constructed of the same steel and concrete, with a similar layout of sleeping, meeting, eating, storage, and medical rooms.

His handlers took him directly to the latter facility, where one of the other Djinni launched into what turned out to be a very thorough examination.

An hour later, as the doctor was finally finishing up his tests, Narayan arrived. "Leave us," he ordered the doctor.

"Yes, Ifrit," the other said. Setting his instruments aside, he slipped past Narayan and disappeared out the door.

For a moment Narayan eyed Daulo in silence. "I understand from Marid Akim," he said at last, "that you may be a traitor."

Daulo sighed, suddenly unbearably tired of this whole thing. "Marid Akim may believe that," he said. "But he's wrong."

"More importantly—and more interestingly—Shahni Haafiz believes it, too," Narayan continued. "Tell me, what have you done to make an enemy of the Shahni?"

"I don't know," Daulo said. "Maybe because I'm a villager, and he doesn't like villagers. Maybe because I helped defend Sollas, and he thinks that somehow makes the city dwellers look bad. Though I can't imagine why he would think that."

"Or maybe because you're a friend and ally of the Cobra warrior Jasmine Moreau and her son Merrick Moreau." Narayan's lip twisted. "Whom Shahni Haafiz tried his best to kill."

Daulo felt his eyes widen. "He *what*? I hadn't heard that."

"We took great pains to keep it quiet," Narayan said grimly.

"But it's true. Shahni Haafiz stabbed Merrick Moreau while he was attempting to rescue him and Shahni Melcha from the Palace. Apparently, he believed the Cobras were in collusion with the invaders. He probably still does."

"That's completely untrue," Daulo said firmly.

"I know," Narayan said. "So do all of us who fought alongside them. But Shahni Haafiz has a reputation for stubbornness, as well as a reputation for never admitting an error if he can avoid it. He prefers to cover over his mistakes, either with words or with diversions."

Daulo sighed. And here he was, Daulo Sammon, a living reminder of the service Jin Moreau had done for Qasama. Not just in this war, but also thirty years ago when she and Daulo helped destroy a quieter but no less insidious threat to their world. "He plans to destroy me, doesn't he?" he murmured. "And my son." Tears abruptly blurred his vision. "What's left of my son."

"It does look that way," Narayan admitted. "For whatever it's worth, I think Advisor Omnathi's willing to hold off judgment until all the facts have been assembled and presented. Still, he's only an advisor, not one of the Shahni. His opinions may or may not carry much weight."

"Against Shahni Haafiz," Daulo murmured, "I suspect they won't."

"No," Narayan said. "But whatever the final outcome, it won't happen for a while. The law states that a trial for the charge of treason must be overseen by one of the Shahni. And since Marid Akim believes your son is a vital part of the charges against you, he's insisted that he be brought here before that trial can begin."

"Insanity," Daulo ground out. "A poor, sick, paralyzed man, and he's going to drag him halfway across Qasama? He can't be serious."

"He's very serious," Narayan said, his voice turning dark. "Eighteen of my Djinn and two of the group Marid Akim brought from Sollas have already set off through the forest toward Milika."

Daulo stared at him. "He sent *twenty* Djinn? How dangerous does he think my son is?"

"I have no idea," Narayan said. "All I know is that he told us he needed as many Djinn as possible for a special mission, then interviewed each of us in private before selecting the twenty." He snorted gently. "Which, considering the questions he was asking, he might as well have done by random calling of names."

"What kind of questions were they?" Daulo asked, intrigued despite his fear and frustration.

"Strange ones," Narayan told him. "More psychological than operational. How we felt about villagers, what we thought of Jasmine and Merrick Moreau and the Cobra Worlds. That sort of thing."

"Finding out which Djinn already share his preconceptions about my guilt."

"Possibly," Narayan conceded. "I myself have no problem with either villagers or the Moreaus, and I was chosen to remain behind." He pursed his lips thoughtfully. "Yet several of those who were sent also fought alongside Merrick Moreau and have the highest respect for him and his mother. One of them, in fact, Domo Paneka, has even suggested that a new Qasaman award of honor be established in their name when the war is over."

"So what qualities *was* Marid Akim looking for?" Daulo asked.

Narayan shook his head. "To be honest, I have no idea."

"No," Daulo murmured. "I just hope . . ." He trailed off, not wanting to even think the thought, let alone state it.

Narayan picked up on it anyway. "He'll be all right," he assured Daulo. "A man is not condemned without cause and proof. Not even in the midst of a war, not even if the charge is treason, not even if the Shahni who sits in judgment has already made up his mind. My Djinn know that. If it's within their power to bring your son here safely, they will."

And as Daulo looked into Narayan's eyes, he knew the other meant it. "Thank you," he said. "I suppose I can accept that Shahni Haafiz wants to execute me, for whatever real or fancied reason he believes. But I wish he'd do it without disturbing my son."

"The ways of the Shahni are often unclear to ordinary men," Narayan said philosophically. "In the meantime, I have work to do, and you need to rest and heal. I'll send the doctor back in to finish his tests, then have you moved to the recovery room."

"Again, thank you," Daulo said.

"No thanks needed," Narayan said. "It's my honor to assist a friend of Merrick Moreau. And don't give up hope. Events will unfold as they will, in their own way and with their own timing."

He considered. "And never forget that the universe always has a few surprises of its own to deliver. Surprises that are always worth the wait."

CHAPTER EIGHT

Merrick's first impression as he came slowly out of the gray fog filling his brain was that he was uncomfortable.

Really uncomfortable. The air around him was cold and dry, his body ached in at least a dozen places, and a half-reflexive attempt to shift position showed his arms, hands, and legs inexplicably incapable of movement.

And then, abruptly, he remembered.

Carefully, keeping his eyes closed, he activated his opticals. He was in a small room, about three meters square, with a single metal door to his right and no windows that he could see from his current angle. The ceiling light was something of a surprise: soft and diffuse instead of the white-hot blaze that Merrick would have expected in an interrogation cell. The ceiling behind the light was also a surprise: textured, reinforced concrete instead of metal. Did that mean he was on the ground instead of inside one of the invaders' warships? Possibly in what was left of the Sollas subcity—what he could see of the room he was in looked very much like the holding cell the Qasamans had had him locked in for a few hours.

Unless he wasn't on Qasama at all. There was no reason why the invaders couldn't have taken him to one of their own worlds instead.

And if they had, not only would he probably never escape, but his remains would probably never even be found.

It was a somber and embarrassing demonstration of his still shaky thought process that it took him another few seconds of swirling panic to recognize the obvious way to answer that question. And with his nanocomputer's clock circuit showing only a little over three days since his capture, it was almost certain that he was still somewhere on Qasama.

He was listening to his thudding heart as it started to slow down when there was a soft click from the door.

He froze, his brain finally kicking into full gear. Now, when his captors thought he was still unconscious, would be his best chance to make his move.

Only an instant later he realized to his chagrin that he couldn't. The immobility of his arms, hands, and legs wasn't because of fatigue, but because they were encased in heavy cast-like wraps bolted to the frame of the bed on which he was lying. Even if he'd had better leverage, it was unlikely he could break the bolts free. He still had his sonic weapons, but there was no advantage in stunning his visitors if all he could do afterward was lie here while other Trofts strolled over and locked the door on him again.

No, all he could realistically hope for right now was to gain some information. Opening his eyes, he turned his face toward the door as the lock clicked again and the heavy metal panel swung open.

A Troft stepped into the room, his clothing a civilian-type leotard instead of the armored ones the invaders' soldiers typically wore. He had a small case in his hand, similar to the sort that Merrick had seen doctors from the Tlossie demesne carrying. Behind the alien he caught a glimpse of a long corridor, its ceiling bowed and battered in places. As the door closed behind the Troft, there was movement behind him and a second figure stepped into view.

Merrick caught his breath. The second person wasn't another Troft. It was a human female.

She was young, he noted in that first glance, probably a few years younger than he was, with a slim but muscular build and the slightly darkened skin of a lifetime spent out in the sun. Her expression was as odd as the rest of her, blank for the most part, yet edged by a hint of wariness.

And framing that unfamiliar face and strange expression was a swirling halo of the brightest blond hair Merrick had ever seen.

The Troft stepped to the bed, set his case down and opened it, and as he reached inside he jabbered out a stream of cattertalk.

Not a single word of which Merrick understood.

Merrick felt his heart picking up its pace again. Like everyone else in the Cobra Worlds, he'd slogged his way through four years of cattertalk lessons in school. While he'd never really cared for those classes—he'd found Qasaman much easier to learn—he'd nevertheless gotten through them, and had even placed in the top half of his class.

Now, it was as if that whole section of his memory had been wiped clean. Was his brain still not functioning at full capacity yet?

Or had the Trofts done something to him in the seventy-five hours he'd been their prisoner? [Your words, I do not understand them,] he said. At least he still remembered how to speak cattertalk. Assuming he *was* actually speaking it right now. [Your comment, will you repeat it?]

The Troft's radiator membranes fluttered as he held a small sensor over Merrick's chest, his eyes flicking sideways to the young woman. "He said that he is your doctor," the woman said in Anglic. "He asks how you feel."

It took another few seconds for Merrick to find his voice. Her faint accent was like nothing he'd ever heard before. "I'm a little groggy," he told her. "Otherwise, I think I'm all right."

The woman looked at the doctor and rattled off some cattertalk of her own. The words were just as incomprehensible as the Troft's had been. The alien made a sort of clucking noise deep in his throat, pointed a finger at Merrick's torso, and said something back to her. "The doctor says you are wrong," she translated. "You have injuries to your spleen, your right kidney, and your stomach which as yet are only partially healed. You also have several areas of torn muscle and strained tendons."

Which were the same injuries Dr. Krites had listed back in

Milika. At least the Troft doctor knew what he was doing.

Or at least he could read a medical scanner. "You only asked how I *felt*," Merrick reminded the woman. "You didn't ask what my actual condition was." He started to gesture, but with his arms pinioned all he could manage was a little wiggling of his fingertips. "So what's the prognosis?"

The woman again spoke to the Troft, and there was another brief exchange between them. "A few days more of treatment and you will be sufficiently healed," she said.

Merrick frowned. "Sufficiently healed for what?"

"For the Games." She waved a hand in a way that reminded him of a stage magician preparing to make his assistant disappear. "Rest now, and heal."

"I'd heal more comfortably if you'd get all these restraints off me," Merrick said, again wiggling his fingers. "Would you ask the doctor if he could please do that?"

The woman's forehead wrinkled slightly, but she launched into more cattertalk. The doctor replied, and the woman shook her head. "The doctor says that you would kill us if he did that. It is not his wish to die that way."

"What if I promise not to kill him?" Merrick offered.

The woman looked him straight in the eye. "*Do* you so promise?"

Merrick held her gaze without flinching. "Yes," he said firmly, and meant it. He wasn't here to kill non-combat personnel.

Besides, between his sonics and his stunner he already had plenty of non-lethal weapons in his arsenal.

But either the doctor already knew that or simply didn't believe him. "No," the woman said. "You will heal as you are, until the Games."

"I'll do my best," Merrick said. It had still been worth a try. "What kind of games are we talking about, exactly?"

"*The* Games," the woman said, as if the word itself was definition enough.

The doctor put his scanner back in the bag and pulled out a hypo. "The doctor will now give you something to help you sleep," the woman continued. "It will also stimulate healing."

"How about if we just stimulate the healing and let me stay awake?" Merrick suggested. "I'm getting really tired of sleeping."

"Without the sleeping there cannot be the healing." Some of the severity seemed to slip from the woman's face. "Have no fear, Merrick Moreau Broom," she added in a marginally kinder tone. "We have all felt this medicine. It will not harm you."

"Thank you," Merrick said. His words struck him as slightly stupid sounding, but on the spur of the moment he couldn't come up with anything better. "I see you know my name," he said, wincing as the doctor slipped the hypo into his arm above the shackle and injected the contents. "May I ask yours?"

"My name is not for strangers to know," the woman said. "But among the common I am known as Anya Winghunter."

"Anya Winghunter," Merrick repeated, nodding his head. It sure sounded like a name to him. There must be some subtlety here that he was missing. "Will I see you again?"

"If the doctor so chooses," she said as the Troft returned the hypo to its place and closed the bag. "I come and go at his pleasure."

"Ah," Merrick said. Was the room starting to go foggy again? "You're his assistant?"

She shook her head. "I am his slave."

Merrick's last view before the room faded into darkness was that of Anya's face framed by her impossibly blond hair.

His last thought before that darkness was *what the hell?*

When he again awoke, his nanocomputer indicated that he'd slept for another seven hours. His head was aching, possibly with dehydration, and his stomach was rumbling with the reminder that that he hadn't eaten since Milika, over three days ago.

It was another handful of seconds before he noticed that the shackles that had been on his arms and legs were gone.

He sat up carefully, mindful of his low blood sugar, wondering where the hook was for this particular gambit. But no lasers blazed at him, no antipersonnel explosives shattered the silence, and there were no hungry predators waiting on the floor beneath his table in hopes of a quick snack.

Maybe that would come later. For now, he could focus on his hunger, his imprisonment, and this new mystery of why his captors apparently no longer feared him enough to nail him to the bed.

And, swirling through all of it, the puzzle that was Anya Winghunter.

She wasn't Qasaman, not with that hair. He'd seen Qasamans with hair as light as a dark reddish brown, but the vast majority of the people he'd met here had black or very dark brown hair. The official records of the Cobra Worlds' other incursions onto Qasama backed up that assessment. She wasn't from the Worlds, either, not with that accent.

Had someone hauled her all the way across the Troft Assemblage from the Dominion of Man? Or had the Trofts found another lost human colony somewhere closer, another colony like Qasama itself?

And what the *hell* was this slave thing?

The Assemblage, he knew, was in fact little more than a loose confederation of three- to five-system demesnes, most of which were in continual low-level and mostly polite conflict with each other, whether for influence, real estate, or trade advantage. The various demesnes had different customs, different goals and viewpoints and, as the Troft doctor had shown a few hours ago, occasionally some interesting and nearly incomprehensible dialects.

But never had he heard any hint that some Troft demesne kept slaves. Especially *human* slaves.

Could it all be a lie? Had they taken some woman, from wherever, tricked her up to look exotic and vulnerable, and dropped her in front of him to try to mess with his emotions? The Trofts a hundred years ago had tried that gambit with Jonny Moreau, he remembered, sending a woman into his cell in hopes that her presence and helplessness would induce him to help her escape and thereby reveal his abilities under controlled conditions and close observation.

If that was the plan, they were going to be sorely disappointed. Now that Merrick was on to them, he knew better than to fall for the trick.

He had just about concluded that the only way he was going

to get food was to pound on the door and demand it when the lock again gave its distinctive double click. Getting a grip on the edge of the bed, ready to move in any direction he might need to go, Merrick braced himself. The door swung open.

To reveal Anya standing in the doorway, a covered tray in her hands. "I was told to bring you food," she said.

"Finally," Merrick said, glancing at the slot in the bottom of the door. There was no reason why she couldn't just have taken off the tray's cover and slid it in to him. Unless there was some reason she thought she should deliver it personally. "Thank you."

But instead of coming in, the woman just stood there. Just waiting.

Merrick frowned. Was he supposed to go over there and take the tray from her? Were the Trofts hoping that luring him that close to an open door would tempt him into an escape attempt that they could watch?

And then, belatedly, he got it. *Slave* . . . "Come in," he invited. "Just put the tray down here on the bed."

Silently, she crossed the cell and set the tray down where he'd indicated. Merrick watched her face closely, but he could see no hint of resentment at having just been ordered around like a child. In fact, she seemed almost relieved that he hadn't left her standing there without telling her what to do.

Maybe she really *was* a slave.

Was that what this invasion of Qasama and the Cobra Worlds was all about? Could all this death and destruction be because some group of Troft demesnes had developed a taste for human slaves and was looking to expand their stock?

If so, they'd badly miscalculated. Merrick had seen how hard the Qasamans fought to keep from being subjugated. They would fight even harder to keep from becoming slaves. Needless to say, so would the Cobra Worlds.

"Will there be anything more?" Anya asked, straightening up and looking emotionlessly at him.

"No, I think that will do it," Merrick said, forcing back a sudden flush of anger at whoever had done this to her. "Thank you."

A brief hint of something flickered across her face. Maybe she wasn't used to being thanked for her service. But she merely nodded, turned, and strode out of the room. "You want to stay and eat with me?" Merrick called impulsively after her.

She turned back, the same odd look briefly crossing her face. "I cannot," she said. "I must return to my master."

She was still facing him when some unseen warden swung the door shut in front of her.

For a few seconds Merrick frowned in puzzlement at the closed door. First a doctor's assistant, then a waitress. On the surface, it looked like whoever was pulling her strings was trying to create opportunities for the slave and the prisoner to interact.

But in that case, shouldn't the hidden puppet master have had her jump at Merrick's invitation to join him for a snack, thereby giving them even more time together? Either the Trofts were slow on the draw, or else Merrick was reading this whole thing completely wrong.

Which was, admittedly, the more likely scenario. Who really knew how Troft minds worked, anyway?

His stomach gave a long growl. "Right," Merrick muttered. "First things first." Turning to the tray, he lifted the cover and set it aside.

He wasn't really sure what he'd been expecting for his first meal as a Troft prisoner. But whatever that unformed anticipation was, this definitely wasn't it. There were three items on the oval plate: an angled piece of bone-in meat that might have been part of some creature's leg or wing, a greenish-yellow vegetable paste with red and off-white specks floating in it, and a small, lumpy loaf of bread shaped rather like a seashell.

Most of Merrick's brief time on Qasama had been spent in Sollas, eating ration bars or light and quickly prepared wartime meals. But he'd also had a slightly more leisurely meal at the Sammon residence in Milika, which had given him a general idea of what Qasaman cuisine was like. More importantly, he'd passed among the mix of cooking aromas in both Milika and Sollas, which had offered his self-trained cook's nose a range of the locals' cooking spices and condiments.

The aromas rising from his tray smelled nothing like any of those spices. And it was for certain that he'd never seen or smelled anything remotely like this with even the most exotic Cobra Worlds fare.

Either the Trofts were putting way more effort into this operation than anyone had any business doing, or else Merrick had been right the first time about Anya being from some distant and unknown world.

And if the meal sitting in front of him was from that same world, and if it contained spices or bacteria that didn't work and play well with his digestive system, this could be a very unpleasant evening.

The survival unit at the Cobra Academy had included a step-by-step procedure for finding non-poisonous plants in unfamiliar territory. But given that the Trofts obviously thought he would be able to handle this meal—and since they could poison him any time they wanted—it didn't seem worth the effort to run the checklist.

The Trofts hadn't provided any flatware with the meal, perhaps forgetting that keeping potential weapons away from a Cobra was wasted effort. The first challenge, therefore, was figuring out how to eat the meal while still maintaining a modicum of etiquette. After some trial and error he settled on the technique of tearing off chunks of the meat, picnic style, and using pieces of bread to scoop up the vegetable paste.

The blend of tastes was good and definitely exotic, reminiscent of various dishes Merrick had tried elsewhere but with enough of a twist to underscore the meal's alien origin. The effect on his digestive system was somewhat less positive, and he spent the next couple of hours lying on his bed listening to rumbles from his stomach and wondering if perhaps he should have gone through the food-testing procedure after all.

But nothing came back up, and his system eventually settled down. Merrick stayed awake for another two hours, just to be sure, before finally and wearily settling down for the night.

He'd been asleep for three and a half hours when he woke to stealthy sounds and the touch of surreptitious fingers on his forearms and shins. Before he could activate his opticals, he felt something close around his left forearm and heard the *snick* of a locking mechanism. The Trofts had apparently decided to put his restraints back on.

Merrick felt a snarl rising in his throat. Like hell they were.

With a jerk, he sat upright, simultaneously snapping open his eyes. The Troft who had been gently working his right arm toward its restraint made a desperate grab for the limb, missed, and gave an agonized grunt as Merrick hit him with a hard backhand punch across the helmet. The two Trofts at Merrick's feet likewise made desperate attempts to grab his legs. One of them flew backward as Merrick kicked him, the other jumped back before he could be hit. The latter grabbed for a belted laser—

And collapsed to the floor as a burst from Merrick's sonic slammed into him. The backwash bounced off the wall and echoed across Merrick, and he had a brief battle of his own for equilibrium as he turned to the two guards flanking the open door. Both were in motion, grabbing at their weapons as they sidled away from each other in an attempt to avoid a quick one-two attack.

Merrick tried to twist the sonic in his torso toward them, but with his left arm pinioned he couldn't turn far enough in that direction. Instead, he activated the capacitor connected to his right fingertip laser, firing a quick laser burst to ionize the air between him and the first guard and then sending a low-level jolt of current along the pathway. The Troft toppled unconscious to the floor just as his weapon cleared its holster, and Merrick's second stun blast took down the second Troft before he could bring his laser up into firing position. As the second guard hit the floor Merrick turned back to the restraint on his left forearm and fired a full-power fingertip laser burst at the clamps, blasting them into sprays of half-molten metal. He twisted his arm free, swung his legs around, and leaped off the bed onto the floor.

And as he finally paused from his reflexive attack in order to take stock of his situation, the possibilities of the open door and the deserted corridor beyond it abruptly flooded in on him.

This was probably the best chance he would ever have to escape.

But even as he lunged toward the door he discovered that he'd already missed his window of opportunity. From three different doorways down the corridor a Troft soldier leaned out into view, his helmet turned toward Merrick, his laser coming up to aim.

Cursing under his breath, Merrick ducked to the side of the door, using his last half-second of view to flick a target lock onto each of the weapons trained at him. So much for an easy exit. Now, he'd have to do it the hard way. He leaned out, keying his fingertip lasers.

Only to discover that all three Trofts had disappeared.

He had just enough time to frown in confusion when three more aliens poked their heads and weapons through an entirely different set of doorways. Quickly, Merrick cancelled his original lock and targeted this new group of weapons.

Only to have the Trofts again duck back through their doorways before he could fire. As they vanished, they were replaced by another trio, this group including one of the original three soldiers.

And Merrick finally got it. The target-lock system enabled his nanocomputer to aim and fire sequentially with a speed and accuracy no human gunner could ever hope to achieve. But it presupposed that all the targets in the sequence were still within firing range. If any one of them was no longer visible or accessible, the lock would simply pause and wait for it to reappear.

Which meant that by popping new targets in and out at random, the Trofts had effectively eliminated that particular tool from Merrick's arsenal. If he wanted to take out those soldiers or their weapons, he was going to have to do it without his nano-computer's help.

Only it was already too late for that, he realized with a sinking heart. Whatever momentum and initiative his surprise attack had gained for him was now gone, and his captors' countermove was already up and running. Trying to escape now would do nothing but get him and a whole bunch of Trofts killed.

[Merrick Moreau Broom, I would have words with him,] an amplified Troft voice called from somewhere down the corridor.

Merrick sighed. It was over, all right. [Merrick Moreau Broom, he hears you,] he called back.

[Your captivity, you cannot end it this way,] the disembodied voice said. [Your cell, you will remain in it. Punishment for your actions, it will be not be given to you.]

Merrick pursed his lips. He already knew that his attempt had failed. But maybe the Trofts didn't. In that case, maybe he could still wangle a concession or two out of them. [The restraints, I do not want them,] he called. [Your pledge to not impose them on me, I seek it.]

There was a short silence. [Your pledge to not attempt escape, I seek it in return.]

Merrick felt his stomach tighten around his alien meal. His life literally depended on him finding a way to eventually get out of here. There was no way he could give the Troft that kind of promise.

Unless he did so knowing full well that he was lying.

Only he couldn't. Not just because it was unethical, but because a lie like that could come back to haunt him in a big and devastating way. Unless he could guarantee that his next escape attempt was successful, breaking his word would not only bring harsh reprisals but would forever eliminate any chance of making future deals with his captors.

He hunched his shoulders, feeling a brief ache from one of his still tender muscle groups. On the other hand, if he was clever, maybe he could have this both ways. [My pledge not to attempt escape until the Games, I give it,] he offered.

There was another pause. [Your pledge, I accept it,] the Troft said. [The restraints, until then they will not be used. Soldiers: the restraints, you will remove them from the prisoner's cell.]

Merrick eased an eye around the door jamb. Down the corridor, at least twenty armored Trofts had emerged from doorways, their lasers at the ready, while another smaller group of unarmed aliens marched in single file down the center of the hallway toward Merrick's cell. Merrick stepped away from the door, moving to the side of the room and placing his back against the wall. He kept his hands at his sides, but made sure his thumbs were resting on the fingertip laser triggers.

The caution proved unnecessary. In complete silence the Trofts unfastened the restraints from the bed and tucked them under their arms. Then they collected their injured and unconscious comrades, and the whole bunch retreated through the doorway.

And as the last Troft left the cell, Anya walked in. "What are *you* doing here?" Merrick asked, frowning.

"I brought you this," she said, holding out a small vial containing a light brown liquid. "It will aid in your healing process."

"Thanks, but the doctor already gave me stuff for that," Merrick reminded her.

"This will help more," she said. "Also, I have been sent to stay with you."

"Oh, no," Merrick said firmly, belatedly noticing the small bag slung over her shoulder and the bedroll bandoleered across her back. "No, no. This place is barely big enough—" He raised his voice. "This place is barely big enough for me," he shouted out into the corridor as he returned to the doorway. [This woman, she cannot—]

He broke off as the door slammed shut in his face.

For a moment he glared at the dull metal, wondering briefly how long it would take to slag the lock with his antiarmor laser.

Unfortunately, there was no point in trying. If he wrecked this cell, they'd just find somewhere else to move him.

Or to move *them*.

Slowly, he turned around. Anya was standing quietly by the bed, apparently waiting for orders. "So what now?" Merrick asked, for lack of anything better to say.

"You should take a few drops of the medicine," she said, again holding up the vial. "It will aid in—"

"In the healing process," Merrick cut her off. "Yes, I remember. I meant after that."

"I have been sent to stay here," Anya repeated. "I have been given to you, to serve you however you choose."

The obvious method by which a young woman could serve a young man flashed into Merrick's mind. Ruthlessly, he forced it back, feeling an unpleasant rush of heat in his cheeks. Getting involved in the middle of a war with someone—*anyone*—would be bad enough. But the absolute worst thing he could do would be to let himself get entangled with someone who was under Troft control. The minute he let that happen, they would have a lever they could use against him however they chose.

"Not much call for servants in a prison cell," he told her, trying to keep his voice light. "I could use a snack, though. Any chance they'll let you out to go get me something?"

"I will ask." Lowering her bag to the floor, she walked toward him. He stepped to the side out of her way and watched as she rapped lightly on the door. She called out, again using the strange cattertalk dialect she'd used earlier. This time, though, Merrick was able to pick out the words *master* and *food*. Maybe a little practice was all he needed to learn how to understand it.

There was no response to her question. She knocked twice more, repeating the message each time, and then turned to Merrick. "They do not seem willing to grant your request," she said.

"I'm not surprised," Merrick said. Bracing himself, he stepped up to her and held out his hand. "Your bedroll, please."

Silently, she slid it off her shoulder and handed it to him. "You can have the bed," he told her, moving to the narrow space at the foot of the bed and fumbling with the bedroll's fasteners. Like Anya herself, the clasps weren't quite like anything he'd ever seen before. "I'll sleep over here."

"Please," she said, crossing to him and taking the bedroll back. With three casually deft flicks of her fingers she undid the fasteners and spread the bedroll on the floor. A small hand pump was fastened to one side, and he watched in fascination as she gave it a few quick squeezes, inflating the roll into something that looked at least marginally comfortable.

And then, before he could do or say anything, she lowered herself onto the roll, stretching out across it. "Is there anything more you wish before I sleep?" she asked, looking up at him.

"No, no," Merrick said, pointing to the bed. "You sleep *there*. *I* sleep here."

Anya didn't move. "Is there anything more you wish from me?"

"Anya—"

"That is a master's bed," she said quietly. "This is a slave's bed. I will sleep here."

Merrick took a deep breath. He could argue with her, he knew. Better yet, he could simply order her to the more comfortable bed. He was the master, after all. He could do that.

But even if she obeyed, she would undoubtedly feel guilty about it the rest of the night. That would probably keep her awake, which would pretty well negate the whole point of giving her the more comfortable bed in the first place.

Worse, making any kind of self-sacrifice for her, even one this small, might be exactly what his captors were banking on. Even so mild an emotional interaction would start him on the road he'd already decided he couldn't take.

"Fine," he said shortly. Turning his back on her, he crossed over to the bed. "Maybe by morning they'll let you get me some food."

"I will ask when I awaken," she promised. "Will you take the medicine now?"

"Maybe tomorrow," he said. "I've had about enough Troft generosity for one day."

"As you wish." If she was annoyed at his refusal or his sarcastic tone, she gave no indication of it. "Sleep well, and call if you need anything."

Suppressing a sigh, Merrick lay down on the bed, wishing he could turn off the overhead light. Wishing even more that he could shut out the sound of her breathing.

It was, he suspected, going to be a very long night.

CHAPTER NINE

According to the tentative schedule Jody had seen the night before, the downed Troft warship had been due to be raised that morning. But as she and Geoff headed across Stronghold, she could see that the damaged ship was still lying across the broken wall.

"Uh-oh," Geoff muttered. "That doesn't look good."

"They're probably just behind schedule," Jody said. "I can't imagine that using Troft slave labor is the most efficient way to run a business."

"I was talking about that," Geoff said, pointing toward the wall ten meters away from the bow of the downed ship. "Isn't that Nissa Gendreves talking to Harli?"

Jody made a face. Two weeks ago, back on Aventine, Nissa Gendreves had been a lowly secondary assistant to Governor-General Chintawa, a career bureaucrat moving her slow but steady way up the Cobra Worlds' political ladder.

But all that had changed with the Troft invasion. Jody's brother Lorne had been tasked with the job of getting Senior Governor Tomo Treakness and his two companions clear of the Trofts, out of Capitalia, and off Aventine. At the height of their mad scramble to take refuge aboard the Tloss demesne heir ship where their more-or-less ally Warrior was waiting for them, a badly injured Treakness had given Nissa full authority of negotiation and treaty for the beleaguered Cobra Worlds.

Unfortunately, the woman was nowhere near ready to handle that kind of power. She'd quickly shown herself to be just another pre-machined and pre-formed cog from Capitalia's political machinery, unable to grasp the desperate new reality the Cobra Worlds faced and incapable of thinking or functioning outside the lines.

So Jody's father had been forced to do that offline thinking for her. His reward for that initiative had been Nissa's furious promise that he would one day stand trial for treason, along with his entire family and probably most of the Caelian government.

Nissa had kept mostly to herself for the past thirteen days, ever since Jody's parents and brother had headed for Qasama with Dr. Croi and the Isis equipment. She'd stayed holed up in the apartment Uy had assigned her—plotting or sulking, Jody didn't know which—coming out only for food and the occasional glowering walking tour of the war-torn city. Whatever it was that had lured her out into the fresh air today and over to the wrecked Troft ship, Jody was pretty sure she wasn't going to like it.

"Maybe we should take a little walk around the block," Geoff suggested. "Let the air clear out a little."

Jody squared her shoulders. If Nissa was hoping that Jody and the others would avoid her out of fear or anything else, the girl was sadly mistaken.

Besides, if there was one thing Jody's parents had taught her it was to hold loosely to any preconceptions, particularly preconceptions backed up by limited numbers of data points. Maybe instead of brooding, Nissa had spent some of her self-imposed exile thinking. "People can change," she reminded Geoff. "Maybe Nissa's thought it through and is ready to see things our way."

"Right," Geoff growled. "That's exactly what *I'd* expect from a mindless government lock-stepper."

"She deserves the benefit of the doubt," Jody said firmly. "Anyway, what have you got to worry about? You've charmed the socks off dozens of reluctant investors. You can certainly stand around and smile nicely enough to keep yourself off Nissa's hit list."

"It's not her hit list I'm worried about," Geoff said sourly. "I'm more worried about Harli. If whatever they're arguing about escalates past words, I don't want to be in the line of fire when he offers to send her into orbit."

"Now you're just being silly," Jody chided. Though now that they were closer and Harli's expression was easier to read, she saw that Geoff's fears might not be all that exaggerated. "Anyway, Harli's way more accurate than that. Just stay behind me and you'll be fine."

Geoff grunted. "Yeah."

The argument had clearly been going back and forth, but it was Nissa who was the one speaking when Jody and Geoff came into earshot. "—can't wait any longer," she said, her tone the exact mixture of bombastic and whiny that always drove Jody crazy. "What if that courier ship didn't have to go all the way to Qasama to get help? What if they have reserves sitting somewhere out in space where they can jump anywhere quickly? In that case, they could be here any time."

"Why would they waste the resources to plant a force out in the middle of nowhere?" Harli asked, his expression stiff but his voice still well back from the breaking point. Maybe his parents had taught him about offering the benefit of the doubt, too. "It makes no sense."

"It's called a flying squad," Nissa said. "That's a unit that can move quickly to—"

"Yes, I know what it is," Harli interrupted. "My question is why the Trofts would bother setting up a flying squad that might need to come to Caelian."

"Because—" Nissa broke off, glowering at Jody and Geoff as they came up. "Aren't you two supposed to be working on something?"

"We are," Jody said coolly. "What seems to be the trouble?"

"It's a policy issue," Nissa said. "Not really any of your business."

"Ms. Gendreves is trying to convince me to move all the Troft prisoners out of Stronghold," Harli said. "What she apparently fails to grasp is that I already agree with her. The problem is where to put them where they won't be a threat to us *and* won't just end up as gigger snacks."

"I've given you three alternatives," Nissa said stiffly.

"Right—Essbend, Aerie, or the downed ship," Harli countered. "And if any of those was actually viable, I'd be happy to consider it."

"They're *all* viable," Nissa insisted. "You can put restraints on the prisoners or else drug them while you fly them to one of the two villages—that lets you transport at least four per aircar. Pull in all twenty aircars you have on Caelian, and you can do it in two and a half trips."

"And then we just clear out whatever town you want to put them in?" Harli countered. "Move all the rightful residents out and let the Trofts do whatever they want with people's homes and property? Not a chance."

"Then put them in there," Nissa said, jabbing a finger toward the downed warship. "I've already told you how you can eliminate any possibility that they'll find something to use against us."

"Really?" Jody asked, intrigued in spite of herself. There'd been endless discussions and arguments across Stronghold over the past few days on how they could assure that any prisoners locked inside the warships couldn't access hidden weapons or equipment. "How?"

"Basically, by blowing it up," Harli growled. "No, seriously. She wants us to take one of the remaining missiles off the wing, set up the warhead on the command deck, and let it blow. Then we move the prisoners into an essentially empty shell."

"And again I ask, what's wrong with that?" Nissa challenged. "That much hullmetal should be strong enough to contain the blast."

"The key word being *should*," Harli said. "We don't know that even a completely intact hull will contain that kind of blast. We also don't know if this particular hull is, in fact, intact. There could be all kinds of damage to the plates, seams, or supports that we don't have the equipment to detect."

"Which is why you first move the ship away from Stronghold," Nissa said.

"Which we may not be able to do," Harli snapped, his voice starting to teeter on the edge.

"Wait a minute," Jody said, frowning. "You can't move the ship? I thought you had all the grav lifts in place and calibrated last night."

"The problem isn't the grav lifts," Harli said. "It's the question of what we do once the downed ship isn't filling in most of the gap where the wall used to be."

"I thought the plan was to raise it up off its side and then just move it back into the gap," Geoff said.

"It was," Harli said heavily. "Problem is, we've taken another look at how we've attached the grav lifts, and we're not sure anymore that we'll be able to move the ship once it's upright. There's apparently a whole raft of angle and lift-vector calculations no one bothered to do."

Jody winced. The broken wall already had an open three-meter gap at either end of the downed ship, which had to be guarded around the clock against gigger and screech tiger incursions. If those smaller gaps suddenly became a single, huge, seventy-meter opening, there would be no way to keep the predators out.

"What about the other ship?" Geoff asked, gesturing to the warship looming over the downed one. "Could that one be moved into the gap once the damaged one's out of the way?"

"That's currently our Plan B," Harli said. "Whether we can move it or not will depend on whether there'll be room to lower it into place once the other one is standing upright again. We're doing some calculations on that one, too."

"Can't we just try it?" Jody suggested. "If it doesn't work, you can always lower the wrecked ship back into place, can't you?"

"In theory, yes," Harli said. "But again, it boils down to the angles we've set the grav lifts at. They can lift it all right, but they may or may not be able to lower it again, at least not in a controlled fashion."

"How about this?" Nissa said, her forehead wrinkled in thought. "We take the grav lifts off the standing ship and put them in the correct lower-hull positions on the wrecked one. We use the first set to raise it up off the ground, then use the second set to move it back into the gap in the wall."

"That's not bad," Jody said, her opinion of Nissa going up a notch. Maybe she *had* spent some of her self-imposed isolation thinking. "That might be the answer."

"It might," Harli agreed, a bit grudgingly. "Problem is, I don't think we've got the time and resources to pull it off. Especially since that would leave the upright ship sitting there with no way to move it."

"Can't we put the grav lifts back after we've lifted and moved the first ship?" Jody asked.

"Again, not in the time we've got," Harli said. "The reinforcements could be here in as little as eight days." He grimaced. "And our available labor force isn't exactly enthusiastic about working fast."

"So let's try thinking outside the lines," Geoff suggested, a sudden, cautious excitement in his voice. "What exactly do we need the wall for, anyway?"

Harli snorted. "I don't have time for this," he growled, starting to turn around.

"No, no, I mean it," Geoff said, grabbing his arm. "Walk with me here. We need the wall mainly to keep out the organics and all the rest of the unpleasant ecology that comes rushing in after them. Right?"

Jody snapped her fingers as she finally figured out where he was going. "The Qasamans' combat suits," she said. "We already know that current flowing through the stiffeners and servos repels the organics, or at least prevents them from attaching. If we can build a curtain across the gap that can do that, it should keep out everything but the larger predators."

"Not much comfort to the citizens who end up being eaten," Nissa muttered.

"Actually, if the smaller animals stay away, most of the predators should, too," Harli said thoughtfully. "The few who get curious enough to come in should be easy enough to deal with. Problem is, unless those suits are a hell of a lot stretchier than they look, they're not going to begin to fill the gap."

"Right, but we don't need the combat suits per se," Geoff said. "We just need the electric fields they generate. If we can duplicate those in or around some other material, we should be able to pull it off. It's at least worth a try."

Harli turned toward the crushed wall, and for a moment gazed at it in silence. Then, abruptly, he turned back and nodded. "What do you need?" he asked.

"Freylan's running the final readings on the electric field right now," Geoff said. "Once he's done—"

"*Freylan's* doing the readings?" Harli said, frowning. "I thought he was still in the hospital."

"He was," Jody said. "He checked himself out early this morning."

"Said there was no way he was going to just sit around and listen to his ribs mend when there was work to be done," Geoff told him. "Anyway, once he's got the final specs, it should be easy to program a generator to duplicate the field."

"So you'll need a generator," Harli said, nodding. "What else?"

"Access to everything Stronghold's got in the way of electronics supplies," Geoff said. "Depending on what we end up needing, we might have to disassemble some of your entertainment or computer systems."

"We'll also need samples of cloth to try out," Jody said. "Drapes, extra clothing—anything we can attach the electronics to that won't block the electric fields."

"And once we figure out which material works best, we'll need probably every bit of it you've got," Geoff said. "In Stronghold, and possibly everywhere else on the planet."

"Plus you'll need a lot of hands to put it all together," Harli concluded.

Jody winced. Between the work on the warship, the general cleanup, and keeping everyone fed and safe, Stronghold's resources and personnel were already stretched dangerously thin. "Unfortunately, yes," she admitted. "I'm sorry."

"Don't worry about it," Harli assured her. "There are plenty of people out there sitting around loafing. A little real work will do them good. I'll have the orders cut by the time you know what you need." Abruptly, he held up his hand. "Quiet a minute." He turned around toward the downed warship.

Jody frowned, trying to figure out what he was looking at. A movement above the crowd of Trofts caught her eye: one of the other Cobras—Popescu, she tentatively identified him—was standing beside the ship's upper stern weapons wing, gesturing toward Harli, his mouth moving. Jody strained her ears, but without Cobra audio enhancements she couldn't tell what he was saying.

But Harli could. And it was clear he didn't like what he was hearing. "You two get back to work," he told Jody and Geoff. His eyes flicked to Nissa. "If you really want to make yourself useful, you can go with them."

Nissa's eyes narrowed— "We could certainly use your help," Geoff seconded quickly. "Freylan's basically glued to his chair right now, with his ribs and all. He could use someone to get equipment and lift things for him."

Nissa's eyes flicked to Jody. "Seems to me you've got plenty of help already."

"We will later," Geoff assured her. "Right now, Jody needs to go talk to Rashida Vil."

Nissa frowned. "The Qasaman woman?"

"Yes, that's what I came out here to ask you," Jody improvised, turning to Harli. She hadn't actually planned on talking to Rashida until later today after they'd finished their work on the combat suits. But Geoff was clearly angling to keep her and Nissa apart for a while, and she could easily readjust that part of her tentative schedule. "Any idea where she is?"

"She's over in the other warship," Harli said, eyeing Jody thoughtfully. "Come on—I need to head over there anyway. I'll walk you through the crowd." He flicked a finger at Geoff. "And *you* go get busy."

He took Jody's arm and led the way toward the broken wall and the Trofts swarming around it. "Well, *that* was interesting," he murmured as they walked. "I wouldn't have thought Gendreves was his type."

"I'm sure it's nothing like that," Jody assured him. "Geoff's always been good at politics and basic old-fashioned charm—it's how we got the funding to come to Caelian in the first place. I think he's decided she's a challenge he can't pass up."

"Maybe." Harli looked sideways at her. "Next question: how did you know I was going to ask you to talk to Ms. Vil?"

"I didn't," Jody said, frowning at him. "I just wanted to check in with her and see how she's doing. What did you want me to talk to her about?"

Harli made a face. "I wish I knew. There's just something . . . she's polite and all, and she takes orders just fine. But there's something going on behind those eyes I can't figure out. I figure since you're the closest thing she's got to a friend here, maybe you could get it out of her."

"Not sure I qualify as a friend, exactly," Jody warned. "But I'll be happy to give it a try."

"Thanks." Harli gestured ahead. "I need to talk to Popescu for a second. If you want, I can get one of the others to walk you the rest of the way."

"That's all right," Jody said. "I'd like to hear what he has to say, too."

Harli grunted. "Fine," he said. "But you aren't going to like it."

He was right.

"I found it wedged behind the number eight grav lift," Popescu said, showing Harli a small, gleaming wrench. "Right where we ran the connections to the ship's power system."

"Exactly where you'd put something metal if you wanted to short the whole thing out," Harli said.

"Yeah, pretty much," Popescu growled. "Sorry, Harli. Someone really dropped the ball on this one."

"Not your fault," Harli said, peering up at the ship. "You never had nearly enough men to ride herd on a work gang this big."

"Yeah, excuses always look so good on your gravestone," Popescu said sourly. "Anyway, I've got Brady pulling together a team to start rechecking everything."

"Good," Harli said. "Any guess as to how soon they'll be done?"

"Depends on how many men he can pull away from other duties," Popescu said. "No earlier than this afternoon, though. Maybe not until tomorrow."

"Damn," Harli said. "Well, if it's tomorrow, it's tomorrow. Just make sure to remind Brady that speed is good, but accuracy is better."

"Be nice if we could have both, though," Popescu reminded him. "What would you think about pulling the Cobras off out-rim guard duty to help out? If the Trofts are going to play games, there's no reason we should knock ourselves out protecting them from giggers and screech tigers."

"Good point," Harli said. "You can take a few, but you need to leave at least half the current number of guards out there." He gestured to Jody. "You know the Tlossies better than I do. Does it make sense to keep the prisoners safe—you know, holding onto the moral high ground, and all that—if we want to get them in as allies?"

"Absolutely," Jody assured him. "The Tlossies put a high premium on playing by the rules."

"Yeah, fine," Popescu said. "But high moral ground isn't much use if all it does is open you to more enemy fire."

"Don't worry, I'm also going to have a little chat with Captain Eubujak," Harli assured him grimly. "I'm going to tell him that if we find any more sabotage from his troops I might just take Ms. Gendreves up on her suggestion to set off a warhead inside the downed ship." He glowered at the Trofts working at the edges of the wall. "And I might not wait until after the explosion to move him and his troops inside."

Jody felt her eyes widen. "You wouldn't."

"No, but Eubujak doesn't know that," Harli said. "Popescu, go help Brady form his crew and get to work. As soon as I've get Jody to the other ship, I'll come back and give you a hand."

They reached the second Troft warship without further incident. The Cobra guard passed them through, and Harli led Jody to the top deck. Rashida was right where Jody had expected to find her: seated at the helm and studying the angled control board.

"Ms. Vil," Harli greeted her as he and Jody walked past two small groups of techs testing the circuits in some of the other boards. "How are things going?"

"They go well," Rashida said, looking up at them.

Only they weren't going well, Jody realized as she studied the other woman's face. There was a tension behind Rashida's eyes, a tautness at odds with her confident words.

Harli was right. Something was wrong.

"Good," Harli said, and Jody could hear the false cheerfulness in his voice, as well. "I'll leave you two alone, then." He glanced at the techs, as if only then realizing how relative solitude was right now. "Just let the guard downstairs know when you want to leave, Jody, and he'll arrange an escort."

"Thank you," Jody said. "Good hunting."

Harli nodded to her, then to Rashida, then turned and strode out of the room.

"What is he hunting?" Rashida asked.

"Sabotage," Jody said, pulling up a chair and sitting down. "One of the Trofts working on the downed ship jammed a wrench where it would short out the power conduits. So now they have to check over everything before they can try to move it."

"Yes, I see," Rashida said, lowering her eyes back to the control panel in front of her. "How much will that put them behind schedule?"

"Don't know for sure," Jody said. "Several hours at least. Maybe a day or more if they find more sabotage."

"Which will then delay the moving of this ship?" Rashida asked.

"I'd say so, yes," Jody said, studying the woman's profile. "Is that a good thing, or a bad thing?"

A muscle in Rashida's cheek twitched. "Does it need to be either?" she countered evasively.

"No, but it usually is," Jody said, lowering her voice. "What's wrong, Rashida?"

Rashida's throat worked. "I..." Her eyes flicked to the side. "I can't tell you. Not here. Not now."

Jody felt a sudden stirring of anger. "Is someone bothering you?" she asked softly. "One of these men?"

"No, not at all," Rashida said quickly. "It's...there's trouble. I should have spoken of it sooner, but..." She trailed off.

Jody chewed at her lip. The techs working on the other side of the room were theoretically out of earshot, especially if Jody and Rashida kept their voices low.

But there was at least one Cobra in the group, and maybe more who Jody didn't know, and distance didn't mean much where Cobra audios were involved.

Still, there was distance, and then there was *distance*. "Come on," Jody said, standing up and offering the other woman her hand. "Let's take a walk."

Rashida shook her head. "I was told to stay here."

"That's okay," Jody said, still holding out her hand. "I'll take responsibility."

Rashida seemed to draw back. "You can do that?"

Jody felt her lip twitch. For a moment she'd almost forgotten how male-dominated the Qasaman culture was.

And it suddenly occurred to her that the Caelian society Rashida was experiencing probably looked a lot like the one she'd left at home. Of course, that was really only because Governor Uy had declared the planet to be on a war footing, which meant that the Cobras—all of whom were men—were basically running everything.

But Rashida wouldn't know that. And whatever her world's rules were about women speaking out or approaching superiors with questions or problems, that system was what she was working under right now. "Of course," she said, trying to keep her voice light. "Come on. A little fresh air will do you good."

Rashida hesitated another moment. Then, almost gingerly, she got to her feet. "All right," she said, still sounding uncertain.

"Wait a second," the Cobra spoke up, frowning at them. "Maybe you missed it, but the fresh air down there is contaminated with Trofts."

"That's okay," Jody assured him. "That's not the direction we're going."

Two minutes later, she pushed open the ship's rear dorsal hatch and climbed up the narrow stairway onto the hull crest. "Here we are," she said cheerfully, offering Rashida a hand up. "Fresh air, no predators, and no Trofts. And a pretty nice view."

"Yes," Rashida said coming gingerly up onto the hull crest. "It's . . . a little high, though."

"You're afraid of heights?" Jody asked, frowning. "But you're a pilot."

"I don't mind heights when I'm encased in a flying vehicle," Rashida said. "Here, there's a chance I might fall." She craned her neck gingerly. "And it's a *very* long way down."

"That it is," Jody agreed, peering at the Trofts, the humans, and the town thirty meters below them. "So tell me what the problem is."

Rashida hesitated. "Can I trust you?" she asked. "I need to trust you. I need you to not tell them."

"Okay," Jody agreed cautiously. "Tell them what?"

"Tell them . . ." Rashida closed her eyes. "I was left here as a hostage, Jody Broom."

Jody felt her eyes narrow. "A *hostage*?"

"You weren't supposed to know," Rashida said. "None of you were. Djinni Ghofl Khatir wanted to show our determination to abide by the terms of our agreement. I'm that guarantee of our honor."

"There wasn't any need for that," Jody assured her. "We know you're honorable. Besides, we don't do the whole hostage thing."

"It was nevertheless Ghofl Khatir's wish that I remain," Rashida said. "From his discussions with Cobra Harli Uy, I believe your leaders accepted my presence because they thought my Troft language skills might prove useful."

"Which they have," Jody said, suppressing the urge to tell her to get to the point. Clearly, she had to do this her way.

"But I believe Cobra Harli Uy also thought my piloting abilities might prove useful." Rashida swallowed hard. "He still believes that."

Jody felt her stomach knot up as she finally saw where Rashida was going. "He wants you to fly the warships away from here," she said. "Only you can't, can you?"

"No," Rashida said, almost too quietly to hear.

Jody looked down at the town again. "But I thought Djinni Khatir said you were a better pilot than he was. Was he lying?"

"No, not a lie," Rashida hastened to assure her. "But certainly a mischaracterization. I can fly most Qasaman aircraft, most likely better than he. I was also the more capable pilot on the freighter we used to travel here from our home. But *this*—" she waved a hand helplessly downward at the ship they were standing on "—this is far beyond my capabilities."

Jody hissed gently between her teeth. Practically every plan she'd heard Harli or the others discuss over the past few days had included the unspoken assumption that they could move the two Troft warships wherever they needed to go. If Rashida couldn't do that, there was certainly no one else on Caelian who could. "But you can learn, right?" she asked. "I know the warship's bigger, and probably has a gazillion times as many controls as the freighter. But the principles are still the same. In theory, all you have to do is apply what you were taught and ratchet it up a bit."

"You don't understand," Rashida said with a tired sigh. "Djinni Khatir and I weren't actually *taught* how to fly the freighter. The invader pilot was drugged and made to believe he was performing various maneuvers under various circumstances. Djinni Khatir and I merely watched and memorized his movements."

Under the influence of memory-enhancement drugs of their own, no doubt. "So you watched him working the controls—"

"There were no controls," Rashida interrupted. "There was no freighter. We memorized his movements as he sat at a long dining table in a Qasaman village and imagined himself aboard his ship. We watched where his fingers and hands worked the controls that he believed he was seeing."

Jody felt a shiver run through her. She'd had no idea Qasaman drugs could do anything like *that*. "I see," she said, trying to keep her voice calm. "So you're saying you never actually *looked* at the controls when you were flying the freighter?"

Rashida shrugged slightly. "I saw them," she said. "I could read their labels, and understand a little of what they said. But the control boards here are an entirely different layout. I can't translate my sequences and control movements to them."

"Got it," Jody said, wincing. Harli was *not* going to be happy about this. "Okay. We'd better go down and find Harli."

"No," Rashida gasped, grabbing Jody's arm. "You can't. If he learns that we lied to him, all will be lost."

"It was a mischaracterization, not a lie," Jody reminded her. "Regardless, he has to know, and he has to know now. His whole strategy's going to need revision, and he's only got eight days to revise it."

"I beg of you," Rashida said, her voice desperate, her fingers digging into Jody's skin. "You must not tell him. I cannot fail him, and you, and my own people. The dishonor would be too much to bear."

"Well, then, you'd better figure out how to fly this thing," Jody said bluntly. "Because those are your only two options."

Rashida stared into Jody's eyes ... and then, to Jody's surprise, the tension seemed to melt out of her face. "No," she said quietly as she let go and let her hand fall to her side. "There is one other choice."

Jody frowned. "What do you—?"

And then, suddenly, she understood. "Whoa!" she said, taking a quick step forward and grabbing Rashida's wrist. "Don't do anything stupid. We need you."

"No, you don't," Rashida said, twisting her arm and freeing it from Jody's grip. "You understand the invaders' language better than I do. You can do whatever translation is necessary. That ability and my presence as a symbol of Qasaman honor are my only value."

"That's not true," Jody insisted, wondering if she should try again to grab the other woman's arm. But their footing was precarious enough up here, and if they ended up in a struggle there was a good chance both of them would fall to their deaths. "Neither of them is true. You speak cattertalk way better than I do."

"My speaking did not prevent the invaders' courier ship from obtaining information of our situation and escaping with it." Rashida gestured again at the ship stretching out beneath them. "No, their writing is what's important now. And you read far better than I do."

"We need you," Jody repeated desperately. "Look, at least you've *flown* a Troft ship. That's more than any of the rest of us have done. Let's put our heads together and figure out—"

She broke off as the hint of an idea suddenly came to her. "Wait a second. You say you flew the freighter on pure touch and kinesthetic positioning, right? What if we go to the freighter, *you* show me what you did, *I* translate the control labels, and we work out together how to adapt everything to the warships' control boards?"

Rashida stared at her, a cautious flicker of hope in her eyes. "But the warship controls are far more complex."

"Sure, because this thing can do a lot more than a freighter can," Jody said. "For starters, the helm probably has a weapons section so that the pilot or copilot can fire the lasers and missiles if the regular gunners are incapacitated. That's how Dominion of

Man warships work. Or at least, that's how they worked the last time we saw one a century ago."

"What if you're wrong?" Rashida persisted. "What if we can't learn to fly the warship that way?"

"Then we won't be any worse off than we are already," Jody pointed out. "Are you at least willing to give it a try?"

Rashida's gaze dipped once to the ground far below and she took a deep breath. Then, she looked back up at Jody and nodded. "Yes," she said firmly. "How do we proceed?"

Jody took a deep breath of her own. The thought of having to watch while Rashida satisfied her Qasaman view of honor had terrified her more than she'd realized. "We go to Harli," she said. "We tell him—"

"No!" Rashida interrupted. "We can't tell him about this. My honor—"

"No, no, no," Jody said hastily. "What we're going to tell him is that we want to go back to the freighter. To, I don't know, check its control systems or something. Maybe say we have to double-check how the navigation system and history readout work—that's something we could only do back there. Once he gives the okay, we can check out an aircar and be at the wreck by mid-afternoon."

"I don't think Cobra Uy will let us use an aircar," Rashida said. "I overheard the other Cobras talking. Most are out on search or transport duty, and he's keeping the rest in reserve."

"Then we'll borrow a spooker," Jody said.

"You can drive one of those vehicles?" Rashida asked, sounding doubtful.

"Sure," Jody said. "I mean, how hard can it be?"

"I'll *tell* you how hard it can be," Harli growled. "Picture a typical grav-lift cycle and multiply it by about ten. Add in unfamiliar terrain, multiply *that* by ten. Then add in nasty, hungry predators and multiply *that* by fifty."

"You don't have to be so dramatic," Jody said stiffly. "I *do* know something about the forest, you know. I spent a full day tromping through it."

"And damn near got yourself killed in the process," Harli retorted. "What am I wasting time arguing about this for? No. The answer is no."

Jody braced herself. "Harli—"

"If you think you need to study the wreck, fine," Harli continued, "I'll have Kemp and Smitty drive you out there."

"Oh," Jody said, feeling the argumentative wind snapped straight out of her sails. She should have realized that was where Harli was going.

Only now, instead of pulling just herself and Rashida out of the already critically short labor pool, they were going to rob Harli of the use of a pair of Cobras, too. That hadn't been part of her original calculation. "Or we could make it simpler and just take an aircar," she suggested.

"The aircars stay put," he said tartly. "They're the only things we've got that can pull any altitude, and you never know when you might need that." He gestured to an older man, one of the non-Cobras, busily digging vegetables from one of the gardens by the broken wall. "Yamara, Kemp should be somewhere around the circle over there. Go get him, will you?"

"Sure," Yamara said. Laying down his shovel, he hurried away.

"He should be here in a minute," Harli said, taking Jody's arm and casually walking her a few steps farther away from Rashida. "You sure this trip is necessary?" he asked quietly. "It's not exactly safe out there."

"I'm sure," Jody told him. "I hadn't thought about taking two of your Cobras away, though. Maybe they could just drop us off, make sure we get inside the freighter, and then come back here. We could set a time for them to come get us tomorrow or the next day."

Harli shook his head. "That ship went through the wringer, and from what Kemp said the hull has a whole bunch of cracks and broken seams. Any number of nasties could already be inside, and if they aren't now they will be once they smell fresh meat." He cocked his head. "But come to think of it, there's no reason why *you* have to go. Kemp and Smitty could take Rashida, and you could stay here and help with this fancy curtain you and Geoff sold me on this morning."

"Thanks, but I'd better go with her," Jody said. "As far as I know, I'm the only other person left on Qasama who reads cattertalk script. She might need me."

Harli grunted. "Fine," he said. "But you've got *one day* to find whatever you think you need. After that, you're back here, even if Kemp has to nail you to the back of his spooker for the ride. Got it?"

"Yes," Jody said. After all, it shouldn't take long for Rashida to run through her flight simulations and for Jody to record it all. After that, whatever analysis they needed to do could be handled here in Stronghold.

"Okay," Harli said. "And the two of you should probably wear the combat suits, too, assuming your friends are through testing them by then. In fact, once they're done you might as well just hang on to them. They'll give you an edge if you need to get near the prisoners, and they fit you better than anyone else around anyway."

"All right," Jody said. The suits were a little uncomfortable, but the built-in strength enhancements would certainly be nice to have. Not having to scrape spores and other organics off them every morning would be a nice bonus, too. "I'll check with Geoff and Freylan and find out when they'll be finished."

"There's no hurry—it's too late for you to head out today anyway," Harli said. "We'll set it up for first light tomorrow morning. You think that'll give Rashida enough time?"

Jody grimaced. "I hope so. Yes, I'll make sure it is."

"Good," Harli said. "And watch her. That whatever-it-is is still bothering her—I can see it in her face." He looked over Jody's shoulder at Rashida. "And don't forget that whatever crazy relationship your family has with the Qasamans, it may not be nearly as solid and secure as you think. Be sure you watch your back."

"Don't worry," Jody said, a shiver running through her. "I will."

CHAPTER TEN

"All right," Lorne called, looking over the twenty men standing at quiet attention in front of him, the sleek gray wraparound computers snugged around their necks making an odd contrast to their simple villager clothing. "This is where it begins. This is where we decide whether you have what it takes to be called Cobras."

The word seemed to echo through the forest. Or maybe it was just echoing through Lorne's own mind.

Because there was certainly good reason for him to pause and consider both the word and the men. This was the most unprecedented group of human beings Lorne had never in his wildest dreams expected to see. Men who only a week ago had been standing restlessly in line waiting for their psychological interviews were now Cobra trainees.

They weren't just any men, either. They were *Qasaman* men.

He looked across the group again, a shiver running through him. Their backs were straight and firm, with no hint of pain or even discomfort despite having had forty hours of surgery over the past five days. Their eyes were shiny with the effects of the learning-enhancement drugs they'd been dosed with this morning, drugs that Fadil Sammon had assured Lorne would cut the usual training period from weeks down to mere days.

And behind the studied calmness of their expressions, Lorne

738

could see the burning fire of men with a mission. Men who'd had their home invaded, and were ready and eager to shove the war back down the invaders' throats.

Back in Stronghold, in the heat and excitement of their victory over the Caelian invaders, Lorne had brushed aside Nissa Gendreves's objections to bringing Isis to Qasama. He'd seen her concerns as merely more of the same unimaginative and inflexible bureaucratic thinking that he and the other Cobras on Aventine had been putting up with for too many years.

Now, as he gazed into the Qasamans' faces, he wondered uneasily if maybe she'd had a legitimate point.

"Cobra Broom?"

Lorne shook away his thoughts. There was work to be done, and it was way too late to indulge in second-guessing. "Yes, Trainee Yithtra?"

"I once again question these," Yithtra said, reaching up to tap the computer around his neck. "It may be both necessary and prudent for those of your worlds to learn their new abilities in slow and controlled stages. But we're Qasamans. We're faster than that."

"That's good to hear," Lorne said. "Because you're absolutely not going to get the slow, controlled course. You're going to get the full-bore, hammer-head, bone-bending version. We're in a war, remember?"

"Exactly my point," Yithtra said. "We were told we would only be given our full capabilities once the training was over. I respectfully request that you give them to us now, so that we may learn all the more quickly how to use them."

Lorne suppressed a grimace. Fadil had warned them during the screening process that the Yithtra family had far more arrogance and self-confidence than was probably good for them, and that first-son Gama was definitely a product of that attitude.

But the Yithtras were also one of the strongest families in the village, and moreover had a long history of rivalry with the Sammon family as the two of them jockeyed for power and influence. Fadil had warned that cutting them out of the Cobra project would probably lead to dangerous accusations and turmoil that no one on Qasama could afford right now, least of all a small village like Milika.

In Lorne's opinion, that wasn't much of a reason to accept someone into a program that was already charged with psychological and physical land mines. But Jin had insisted that Fadil have final say on which of his fellow villagers were fit to become Cobras, and Fadil had recommended Yithtra, and so here he was.

But Fadil only had final say on entry to the program. It would be up to Lorne and his fellow Cobras as to which of the candidates ultimately passed the course.

Which was, after all, the true reason why wraparound computer collars were used to control their equipment during training. The Qasamans' nanocomputers were already in place beneath their brains, but for now they were dormant, awaiting the final induction-field signal that would activate them. Whether that activation gave the trainees full access to their implanted weapons and strength-enhancing servos, or whether they got only the stripped-down version of the programming that would turn them into merely extra-strong civilians, was a decision that still lay down the road.

A road that started right now. "The collars stay," Lorne told him shortly. "Let me introduce you to your trainers." He gestured to his left. "This is Cobra Everette Beach; beside him is Cobra Wendell McCollom. Both have experience in training Cobras, and both have survived many years on the intensely dangerous world of Caelian. If anyone can teach you to handle the pressures of war, they're the ones who can do it."

He paused and tried to watch all twenty faces at once. "Next to Cobra McCollom is Jennifer McCollom," he continued. "As Cobras Beach and McCollom are only marginally familiar with the Qasaman language, she'll be translating all of their instructions and orders to you."

The facial twitches were small, and for the most part were hastily covered up. But they were there, once again exactly as Fadil had predicted.

Fully half of the Cobra trainees were not at all happy at the prospect of taking orders from a woman.

Fadil had warned about this. So had Jin. But there was nothing either of them could do about it. The unforgiving realities of life on Caelian left little time for leisure, and few on that world chose to squander that precious time on something as theoretical as foreign language studies. Particularly foreign languages no one ever expected to need.

Jennifer McCollom was a rare exception, a woman who loved the challenge of new languages and had mastered at least four of them over the years, including Qasaman and Troft cattertalk. She'd been a great help to Lorne's parents over the past two weeks as they tried to give Wendell and Beach at least a working knowledge of the language.

But while the two men could now probably navigate their way through the Milika marketplace, neither had the fluency and vocabulary necessary for a military training regimen.

Hence, the need for a translator. And with everyone else who spoke both Anglic and Qasaman already tied up with other duties, Jennifer was going to be it.

Still, as Jin had pointed out, the slightly awkward situation might have a silver lining. Watching how the recruits accepted being ordered around by a woman might give an indication as to how they would accept being ordered around in combat situations by the Qasaman military hierarchy, most of whom were city dwellers.

It might also give Lorne some idea of how determined they really were to become Cobras. "Anyone have a problem with that?" he invited.

"Our only problem is the invaders occupying our world," Yithtra said shortly. "We waste time, Cobra Broom. Train us, and let us fight."

Lorne looked at McCollom and Beach, caught their microscopic nods. "Very well," he said. "Cobra Beach?"

"We're going to begin by teaching you how to run," Beach announced. He waited for Jennifer to translate, then continued, "Not normal running, of course, but the techniques of letting your new servos take all the strain and do most of the work. Once you've mastered the method, you'll be able to run for fifty kilometers without even working up a sweat. The first thing to remember—"

"Hold it," McCollom cut him off, holding up his hand as he frowned somewhere past Lorne's shoulder. "Someone's coming."

Frowning, Lorne keyed up his own audios.

And stiffened. It wasn't just some*one* jogging through the forest toward them. It was an entire group of someones, ten or fifteen at least, all of them marking the same brisk, almost mechanical pace.

He hadn't heard any reports of Trofts traveling through the forest on foot. But there was a first time for everything. "Cobras, spread out," he murmured to McCollom and Beach. "The rest of you, stay put." He took a few quiet steps to his right, peripherally aware that McCollom and Beach were drifting the other direction toward possible cover. The jogging footsteps were getting closer, and Lorne estimated the unknowns would pass a little to the east. He took another step, wincing as a particularly brittle dead branch snapped beneath his foot.

And within the space of two seconds, the footsteps suddenly came to a halt.

Lorne held his breath, notching up his audios again. There were new sounds coming from that direction now, murmured voices speaking words his enhancements couldn't quite make out. The voices appeared human, but he remembered that the Caelian invaders' translators had also sounded reasonably human.

The voices stopped. A moment later, he heard the faint sound of stealthy footsteps coming toward him.

Despite the tension, he had to smile at that one. Sneaking up on a Cobra was generally a pretty futile endeavor. Lorne glanced back, caught Beach's eye and gestured him to move further out of range of a quick one-two shot. The newcomers were splitting up, Lorne could hear now, moving to try to flank him.

It was actually a decent tracking challenge, it occurred to him, and if the recruits had been farther along in their training he might have been tempted to take advantage of the unexpected opportunity. As it was, though, they really didn't have time for this. "Come on out," he called. "Don't worry—we won't hurt you."

The whole group of footsteps again stopped, and there was a moment of silence. Then, the first set Lorne had heard resumed, this time with no attempt at stealth. Lorne adjusted his position slightly, making sure he was facing the figure that emerged from the forest cover.

It was, indeed, a Qasaman. A male, about Lorne's age, wrapped in badly rumpled clothing. "I greet you," Lorne said, making the sign of respect. "What brings you and your companions out into the middle of nowhere?"

"I could ask the same question of you," the other said, flashing a suspicious look at the silent crowd of trainees.

"We're hunters from Milika," Lorne told him. "We came out to practice our strategy for attacking the invaders' hunting parties."

"I see," the man said. "Your name?"

"This is our home territory," Lorne pointed out. "I believe it's customary for the stranger to first introduce himself."

The other smiled thinly. "It is indeed," he said. "And were you a genuine Qasaman, you would have had no hesitation about stating the custom as such." He drew himself up. "But no matter. I am Kaml Ghushtre, Ifrit of Qasama. And you, from your family likeness, I guess are the brother of Cobra Merrick Moreau."

"Correct," Lorne said, quickly covering his surprise. This man knew Merrick? "Cobra Lorne Moreau Broom. Are those with you more Djinn?"

"They are." Ghushtre gave a set of trilling whistles, and with a rustling of grass and branches a wide spread of silent men emerged into view on either side of him.

"We're pleased to see you," Lorne said, doing a quick count. Twenty in all, unless Ghushtre had decided to keep a few back in reserve. "Your help will be greatly appreciated."

"Yes," Ghushtre said, his voice studiously noncommittal. "We first have an errand in Milika. Can you direct us to the village?"

"I would be honored to escort you there personally," Lorne offered. "May I ask the nature of this errand?"

"No." Ghushtre took a second look at him, and something in his face subtly changed. "But I can tell you that it concerns Fadil Sammon, son of Daulo Sammon."

Lorne felt his stomach tighten. "I'm afraid Fadil Sammon is unwell."

"His condition is known to us," Ghushtre said. "Please take us to him."

"If you know his condition, you also know that he can be of only limited assistance to you," Lorne persisted. "Perhaps I can serve in his place."

"We will speak to Fadil Sammon, and no other," Ghushtre said, his voice darkening. "If you no longer feel able to take us to him, then give us a direction and we'll find the village ourselves."

"No, of course I can take you," Lorne said. And he'd thought villagers could be pushy and condescending. "Beach, McCollom—continue with the exercise. I'll be back as soon as I can."

He gestured. "If you'll follow me, Ifrit Ghushtre?"

"Rook to knight's seventh," Paul announced, moving one of his pieces on the chessboard set out in front of him. "Check."

"Interesting," Fadil murmured, gazing up at the implanted star-like gemstones in the ceiling above his medical bed. "I was certain you would move your bishop. I'll have to think a moment."

"Take your time," Paul said. "Would you like me to move the board to where you can see it?"

"No, thank you," Fadil said, a bit of sadness edging into his tone. "I have little else to occupy my mind these days. I appreciate the challenge of having to keep track of the board."

"As you wish." Paul looked across the room at Jin and smiled. "You're beating me soundly enough as it is."

Jin smiled back, trying to keep her face as unconcerned as possible as she lounged casually on the comfortable cushions in Fadil's meditation nook, watching her crippled husband and the paralyzed Qasaman as they tried to fill the long, increasingly tiresome hours.

And as she herself waited for her head, and the room around her, to stop spinning.

It was getting worse. All of it—the dizzy spells, the lapses of logic and reasoning, the disconcerting derailing of her train of thought. The tumor in her brain, which the Qasaman doctors had temporarily shrunk before she and Siraj Akim's team had headed out for Aventine, was starting to come back. And it was coming back with a vengeance.

How long did she have? She had no idea. At her last treatment the doctors had guessed that without surgery she still had three months to live. But that had been only three weeks ago, and it was clear that things were progressing far quicker than anyone had thought. Even if she made it the full three months, she suspected she would be incapacitated long before her actual death. If she was going to survive this, she needed to get to a properly equipped Qasaman hospital, with properly trained Qasaman surgeons, and soon.

The problem was that every such hospital was either occupied or besieged by the Troft invaders.

She clenched her teeth, fighting against a sudden wave of nausea as she continued smiling at her husband. They didn't need the hospital just for her, either. The skin and muscle that had been burned away from Paul's leg could also be fixed, but Dr. Krites had warned her that the window of opportunity on that was rapidly closing as well. If he didn't start the treatments within another week or two the nerves would never properly reconnect. Even if they were later successful in regrowing the leg, he would end up with no feeling in the new sections of the limb.

"Are you expecting company?" Paul asked. "I hear someone coming."

Shaking away her morose thoughts, Jin keyed her audio enhancements. He was right. There were footsteps in the corridor, lots of them, all coming this way.

"I have nothing scheduled," Fadil said. "Perhaps Lorne Moreau is bringing the new Cobra trainees to visit."

Jin frowned. There was something about the footsteps that brought up the image of determined, resolute men. "They don't sound like villagers," she said, climbing awkwardly out of the pile of cushions and taking up position between the door and Fadil. The footsteps reached the door—

The door swung open, and Jin found herself facing her son. "Lorne," she said, her eyes flicking across the hard-faced young men lined up behind him. The face just over his shoulder seemed to jump out at her—it was a face she'd seen somewhere before—

And then the semi-familiar man pushed past Lorne through the doorway and into the room. "I greet you, Fadil Sammon," he said formally. "I am Kaml Ghushtre, Ifrit of Qasama."

Jin felt her lungs freeze. *That* was where she'd seen him before: in the Sollas subcity, when she and Merrick had first arrived and been hauled before Miron Akim under suspicion of collusion with the Trofts who had just landed on Qasama. Merrick had offered to show the Cobras' power as a way of proving their goodwill toward the Qasamans, and had instantly earned Ghushtre's ill will by not playing according to the young Djinni's expectations of how the demonstrations should go.

And given the icy temperature of Ghushtre's single glance at Jin as he came into Fadil's room, it was clear he hadn't forgotten the incident, either.

"I greet you, Ifrit Ghushtre," Fadil answered the other calmly. "How may I serve you?"

"We would speak with you." Ghushtre looked again at Jin. "Alone."

"May I ask what this is about?" Jin asked, making no effort to move out of his way.

"No, you may not," Ghushtre said. "The matter is a private one, between Qasamans only."

"Fadil Sammon's condition requires extra care," Paul pointed out. "One of us should remain in case he needs assistance."

"He will not need assistance during the brief period of our conversation," Ghushtre countered. "We are at war, Cobra Jin Moreau. We have no time to spare for foolish chatter. You and your family will leave this room. Now."

Jin focused on the other Djinn, still standing in orderly lines in the corridor behind Lorne. If she could signal her son, and if he could spin around and hit them with his sonic before they could react . . .

"It's all right, Jin Moreau," Fadil said quietly. "You may leave. I'll be all right."

Jin turned to look at him. His face was calm, but the tranquility had tension lurking beneath it. "Do you know what this is about?" she asked.

He looked away from her gaze. "For the most part, yes," he said, and she had the impression that he was choosing his words carefully. "Please go now. Ifrit Ghushtre and I must speak."

Jin took a deep breath. "We'll be outside if you need us," she said. "Paul? Do you need a hand?"

"I've got it," Paul said. Standing up on his one good leg, he got the crutches Dr. Krites had given him into position under his arms and made his awkward way across the room to the door. Jin joined him, and with Lorne bringing up the rear they stepped out into the corridor. At a terse command from Ghushtre the rest of the Djinn filed silently past them into the room, the last one closing the door behind him.

"Are you okay?" Jin asked, eyeing her husband. "You looked like a decrepit ninety-year-old in there."

"You mean with these?" Paul asked, twirling one of his crutches. "No, I'm fine. Just part of my on-going philosophy of looking as harmless as possible in front of potential enemies."

"The Djinn aren't potential enemies," Jin said firmly, wishing she completely believed that. Most of them, like Siraj Akim and Carsh Zoshak, had come around quickly enough. But there were a few like Ghushtre who were still question marks.

"If you say so," Paul said. "Lorne? Don't."

"Don't what?" Lorne asked.

"You know perfectly well," Paul said with mild reproof. "You were about to casually lean your ear against the door. But don't. They asked for privacy—both of them did—and we need to honor that request."

"Even if Fadil's in trouble?" Lorne countered. "There's something about that Ghushtre guy that sets my teeth on edge."

"Probably because he doesn't like us," Jin told him. "Or at least he doesn't like me. Doesn't mean he won't be perfectly civil to Fadil."

"Yeah, right," Lorne growled. "How does he know us well enough not to like us?"

"He came in for a bit of embarrassment in front of his peers when Merrick and I first arrived," Jin said. "Not much—on a heat scale, no more than a light singeing."

"Though of course he might remember it differently," Paul pointed out. "How did you happen across them, Lorne? I thought you were out in the forest with the new recruits."

"I was," Lorne said. "They were heading through on a quick-march and ran into us in one of the clearings northeast of town."

"They were heading *through* the forest?" Paul asked, frowning. "And from the northeast?"

"Yes, and I don't blame them," Lorne said. "The latest scout reports say all the main roads are under constant Troft surveillance, with everything from drones flying overhead to those armored trucks parked outside the towns and at all the major intersections."

"It's the northeast part that interests me," Paul said. "That implies they didn't come from Azras or one of the other southerly cities. Sollas, perhaps?"

Lorne made a face. "There wasn't much left of Sollas when we flew in last week. There's probably even less now."

"Which would make it a good place to be running from," Paul said thoughtfully. "The question is, why come *here*? What in the Worlds would make Fadil so important that anyone would send twenty Djinn to talk to him?"

"Unless they're not just talking," Lorne said, moving toward the door again. "Dad, for Fadil's sake we need to find out what's going on in there."

"Lorne—"

"Hold it—they're coming," Jin interrupted. "Lorne?"

He nodded and took a long step back.

Just in time. A second later the door was flung open and a glowering Ghushtre strode out of the room. He stopped short, as if surprised to find the three Brooms still there, and for a moment he looked back and forth between Jin and Paul. Then, he drew himself up. "I've decided that my Djinn and I will avail ourselves of the alien equipment that now resides in the Sammon family mine," he said.

"What equipment is that?" Paul asked cautiously.

"Foolish games do not become you, Cobra Paul Broom," Ghush-tre growled. "I refer to the Isis equipment which you and your countrymen brought from the Cobra World called Caelian." He turned to Jin and seemed to brace himself. "You'll take us there at once, that I and my Djinn may become Cobras."

"Well, *that's* new," Lorne murmured.

Jin felt her mouth go suddenly dry. If Ghushtre decided to take that as an insult, or worse, as a challenge...

But the Djinni didn't even twitch. "You will take us to Isis, Jasmine Moreau," he said.

"My mother's not well," Lorne said, stepping forward. "I can take you."

"You have duties elsewhere, Lorne Moreau," Ghushtre said. "You have Cobra soldiers of your own to train. Go."

Lorne's eyes narrowed— "It's all right, Lorne," Jin said quickly. "I can take them to Isis. Go back and assist Beach and McCollom."

She could see the objections flicker across his face: how there were still unpleasant levels of dust in the parts of the mine they had to pass through to reach the Isis setup, how her dizzy spells could lead to serious injury if she stumbled against a stone wall, how suddenly fainting in the partially open lift could be even more disastrous.

But while Lorne was her son, he was also a Cobra. He knew how to take orders, whether he liked those orders or not. "Fine," he said. "I'll see you later." With a last lingering look at Ghushtre, he turned and strode down the corridor.

"And you, I believe," Ghushtre added, turning to Paul, "have a position of assistance to return to."

"That's all right," Paul said. "As you said, Fadil Sammon can do without assistance for a short time. I'll come with you."

Ghushtre's eyes lowered pointedly to his injured leg. "He may need you," he said. "You will return to him." He looked at Jin. "At your convenience, Jasmine Moreau."

"Let me first make sure Fadil Sammon's comfortable," she told him. Without waiting for an answer, she slipped past him and Paul and hurried back into the room. The other Djinn, lined up as before behind their leader, moved out of her way without comment or complaint.

Fadil watched her as she crossed over to him. "Are you all right, Jin Moreau?" he asked as she stopped beside his bed.

"I was going to ask *you* that," Jin said, studying his face. The tension she'd noticed when Ghushtre first arrived had abated somewhat, but lingering bits of it were still present. "What's happened? What do they want?"

He smiled, his expression touched with sudden sadness. "What we all want," he said. "Victory."

Jin glanced over her shoulder. "On whose terms?"

"That's always the question," Fadil agreed. "For now, certain things must remain a mystery to you, Jin Moreau." He looked past her shoulder toward Ghushtre. "And now you must go."

Jin sighed. "All right," she said. "But you should know that I really hate mysteries. I'll probably be worrying about it the entire rest of the day."

"My apologies." Fadil smiled again, a more genuine one this time, then sobered. "In that case, perhaps you'll allow me to offer a more interesting puzzle. You told me earlier that the invaders had also invaded your home world of Aventine, where they released razorarms taken from Qasama into the cities. Tell me, have the forests of Aventine been emptied of similar predators?"

"Hardly," Jin said grimly. "Those razorarms are probably the only thing that's kept the government from cancelling the Cobra project entirely."

"Then tell me," Fadil said. "If there are razorarms available for the taking on Aventine, *why are the invaders still hunting them here in the Qasaman forest?*"

Jin stared down at him. Somehow, that thought hadn't even occurred to her.

But he was right. Why would anyone bother transporting dangerous animals all the way from Qasama to the Cobra Worlds when they had all they could ever want right there in Aventine's own expansion regions? "I don't know," she said.

"Nor do I," Fadil said. "But I very much fear that there is more to this invasion than meets the eye. And until we know the invaders' secrets—*all* of their secrets—we may never fully defeat them."

"Then I guess we'd better get busy and learn those secrets," Jin said. "Because I have no intention of letting any of the sons of chickens just walk away."

She reached down and squeezed his hand. "Take care, and I'll see you later."

"I'll look forward to it," Fadil said. "In the meantime, please ask Paul Broom to come in." He smiled. "We still have a chess game to finish."

Carsh Zoshak was lounging casually in an open-air café near the mine entrance when Lorne tracked him down. "Ah—Lorne Moreau," Zoshak said, waving in greeting as Lorne came up to him. "I thought you were out in the forest."

"I was, and I have to get back," Lorne said, pulling up a chair and sitting down. "But first I wanted to give you a heads-up. You know a Djinni named Kaml Ghushtre?"

"He was one of the Sollas contingent," Zoshak said, nodding. "Why do you ask?"

"Because he's here," Lorne told him. "He and a squad of twenty blew into Milika about an hour ago, had a short chat with Fadil Sammon, and are now on their way to meet Isis."

Zoshak's eyes widened. "They're coming *here*?"

"And apparently planning to undergo the treatment," Lorne said. "My question is, are they sincere, or could this be a plan to destroy Isis and rid Qasama of alien influences, or some such insanity?"

"Wait, wait, I'm losing the line of your logic," Zoshak protested. "There's no possibility that Djinni Ghushtre would make such a decision on his own. Isis is part of the treaty between Qasama and the Cobra Worlds. Only the Shahni have the power to repudiate any aspect of the treaty, including Isis."

"That assumes there are members of the Shahni still around," Lorne pointed out. "What if there aren't?"

"Then rule would fall to the military commanders," Zoshak said, frowning in thought. "But your question raises a second, more interesting one. If Djinni Ghushtre wouldn't dare interfere with Isis without orders, so also wouldn't he dare undergo the procedure without orders."

"Unless, as you said, the military has taken over," Lorne pointed out grimly. "In that case, team and unit officers might have been given more autonomy than they used to have."

"Except that Djinni Ghushtre isn't an officer," Zoshak said. "He would need to be an Ifrit to even have unit command."

Lorne frowned. "He *is* an Ifrit. At least, that's how he introduced himself."

"Really," Zoshak said, an odd tone to his voice. "Djinni *Ghushtre* has been made an Ifrit?"

"That he has," Lorne confirmed. "Unless you think the rank might have been self-awarded."

"No," Zoshak said firmly. "The other Djinn in the unit would never stand for that. He must have been granted the rank, and only Marid Miron Akim or one of the Shahni could do that. Tell me, did he know about Isis before he arrived here?"

"I don't know," Lorne said. "But he didn't say anything about it before his chat with Fadil. *And* he definitely came out of the meeting looking annoyed."

"Still, my guess is that he already knew," Zoshak said slowly. "Which would imply in turn that Siraj Akim and Ghofl Khatir did indeed make it safely to Azras."

Lorne grimaced. Siraj and Khatir had disappeared the minute all the Isis crates were safely inside Milika, taking a small car and heading for Azras, the nearest large city, to try and make contact with whatever was left of the Qasaman government.

But that had been eight days ago, and neither man had been heard from since. Given the scout reports of the Troft activity in and around Azras, Lorne considered their silence to be ominous in the extreme.

Still, maybe Zoshak was right. Maybe the two Djinn had made it to Azras and were able to touch base with the Shahni remnant on the Qasamans' fancy underground communications system.

He hoped so, anyway. The idea of Qasaman rule dispersing to individual unit commanders sounded like the quick path to complete chaos. And Zoshak was right—even a freshly-minted Ifrit like Ghushtre was surely smart enough not to make critical decisions on things like Isis without some serious thought.

So then why had he looked so angry when he came out of his meeting with Fadil?

"Here they come."

Lorne looked furtively behind him. In the distance he saw his mother come into view around a vendor's stall with Ghushtre and the rest of the Djinn striding along behind her. "I'd better go before he spots me," he told Zoshak, getting up from his chair. "Keep an extra close eye on the mine from now on, will you?"

"I always take my duty seriously." Zoshak stood up, too. "In fact, I believe it's nearly time for me to do my prescribed check of the mine itself. I think perhaps I'll join your mother in escorting Ifrit Ghushtre and his men in to Isis."

"Do that," Lorne said. "And watch him, Carsh Zoshak. Watch him closely. He's up to something. We need to find out what that something is."

CHAPTER ELEVEN

When Harli had said that the group would be leaving Stronghold at first light, Jody had naturally assumed that he meant there would actually be light in the sky.

He hadn't. She was still waiting for her alarm to go off when Kemp's pounding at her door jolted her awake. By the time she settled herself groggily onto the spooker saddle behind him there was still not a single hint of glow in the eastern sky that she could detect. Apparently, first light was something that related only to Cobra optical enhancements.

Spooker travel, she'd learned the first time she experienced it, was simultaneously one of the fastest and yet one of the slowest methods of transportation ever invented. Fastest, because the sheer speed of the spike-covered grav-lift cycles chewed up the fifty kilometers to the wrecked freighter in less than an hour. Slowest, because the sheer terror of watching the landscape shoot toward and past them at that speed stretched every millisecond of the ride into its own sizeable fraction of eternity.

Only once during the trip did she find herself wondering how Rashida was taking it. After that, she focused her full attention on getting through it herself.

By the time they reached the crash site there was enough of a glow in the eastern sky for her to see both the wrecked freighter and the long gouge through the forest it had created when it plowed its way to a stop. As was typical of Caelian, of course, while the demolished trees remained demolished, the rest of the undergrowth had already started retaking the scarred ground.

And where there was Caelian undergrowth, she knew, there were also Caelian predators. It was just as well, she reflected as Kemp and Smitty let the spookers coast to a halt beside the entry ramp, that she hadn't insisted that she and Rashida come alone.

"Well, there it is," Kemp said as he hopped off the spooker and offered a helping hand to Jody. "Not exactly in prime working condition."

"Looks better than the wrecked warship back at Stronghold," Jody said, taking his hand for balance as she climbed out of the saddle. She didn't really need the help, but it seemed impolite to refuse the offer.

"It also looks worse on the inside," Rashida warned as she took Jody's cue and accepted Smitty's help to the ground. "I don't think Ghofl Khatir locked the hatch when we left, so we should be able to get in easily enough."

"Whoa, there—not so fast," Kemp said, putting out a hand as she started up the ramp. "You and Jody are staying out here while I check for predators. Smitty, keep an eye on them."

They'd been waiting for over twenty minutes, and Smitty had killed two giggers and a screech tiger, when the freighter's hatch finally opened again. "Clear," Kemp called. "Sorry it took so long. On the plus side, it looks like we aren't going to have to go hunt for lunch."

"Gigger?" Jody hazarded as she and the others headed up the ramp.

"Hooded cloven, actually," Kemp said. "A small one—I'm still not sure how he managed to get in. Plus ribbon vine salad on the side, of course. Afraid the blue treacle's a bit overdone—I had to burn it off to get the command room door open."

"It all sounds delicious," Jody murmured. "I can hardly wait."

"Trust me," Kemp said with a sly smile. "Come on—I've got the power going."

Rashida had been right, Jody noted soberly as she followed Kemp through the narrow corridors toward the bow. The beating the freighter had taken, first from the invaders' brief attack and then from the crash landing, had seriously messed up the interior. Walls and bulkheads were buckled, floors were canted, and there was broken equipment everywhere. The vines and other plants already starting to fill the open areas merely added a bizarre aspect to the ship instead of hiding any of the damage.

"So now what?" Kemp asked when they were finally standing in the command room.

"Rashida and I need to do some reconstruction of the course," Jody said, a shiver running through her as she stared at the lumpy gray hull sealant running in a jagged line across the wall. Her mother had nearly died right here . . .

"What can we do to help?"

"Nothing, really," Jody said. "It's pretty much a job for us cattertalk-readers."

"There's a lounge just aft of the hatch, if you'd like to rest," Rashida offered.

"And if you get bored with that, you can poke around and see if there's anything aboard worth taking back to Stronghold," Jody added.

"Yeah, keeping busy sounds good," Kemp said. "Smitty, you stay here and keep an eye on them. I'll go start opening cabinets."

Jody looked at Rashida's suddenly tense face. If Smitty figured out what they were doing, they were going to be in big trouble with Harli. "It would be safer if you stuck together," she told Kemp. "Remember, you still don't know how that hooded cloven got in. The command room looks pretty secure—we'll be fine here on our own."

"Besides, we have these," Rashida added, holding up her arms to show the glove lasers on their combat suits.

For a moment Kemp eyed her thoughtfully. Then he shifted his gaze to the walls and floor, his eyes moving methodically across every centimeter of the command room's surfaces. "Okay," he said at last, pulling out a field radio and handing it to her. "We'll seal up behind us—call me immediately if you see anything that even looks like it might be trouble. And *don't* open the door until we get back, for any reason. Got it?"

"Got it," Jody said, clipping the radio to her belt. "Happy hunting."

Kemp gave the room a final sweep, then strode out. Smitty gave a last look at Rashida and then followed, sealing the door behind him.

Jody took a deep breath and pulled her recorder from her inside pocket. "Okay," she said, gesturing Rashida toward the helm. "Let's see what we've got."

After the way Rashida had talked, Jody had fully expected the script on the helm controls to be faded or scratched or otherwise difficult to read.

She hadn't expected for it to be completely incomprehensible.

Steady, girl, she told herself firmly as she studied the flowing characters. *These are Trofts. They speak cattertalk, and they write cattertalk. This has to be understandable.*

But the characters refused to resolve themselves into anything she was familiar with.

"You can't read it either?" Rashida asked anxiously as the silence lengthened. "What do we do?"

"We start by not panicking," Jody told her. "The Troft Assemblage is made up of hundreds of small demesnes, with probably dozens of different dialects and tonal shadings among them. This has got to be one of those differences. We just have to figure out how it...wait a minute."

"You have something?"

Jody smiled lopsidedly. Of course. "Got it," she said. "It's normal script, except with a bunch of extra twiggings and some really strange angles. Sort of like—let's see; what did they call it?—like Earth Gothic script. Something like that."

"Yes," Rashida said slowly, peering closely at the script. "Yes, I think I see it now. But don't these differences make communication difficult?"

"Apparently not to the Trofts," Jody said. "I've heard that groups who normally speak even extremely different dialects usually don't have any trouble understanding each other's cattertalk. I guess reading each other's script works the same way."

She took a deep breath and let it out in a relieved *whoof*. Now, with that realization, the whole board made sense again. Deciphering it would be slow and tricky, but at least it would be possible. "So okay," she continued briskly. "How do you want to work this?"

"I thought we could go down the same list of situations and responses that the interrogator used back on Qasama," Rashida said, sitting down in the main helm seat and flexing her fingers. "You can record both, and hopefully we can then adapt all the movements to the warship's controls after we return to Stronghold."

"Sounds reasonable," Jody said. "You think you can remember all the questions?"

Rashida frowned up at her. "Of course."

"Right," Jody murmured. Settling herself at Rashida's side, she aimed the recorder's lens over the board. "Whenever you're ready."

[The main drive engines, they are to be activated,] Rashida said, slipping into cattertalk as her hands traced out a sequence of eight different controls. [The grav lifts, they are to be activated...]

They'd been at it for four hours straight when Kemp and Smitty finally returned to the command room. "How's it going?" Smitty asked as the two Cobras again made sure to seal the door behind them.

"We're making progress," Jody confirmed. "You?"

"The same," Smitty said, pulling over one of the chairs and sitting down. "There's a lot more stuff back there than we realized."

"A little too much, in fact," Kemp said, passing Smitty and coming up beside the two women. "Rashida, how long did it take you to fly from Qasama to Aventine in this thing?"

"About five days," Rashida said. "That was the freighter's highest speed."

"Why, were you thinking they should have gotten there faster?" Jody asked.

"No, just the opposite," Kemp said, frowning down at the control board. "It looks like there was space for twelve spine leopards in the main hold. That sound about right?"

"Yes, I believe so," Rashida said. "I know Miron Akim removed ten, and there was room for one or two more."

"So ten to twelve of the beasts," Kemp said. "But the amount of food they had stored up for them—some kind of frozen carcasses, I think—looks like enough for a good three-week trip."

"'Course, we don't know how much Qasaman spinies usually eat," Smitty warned. "Could be they chow down more than their Aventinian cousins."

"No, they should be pretty much the same," Jody said, frowning. "I think Governor Telek made sure they did food compatibility tests before they released the first of them onto the planet." Rashida stirred, but didn't speak. "They were probably just planning a slower trip, that's all."

"Yeah, we thought of that," Kemp said. "Problem is, it brings up an even thornier question. Your mother and brother both told us that the Trofts had already invaded Aventine when your mother and the Qasamans arrived. That means that if the original Troft crew had still been in charge, they'd have been barely in time to offload their load of spinies before the first invasion wave finished consolidating their gains. If they'd been running at fuel-saver speeds, there's no way they would have arrived until the party was pretty much over."

"Maybe they were supposed to be part of the second wave," Jody suggested. "They were to bring in the next batch of spinies to replace the ones the Aventine Cobras would have killed."

"And they wanted to bring them all the way from Qasama?" Kemp asked. "Think about it—once the Trofts have Aventine, they can zip out to the expansion regions whenever they want and pick up as many spinies as they want."

"*And* they can get the things without having Qasamans shooting at them the whole time," Smitty added.

Jody frowned. They had a point. An extremely good point. "Okay," she said slowly. "So maybe the carcasses were also for the crew to eat?"

Kemp snorted. "You see a butcher shop or carving station on your way in?" he asked. "Come on—a simple freighter crew's not going to load a bunch of whole carcasses aboard a ship when pre-packaged meals are a hell of a lot easier to deal with."

"No, I suppose not." Jody looked at Rashida. "Feel free to jump in with any ideas," she invited.

"I have one thought," Rashida said slowly. "But I'm not sure it makes sense."

"Well, the one we came up with doesn't make sense, either," Smitty said. "How bad can yours be?"

"Go ahead, Rashida," Jody said encouragingly.

Rashida hunched her shoulders. "Perhaps the presence of extra supplies means the invaders never intended to bring these particular razorarms to your worlds. Perhaps the plan was to take them somewhere else."

"Congratulations," Kemp said sourly. "Looks like we're all going crazy together, because that's the same conclusion *we* came to. Problem is, we can't figure out where or why anyone would want to do that."

"I don't suppose the pilot your people interrogated might still be alive," Smitty said. "If he is, we might be able to ask him when this is all over."

"I don't know what happened to him," Rashida said, frowning into the distance. "That would have been Senior Advisor Omnathi's decision. But there may be another way."

She swiveled back to the board. "There should be a history of previous travel in the ship's log," she continued, keying the navigational section. "If we can find out where the ship has been, we may find a clue to where it was going."

"Good idea," Smitty said approvingly, getting up and stepping to her side. "Do we have some kind of—? Oh, you've got a recorder, Jody. Great. Does it have a Troft jack?"

"It has a standard one," Jody said, looking around. "But I didn't bring a cable for it."

"I'll look in here," Kemp offered, heading toward a cabinet fastened to the side wall. "Smitty, see if you can find any drawers under the control boards."

"There's another spare-parts cabinet in the anteroom," Rashida said.

"I'll check it," Jody said, turning toward the door.

"*I'll* check it," Kemp said firmly, changing direction. "You can look in this one."

They'd collected a total of five data cables by the time Rashida found the freighter's course history. Three of the cables were of an odd and non-standard configuration, which Jody suspected went along with the script variant used by the ship's owners. Fortunately, the control board had several different jacks, one of which was the kind Jody was used to and that her recorder could take. Even more fortunately, the other two cables were of that same type.

Three minutes later, she had a full recording of everywhere the wrecked freighter had been in the past eight Troft standard months.

"For all the good it'll do us," Kemp said with a grunt as Jody disconnected the cable. "If it's been flying someplace off our charts, we won't know where any of those planets is anyway."

"There are more extensive maps back on Aventine," Jody said, double-checking the download. It would be embarrassing to get back to Stronghold and only then discover that her recorder hadn't encoded the data properly. But everything seemed to be there. "And the Tlossies should be able to pull up data on everything any group of Trofts have ever put their status curlies on. When Warrior's people get here we can have him take a look."

"Let's hope *they're* not running at fuel-saver speeds," Kemp said. "So what now?"

"We still have some work to do in here," Jody said, looking at Rashida and getting a small nod of confirmation in return. "You said something earlier about lunch?"

"That we did," Kemp agreed. "Come on, Smitty, let's go outside and get a fire going. Might as well give our guests the full Wonderland experience."

"Sure," Smitty said. "Rashida, how do you like your hooded cloven steaks?"

For a moment Rashida looked uncertainly at him, as if trying to figure out if he was making fun of her. She must have seen something in his face, though, because Jody saw her tense muscles relax. "Not too deeply cooked," she told him. "The very center part should remain the color of the original meat."

"We'll call that a rare," Smitty said, looking at Jody. "Jody?"

"Medium rare," Jody told him. "And char the outside, if you don't think it'll make the meat too tough."

"It won't," Smitty promised. "You two get back to work. One of us will come get you when it's ready."

By the time Smitty came to get them, Rashida and Jody were nearly finished with the read-through on the piloting instructions Rashida and Khatir had received back on Qasama. Long before that point was reached Jody found herself utterly astonished by the sheer amount of information the Qasaman treatments had enabled Rashida to retain.

And not just information, either, but also the detailed muscle memory that had allowed her to pilot an alien ship across the stars to Aventine and then to Caelian.

Khatir and Siraj had assured Governor Uy that the Qasamans would be able to learn how to be Cobras in days rather than weeks. At the time, Jody had assumed that was fifty percent boasting and fifty percent finger-crossed hope. Now, she wasn't so sure it wasn't a hundred percent truth.

The lunch the two Cobras had prepared was excellent, far better than Jody had expected untreated and unseasoned meat cooked on an open fire could ever be. Kemp hadn't been kidding about including a ribbon-vine salad, either, which was also delicious. The fact that they had to eat everything with their field knives only added a dash of adventure to the whole experience.

The rest of the piloting read-through took less than an hour. By the time Jody announced they were ready to leave, Kemp and Smitty had finished searching the ship and had assembled a small collection of electronics and other small items they thought might be useable and that could be carried on the spookers.

By the time the sun had reached the tops of the tallest western trees, they were back in Stronghold.

Jody's plan had been to head immediately to her house and see how Freylan and Geoff were doing with the spore-repellant cloth. But Rashida insisted on first going to the Troft warship to look over the helm board again and run a quick comparison with the records Jody had made of the freighter's controls. Reluctantly, Jody agreed.

It was just as well that she had.

"The good news is that we should be able to translate everything you did in the freighter to here," she told Rashida after a quick but careful study of the boards. "The bad news is that you're not going to be able to do it alone."

"What?" Rashida asked, looking stunned. "But you said the pilot should be able to fly the ship alone."

"Under normal circumstances, he probably could," Jody said grimly. "But that didn't count on Captain Eubujak having five last minutes in here before the Cobras broke in."

Rashida's eyes widened some more. "Sabotage?"

"Yes, of a very clever sort," Jody said. "See here, how the power section and sensor monitor sections of the helm board are dark? Looks like he had just enough time to cut the cables that echoed those control systems from those particular boards over to here."

Rashida looked at the areas Jody had pointed out. "I don't understand," she said. "If he wished to completely disable the ship, why didn't he just destroy the entire board? I was told he and those with him were armed with lasers when they surrendered."

"Because he *didn't* want to completely disable the ship," Jody said. "A wrecked board would have meant no one would ever get the thing off the ground, at least not without a lot of work. What he did was make sure it took three people who knew what they were doing to fly the thing."

"His thought being that there wouldn't be that many humans on Caelian with such knowledge?"

"Exactly," Jody said. "Besides which, I don't think he'd given up hope of pulling a last-minute run for it. I'm guessing they had the grav lifts coming up to power when the Cobras came charging through that door."

Rashida let out a long, thoughtful breath. "All right," she said, still staring at the board. "You say three people can fly it. What about two?"

"Like who?" Jody countered. "Eubujak was right, you know. No one else on Caelian has even a clue how to run systems like this."

Rashida turned her gaze on Jody. "Except you."

"*Including* me," Jody retorted. "I've never flown anything more complicated than an aircar in my life. I've never even *watched* anyone fly something this big."

"But you understand the language," Rashida reminded her, gesturing at the cattertalk script. "You watched while I ran through the procedures for flying the freighter, and you've already promised to help me adapt the procedures here. How much more complicated can it be for you to learn while you also teach me?"

"Rashida—" Jody held out her hands, palms upward. "I can't do this. I'm sorry. It's not that I *won't* do it. It's that I *can't*."

"You're wrong," Rashida said quietly. "I've seen your family in action, Jody Moreau Broom. I've seen what your parents and brothers can do. You're part of a remarkable family, more remarkable even than the rest of your people. Whatever you choose to do, you *can* do it. I know you can."

Jody shook her head. "My family is Cobras, Rashida," she said. "The parents and brothers you so admire—they're all Cobras. That's the reason they're special, not some historical or mystical family name." She sighed. "But that being said, if we don't get this thing off the ground, it's going to sit here until the invaders' reinforcements arrive, at which point it probably gets turned back around against us."

"Yes, it does," Rashida said. "Which leaves us only two choices: fly it, or destroy it."

"And we can't destroy it this close to Stronghold without risking the city," Jody concluded reluctantly. "Which means that either way we have to learn how to fly the damn thing." She sighed again. "Sometimes I hate logic. Okay, fine. I'm in."

"Thank you," Rashida said. "You said the power and sensor functions have been detached?"

"Yes," Jody said. "And since power is probably more important than sensors, I'll have to handle that board."

"But won't we need the sensors, too?"

"Given that Eubujak made a point of disconnecting them, I'd say we probably will," Jody conceded. "We'll just have to hope we can find a way to preset them."

"Or," a voice said calmly from the doorway behind them, "you get a third person to run them."

Jody spun around, nearly wrenching her back in the process, a taste of bile welling suddenly into her throat. Kemp and Smitty stood just inside the doorway, their faces expressionless.

A brittle silence filled the room. "I don't suppose," Jody said, just to try to spark some reaction from those stone faces, "that we can convince you we were just goofing around."

"No," Kemp said with a simple, cold flatness that made her wince. "What the *hell* were you thinking, Broom?"

"She's not to blame," Rashida cut in before Jody could find an answer to that. "I insisted she not tell anyone."

"You can insist all you want," Kemp growled back, glowering openly at her now. "She's under no obligation to baby-sit your feelings or your honor or anything else." He shifted the glower to Jody. "She *is* under obligation to keep the people in charge up to date on everything that in any way impinges on our plans for the defense of Caelian."

"I'm sorry," Jody said between stiff lips, her stomach knotted painfully. It was one thing, she realized dimly, to talk with casual unconcern about her family's name when that name wasn't on the line. Only now, with it in danger of being dragged into public shame, did she realize how much it truly meant to her.

And yet, paradoxically, in that same instant she realized how little a name meant. Not when it was weighed against such things as life and freedom and victory. "I'm sorry," she said again. "But assuming you've been listening the whole time, you know that we're right. We have to move this ship, and Rashida's the only one who can do that. You want to lock me away, or whatever you do to prisoners, fine. I'll take whatever punishment you or Harli want to throw at me."

Bracing herself, she sent as stern a look as she could manage upstream against Kemp's glare. "But Rashida has to stay free and able to work."

Kemp's eyebrows rose slightly on his forehead. "Are you bargaining with me, Broom?" he demanded. "*You*, of all people?"

Jody took a deep breath—

"*Especially* you, who needs a third person to help you fly this
bird?" he added in the same gruff tone.

Jody blinked, feeling the sudden discomfiting sensation of having
been leaning against a wind that had suddenly stopped blowing.
"Excuse me?" she asked cautiously. "Are you saying...?"

"That we're going to join the crazy offworlders who can't seem
to understand basic simple orders?" Smitty suggested. "Yeah, I
guess we are."

"Don't misunderstand," Kemp warned. "I'm still mad as hell
that you didn't go to Harli the minute you realized there was a
problem. But that's water long under the bridge. You're right, we
have to move this damn chunk of alien hardware."

He looked at Rashida. "And *she's* right that you're going to need
a third person. Smitty?"

"I'll do it," Smitty said without hesitation. "You've got enough
on your own plate already. Besides, I can make myself scarce easier
than you can. Just switch me to Babool's roving-patrol shift, and I'll
have an excuse to be in here while Rashida and Jody are working."

"Safer to just assign you to guard and assist them," Kemp said,
eyeing Jody thoughtfully. "A more critical question is whether they
can spare Jody from work on that fancy curtain they're putting
together."

"Easily," Jody assured him. "My degrees are in animal physiology
and management—Geoff and Freylan only brought me in on this
job to deal with the fauna we were going to capture and study.
All the electrical and mechanical stuff was their department. Once
they figure out how to build the curtain, all they'll need is extra
hands for the grunt work. Anyone in Stronghold can do that as
well as I can. Probably better."

"Well, we'll see," Kemp said. "And for the record, they've already
started work on the curtain, along with about thirty of Stronghold's
finest. If no one starts screaming in panic for your help, I guess
we'll be okay with leaving you here."

He took a step closer to Jody. "But let me make one thing *very* clear. From now on everything you do gets reported. Every success, every failure, every strange thought or idea—*everything*. Understood?"

"Understood," Jody said. "Do we report to you, or to Harli?"

Kemp looked sideways at Smitty. "What do you think?"

"Harli's way too busy with everything else he has to do," Smitty said. "And since I'll already be here, you can just report to me."

"Yeah, let's keep the chain of command simple," Kemp agreed with a hint of sarcasm. "Wouldn't want you to get all confused again."

"We appreciate that," Jody said, finally starting to breathe again. "Thank you."

"Thank me after you get this bird off the ground," Kemp growled. "*And* you've put it down again where Harli's told you to."

He took a deep breath, let it out in a huff. "Okay. Logistics. Your house is going to be the center of a round-the-clock sewing and soldering marathon for a while, so you might as well move into the governor's spare room with Rashida. Smitty will pick you both up there at oh-five-thirty tomorrow, and the three of you will get to work. Any questions?"

"Just one," Rashida said, a bit timidly. "We had a late and very filling lunch, and I'm not yet tired."

"Neither am I," Jody agreed.

"I could stick around another hour or two myself," Smitty offered. "In case they find something for me to do."

Kemp hesitated, then gave a reluctant nod. "Fine," he said. "But no more than a couple of hours. The next guard shift starts about then, and I'd just as soon avoid any awkward questions as long as possible." He turned and headed across the room. "Just be careful," he called over his shoulder, "and try not to fire any thrusters or whatever else this thing's got."

He reached the door and turned back. "And no matter what you do tonight," he added, "tomorrow will *still* start at oh-five thirty."

CHAPTER TWELVE

The first night with Anya in his cell was rough on Merrick. Every time she rolled over, it seemed, or made any kind of unexpected noise or strange movement he snapped awake, his brain and reflexes on hair trigger, his body in full fight-or-flight mode. By the time the guard delivered the breakfast tray through the slot at the bottom of the door, he felt almost as tired as when he'd gone to bed.

Fortunately, the day itself turned out to be uneventful. The Troft doctor came by once with another injection, but aside from that Merrick didn't see any of the aliens. Every half hour or so Anya asked if there was anything she could do for him, subsiding without comment or complaint when he told her there wasn't. He tried faking a nap after lunch, just to see if she or the Trofts would try to pull something when he wasn't watching. Nothing had happened by the time he did accidentally fall asleep, nor did anything seem changed when he woke up.

At bedtime Anya again offered him a dose from her medicine vial. Again, he turned her down.

And life settled into an odd but not unpleasant routine.

Merrick had told himself firmly that he wasn't going to get emotionally involved with Anya, no matter what she did to encourage such a relationship. To his mild surprise, she did absolutely nothing in that direction. She never spoke to him unless she was asking if he had any orders, or was answering one of his infrequent questions. She was always first at the door when meals arrived, retrieving the tray and bringing it to Merrick, then retreating to her bed to sit silently and patiently until he turned over her half of the food to her. When it was time to sleep, she asked one final time what she could do for him, offered him some of her medicine, then retreated again to her bed. She never joined Merrick in his daily workout regimen, but he often noticed her doing quiet isometric exercises of her own. Once, when he woke up in the middle of the night, he spotted her doing some stretching and limbering and something that looked like a combination of tai chi chuan and ballet.

Once, out of a sudden sheer desperation for human companionship, he invited her to eat with him. As she had with his offer of the room's bed that first night, she reminded him that he was the master and she was the slave, and that she would eat only what he didn't want, and only after he'd decided what that portion was. The strangest part of the conversation was the sense Merrick had afterward that Anya had made the same decision he had about not becoming emotionally entangled with her unasked-for roommate.

All of which, to Merrick's mind, made her a most unlikely Troft spy. So who was she? And why had they put her in his cell?

By the fourth day of their captivity together, he'd still come up with only one answer.

She really was, in fact, nothing more or less than a slave.

And it was frightening how easy it was to get used to having such a person around.

It was on the sixth day, an hour after Anya had sent the empty lunch tray out through the door slot, when the routine changed.

It began with the usual double click of the lock. But this time, instead of the Troft doctor, a pair of armored soldiers stepped through the doorway. [The Games, you are ordered to accompany us to them,] one of them announced.

"Am I, now," Merrick murmured, eyeing the aliens. Both carried small lasers, but the weapons were belted at their sides, with the security straps still attached. Apparently, they weren't expecting trouble from the prisoner.

What they *were* clearly expecting was an uneventful trip to wherever they were going. Each of the aliens was carrying a set of shackles, thick metal cuffs connected by thirty centimeters of heavy-looking chain. One set was probably for Merrick's wrists, those cuffs including fan-shaped palm pieces he assumed were designed to limit the use of his fingertip lasers. The other set was probably ankle cuffs, a bit larger than the wrist versions but just as sturdy-looking.

Merrick suppressed a cynical smile. If they thought that was all they needed to immobilize a Cobra, they were in for a rude awakening. [The Games, of what do they consist?] he asked in cattertalk.

[The truth about them, you will learn it soon,] the guard said. [The shackles, you will submit to them.]

Merrick flicked a glance over their shoulders at the corridor beyond. Once again, whoever was in charge had set up the pop-in/pop-out arrangement of gunners in the various doorways near Merrick's cell. Even if he barreled through the two guards standing in front of him, he wouldn't get very far.

But if he went along with the shackles another opportunity might present itself along the way. Even alert people sometimes got sloppy when they thought they were holding all the cards. [The shackles, I will submit to them,] he agreed, hopping off the bed and offering his wrists. [The shackles, you may attach them.]

The two Trofts stepped warily forward, one of them fastening the wrist cuffs around Merrick's arms, the other squatting down and doing the same with the ankle cuffs. All four of the cuffs, Merrick noticed as they were locked in place, had thick round rings welded to their sides, too sturdy to be simple hanging rings. Perhaps they were planning to transport him by vehicle and the rings would be attached to more chains to anchor him to the floor or walls.

The guards finished and stepped back. [To the arena, you will follow us,] the first guard said. He turned and gestured to Anya. [Merrick Moreau, you will also accompany him.]

[Obedience, I give it,] Anya said, standing up and coming to Merrick's side.

[Behind him, you will walk there,] the guard said, gesturing again.

Silently, Anya took two steps back, stopping a meter behind Merrick. The guard took up position behind her, the other guard settled in two meters in front of Merrick, and at a curt order the whole procession trooped off together out of the cell and down the corridor in parade-style single file.

With the prisoner now theoretically helpless, Merrick had assumed the randomized guard rotation would end after they passed the first group of doorways. But the Troft commander was smarter or warier than that. As they continued on, more doorways ahead began sprouting soldiers, running the same target-lock-defeating pattern as the first group.

Still, sooner or later the Trofts were bound to make a mistake.

And then, twenty meters dead ahead, there it was. In the center of a cross-corridor a large, heavy-looking metal ring had been set up in front of their procession. The structure was about a meter and a half in diameter, standing vertically on a wide, flat stand, with the look of a security metal detector about it. Power cables snaked away to the left, while a small control board on the right glowed with blue and green status lights.

Mentally, Merrick shook his head. What in the Worlds they thought a metal detector would teach them at this stage he couldn't imagine.

What it *was* going to teach them, though, was that powered electrical equipment and Cobras were a very bad mix.

It would have to be quick, he knew. But he could do it. He would wait until the first three of their group had passed through the detector, and as the Troft bringing up the rear stepped into the ring Merrick would turn and trigger his arcthrower, flash-vaporizing the electronics and electrical components inside the ring and blowing the whole device, hopefully with enough force to take out the guard. At the same instant, he would stun the Troft in front of him with a blast from his sonic. A fingertip laser burst at his ankle chain to free his legs, a pretzel-twisted leg and antiarmor blast into his wrist chain, and he and Anya would be clear to make a run for it.

If Anya was interested in escape, that is. If she wasn't . . .

Merrick set his jaw. If she wasn't, he told himself firmly, he wouldn't waste precious seconds trying to argue or reason with her. She came with him the instant he was free, or he would have no choice but to leave her to her own devices.

The lead Troft reached the ring and passed through it. Merrick frowned, flicking a glance at the status board. As far as he could tell, none of the lights had changed. Yet the Troft was obviously loaded with metal, electronics, power supplies, and everything else that a security detector might be programmed to search for. Could the ring be something else instead? He stepped into it, momentarily dismissing the question as he readied his arcthrower.

And in a violent fraction of a second he was yanked to a halt, his arms snapping to either side to slam into the ring, the chain between his wrists breaking with barely even a sound or a tug. Simultaneously, his legs were pulled forcibly together, that chain not breaking but simply bunching together between his ankles with links digging painfully into his skin.

The ring wasn't a security detector at all. It was a giant, electromagnetic trap.

And Merrick had literally walked right into it.

He flexed his chest and arm muscles with all his strength, adding full servo power to the effort. But with his arms spread-eagled to the sides his leverage was effectively zero. He looked up at his right hand, peripherally noticing the breakaway link that had been coyly nestled in amidst the real ones in his wrist chain, wondering if he could still fire his arcthrower. But with the cuff pinned to the ring, his little finger was now pointed along the side of the metal arc instead of directly at it. Triggering the arcthrower would just send the bulk of the current away from the mechanism instead of directly into it.

And even if enough of the charge got into the ring to do some damage, with his cuff pinned to the metal there was a good chance that much of the jolt would flow into his own arm. There were, he reflected bitterly, few more humiliating ways to die than by the careless use of his own weapons.

From behind him came the sound of hurrying feet. He tried

twisting his torso against his wrists, hoping he could at least turn the edge of his sonic toward whatever was about to happen back there. But again, his lack of leverage defeated the attempt.

A pair of Troft hands appeared at his right and deftly slid a sturdy-looking rod into the small ring he'd noticed earlier welded onto his right wrist cuff. A quick turn of his head to the left showed the other end of the rod now being attached to that cuff. A second rod was fastened to the horizontal bar near his left wrist, and he glanced down to see the other end sliding into the ring on his left ankle cuff. A third rod mirrored the second by linking his right wrist and ankle.

And with that the activity ceased. A hum Merrick hadn't noticed faded, and the pull on his wrists and ankles vanished as the electromagnets were powered down.

For all the good it did him. With a yoke-style bar across his shoulders keeping his arms rigidly apart, and with his legs able to move only forward and backward, and then only a few centimeters at time, he was as thoroughly trapped as if he was still pinned to the ring.

But if his lasers and arcthrower were now useless, he still had his sonics. He focused on the Troft guard in front of him, who had stopped and turned to face the operation. It would be a useless and fairly juvenile gesture to flatten the soldier, Merrick knew. But at the moment he was in the insanely frustrated mood to do it anyway.

And then, even that small token act of defiance was taken away from him. With a Troft hand gripping her wrist, Anya stumbled under Merrick's pinioned right arm and was hauled to a stop directly in front of him, right exactly where she would take the brunt of his sonic.

Merrick took a deep breath. [My cooperation, you could have simply asked for it,] he called.

[Your forgiveness, I ask it,] the same disembodied Troft voice he'd heard that first day replied. [Your pledge of cooperation, you only gave it until the Games. The risk, I could not take it.]

[A drug, you could have used it instead,] Merrick pointed out. [Unless such elaborate schemes as this, you enjoy them.]

[A drug, it might dangerously slow your reactions in the Games,] the Troft said. [A point, it was also necessary to make. This demonstration, it is intended to teach you truth.]

Merrick grimaced. [The truth, that my mind and intentions can be read in advance?]

[The truth, you recognize it,] the Troft confirmed. [A transport dolly, it will now be brought to take you to the Games.]

Merrick squared his shoulders as best as he could with a pole digging into his back. [Your offer, I acknowledge it,] he said. [The Games, I will travel there under my own strength.]

There was a pause, and then something that sounded like a rasping chuckle. [Your spirit of rebellion, I approve of it,] the disembodied voice said. [Your destination, the soldiers will lead you to it.]

Traveling in his current situation, Merrick quickly discovered, was easier said than done. The rods allowed him less than half his usual stride, and even those small steps transmitted an awkward and unpleasant torsion to the shoulder rod with each movement.

But there was no way he was going to change his mind and ask the Trofts for a ride. Not now. Especially not when he had a sneaking suspicion that the alien commander was hoping that he would do so.

Besides, the leisurely pace forced by his restraints gave him a better opportunity to study the layout of the maze of corridors as they passed through it.

And for the first time since his capture, he finally knew beyond the shadow of a doubt where he was.

The Trofts had indeed locked him in the Sollas subcity. And not only in the subcity, but in the southwest area, the part of the labyrinth he was most familiar with.

Like Merrick himself, though, the place was no longer in pristine shape. The walls and ceilings showed signs of stress or battering, as if the Trofts had been at them with giant sledgehammers. Or, more likely, that someone had been busy at ground level with explosives and bulldozers, pummeling the subcity with random shock waves and toppling buildings across areas that hadn't been properly prepared to take that kind of weight.

Finally, after fifteen minutes of plodding through increasingly familiar territory, they arrived at their destination: the very arena where Merrick and the Djinn had planned and trained for that final attack on the invaders' warships.

The battle in which Merrick had nearly been killed.

He looked around the room, the memories of those long hours of practice mixing with the remembered stress and agony of the battle itself. The arena was good-sized, fifty meters by thirty, with an eight-meter-high ceiling. The walls were lined with doors of various sizes, six of them exits, the others leading to storage for the equipment, ramps, and prefab structures that could be used to turn the empty room into a duplicate of whatever the Djinn would be facing on their next mission. Near the ceiling were a set of catwalks and projectors that could handle lighting and other optical and audio effects. Lower down were display screens that could add further visual details and cues that the team might need to know.

The arena hadn't escaped the general subcity damage. One of the catwalks had lost its supports at one end and was hanging at an angle, its lower end suspended in midair about three meters above the floor. Two of the exit doors had been shattered, with the pieces still lying nearby, and the walls near all the other exits were pitted with laser marks. Behind the broken doors he could see stacks of rubble that blocked any chance of movement in those directions. In the center of the room the entire ceiling had been bowed downward, with several square meters of the concrete broken away and the exposed rebar hanging open like a strange abstract sculpture.

More ominous were the dark stains of dried blood scattered across the floor. Whatever had happened here, the Qasamans hadn't given up without a fight.

[Ten more steps, you will take them,] the unseen Troft ordered, his voice coming now from one of the speakers in the arena's upper walls.

Merrick grimaced. Another ten steps with this stupid rig he was wearing? [The Games, what do they consist of?] he called as he obediently set off toward the center of the arena.

[The Games, they are from Anya Winghunter's culture,] the Troft said. [Their purpose, she will explain it.]

Merrick focused on the woman still walking in front of him. The Games were *her* idea? "Anya?" he prompted.

"Commander Ukuthi speaks truth," Anya said over her shoulder. "The Games are the way my people test our young ones."

"I thought you said you were slaves," Merrick said. At least now he had a name for the Troft who'd been running him in rings ever since he was brought here. The question was, how did Anya know him? "What do you test them for?"

Anya stopped and turned around, her eyes cool and measuring as she looked at him. "For skills of combat," she said, as if it was obvious. "Our masters enjoy watching us fight."

Merrick was still trying to find a response to that when there was a multiple *snick* from his wrists and ankles. The cuffs popped free and dropped clattering to the floor, the three connecting rods dropping with them.

He turned around, flexing his arms and fingers, just in time to see the last of their two Troft escorts hurriedly disappear through the doorway they'd entered by. The door swung shut with a thud, and he heard a double click as it was locked.

Locked; but not for long. Merrick's cell door had been specifically designed to keep people from getting through it. The arena's doors hadn't. Flicking a target lock onto the bolted side, he shifted his weight onto his right leg—

[The exits from the room, explosives have been attached to them,] Commander Ukuthi's voice drifted down from the ceiling. [A devastating blast, it will occur if you attempt to escape.]

Merrick hesitated, still balanced on one foot. The Troft might be bluffing, though from what Merrick had seen of him so far that didn't seem likely. But even if he wasn't, Merrick and Anya were a good five meters back from the door. There would have to be a hell of a lot of explosives back there to reach them at this distance. The gamble was probably worth taking.

He looked up at the cracked ceiling. On the other hand, he had no idea how much damage this part of the subcity had taken.

It was conceivable that an explosion of any size would bring the whole arena down on top of them.

His programmed Cobra reflexes might still get him safely through a catastrophe like that. But they wouldn't help Anya.

He'd promised himself that he wouldn't get in any way emotionally attached to this mysterious woman. But whether he liked it or not, she was a fellow human being, and he couldn't risk her life so casually. Certainly not on a plan that had such a limited chance of ultimate success anyway.

"Fine," he muttered. "Whatever." He raised his voice. [The Games, begin them.]

There was a short pause. Then, across the arena, one of the storage room doors opened, and a razorarm strode into the room. It caught sight of the two humans and broke into a loping run toward them.

Merrick frowned. Was Ukuthi kidding? Razorarms had decentralized nervous systems that made them tricky to kill, but Aventine's Cobras had long since learned the necessary tricks. Targeting three of the easiest kill points, he waited for the predator to get closer.

And as it closed to within ten meters and threw itself into an attack sprint, he swiveled his left leg up and fired his antiarmor laser. There were three brilliant bursts of light, and the spine leopard slammed into the floor and skidded to a halt at Merrick's feet.

Merrick gave it a few seconds, just to make sure, then looked up at the speaker. "Is that it?" he called. "Can we go home now?"

"There will be more," Anya murmured into the silence, her voice odd. "They will not stop with just one."

Merrick looked at her, frowning. The oddness of her voice, he saw now, was matched by the oddness in her face. In place of the wooden, distant expression he'd become accustomed to was a mixture of surprise, disbelief, and a touch of fear.

Only then did it occur to Merrick that she'd probably never seen what a Cobra could do.

"Don't worry about it," he said as soothingly as he could. There was something disconcerting about being looked at in that way. "Whatever they throw at me, I can handle it."

[The next predator, it will not be the same,] Commander Uku-thi's voice came over the speaker. [Concussion charges, they will be attached to its hide. Detonation of the charges, your lasers will cause. Understanding, do you have it?]

Merrick looked at Anya again. This one seemed new to her, too. [Understanding, I have it,] he called. [Danger to us, do the charges possess it?]

[Danger, they certainly possess it,] Ukuthi assured him. [The charges, they are shaped to spread their force outward. The preda-tor, it will not be harmed.]

[Understanding, I have it,] Merrick repeated sourly. In other words, if the concussion charges were close enough when they detonated, they would stun or otherwise disable Merrick and Anya but not the razorarm, leaving the predator free to maul them at its leisure.

But that shouldn't be a problem. He knew at least four different ways to kill a razorarm, and if this was Ukuthi's way of learning the full range of Merrick's Cobra weaponry he was going to be disappointed. All four ways involved his lasers, which the Trofts had already seen.

To Merrick's left another of the storage room doors swung open and a second razorarm bounded out. This one, he saw, was noticeably more agitated than the first had been.

Small wonder. Attached to its head, looking like some sort of strange lily pads floating on a misshapen pond, were three cup-like devices about ten centimeters across.

And they were positioned precisely over the three spots where Merrick had shot the first razorarm.

This time Merrick didn't bother to let the predator find and identify its potential prey and launch itself into a charge. With three more rapid-fire laser shots, he dropped it where it stood.

"Amazing," Anya murmured from his side.

"It's all in the wrist," Merrick told her, glancing around the room. The rest of the arena's doors were still closed. "Stay here," he ordered. Warily, he crossed to the dead razorarm and squatted down beside it.

The devices fastened to the animal's hide weren't anything he was familiar with. But the trigger mechanism did indeed look like a temperature fuse, which meant Ukuthi hadn't been lying about the risk if Merrick's aim went awry.

What was interesting was that a temperature fuse would also be triggered by Merrick's arcthrower or possibly even the lower-intensity current of his stunner. Yet Ukuthi had only warned him against laser misfires. Did that mean Ukuthi didn't know about those weapons? Or had that been a test to see if Merrick was smart enough to extrapolate to such conclusions on his own?

He was pondering that question, and trying to figure out what he might be able to do to the concussion charges without setting them off, when a third door swung open across the room. This time, the razorarm sported six of the concussion-charge lily pads, the collection covering both sets of Merrick's earlier kill points.

Merrick sighed as he got back to his feet. Now it was just getting ridiculous.

He killed the razorarm, and the one after that, and the one after that. Each time, the next predator emerged with more and more of the concussion charges in place, until the last one came out looking like some high-fashion satire.

But there was nothing amusing about the fact that all the predator's best target zones were now off-limits. Merrick wound up lasering its legs to bring it to a halt, then moving right up beside it and carefully lasering three shots into its head beneath the charges. Once again he confirmed that the predator was dead, then returned to Anya's side to wait for whatever Ukuthi and the Games had planned for him next. Another door opened, much earlier than Merrick had expected, and he turned to face it.

And felt his mouth drop open. It wasn't a razorarm this time, but a creature like nothing he'd ever seen before.

Its basic shape was that of a tapered cylinder, five meters long and half a meter in diameter at its largest, heavily scaled, with no legs and a barely discernable head with tiny eyes and a wide slit of a mouth. It rippled its way out of the storage room onto the arena floor in a fluid, snake-like motion, its movement accompanied by the muted crackle of hard scales against concrete floor. Its front segment swayed back and forth a few times, as if the creature was surveying its new territory. Then, with almost arrogant leisure, it turned to face Merrick and Anya.

"What the *hell* is that?" Merrick muttered, taking Anya's arm and backing them slowly away from the creature.

"It is called a jormungand," she said, her voice trembling. Merrick spared her a quick glance, his stomach tightening at the sight of her wide eyes and suddenly pale face. Whatever this thing was, she was very unhappy to see it. "How did he find—?"

"Save it," Merrick cut her off. The armored snake was on the move, rippling toward them with deceptive speed.

There was no time for finesse. Swiveling on his right leg, Merrick brought up his left and fired his antiarmor laser into the creature's head. The shot sent a burst of thick green smoke from the impact point, momentarily hiding the jormungand from sight.

The smoke cleared away to reveal the creature still slithering toward them as if nothing had happened.

"You have to kill it!" Anya said frantically. "Please."

"I'm trying, I'm trying," Merrick snarled, wrinkling his nose as the fetid odor from the smoke reached him. He fired again, still targeting the head, then again, and again. The results were the same: clouds of smoke, some charring of the scales where the shots hit, but no serious damage and no obvious effect on the jormungand's ability to function. The scales were ablative, Merrick realized with a sinking feeling, the first microsecond of the laser's heat vaporizing a thin layer, with the resulting smoke then diffusing the rest of the shot and probably also carrying away most of the energy. If the scales were thick enough, he could probably pump fifty shots into the damn thing and still not kill it.

He didn't have time for fifty shots. And he definitely didn't have time to experiment. Angered or stung by Merrick's useless attacks, the jormungand had picked up speed and was now coming at them at the pace of a brisk jog. "Go," Merrick told Anya, giving her a push back behind him. "Go. Run!"

"Run where?" she asked, taking a few steps and then stopping. Merrick glanced around. Aside from the dead razorarms the arena was bare, with no cover anywhere. The catwalks would be safe enough from something that couldn't jump, but they were all too high to reach.

Except for the broken one hanging precariously from one end.

It would be dangerous, Merrick knew—the supports might be in bad enough shape that any extra weight would bring the whole thing crashing down. But it was all they had. "Over by the catwalk's lower end," he ordered, jabbing a finger toward it. "Go there and wait for me."

"Be careful," Anya said, and took off running.

Merrick turned back to the jormungand slithering toward him and tried to think. Distance shots weren't working. Maybe something a little closer would be more effective.

The problem was that closer also meant more dangerous. He hadn't seen what kind of teeth the thing had, but he had no doubt they were as formidable as the rest of it. But he had to risk it. Bending his knees, he stretched out his right hand toward the creature and braced himself.

And as the jormungand got to within two meters he fired his arcthrower, sending a bolt of high-voltage current into the creature's head. As the thunderclap echoed across the arena he shoved off the floor, leaping up and over the armored snake.

He nearly died right there. The entire lower half of the jormungand's body whipped upward like a thick, scaled whip as he jumped, barely missing him as he soared past overhead. He hit the floor and spun around.

To find that the arcthrower hadn't done any better than the laser.

Or maybe it had, just a little. The jormungand seemed fractionally more sluggish as it turned around toward him again. Fifty shots with the arcthrower, maybe, would do as well as fifty with the antiarmor laser.

Across the room, Anya had reached the hanging catwalk and turned back to watch the drama. Merrick gave the jormungand a wide berth and sprinted over to join her.

"Are we going up there?" she asked, pointing at the catwalk as he braked to a halt.

"*You* are," Merrick said, crouching down in front of her and holding his hand, palm-upward, beside her foot. "Step on my hand. Come on—do it."

Hesitantly, she did as ordered. Merrick straightened, hearing the faint whine as his servos took the woman's weight, and lifted her up to the catwalk. "Grab the rail and pull yourself up," he instructed. "If it feels safe, try climbing another meter or so—we don't want the snake thinking you're close enough to be worth making a snatch for."

"What about you?" Anya asked as she eased herself onto the catwalk. The structure swayed ominously, but the anchors at the upper end seemed to be holding.

"I'll be back soon," Merrick said, giving the catwalk one last look and then turning back around.

And leaping instantly to the side as his nanocomputer took over, the jormungand's snapping jaws nearly catching his leg as he flew away out of its reach. It had teeth, all right, lots of big, sharp ones. Merrick hit the floor, rolled, and came back up onto his feet.

His first fear was that the jormungand might decide to try for the low-hanging catwalk and the stationary prey clinging to it. But apparently it was smart enough to recognize that Merrick posed the more immediate threat. It had already turned again and was slithering toward him, its beady eyes barely visible beneath the scaled brow ridges. Briefly, Merrick considered trying to blind it, decided his better option right now would be to get the hell out of there, and took off running.

He reached the far wall and again turned around. The jormungand was still charging toward him, but his sprint had opened up a wide enough gap to give him some breathing space. Time to breathe, and time to think.

The snake could be killed. Everything could. He just had to find the right way to do it.

Glancing up at the ceiling, wondering if Ukuthi was enjoying the show, he keyed his infrareds.

The facial-mapping system his generation of Cobras had been fitted with had been designed mainly to study human faces, with the goal of detecting stress, fatigue, and possible bald-faced lies. But it should work equally well on large armored snakes. Warm spots, Merrick knew, would indicate places where the scaling was thinner, or where the jormungand's blood vessels were closer to the surface, which might give him a clue as to where his weapons would be most effective.

Only there weren't any such warm spots, not anywhere on the creature's head, back, or sides. There was heat there, certainly, but it seemed to be radiating pretty uniformly across the whole of the jormungand's hide.

But there had to be *someplace* that was less protected. At the very least, the snake had to have an opening for dumping its wastes. Probably somewhere in the tail area, either underneath the animal or otherwise blocked from Merrick's current vantage point. He waited for it to slither closer, then leaped over it, making sure this time that he went high enough to avoid its lunge.

And as he reached the top of his arc and started back to the floor, he finally spotted it. The whole tip of the jormungand's tail was blazing with infrared. Thinner, possibly newer scales, and the place where he was going to have to nail it.

He hit the floor and spun around, readying his laser. But it was too late. The jormungand had already twisted around and was heading for him again. Clearly, the first challenge was going to be getting the damn thing to hold still.

He glanced around the room, looking for inspiration. Could he get Anya to somehow hold the jormungand's attention long enough for him to get behind it? But the snake had already shown it was more interested in Merrick than it was in her.

Could he lure it close to one of the dead razorarms and then laser some of the concussion charges? But fine-tuning the snake's positioning that way would require Merrick to be dangerously close himself, and there was a fair chance the concussion would affect him more than it did the jormungand.

But there was one other option.

He set off across the room again, keeping an eye over his shoulder and adjusting his pace to let the jormungand slowly gain on him. This was going to require careful timing, and be horrendously risky even if he nailed it precisely. He checked the distance in front of him, slowed down a bit, then looked back again. The jormungand, perhaps concluding its prey was starting to tire, had put on an impressive burst of speed, closing to within a meter of his heels as Merrick neared the wall. Again, he adjusted his pace to maintain his lead. He reached his jump-off point, two meters from the wall, and leaped up and forward, throwing out his hands to catch the wall that was now rushing toward him.

And as he soared above the exit door directly beneath him, the door Commander Ukuthi had warned had been wired with explosives, he sent an antiarmor shot straight through the panel.

The explosion was every bit as powerful as Merrick had expected, the blast hammering into his ears as the shock wave buffeted him. He slammed palms-first into the wall, his arm servos absorbing the impact, his hooked fingers finding a tenuous grip in cracks in the masonry.

But Ukuthi's explosives experts had done their job right. As hard as Merrick had been hit by the edge of the blast, the main force had been straight outward, disintegrating the door and hurling the pieces across the room like multiple champagne corks as a gigantic fireball burst out behind them. Merrick peered down through the swirling dust and superheated air to see a wide section of blackened and newly cracked floor.

And in the center of the destruction, the charred and motionless form of the jormungand.

The best-case scenario had been that the explosion would kill the thing outright. Incredibly, though, it was still alive, its tail making small twitching movements, its whole body shaking with the shock of the damage. Merrick had no idea how extensive the creature's injuries were or if, left to itself, it might survive and recover.

He also had no intention of finding out.

It took five long antiarmor blasts to finally burn a small hole through the scales in the very tip of the jormungand's tail. But once that was done, the rest was straightforward. Sitting down behind the snake, he lined up his left leg with the opening and opened fire.

The snake could have all the armor it wanted on the outside. But its insides should cook just as well as those of any other living being.

The flexible laser conduit across Merrick's ankle was starting to become uncomfortably hot when the jormungand's twitching and shaking finally stopped.

Taking a shaking breath, Merrick got back to his feet, wincing as the assorted aches and pains he'd collected started making themselves felt through the fading adrenaline in his system. He looked across the room, wondering if the shock of the blast had knocked the dangling catwalk the rest of the way off the wall. But it was still hanging on.

So, to his quiet relief, was Anya. "You okay?" he called.

She nodded, a jerky movement. "Hang on," he said, starting toward her. "I'm coming."

He'd taken three steps when he heard a scurrying sound behind him. Instantly, he spun around, snapping his hands up into firing position.

But it wasn't another razorarm or jormungand. It was just a few Troft soldiers, scrambling madly to guard the corridor that now lay wide open in front of him.

An hour ago, Merrick might have been tempted. But not now. [The effort, don't bother with it,] he called. Turning around again, he continued walking toward the catwalk.

A minute later, he had Anya safely down. [The Games, do they now continue?] he called toward the ceiling.

[The Games, they are over,] Ukuthi said. [Your abilities, they are beyond even my expectations.]

[My satisfaction, it swells with your enjoyment,] Merrick said sarcastically. [Your associates, did they also enjoy the show?]

There was no answer. But across the room, one of the large display panels came to life.

And Merrick saw a row of silent Trofts seated in a small room. All were in uniforms, and most were wearing what the Qasaman military had tentatively identified as senior officer insignia. The one in the center was also wearing the distinctive red sash of a demesne-heir.

Merrick had just enough time to wonder what that was all about when the image winked off. [The demonstration, my associates did indeed enjoy it,] Ukuthi confirmed calmly. [Rest and food, you may now have them.]

Merrick grimaced. [The shackles, must I submit to them?]

[The shackles, there will be no need for them.] Behind Anya, a door swung open to reveal another of the arena's storage rooms, this one furnished like Merrick's old cell. [The doctor, I will also send him to you,] Ukuthi added.

[A doctor, I do not need one,] Merrick said.

[The doctor, I will send him,] Ukuthi said, his tone making it clear that it was an order. [A conversation, we will have one soon.]

"Sure," Merrick said under his breath. [The woman, her services I also no longer need.]

[The woman, she will remain with you.]

Merrick snorted. With Ukuthi no doubt hoping the two captive humans would bond even more closely.

But it was already too late, and Merrick knew it. He'd put his life on the line to get Anya to safety. Despite his best efforts to keep his distance, he was already emotionally entangled with her.

What Ukuthi was planning to do with that connection he didn't know. But he knew it wouldn't be good.

Anya was standing quietly, watching Merrick. Waiting for orders. "Come on," he said, trudging toward his new cell. "Let's get some rest."

CHAPTER THIRTEEN

It had been five days since Jody, Rashida, and Smitty had started poring over the Troft warship's control boards. They had translated everything, relabeled most of the controls, especially the ones Smitty would need to use, and painstakingly applied Rashida's freighter techniques to the larger ship. As far as Jody could tell, they had everything down cold.

But ultimately, the only way to know whether they did or not was to actually try it.

Kemp had strongly urged that they finally tell Harli the whole truth about what they'd been doing before the test. But Rashida was still terrified of the consequences of admitting her earlier evasions, and Jody had backed her up. Both women readily agreed, though, that they should warn Harli to move the Caelians still working on the downed ship to a safe distance.

And with that now done, it was finally the moment of truth.

"Grav-lift power levels?" Rashida called across the control room.

"Ready," Jody reported, eyeing the proper displays and then checking the main drive registers. "Drive's still coming up. Probably two more minutes."

"Everything outside looks good," Smitty added from the sensor station. "Everyone's back far enough. Temp and oscillation-resonance readings on the engines are holding."

Standing out of the way by the door, Kemp keyed his field radio. "We're about ready," he reported. "Grav lifts are at power; Jody says two more minutes on the drive."

"Acknowledged," Harli's voice came back. "Remind them to take it easy. We've got plenty of time, and the last thing we need is *two* Troft warships lying on their sides."

"Right," Kemp said. "You get that, Rashida?"

"Yes," Rashida said. Her voice seemed steady enough, but Jody could sense the tension beneath it. "Let me know when the drive power—"

"I've got movement," Smitty said suddenly, leaning toward one of his displays. "A Troft—make that *two* Trofts—running toward the downed ship."

"Harli, you've got runners," Kemp snapped into the radio. "Vector ninety, heading for the downed ship."

"We're on them," Harli said tightly. "We've got three—oh, *hell*."

"What is it?" Jody demanded, craning her neck and trying to see Smitty's monitors. But from her angle she could barely even tell which ones were active and which ones weren't. "Smitty? What's going on?"

"I can't tell," Smitty said tautly. "Got some smoke—where the *hell* did they get smoke bombs?—laser flashes—okay; one of them's down. The other's still running—wait a minute, there are two more now. Still going all-out for the downed ship—"

"Get that ship out of there," Harli's voice barked suddenly from the radio. "Kemp? You copy?"

"We copy," Kemp said. "Where do you want them to put it?"

"Anywhere!" Harli snarled. "Just *get it out of there!*"

"You heard him, Rashida," Jody put in. "Do it."

For a second nothing happened. Then, with a sudden lurch, the warship lifted into the sky. "You did it!" Jody called. "Rashida—"

She broke off, grabbing for the edge of her control board as the ship tilted forward. "Straighten up!" she snapped. "Rashida—we're falling! You have to straighten up."

"No, no, she's right," Smitty said. "She's leaning us forward so the grav lifts can buy us some distance."

Distance from what? Jody clamped down hard on the question.

Whatever was going on, at least Rashida and Smitty seemed to be on the same page about it.

"Drive power?" Rashida called.

With an effort, Jody focused on the display. "Low but functional."

"Smitty?" Rashida asked.

"Right," Smitty said. "Tip 'er back three degrees and give it a try."

"Wait a second," Jody protested, grabbing for her board again as the ship leveled itself. "What are we—?"

"Now!" Smitty barked.

And with another, even more violent lurch the ship shot forward.

"Good," Smitty said, raising his voice over the laboring rumble of the engines. "Ease 'er back—straighten up—that's good. A little more..."

"Kemp?" Harli called.

"We're here," Kemp said. "Situation?"

"Resolved," Harli bit out. "Mostly. How's the ship doing?"

"Seems fine," Kemp said. "Rashida and the others are running it like pros. You want us to bring it back?"

"Yes," Harli said. "No, wait. Can you maneuver it over to the landing field?"

"Rashida?" Kemp asked.

For a moment nothing happened. Then, the ship began to turn, slowly and gently enough that only Jody's inner ear was aware of the motion. "Yes, I think so," Rashida said.

"She says yes," Kemp relayed. "As close to the wall as possible, I assume?"

"Without actually hitting it, yes," Harli said sourly. "Actually, give it a few meters farther than she thinks she can do without hitting it. I've had enough disasters and near-disasters for one day."

"What happened?" Jody called. "Harli?"

"You just concentrate on landing the damn warship," Harli called back. "There'll be time for talk later. I'll send an aircar to meet you."

"We can walk it if you'd rather," Kemp offered.

"I wouldn't," Harli said flatly. "Not with the shape the field's in. When you're down, just wait inside until the aircar gets there." There was a click and the radio went dead.

"Okay," Kemp said. "Nice and easy, now. Like he said, we've got time."

The ship began to turn again. "What did he mean by the shape the field's in?" Rashida asked.

"It's like the clear zone around Stronghold, only more so," Smitty said. "As in, seriously on the overgrown side."

Jody grimaced. *Overgrown* was putting it mildly. Three weeks of neglect had allowed Caelian's aggressive plant life a head start on reclaiming the fifty-meter zone around the city that was normally kept clear of such intrusions. The rectangular landing field south of the city, without even the continual human and Troft trampling that was currently taking place in the area around the two warships, would be even worse. "He means knee-deep in hookgrass and razor fern," she told Rashida.

"And all the other delightful things that live there," Smitty said. "Waiting for an aircar will be a lot simpler."

"Not to mention that it'll get us back across town faster," Kemp said grimly. "I for one want to find out what the hell just happened back there."

"And whether it's going to complicate our lives?" Smitty asked.

Kemp snorted. "Oh, well, that's pretty much a given. The only question is how badly."

"This," Harli said, holding up a double-fist-sized piece of smashed electronics, "is what the ship techs call a grav-lift cascade regulator. Or at least, that's what it used to be. Now, it's a desktop junk sculpture."

"Any chance of fixing it?" Kemp asked, taking the device and turning it over in his hands.

"Anything can be fixed if you have spare parts and know how to put them together," Harli growled. "Which means, no, we can't. Not a chance." He gestured toward the downed ship. "We're just damned lucky you got the other ship out of there in time."

Jody gazed at the downed warship, a shiver running through her. "So it really would have flipped all the way over if they'd gotten to the generators and started up the grav lifts?"

"We don't know for sure," Harli said. "But the techs say there's a good chance that it would have. Straight up, straight over, and a nice little domino effect when it slammed into yours." He gestured to Jody. "That was fast thinking, by the way, using a drive pulse to blow away the smoke once you were clear. Made it a lot easier to spot and laser them."

"Actually, it was Rashida's idea," Jody told him. "She and Smitty coordinated it together."

"In that case, good job, Rashida and Smitty," Harli said, a little testily. "As long as you two are brimming with ideas, you got one for making sure the Trofts don't pull another stunt like this?"

"You know my views," Smitty muttered. "Shoot them all and be done with it."

"We've been through this," Jody said firmly. "Moral high ground, remember?"

"Yeah, I know," Smitty said. "It just feels good to say it every so often, that's all."

"Harli's right, though," Kemp said. "A homemade smoke bomb's reasonably harmless, and even with that Eubujak nearly caused a catastrophe. The next gadget he comes up with will be a lot nastier."

"Bet on it," Harli said grimly. He hissed out a sigh. "And that about wraps things up for your fancy curtain, too, Jody. I'm sorry, but we're going to have to leave the downed ship right where it is. There's no way we can risk trying to lift it now."

"Why not?" Smitty asked, frowning. "If the lifts flip it over, so what? In fact, that'll put it even more out of the way of the wall gap."

"The *so what* is that we don't know what a second impact might do to the internal workings," Harli said. "Especially the fuel and other fluids that we'd just as soon keep inside. We were lucky the first time—warships are built tough, and the impact with the wall may have cushioned the fall a little. But we can't count on being that lucky twice."

Jody looked away from the ship, focusing on the partially trampled hookgrass and other plants outside the wall. "So we're not going to use the curtain at all?" she asked, an idea starting to take shape in the back of her mind.

"I don't think we can risk it," Harli said. "I know your friends put a lot of work into it, but—"

"Hold it," Kemp said, lifting a hand. "I don't think that's where she was going. You have something, Jody?"

"Maybe," Jody said slowly. "We can't just drive the Trofts into the forest, because that would be the same as shooting them. But what if we could put them out there and at the same time keep most of the wildlife away?"

"You mean like a bunker?" Smitty asked.

"She means like a spore-repellent curtain," Kemp said. "Right?"

"Right," Jody said. "We were planning on, what, seventy or eighty meters to cover the gap in the wall?"

"I told them we needed seventy-five," Harli said, eyeing her closely. "And three meters high."

"Okay," Jody said, running a quick mental calculation. "So if we lay the curtain out in a ring seventy-five meters in circumference, that makes the area inside something like four hundred thirty square meters. Right?"

"Closer to four-forty, I think," Harli said.

"Either way, with a hundred ninety prisoners that comes to over two square meters each," Jody said. "Not comfortable, but feasible. They'll be mostly safe, *and* they'll be out of our hair."

"What about the big predators?" Smitty asked. "The curtain's not going to keep them out."

"But most of them won't bother to investigate," Harli said thoughtfully. "For those who do, I guess the Trofts are on their own."

"Or we could give them a couple of shotguns with ten rounds each," Kemp suggested.

"If they've got weapons, Eubujak might order them to come back here," Smitty warned.

"Only if he knows where we are," Jody said. "We could burn away a path half a kilometer or so into the forest, burn out a clearing, and march them there under the curtain to keep them from seeing where they're going."

"Couldn't they just follow the burned path back?" Smitty asked.

"We could burn two or three of them," Jody said.

"Probably not necessary," Kemp said. "They head through any part of the forest and the giggers'll get them before they get fifty meters. We just nail the generator to a tree so they can't take the curtain with them, and they'll be stuck there."

"That's a lot of burning," Harli pointed out. "Don't know if we have time for that." He looked at Jody, his lips twisting in a slightly evil smile as he pulled out his radio. "But I think we can come up with something simpler, *and* maybe even a bit more elegant." He keyed the radio. "Nissa? You there?"

"I'm here," the woman's cool voice came back.

"Any update on the curtain timeline?"

"Just a minute." There was a brief pause filled with muffled and distant voices. "They say it'll be ready by tomorrow morning," Nissa reported. "Possibly tonight, if they hurry."

"Then tell them to hurry," Harli told her. "I want to know the minute it's ready."

"You will," Nissa said.

"Good. Get back to work." Harli keyed off the radio and put it away. "We'll need to rig some stands to hold the thing up," he said, almost as if talking to himself. "But we were going to have to do that anyway. I figure we should be ready to march them out by mid-morning at the latest."

"We're never going to burn them a clearing by then," Kemp warned.

"No clearing needed," Harli assured him. "We're going to put them at the far end of the landing field."

"That close to Stronghold?" Kemp asked, frowning. "How do you expect to keep them there?"

"You'll see." Harli smiled tightly, then sobered. "I'm glad you've got the ship running. We need to start the evacuation this afternoon, and this'll make it a lot easier than running a line of overloaded aircars back and forth across the forest."

"Be easier on the wounded, too," Kemp said. "At least they'll get to stretch out for the trip. You and the governor still going to put everyone in Aerie?"

"No, we thought about it and decided that an influx of nine hundred new citizens would strain even their traditional hospitality,"

Harli said. "We're now figuring three hundred each to Aerie, Essbend, and Rockhouse."

"Even that's going to be pushing it," Kemp warned. "Especially for Rockhouse."

"I know," Harli conceded. "But I don't see any other way. When those Troft reinforcements come, they'll be coming to Stronghold first. We have to get the citizens out of harm's way, and dividing them up is the best way to do that."

"Unless you moved everyone into the Octagon Caves," Smitty said suddenly. "I didn't think about that earlier, but there's plenty of room in there for a mass camp-out. Or they could split up into smaller rooms—Danny and Kirstin and I found dozens of them back when we used to poke around in there."

"Actually, I'm thinking we might use the caves for something else," Harli said. "I'll want to talk to you about that later."

"Perhaps Smitty's right about hiding away in caverns," Rashida spoke up hesitantly. "Even if the invaders come here first, they'll surely travel afterward to the other towns you spoke of."

"Yes, that'll probably be their plan," Harli agreed. "Our job is to make sure that doesn't happen." He gestured to her. "Your job is to get better at flying that thing. The Trofts could arrive in anywhere from two to three days. In six hours I'm going to start moving people out of Stronghold. Think you'll be ready to start taking passengers by then?"

Rashida looked at Jody and Smitty, then back at Harli. "We'll be ready in three," she promised.

"Good," Harli said. "Kemp, go grab Popescu and Brady and get them working on support frames for that curtain. I'll go tell Dad to alert the first evacuee list."

He looked up at the sun. "We're burning daylight. Let's get to work."

Nine weeks.

The words swirled through Jin's mind, disturbing and mocking, as the car bounced along the wide road leading toward Azras. *Nine weeks.*

That was how long it took on Aventine to turn a new recruit into a full Cobra. That was always how long it had taken, ever since Jin could remember. The exact regimen had been adjusted over the years, as the instructors experimented with new techniques or as the implanted equipment itself was tweaked. But the total length of the training period never wavered. *Nine weeks*.

Yiththra and the Milika villagers had had six days.

Ghushtre and his fellow Djinn had had one.

She focused on the back of Yiththra's head as he steered the car along the winding forest road, smelling the very Qasaman scent of the two others in the front seat and the one on Paul's other side here in the back. Beach and McCollom thought the group was ready, though both of them had expressed varying degrees of astonishment at that fact. Certainly the villagers and Djinn themselves thought they were ready.

But were they? That was the question that had been nagging at Jin since the convoy left Milika two hours ago. Were they really ready for war?

But then, was anyone ever really ready for war? Or did everyone just do what they could with what they had, struggling along and hoping for the best?

"There," Gama Yiththra said, taking one hand from the wheel and pointing ahead. "That's Azras."

Jin leaned across Paul's chest to look past Yiththra's head. Ahead and to the right, she could see the top edge of a city wall above the rolling hills a couple of kilometers beyond the edge of the forest.

On the other side of the road, a kilometer from the city itself, she could see the top of another of the tall, narrow Troft warships.

"I see they've learned from their Sollas drubbing," Paul murmured. "Sitting way out there, they can shoot down any SkyJos the Qasamans launch from Azras before they get into their own attack range."

"Their cunning goes far deeper than that," Yiththra said. "They have the entire city under siege, with eight of their armored troop trucks roaming the streets at all times. They also have drones overhead, watching every gathering of citizens and tracking where they come from and where they go."

"Trying to find a way into the subcity," Jin said, nodding. "Still, if they're waiting for someone to get sloppy, they're going to have a long wait."

"Ah, but they *aren't* merely hoping for carelessness," Yithtra said grimly. "They hope also to elicit treason."

Jin snorted. "Good luck with that one."

"Perhaps," Yithtra said. "But as you'll see, we and the food we bring to the blockaded citizens will be readily allowed in. But we'll find that we're then forbidden to leave."

Jin frowned; and then she got it. "Thereby increasing the number of mouths that need to be fed, which adds more strain on the city's resources."

"And adds more to the usual tension existing between city dwellers and villagers," Yithtra said. "Especially as the villagers now trapped by their errand of mercy will be increasingly frantic to return to their homes and families."

"Let me guess," Paul murmured. "Point out an entrance to the subcity and you can go home."

"Exactly," Yithtra said. "Or deliver a military weapon to them, or identify a Djinn or soldier to the invaders, and likewise buy your escape." Yithtra made a spitting sound. "A futile hope, of course, that any villager would betray our world. We aren't city dwellers, who might—"

"Enough of that," Jin interrupted firmly. "You're not a villager anymore, Gama Yithtra, any more than the Djinn riding behind us and the people you'll meet in Azras are city dwellers. You're Qasamans. Nothing more, nothing less."

"Of course," Yithtra said. But he didn't say it like he really believed it. Or meant it.

Jin looked sideways at Paul. He grimaced, but merely gave a small shrug.

Even under the pressures of war, the old rivalries remained.

There were four of the Troft armored trucks arrayed around the main gate into Azras: two of them flanking the road, facing opposite directions with their roof-mounted swivel guns guarding both approaches to the city. The other two trucks flanked the short access spur that led from the main road to the gate, their swivel guns both pointed into the city.

There were also Troft soldiers on duty, at least twenty of them, standing guard at the gate, perched on top of the trucks, or manning the checkpoint barrier that had been set up along the road. All were dressed in the enemy's familiar armored leotards and full-face helmets, all carried big hand-and-a-half lasers, and all had their full attention on the eight-car convoy now rolling toward the checkpoint.

As a no doubt unintentional touch of irony, the Azras gate itself stood wide open.

One of the Trofts strode toward their car as Yithtra brought the vehicle to a halt. "State your name, point of origin, and business," the translator pin on the alien's left shoulder said in a flat voice.

"Gama Yithtra, son of Bejran Yithtra of Milika," Yithtra identified himself. "We bring aid and food for the besieged citizens of Azras."

The Troft looked back at the other seven cars now stopped in a line behind them. "You will leave your vehicles," he ordered, stepping back and leveling his laser at Yithtra. "All will remove their tunics and upper robes."

"Our group includes two women," Yithtra objected. "Such public exposure is shameful and cannot be allowed."

For a moment the Troft regarded him silently, his mouth moving behind his faceplate as he either discussed it with his fellow guards or else checked in with higher authority. Jin watched him closely, mentally crossing her fingers. Stripping to their underwear, she knew, wouldn't bother either her or Jennifer nearly as much as it would a typical Qasaman woman. But that was the point: they were supposed to *be* Qasaman women, with typical Qasaman sensibilities. If the Trofts refused to grant them an exemption, they would have to leave the men here and hope they could figure out another way into the city.

Fortunately, it wasn't going to come to that. "The females will pull back their sleeves and show their arms to be bare," the Troft ordered. "The males will remove their tunics and upper robes."

Jin gave a silent sigh of relief. Still, the concession to modesty wasn't all that unexpected. The Trofts were clearly looking for Djinni combat suits, and the Qasamans were even worse at permitting women into the ranks of their elite soldiers as Aventine was at accepting female Cobras.

"Understood," Yithtra said. He opened the door and started to get out of the car.

"And after you have done that," the Troft continued, "you will leave your vehicles and carry your supplies by hand through the gate."

Jin had never done any acting herself, and didn't know the first thing about the art or science of that craft. But she knew a good performance when she saw it, and Yithtra's was definitely it. He froze in mid-step, his eyes widening as he looked sharply at the Troft. "What?" he asked, his tone more bewildered than anything else.

"You will carry your supplies in through the gate," the Troft repeated. "Your vehicles will remain here."

Yithtra shot a disbelieving look back down the line of cars, then turned back to the guard. "Why?" he asked. "What's wrong with the cars?"

"You will carry your supplies—"

"Yes, I heard you the first two times," Yithtra cut him off, outrage starting to replace bewilderment in his voice. "That makes no sense. You have any idea how *heavy* those parcels are? And one of our doctors is on crutches—you expect him to *walk* the whole way to the aid center?"

The Troft lifted his laser warningly. "You will go into the city now," he said, the flat translator voice somehow managing to carry an edge of menace. "If you leave the supplies, they will be confiscated along with the vehicles."

Yithtra glared at him. But there was no power behind the defiance, only frustration and anger. He looked through the window at Jin, looked back along the cars again, and muttered a long, feeling curse. "Everybody out!" he shouted, waving his arm over his head. "And—" He grimaced. "Take off your tunics."

Five minutes later, with their tunics now tied around their waists and stacks of food and medical supplies in their arms, they all marched silently between the sentries and through the open city gate. There was another sentry line of Trofts inside, apparently positioned to keep the city dwellers back.

After all, Jin thought cynically, the invaders wouldn't want anyone shouting a warning to all those well-meaning visitors about the trap they were walking into.

Given what newcomers meant to the supply situation within the city, Jin had wondered if the citizens would greet the newcomers with disdain or even hostility. But as they passed the inner sentry line and approached the line of onlookers who'd gathered to watch this latest version of the oft-repeated drama, she saw nothing but resolve and solidarity in their faces. In fact, as she and the others approached, many of the citizens broke ranks and stepped forward, probably risking Troft laser fire, quietly greeting the villagers and gently but firmly relieving them of their burdens. Two of them, spotting Paul lurching along on his crutches, found a wheelchair somewhere and had it ready by the time he reached the edge of the crowd. Another of the citizens, this one a well-dressed man in his sixties, gestured toward a store a block away, which from the stacks of boxes around it had apparently been set up as a distribution center, and led the way toward it.

They had covered half the distance, and the Trofts at the gate were no longer visible through the crowd, when a slightly scruffy-looking man sidled up beside Jin and took her last remaining package. "Welcome to Azras, Jin Moreau," he murmured. "We're pleased you arrived safely."

Jin smiled. "Thank you, Siraj Akim," she greeted him in turn. "I'm pleased to find you also safe and well. I was told you and Ghofl Khatir had come here, but I never heard what happened after that."

"Like everyone else on Qasama, we've been busy," he said with a touch of dry humor. "As you clearly have also been." He threw a glance behind them at the rest of the group. "The recruits seem eager for combat."

"They are," Jin agreed heavily. "And their instructors also seem to think they're ready. But whether they actually are..." She shook her head. "I'm hoping we'll have a few days before we leave here so that Beach and McCollom can run them through a few more drills."

"You weren't told?" Siraj asked, an odd tone to his voice.

"Told what?"

Siraj moved a little closer and lowered his voice. "We won't be going to Purma or elsewhere," he said. "The attack will be here. And it'll be launched tomorrow."

Jin felt her eyes widen. "*Tomorrow?* But—" she broke off. "I thought we'd want to run at least a few more groups through Isis first."

"Such was indeed the original plan," Siraj said grimly. "But it's not to be. Five days ago a Drim courier ship arrived at the invaders' Sollas encampment, carrying what our spotters described as a highly agitated commander and crew. They were taken into one of their demesne's warships, where they stayed for two hours. Four hours after that, two other Drim warships lifted from the encampment and left Qasama."

Jin's stomach tightened. "They found out about Caelian."

"So we believe," Siraj agreed. "We feared our new ally was about to come under renewed attack."

Jin nodded, feeling suddenly ill. And when that happened, the Caelians wouldn't have a chance. Not a second time. Not with the Trofts knowing what they were flying into.

And Jody was there with them.

"There was nothing we could do directly to help them," Siraj continued. "But what we *could* attempt to do was create the conditions that would hopefully end the entire war, our part as well as Caelian's."

Jin nodded again as she understood. "By handing the invaders a massive defeat," she said. "Thereby giving the Tlossies and the other local demesnes the leverage they need to step in and force the Drims and their allies to back off."

"Exactly," Siraj agreed. "Even at that we may have waited too long—our estimate is that the Drim ships are now only a day removed from Caelian. But we needed all the new warriors we could get, and it was decided to wait until Ifrit Ghushtre and his Djinn had completed the Isis transformation."

"So that's why they were so adamant about leaving Milika with us," Jin said, the past few days' worth of puzzling conversations suddenly coming clear. "And why they insisted they didn't need any further training."

"Which may in fact be the truth," Siraj said. "Their combat suit capabilities in many ways parallel their new internal ones. That expertise combined with the learning drugs makes it quite possible that a few hours of practice with the attack plan will be all the further training they need. We'll find out shortly."

"I hope we're not all going to the subcity together," Jin warned. "I'm told the Trofts are watching for that kind of parade."

Siraj chuckled. "Never fear, Jin Moreau. After we deliver the supplies to the distribution center, your group will be broken up into three-man teams and escorted by different routes to the sub-city and the designated practice arena."

"Good," Jin said, forcing her mind away from Jody and Caelian. "I trust that Paul will instead be taken directly to the hospital?"

"He and you both," Siraj said, nodding. "The doctors have been briefed about his leg and your tumor, and are already prepared to begin their work."

"Thank you." Jin glanced behind her. Paul was far enough back to be safely out of earshot. "But they'll only be working on Paul. I'll be coming with you to the briefing."

"We appreciate your courage and your commitment to Qasama," Siraj said gravely. "More than you can imagine. But your part of the war is over."

"No," Jin said firmly. "My husband's may be, but mine isn't. Not as long as Lorne is still fighting. Certainly not as long as Merrick is a prisoner of the invaders and Jody is in their crosshairs."

"Jin Moreau—"

"And whether you like it or not, you need me," Jin said. "You said it yourself: you need all of us that you can get."

"We'll have enough," Siraj assured her.

"Will you?" Jin countered. "By my count, you have exactly four—Lorne, Beach, McCollom, and me—who've fought as Cobras, plus ten who've only fought as Djinn, plus ten who've never fought at all. So tell me again how you've got all the warriors you need."

Siraj was silent a few more steps. "If I were braver, I'd stand up to you and simply tell you no," he said. "If I were more like my father, I'd find a clever way to make you think you were getting what you want while also achieving my own goals. But I'm neither. Besides, I suspect far too many of those marching with you would come to your support, and I have no interest in fighting all of them."

"Thank you," Jin said quietly.

"Just promise you'll come to *my* defense when your husband learns of your decision." Siraj gave a gentle snort. "Do you recall, back when you and your son were first brought into the Sollas subcity, Kaml Ghushtre questioned my father on the place of honor and pride in warfare?"

"Very well," Jin assured him, wincing at the memory. She and Merrick had come very close to dying that day. "Your father told him that victory was more important even than honor."

"Yes," Siraj said. "I find it supremely ironic that the choice he presented Djinn Ghushtre has not, in fact, been made. Nor has it been required to be made. Whatever happens tomorrow, whether we succeed or fall, honor nevertheless remains ours."

He half turned; and to Jin's surprise he made the sign of respect to her. "Ours," he added, "and yours."

Jin swallowed hard as she returned the sign. "Thank you, Siraj Akim. Whatever happens tomorrow, it's been a privilege to serve with you. And with all of Qasama."

"As it has been for us to serve with you." Siraj smiled tightly. "But I also have no doubt that honor in victory is better than honor in defeat. Let us go and prepare ourselves as best we can for the challenges we will soon face."

"Absolutely," Jin agreed. "Lead the way."

CHAPTER FOURTEEN

From the very beginning of his incarceration in the Djinn command post, Daulo had tried to keep to himself as much as possible.

It had turned out to be surprisingly easy. Much easier than he'd expected given the post's compact size. But with Miron Akim having sent twenty of the Djinn to Milika, and with at least six of the remaining fourteen on patrol in the forest at any given time, the post sometimes felt almost like the Sammon family mine on a workers' holiday.

Most days the only person he saw was the doctor, and he usually only stayed long enough to check the progress of Daulo's recovery and occasionally adjust the level of his medications. As long as Daulo took his meals from the self-service galley at non-standard hours, his chances of avoiding everyone else were really quite high.

Fortunately, the one person he most urgently wanted to avoid seemed to also be trying to keep to himself. Daulo only saw Shahni Haafiz twice during those first few days, both of them chance encounters as Daulo was entering the galley and Haafiz was leaving.

The first of those times, Haafiz had demanded to know why Daulo wasn't under direct guard, and had warned he would be asking Ifrit Narayan the same question. The second time, he simply glared at Daulo and passed by without a word. Apparently, whatever answer he'd gotten from Narayan hadn't been the one he wanted.

As to Omnathi and Akim, Daulo didn't see either of them at all. He asked the doctor about it once, concerned that they might have taken ill, and was assured that both men were simply busy elsewhere on the post. That was all the doctor would say, and Daulo hadn't asked since.

The disadvantage of Daulo's self-imposed isolation was that the silence gave him that much more time to brood about the false charges against him and his son, and to worry about Fadil's safety as the Djinn transported him through the forest.

But he knew down deep that surrounding himself with company wouldn't have distracted his mind from those issues, either. Better not to have to gaze into other people's faces and wonder if they believed Akim's charges against him.

It was on the tenth day after his arrival when it all suddenly came apart.

He was alone in the galley, finishing up the late breakfast/early lunch meal he'd become accustomed to, when Haafiz entered. "There you are," the Shahni said, his voice cold and stiff. "I've been looking all over for you."

Which was probably a lie, Daulo knew, or at least an overly dramatic overstatement. There were only three places he ever went: his quarters, the galley, and the shower room. If Haafiz hadn't figured that out by now, he had no business being a Shahni.

But it wasn't Daulo's place to make such points, at least not out loud. "Can I help you, Shahni Haafiz?" he asked instead, making the sign of respect.

And caught his breath. Nestled in the Shahni's hand was a small but nasty-looking handgun.

"I don't know, Daulo Sammon," Haafiz said darkly as he strode across the galley. "Can you tell me why you, accused of treason, still walk free and unhindered around a secret base of the Djinn? Can you tell me why there's been no movement on any trial or interrogation, which is supposedly why I'm still here instead of at Purma?"

He stopped two meters from Daulo and lifted the gun to point squarely at Daulo's face. "And why," he added, his voice suddenly deadly, "your son is still not here?"

Daulo's whole body suddenly felt cold. "It's only been ten days," he managed, trying not to stare at the gun. "Ifrit Akim said it would take a week in both directions."

"Miron Akim lied," Haafiz said flatly. "I've calculated the numbers. A Djinni with combat suit assistance should be able to cover the distance to Milika in no more than five days. Four, if they chose to push themselves." He lifted the gun slightly. "So I ask you again, Daulo Sammon: where is your son?"

"You don't really expect him to know that, do you?" a voice called from the doorway.

Daulo tore his gaze from the gun and looked over Haafiz's shoulder. It was Narayan, walking casually across the galley toward them.

But there was nothing casual about the tight expression on his face. Nor was there anything casual about the way his gloved hands, still swinging at his sides, were already curled into laser-firing positions.

Only Haafiz, with his glare on Daulo, couldn't see that. "Why not?" Haafiz bit out over his shoulder. "Everyone else claims to know nothing. Perhaps only Daulo Sammon knows the truth. Shall we not ask him?"

"How could he possibly know things that are happening hundreds of kilometers away?" Narayan asked reasonably. "He's been locked up in here ever since he arrived."

"One radio has already been found in his possession," Haafiz reminded him. "Perhaps he had two."

Abruptly, the Shahni spun around, his gun now leveled at Narayan's chest. "Or perhaps," Haafiz said softly, "he's not the only traitor here."

Narayan stopped. "Perhaps he's not," he said, his voice as soft as Haafiz's.

Haafiz seemed taken aback by the other's response. "Then you agree," he said, lowering his gun barrel a few degrees. "Using the excuse of Daulo Sammon to keep me trapped here can only be attributed to cowardice, incompetence, or treason. And I know neither Moffren Omnathi nor Miron Akim is incompetent or a coward."

"Is *that* what you referred to?" Narayan said, his forehead wrinkling as if in confusion. "Your pardon, Shahni Haafiz. I misunderstood what you meant by treason."

"What did you *think* I meant?" Haafiz countered.

Narayan shrugged. "I assumed you were speaking of attempted murder," he said.

And suddenly his hands came up, the lasers in his gloves pointing at Haafiz's chest. "The attempted murders," he continued quietly, "of Senior Advisor Moffren Omnathi and Marid Siraj Akim."

Daulo felt his jaw drop. Haafiz had been planning to *murder* Omnathi and Akim? He opened his mouth to demand an explanation.

And closed it again. This was nothing he wanted to get in the middle of.

But if Haafiz was thrown by the accusation, he didn't show it. "Moffren Omnathi is a traitor," the Shahni spat. "With utter contempt for the rule of the Shahni he sent an emissary to make a devil's bargain with our enemies."

"He *had* approval from the Shahni," Narayan said.

"Not *all* the Shahni," Haafiz retorted.

"All the Shahni who were present."

"Yes, and how very convenient that was for him," Haafiz bit out. "I was available. I should have been called. And his treason was then compounded by Siraj Akim, who went so far as to send his own son on the mission. All of them are traitors. All of them deserve to die."

"If you believed that you should have brought formal charges against them," Narayan countered. "Instead, like a coward, you ordered them on a mission which would leave them dead." He took a step closer to the Shahni. "And then ordered six good and loyal men to die alongside them."

Daulo caught his breath, that confrontation in the Sollas subcity suddenly coming clear. Haafiz hadn't cared about slowing the invaders' penetration into the city's last remaining stronghold. The sole purpose of his proposed ambush had been to put Omnathi and Akim in front of enemy lasers where they would die.

"And how useful do you think it would have been to bring

charges?" Haafiz asked scornfully. "You know what happened—those good and loyal men, as you call them, defied my direct orders. What use is it to follow the rule of law when the Djinn have chosen to put themselves above both the law and the Shahni?"

"We're at war," Narayan said. "Sometimes rules must be broken if we're to throw the invaders off our soil."

"The rule of law and the Shahni cannot and will not be broken," Haafiz insisted. "*We* are the leaders of the Qasaman people, Ifrit Narayan. *We* are the ones who make the decisions for our world."

He lifted his gun higher, ignoring the lasers pointed at him and leveling the weapon at Narayan's chest. "And if I make the decision to dispense justice here and now," he said, "you *will* stand aside and permit it."

Narayan drew himself up. "No, I will not," he said flatly. "You have no evidence, and without evidence there cannot be justice."

"The evidence is that I'm still here, which proves a conspiracy to keep me here," Haafiz said. "For the good of Qasama, I must return at once to the business of saving my world."

Narayan spat a curse under his breath. "Do you think you're the only one who hates this place?" he bit out. "You think that none of the rest of us teeter at the edge of insanity at being forced to remain idle while—?" He broke off abruptly.

But too late. "While what?" Haafiz demanded. "What's going on out there that I should know about?"

"The war is going on," Narayan said. "You already know that."

But the words were an evasion. Daulo knew it, and so did Haafiz. "I'm leaving now, Ifrit Narayan," the Shahni said, his voice quiet but as unyielding as granite. "Assign your Djinn to escort me, or let me go alone. But I will not spend another day here. I *will* know what is going on across my world."

Narayan's eyes flicked down to the gun pointed at his chest. "I have my orders, Shahni Haafiz," he said. "I can't allow you to leave. Not yet."

"Move aside," Haafiz ordered in the same stony voice. "Or I kill you where you stand."

Slowly, Narayan shook his head. "I can't."

Daulo curled his hands into helpless fists. And with that, he knew, Narayan was dead. Haafiz wouldn't back away from his order and his threat. Not Haafiz. Narayan would stand there until the Shahni pulled the trigger. Then Haafiz would walk over the body, leave the outpost and head out into the forest, and start the long journey toward Purma.

And alone in a swirl of dangerous predators and even more dangerous Troft invaders, he too would almost certainly die.

Daulo had to stop this. Somehow, he had to break the impasse.

And there was only one way to do that. "Then let the trial begin," he said. "Right now."

"Be quiet, Daulo Sammon," Narayan said, his eyes still on Haafiz's face. "This isn't your fight."

"It's every bit my fight," Daulo retorted. "Shahni Haafiz is right—I'm the reason he's been stuck here all this time. Very well, then. Try me, acquit or convict me, and allow Shahni Haafiz to travel to Purma."

For the first time Narayan's eyes shifted to Daulo's face. "You have no idea what you're saying," he said. "You have no evidence of your innocence, only your word against Marid Akim's. We need to wait until your son arrives to speak on your behalf."

"My son has apparently been delayed," Daulo said, his heart tearing yet again at the thought of what might have happened to Fadil. "Enough time has been wasted. One way or the other, it ends now."

"Not now," a new voice said quietly from across the galley. "But it ends tomorrow."

Daulo leaned to the side to see around Haafiz and Narayan. Miron Akim was standing calmly in the doorway. "What did you say?" he asked.

"I said you will have your wish, Daulo Sammon," Akim said. "And you will have yours, Shahni Haafiz. Daulo Sammon's trial for treason will begin tomorrow."

His eyes seemed to glitter. "And it will end tomorrow."

"And I'll finally be permitted to leave this place?" Haafiz demanded suspiciously.

Akim nodded. "With a full Djinn escort, if you wish."

Haafiz hesitated, then lowered his gun. "Very well," he said. "But I warn you: I'll stand for no further delays."

"There will be none," Akim promised. "Have you finished your meal, Daulo Sammon?"

Daulo nodded. "I have."

"Then return to your quarters," Akim ordered. "The computer will have the necessary legal guides for preparing your defense. I suggest you study them."

Daulo swallowed. "I will, Miron Akim."

"Good," Akim said. "Then go."

Gingerly, Daulo eased past Haafiz and Narayan and headed across the galley. Narayan, he noted in passing, had also lowered his arms and lasers.

The confrontation had been defused. For the moment, at least, both men were safe.

Leaving Daulo alone facing the risk of death.

He started to walk past Akim, stopped as the other caught his arm. "And don't give up hope," Akim murmured. "It may still be that your son will come to your rescue."

Daulo took a deep breath. "I fear that my son can no longer come to anyone's rescue," he said.

"Perhaps," Akim said. "We shall see."

Three days earlier, at the close of the cat-and-rat survival contest that Anya and Commander Ukuthi had euphemistically called the Games, Ukuthi had said that he and Merrick would be having a conversation soon. Now, three days later, the Troft had yet to summon Merrick to that promised conference. Perhaps, Merrick thought sourly, he was spending his time trying to dig up a few more jormungands to amuse his guests with.

Personally, Merrick was in no hurry for either talk or combat. The physical exertion in the arena hadn't reopened any of his old injuries, but he'd collected a fresh assortment of scrapes, bruises, and small cuts along the way. Nothing that the Troft doctor seemed concerned about, at least not according to Anya's translation of his

still indecipherable dialect. But then, the doctor could afford to
be unconcerned. It wasn't his skin that had taken all the abuse.

It was an hour after lunch on that third day when the lock clicked
and the door swung open to reveal a middle-aged Troft wearing a
non-armored leotard, a senior officer's insignia, and—most surprising of all—a red heir sash. [Merrick Moreau, I greet him,] he said.

[Merrick Moreau, he greets you in return,] Merrick said, slipping off the bed and standing up. He'd been given only a glimpse
of his audience back in the arena, but he was pretty sure this was
the same Troft he'd seen in the center of the group of observers.
[A demesne-heir, to which am I honored to speak?]

[Commander Ukuthi, I am he,] the Troft said. His radiator
membranes fluttered and his beak cracked slightly open. [Surprise,
you have it.]

[Surprise, I have it,] Merrick conceded with a flush of embarrassment. It was double surprise, actually: first that a demesne-heir
would risk facing a dangerous prisoner with his guards standing
uselessly outside the door behind him, and second that the heir
in question could actually read human expressions well enough to
have picked up on Merrick's emotion. [Your forgiveness, I ask it.]

[My forgiveness, it is unnecessary,] Ukuthi assured him. He
lifted a hand and made a gesture.

And to Merrick's even greater surprise, the cell door closed
behind him, leaving the guards outside. [Privacy, we now have
it,] Ukuthi said calmly.

[Surprises, you are filled with them,] Merrick said, glancing at
Anya. She was sitting cross-legged on her bed, her face expressionless. Either she wasn't surprised by Ukuthi's actions or she hid
it very well. [Serious risks, you take them.]

[Surprises, I have even more of them,] Ukuthi said, his beak
cracking open again. Was that supposed to be an attempt at a
human-type smile? He ruffled his shoulders and seemed to clear
his throat— "As for risks," he said, in an accent that closely mim-
icked Anya's own inflections, "I do not believe I am taking one."

It took Merrick three tries to get his own voice working again.
In all his years of dealing with Troft merchants and diplomats,

he'd never, ever had one speak to him in Anglic. He wasn't even sure anyone in the Cobra Worlds knew they *could* speak Anglic. "You're—yes, very surprising," he managed. "I've never heard a Troft speak our language before."

"It is not easy for us to do," Ukuthi conceded. "Much easier for your vocal apparatus to speak cattertalk."

"We can return to that if you'd like," Merrick offered.

"This is better." Ukuthi's beak cracked open again. "The practice, it is useful. Tell me, what are your feelings toward Anya Winghunter?"

The intellectual curiosity Merrick had been feeling at this new revelation vanished. "I have no feelings toward her," he said, letting his voice go dark and rigid.

"Yet she is human like yourself," Ukuthi pointed out. "Have you no consideration at all for her?"

Merrick looked over at Anya. She was looking back at him, her face still expressionless.

Expressionless, but perhaps not emotionless? On sudden impulse, Merrick activated his infrareds.

To discover that the woman was anything but emotionless. Her face was a swirl of heat, a pattern that seemed to indicate both fear and hope. "We call this beating around the bush," Merrick said, keying off the infrareds and turning back to Ukuthi. "Get to the point, and tell me what you want."

"I am unfamiliar with that turn of phrase," Ukuthi said. "You must tell me its origin someday. What do you know about this war?"

"I know we didn't start it," Merrick said. "I also think we're going to win it. Aside from that, not much."

"You may be correct on the second point," Ukuthi said. "But you are not correct on the first. The war *was* begun by humans. Specifically, the humans of the Dominion of Man."

Merrick felt his stomach tighten. He and his mother had speculated that the invasion of their worlds might have been a response to something happening on the far side of the Troft Assemblage. "The Dominion of Man is a hundred thirty light-years away, and we haven't had contact with them in seven decades," he said. "Why are we being punished for their actions?"

"That I cannot say," Ukuthi admitted. "All I know is that the demesnes fighting that war have contracted with the Tua'lanek'zia demesne to conquer and subdue the human worlds at this side of the Trof'te Assemblage. The Tua'lanek'zia contracted further with the Drim'hco'plai, the Gla'lupt'flae, and my own Balin'ekha'spmi for our assistance."

"I see," Merrick said sourly. Four entire Troft demesnes, plus the implied threat of whoever had organized this military dogpile in the first place. No wonder the Tlossies and the Cobra Worlds' other trading parties hadn't lifted a finger to stop them. "I hope you're at least making a decent profit."

"Our profit is not to be made in currency," Ukuthi assured him. "My demesne-lord has other objectives in sight." He gestured to Anya. "Anya Winghunter, tell Merrick Moreau of your people."

Anya hesitated. Then, she got to her feet, bowed once to Ukuthi, and turned to Merrick. "We are slaves," she said. "We create sculptures, which our masters take for their enjoyment. We hunt rare animals and find rare plants, which our masters take for their tables." She lowered her gaze to the floor, then looked back up at Merrick. "But mostly we fight in the Games."

"What do you fight?" Merrick asked. "Animals like that jormungand?"

"Sometimes," Anya said. "Most times, we fight each other."

Merrick looked at Ukuthi, his hands dropping into laser-firing position. "For you?"

Ukuthi's radiator membranes fluttered. "Not us," he said. "The Drim'hco'plai are their masters."

Merrick pointed to Anya. "Yet she's here. With you."

"She is," Ukuthi acknowledged. "Some years ago the Drim'hco'plai began selling human slaves to other demesne-lords for their amusement. My demesne-lord was intrigued, so he bought several to study." He cocked his head. "Yet now, within the past two months, the Drim'hco'plai demesne-lord has suddenly and urgently requested that all slaves be returned to him."

Merrick frowned. "Why?"

"We do not know," Ukuthi said. "I also note two other curious happenstances. First, the invasion of the Cobra Worlds is well advanced, yet the Drim'hco'plai continue to take razorarms from Qasama. Where do they take them? Second, their demesne-lord insisted that the Drim'hco'plai be solely responsible for the subjugation of the Cobra World of Caelian."

Where there were dozens of predators every bit as dangerous as razorarms. "Sounds like they're looking for new animals to throw at Anya's people on Game night," he said.

"That was also my thought," Ukuthi said. "But why keep that goal secret from the other demesne-lords? All four demesnes involved in this war have bought Drim'hco'plai slaves. Why not simply state that refreshed games are the purpose? And again, why does the demesne-lord spend the money necessary to buy back all his slaves?"

Merrick scratched his cheek. "Maybe they're worried that the Tua demesne won't like the Drim playing animal hunting games when they're supposed to be concentrating on fighting a war," he said slowly. "But that doesn't explain the slave recall."

"It does not," Ukuthi agreed. "It is a puzzle, one which my demesne-lord wishes to solve."

"Okay," Merrick said. "So why are you telling me this?"

Ukuthi cocked his head to the side. "I wish you to travel to Anya's world with her and seek truth for my demesne-lord."

Merrick felt his eyes bulge. "You *what*?"

"But we do not send you merely for information." Ukuthi gestured to Anya. "Anya Winghunter?"

"We need your help, Merrick Moreau," Anya said quietly. "My people do not wish to be slaves anymore."

"I sympathize," Merrick said. "But you're asking me—I don't even know *what* you're asking me."

"You are a *koubrah*-soldier," Ukuthi said. "I have seen you do remarkable feats."

"I'm *one* Cobra soldier," Merrick said tartly. "What you need is a battalion of us. Better yet, you need a battalion of armored troops and a Dominion of Man war fleet." He waved a hand. "Why are we even discussing this? The Drim will know what all their slaves look like. How do you expect to slip me into that group?"

"You are wrong," Ukuthi said. "They will not know each slave's appearance. Nor will they care. To them, one human slave is no different than any other."

"Well, then, the other slaves will know I'm not one of them."

"You will have nothing to fear from the other slaves," Ukuthi said. "They will listen to Anya, and will keep their silence concerning your true identity."

"The doctor might not," Merrick persisted. "The one who's been treating me. He comes from Anya's world, doesn't he?"

"No," Ukuthi said. "He is my personal physician. He spoke in the dialect of those of Anya's world because I wished to know if you understood that dialog, or could learn to understand it. Can you?"

"I don't know," Merrick said. "Probably. But that's not the point. The point is that there's no way I can fight a whole planetful of slave-owning Trofts alone."

"You will not be fighting alone," Anya said. "We too are fighters, and we yearn for freedom. We will fight at your side."

"With what, sticks and rocks?" Merrick demanded. "Swords and spears? No offense, Anya, but whatever you've got isn't going to be much good against Troft lasers and body armor." He shook his head. "I'm sorry, but it can't be done."

"It can be done," Ukuthi said firmly. "History has shown how successful revolutions are often started by a single spark. Anya's people are strong, but they require a leader who can fight. A leader with vision and the knowledge of strategy and tactics. You can be that leader."

"You don't know that," Merrick insisted. "You don't know that I have any of those skills."

"I am confident that you do," Ukuthi said.

"But you ran me through the Games to make sure anyway?"

"You misunderstand," Ukuthi said. "The test was not for my benefit, but for Anya's. It was she who needed to see your skills."

"Really." Merrick glared at the woman. "Are you satisfied?"

"I am," she said quietly.

"But more important than combat skill is an honorable character," Ukuthi continued. "That too is a quality I know you possess."

Merrick snorted. "Why? Because I haven't killed you yet?"

"Because you risked yourself to protect Anya in the arena," the Troft said. "And because you targeted the weapons and not the soldiers when you attacked them in the forest near Milika."

Merrick frowned. He'd forgotten all about that incident. He'd also forgotten Fadil Sammon's intriguing questions about it. "It seemed only fair, given that their missile launcher was aimed over our heads."

"Did you know they were on mercy setting before you chose to attack only the weapons?"

Merrick thought back. "No, I guess not," he admitted, frowning suddenly. "Wait a minute. I thought you said that was a Drim ship out there hunting for razorarms."

"The ship was Drim'hco'plai," Ukuthi confirmed. "But the tactics and weapons settings were mine." His beak cracked open. "After our coalition was temporarily thrown off Qasama, the Tua'lanek'zia ordered that tactical leadership on this world would henceforth be provided by the Balin'ekha'spmi."

"In other words, by you," Merrick said, nodding. He'd thought he'd sensed a new skill and subtlety in the invaders' techniques since their return to Qasama. Now he knew why. "So the Tua just handed their command over to you? Risky of them."

"The Tua'lanek'zia decision had little effect on their forces," Ukuthi said. "Their main strength is on the Cobra Worlds capital of Aventine, with only an observer force on Qasama. It is the Drim'hco'plai who have the strongest presence here, and it was they who spoke the strongest objections against the Tua'lanek'zia decision."

Merrick's mind flicked back to some of the conflicts he and his mother had had early in the campaign with Miron Akim and the rest of the Qasaman military. "I'm not surprised," he said. "No one likes to have someone else telling him what to do."

"Indeed," Ukuthi said. "Unfortunately, that is the situation a slave faces every day of his life."

Merrick sighed. "Look, it's not that I don't feel for them. I do. It's just that—"

"Will you at least think on my offer?" Ukuthi asked.

"Like I've got anything else to do," Merrick growled. "Fine, I'll think. How long do I have?"

"You have one day."

Merrick stared at him. "One *day*?"

"I am convinced that the decisive battle will take place tomorrow in the city of Azras," Ukuthi said. "Whether the Qasamans succeed or fail, the Trof'te forces will be thrown into disarray. That confusion will give us the opportunity to collect whatever equipment from Qasaman stores that you wish to take with you when my demesne-lord returns you and the rest of his slaves to the Drim'hco'plai."

Merrick snorted. "Right. You're expecting the Drim to let their slaves just march back home lugging satchels full of weapons and explosives?"

"Grant the Drim'hco'plai a higher intelligence," Ukuthi said, and for the first time there was a hint of annoyance in his tone. "But also grant us the same. Our weapons smiths and technicians will naturally camouflage them first."

"You think there'll be time for that?"

"The Drim'hco'plai request specified all slaves would be returned within the next six weeks," Ukuthi said. "That will permit us adequate time."

"Probably," Merrick said, a sudden strange thought drifting up through the utter insanity of this whole thing. If Ukuthi was willing to collect weapons and supplies from Qasama . . . "What about more people?" he asked. "More soldiers, I mean. If you can slip one non-slave ringer into the Drim shipment, why not five or six or twenty?"

"That may be possible," Ukuthi said, eyeing Merrick thoughtfully. "Are there Qasamans here who you trust with such a mission?"

Merrick looked at Anya again. At her wooden, hopeful face. "There are a few," he said. "The question is whether you could camouflage their combat suits well enough to get them past the Drim."

"I am confident that can be done," Ukuthi said. "Do you then accept the mission?"

"Not so fast," Merrick warned. "So far all I'm accepting is the job of thinking about it. *And* my answer will probably also depend on the outcome of tomorrow's activity. If the particular Qasamans I'm thinking about inviting are killed, that'll change things. You'll want to keep that in mind when you're preparing your strategy."

"My strategy will be the same whether you accept or not," Ukuthi said. "The soldiers and warships of the Balin'ekha'spmi will remain at their current stations at Sollas and Purma. The Drim'hco'plai at Azras will be left to succeed or fail on their own strength."

"Or you could help the Qasamans more actively," Merrick suggested, feeling his heart beating harder. If he could actually create a rift in the Troft coalition and bring the Balins onto the human side, the Azras battle Ukuthi was anticipating might not even have to be fought.

But the Troft shook his head. "I cannot," he said in a voice that left no room for argument. "The Drim'hco'plai are still our contractual allies. Furthermore, they outnumber us greatly. I cannot and will not actively fight them. I can only deny them my skills and the resources of the Balin'ekha'spmi."

Merrick nodded. Not as good as he'd hoped, but better than he could have expected. "I have your pledge of that?" he asked.

"My pledge, I give it," Ukuthi said without hesitation. "And I will do more. If you wish, you may watch the battle unfold at my side in my warship's command center. You will see for yourself that I and the Balin'ekha'spmi are not aiding the Drim'hco'plai."

"You'd let me aboard your ship?" Merrick asked carefully, trying to keep his voice casual. To be inside a Troft warship's command center, with its weaponry right there at his fingertips...

"You will be required to pledge that you will attempt neither escape nor sabotage," Ukuthi added.

"Of course," Merrick said, suppressing a sigh. Once again, the temptation to lie tugged at him. Once again, he knew he couldn't. "Very well. I so pledge."

"Then I shall see you again tomorrow," Ukuthi said, taking a step back toward the door. "Together we shall watch the Qasamans make their final bid for victory."

Merrick grimaced. "Yes," he murmured.

Ukuthi paused with his hand raised to the door. "You fear for their lives," he said, almost gently. "And so you should, for warfare is too often a random destroyer. But I do not think you need worry about the final outcome. You humans are an inventive and determined and resilient species, superior in many ways even to the Trof'te."

"Maybe," Merrick said. "But we also play politics among ourselves at least as well as you do. Our internal conflicts and power games often weaken us and destroy that determination and resilience. Sometimes they even bring about our defeat without the actions of an external enemy."

"Let us both hope that will not be the case here," Ukuthi said. "For I feel in the deepest core of my being that whatever the Drim'hco'plai are planning will be of great evil, for human and Trof'te alike."

He rapped sharply, three times, on the door. [That danger, think on it as well,] he added in cattertalk as the door swung open. [Your presence, I will request it at the proper time tomorrow.]

[My presence, you will have it,] Merrick promised.

His last view of Ukuthi as the door swung closed was the commander standing firm and tall, with only a small flutter in his radiator membranes showing the stresses of his position and command.

And, perhaps, the looming betrayal that he was planning of his fellow Trofts.

"You will think on this?" Anya asked hopefully.

Merrick nodded. "As I promised."

He expected her to say more, either to continue Ukuthi's pleading of her people's case or else to launch into a showering of thanks they both knew was as yet underserved. But she merely nodded and sat down again on her bed.

With a sigh, Merrick climbed back onto his own bed and stretched out, staring at the plain concrete ceiling above him. Ukuthi wanted an answer by tomorrow. Merrick would give him that answer.

He just wished he had some idea what the hell that answer would be.

✧   ✧   ✧

"Fadil Sammon?"

With an effort, Fadil forced his way out of the tortured dream and clawed his way toward consciousness. It was the same dream, the one he'd had so many times since the mind-enhancing drug had robbed him of the use of his body. He opened his eyes and turned his head, the only part of him he could still move.

Carsh Zoshak stood beside his medical bed, gazing at him with an odd expression. A few paces behind him was Dr. Krites. "Yes?" Fadil asked. "What do you want?"

Zoshak's forehead furrowed, and he looked back at Krites. "You don't already know?" Krites asked.

Fadil frowned in turn... and slowly—far too slowly—the truth dawned on him. "It's gone, isn't it?" he said.

Krites shrugged. "You've been all but reading everyone's expressions ever since your return to this house," he reminded Fadil. "If those powers of observation and analysis have left you, the rest probably has also."

Fadil swallowed hard. And so the glory passed. Fadil Sammon, super-genius, was no more. Only Fadil Sammon, cripple, remained.

In his mind, he closed his hands into fists. Laying motionless beside his body, his hands didn't even twitch. "Why have you awakened me?"

"Forgive me," Zoshak said. "I just wanted to tell you that they've arrived at Azras."

Fadil stared at him in disbelief, then shifted his eyes to the clock on the wall. He'd had no idea that he'd slept that long. "And Paul Broom has been taken to the hospital?"

"He has," Zoshak confirmed. "The regrowth treatments for his leg will begin shortly."

Fadil felt a cheek muscle twitch. And in two or three weeks, Paul Broom would have a brand-new, fully functional leg. For a moment, he felt a spark of envy.

But envy was a trap, and a sin, and an utter waste of energy. Ruthlessly, Fadil pushed it aside. "Jin Moreau is there with him?"

"The report didn't say, but I assume so," Zoshak said. "That *was* the arrangement you made with Ifrit Ghushtre, was it not?"

Despite the seriousness of the situation, Fadil had to smile. Zoshak was working hard at looking all solemn and professional now, but Fadil remembered the staggered expression on his face two days ago when Ghushtre first told him what Fadil had done. That look alone had almost made it worth what it had cost him.

But all that was in the past. This was the present. Miron Akim had done as he promised, sending Jin Moreau and Paul Broom to Azras with the new Cobras so that they could begin their healing. Now, it was time for Fadil to fulfill his part of the bargain.

And despite Zoshak's emotionless expression it was clear he was ready, even eager, to carry it out.

"And Gama Yithtra played his part adequately?" Fadil asked.

"Again, the report didn't say," Zoshak said. "But since the passage at the Azras gate went smoothly, I think we can assume he did."

"Good," Fadil said, his final twinge of uncertainty fading away. "That's why I chose him to be one of the recruits, you know."

"Not because his father is an important village leader?"

"Partially," Fadil conceded. "But mainly because I knew what an accomplished liar he is. I knew he could manage any deception that was required of him."

"Apparently so," Zoshak said. "And now, it's time to go."

Fadil sighed. He'd argued against this path, argued and pleaded both. It was wrong to waste Qasaman resources like this, especially in the midst of war. But Miron Akim had refused to listen to reason.

And as Fadil had already noted, the Marid had fulfilled his part of the bargain.

"Could I wait one more day?" Fadil asked Zoshak, trying one last time. "I'd like to see the outcome of tomorrow's battle."

"No," Krites said firmly before Zoshak could answer. "I sympathize, Fadil Sammon. But we have our orders."

"And those orders state that the time is now," Zoshak said. "Is there anything you'd like before we go?"

Fadil turned his head back and gazed up at the ceiling. He'd seen that ceiling thousands of times growing up. Yet it was only now, in the three and a half weeks since his return from Sollas, that he'd actually *looked* at it.

And only at this moment did he suddenly realize that, in the midst of war and the lurking threat of despair, things of beauty were somehow made even more beautiful.

He took a deep breath. "No, thank you," he said.

He gave the ceiling one final lingering look, then turned back to Zoshak. "I'm ready."

CHAPTER FIFTEEN

"There," Siraj said, nodding along the crowded street as he and Lorne pretended to examine the sparse wares at a vegetable stand. "That one's ours."

Lorne half turned to bring the tomato he was holding more fully into the mid-morning sunlight streaming down across the Azras buildings. Half a block away, parked squarely in the middle of the road, was one of the Troft armored trucks he'd had way too much experience with lately. Its swivel gun was pointed more or less in their direction, but the five armored soldiers sitting on the roof were arrayed in a tight circle, all facing outward, where they could watch all approaches. On both sides of the vehicle, citizens streamed sullenly or nervously past as they went about their daily lives. "Any idea how many more are inside?" he asked, replacing the tomato in its tray and selecting another one.

"Typically, each truck carries ten of the invaders," Siraj said. "That would indicate a driver, gunner, and three more soldiers inside."

"Not too bad," Lorne said, trying to sound casual. He'd tackled the things twice, but neither time had been exactly easy. "The open-sesame is...?"

"Is ready," Siraj said with a touch of amusement. "Don't concern yourself with the opening, Lorne Moreau. Concern yourself with the task once the opening has occurred."

"I know," Lorne said with a touch of offended dignity. "I'm just a bit concerned about what happens if the opening *doesn't* occur. Like, for example, if the rotating password pattern got reset this morning."

"The rotation is unchanged," Siraj assured him. "We've monitored two to three openings for each truck since dawn, and all are still running the same system they were when they first came into Azras."

"Okay," Lorne said, still unable to shake his nervousness about this whole scheme. "And you're sure about these radios?"

"Very sure," Siraj said. "My father himself has vouched for their safety and security."

Lorne took a deep breath and returned the tomato to the tray. "Okay, then," he said, doing a quick check of his nanocomputer's clock circuit. "Three minutes ten to go."

"There," Siraj said, putting down the vegetable he'd been examining and nodding toward the sky. Lorne looked up, to see three hovering Troft drones suddenly begin moving toward the eastern part of the city. "The Brigane Street road work has caught their attention."

"Looks like it," Lorne agreed, watching the drones as they disappeared from sight behind the buildings. "Let's hope they can hold their audience for the next six minutes. *And* that we can get in fast enough to keep any of their friends from calling them back here."

"We will," Siraj assured him. "We should begin walking now."

Lorne checked his clock circuit again. "Right," he confirmed.

"And remember to keep your sleeves pushed up," Siraj added as they joined the stream of pedestrians walking down the street. "The invaders insist on seeing bare arms, and we don't want to give them any reason for concern."

Lorne nodded and pushed his sleeves up, tucking them into large, ungainly knots on his shoulders. It still felt awkward, but after all the practice yesterday afternoon and evening at least he knew how to function with them that way. "Okay," he said, taking a deep breath and letting it out slowly. "Ready or not, here we come."

"We are gathered here," Shahni Haafiz intoned from his place at the center of the briefing room table, "for the trial of Daulo Sammon, son of Kruin Sammon, of the village of Milika. The charge is treason in the highest degree."

Treason. The word echoed through Daulo's mind as he stood stiffly before the three men at the table, sending weakness into his knees and a trembling blackness into his soul. His life was on the line here, and his family holdings, and his sacred honor.

But at least Fadil wasn't going to have to brave the dangers of the forest in order to stand trial alongside him. Miron Akim had come to him privately yesterday and assured him that his son was still in Milika, and that he would be permitted to remain there.

"The charge has two points," Haafiz continued in the same solemn voice. "First, that Daulo Sammon was in possession of a radio, as forbidden by the Shahni since the invasion of our world." He waved a hand over the cylindrical device sitting on the table in front of Akim, his fingers stopping short of actually touching it. "Second, that Daulo Sammon used this same radio to contact the invaders and make an as-yet unknown bargain of betrayal against the Shahni and the people of Qasama."

Daulo caught his breath, his eyes suddenly frozen on the radio. The radio Akim claimed to have found in his wheelchair carrier bag. The radio that had been the reason he'd been locked underground in the command post for the past thirteen days.

Akim had told him yesterday that Fadil was still in Milika. *How could he possibly have known that?*

Had the Djinn he'd sent to the village returned with that news? But Daulo had heard nothing about new arrivals, nor had he seen Ghushtre or any of the others since their departure. Had some other messenger or courier arrived? But why would a courier waste time traveling around the outlying villages when the cities of Qasama were under siege?

There was only one answer. One horrible, terrifying answer.

Slowly, Daulo raised his eyes to Akim. The other was watching him, a faint smile at the corners of his lips.

"—is the procedure we will follow," Haafiz was saying. "The first statement—"

"Forgive me," Daulo interrupted, his knees suddenly shaking so hard he could barely stand. "Forgive me, Your Excellency, but it's urgent that I speak."

"You dare make a mockery of these proceedings?" Haafiz bit out. "You will remain silent—"

"No," Moffren Omnathi interrupted mildly from his seat at Haafiz's other side. "Let the accused speak."

Daulo stared into Omnathi's calm, unconcerned face. Was he in this along with Akim?

His mouth went dry. Of course he was. It had been both men, working together, who had kept Daulo trapped here, unable to communicate with the outside world. It had to be both of them.

But why?

And then, his eyes shifted back to Haafiz. The Shahni's expression, in sharp contrast with Omnathi's, was brimming with anger, frustration, and impatience.

And with that, it was suddenly obvious.

"As I told you before, Your Excellency, the radio isn't mine," Daulo said, the words stumbling over themselves as he hurried to get them out before one or the other of the traitors could stop him. "It's Miron Akim's, and always was. Miron Akim is the one who accused me of treason, using that excuse to force us all to remain here."

"To what end?" Akim asked, his voice perfectly calm.

"To keep His Excellency Shahni Haafiz away from Purma," Daulo said, glancing to both sides of the room where Narayan and the other Djinn stood ceremonial guard. Could he convince them of the truth before Akim ordered him and Haafiz both murdered? "To keep him from all communication with the remaining Shahni."

"But to what end?" Akim persisted. "Why would I wish that His Excellency not communicate with Purma?"

"I don't know," Daulo said, looking desperately at Narayan. But the Djinni was just standing there. "Perhaps he knows something you didn't want becoming known. Perhaps—" He broke off, looking sharply back at Akim. "Because he tried to have you and Moffren Omnathi condemned as traitors," he breathed. "You knew that if he went to Purma he would tell the rest of the Shahni what had happened and might persuade them to confirm his charges against you."

Akim shook his head. But to Daulo's dismay, it was more a gesture of admiration than one of denial. "You're amazing, Daulo

Sammon," he said. "I see where your son Fadil got his intellect and perception."

"Are you saying he's *right*?" Haafiz asked, sending an uncertain glare toward Akim.

"Only partially," Akim said. "But he deduced all the parts that he reasonably could have."

Haafiz shot a look at Daulo. "Which parts? What are you talking about?"

"The parts about my accusation being nothing more than an excuse for keeping you here, Your Excellency." Akim inclined his head. "But thankfully, it wasn't for the purpose he supposes."

"Whatever the purpose," Haafiz bit out, "restraining a Shahni against his will is still treason."

"Perhaps," Akim said. "But it was for a higher good."

Haafiz snorted. "What higher good can treason possibly serve?"

"The higher good," Akim said quietly, "of protecting our world. Of preventing you, Your Excellency, from destroying it."

Two of the five Trofts sitting on top of the armored truck turned their faceplates toward Lorne and Siraj as they walked toward the vehicle. But they apparently looked no more dangerous than the rest of the citizens passing by. By the time the two men came alongside the vehicle the aliens had shifted their attention elsewhere in the milling crowd.

They were passing the truck, and Lorne had just finished putting target locks on the five soldiers, when the short, sharp warning whistle came from one of the buildings above them.

Out of the corner of his eye he saw the Trofts look up, probably trying to locate the sound. In three seconds, Lorne's mother would be calling the password into a radio transmitter in hopes of getting the soldiers inside the truck to open the rear door. If they did, this should be a straightforward exercise in combat timing.

If they didn't, he and Siraj were going to have to do this the hard way.

Fortunately, they did. Lorne had just reached the rear of the truck when there was a thunk from the lock mechanism and the door swung open.

And as Siraj lobbed a concussion grenade past the shocked Troft and in through the opening, Lorne spun around and leaped for the top of the truck, his stunner spitting bursts of current into the soldiers scrambling madly to bring their weapons around.

Like the soldiers inside the truck, they were far too late. Even as Lorne landed in a crouch in the middle of the sprawled bodies the truck shuddered beneath him with the muffled thud of the grenade's detonation. A quick check to make sure all five Trofts were well and truly unconscious, and he hopped back down to the street.

Siraj was holding the rear door open a crack and peering cautiously inside. "Looks clear," he said.

"I'll check," Lorne told him, keying his infrareds and looking inside. It was impossible to read the three soldiers through their armor and helmets, but the unhelmeted driver and swivel gunner were definitely unconscious.

"Clear," he told Siraj. "Get the welders started and get into your combat suit. We've got exactly two minutes and thirty-five seconds to get moving."

"How *dare* you?" Haafiz demanded, his face darkening with barely-controlled fury. "You overstep your bounds for the final time, Miron Akim." He stabbed a finger at Narayan. "Ifrit Narayan, you are ordered to place Miron Akim under immediate arrest."

Daulo tensed. But to his astonishment, neither Narayan nor any of the rest of the Djinn stirred from their places. "Ifrit Narayan!" Haafiz snapped. "That's a direct order."

"They won't obey you," Akim said quietly. "As of this morning, they know the truth. They know what you would have done if you'd been permitted to travel to Purma."

"And what would I have done?" Haafiz retorted. "Destroyed Qasama with my own hand?"

"Yes," Akim said. "Because you would have ordered the Djinn to turn against our allies."

"Our—?" Haafiz broke off. "So it was done," he said, his voice turning even colder. "Ghofl Khatir brought demon warriors from the worlds of our enemies."

"From the worlds of our allies," Akim corrected. "We now have a treaty with them."

Haafiz spat. "Treason."

"They've brought resources for our war against the invaders," Akim said.

"Treason."

"Even now, they fight alongside our forces in Azras."

Haafiz slammed his fist on the table. *"Treason!"* he snarled. "Treason and madness. They'll turn on us, Miron Akim—if not today, then the moment the other invaders have been thrown off our world. They must be stopped *now*, before they know all our secrets. We don't need their so-called help, and we don't *want* it."

"You're wrong, Your Excellency, on both counts," Akim said. "Besides, it's too late. The battle for our world has already begun." He picked up the radio from the table in front of him. "I received the word from the military commander of Azras fifteen minutes ago."

Haafiz's eyes dropped to the radio, his glare slipping a bit. "So it's true," he said bitterly. "The radio was yours. *You're* the traitor communicating with the invaders."

"The radio is mine," Akim acknowledged. "But I'm not in communication with the invaders. In fact, the invaders don't even know these exist. They operate in a special and undetectable way, piggybacking their signal onto the invaders' own radio communications. They can thus send messages back and forth without the invaders ever noticing a transmission or being able to search and lock onto it."

And then, to Daulo's amazement, Akim looked at Daulo and smiled. "The technique, and the radios themselves," he added, "were created in large part by Fadil Sammon, son of Daulo Sammon."

Daulo felt his mouth drop open. Fadil had done *that*? "But you said..."

"I said you and your son were traitors," Akim said, "and for that I beg your forgiveness. But it was necessary that we prevent Shahni Haafiz from traveling to Purma, and you were the only excuse I could think of to give him."

"But how could he have stopped Jin Moreau and the Cobras

from aiding us?" Daulo asked in bewilderment. There was something here he still wasn't getting. "He's only one voice of many, and you said the Shahni had already approved the treaty. Wouldn't it require all the Shahni together to abrogate it?"

"It would," Omnathi said quietly. "If there were any Shahni left."

"God above," Haafiz said, his voice sounding shaken, his anger gone for the first time since the meeting began. "They're dead? *All* of them?"

"All of them," Omnathi said. "Killed during the defense of our world."

"And even you escaped Sollas only by the barest of margins," Akim added. "Either the soldiers who confronted us didn't recognize you, or else they deliberately let you leave in hopes that you would travel to Purma and unwittingly identify the military leaders to their drones." He waved a hand around them. "Yet another reason Moffren Omnathi and I felt it vital to hide you here."

Haafiz looked at him, then at Daulo, and finally at Narayan. "Then Qasama is gone," he said. "We have enemies on all sides, and you've deliberately prevented the one remaining leader from resuming command of our defense."

"There are other leaders, Your Excellency," Omnathi assured him. "Military leaders, who can see past old memories to what must be done for our world."

"If you believe that, then you're a fool," Haafiz said bluntly. "The Cobra Worlds care nothing for us beyond our destruction."

"I think not," Akim said. "They have, in fact, already given us a great gift."

Haafiz snorted. "The *gift* of demon warriors who will soon stab us in the back?"

"You may not like this, Your Excellency," Akim warned. "In fact, I'm quite certain you won't. But it's now time for you to know the rest of it."

He gestured. "So if Ifrit Narayan will take his Djinn and Daulo Sammon out of the room, Moffren Omnathi and I will tell you about a project called *Isis.*"

❖   ❖   ❖

Merrick's usual morning routine involved sleeping or at least dozing until the breakfast tray arrived at his cell, then doing some exercises and plotting escape until lunch. But not this morning. He and Anya were awakened an hour after dawn by a pair of soldiers whose armor bore the curlies, highlighted in red, of the Balin'ekha'spmi demesne. Ukuthi's personal guard, Merrick tentatively concluded. The soldiers brought new clothing for both humans—simple, unadorned gray jumpsuits—and an order from Ukuthi to dress quickly and accompany the soldiers to his warship.

Merrick also noted with some dark amusement that the soldiers seemed a bit jumpier than the other soldiers he'd encountered so far in this war. Ukuthi had probably alerted them as to exactly who and what they were dealing with.

They needn't have worried. Merrick had already given his word.

More than that, he'd done some serious thinking since yesterday's conversation. And while he wasn't yet ready to commit to Ukuthi's insane mission he had some definite ideas of how it might be done.

He would need help, of course. Five to ten Qasamans, or an equal number of Cobras if he could get his hands on them. His father hadn't specified in that hurried Dida conversation back at Milika how many Cobras he and Jin had brought from Caelian, but surely they'd brought at least that many. Assuming they could spare a few, and assuming Ukuthi had been right about being able to disguise any equipment they wanted to smuggle onto Anya's world, this whole thing might actually be possible.

The soldiers had a ground vehicle waiting at the subcity exit when they emerged into the sunlight. Merrick winced as they rode across the battered landscape, both at the horrible wasteland Sollas had become and also at the sheer number of Troft warships gathered on the plains north of where the city had once stood. Whatever the Qasamans were planning at Azras, it had better be good.

The Balin ships, as best as Merrick could read the curlies, were gathered together at the eastern end of the group. The driver steered the car to the base of one of them and tapped a signaling button on the control board.

And to Merrick's surprise, one of the warship's bow doors opened and Ukuthi stepped out. [The vehicle, remain in it,] he called to Merrick as he strode up to the car. [The Drim'hco'plai command ship, I am ordered to report to it.]

An unpleasant tingle ran up Merrick's back. [The battle, it has begun?] he asked as he slid hastily across the seat to give Ukuthi room to get in.

[The battle, I have yet seen no signs of it,] the other said. [Commander Inxeba, I believe he merely wishes to consult with his colleagues.]

Merrick grabbed for a handrail as the car lurched forward again. [Slaves, are they also invited to this meeting?] he asked pointedly.

[A problem, it will not be one.] Ukuthi paused. [My proposal, have you given more thought to it?]

[The proposal, I have given a great deal of thought to it,] Merrick assured him. [The details, I will wish to discuss them further.]

[Further discussion, I will look forward to it.] Ukuthi gestured to Anya. [A slave, you must now behave as one. Anya Winghunter's behavior and manner, you must imitate them.]

Merrick grimaced. He hadn't thought about that aspect of this masquerade. If the other Trofts tumbled to the fact that he wasn't, in fact, one of Ukuthi's slaves, there would be serious hell to pay.

Still, if he wanted to monitor Ukuthi's behavior during the upcoming action and confirm he wasn't helping the Drim against the Qasamans, this was where he needed to be. [My best, I will do it,] he told the other.

There were four soldiers waiting at the base of the Drim command ship when the Balin car arrived. Merrick thought he saw some surprise in their faces when Ukuthi strode toward them with a pair of human slaves in tow, but it might have been his imagination. Certainly neither of them said anything. Two of the soldiers ushered the visitors through the bow door into what seemed to be a guard room, then led the way up a switchback stairway to the ship's top deck. There, they were shown into a conference room where four Trofts wearing senior officers' insignia and identical sets of curlies were already seated on upholstered couches.

The couches, Merrick noted, came equipped with small control boards and tables to hold the Trofts' drinks. A fifth couch, currently unoccupied, had a drink poured and waiting.

The soldiers had been too polite or too discreet to mention Ukuthi's slave entourage. But one of the officers had no such compunctions. [The meaning, what is this?] he demanded, glaring at Merrick and Anya. [Commander Ukuthi, does he now bring slaves to military conferences?]

[Commander Ukuthi, he is training them to military capabilities,] Ukuthi said calmly. [Constant service, I require them to learn it.]

[Unseemly, it is,] the other Troft growled. [Commander Inxeba's slaves, he has not brought them.] He gestured to the other Drim officers. [My officers, their slaves they have also left elsewhere.]

[Commander Inxeba's forgiveness, I ask it,] Ukuthi said. [My departure, do you wish it?]

Inxeba sent Merrick another glare, but pointed to the empty couch. [Your presence, I request it,] he said tartly. [The slaves, they will stand silently.]

Ukuthi looked at Merrick as he settled onto his couch. [Silence, you will maintain it,] he ordered.

Anya bowed. Merrick caught the beginning of the gesture in time to follow suit. [The order, we obey it,] she said. She looked sideways at Merrick and gave a small warning shake of her head.

Merrick nodded back and remained silent. Apparently, all the members of a group of slaves were to bow, but it was sufficient for only one of them to acknowledge a general order.

[The purpose of this meeting, what is it?] Ukuthi asked as he sampled his drink.

[Activity in Purma, it has suddenly increased,] Inxeba said, pointing to one of a bank of sixty small monitors arrayed across two of the room's walls. That particular display showed an aerial view of a city intersection, with twenty Qasamans moving purposefully around the area. At the bottom of the image were the words *Purma/Five* in cattertalk script. [A SkyJo lair, it is,] Inxeba identified the view. [The Qasamans' attack helicopters, they are about to deploy them.]

Merrick frowned. Ukuthi had predicted an attack, but in Azras, not Purma. Had he been wrong? Or was Purma just a diversion?

Ukuthi was apparently wondering along the same lines. [The SkyJos, have you yet seen one?] he asked.

[The SkyJos, I have not seen them,] Inxeba admitted. [A SkyJo lair, I am still convinced it is.]

[The truth, perhaps you speak it,] Ukuthi said. [Azras, is there activity there?]

[Activity, it is also occurring in Azras,] Inxeba said, a note of impatience in his voice. [But the activity, it is less urgent. Purma, the center of enemy government it is. Purma, from there will the enemy's next attack arise.]

[Purma, the attack will perhaps arise from there,] Ukuthi said noncommittally. [The truth, you appear to have it. My presence, why have you requested it?]

[Strategic command, the Drim'hco'plai have given you,] Inxeba said, and there was no mistaking the resentment in his tone. [Commander Goqana, he requests your approval for my action.]

[Your action, what form does it take?] Ukuthi asked.

The Drim commander launched into a convoluted explanation, much of it involving military terms that Merrick didn't know. As he listened with half an ear, he looked across the rest of the monitor bank until he found the set of eight images that were marked with the identifying word *Azras*. Like the Purma cityscape, all the Azras images were coming from hovering drones. All eight showed the same sort of street activity that the Purma drones were watching, though as Inxeba had said the Azras version didn't seem nearly as intense or surreptitious.

He frowned as something odd caught his eye. The eight Azras monitors showed street activity; but it was the *same* street activity. Whoever was directing operations had apparently been intrigued enough by what was happening on that particular street to gather all the drones together to monitor it.

Leaving the rest of the city completely unwatched.

Merrick's guess had been right. Purma was a diversion.

He stole a look at Inxeba. The Drim commander was still gazing intently at the wrong displays, his radiator membranes fluttering slowly with anticipation of the coup he was fully expecting to achieve today.

[Slave.]

Startled, Merrick looked at Ukuthi. The Balin commander was pointing at his empty glass.

[Your wish, we obey it,] Anya said. Nudging Merrick, she nodded across the room to a sideboard where a large, half-full pitcher sat on a cooling plate.

Merrick nodded back and crossed to the pitcher. It was heavier than it looked, but his arm servos were more than up to the task. Returning to Ukuthi's couch, he carefully refilled the glass. [The others, you will serve them,] Ukuthi said when he'd finished.

[The order, I obey it,] Merrick said, wincing. Here he was, trying to hold still and remain invisible; and here Ukuthi was, thrusting him squarely into the center of attention.

But for all he didn't know about proper slave protocol, he *did* know that he wasn't supposed to argue with his master. Steeling himself, he set off around the room, stopping at each of the occupied couches and topping off the other Trofts' drinks.

To his mild surprise, none of them looked at him. Certainly none of them thanked him. It was entirely possible, in fact, that they didn't even notice him. Perhaps that was the point Ukuthi had intended to make.

Still, Merrick didn't breathe easy again until he'd finished his task, returned the pitcher to the sideboard, and resumed his place at Anya's side.

[My thought, I will give it to your proposal,] Ukuthi continued, gesturing to the Purma displays. [My attention, I will now give it to the situation.]

His eyes flicked to Merrick. [Useful knowledge, I will hope to gain it.]

Merrick swallowed hard, his eyes on the Azras displays. There was useful knowledge out there, all right. Ukuthi seemed to have already spotted it.

The question was whether Inxeba would also pick up on it in time. Merrick would bet heavily that he wouldn't.

The Qasamans of Azras were betting, too. Only they were betting their lives.

CHAPTER SIXTEEN

The first task, once the eight armored trucks had been captured and their crews neutralized, was to get the vehicles out of Azras.

That part was more or less easy. Lorne had driven one of the trucks back on Aventine and had spent an hour the previous night coaching the Djinn who would be in charge of that part of the operation. The relative simplicity of the task, combined with the learning-enhancement drugs the Qasamans had been given during the session, pretty much guaranteed they'd do a decent job.

And they did. Lorne watched with only mild trepidation as their driver maneuvered his truck through the city streets with a minimum of hesitation and only a single badly-taken corner. Along the way the other captured trucks swung out of other streets to join them, and by the time they came in sight of the main city gate the full eight-truck convoy was running together in a tight battle-phalanx array.

The second task was to get past the Trofts guarding the gate. That one was slightly less easy. The individual soldiers weren't a problem—most of them goggled at the armored column bearing down on them, made frantic radio calls back to the warship for help or fired a useless shot or two before diving out of the way to the sides of the road. The four armored trucks, though their occupants were obviously as startled as the soldiers, stood their ground, their swivel guns turning toward the attackers and opening fire.

They got off perhaps two shots each before the missiles the Djinn had set up in concealed launch tubes on top of the wall blasted down on them, destroying all four trucks and sending mushroom clouds of fire and debris curling high into the air.

But with that, the real job began...because while the truck crews and the gate guards had been taken more or less by surprise, the warship a kilometer away was now on full alert. As the trucks set off toward it across the empty field, their swivel guns firing madly, the heavy lasers on the pylons beneath the warship's stubby wings began returning fire.

And suddenly the landscape around the trucks became a blazing hell of fire and smoke.

Beside Lorne, Siraj was quietly cursing through clenched teeth, anger and fear mixing together in his voice. Not fear for himself, Lorne knew. Hanging underneath the truck on the hand- and footholds that had been quick-welded into place before they drove out of the city, and with the entire bulk of the truck between them and the warship's lasers, he and the rest of the strike team were as safe as it was possible to be.

But the drivers and gunners inside the trucks didn't have nearly as much protection. They were heading straight into the deadly fire, fully aware of the danger, fully aware that most or all of them would probably die in the next ninety seconds, but fully committed to getting the strike team as close to the warship as they possibly could.

A fresh wave of smoke billowed across the ground beneath the truck as a near-miss ignited a patch of low bushes. Lorne squeezed his eyes closed against the sting, relying on his implanted opticals to see what was happening. They'd made it across the first small ridge, he could tell, and he could hear the *crack* of the relays through the thick metal above him that meant their swivel gun was still sending laser fire back at the warship's weapons clusters. The assumption had been that the warship would target the swivel guns first, trying to knock them out before they could do serious damage to the ship's own lasers, missiles, and point-defense systems, and only then concentrate on disabling the trucks themselves.

The truck lurched and seemed briefly to float in midair before crashing heavily to the ground again. Second ridge passed. Two more to go, then a shallow dip twenty meters wide that led right up to the warship's base and the two bow doors that were the strike team's hoped-for way in. Third ridge should be coming up...

And then, with a final sputtering *snap* from the capacitors, the swivel gun above them went silent. "Siraj Akim?" Lorne called.

"Our gun's been silenced," Siraj confirmed, his head tilted sideways as he listened to the small radio attached to his right shoulder. "Three of the others have also lost their guns. The others are still firing."

Lorne grimaced. The assumption that the warship would take out the trucks' guns first was a reasonable one. But it *was* only an assumption. If the Troft commander decided he'd rather keep the stolen vehicles at arm's length than disarm them, the strike team could find themselves hanging under broken vehicles too far away from the warship to have any chance of breaching it.

And then, to Lorne's dismay, a new sound joined the snapping of displaced air and the louder crackling of stressed metal and burning vegetation: the sizzle-roar of missiles. Had the Trofts decided it was time to escalate from lasers to missiles? "Siraj Akim?"

"It's all right," Siraj said, his lips pulling back into an evil-looking smile. "Ghofl Khatir has ordered more missiles to be launched from the Azras wall."

Lorne felt his own lips curl back. And now the Trofts were being forced to deal with the more immediate threat of a missile attack before they could return to the task of disabling or destroying the approaching trucks. Khatir had just bought them a few more precious seconds.

His smile turned into a grimace...because the strike team's extra seconds were being bought with Qasaman lives. Back in Sollas, during the first invasion, the Trofts had dealt with incoming fire by blanketing the area with laser and missile fire, taking out the enemy positions as well as much of the architecture around them. If they kept to that pattern, many of the men manning the Azras missile launchers would be killed, along with probably dozens of civilians.

The truck shot up and lofted itself down from another ridge. Lorne held on grimly, trying to figure out which of the five ridges that had been. To his embarrassed chagrin, he realized that in the confusion of the moment he'd lost count.

But his nanocomputer clock circuit showed a minute twenty had passed since they'd blown out of Azras. It should only be another ten seconds to the ship.

And then, with an ear-hammering blast and a jolt that nearly wrenched Lorne's hands from the bars, the truck ground to a halt.

"Are we there?" the Djinni on Siraj's far side asked.

"Either there or as close as we're going to get," Lorne told him. He lowered himself onto the ground, wincing at the heat from the burned grass against his back, and made his way to the front of the truck.

The gamble had worked. The Troft warship was right in front of them, the nearest of the bow doors no more than five meters away.

And now came the *really* hard part.

"We're here," he confirmed, looking both directions. "We're five meters out—the rest are no farther than seven or eight. If we all hurry, we should be able to make it before they notice us and open fire from the wing clusters."

"Assuming the invaders are foolish enough to open the doors," Siraj warned, crawling up beside him.

Lorne nodded silently. Again, the assumption was sound: the Trofts would want to quickly deal with whoever might still be alive inside the trucks, but deal with them in a way that wouldn't require them to expend energy or missiles and also wouldn't end up with the utter destruction of their trucks. But again, it was only an assumption. "They will," he assured Siraj. "Anyone still alive in here will by definition be military, and the Trofts will want to question any survivors about Azras's SkyJo contingent."

"Or if not question him, at least identify his face," Siraj said. "If they've been recording their drone observations, they may try to backtrack their prisoners and see which buildings they've been using."

Lorne looked at Siraj in mild surprise. That one hadn't even occurred to him. "That *would* be clever, wouldn't it?"

"One of my father's thoughts," Siraj explained with a tight smile. "He *is* the Marid of Djinn, after all. One should expect him to have an occasional good idea or flash of wisdom."

"One should," Lorne agreed, looking back at the still sealed bow door. "Come on," he muttered. "Come *on*."

"Give them a moment," Gama Yithtra advised as he crawled up beside Siraj. "They were taken by surprise. They may still be rushing madly to don their armor."

Lorne nodded, looking down at the device clutched in Yithtra's hand. Its cross shape and flat sides, he'd been told, harkened back to an ancient hunting weapon called a *chalip*, which had long ago been relegated to the status of children's toy.

But this version, consisting of four metal crossarms thirty centimeters across, was considerably more sophisticated. "Just stay alert," Lorne cautioned. "There won't be much time once they charge out."

"Don't worry, Lorne Moreau," Yithtra said, wiggling the *chalip* for emphasis. "You may be an expert on hunting Troft invaders, but *I'm* the expert with this."

And then, abruptly, the warship door swung open and a double line of armored Troft soldiers charged out, lasers held ready. The first four broke to their left, heading for the farthest of the stalled and battered trucks, while the next four split into pairs and headed toward Lorne's vehicle.

Lorne froze, pressing himself against the ground. But the soldiers' eyes were on the truck's partially blackened windshield and side windows, clearly expecting any further attack to come from one of those directions. Quickly, Lorne flicked a target lock onto the two on his side of the truck as they strode around the front and headed warily toward the rear. Behind them, more Trofts filed from the warship, breaking into more foursomes and heading for the other trucks. The flow stopped, and Lorne got a glimpse of two more Trofts inside the ship, keying the control that started the bow door swinging shut.

Lurching his torso up off the ground, Yithtra hurled the *chalip* low over the ground toward the closing door, sailing it like a horizontal pinwheel firespitter through the smoky air. It reached the gap just as the door closed on it, getting caught between door and jamb and blocking the door open a few centimeters. There was a flash of bright yellow where the crossarms touched the door and the jamb—

"Attack!" Ghushtre shouted.

Grabbing the wide bar at the front of the truck, Lorne pulled hard, flinging himself out into the open like a missile from its launch tube. He flipped over onto his back, catching a glimpse of the Trofts who'd been heading toward the rear, now trying desperately to bring their weapons around to face this unexpected threat that had appeared behind them.

They were still trying when Lorne's antiarmor laser flashed twice, sending both soldiers sprawling to the smoldering ground.

Lorne kicked his legs over his head, flipping himself back to his feet as more flashes of laser fire lit up the area between the trucks. He glanced around, confirmed that the Cobras and Djinn of the strike force were all emerging from beneath their vehicles, then turned back to the warship.

The two Trofts he'd seen inside hadn't been caught as thoroughly by surprise as their late comrades outside had been. Both aliens were at the jammed door, struggling with the *chalip* as they tried to pry it loose so that they could seal the door against this unexpected attack.

But the exothermic fast-setting adhesive pellets spaced along the crossarms had fastened it in place as effectively as if it had been welded there. The Trofts were still trying to get it free when Siraj reached the door and took them out with two quick shots from his glove lasers.

Yithtra was already on his knees by the *chalip*, working the hidden catch that broke the weapon apart, finally freeing the door. Grabbing the door edge with one hand and the jamb with the other, he started trying to force the door open again. Standing braced above him, Siraj and his combat suit servos were pushing at it as well.

Braking to a halt beside them, Lorne grabbed the edge of the door below Siraj's hands, adding his own servos to the task. It was surprisingly difficult, more difficult than he'd expected. "Motor's still trying to close it," Siraj grunted. "You have hold? Good—keep pulling."

Resettling his grip on the edge of the door, the Qasaman flipped himself up above Lorne's head into a horizontal position, his hands shifting to a hold on the top of the door with his feet braced against the side of the ship. "Now," he grunted.

For a moment all three of them continued to strain. Then, abruptly, there was the soft *snap* of a burned-out motor, and the door swung free, nearly sending Siraj tumbling to the ground before he could catch himself. "Clear!" Lorne shouted. "Everyone in!"

Siraj was already inside, Yiththra right behind him. Ghushtre ran up at the head of the next group, gesturing Lorne through the door. "Inside," he ordered. "Wait in the guard room until the stairway's clear."

Lorne made a face, but nodded and ducked inside. Part of him wanted to be at the forefront of the attack, an even larger part of him knowing that he *should* be at the forefront. He was, after all, one of only four people in the strike force who'd ever been inside one of these ships.

Which was, of course, the exact reason why the mission's planners had insisted that he stay out of the assault's main spearhead. Not only was he one of the few who knew the ship's layout, but he was the only one who'd had experience controlling the drones.

Lorne understood the logic, and he agreed with it. But he didn't have to like it.

The sounds of combat were starting to come from the stairwell by the time the last of the strike force slipped in through the door. A *lot* of combat, too, Lorne realized uneasily as he notched up his audio enhancements. There was the hiss and small thuds of laser fire and the heavier thuds of falling bodies, all mixed with grunts and moans and stifled screams, both human and Troft.

And none of that was supposed to be happening. Not yet.

The rest of the strike force knew it, too. The Djinn and Cobras still waiting in the guard room were standing tensely in their individual groups, their eyes on the door or else raised to the ceiling, their hands or mouths twitching with suppressed nervousness as they listened to the sounds coming from the stairway.

A few meters away, Siraj was standing with Wendell and Jennifer McCollom, his lips compressed into a tight line as he pressed his radio to his ear. Lorne worked his way over to him and touched his arm. "What's going on?" he asked quietly.

"They've learned from their experience in Sollas," Siraj said tautly.

"Their helmets are now equipped with air filters. The spearhead's gas grenades aren't affecting them."

Lorne chewed at his lip, feeling a small throbbing in his still-tender nose from the nostril filters the doctors had implanted yesterday. The quick-acting sleep gas was one of the Qasamans' most effective weapons, and had figured heavily in the mission's planning.

Worse, the mission had banked on the Qasamans keeping the initiative all the way to the command deck. With the attack bogged down in the stairway, that momentum was gone. "How far up are they?" he asked.

"They've pushed back the invaders to Deck Four," Siraj said. "One more deck, and it should be safe to breach the door and try to get you to the drone control room."

Unless the Trofts had already set up their defenses in the corridor. If Lorne had been in charge, that was certainly what he would have done.

But there might be another way. Maybe. "Never mind Deck Four," he said. "Let's see if we can breach Deck Six."

"The vehicle bay?" Siraj asked, frowning. "What do you expect to find in there?"

"I don't know yet," Lorne said. "Let's grab a squad and go look for inspiration."

The stairway battle was even louder as Lorne, Siraj, and the six other Djinn Siraj had commandeered slipped through the door and headed up. But it was also clearly winding down, and as they reached the Deck Six doorway Lorne heard the final Troft body tumble down one of the upper flights of stairs as the laser fire finally ceased. "Stairway's secured," one of the other Djinn said. "We're needed at Deck One."

"We'll do this first," Siraj told him as Lorne pressed his ear against the door. "As soon as the bay's secured, you can join the rest of the spearhead."

"Our orders are to—"

"Your orders have been changed," Siraj cut him off. "Now be quiet. Lorne Moreau?"

Lorne held his breath, keying his audios all the way up. There was plenty of noise being conducted through the metal walls and floors, but it didn't sound like there was anything coming from the bay itself. "It's either clear, or else they're set up and ready for us."

"I suspect the former," Siraj said, pointing to the edge of the door. "The door's been welded shut."

Lorne nodded as he saw the rippling and faint discoloration. "I can fix that. Everyone get back."

The welding had apparently been part of a general order. As Lorne began cutting at the metal, he could see more reflected laser light from the Cobras and Djinn on the landings above him. Whoever was calling the shots for the Trofts these days, he at least knew how to generate delaying tactics.

Unfortunately, he also knew what to do with the time those tactics bought him. As Lorne turned his antiarmor laser on the last section of weld he suddenly noticed that the warship was rumbling with a deep, almost subsonic vibration. The warship's engines were in startup mode, working their slow but steady way toward full power.

And if there was one thing no one in the strike team wanted, it was to fight the rest of this battle while the ship was flying over the Qasaman landscape toward the bulk of the invaders' forces at Sollas.

The last bit of weld sputtered and disintegrated in a shower of liquid metal droplets. "Done," Lorne announced. "Stay back, and let me—"

He broke off as Siraj brushed past him, shoved the door open, and leaped inside, his combat suit's low-power sonic blasting across the bay. The other six Djinn were right behind him. Swearing under his breath, Lorne lunged through the opening after them.

To find the bay deserted.

"Incredible," Siraj murmured as they spread out across the open space. "They haven't even bothered to defend this place?"

"What's there to defend?" one of the Djinn growled, looking around.

He had a point, Lorne had to admit. There were no vehicles, all apparently having been deployed into and around Azras. There were tools and spare parts racked neatly along the walls on either side of the wide vehicle ramp, but nothing that looked like it might be a heavy laser or other weapon.

Outside in the stairway, the laser fire was suddenly joined by the sounds of explosives and rapid-fire projectile weapons. "They're through the doors," the Djinni said urgently. "We're needed up there, Ifrit."

"Go," Siraj ordered, still looking around.

The Djinni gestured, and he and the others took off toward the stairwell. "On your way," Lorne called after him, "give a shout to the guard room and have Wendell and Jennifer McCollom join us."

There was no response, but a second later Lorne heard the Djinni's booming voice as he delivered the message.

"What do you want them for?" Siraj asked.

"Jennifer's the only other one in the team who can read cattertalk script," Lorne told him. "She's going to help me look through all this stuff and see if there's something we can use."

"And if there isn't?"

Lorne felt his stomach tighten. "There will be," he said. "There has to be."

[My ship, the enemy has penetrated it!] a taut voice came from the speaker in Commander Inxeba's conference room. [New weapons, the enemy has them.]

Inxeba spat a phrase that had never shown up in Merrick's cattertalk classes. [The enemy, you must destroy them,] he snarled. [Our ridicule, it must not be seen.]

Merrick frowned. Seen by whom? The Qasamans?

No. Not by the Qasamans, but by the rest of the Trofts. The force that the Azras Djinn had attacked were, like Inxeba, members of the Drim demesne. Inxeba desperately wanted to keep his allies from finding out that enemy soldiers had basically just strolled aboard one of his warships.

And that shyness might work to the Qasamans' advantage. Keeping the other Troft demesnes in the dark meant Inxeba wouldn't be able to call on their ships and soldiers to support his.

Unfortunately, it might also mean that Inxeba would decide to cover his embarrassment by eliminating all witnesses to the fiasco. Even if it meant ignoring the normal Troft military policy against mass slaughter of civilians.

Merrick's hands curled almost unconsciously into fingertip laser firing position. He could stop that from happening, he knew. There were only two guards at the door, with danger probably the last thing on either of their minds. A set of targeting locks on them, Inxeba, and Inxeba's officers, and with six quick shots Merrick would effectively cut the head off the Qasaman invasion force.

Then he would die, of course, because there was no way he could get out of a ship full of enemy soldiers alive. But his death might buy a chance for the Azras team to pull out a victory.

Only it wouldn't be just *his* death, he realized with a sinking feeling. Anya would die, too, whether Merrick tried to take her with him or left her here. The Drim would certainly take revenge for their commander's death, and she was after all only a human and a slave. Commander Ukuthi would die, too. He was the one who'd brought the assassin aboard.

He was also the one to whom Merrick had given his pledge.

Slowly, he straightened his hands again, the flash of uncertainty and courage fading away into quiet frustration. What could he do? What *should* he do?

He had no idea.

[Your courage, I am impressed by it,] Ukuthi said quietly.

Merrick shifted his eyes to the Troft. Ukuthi was gazing at him, ignoring the sound and fury going on between Inxeba and the Azras ship commander, a knowing look on his face. [My courage, I have none,] Merrick said bitterly.

[Courage, you do have it,] Ukuthi insisted. [Inaction, the hardest task it always is. Yet inaction, the proper course it often is.]

[Commander Ukuthi, his attention I would have it,] Inxeba called angrily.

[Commander Ukuthi, his attention you have it,] Ukuthi said, turning away from Merrick.

[Balin'ekha'spmi warships, I request them,] Inxeba said. [A new force, I would send it to Azras.]

It seemed to Merrick that Ukuthi sent a small glance over his shoulder at the two humans. [Balin'ekha'spmi warships, I will not send them,] he said.

Inxeba's radiator membranes snapped rigid with surprise. [Your statement, repeat it,] he demanded.

[Balin'ekha'spmi warships, I will not send them,] Ukuthi repeated. [A trap, I believe this is one. Balin'ekha'spmi warships, I will not send them into ambush.]

Slowly, deliberately, Inxeba rose from his couch. [Balin'ekha'spmi warships, I demand them,] he said, his voice dark, his radiator membranes stretched to their limit. [Balin'ekha'spmi warships, I demand them *now*.]

[My answer, you already have it,] Ukuthi said calmly. [Drim'hco'plai warships, you may send them if you wish.]

For a long moment the room was silent except for the muffled sounds of battle coming from the speaker. Even the Azras commander had stopped talking. Keeping his head and body motionless, Merrick put target locks on both guards and on the small pistol holstered at Inxeba's side. His pledge to Ukuthi hadn't included defending the Balin commander from his own people.

Slowly, Inxeba's membranes folded back against his upper arms. [Glory, this operation will yet bring it,] he said, stepping back to his couch. [Glory, it will belong wholly to the Drim'hco'plai.]

He dropped onto the couch and gestured to one of his officers. [Two warships from Purma, they will travel to Azras,] he ordered. [Arrival, what is the time until it?]

[Floatator activation, there will be seventeen minutes until it,] the officer said. [Travel to Azras, eleven minutes will be required for it.]

[The order, give it,] Inxeba said. [Captain Vuma, his courage and determination are required. Assistance, in twenty-eight minutes it will arrive.]

[Captain Vuma, his strength and determination will be sufficient,] the voice from the speaker promised. [The attackers, we will hold them.]

[Commander Inxeba, he is pleased.] Inxeba's membranes fluttered. [Death, the enemy shall have it.] He looked balefully at Ukuthi. [And then glory, *we* shall have it.]

❖   ❖   ❖

They'd been searching the vehicle bay for five solid minutes, and Lorne was sifting rapidly and uselessly through a collection of laser actuators and cooling modules when he heard a short, sharp whistle from the small machine shop at the rear of the bay. "Broom? Akim?" McCollom called. "Got something."

They found McCollom and Jennifer leaning over a workbench tucked away between two stacks of meter-square metal plates that were strapped securely to the wall. The bench and the storage shelf behind it held a bewildering collection of tools and equipment. "What did you find?" Siraj asked as he and Lorne came up to the bench.

"For starters, these," Jennifer said, pointing to the plates. "They look to me like replacement hull plates."

"Yes, that makes sense," Lorne said, eyeing the plates. "And?"

She gave him an odd look. "*And* whatever weapons the Trofts are using against the Qasamans probably aren't designed to handle hullmetal," she said with exaggerated patience.

"She's right," Siraj said, keying his radio. "Ifrit Ghushtre? Send three men to the vehicle bay immediately, and then pull back to harassment positions. We've found something the spearheads can use as shields."

He got an acknowledgment and started unfastening the straps securing the plates to the wall. "I'll get these," he said. "McCollom?"

"On it," McCollom said, starting on the other set of plates.

"Hang on, I'm not done," Jennifer said. "If they want to put in replacement plates, they first have to take out the damaged ones, right? So I figure—"

"They must have a cutting torch somewhere," Lorne interrupted, stepping to her side and scanning the equipment at the back of the bench.

"And I figure something designed for hull plates should cut through deck plates like a laser through blue treacle," Jennifer continued. "You might be able to cut through the ceiling and climb up behind the Trofts while they're concentrating on the Djinn coming in the stairway."

"Can't do it from down here," McCollom told her, glancing

up at the bay's high ceiling. "That's too far for a cutting torch to reach."

Lorne felt his breath catch as an idea suddenly popped into his mind. "Not *up*," he said. "*Down*. We get on top of the ship, cut through the hatch up there, and *then* come in behind them."

"Nice," McCollom complimented him. "Problem: we're on Deck Six, the top of the ship is above Deck One. How exactly do you plan to get up there?"

"You'll see," Lorne said. "Siraj Akim, what happened to Gama Yithtra's *chalip*?"

"Still glued to the entry door," Siraj said, his eyes hard on Lorne's face. "You're not serious."

"Why not?" Lorne countered. "There were four adhesive pellets on each of the *chalip*'s cross-arms, and only two of the arms got triggered. That leaves eight pellets still available."

"That's not enough," Siraj said. "Wendell McCollom is right—it's a climb of nearly twenty meters. You can't do it in eight steps."

"Wait a minute," Jennifer said, frowning back and forth between them. "*Climb*? Climb where?"

"Along the outside of the ship," McCollom told her. "He's right, Broom. And you're not going to be able to jump from one and attach the next one in midair. The glue can't possibly set *that* fast."

"Trust me," Lorne said with a tight smile. "The trick is that once we get going, it'll be *ten* meters, not twenty."

McCollom huffed out a breath. "Okay, *this* one I have to see."

"Three minutes," Lorne promised. "Siraj, get someone to bring that *chalip* up here. McCollom, you and Jennifer find and assemble the torch. You know how to use one?"

"Probably better than you do," McCollom assured him.

"No argument there," Lorne agreed. "I'll go find something we can use as hand- and footholds."

There was a rattling sound from the main bay. Lorne tensed, then relaxed as he saw it was just the three Djinn Siraj had sent for. "And let's get it done before the grav lifts come on line. I don't want to do this from a thousand meters in the air."

❖   ❖   ❖

Three minutes later, right on schedule, they were standing at the bow end of the bay, watching as Lorne lowered the wide vehicle ramp.

But not all the way to the ground. In fact, he hardly lowered it at all, but only opened it enough to leave a meter-wide gap at the top.

A gap big enough for them to crawl through.

"I'll go first," Lorne said, sliding the makeshift pouch bouncing against his left to ride farther around his back. "Then Siraj, then McCollom. Jennifer, you stay here and watch the ramp. If it starts to drift—open *or* closed—give us a shout and try to get it back to where it is right now. Everyone ready? Let's go."

Lorne's initial worry was that the ramp would prove unclimbable. Fortunately, that turned out not to be the case. Not only did it have low ridges to aid with traction, but it had also collected a number of pits and cracks over the years that provided plenty of fingerholds. His second worry was that Siraj, who lacked both Cobra climbing training and lockable fingers, would have to be hauled up by one of the others. But apparently his Djinn instructors had recognized the possible need for scaling nearly sheer walls, and Siraj made it up the ramp with nearly as much ease as Lorne and McCollom. Within half a minute, all three of them were perched on the end of the ramp, gazing up the smooth hullmetal of the warship's bow.

"Nice view," McCollom grunted as Lorne pulled out the first of the wide, long armored-truck door hinges that he'd taken from the vehicle bay's collection of spare parts. "Especially the part of the view where we can't see the weapons pylons."

"If we can't see them, they can't shoot us," Lorne agreed. Getting to his feet on the end of the ramp, balancing himself cautiously, he reached as far up as he could and slammed the edge of the hinge firmly against the hull.

There was a yellow flash, and Lorne felt a brief wave of heat on his hand as the highly exothermic adhesive inside the pellet was exposed to the air. He held the hinge in place a few seconds, then cautiously gave it a pull.

The hinge didn't budge. He pulled harder, and harder, until he was hanging free with his full weight being supported. "We're in business," he told the others. "I'm heading up. Follow as you can."

Pulling himself up, he worked his way into a crouching position on the hinge, stood upright, and reached up to glue his second hinge to the hull.

Four minutes later, he'd made it to the crest of the ship.

He was at the stern, using his antiarmor laser to burn away the radar-absorption coating from around the dorsal hatch, when the others caught up to him. "Okay, the rest should be just standard hullmetal," he said as McCollom laid the torch's fuel tank on the crest. "Anything we can do to help?"

"Just stand clear," McCollom said, lowering a set of slightly-too-small goggles over his eyes and igniting the torch.

Lorne stepped back, wincing as a glimpse of the cutting jet tried to burn its way into his retinas before he could look away. Blinking against the afterimage, he peered out toward Azras.

And felt his stomach tighten. The city had paid heavily for those diversionary missiles Ghushtre had launched earlier. A huge section of the outer wall had been disintegrated, turned by the warship's lasers and missiles into a sixty-meter-long ridge of broken steel and masonry. Beyond it, nearly all of the first row of buildings had likewise been turned to rubble.

Lorne and his mother had urged that the Qasamans move the civilians out of that part of the city before the attack. Ghushtre and Siraj had argued in turn that suddenly underpopulated streets could tip off the invaders that something was about to happen.

As usual, the Qasamans had won the argument. Their sole concession had been to agree to put volunteers in the most dangerous zones, and to move them out as quickly as possible once the strike force and their commandeered trucks were on the move.

Distantly, Lorne wondered how many of those volunteers had made it out before the warship's lasers began collapsing the city around them.

Behind him, the acrid blaze of the torch winked out. "We're in," McCollom announced. "Who's going first?"

Lorne turned back, pushing the image of dead civilians out of his mind as best he could. McCollom had carved a groove in the hull around the hatch, burning through all three of its locks, and was carefully levering it open. "Definitely not you," he told the big Cobra, leaning over the open hatchway and listening closely. There were the sounds of laser and projectile fire down there, but it was all reasonably distant. Probably in the command section's main corridor. "You're way too easy a target."

"Besides which, Lorne Moreau and I are the only ones who've already fought inside one of these ships," Siraj added, handing McCollom the radio and starting down the ladder. "We'll be first and second. You'll be backup."

"Typical," McCollom grumbled. "Pick on the big guy, why don't you?"

"If it'll make you feel better, you can have first crack at getting the command room door open after we clear out the corridor," Lorne offered as he headed down behind Siraj. "Give Ifrit Ghushtre a call and warn him we're coming in."

The sounds of battle were much louder down here. As Lorne moved along the short corridor leading to the command area, he was able to pick out individual weapons as well as the sounds of grunted cattertalk, and tried to form a mental map of the enemy's deployment. All of the sound and fury was coming from the left, the direction to the stairwell the Qasamans had secured. He reached the corridor, motioned Siraj to stay back, and eased an eye around the corner.

The Trofts' defense was set up pretty much the way he'd envisioned it: a double row of armored aliens set up a few meters back from the stairway, one standing, the other crouching, all with lasers blazing toward the open door and the shadowy figures visible beyond. In the front-center of the group was a much larger wheel-mounted laser with a wide shield attached to protect its gunner. The Qasamans in the stairway were keeping up what Ghushtre had described during their practice sessions as a random-edge system: Djinn popping out at various places around the door edge, firing their glove lasers, and immediately withdrawing. A half dozen Trofts were lying motionless on the deck among the defenders, some of them surrounded by the scorch marks left by the handful of grenades the Qasamans had brought along. In the stairwell behind the Qasamans, he could see a pair of the hull plates Jennifer had found in the vehicle bay being readied for use as shields.

The right end of the corridor, in contrast, was silent. Lorne gave a quick look in that direction, expecting to find the area empty of both attackers and defenders. To his surprise, he found a mirror-image of the force currently engaging the Qasamans, this second force facing the other stairway with their backs to Lorne. Clearly, the Troft commander was expecting the attackers to eventually make a sortie through that door, and had laid out his forces in anticipation of that second front.

Lorne smiled humorlessly as he drew back again. Right idea. Wrong direction. Motioning Siraj forward, he gestured him to the right. Siraj glanced out, nodded acceptance of his part of the counterattack, and stepped fully out into the corridor, raising his glove lasers to the right. Lorne stepped out behind him, turning to the left, and flicked targeting locks onto the heavy laser's power pack and as many of the Troft hand weapons as he could see from his position.

And as Siraj's glove lasers began spitting fire behind him, he swiveled up on his right leg and fired his antiarmor laser.

The power pack went first, exploding in a burst of shrapnel that staggered the four aliens closest to it. A chopped second later Lorne's next group of shots took out the smaller weapons, their smaller blasts also sending their owners reeling. He heard grunts and screams of pain from behind him as he charged forward, targeting the rest of the aliens' weapons as he ran and firing his fingertip lasers to neutralize them.

And then he was in the middle of the rear line, jabbing at chests and throats with servo-powered fists and forearms, scattering the soldiers like sticks in a gale as they fell to the deck or first bounced off the walls before collapsing into individual heaps. There was a shout from in front of him, and he saw the Djinn from the stairwell rushing to his aid.

Bravely, but unnecessarily. By the time they reached him, it was all over.

"Very courageous," Ghushtre growled as he stepped over the stunned or unconscious Trofts. "Also very foolish. You have your lasers—why didn't you just kill them?"

"Because I'm hoping to talk the captain into surrendering," Lorne told him, breathing hard. His servos had done most of the actual work during the fight, but the adrenaline rush was still tingling through him. "Easier to do if we've demonstrated some restraint." There was the sizzle of a laser behind him, and he turned around.

Just in time to see McCollom vaporize the last of the hinges and throw himself shoulder-first against the command room door. With a teeth-aching sound of tearing metal the door collapsed inward and crashed to the deck.

And from the opening came a flurry of laser fire that once again lit up the corridor.

Cursing under his breath, Lorne sprinted for the door. He reached the open doorway, wincing at the laser shots flashing around him. Inside the room McCollom was on his back, his knees and torso curled inward toward his belly as he spun around in a circle, his antiarmor laser spitting fire across the command room.

Lorne glanced up, targeted the ceiling, and jumped.

The ceiling jump was one of a Cobra's pre-programmed reflexes, and as usual Lorne's nanocomputer performed the stunt flawlessly. Before his feet even left the floor the computer had taken control of his servos, tucking his head inward and spinning him a hundred eighty degrees around just in time for his feet to be uppermost as he reached the ceiling. His knees bent, absorbing the impact, then straightened again, shoving him off at a new angle with enough spin to turn him upright again as he hit the deck between two banks of monitor displays. As his knees bent again with the impact, he glanced around the room, putting quick targeting locks on the weapons trying to track toward him. His fingertip lasers fired their scattered shots, and once again broken weapons went flying. [Your firing, cease it!] he shouted into the chaos.

For a moment the Trofts froze, their lasers still held ready, their radiator fins fluttering with stress. Lorne took advantage of the pause to target the rest of the weapons in sight, knowing that McCollom would be doing the same. [Your captain, I would speak with him,] he said into the frozen silence. [His surrender, I demand it.]

One of the Trofts stepped forward, senior officer insignia on his leotard, his radiator membranes stretched fully out. [Captain Vuma, his surrender you will not have it,] he bit out. [The Drim'hco'plai, they do not surrender to aliens.]

[Then the Drim'hco'plai, they will die at the hand of aliens,] Lorne said flatly.

Vuma looked at the line of Qasamans now standing just inside the door, their own weapons aimed and ready. [The disgrace of surrender, I will not accept it,] he insisted.

Defiant words...and yet he was still talking. If he'd really been insistent on going out in a blaze of glory, he should have already done so. [Useless deaths, they also bring disgrace,] Lorne pointed out. [Courage, a good warrior must have it. Wisdom, a warrior must also have it.]

Vuma looked at the Qasamans again. [Our lives, do you guarantee them?] he asked.

[Your lives, I guarantee them,] Lorne promised. [Your weapons, your soldiers will lay them down. The nearest quarters, they will go immediately to them.]

[The exits, we will instead leave by them,] Vuma offered. [The ship, we will give it to you.]

[The nearest quarters, your soldiers will go immediately to them,] Lorne said firmly. [Three minutes, they have only them.]

Vuma's membranes fluttered. But he bowed his head and gestured to a Troft standing beside one of the consoles. [My words, broadcast them,] he ordered. [Soldiers of the Drim'hco'plai demesne, my surrender, I have given it. Your weapons, you must lay them down. Your quarters, you will return immediately to them.]

He gestured again. Silently, the Trofts in the command room laid their weapons on the deck. [Three minutes, you have only them,] Lorne reminded him. [Death, a Troft outside the quarters will receive it.]

[Your orders, we will obey them.] Turning, Vuma strode past the Qasamans and out into the corridor, the other Trofts following.

Lorne waited until they were all gone. Then, circling the console, he walked over to McCollom, who was still on his back on the floor. "I think that was the definition of damn fool," he commented, offering the big Cobra a hand.

"Hey, you *said* I could take out the door," McCollom reminded him, not taking the hand or getting up on his own. "Why should I let you and Akim have all the fun?"

"As long as you had a good reason," Lorne said, frowning down at him. "You all right?"

"Mostly," McCollom said. "A few small burns. Nothing serious."

"Except that you can't get up?"

"I'm sure I could," McCollom said in a dignified tone. "I just think it would probably hurt, and I don't want you to hear me swear."

Lorne looked over at Ghushtre. "Ifrit?"

"The medical area has been alerted," Ghushtre confirmed as he stepped to Lorne's side. "I'll have him carried there as soon as the invaders are clear of the corridors."

"Thank you," Lorne said, wincing as some of the pain from his own collection of laser burns started to throb their way through the fading adrenaline. "What do you think?"

Ghushtre looked down at McCollom, then back up at Lorne. "Too easy," he said darkly. "Far too easy."

"Agreed," Lorne said, nodding. "I'm guessing that he expects reinforcements any time now, and figures there's no point getting himself killed for nothing. Probably why he wanted to get out of the ship—he wanted the reinforcements to be able to come aboard with lasers blazing and not have to worry about hitting friendlies."

"Yes," Ghushtre said. "But as yet no other warships have left their positions."

"Probably still warming up," Lorne said. "If we hurry, we should still have time. I'll get downstairs and deal with the drones. You'd better call Azras and tell them phase two is on."

"Already done," Ghushtre said. "The explosives will be ready when you are."

"Good," Lorne said. "And have someone get Jennifer McCollom

up here. I want someone who reads cattertalk script to look over the weapon firing systems."

"I'll send for her," Ghushtre said, frowning. "You *do* remember that we can't use those weapons, don't you?"

"Of course," Lorne assured him. "But we may be able to at least get the lasers and missile tubes to swivel a little." He shrugged. "With a plan like this, it's all in the perception."

"Perhaps," Ghushtre said. "Just don't forget that once the warships leave Purma you'll have no more than ten or twelve minutes until their arrival."

"Don't worry," Lorne said grimly. "We'll be ready."

CHAPTER SEVENTEEN

It had taken a full day to get the new spore-repellent curtain set up at the south end of Stronghold's landing area, and Jody Broom's friends Geoff and Freylan had insisted on giving it another two hours of testing to make sure that the transportation and setup hadn't knocked anything loose. Harli had had a chance to examine it as he oversaw the operation, and had quickly concluded that the curtain was the ugliest stretch of cloth he'd ever seen in his life.

It was even uglier on the inside, where the Trofts were now gathered. But it worked, and that was all that mattered.

Not that he was expecting Captain Eubujak to comment on either the aesthetics or the practicality. He was expecting Eubujak to be sputtering mad about the prisoners' new accommodations, and he was right.

"This is unacceptable," Eubujak said, the emotionless tone of his translator pin in sharp contrast to the violent fluttering of his radiator membranes. "It is barbaric. There is no space, there are no sanitary facilities, there is no proper bedding—"

"There are two square meters of space each," Harli interrupted the tirade. He really didn't have time for this. "Sanitary facilities are right outside the curtain if you want them. As for the rest of it, there should be Tlossie ships arriving any time now to take you to a proper prisoner-of-war camp."

Eubujak glared at him a moment, probably waiting for the running translation to finish. "There will be consequences," he warned, gesturing toward the crazy-quilt patchwork rising over the Caelian greenery behind him. "The Drim'hco'plai demesne will not accept such treatment of its citizens."

"The Drim'hco'plai demesne should have thought of that before they decided to invade other people's worlds," Harli said bluntly.

Eubujak continued to glare. But as his eyes shifted from Harli to the Stronghold wall, half a kilometer to the north, his radiator membranes settled lower against his upper arms.

Harli smiled cynically. The Troft had certainly noticed their warship ferrying the civilians out of the city over the past few hours. The final group, in fact, had left just as the prisoners were being marched across the overgrown field to their new open-air quarters. Apparently, Eubujak had just put the pieces together and realized that once the last few Cobras had also left he could simply march his troops back to the deserted city and settle into the far more comfortable homes of its residents.

It was almost a shame to have to burst his bubble. Almost.

"Oh, and there's one other thing," Harli said, keying on his field radio. "Popescu? You ready?"

"We're ready," Popescu's voice came, sounding every bit as pleased as Harli was feeling. "Got a really nice load, too."

"Great," Harli said. "Go ahead and drop 'em."

From one of the clearings east of the city, one of Caelian's two air-transport vans lifted into view. It flew across the forest to the field of knee-high hookgrass and razor fern that the Trofts had just slogged through to their new quarters. As it reached the area between the curtain and Stronghold, the rear doors opened and one of the Cobras started tossing out objects that sent ripples through the grasses as they thudded to the ground.

Out of the corner of his eye, Harli saw Eubujak's radiator membranes starting to stretch out again. "What is this?" the Troft asked. "What do they throw from the vehicle?"

"Carcasses," Harli told him. "Dead animals. Hooded clovens, orctangs, giggers, maybe a saberclaw or two. Basically, everything they were able to hunt down and kill over the past couple of hours."

Eubujak looked at the transport, then at the ground, then back at Harli. "Explain," he demanded.

"Give it a minute," Harli said, keying his audios. Over the hum of the transport's grav lifts, he could hear the quiet whispering of small creatures moving through the flora around them.

And then, one of the bodies twenty meters away suddenly began writhing violently.

Eubujak's membranes snapped all the way out. "You said they were dead!"

"They are," Harli said as two of the other carcasses also began twitching. "Those are some of Caelian's scavenger animals—ratteeth and scrimmers, mostly, with probably some picklenose and a *lot* of different insects thrown in. We've just laid out the best buffet they've ever seen in their short, violent, miserable little lives."

He pointed to the edge of the forest, where his infrareds now spotted the tell-tale profile of a screech tiger. "And speaking of buffets..."

Right on cue, the screech tiger bounded from cover, driving a rippling shock wave through the grasses as it raced toward one of the twitching carcasses. From the other side of the forest, a pair of smaller wakes marked the arrival of giggers or saberclaws.

"It's kind of like those museum dioramas I used to see pictures of when I was a kid," Harli said as a flock of split-tails appeared and made a diving run over one of the shaking carcasses. Two of them shot back out of the grass a second later with mouse-whiskers clutched in their talons. "Pretty much the whole Caelian ecosystem is about to settle in right here in front of you. It'll be great fun—and *very* educational—for you to watch. Though I strongly recommend you do so from *inside* the curtain."

He looked significantly at Eubujak. "Out here, it's not going to be very healthy." He tapped the greenish patina of spores already collecting on the Troft's leotard sleeve. "Especially since you're starting to look a lot like lunch."

Eubujak looked down at his sleeve, then at the increasingly

active kill zone between him and the city wall. "There will be consequences," he warned again, and stepped back toward the curtain.

"Only if you try to come out," Harli said. "But don't take my word for it. Feel free to—"

"Harli!" Popescu's voice came urgently from the radio. "Harli, you there?"

Frowning, Harli keyed the transmitter. "I'm here," he said. "What's up?"

"Whistler just picked up visual on two bogies coming in from the east," Popescu said tautly. "Still too far away for a positive ID, but they sure as hell look like Drim warships."

Harli felt his throat tighten. "You sure?"

"Whistler is," Popescu said. "He said he tried hailing, but there was no answer."

Harli looked toward the east, cursing under his breath. The ships that the Tlossie demesne-heir Warrior had promised to send for the prisoners would be transports, not warships. And they definitely wouldn't ignore a hail.

The Drim reinforcements had arrived.

Only they'd arrived a whole damn day too early.

"Get inside," he ordered Eubujak, hooking a thumb toward the curtain. "Get *inside*. Now."

Eubujak flicked a look of his own toward the east. Then, without a word, he stepped back, pulled up the lower edge of the curtain and ducked down, and disappeared into the enclosure.

"What do you want us to do?" Popescu asked.

For a pair of heartbeats Harli gazed into the eastern sky, trying to think. Rashida and their one functional Troft warship should have dropped off the last load of civilians by now and be heading back to Stronghold to collect the rest of the Cobras. Probably no way they could make it before the new ships arrived.

Or maybe they could. Warrior had said that Drim warships couldn't fire on each other. If he was right about that, Rashida might just barely be able to bring the warship in, grab the remaining twenty Cobras, and hightail it out of here.

But hightail it to where? One of the other settlements, where the invaders would be sure to follow? Somewhere out into Wonderland, where the Cobras would have the lethal Caelian ecology to help take them out?

He glanced over his shoulder at the curtain. Whatever he decided, he realized suddenly, he first needed to move out of Troft earshot. He'd already seen how inventive Eubujak was at getting messages to his fellow Drims.

Unless Harli could come up with something he *wanted* the incoming warships to know about...

"Here's what you do," he told Popescu. Actually, now that he thought about it, the warships were probably monitoring their radio transmissions anyway. Still, better to double down on this one and stay close to the curtain. "First, get a message to Smitty and have him divert Rashida to the Octagon Caves. Tell him to forget the booby-trap. He's to get the missiles and the rest of the gear out of the chimney, load 'em aboard, and get 'em back here. Got it?"

"Whoa, whoa," Popescu protested, sounding thoroughly confused. "What—?"

"Shut up and listen, you stupid spelunker," Harli snarled. "Don't worry—between the construction crew and the ordnance team he'll have at least fifty Cobras to help him with the loading. While he does that, we're going to fire up the weapons on the downed ship. Our new guests should be flying pretty much straight over us, so we should be able to take out at least one of them before they know what's up. Got all that?"

"Yeah, I got it," Popescu growled. "And lay off calling me a spelunker. Do it again and I'll come over there and pop your wings off."

Harli smiled grimly. Popescu had gotten the message, all right. "I'd like to see you try it," he growled back. "Go on, get moving."

The predators were still churning up the hookgrass. Harli ran as close as he dared to the frenzy, then did a full-servo flying leap that took him safely over the feeding melee. He hit the ground running and headed for Stronghold.

Popescu was waiting for him at the broken section of wall, along with the last of the Cobras still in the city. "I hope that was an act," he said as Harli came up to them. "If it wasn't, I have no idea what you're up to."

"You got it just fine," Harli assured him. "You relay all that to Smitty?"

"Word for word," Popescu said. "So what's our part of the plan?"

Harli pointed at the Troft ship lying on its side. "Basically, we get inside the ship and wait," he said. "I'm figuring that between Eubujak and the newcomers' own eavesdropping they'll get the word that we're going to try to ambush him."

"I thought we couldn't do that," Popescu said. "Didn't Warrior tell you there was an IFF setup on the lasers that would keep us from shooting at other Drim warships?"

"Right, but Eubujak doesn't know we haven't found a way around that," Harli said, gesturing the others to follow and heading at a fast jog toward the downed ship. "I'm hoping one or both of the Drims will land and try to get to us before we can get the weapons activated."

"And when they come charging in we ambush them?" Popescu asked doubtfully.

"I know it's not much of a plan," Harli said, "but with something like seven to one odds against, making them come at us in mostly single file is the best we're going to get."

"Especially since they're not going to have any more experience than we do fighting inside a sideways spaceship." Popescu lifted his radio. "Torrance? We're making our stand in there. Kick everything off standby and run it to full power. Might as well make a good show of it for them."

"Got it," Torrance's voice came back. "I'll start making a list of good places to set up traps."

"Thanks." Popescu lowered the radio and pointed east. "Whistler estimated another ten minutes before they get here. That's not much time."

"We'll make it," Harli assured him. "I just hope Smitty and his crew can figure out what it was I was trying to tell them."

"And can pull it off?"

Harli grimaced. "Yeah. And can pull it off."

"Got it," Smitty said into the radio. "Going silent now. Good luck."

"You too," Popescu said.

Smitty keyed off the radio and busied himself at the control board. "Well," he said. "Nothing brightens up a dull day like an alien invasion. You two doing all right?"

"Sure," Jody said, trying to keep her voice from shaking as her heart thudded in her throat and her stomach tried to do pole-spins around her esophagus. The Drim reinforcements were a day early. A whole day early.

And she wasn't prepared yet. None of them were.

"I'm fine," Rashida said, and Jody felt a flash of envy at how much calmer the other woman sounded than she did. "But I'm confused by Harli Uy's message. I'm also not familiar with the word *verbatim*."

"That means Popescu gave us Harli's exact words," Smitty told her, tapping one final key. "Okay, I think I've sent you the course heading for the Octagon Caves. Did it come through?"

"Yes, I have it," Rashida confirmed, and Jody's inner ear registered the change as the ship angled onto a new vector. "We'll be there in approximately eight minutes. But I still don't understand the message. When did Harli Uy send fifty Cobras to the cave?"

"He didn't," Smitty said. "He and Popescu must have figured the Trofts were listening in on the conversation and had to make up a code on the fly. We just have to connect the dots to translate from what he *said* to what he *meant*."

Jody winced. And they probably had to do it in the next eight minutes, before they reached the caves.

"For instance," Smitty continued, holding up a finger. "Popescu's not a spelunker, which is a person who likes exploring caves. But I am. That says Harli's counting on my knowledge of the caves, and my skill at moving around in them."

"Right," Jody said, her brain starting to work again "He talked about a chimney, too. That's some kind of cave formation, isn't it?"

"A rock formation in general, yes," Smitty confirmed. "I know of at least three in the caves that can be climbed, the best one right off the rear of the main chamber."

"But there are no missiles there, correct?" Rashida asked, still sounding bemused.

"No missiles, and no fifty Cobras," Smitty confirmed. "I'm guessing both of those were Harli's attempt to dangle enough bait in front of the Drims so that at least one of the ships ignores Stronghold and the other towns and comes after us instead."

Jody winced. "Wonderful," she murmured.

"Hey, that's our job, Jody," Smitty reminded her soberly. "Well, maybe not *your* job, or Rashida's—"

"It's our job now," Rashida said firmly. "What about the rest of the message?"

"Right," Jody seconded, ashamed of her momentary twinge of self-pity. They had a job to do. Besides, her parents and brothers were undoubtedly in far worse danger on Qasama than she was here. "Harli talked about booby-traps. Was anything set up?"

"Not yet," Smitty said, and Jody thought she could hear a new note of respect in his voice. Probably for Rashida—she was certainly behaving more like a Cobra than Jody was. "That work was supposed to start tonight, after Stronghold was evacuated and the prisoners had been settled in their new home and we had a little breathing space."

"He also talked about the weapons in the downed ship," Rashida said. "But he can't actually use those, can he?"

"Not unless he's got a miracle up his sleeve," Smitty said. "That must be the same window-dressing as the missiles in the chimney—he's giving the invaders another target to go after."

"So if they're smart, they'll assign one ship to each of us," Rashida concluded. "And with the implied threat of immediate attack, we may hope they'll come after us quickly, without careful tactical thought."

"Exactly," Smitty said, nodding. "Your best chance when you're outnumbered this badly is to get the other side moving faster than they can think."

"Hopefully, that means he already has a plan for Stronghold," Jody said.

"Or else he's making it up as he goes," Smitty said. "Of course, he's also got twenty Cobras to work with. We've just got you two and me."

"*And* these," Rashida reminded him, lifting her arm to show the sleeve of her Djinni combat suit.

"For whatever that's worth," Jody said.

"Oh, it's worth a lot," Smitty said. "More than that—" He tapped the edge of his control board. "We've got this."

Jody frowned. "The sensors?"

"The ship," Smitty said. "You're forgetting Popescu's threat to pop Harli's wings off."

Jody felt her back stiffen. "*And* Harli saying he'd like to see Popescu do it."

"Exactly," Smitty said as he got to his feet. "I'll be right back. Jody, you'll have to keep an eye on the sensors."

"Where are you going?" Rashida asked.

"We've got everything we need to make one hell of a booby-trap," Smitty told her as he headed for the door. "Namely, a bunch of high-explosive missiles tucked under our wings."

He threw her a tight smile. "We just have to figure out a way to set them off."

[The images, what has become of them?] Inxeba demanded, gesturing angrily at the dark displays where the views from Azras had been up until thirty seconds ago. [Their return, I demand it.]

[The images, they cannot be returned,] one of the Drim officers reported, peering at his couch's board. [The images, they have been shut off at the source.]

Inxeba swore viciously. [Captain Vuma, I would speak with him.]

[Captain Vuma, he is not responding,] the officer told him. [Captain Vuma, I fear he has been taken prisoner.]

[Captain Vuma, you believe he has been taken prisoner?] Ukuthi asked. [Captain Vuma, you do not believe he has been killed?]

[Officer Cebed, he has misspoken,] Inxeba bit out, sending a glare at the Troft who'd just spoken. [Captain Vuma, he has most likely been killed.]

[The enemy war pattern, perhaps you know more of it than I

do?] Ukuthi suggested politely. [News from Caelian, the courier ship brought it?]

Deliberately, Inxeba turned to look at him. [News from Caelian, what would you know of it?] he demanded in a low voice.

[News from Caelian, I know nothing of it,] Ukuthi assured him. [Captain Vuma, I merely observe Officer Cebed assumed his capture. The enemy war pattern, I therefore conclude it to favor capture over death.]

[Captain Vuma's fate, it will ultimately reveal the enemy war pattern,] Inxeba said stiffly.

[The choice of capture, it reveals an enemy's confidence,] Ukuthi continued, as if talking to himself. [Such restraint, it has a strong appeal to the ethos of other Trof'te demesnes.]

[Your silence, I will have it,] Inxeba snarled off. He spun half around on his couch and glared again at Cebed. [The two Purma warships, what is their status?]

[The two Purma warships, they are ready to lift,] Cebed reported, sounding like he wished he was somewhere else.

[The delay, what then is its purpose?] Inxeba demanded. [The ships, send them at once.]

[The order, I obey it.] Hurriedly, Cebed keyed his board. [The ships, they are sent. Their arrival at Azras, eleven minutes there will be until it.]

[The time, perhaps it can be put to use,] Ukuthi suggested. [The situation at Caelian, I would like to learn of it.]

[The situation at Caelian, it is not your concern,] Inxeba said tartly. [The control of Caelian, the Drim'hco'plai were assigned it.]

[The truth, you speak it,] Ukuthi acknowledged. [Yet the enemy's war patterns, they would be useful to know.]

[The war patterns, those of the two human demesnes are different,] Inxeba said. [Your supremacy, only on Qasama have the Tua'lanek'zia granted it to the Balin'ekha'spmi.]

[The Tua'lanek'zia, perhaps they would believe it otherwise,] Ukuthi suggested.

[The Tua'lanek'zia, do you wish to ask it of them?] Inxeba countered.

For a dozen seconds the two Trofts stared at each other, their radiator membranes half extended. It was clearly some kind of confrontation, but like nothing Merrick had ever seen before.

It was also clear that there were high stakes being played for. He kept himself as motionless and unobtrusive as possible, wondering if Ukuthi was going to get caught up in the moment and forget his larger plan.

To Merrick's relief, he didn't. [The Tua'lanek'zia, I do not wish to ask it of them,] Ukuthi said, lowering his head in an abbreviated bow as his membranes folded themselves back onto his upper arms.

[The subject, it is then closed.] Inxeba shut his beak with an audible click, then turned back to the displays.

The minutes crept past. Merrick spent the time looking back and forth across the various city views, trying to guess what the Qasamans might be up to. But aside from the blank screens and the still suspicious-looking street work in Purma everything looked normal.

There were still two minutes to go until the Purma warships' arrival at Azras when the eight blank displays suddenly came to life again. [The enemy, their ignorance is now revealed,] Inxeba said with malicious satisfaction. [The drone sensors, that they can be activated by other Drim'hco'plai warships was unknown to them.]

Merrick studied the displays. They seemed to be in the same positions they'd been in when the cameras were cut off, hovering about fifty meters above the Azras cityscape. In contrast with the earlier shots, though, six of the eight monitors now showed streets that were largely deserted, with only a few people still visible. Only on the two that gave a view of the main gate—or rather, where the main gate had once been—was there any human activity.

And surrounding that activity was utter devastation.

Merrick felt his stomach churn. He'd gotten a glimpse of the destruction earlier, but the probes' cameras hadn't really been focused on that area before. Now, they were showing the Trofts' handiwork in all its terrible glory. A long section of the wall had been leveled, along with an entire row of the buildings just behind it. Dozens of people lay unmoving among the rubble, most

of them men but a few of them women. All were battered and
bloody, and all still had the bare arms and shoulders that had been
mandated by the occupying forces in their effort to thwart attacks
by combat-suited Djinn.

[The pavement, to the right look at it!] one of the officers said
abruptly, jabbing a finger at the edge of the monitor.

Merrick felt his stomach tighten. Barely visible amid the broken
stone and twisted metal was a crack in the street, perhaps half a
meter wide.

But it wasn't like the other cracks he could see, the ones presumably created by the falling buildings. This one was straight and
smooth, cutting across the pavement at perfect right angles. And
the men he could see working feverishly at its edges weren't digging out bodies, but seemed to be trying to remove a pair of long
girders, probably pieces of the wall, that had wedged themselves
into the opening.

Somehow, the attack by the warship had popped open one
of the entrances to the Azras subcity. Not only opened it, but
jammed it open.

With a pair of Troft warships only a minute away.

An unpleasant tingle ran through Merrick's skin. It was still
possible that the ships hadn't noticed the security breach. If Merrick acted right now, if he killed Inxeba and the officers in this
room before they could sound the alert, the Qasamans might have
a chance to get the gap sealed in time.

Once again, Merrick felt his hands curl into laser firing positions. Once again, hesitation at the thought of betraying his pledge
to Ukuthi slowed his resolve.

And then it was too late. [An opening, in the pavement there
is one!] the officer continued excitedly. [The subcity, it lies open
before us!]

[The opening, we see it,] someone on the warship acknowledged. [The soldiers, I am preparing them. A landing site, I have
located one.]

One of the display images scrolled sideways as the drone shifted
position, its sensors zeroing in on a spot of pavement twenty meters

back from the subcity entrance that had somehow managed to stay clear of rubble. The camera zoomed in on the site, touching momentarily on yet another group of bedraggled, bloodstained bodies lying amid the chunks of concrete as it panned across the area.

And Merrick felt his blood suddenly turn to ice. For a fraction of a second the camera had touched the casualties' faces...

Anya must have sensed Merrick's reaction. "What is it?" she murmured, leaning closer to him. "Merrick?"

Merrick took a deep breath, the air freezing in his lungs, his mind swirling with horror and helplessness, with unbearable pain and murderous rage. "One of the bodies," he murmured back, his voice shaking. "In the group there by all the rubble.

"It was my mother."

The dark spot was clearly visible in the cliffs rising in front of them when Smitty returned. "We there yet?" he asked as he crossed to the sensor station.

"I think so," Jody said, stepping away from his chair with a twinge of relief. Keeping tabs on his station and her own had been harder than she'd expected. More than ever she was glad he'd talked her and Rashida into letting him join their little piloting group. "As far as I can tell, it's the only cave around."

"Yep, that's it," Smitty confirmed as he resumed his seat. "The Octagon Cave complex. Thirty kilometers of the most beautiful caverns on Caelian."

"Never mind how they look," Jody said as she sat down and strapped in, giving the power displays a quick check. "My question is whether this thing will actually fit inside. That opening looks pretty small."

"Don't worry, it's big enough," Smitty assured her. "If not, I'm sure we can make it big enough."

"Oh, *that's* encouraging," Jody said. "I don't suppose you've actually measured it?"

"Not officially," Smitty conceded. "But I've walked in there a hundred times." He waved at his board. "Besides, I'm pretty sure the sensor readings are on my side."

Timothy Zahn

"I guess we'll find out," Jody said. "Rashida, if you turn out having to shave off something, shave off the topside. The bottom—"

Without warning the whole ship jerked hard, twisting and shuddering violently. Jody grabbed at her straps with one hand and the edge of her board with the other, clamping her mouth tightly to keep from accidentally biting down on her tongue. For a second the ship straightened out, only to start rocking again.

And suddenly, it lurched forward and to the right and then came to a halt at a forty-five-degree angle.

For a moment all three of them just sat there. Then, Jody exhaled a breath she'd somewhere along the line decided to hold. "I was about to say, the bottom is where most of the grav lifts are," she said into the sudden silence. "But never mind—I don't think we're flying this thing any farther today anyway."

"It would seem not," Rashida agreed. For once, even her usually calm demeanor sounded a little shaken. "I don't believe the opening was quite as large as you thought, Smitty."

"Well, it is now," Smitty said calmly. "Good flying, Rashida. You two sit tight while I get what's left of our cameras online and see what we've got to work with."

"Do we have any idea what's happening with the incoming ships?" Jody asked as she unstrapped and eased herself gingerly out of her canted chair and onto the canted deck. Everything seemed more or less steady, but she couldn't shake the feeling that the whole ship was teetering on a precipice, that it might suddenly break loose from wherever it was pinned and topple into some dark chasm looming beneath them. "I didn't want to mess with your settings while you were on your scavenger hunt."

"Yeah, I checked just before we hit the cave," Smitty said. "It looks like one of them landed at Stronghold, and the other one's heading our direction. I guess the chance to deal with some missiles and fifty Cobras was too tempting to pass up."

Jody looked at Rashida. The Qasaman had her calm expression on again, but her face looked a little pale. "Sounds like fun," Jody murmured.

"Don't worry, we can take them," Smitty assured her. "Remember,

I know these caves and they don't. Okay, here's the deal. The whole lower part of the ship is jammed into the floor, so the bow exits are out. The good news is that I was planning to use the dorsal hatch anyway. The even *better* news is that we're not going to have to jump or find ourselves a thirty-meter rope, because there's a big snake trail no more than three meters from the forward wing that'll take us the direction we want to go."

"What's a snake trail?" Rashida asked.

"A partially-open rock tube that runs along a cave's wall or ceiling," Smitty explained, getting to his feet. "I've never traveled this particular one, but it looks sturdy enough to hold our weight, and it's even big enough to stand up in."

"Where does it go?" Jody asked.

"Don't know yet," Smitty said. "Rashida, give me that other radio."

Rashida nodded and unclipped it from her belt. Smitty took it, turned it off, and fastened it beside his own radio. "Let's go."

He led the way down the corridor to the stairway leading to the dorsal hatch. Lying at the foot of the stairway was a large silliweave bag. "I found an arc welder down in the vehicle bay that someone missed," Smitty said, picking up the bag. "You two might want to stay here while I go rig it up to the missiles on the wing."

"We'll come with you," Rashida said firmly. "You may need a hand."

Smitty eyed her for a second, then nodded. "Okay," he said, starting up the stairs. "Watch your footing."

He reached the top, unfastened the hatch, and climbed out. Rashida was right behind him. Taking a deep breath, Jody followed.

It wasn't as bad as she'd expected. The hull crest was as badly tilted as the rest of the ship, but with the cavern roof pressing down to within a meter or two of the ship it was more like being in a sloping tunnel than being thirty meters above an unyielding stone floor. She eased over to one of the lower ceiling sections, got a reassuringly firm grip on a section of pockmarked rock, and looked around.

There wasn't a lot of sunlight seeping through the opening they'd just battered their way into. But there was enough for her to see that the chamber included a wide variety of different formations: curtains, stalactites, hourglass-shaped columns, and some hanging vine-shaped things she didn't have a name for. Most of the rock was dark, possibly some kind of basalt, but she could see a few layers of lighter stone, plus a generous sprinkling of glittering gem-like objects that added an eerie night-sky effect.

"Ready," Smitty called, and Jody looked over to see him walking carefully back from the aft wing onto the hull crest, Rashida beside him clutching his arm, the now empty bag tucked into her belt. One of Smitty's two radios, Jody noted, was gone. "Snake trail's over here."

The snake trail was just as Smitty had described it: a two-meter-diameter horizontal tube running along the ceiling near the ship's bow, with a section of its side wall open to the air. "You two feel comfortable enough with those suits' servos to jump on your own?" Smitty asked as they eased their way out onto the slanting forward wing. "If not, I can throw you over to it."

"No, we can do it," Rashida assured him.

"Okay," Smitty said. "I'll go first. Just watch me and do what I do."

He bent his knees slightly and jumped, ducking his head and drawing his knees up toward his chest as he arced through the air toward the tube. He slipped through the gap with a good half meter to spare and straightened out his knees again just in time to land upright. "Your turn," he said, turning and holding out his hand. "Nice and easy."

The jump was one of the most nerve-wracking things Jody had ever had to do. But she made it, and a minute later Smitty was leading them down the snake trail toward the rear of the chamber.

They were nearly to the back wall, and Jody had just noticed that their conduit abruptly narrowed a few meters ahead, when she heard the faint sound of approaching grav lifts. "Smitty?" she murmured.

"Yeah, I hear them," Smitty murmured back. "Okay, snake trail's ending. Looks like we're going to have to jump."

Gingerly, Jody eased her head out through the gap in the wall and looked down. The cavern floor had gradually risen as they'd neared the back wall, but there was still a good five meters of empty space beneath them. "You mean down, right?"

"Don't worry, your servos can handle the landing," Smitty assured her. "We drop, cross that ridge ahead, and the entrance to the chimney is just past that soda-straw formation to the left."

Abruptly, the edges of the cavern lit up with reflected light. Jody twisted her head around and saw a hint of crackling flame in the distance behind the wrecked warship. "Looks like they're laser-burning the foliage around the edge of the entrance," Smitty said. "Making sure we don't launch an ambush from out there."

He touched Jody's arm. "Come on. I'll go first."

CHAPTER EIGHTEEN

The two Troft warships had raced up toward Azras with almost frightening speed, fast enough that Lorne thought for a very bad few seconds that he'd cut his margins too close and that he wouldn't have enough time to pull this off. But then, to his surprise and relief, they coasted to a halt, one settling into position twenty meters above the broken section of wall, the other a hundred meters higher and fifty meters back.

And for the past minute and a half, they'd held those exact same positions.

"They're not going for it," he murmured to Ghushtre, standing behind him in the drone control/monitor room. "They smell a trap."

"Not necessarily," Ghushtre said, leaning over Lorne's seat and studying the displays. "Remember, they were coming to give battle to us in this warship. Now, they've suddenly been presented with a new goal. This may simply be the delay necessary for them to dress their soldiers in their armor."

"I hope so," Lorne said. "If whoever's in charge has come up with something clever, we could be in trouble."

"Whatever they hand us, we'll send it back down their throats," Ghushtre said with a deadliness in his voice that sent a tingle across the back of Lorne's neck. "What's the situation with the drones?"

"They're on their way," Lorne assured him, turning to the drone displays. The incoming ships had taken command of the drones long enough to turn their cameras back on, just as the Qasaman analysis of the invaders' radio operations in Sollas had guessed they could do. But the minute the Trofts had spotted the open SkyJo lair they'd apparently lost all interest in the drones.

Now, with the eight drones again under Lorne's control, the six that had been watching the deserted parts of Azras—the areas the invaders had presumably glanced at and dismissed—were drifting toward their new positions. Two of them were heading toward the warship still hovering low over the gate, moving as if to support the two drones currently feeding the invaders their view of the SkyJo lair. The other four drones were moving back and up, rising into the air above the second, higher warship.

"Movement," Ghushtre said.

Lorne turned back to the other bank of monitors. The lower of the two warships had stopped hovering and was sinking down into the clear spot the Qasamans had carefully prepared for it between the stacks of wall and building rubble. "Okay," he said, part of him relaxing a bit even as, paradoxically, another part of him felt the tension ratcheting up. The Trofts were back on track, which meant that the phase two strike team was that much closer to risking their lives in battle.

But there was nothing Lorne could do except make sure he gave them the best possible chance of living through the next hour. He watched the warship settle to the ground, then turned back to the drone controls, making sure the drones were on schedule—

"Game change!" an urgent voice came from the radio on the board in front of him. "The invaders are lowering the ramp. Repeat, the invaders are lowering the ramp."

Lorne spun back around, his breath catching in his throat. Lowering the vehicle ramp meant the Trofts had decided to roll out their armored trucks instead of coming out on foot through the bow doors.

Only that wasn't what the strike team was prepared for. And

unless they came up with a new plan, and fast, they were going
to be slaughtered right there in the Azras streets.

And Lorne's mother was right in the middle of it.

"Game change!" a barely audible voice came from the radio
lying half hidden beneath a thin piece of stone at Jin's head. "The
invaders are lowering the ramp. Repeat, the invaders are lowering
the ramp."

"God in heaven," one of the Qasaman Cobras murmured from
the pile of stone behind her. "Jin Moreau? What do we do?"

Keeping her eyes closed, knowing that the cameras in the warships' weapons wings would be watching everything, Jin slowly
turned her head just far enough for her opticals to see up along
the ship's bow. Sure enough, the ramp had been unfastened and
was starting to swing ponderously down toward the ground.

Only that wasn't what she and the strike team had planned
for. The Trofts were supposed to have seen all the rubble in the
area around the SkyJo lair, correctly concluded that their armored
trucks wouldn't make it five meters without getting hung up, and
sent the soldiers out on foot instead through the bow doors three
meters from her and the rest of the team. This was supposed to be
a variation of the operation Lorne's strike team had already pulled
off: a fast-break incursion and neutralization, only this one with
the added advantages that Lorne and the others in the captured
ship could provide.

"We can't let them get those trucks out," a new voice murmured
from the radio.

Jin shifted her attention to the other side of the warship's bow.
Beach was lying there with his half of the strike team, his face
grim behind the fake blood staining his forehead. "Agreed," she
said. "I'm reading five meters to the top of the ramp. How many
do we want to take with us?"

"I don't think anyone," Beach said. "Not until the portside wings
are down. Too big a chance they'll get blasted on their way in."

Jin grimaced. But it made sense. Just the two of them, her and

Beach, leaping suddenly to the top of the ramp before the gunners inside the warship could react, might make it inside. A whole squad trying it would be mass suicide. "We move just before the ramp hits ground and try to knock out the first truck in line," she said. "That'll block in all the others."

"Sounds good," Beach agreed. "Lorne, you said a few arcthrower shots up beneath the engine compartment would do it?"

"I said that that trick worked *once*," Lorne's tight voice cut into the conversation. "There's no guarantee I didn't just get lucky."

"It's still our best shot," Beach said.

"There's another solution," the Qasaman behind Jin said. "You two stay here and Domo Pareka and I will go in."

"No," Beach said. "I mean, you can take Jin's place if you want—that would be fine—but I have to go along. Arcthrowers are notoriously tricky, and none of you has had nearly enough practice with them."

"Which is why it has to be Beach and me," Jin agreed reluctantly. "Okay. Here it comes..."

"Wait a second," Lorne said suddenly. "How about if I put one of the drones in there instead? Neat and clean, and no one has to get shot at."

For a second Jin was sorely tempted. Going up against a whole vehicle bay's worth of Trofts and armored vehicles, just her and Beach, wasn't a plan with a huge margin for error.

But it wouldn't work, and she and Lorne both knew it. "No good," she said. "If you don't take out both portside wings the SkyJos won't be able to launch. If they can't disable the ship before it lifts and heads for the hills, we won't get the drones we need for phase three."

"So we don't get the drones," Lorne said doggedly. "Maybe if we—"

"No maybes," Jin said firmly. "There's no time for a whole new plan. We have to go, and we have to go now."

"But feel free to blow the wings as soon as we're clear of the blast zone," Beach added. "Jin?"

"Ready," Jin said. "On three?"

"On three," Beach confirmed. "One, two, *three.*"

Jin surged to her feet, trying not to think of the heavy lasers looming over her and sprinted the half dozen steps to the edge of the ramp. Bending her knees, she leaped straight up, caught the edge of the sloping metal right where it joined the hull and swung herself up onto her side. The first armored truck in line was waiting at the edge of the ramp, and a quick roll took her past the massive front wheel and underneath the vehicle.

Beach was already there, running his fingers along the smooth metal overhead as he looked for a likely target. "Watch your eyes," he warned, and triggered his arcthrower.

The brilliant lightning bolt lashed out from his little finger, lighting up the underside of the truck. Jin squeezed her eyes shut, again shifting her vision to her opticals. Picking a spot half a meter from where Beach was sending his fire, she added her arcthrower's high-voltage current to his.

For a second nothing happened. The truck didn't move, its driver possibly frozen with astonishment at having seen two dead bodies suddenly appear five meters off the ground and disappear under his vehicle. But she could hear the low rumble that meant the engine was still functioning. Clenching her teeth, she shifted her aim to a different spot and again fired the arcthrower.

"Keep at it!" Beach called over the roar. "I'm going to try something else." Before Jin could reply he swiveled around on his back, lined up his left leg on the inside of the front right wheel, and triggered his antiarmor laser. Trying to wreck or fuse the wheel mechanism? There was a flicker of movement to her left, and she turned her head to look.

Just in time to see an armored Troft crouch down and poke the muzzle of his laser under the truck.

Instantly, Jin flicked a target lock on the weapon and triggered her antiarmor laser. Her nanocomputer responded to the order by rolling her up onto her right hip and twisting her left leg around to line up the laser, then sending a flash of blue fire into the alien's weapon. It shattered in his hand, staggering him back. Jin fired again, this time into his torso, and he fell backward onto the deck and didn't move.

She grimaced. One down. Dozens, maybe hundreds to go.

And until she and Beach managed to immobilize the truck, they were going to be trapped under here, with a limited firing range and near zero maneuverability. All the Trofts had to do was line up along the sides and start shooting, and it would be all over.

"Blast it, Lorne," she snarled under her breath. "Where *are* you?"

"They're in!" the radio announced. "In, and under."

Ghushtre slapped Lorne on the shoulder. "Go."

"Already going," Lorne snapped, his tension crackling all the way to his fingertips as he keyed the controls. Like he needed Ghushtre or anyone else to tell him.

The four drones that had been hovering innocently above the backup ship, out of view of its mostly downward-looking cameras, were dropping now toward the weapons wings. At the same time, the two drones that had been flanking the grounded ship were drifting more subtly toward its portside wings, the ones that pointed into the city and had the best angle on the half-open SkyJo lair.

A sudden, odd thought flicked across the back of Lorne's mind: whether in the urgency of the moment it had ever occurred to the Troft commanders in Sollas to wonder what the Qasamans might have done to the drones during the minutes when Lorne had been blacking out their transmissions. With a sudden, final surge all six drones rounded their designated wings and came up beneath them, nestling in close to the weapons clusters— "Now," Lorne said. Behind him, he heard the click as Ghushtre triggered the radio transmitter.

And with a multiple, stuttering roar, the bombs the Qasamans had packed aboard the drones exploded.

"*Yes*," Lorne hissed under his breath, curling his hands into tight fists. The brilliant yellow-white of the blasts quickly turned to reddish black as the fireballs faded and mixed with bits of shattered warship. The last bits of fire vanished into the expanding cloud of debris, and Lorne tightened his fists even harder as he waited anxiously to see if the Qasamans' gamble had paid off.

It had. The upper backup ship was reeling violently, wobbling like a drunken politician as it fought to maintain altitude after the multiple shocks to its hydraulic, control, and power systems. As it twisted around, Lorne got a clear view of both sides, enough to see that all four of its weapons wings had been disintegrated.

"Misfire!" the radio barked suddenly. "Forward-portside-beta has not triggered. Repeat, forward-portside-beta has not triggered."

Lorne's heart seemed to freeze. The forward portside weapons cluster on the lower ship covered the side of the ramp that Lorne's mother had just jumped up onto. That was also the side any Qasaman reinforcements would have to use to follow her and Beach inside. If that cluster was still active— "Ghushtre!" he snapped.

"Trying," Ghushtre said tightly, toggling the firing switch again and again. "It's not working. A connection must have been lost."

"We have to do something," Lorne insisted, his stomach churning as he stared at the ship squatting at the edge of the city a kilometer away.

But there wasn't anything that could be done. With both forward weapons clusters still intact, the warship had the ramp completely covered, blocking any chance for Jin or Beach to escape or for any Qasamans to reinforce them. Even worse, the fire zone of the undamaged portside cluster covered the two closest SkyJo lairs, the ones that should even now be disgorging a stream of attack helicopters that could quickly batter the alien warships to rubble.

And unless the commanders in Azras could make that happen, and fast, Lorne's mother would die. This final gamble would be lost, and Qasama and the Cobra Worlds would remain under Troft domination. Maybe forever.

"Don't underestimate them, Lorne Moreau," Ghushtre said quietly. "You and I may be out of the fight in here. But they aren't. They *will* find a way."

"They who?" Lorne asked, his frozen mind barely even registering Ghushtre's words. "My mom and Beach?"

Ghushtre rested his hand reassuringly on Lorne's shoulder. "Your mother and Everette Beach... and the Qasamans."

[The three Purma warships, they will proceed immediately to Azras,] Inxeba snarled, his radiator membranes fluttering with

consternation or surprise or rage. Probably, Merrick thought, mostly
rage. [Captain Geceg, he will be in command of them. Captain
Zimise and Captain Dinga, they will withdraw immediately to
rendezvous with him.]

[Captain Zimise, his floatators are malfunctioning,] Officer Cebed
reported, his membranes showing even more agitation than his
commander's. [Captain Zimise, he warns his warship may need
to be grounded for safety.]

[Safety, there is none of it in war,] Inxeba retorted. [Captain
Zimise, he *will* withdraw toward Purma. The order, you will send it.]

[The order, I obey it,] Cebed said reluctantly. [Captain Dinga,
his floatators are also malfunctioning. The floatators, they must
be restarted.]

[The floatators, they will *not* be restarted,] Inxeba snarled. [Cap-
tain Dinga, he *will* seal his ramp and lift his ship. Captain Dinga,
he will then kill the enemies in his vehicle bay.]

He turned challenging eyes to Ukuthi. [Commander Ukuthi,
has he objections to this path?] he demanded.

[Commander Ukuthi, he is content to allow you to choose
the path,] Ukuthi said calmly. [The results, I will be interested in
seeing them.]

Merrick swallowed hard. If the warship lifted with his mother
and Beach still inside, all hope for them would be lost. Did Ukuthi
realize that? Or did he simply not care?

Or could it be that he had some inkling of what the Qasamans were
planning, and had no intention of sharing that insight with Inxeba?

[The results, you will see them soon,] Inxeba promised, turning back to the displays. [The order, give it. The victory, it will
soon be ours.]

Beach's antiarmor laser stopped firing, and Jin glanced over to
see a reddish glow coming from the wheel mechanism he'd been
firing at. If he hadn't slagged the mechanism into uselessness, she
guessed, it wasn't ever going to happen.

Still, it wouldn't hurt to be sure. She fired another arcthrower
burst into the engine, and then another.

And with a violent shudder, the engine finally went silent.

Jin took a deep breath. They'd done it. The truck was disabled, and the other four vehicles lined up behind it were now well and truly trapped.

Only as she paused to evaluate the situation, she realized with a sinking sensation that the risk she and Beach had taken had been rendered moot. Outside the bay, she could see the flashes of laser fire coming from above—not the fire of SkyJos, with their distinctive rotor sound, but fire from one of the warship's weapons clusters. Somehow, the Qasamans' drone attack had failed.

And with that failure, she and Beach were dead.

She looked at Beach, found him looking back at her. "I think," he said, "we'd better find a way out of here."

"Agreed," Jin said, shifting her eyes again to scan what she could of the rest of the bay.

Only there wasn't anywhere to go. Armored Troft feet were hitting the deck all across the bay as the soldiers who'd been inside the trucks scrambled out to deal with this new threat to their ship. Even if Jin and Beach had time to get out into the open before the Trofts began firing, there was only so much their nanocomputers and programmed reflexes could do. In an enclosed space, even this large an enclosed space, the kind of firepower about to be brought to bear would kill them within seconds.

Outside, the flashes of laser fire seemed to intensify, and Jin felt a new vibration against her back as the ramp started rising again from the ground. With all hope of an armored sortie now thwarted, the Trofts were sealing the ship, probably in preparation for getting the hell out of Azras.

And once the ramp was closed, there would literally be nowhere for Jin and Beach to go.

A pair of Trofts moved suddenly into view alongside the truck. Jin rolled partially over and gave them each a shot from her anti-armor laser. Not that the ramp had ever offered any real chance anyway. With one weapons clusters on each side of the ship still intact, the whole ramp area would be open to Troft attack.

Or rather, most of it would be. Abruptly, Jin's mind flashed back to Lorne's own daring climb up the outside of the other warship during the phase one attack. He and McCollom had shown that there was a blind spot at the very end of the ramp just as it rose into its closed position.

Of course, here there would be no chance of stopping it partially open the way Lorne and McCollom had. There would certainly be no time to climb it like they had.

But if she and Beach could get out from under the truck without getting themselves killed, there should be enough time for Jin to throw Beach up the ramp to the far end before it sealed itself shut. From there he might be able to jump all the way to the top of the ship, or possibly to one of the nearby Qasaman buildings.

Or maybe he could get onto the wing and destroy the remaining portside weapons cluster.

A rush of painful memory flooded back in on her as she thought back to Caelian and her own attempt to pull that stunt. She'd succeeded, but had nearly died in the process.

But if she could survive, there was a chance Beach could, too. And even the small odds out there were better than the nonexistent ones in here. "Beach—"

"Ramp's closing," he cut her off. "Roll over here, will you?"

"There's no time—"

"When I give the word, we're going to get out from under here, and I'm going to throw you up onto the end of the ramp," Beach continued. "Got it?"

Jin felt her mouth drop open. "That was *my* idea."

"It's mine now," Beach said. "No time to argue. Get over here—" He broke off, spinning to the side and sending a Troft sprawling to the deck with an arcthrower jolt. "Get over here and let's do it."

There was a movement beside Jin, and she again turned up onto her side as a trio of Trofts sprinted toward her. "All right," she called to Beach, targeting the attackers. "I'll be right—"

She jerked violently back as, without warning, a huge slab of concrete dropped out of nowhere, slamming into the Trofts she'd been about to shoot and throwing them to the deck amid a cloud of white dust and an impact that seemed to shake the whole ship.

Jin had just enough time to blink at the slab in disbelief when, all around her, she heard and felt the heavy thuds of a dozen more impacts. Somewhere behind her a Troft shouted in rage or agony—

And from the direction of the still-rising ramp came a firestorm of laser bolts, crackling the air and throwing a flickering blue glow across the walls and deck.

Against all odds, against the awesome firepower of the warship's heavy lasers, the Qasamans had arrived.

And as the firestorm continued against the screams and panicked footsteps of the Troft soldiers, Jin finally focused her full attention on the slab of concrete lying on the deck beside her. On the heat-stress cracks all through it, on its burned and blistered upper side...

"Jin Moreau?" a Qasaman voice called anxiously.

"We're here, Domo Pareka," Jin called back. "Under the truck."

"Stay there," Pareka ordered, and as Jin lifted her gaze from the half-melted concrete she could see from the reflected laser light that the Cobras' attack was moving back through the bay. "Give us a moment to clear them out."

"Nice to have someone else take point for a change," Beach murmured from his side of the truck. "I just hope they didn't lose too many getting in here."

"I don't think so," Jin said. "It looks like they grabbed chunks of the broken buildings and wall and used them as shields while they ran up the ramp."

"Nicely done," Beach said approvingly. "Also amazingly done. Those slabs are heavy as hell."

"You'd be amazed at how far sheer stubbornness will take someone," Jin said, listening with half an ear to the battle. It was all the way in the back now, and was definitely winding down. "But all the stubbornness in the world won't help the SkyJos," she added. "We still have to knock out that weapon cluster."

"Yeah, well, I've got an idea on that one," Beach said.

Jin's stomach tightened. "Just bear in mind that I'm the only one who's ever actually pulled it off," she warned him. "If anyone's going to do it, I am."

"Actually, I've got something a little safer in mind," Beach said. "Come on—sounds like the fighting's about over."

They crawled out from under the truck to find that the fighting was indeed over. A few of the Qasaman Cobras were at each of the two stairwell doors, listening closely or else firing at the door jambs with their fingertip lasers. The rest were going methodically through the trucks and other vehicles, checking to make sure no one was still hiding inside. "Are you all right?" Pareka asked, hurrying toward them. "There's no time to lose—we have to find a way to get you out and to safety."

"What happened out there?" Jin asked. "It sounded like only one of the drones exploded."

"Yes, the one planned for the forward cluster failed," Pareka said. "And with weapons still on both sides of the warship, the SkyJos can't lift from their lairs without risking destruction. The warship is preparing to lift, and we find that the retreating invaders have welded the stairway doors against us."

"Not a problem," Beach assured him. "We have—"

"You don't understand," Pareka said sharply, changing direction toward the ramp controls and waving Jin and Beach to join him. "Once you're safely outside—we'll detach two of the truck doors for you to use as shields—we'll need to force the stairway doors and try to reach the control room before the ship escapes."

"And you think we're just going to run off and leave you?" Jin asked.

"You of the Cobra Worlds have done your share, Jasmine Moreau," Pareka said firmly. "In truth, you've done far more than your share. The rest of the fighting—and the dying—will be ours."

"Or we could do it without any dying at all," Beach suggested, extending a finger to point at the nearest truck. "You see those trucks, Cobra Pareka? You see those swivel guns on their roofs?"

"Of course," Pareka said impatiently. "How else do you think we plan to breach the stairwell doors?"

"And do you see *that*?" Beach continued, turning his finger to point at the machine shop at the far end of the bay. "Behind that bulkhead—behind, above and below—is the ship's engineering section. Where all the generators are. Including the ones that power the grav lifts and the weapons clusters."

For a second Pareka just stared at him. Then, his lips twisted in a tight smile. "And you think the swivel guns can penetrate the bulkheads?"

"All I know is that even warships have to save weight somewhere," Beach said, setting off at a fast stride toward the rear of the bay. "I see eight trucks and eight swivel guns," he added over his shoulder. "I've got dibs on the one at the rear. Get your people inside the others, and let's give it a try. Sooner or later, if we keep at it, we're bound to hit something vital."

Three and a half minutes later, they did.

[Captain Dinga, he urgently requests assistance,] Officer Cebed reported tightly. [Emergency battery power, his ship relies now upon it. His weapons, they are no longer functional.]

[Captain Dinga, do his soldiers do battle with the enemy?] Inxeba demanded.

[The enemy, they are barricaded inside the vehicle bay,] Cebed said. [The enemy, they have contented themselves with crippling his ship.] His membranes twitched abruptly as he leaned closer to his board. [The drones, the enemy has remote-accessed them,] he said, sounding bewildered. [The drones, the enemy has flown all twelve from Captain Dinga's ship.]

[Captain Zimise, he reports the Azras SkyJos have risen from their lairs,] one of the other officers spoke up. [Six SkyJos, they are flying toward Purma.]

[Captain Dinga, he confirms the report,] Cebed said, still sounding confused by the drones' mass exodus. [Two drones, they are now being flown in point before each of the SkyJos.]

Inxeba gave a rasping snort. [Foolishness, the enemy has it,] he said contemptuously. [Their plan, I see it. The ally-identification system, they believe the drones to be connected with it. The drones, the enemy expects them to prevent the warships from firing upon the SkyJos.]

[Captain Geceg, he reports his warships are in visual range of

Azras and the approaching SkyJos,] the third officer spoke up. [The SkyJos, do you wish them destroyed?]

[Their destruction, it will not be yet,] Inxeba said. [The SkyJos, they will be allowed to fly closer. The enemy's hopes, I will allow them to remain a few minutes longer. The enemy's confidence, I will then shatter it in a single thrust.]

He turned to Ukuthi, seated quietly on his couch. [And the honor of the Drim'hco'plai, it *will* be restored.]

CHAPTER NINETEEN

"There they go," Popescu announced, craning his neck and looking up at the display hanging in midair over them in the sideways control room. "Rather, here they come. I guess they're done talking to Eubujak."

"They stayed in the air the whole time?" Kemp asked.

"Yeah," Popescu said. "Too bad, too. I was hoping they'd put down in the middle of our Wonderland buffet and try to walk over to the cage. Or better yet, land right on top of the curtain and let Wonderland in."

"You couldn't have seen anything anyway," Harli pointed out, resting his hand on the edge of the command room's power-control console and trying not to let the weirdness of the sideways room get to him. He hadn't spent much time inside the downed ship, and he'd never gotten used to walking on bulkheads while decks and ceilings pretended to be walls. Or looking up at consoles and control panels jutting out from those walls, or maneuvering through doors that were now wide slits halfway up the walls. "The wing would have blocked your view."

"I know," Popescu said. "But it would have been nice to think about."

"Dream on," Kemp said, stepping around a circuit-test setup that someone had left behind and crossing over to Harli. "Everyone ready?" he asked quietly.

"As ready as we can be," Harli said. Which, he admitted silently, wasn't very much. "There's really only one door they can come at us through, assuming they don't want to launch their assault from hovering aircars or long ladders. I've got a layered defense down there, and Whistler's doing what he can to put a few barriers in place. I've also got some small booby-traps on the other two doors, just in case they decide they like aircar assaults."

"Sounds good," Kemp said. "Though of course you realize that with their numerical advantage we could take out the first four waves and still end up on the short end."

"Yes, I used to get medals in simple math," Harli said dryly. "Not to mention that even if by some miracle we were able to clean out this one there's another whole ship over at the Octagon Caves. Unless Smitty pulls off his own class-A miracle, we'll eventually have that bunch to deal with, too."

"Maybe," Kemp said. "But don't sell Smitty short. Between him, Jody, Rashida, and the caves, he could pull it off."

"Here they come," Popescu reported. "Making a long circle back over Stronghold. Maybe they bought your bluff about being able to shoot them down."

"We'll find out soon enough," Harli said, mentally running through the traps and blocks he'd put around the dorsal hatch. That was the only way in that didn't involve coming in under the downed warship's weapons.

Of course, that entrance was also seven meters above the ground, with all the tricky aircar or ladder logistics.

Unless the newcomer put his ship right up against the downed ship's upper side and rigged some kind of ramp from somewhere to the dorsal hatch. Harli hadn't thought about that possibility.

But that would require the ship to land inside Stronghold, and there wasn't a lot of room to spare inside the wall. They would probably have to level a few buildings first, which would give the Cobras plenty of time to shift more of their defenses to that end of their refuge.

"Whoa—there they are," Popescu said suddenly. "Coming across straight overhead."

And without warning the ship suddenly bucked like a stung horse, sending equipment flying as a muffled double explosion rocked the room.

Harli grabbed for the console beside him, shaking his head sharply against the ringing sensation echoing through his ears. He swallowed once, swallowed again—

"—completely gone," Popescu's distant voice faded in through the aftershock. "Say again: both wings are blown to hell."

A hand grabbed at Harli's arm, and he looked down to see Kemp struggling to his feet, a trickle of blood running down the side of his head. Beside him, a circuit multitester with a freshly cracked display and torn wire connecters had a spot of the same bright red on one corner. "You okay?" Harli called as he helped Kemp back to his feet.

"Sure—fine," Kemp called back, wincing as he wiped away the blood. "I guess you *can* fire on another Troft ship."

"Yeah, but you probably need a special passkey to do it," Harli said. There was another, smaller thud, a vibration mostly felt through the bulkhead they were standing on. "Sounds like he's down," he said. "Any idea where he landed?"

"Nope—the cameras went when he blew up the wings," Popescu said. "You want me to call down to Whistler and have him send someone outside to look?"

"No, don't bother," Harli told him. "It doesn't really matter—"

He broke off, a sudden surge of adrenaline flooding into him.

He was wrong. It *did* matter where the invaders had put down. It mattered a hell of a lot. "Kemp, take command," he said, heading for the horizontal door. "Make sure Whistler's ready to receive company."

"Where are you going?" Kemp called after him as Harli grabbed the door jamb and pulled himself through.

"Out," Harli called back through the door. "Back in five."

The traps he'd set up at the dorsal hatch were simple ones, and it took him only a minute to deactivate them. For a moment he held his ear against the hatch itself, his audios at full power as he listened for any sound of activity.

Nothing. Unfastening the hatch, he pushed it open, and eased his head through the opening.

The broken and battle-scarred city lay stretched out before him in the afternoon sun. Fortunately, the scene wasn't further blighted by the presence of armed Trofts, either on the ground or patrolling the sky. Getting a grip on the upper edge of the hatchway, he ducked through the opening, standing precariously on the lower edge. Above him, the starboard side of the hull crest rose another seven meters into the sky, tall enough to block his view of the newly arrived ship.

He focused on the hull. It was fairly smooth, certainly comfortable enough to walk on in the ship's usual upright position, but hardly designed for climbing. But at the very top of his view was a monstrous tangle of broken and twisted metal where the aft weapons wing had been before the incoming Trofts blew it to shrapnel. If he could jump up there and get a handhold on one of those pieces, he should be able to see exactly where the other ship had put down.

Assuming, of course, that he didn't slice his fingers off on the torn metal. But it was the only way. Putting a targeting lock on the sturdiest-looking ribbon to give his nanocomputer the range, he carefully bent his knees—

"So when you said *out*," Kemp's voice came from the direction of his shins, "you really meant it."

Harli jerked, nearly losing his grip, and peered into the hatchway. Kemp was standing there, looking out at him. "What the hell are you doing here?" he demanded. "I gave you an order."

"I wrote myself a medical excuse," Kemp said, pointing at the blood still trickling down his head. "Popescu and I thought someone should see what you were up to and find out if you needed a hand."

"I had an idea, that's all," Harli said, gesturing up the side of the hull crest. "It suddenly occurred to me that Eubujak probably told the other Troft captain that we'd been setting up booby-traps."

"Which we hadn't gotten around to yet."

"Which Eubujak doesn't know," Harli reminded him. "More importantly, he doesn't know whether these supposed traps are in the ship, in Stronghold, or out in Wonderland. Given all that uncertainty, where's the absolute safest spot for a clever and cautious captain to land his ship?"

Kemp shook his head. "No idea."

"Come on, it's obvious," Harli said, hoping desperately that it really *was* obvious, that his mind wasn't playing some macabre trick on him. "The one place where he can actually see the ground, and not a waving field of hookgrass that could be hiding a collection of pressure mines—"

"Is right where the other ship was before Rashida flew off with it," Kemp interrupted, his eyes going wide. "You're right. Hell in a handbasket. You got confirmation?"

"I'm about to," Harli told him, stepping out of the opening and up onto the edge of the hatch. "As long as you're here anyway, make yourself useful. Lean out here and catch me if I don't stick the landing on my way back."

He looked up at the broken metal, took a deep breath, and jumped.

Survival on Caelian, his Cobra instructors had often told him, was less a matter of courage or brute strength than it was a matter of timing and precision. Over the years Harli had taken that advice to heart, and he reached the top of his leap with his outstretched hands precisely at the torn metal ribbon he'd been aiming for. He hooked his fingers gingerly around it and held on as he let his residual momentum and swaying dampen out. Then, slowly and carefully, he pulled himself up until he could see the top of the alien ship.

And for the first time in days, he smiled.

Kemp was holding the hatch steady as Harli slid back down the hull crest and landed on its edge. "Well?" he asked, holding his other hand where Harli could grab it for balance if necessary.

"He is indeed clever and cautious," Harli confirmed. "I think we're in."

"Terrific," Kemp said. "Assuming it's still set up."

"It is." Harli turned and looked at the work station a hundred meters away beside the broken wall, a sobering thought suddenly occurring to him. "Of course, we *will* be visible to the other ship's wing cameras over there."

"You're right," Kemp muttered. "Ouch. Any thoughts?"

Harli looked down at the hatch cover he was balancing on. Too small to be a useful shield, even if they could get it off quickly enough. There were other, heftier slabs of metal inside the ship, but it would take equal amounts of time to get them free and most wouldn't pass through the hatch opening anyway.

He shifted his focus to the ground below them. The matted hookgrass was a good sixty centimeters tall and completely filled the space between them and the work station. It could theoretically be crawled through if they didn't mind running into a few unpleasant animals and insect nests along the way.

Unfortunately, sixty centimeters wasn't nearly tall enough to hide them, especially from cameras that would be looking more or less straight down.

On the other hand, it wasn't *just* hookgrass down there. "You've been tramping back and forth through that stuff more than I have," he said, keying in his telescopics for a closer look at the tangled plants. "How much blue lettros did you spot mixed in?"

"Enough," Kemp said thoughtfully. "It'll be risky, though. The stuff burns like hell once you get it going, and the razor fern is even worse. It's also growing right through where the wall used to be, which means there's a fair chance we could burn down the whole town."

"Noted," Harli said. "But it's still our best shot. You'd better get back and warn Popescu and the others."

"Popescu and the others will figure it out for themselves," Kemp said firmly, swiveling around to dangle his legs out the hatchway. "Ready?"

"Ready," Harli said. "You take north; I'll take south."

Their antiarmor lasers flashed in unison, blazing across the landscape as they traced out patterns through the mix of grasses below. Harli keyed in his infrareds, spotted the hot spots he'd created, and sent another blast into each of those areas. A few seconds later the smoldering blue lettros popped out small yellow flames that began to grow and spread. He shifted his attention to the edges of the fires, located the telltale trail of sub-flashpoint ribbon vine and fired another laser blast into it. More flames popped up, and tendrils of oily black smoke began to rise into the air. Harli kept firing, nurturing the growing flames, watching out of the corner of his eye as Kemp similarly worked his end of the field.

And then, all at once, the whole expanse ignited, the flames leaping up almost instantly obscured by the billowing clouds of smoke.

Harli set his teeth, wincing as the first blast of hot air blew up across his face. This was *not* going to be fun. "Last chance to go warn Popescu," he shouted to Kemp.

"We're wasting time," Kemp shouted back. "Last one to the work station's a cooked egg."

Lurching forward, he dropped off the edge of the hatchway and disappeared into the smoke and flame. Taking a final deep breath, squeezing his eyes shut and keying in his opticals, Harli jumped after him.

He hit the ground hard, the landing sending up a double splash of bright sparks and flaming vegetation as he bent his knees to absorb the impact. The smoke and flames were all around him now, tingling his nostrils and washing waves of heat against his clothes and skin. Through the blaze of infrared he could just barely see Kemp already charging through the inferno.

Belatedly, it occurred to him that if the fire made it to the work station before he or Kemp did, this whole thing would be for nothing. Clenching his teeth against the heat and rapidly increasing pain, he set off at a dead run.

He didn't remember much of the trip afterward. The only thing he was ever able to fully recall was the terrible agony as the fire burned across his skin and hair, the acrid smell of the smoke eating away at his throat and lungs, and the quietly horrifying fear that his eyes would be destroyed despite the forearms he had pressed across his face. His feet pounded against the ground, his servos pushing him along faster than his own muscles could ever manage, the cooling wind that would have normally accompanied such a race turned by the fire into a furnace blast. He struggled

on, knowing it was their only chance, knowing that Kemp wasn't
going to give up and that he damn well wasn't going to either—

And then, suddenly, he was in clear, cool air again. Five meters
ahead, he saw Kemp stumble and collapse to his knees beside the
work station, small flames still burning on the half-melted silliweave fabric on his shoulders and upper thighs. Harli staggered
toward him, blinking his eyes open, wincing at the new wave of
pain that effort cost him.

According to his nanocomputer, the entire run had lasted just
seven point two seconds.

"Kemp?" he croaked. Two meters past the station was an empty
food table with a half-full hundred-liter jug of water in a dispenser
beside it. Limping past Kemp, he headed toward it.

"Got it," Kemp croaked back. "System coming up—activating—
God, don't let the power and control cables have been burned
through—"

"Step back," Harli ordered, pulling the jug from the dispenser
and sloshing a little of the water out onto the ground as he turned
it upright. "Come on, step back."

"It's done," Kemp said, breathing shallowly as he pulled himself
to his feet and staggered back from the control board. "But if it
doesn't work—"

"It'll work," Harli said, directing splashes of water onto the
remaining flames and then, for good measure, pouring some over
Kemp's head. "Trust me. It'll work."

The words were barely out of his mouth when, through the roar
of the fire, he heard the creaking of moving metal.

He looked over at the downed ship. Through the billowing smoke
he could see that it was on the move, rising ponderously up from the
ground as the grav lifts the Troft prisoners had moved to the sides
and broken lower wings ran to full power. The ship continued to rise,
moving faster now as it approached the top of its arc. It reached it,
and for a brief moment it stood proudly upright again for the first
time since Harli and the other Cobras had knocked it over.

But it didn't stay vertical for more than that brief second. The
grav lifts were still pushing, the wrecked cascade regulator was no

longer there to ease back their power, and the huge mass of metal had built up way too much momentum. The ship kept moving and toppled over in the other direction, slamming into the newly-arrived ship with an ear-splitting grinding of metal against metal.

For a moment the two ships seemed to pause, teetering and shaking. Then, with an even louder shriek of grinding metal, they fell over together in a violent crash that shook the ground so hard it nearly knocked Harli off his feet.

For a long moment the only sound was the crackling roar of the frames. Finally, Kemp stirred. "Popescu," he said in a hoarse voice, "is going to be furious."

Harli drew a careful breath into his aching lungs. "I *said* you should go back and warn him."

"He'll get over it." Taking the jug from Harli's blackened hands, he sprayed some of the water onto a smoldering fire on Harli's shoulder that he hadn't even noticed was there. "But we should probably let him know that the Trofts probably won't be up for a fight anytime soon," he added. "Might be a good time for him to call on the captain to surrender."

"Sorry, I didn't think to grab a radio," Harli apologized. He waved wearily at the fire. "And I don't think I'm up to delivering the message in person."

"Me, neither," Kemp conceded. "Well, if Popescu wants us, he'll find us."

"Sure," Harli said. "Come on, let's see if they left any burn salve or painkillers in the hospital when they moved everyone out."

"Sounds like a plan." Kemp peered at his blistered hands. "You really think the Qasamans were able to grow Paul Broom's leg back?"

"They said they could," Harli said. "Don't know how they'll do with burns, but it's worth checking out. When this is over, we'll talk to Rashida about setting us up."

"Assuming she survives," Kemp said quietly.

Harli winced. "Yes," he said. "Assuming she survives."

Jody's original concern had been that the Trofts would come charging into the caves the minute their ship landed, catching her and the others out in the open. But the captain's decision to first burn away any nearby ambush positions had given their prey the time they needed to cross the chamber and get to Smitty's chosen rock chimney.

Getting there, unfortunately, turned out to be only half the battle. Smitty was an expert at that kind of climbing, and Rashida had the method down after her first try. But for some reason it took Jody a dozen attempts and ten minutes of intensive coaching before she finally figured out the necessary technique: back and feet braced on opposite sides of the chimney, hands pushing down to move her back upward, feet simultaneously walking up the other side. She still felt a lot more awkward than either of the others looked, but at least she was able to do it.

And with that, they finally started up.

Smitty, who knew the route and the tricky parts of the chimney, took the lead. Jody came next, a meter behind him, still struggling. Rashida, moving much more gracefully, brought up the rear. Smitty hadn't been able to find any rope aboard the ship during their race to the caves, but Rashida had used Jody's prolonged tutoring time to carefully tear the silliweave bag into strips and then braid them the sturdy-looking lines that now tied the three climbers to each other.

Though *sturdy-looking*, Jody knew, didn't necessarily mean *sturdy*. As they worked their way up the rock tube she found herself staring at the rope hanging loosely between her belt and Smitty's, wondering how much weight the thing could actually take. Hoping fervently that they never had to find out.

They were nearly to the top of the chimney, and Jody could see the glow of diffuse sunlight seeping between Smitty's torso and arms, when she heard the clink of metal on rock beneath her.

She froze, wondering fleetingly if she dared speak up to warn Smitty and Rashida. Fortunately, they'd apparently also heard the noise, and stopped as quickly as she had.

For a moment there was nothing more. Jody peered down over her shoulder, trying to see past Rashida to the bottom. But all she could see was the dark rock of the chimney and the even darker rock far below.

But other sounds were now starting to drift up: the sound of feet shuffling across pebble-strewn rock, an occasional distant and muffled Troft voice, a few more random clinks and thuds. Jody strained her ears, trying to figure out if all of it was getting closer to them, but the natural echo of the huge chamber thwarted her efforts.

And then, without warning, a Troft stepped into view beneath them.

Jody held her breath. He seemed to be looking around, his helmet and laser turning slowly as he surveyed the area.

There was a breath of movement above Jody, and she looked up to see Smitty ease his left leg out of its bracing position against the rock wall and stretch it out along the side of the chimney, aiming his antiarmor laser downward. Clenching her teeth, trying not to dislodge any loose stone from the wall, Jody eased herself as far out of his line of fire as she could. She looked down, hoping Rashida had also spotted Smitty's maneuver and was likewise giving him room to shoot.

She wasn't. Her eyes were still on the Troft, her left hand pointed downward, the glove laser along the little finger lined up on the alien's helmet. Either she hadn't seen what Smitty was doing, or else had decided for some other reason to take this one on herself.

Only she'd apparently forgotten that her laser didn't have enough power to cut through that helmet. In fact, at this range, it might not be able to penetrate even his much more vulnerable faceplate.

Jody reached down, trying to touch Rashida's shoulder, trying to get her attention. But the shoulder was out of her reach. "Rashida, no," she whispered as loudly as she dared.

Rashida didn't respond. The Troft looked around once more and started to step away from the chimney.

And then, almost as if it was an afterthought, he tilted his head back and looked up. His radiator membranes snapped out from his upper arms, and he swung his laser up.

Rashida fired first, her laser sending a bolt squarely into the Troft's faceplate. An instant later, the Troft's much more powerful shot flashed up the chimney, shattering a section of wall near Rashida's feet and sending out a stinging spray of jagged rock chips.

And with that part of Rashida's support suddenly cut out from under her feet, she lost her hold and tumbled down the chimney.

In that first frozen half second the only thing that saved her was the makeshift rope tying her belt to Jody's. The rope jerked taut as she fell, spinning her upright and bouncing her shoulders and back against the chimney wall. The sudden additional weight yanked at Jody, dragging her a few centimeters downward before she and her suit's servos could increase the pressure against the rock and bring her to a halt. Her upper arms were pressed hard against the stone at her back, adding their pressure to help hold her in place. Risking the loss of some of that pressure, she reached down and managed to grab Rashida's arm as the other woman flailed for balance.

Her fingers had barely closed around Rashida's wrist when the silliweave rope snapped.

Jody braced herself. But this latest jolt was too much. With a surge of helpless horror she felt her back being pulled inexorably downward, the rough stone digging grooves into her skin beneath the power suit material. Clenching her teeth, she pressed her feet even harder against the other side, trying to halt her slide.

But she was already too far out of balance. Desperately, she dropped her right foot to a lower section of wall, hoping to reestablish a brace. But even as she tried to get it wedged a second laser blast sizzled up from below, this one shattering a section of wall above her and raining stone fragments into her face. She winced away, reflexively raising her other arm to protect her eyes.

With a wrenching twist, she lost her fight for balance and started to tumble down the chimney, jerking to a halt an instant later as the rope tying her to Smitty snapped taut. Blinking the swirling rock dust from her eyes, she looked up to see Smitty's hand reaching down and grabbed it just as the rope broke. She slammed back-first against the wall, her legs bouncing off Rashida's torso.

And then, even as she tried to catch her breath, a brilliant flash of blue lanced through the air in front of her face.

With Jody and Rashida finally out of his way, Smitty had fired his antiarmor laser.

Jody never actually heard the sound of the Troft hitting the stone. But as she peered down the chimney, trying to look around the afterimage Smitty's shot had burned into her retinas, she could see the alien's smoldering body sprawled on the cavern floor.

"Don't just hang there," Smitty grunted from above her. "Get your feet back up, and let's move it. Jody, you have to go first—Rashida can't move with you in her way."

"Right." Carefully, remembering to let her suit's servos do most of the work, Jody lifted her legs and planted them again on the opposite side of the chimney. "Okay," she said. "Rashida?"

"No," Rashida said quietly.

Jody looked down in surprise. Rashida was still hanging from Jody's grip, making no attempt to get back into climbing position. "What?"

"We can't do it," Rashida said, her voice dark but determined. "Not all of us. The other invaders will surely have seen the battle and even now will be coming."

"So stop jabbering and get moving," Smitty snapped. "Come *on*."

"There's no time," Rashida said. "We can't reach the top this way. Not before they arrive. Our only chance is for me to stay here and hold them off while you try to reach safety."

Jody felt her stomach tighten. "No," she said firmly.

"Absolutely not," Smitty seconded. "We leave together, or we don't leave at all."

"So three die instead of one?" Rashida demanded. "Where's the honor in that?"

"Where's the honor in leaving one of your own behind?" Smitty countered.

"I can't answer for your honor," Rashida said. "I can only answer for my own. Farewell." She reached up her other hand toward where Jody was gripping her wrist—

"Hold it," Smitty said hastily. "Okay—here's what we do. We'll all go back down, but just long enough to change positions. You'll take point, Rashida, with Jody next and me bringing up the rear. That way we'll have my antiarmor laser and target-locks where they can actually do us some good. Okay?"

Rashida hesitated, then nodded. "All right," she said.

"Here's the plan," Smitty said. "Rashida drops first, obviously— your leg servos should be able to handle the landing, but watch your footing. As soon as you're down, move out of the way so Jody can join you. Jody, ditto. Once I'm down, I'll throw you one at a time as high up the chimney as I can—if I do it right, you should be able to just push out with back and legs at the top of your arc and get back to climbing. Got it?"

"Got it," Jody said, frowning. There was something in his tone that was sending warning sirens screaming through her brain.

"Yes," Rashida said.

"Okay, then," Smitty said. "Rashida, bend your knees a little. Jody, let go of her."

And even as Jody started to open her hand the horrible truth flooded in on her. "No!" she snapped, tightening her grip again. "Rashida, it's a trick. He's not planning to come back with us. He's going to stay down there and fight the Trofts so we can get away."

"Oh, for—" Smitty choked off a curse. "*Damn* it, Broom."

"We leave together, or we don't leave at all," Jody reminded him tightly.

He took a deep breath. "Listen to me, Jody," he said. "We have only two choices. One, you let me stay behind and keep the Trofts off your backs. Two, we keep climbing and they blow all three of us out of here in pieces."

"Or three," Rashida put in, "we let *me* go down and do the fighting."

"No," Smitty said flatly. "I can't let a civilian make that kind of sacrifice. Not while I'm still alive and able to fight."

"I'm not a civilian," Rashida said, and Jody shivered at the sudden darkness in her voice. "No Qasaman is. Not anymore. When our world was invaded, we all became soldiers."

"I don't care if you all became cybernetic screech tigers," Smitty retorted. "I'm not leaving you—"

"Wait a second," Jody interrupted as a sudden, crazy, possibly lethal idea struck her. "There may be one more option." She braced herself. "We blow your booby-trap."

"Sorry, but that won't help," Smitty told her. "Not enough, anyway. It'll flatten everyone already in the chamber, but they'll have plenty of soldiers still in reserve on the ship. And there's no way we can make all the way to the top before the reinforcements arrive—" He broke off. "I'll be damned," he said, his voice suddenly thoughtful. "You're right—it's worth a shot. Rashida, get your feet up. *Now.*"

"I don't understand," Rashida said. But she nevertheless pulled her legs up and set them against the far wall. "What are we doing?"

"We're taking the express," Smitty said, and Jody glanced up to see him pull out his radio. "Heads tucked to your chests, eyes closed, and everyone hold tight to each other. Here we go."

Jody pressed her chin against her chest and squeezed her eyes shut. Rashida's arm rotated slightly in her grasp, and she felt the other woman's fingers close around her wrist. Taking the cue, Jody shifted her wrist in Smitty's grip and locked her fingers around his arm. Below them, she could hear the multiple scurrying of feet as the other Trofts in the cavern converged on their refuge. In the near distance there was a violent thundercrack as Smitty's booby-trapped missiles exploded—

And an instant later a blast of hot air slammed into her from below, breaking her friction grip on the chimney wall and throwing her violently upward.

She kept her chin tucked, her hands gripping Rashida's and Smitty's, her teeth clenched against the pain as she was bounced back and forth off the chimney walls. An old memory flashed unexpectedly to mind: the first time she'd ever climbed up on a chair as a toddler and stuck her face over a pan where her mother was boiling water. The buffeting slowed, the heat that had been flowing up around her back and legs fading away. She felt herself slowing—

And with a wrenching of her arm she came to a sudden halt.

She looked up. Smitty was still gripping her arm, but he was no longer twisted like half a pretzel and braced against the sides of the chimney. Instead, he was standing vertically, his legs stretched to either side of her.

For a second it didn't register. Then her mind cleared, and she realized Smitty was vertical because he was no longer inside the chimney. Instead, he was standing in a larger chamber, straddling the chimney opening from above.

The shock wave from the explosion hadn't just sent them flying higher up the chimney. It had thrown them all the way up to the top.

"You all right?" Smitty asked as he pulled her up. "Rashida?"

"I think so," Jody said, frowning. Somewhere along the way on that turbulent ride, Rashida's grip around her arm had loosened. And now, as she looked down, she saw that the other woman's head was hanging limply against her chest. "Smitty!" Jody said.

"I'm on it," Smitty said grimly, pulling her the rest of the way out of the chimney and setting her down on solid rock. As he did so, he reached down with his other hand and took Rashida's arm. "Rashida?" he called, peering anxiously into the woman's face as he set her feet down on the opposite side. "Come on, girl, wake up."

There was no response. He shifted his grip on her, putting his other arm around her shoulders as Jody circled the chimney opening and got a grip on Rashida's head and belt. Together, they eased her into a half-sitting, half-lying position on a slanted rock ledge at the side of the chamber. "Rashida?" Smitty called again, kneeling down beside her, his fingertips gently tapping her cheek. "Rashida?"

And then, to Jody's relief, Rashida's eyes blinked open. She looked at Smitty, then at Jody, then back at Smitty. A frown creased her face, as if she was sifting through jumbled memories trying to figure out what had happened. Then, the creases in her forehead smoothed and the faintest hint of a tentative smile touched her lips. "Ouch," she said.

Smitty chuckled, sounding relieved, amused, and slightly embarrassed at the same time. "That's for sure," he agreed. "And naturally you got the worst of it. I'm sorry."

"I'm not," Rashida said, wincing as she reached a hand down to her ribs. "Whatever injuries I may have received, they were a small price to pay for our survival."

Abruptly, Smitty seemed to realize that his fingertips were still resting against Rashida's cheek, and he dropped his hand to his side. "Okay, then," he said briskly, getting back to his feet. "There's an exit onto the top of the cliff nearby. Jody, why don't you wait here with Rashida while I check it out."

"Wouldn't it be safer for us to stay together?" Rashida asked, putting her hand on the rock wall beside her, her fingers searching for a grip. "I can travel."

"You sure?" Smitty asked, taking her hand and helping her to her feet.

"Yes," Rashida said firmly. "Besides, I want to see with my own eyes what the explosion did to the invaders' other warship."

"Fair enough," Smitty conceded. "Okay. Follow me."

Ten minutes later, they emerged through a ragged opening onto a jumble of small rocks overgrown with ribbon vine and green treacle and dotted with bushy solotropes. Holding both women by the hand, Smitty cautiously led the way to the crumbling edge of the cliff.

Jody had hoped the explosion had been strong enough to tip the newly arrived warship over onto its side. To her mild disappointment, the ship was still upright, squatting on the relatively flat area below the cave with its bow weapons clusters pointed into the entrance. It was hard for Jody to tell through the drifting smoke from the burned-off areas, but it didn't look like the ship had taken any damage at all. "Well, at least we probably took out a few of their soldiers," she said philosophically. "What now?"

"We wait," Smitty said, moving them back from the cliff edge to more secure footing. "Sooner or later someone will come looking for us—that smoke will be visible for dozens of kilometers, and Harli and the others know where we went. Either they'll come, or the Tlossies will whenever they finally get here."

"Or the invaders will," Rashida murmured.

"Let 'em try," Smitty said. "There are places in the upper caves where we could hold out for weeks where even a missile would have a hard time getting to us."

He gestured around them. "In the meantime, this is probably the best place in Wonderland we could have picked to hang out for a while. We've got edible plants, plenty of food animals, and only the smaller predators."

He let go of Jody's hand, holding Rashida's another moment before also releasing it. "Come on. I'll get you back inside, then go hunt us up some dinner."

CHAPTER TWENTY

"Ten seconds," Ghushtre announced from behind Lorne.

"Acknowledged," one of the two Djinn at the weapons board replied. "All missiles armed and ready to go."

Lorne felt a shiver run up his back. Here it was: the final make-or-break moment. The moment when the Qasamans either won their freedom from the Trofts who had invaded their world, or the moment when they settled into a long, bitter war of attrition that might never be won.

"Lorne Moreau?"

Lorne shook away the thoughts. "The drones have closed to within a kilometer of the incoming warships," he reported. "SkyJos holding close formation behind them."

"Two seconds," the Djinni warned.

Lorne closed his hand on the edge of his seat. A moment later, the warship gave a gentle lurch, far gentler than he'd expected. "Missiles away," the Djinni announced. "Two targeted on each SkyJo."

"And yet the invaders hold their fire," Ghushtre murmured, sounding vaguely bemused.

"As Moffren Omnathi predicted they would," Lorne reminded him. "The Troft commanders got to see the SkyJos' capabilities when you chased them out of Sollas, and they know the three incoming warships are still out of their optimal weapons range. They want to make sure there's no chance any of the SkyJos has time or room to maneuver when they finally do open fire."

"And perhaps they think we still believe the drones will protect the SkyJos until they've closed to that range?"

Lorne shrugged uncomfortably. That one had been his parents' prediction, and it was clear Ghushtre didn't have nearly as much confidence in it as he did in Omnathi's own drug-enhanced pronouncements. "Warrior told us the drones carry IFF transponders," he reminded Ghushtre. "It's obvious that something with such a small cross-section won't be able to shield the SkyJos once they're close enough. But again, the invaders don't know we know that."

"Perhaps," Ghushtre said. "We shall know soon enough."

[Missiles, Captain Vuma has launched them,] Officer Cebed said, his radiator membranes fluttering with confusion. [The SkyJos, the missiles are targeting them.]

[Captain Vuma, *he* has launched missiles?] Inxeba demanded, frowning at Cebed. [Captain Vuma, was he not captured by the enemy?]

[The missiles, they have been launched,] Cebed repeated. [Captain Vuma, perhaps he has retaken control of his ship.]

[Captain Vuma, no communication has he made,] one of the other officers objected suspiciously.

[The SkyJos, they have increased speed,] one of the other Trofts spoke up urgently.

[The SkyJos, they seek to escape the missiles,] Inxeba said, his own suspicions fading into anticipation. [The SkyJos, what is their combat status?]

[Their weapons, they will be in optimal firing range in ten seconds,] Cebed said. [Captain Geceg, he reports all of his point defenses are functional.]

[A race, it shall then be,] Inxeba said. [Captain Vuma, his missiles; Captain Geceg, his point defenses. The SkyJos, we shall see which destroys them first.]

And it was at that moment, as he frowned at the drone monitors and the views from Geceg's three-ship task force, that Merrick suddenly understood.

Surreptitiously, he looked at Ukuthi. The Balin commander was looking back at him, and from his expression Merrick knew he'd also figured it out.

For a pair of heartbeats he held Merrick's gaze. Then, calmly and deliberately, he turned back to the displays. Reaching for his drink, he took a sip and then set it back on its table.

Merrick smiled tightly. Ukuthi had figured it out, all right. But Inxeba had demanded the glory of this operation go to his demesne, and Ukuthi had graciously conceded it to him. Only it wouldn't be glory. It would be disaster.

And Inxeba would never even see it coming.

The missiles closed to within two seconds of the SkyJos...and with that, Lorne knew, they had won.

And yet, he still marveled at the Trofts' arrogant blindness. They'd recognized quickly enough the overt part of Omnathi's plan, that the drones' IFF systems would shield the SkyJos from the warships' weapons.

What they still apparently hadn't realized was that such shielding worked both ways.

The missiles from the Qasamans' captured warship couldn't target the three incoming ships. But they *could* target the Qasamans' attack helicopters.

And if those SkyJos happened to be directly between the missiles and the Troft warships when the missiles locked on...

He was gazing at the displays, wondering at the fortunes of war, when the SkyJo pilots ejected. Half a second later, the helicopters' self-destructs went off, shattering them along preset stress lines as the blasts disintegrated them into clouds of dust.

Half a second after that, the incoming missiles, already armed and with no time for a course readjustment, swept through the debris and detonated against the bows and wings of the oncoming warships.

❖   ❖   ❖

And as the entire bank of displays flared and then blanked, the conference room erupted in pandemonium.

Merrick listened to the shouts of rage and disbelief, the demand for information and the demands that someone do something. And as he listened, he felt a warm glow of triumph and relief flow through him.

The Qasamans had pulled it off. Against all odds, they'd pulled it off.

And Inxeba knew it. The fury in his voice was tinged with fear, his shouted demands edged with near panic. In a single day, he'd lost at least three and maybe as many as six of his warships.

And with them, he'd also lost the war.

[Captain Geceg, he reports,] Cebed called out, his voice managing to penetrate Inxeba's ranting and the other officers' scrambling orders. [One warship, it is crippled and has fallen. Two warships, they are still functional.]

[Captain Geceg, he is to retreat immediately to Sollas,] Inxeba ordered, clearly fighting hard to try to calm himself.

[Captain Geceg, he will not arrive,] Ukuthi said, gesturing toward the blank displays. [Blind, his two remaining warships have become.]

[Sensors, Captain Geceg does not require them to locate Sollas,] Inxeba retorted acidly.

[Sollas, Captain Geceg will not reach it,] Ukuthi repeated. He shifted his finger to point at the drone images still coming from Purma. [SkyJos from Purma, they are being launched as we speak. Captain Geceg, they will easily destroy his remaining ships.]

Inxeba stared at the displays, his radiator membranes shaking. [More ships, I will send them from Sollas,] he said. [Commander Ukuthi, the Balin'ekha'spmi ships, you will send them as well.]

[The Balin'ekha'spmi ships, I will not send them,] Ukuthi said quietly. [The war, it can no longer be won.]

Inxeba turned toward him, his hand fumbling for his pistol. [Treason, you speak it,] he snarled. [Warships, the Drim'hco'plai have more than enough to destroy this world.]

[The Drim'hco'plai warships, they will not be permitted to destroy this world,] Ukuthi said flatly. [Warships of the Tlos'khin'fahi and

Chrii'pra'pfwoi demesnes, they wait in the outer system. Your defeat today, they will soon have reports of it.]

Inxeba's hand tightened on his weapon's grip. [Reports, they will *not* receive them,] he warned coldly.

[Reports, they will not be sent by the Balin'ekha'spmi,] Ukuthi said, his voice chilling to match Inxeba's. [Reports, from the Qasaman Shahni they will obtain them.]

Inxeba spat. [The Qasaman Shahni, there are no more of them. Their deaths, they have been achieved.]

[The Qasaman Shahni, there remains one,] Inxeba corrected. [His departure from Sollas, fifteen days ago, I permitted it.]

Inxeba stared at him. [My direct order, you have violated it. The reason, you will explain it at once.]

[An official leader, one must always be left,] Ukuthi said, facing Inxeba's glare without flinching. [The leader, a conquered people may be more easily controlled through him.]

He gestured again to the images of Purma and the SkyJos rising into the sky like a cloud of angry wasplings. [The leader, a truce may also be requested through him.]

[A truce, I will *not* request it,] Inxeba snarled.

[The Drim'hco'plai warships, more of them will then be lost.] Deliberately, Ukuthi stood up. [But the Drim'hco'plai warships, they will be lost alone. The Balin'ekha'spmi warships, I am removing them from Qasama.]

[Treason, you speak it,] Inxeba said again.

But even Merrick could see that the words had no power behind them. Ukuthi had been given tactical command of the Qasaman forces by the overall commander of the invasion forces. If he chose to withdraw, there was nothing Inxeba could do to stop him. Not without declaring war on the whole Balin'ekha'spmi demesne.

Everyone else in the room knew it, too. [Your warship, I now leave it,] Ukuthi said into the silence. Turning, he gestured to the two guards at the door. Without a word, they stepped aside.

[Your departure, I cannot stop it,] Inxeba said bitterly. [Your slaves, you will leave them here.]

Ukuthi turned back to him, and for the first time since Merrick had met him the commander seemed genuinely to have been caught off-balance. [My slaves, they will leave with me,] he said cautiously.

[Your slaves, they are property of the Drim'hco'plai demesne-lord,] Inxeba countered. [All slaves, my demesne-lord has ordered their return. That request, have you not heard it?]

[The request, I have heard it,] Ukuthi said. [These slaves, my demesne-lord will return them with the others.]

[These slaves, they will stay,] Inxeba insisted.

And they would, too, Merrick realized as a hollow feeling settled into his stomach. Inxeba had lost the war and been humiliated in front of his officers. This small and meaningless act of revenge was all he had left to slap Ukuthi with.

For a long moment the two commanders stood facing each other. Merrick once again found his hands curling into firing positions, a hundred plans racing through his mind, each one more impossible and insane than the last.

And in the end, as that long, tense moment drew to a close, he knew he really had only one option. [Anya and I, to her world we will go,] he murmured, low enough for only Ukuthi to hear. So much for leading a team of Cobras equipped with Qasaman weapons to help free Anya's people. So much even for saying good-bye to his family.

Unless, perhaps, Ukuthi was as observant as he was clever. [The drogfowl cacciatore of home, I will look forward to tasting it again soon,] he added. [My family, they will welcome my return.]

For a brief moment Ukuthi continued to stare at Inxeba. Then, he gave a little snort and waved in a gesture of dismissal. [The slaves, you may keep them,] he said contemptuously as he headed for the door. [The slaves, they are of no concern.] Passing between the guards, he disappeared through the door.

For another moment the room was silent. [Commander Inxeba, what are his orders?] Cebed asked carefully.

Inxeba turned and looked back at the displays. [Commander Inxeba, what are his orders?] Cebed repeated.

Inxeba's membranes flared out with a final surge of emotion. Then, almost delicately, they settled back against his arms. [A signal, send it to Captain Geceg,] he said quietly. [Sollas, he will not return to it. High orbit, he will instead rise to it.] He lowered his head. [A signal, you will then send it to all Drim'hco'plai,] he said. [Their immediate departure from this world, I order it.]

The officers looked at each other. [The order, I obey it,] Cebed said.

Inxeba rose from his couch, and as he did so his eyes flicked to Merrick and Anya. [The slaves, you will then put them with the others,] he said.

Turning his back on the other officers, he started for the door. [Clarification, I seek it,] Cebed called hesitantly after him. [The Drim'hco'plai departure, to high orbit is it?]

[Our departure, to the Drim'hco'plai demesne it is,] Inxeba said without turning around. [The war, the Tua'lanek'zia demesne may continue it alone if they choose.]

[Our departure, the Tua'lanek'zia demesne-lord will be angry with it,] Cebed warned.

[The Tua'lanek'zia's demesne-lord, his anger is meaningless,] Inxeba countered. [The anger of his master, it only is to be feared.]

He sent a measuring look at Merrick and Anya. [But his anger, it will soon be soothed,] he added, his voice thoughtful. [Commander Inxeba, he will then be rewarded.]

It had been a long and bitter struggle, full of half-felt pain and strange disorientation, surrounded by hunger and thirst and freakish dreams. But finally, finally, it had come to an end.

The first thing Fadil saw when he opened his eyes was the ceiling of his room, the gem-glittered replica of the night sky that he'd stared at for so many hours from his medical bed, soaked in meaningless perspiration and the helplessness and despair of his broken body. Now he was back, and the thought fleetingly touched his mind that it was as if the past few days had been merely a long nightmare.

But they had indeed been real...because the second thing he saw, looming over him from beside his bed, was his father's face.

For a moment Fadil just stared into those dark eyes, his mind flashing back to all the nightmares, wondering if this was just one last bit of mockery from the depths of a feverish mind.

But then his father smiled; and with that, the fears and misgivings vanished like morning mist. "Hello, Father," Fadil said. His voice sounded strange, cracking with thirst or disuse or perhaps simple emotion. "You're looking well."

"Hello, my son," Daulo said; and his voice, too, had the same strange tone as Fadil's own. "How do you feel?"

Fadil took a deep breath. "I feel well," he said. "I feel...alive. As I thought I'd never feel again." He felt his throat tighten with shame. "As I never should have been allowed to feel."

"It's all right," Daulo soothed as he reached across the bed and took Fadil's hands. "Truly it is. You have no cause for regret or shame."

"Don't I?" Fadil asked, lowering his eyes from his father's gaze. "I've taken resources that Qasama desperately needs for my own selfish ends."

"The decision wasn't yours," Daulo reminded him. "It was Moffren Omnathi's, and was made in honor and thanks for your service to Qasama."

"How can I accept such thanks in the midst of war?" Fadil bit out, more angrily than he'd intended. "How can I let them do this to me when others even now die for our world?"

Daulo shook his head. "You misunderstand, Fadil. No one is dying for Qasama. Not anymore. The war is over."

Fadil stared at him, disbelief and hope churning together in his heart. "Impossible," he said. "It's been only—" He broke off, trying to count. Had it really been only five days?

"Only five days," Daulo confirmed. "But it's the truth. The invaders and their warships are gone. Warships of the Tlos'khin'fahi demesne, allies of the Cobra Worlds, now patrol the skies above Qasama. Even as we speak, their cargo ships bring in food and pre-built structures for those city dwellers who still huddle in tents. Shahni Haafiz and Senior Advisor Moffren Omnathi have had personal discussions with the demesne-heir known as Warrior, with the promise of more assistance to come."

Fadil grimaced. "So despite it all, we still have no choice but to deal with the Trofts?"

Daulo shrugged. "Perhaps that's the way of our future. Perhaps not. Only time will tell." He let go of Fadil's hands and stood up. "I was told you would be extremely hungry when you awoke. Dinner awaits downstairs in the dining hall. Will you come share it with me?"

Fadil took a deep breath. He lowered his eyes to his left hand, and as he had every day since his return from Sollas he silently ordered it to rise.

Only this time, it obeyed him.

He let his breath out in a sound that was half gasp and half laugh. The fingers worked too, he saw as he moved the hand to the bed rail and closed the fingers around it. Still holding onto the rail, he willed his right arm to also move, to the bed beside his torso so that he could lever himself upright.

And his right arm, too, obeyed him.

Carefully, he sat up. Just as carefully, he shifted his legs sideways across the bed, then over the edge, and finally planted his feet on the floor.

And for the first time in nearly a month, he stood upright.

His father stepped forward and gripped his arm, and Fadil could see tears glistening in his eyes. "Welcome back, my son," he said quietly. "Welcome back, Cobra Fadil Sammon."

CHAPTER TWENTY-ONE

It had been a quiet dinner, uncharacteristically quiet for a Moreau family gathering.

Not that any of the six gathered around the table had expected anything like the loud and boisterous celebrations taking place elsewhere across Aventine and the other Cobra Worlds. Not considering the multiple dark clouds hanging over all of them.

Especially not since the six should have been seven.

The meal was over and Jody and Paul had cleared the table—at Paul's insistence and over Jody's and Jin's objections—when the unexpected guest Jin had been expecting all evening finally arrived.

"I'm sorry to crash your family time this way," Governor-General Chintawa apologized as Thena Moreau escorted him into the conversation room. "But I thought someone should unofficially welcome you all back to Aventine." He grimaced. "Especially considering how the official welcome went."

"That's all right," Corwin Moreau said, ever the gracious host, as he waved Chintawa to an empty seat. "So she's actually going through with it?"

Chintawa sighed as he lowered himself into the chair. "I'm sorry, Corwin. All of you. I tried to talk her out of it—I really did. But as you may have discovered, Nissa Gendreves is an extremely stubborn person."

"With, I dare say, more than her share of political ambition?" Paul suggested.

"You don't hang around the Dome putting in long hours for low pay without some of that," Chintawa conceded. "But I don't think she's out to get you simply to make a name for herself. She genuinely believes that all of you—well, you four Brooms, anyway—committed high treason by giving Isis to the Qasamans." He hesitated. "And unfortunately, according to the law, she's right."

"So has she also brought charges against Governor Uy?" Lorne asked. "She was just as mad at him as she was at us."

"I'm sure she'd like to," Chintawa said. "No, that's not fair. She was very clear about his part of the decision in her closed Council testimony, and I know she intends to make those additional charges official as soon as she's been given clearance to do so."

"Only she hasn't," Lorne suggested acidly, "because Uy's one of the Council's own, and you don't throw the big fish to the sharks?"

Jody stirred. "Governor Uy did a lot to help win the war, Governor Chintawa. Everyone on Caelian did."

"As did everyone in this room," Lorne said. "I don't see the Council throwing us parades or hushing up *our* collection of ridiculous charges."

"Easy, Lorne," Corwin murmured. "Governor-General Chintawa's not the enemy here."

"He's right, Cobra Broom," Chintawa agreed. "Believe me, I'd like nothing better than to give you full pardons right now and sweep this whole thing out the door. But the fact is that Governor Treakness *did* give Ms. Gendreves full diplomatic authority, and she *did* order you not to give Isis to the Qasamans. Even you admit that, and we have Dr. Croi's testimony as well."

"And we're sure Governor Treakness never said anything to clarify his authorization?" Thena asked.

Chintawa shook his head. "I doubt the Trofts ever bothered to ask him. I'm not even sure how much of those last few hours he was conscious. The point is that charges have been made and corroborated. Unless the Council reaches deep within itself for understanding and charity—and you know the chances of *that* happening—you're going to have to be arrested and stand trial."

"So much for the Cobra-haters suddenly seeing the light," Paul murmured.

"Not likely," Chintawa said with a sigh. "You can force-read them the reports from Caelian and Qasama all day long, but what they *saw* was our Aventinian Cobras sitting around not doing a damn thing."

"At *their* specific orders," Corwin reminded him.

"Of course," Chintawa said. "You want logic and consistency, get out of politics." His lip twitched in a smile. "As, of course, you did. Sometimes I have to admit I envy you that decision."

Jin looked at Paul, and she could tell he was thinking the same thing she was: that her Uncle Corwin hadn't left politics so much as he'd been booted out. But of course Chintawa knew that.

"And now with Isis in Qasaman hands they've got an even bigger Cobra bugaboo to worry about," Lorne pointed out.

"With more than a little justification," Chintawa said, an edge of annoyance in his tone. "I know how warm and trusting you all are when it comes to the Qasamans, but there's no guarantee that your decision won't someday turn sour on us. And if the Qasamans ever decide they want vengeance for whatever real or imagined wrongs the Worlds have inflicted on them, what we've just gone through with the Trofts will seem like a stroll down the river."

"It won't happen," Lorne said firmly.

"I hope to God it doesn't." Chintawa hesitated, then looked at Jin. "I understand there was a letter," he said, the annoyance gone. "May I see it?"

Jin hesitated. But he probably had a right to see the actual note. Reaching into her tunic, she slipped the envelope out of the inner pocket, the one closest to her heart. She pulled out the single slip of paper, unfolded it, and for the hundred thousandth time in the past three days her eyes traced across the confusing, bleak, hopeful words.

The drogfowl cacciatore of home, I will look forward to tasting it again soon. My family, they will welcome my return. Courage.

Jody was standing quietly beside her when Jin looked up. Blinking back sudden tears, she handed her daughter the note. Holding it like she would a piece of fine crystal, Jody crossed the room and offered it to Chintawa.

For a long moment he gazed down at it. Then, he looked up again. "What do you make of it?"

"We're not sure," Paul admitted. "The words are Anglic, but the grammar form is Troft. The handwriting isn't Merrick's, and I doubt very much it's even human. It was delivered to Jin by the Tlossies, but they claim it didn't originate with them. We've made at least a hundred inquiries, but every one of them has either been ignored or run straight into a steel-core wall."

"*Someone* knows what happened to Merrick," Lorne put in. "But whoever that is, he isn't talking."

"Hmm," Chintawa said, looking at the letter again. "And you're sure the message is from him?"

"We had drogfowl cacciatore the night we got the first letter," Paul said. "The one that took Jin and Merrick to Qasama in the first place. More than that, I used those words as an identifier when I communicated with him just before his capture. No, Merrick's the only one who could have sent this message."

"I see," Chintawa murmured. "*Courage.* That's probably good advice right now. For all of us."

Corwin cleared his throat. "And speaking of drogfowl cacciatore and conspiracies," he said, "I'd like to point out that Thena and I were also at that meeting. If you're going to charge my niece and her family with treason, you'd best put us in the docket along with them."

Chintawa snorted. "If you think I'm going to put any more necks into Ms. Gendreves's noose than I have to, you can forget it." Carefully, reverently, he handed the letter back to Jody and stood up. "At any rate, I should be getting back to the Dome. I just wanted to let you all know that I, personally, am very glad to see you all safe and sound."

Jin's throat tightened. All of them except Merrick.

"I also wanted to let you know that I'm not the only one on the

Council who appreciates what you've done," the governor-general added. "Let's all just hope and pray that the Qasamans are as friendly as you believe."

"We don't need them to be our friends," Corwin said mildly. "All we need is for them to *not* be our enemies."

"Right now, I'd be happy with either," Chintawa said. "Well ... good night, all. Don't get up, Thena—I'll let myself out."

He walked out of the room. Jin keyed in her audio enhancers, following his footsteps as he continued down the hallway and then opened and closed the door. "Any thoughts?" she asked, keying the audios back down. "Uncle Corwin?"

Corwin shrugged. "I think he's sincere, for whatever that's worth."

"Probably not much," Jody said, an edge of bitterness in her voice as she returned the precious letter to her mother. "All we went through on Caelian—and she *saw* all of it—and she *still* turns around and stabs us in the back."

"Don't be too hard on her," Corwin advised. "The first thing a politician learns is not to make threats he isn't willing or able to carry out. Having accused you of treason in front of a room full of witnesses, she really had no choice but to follow through on it."

"Besides, from her point of view she's entirely correct," Paul pointed out. "If we're wrong about the Qasamans, our giving Isis to them is going to get *all* of us stabbed in the back."

"And on that cheery note," Jin said, giving Merrick's note one final lingering look before returning it to its envelope, "we should probably get going. It's been a long day, and tomorrow's likely to be even longer."

"And you two are still recovering from surgery," Lorne added, standing up and stepping to Jin's side. "Let me give you a hand."

"Can I ask one last question?" Jody spoke up suddenly. "It's funny how when you think you're going to die the weirdest questions pop into your head." She turned to Corwin. "Uncle Corwin: why do you call this house the Island?"

Jin looked at her daughter in surprise. But Corwin merely chuckled. "You know, I've been waiting twenty years for one of you to give up on all your private and group speculation and just come out and ask. Well done, Jody. Direct questions are a sign of maturity, you know."

"Hey, I've asked you before," Jin protested. "You would never tell me."

"You hinted broadly, but you never actually asked," Corwin corrected. "Any of you ever hear the old saying *a mind is like a parachute—it only works when it's open?*"

"You've got to be kidding," Lorne said with a snort. "I think that one goes all the way back to DaVinci."

"Granted," Corwin said. "What's often forgotten is that the purpose of a parachute isn't to *stay* open, but to guide you safely to the ground."

"Interesting point," Paul murmured. "You're right; most people don't think it all the way through."

"I always had to keep an open mind in politics, you see," Corwin continued. "Not open in the sense of listening to different ideas and positions, but open in the sense of too often having to compromise my deepest moral and ethical convictions in the name of unity or other high-sounding but usually meaningless concepts."

He reached across to Thena's chair and took his wife's hand. "But then I retired," he said. "Now, I can hold those convictions as tightly as I want. As tightly as I always promised myself I would."

Jin caught her breath. Finally, after all these years, she got it. "Island," she murmured. "I *land.*"

"Exactly," Corwin said. "I'm sorry if the solution isn't nearly as intriguing or interesting as the mystery. But I'm old, you know, and I was never very clever to begin with."

"There's nothing wrong with the solution," Jin assured him. "It's both elegant and clever—"

"Just a moment," Corwin said, lifting a finger as he pulled out his phone. He frowned at the display, then keyed it on and held it to his ear. "Yes?"

For a few seconds he listened in silence, his expression tightening. "We'll be right there," he said at last. "Yes, just as soon as we can."

He keyed off. "That was Chintawa," he told the others. "He just got a call from the Dome, and he wants all of us to join him there right away. Front entrance, he said, and just leave your car at the curb."

"We're going to the Dome *now*?" Lorne echoed, frowning. "What, have they got treason trials on the night shift?"

"Maybe they decided to skip the trial and go straight to the execution," Jody suggested.

"You can write out your impassioned appeal on the way," Corwin said, gesturing toward the front door. "For now, just drive. Thena and I will get our car and meet you there."

To Jin, the Dome looked its usual nighttime self as they drove up to the front entrance—dark, quiet, and peopled mainly by overworked clerks and aides.

But that first look was deceiving. Even as they got out of the car, she could see a dozen other vehicles converging on different parts of the building, plus multiple flashes of headlights from the parking structure across they street. Whatever was happening, she and her family weren't the only ones who'd been called in.

Even more ominously, there were *six* Cobra guards flanking the door instead of the usual two.

An aide was waiting for them just inside the building. He waited in silence with them until Corwin and Thena arrived, then led the whole group to the small communications routing room near the center of the Dome.

Chintawa was already there, his face tight as he gazed at the status display above the two techs seated at the board. "Thank you for coming," he said as the aide ushered the six of them into the room. "I think we may have just gotten an answer to the question of why the Trofts picked this particular moment to try to conquer us and the Qasamans." He gestured to one of the techs. "Put it up."

The tech nodded and touched a switch, and the display became a telescopic view of the sky over Capitalia.

A sky with three huge ships floating against the stars.

Jin gasped. "Are those—?"

"Trofts?" Chintawa shook his head. "Fortunately, no. Or maybe not so fortunately." He took a deep breath. "I asked you here because—well, listen for yourselves."

Stepping to the board, he picked up a mike and keyed the switch. "Commodore Santores, this is Governor-General Michaelo Chintawa," he said. "My apologies for not being here when you first made contact."

"Quite understandable, Governor Chintawa," a booming, cheerful voice came from the speaker. "It *is* night there, after all. Permit me, if you will, to formally introduce myself to you: Commodore Rubo Santores of the Dominion of Man, commanding the Star Cruisers *Megalith*, *Algonquin*, and *Dorian*. After nearly three-quarters of a century of wondering what happened to their grand Cobra Worlds experiment, the Dome finally decided it was time to send someone to see for themselves. That someone would be us."

"We're honored by your presence," Chintawa said cautiously. "As you can see, we're alive and well."

"And from the looks of things, even thriving," Santores agreed. "We're pleased and relieved to find you so."

"Thank you," Chintawa said. "I understand there was also something in your mission profile about bringing us back into the Dominion fold?"

"Oh, I wouldn't worry about that," Santores said off-handedly. "Everything the Dome does has some kind of political subtext, you know. Well, no, of course you don't know that. But we can discuss all that later, perhaps when I come down to formally present my credentials."

"Yes, of course," Chintawa said. "I trust morning will be soon enough? It may take a while to assemble the Council."

"Take whatever time you need," Santores said. "My task force and I are entirely at your disposal."

"Thank you." Chintawa looked over at Jin and the others and visibly braced himself. "I understand there was one other matter one of your officers expressed some interest in?"

"Oh, yes," Santores said. "Though this one's purely unofficial, of course. The commander of the *Dorian*, Captain Barrington Jame Moreau, was hoping that some descendents of his great uncle, the

First Cobra Jonny Moreau, might still be with you. If so, he'd be most interested in meeting them."

"I think we'll be able to find a few family members for him to talk to," Chintawa said. "With your permission, Commodore, we'll continue this conversation tomorrow morning."

"At your convenience, Governor," Santores said. "*Megalith* out."

The radio went silent. For a long moment, the room remained likewise. "You see," Chintawa said at last, "why I asked you all to come here."

"Indeed," Corwin said. "Am I to assume that my retirement from politics has just ended?"

"Yes," Chintawa said soberly. "I'm very much afraid that it has."